OF HUMAN BONDAGE

WILLIAM SOMERSET MAUGHAM was born in 1874 and lived in Paris until he was ten years old. He was educated at The King's School, Canterbury, and at Heidelberg University. He later walked the wards of St. Thomas's Hospital with a view to practicing medicine, but when he had qualified, the success of his first novel, *Liza of Lambeth* (1897), won him over to letters. Some of his hospital experience is reflected in the story, as well as in his later masterpiece, *Of Human Bondage* (1915). With *The Moon and Sixpence* (1919) and *Cakes and Ale* (1930), his reputation as a novelist was further enhanced.

A celebrity by the age of thirty-three, when he became one of the most successful playwrights on the London stage, Maugham's Edwardian comedy *Lady Frederick,* his first hit (1907), was followed by a string of successes just before and then after the First World War. At one point Maugham had four plays running at the same time in London's West End. His theater career ended with *Sheppey* (1933).

His fame as a short-story writer began in 1921 with *The Trembling of a Leaf,* subtitled *Little Stories of the South Sea Islands,* which contained "Rain." After initial magazine publication of each story he wrote, there were ten more collections. Somerset Maugham's general nonfiction books also reflect his love of travel; they include *On a Chinese Screen* (1922) and *Don Fernando* (1935), essays, criticism, and the self-revealing *The Summing Up* (1938) and *A Writer's Notebook* (1949).

He traveled widely in the Far East and throughout Europe. His permanent home since before the Second World War was on the French Riviera, which he vacated temporarily in 1940. He became Companion of Honor in 1954 and he died in 1965.

ROBERT CALDER is Professor of English at the University of Saskatchewan. He is the author of *W. Somerset Maugham and the Quest for Freedom* and *Willie: The Life of W. Somerset Maugham,* which won the 1989 Governor General's Literary Award for Nonfiction.

W. SOMERSET MAUGHAM

Of Human Bondage

With an Introduction by
ROBERT CALDER

PENGUIN BOOKS
Published by the Penguin Group
Penguin Group (USA) Inc., 375 Hudson Street, New York, New York 10014, U.S.A.
Penguin Books Ltd, 80 Strand, London WC2R 0RL, England
Penguin Books Australia Ltd, 250 Camberwell Road, Camberwell, Victoria 3124, Australia
Penguin Books Canada Ltd, 10 Alcorn Avenue, Toronto, Ontario, Canada M4V 3B2
Penguin Books India (P) Ltd, 11 Community Centre, Panchsheel Park, New Delhi – 110 017, India
Penguin Books (N.Z.) Ltd, Cnr Rosedale and Airborne Roads, Albany, Auckland, New Zealand
Penguin Books (South Africa) (Pty) Ltd, 24 Sturdee Avenue,
Rosebank, Johannesburg 2196, South Africa

Penguin Books Ltd, Registered Offices: 80 Strand, London WC2R 0RL, England

First published in Great Britain by William Heinemann Ltd. 1915
First published in the United States of America by
George H. Doran Company 1915
Published in Penguin Books (U.S.A.) 1978
This edition with an introduction by
Robert Calder published in Penguin Books 1992

20 19 18 17 16

Introduction copyright © Robert Calder, 1992
All rights reserved

ISBN 0 14 01.8522 4

(CIP data available)

Printed in the United States of America

CONTENTS

CONTENTS

INTRODUCTION

On its publication in 1915, *Of Human Bondage* became a substantial addition to the genre variously called the novel of adolescence, the novel of apprenticeship, or the *bildungsroman*, the novel of educational or character development. Though its origins lay in the eighteenth century, the form flourished especially vigorously in the first two decades of the present one. Among the more notable examples in this period are Samuel Butler's *The Way of All Flesh* (1903), Henry Handel Richardson's *Maurice Guest* (1908), H.G. Wells's *Tono Bungay* (1909) and *The New Machiavelli* (1911), Arnold Bennett's *Clayhanger* (1910), Compton MacKenzie's *Sinister Street* (1913), D.H. Lawrence's *Sons and Lovers* (1913), and James Joyce's *A Portrait of the Artist as a Young Man* (1913–1915). So common was the genre that William York Tyndall later observed that "from 1903 onwards almost every first novel by a serious novelist was a novel of adolescence."

Of Human Bondage, begun when its author was thirty-seven, was, however, far from being Maugham's first novel. In 1897, following five years of medical study at St. Thomas's Hospital in London, he had published *Liza of Lambeth*, a good, realistic slum novel based on his experiences as a medical student in the mean streets of Lambeth. Deceived by the favorable reviews, he abandoned any idea of practicing medicine to pursue a literary career and then endured ten years of struggle before becoming securely established as a writer. During that time, he produced a volume of short stories and seven novels, but none were as good as *Liza of Lambeth* and few sold well. Hoping as well to become a dramatist, Maugham wrote a number of plays, but except for the very brief run enjoyed by *A Man of Honour* in 1903, none were staged.

It was the theatre, however, that saved Maugham's writing career. When the Court Theatre suddenly needed a play to replace an unexpected failure in October 1907, its manager turned to *Lady Frederick*. It became an enormous success, and by the summer of 1908 Maugham had four plays running in

London, a feat previously unmatched even by Shakespeare. Within eight months he had become a leading British playwright, a position he maintained until he stopped writing for the theatre in 1933. Moreover, having achieved financial security, he resolved never to write another novel.

This was a professional decision, however, and within three years Maugham was driven back to fiction by a stronger, more personal impulse. In his foreword, he describes how he had become obsessed by memories of his past—identified in *The Summing Up* as the death of his mother and the breakup of his home, the misery of his school years, his stammer, and his experiences in Heidelberg and at medical school. Only by writing them down could he free himself from their burden, and so at thirty-seven he began a lengthy work of catharsis.

Maugham had actually written an autobiographical novel, which he called "The Artistic Temperament of Stephen Carey," in 1898, but the loosely constructed and sloppily written work had attracted no publishers. Rather than a candid self-portrait, it was a picture of what the author thought a turn-of-the-century aesthete should be. Its rejection preserved the material for a time when he could explore it with more maturity, but it denied him the emotional release he sought.

Looking at Maugham's early life, one can understand why he needed to purge himself of distressing memories, why in the words of his nephew, Robin Maugham, "he was a person who was crippled by his emotional experiences as a child and from which he never recovered." Born in Paris in 1874, he was the fourth son of an English solicitor attached to the British embassy and his beautiful wife. After his brothers were sent to boarding school in England, the young "Willie" had the exclusive attention and love of his mother, and for four years he was surrounded by emotional warmth and security. Edith Maugham died of tuberculosis, however, six days after his eighth birthday, creating an emotional wound that would never heal. On his ninetieth birthday, he told a reporter: "Perhaps the most vivid memory left to me is the one which has tortured me for more than eighty years—the death of my mother. I was eight when she died and even today the pain of her passing is as keen as when it happened." When Maugham died on December 16, 1965, there were three photographs of Edith Maugham on his bedside table.

Though many details have been changed—Philip is an only child because that is how the young Willie felt when his brothers were away at school—the death of the young boy's mother in the opening pages of *Of Human Bondage* is an accurate rendering of the emotional impact of the author's own loss. When Maugham was asked in the 1940s to make a recording of passages from the novel, he broke down and wept after reading only a dozen lines of the description of Philip's mother.

Two years after the death of Edith Maugham, Willie's father died of cancer, and he was sent to live in Whitstable, in Kent, with his uncle Henry MacDonald Maugham, a vicar, and his wife. Both were in their fifties, childless, and ill-suited to raise a sensitive young boy who had just lost both parents, and Maugham felt like an intruder. The portrait of the vicar in *Of Human Bondage* is caustic—Maugham provided a more sympathetic one in *Cakes and Ale* in 1930—but accurate, and the narrow, circumscribed life of "Blackstable" is drawn from the author's memories of Whitstable.

Similarly, the chapters dealing with Philip's school years in "Tercanbury" are thinly disguised accounts of Maugham's time at King's School, Canterbury. Carefully recreated are the bullying, the insensitivity of many of the masters, the tedium, and the self-consciousness. As well, there is the growing sense of identity—in particular, of being an outsider—which reflects Maugham's own development.

Like Philip, Maugham left school early and spent a number of months as an unregistered student at the University of Heidelberg, and the ferment of ideas described in *Of Human Bondage* records not only his own intellectual growth but many of the intellectual currents swirling around at the end of the nineteenth century: the writings of Goethe, Verlaine, Meredith, and Flaubert, the art of Watts and Burne-Jones, the new drama of Ibsen and Sudermann, the revolutionary music of Wagner, the aestheticism of Pater and Arnold, and the lectures of Kuno Fischer. The religious scepticism planted in Philip by his reading of Renan's *Vie de Jésus* is not only Maugham's own agnosticism but the loss of faith of generations of late Victorians.

Like Philip, Maugham spent some months of drudgery as an apprentice chartered accountant in London, but he never attempted a career in painting. He did, nonetheless, spend a year in Paris (1904–1905) among the art colony, and many of the figures in the Paris section have their origins in those he encountered. Flanagan is based on the American illustrator Penryhn Stanlaws, Clutton on the Irish painter Roderick O'Connor, Cronshaw on the Canadian artist J.W. Morrice, and Lawson on Gerald Kelly, who later became president of the Royal Academy and one of Maugham's most loyal friends.

Philip's life in medical school is a vivid record of Maugham's own experiences at St. Thomas's Hospital, though the author suffered neither the failures nor the economic setbacks he gives his protagonist. He did not have the clubfoot, which makes Philip an object of curiosity at school and in the hospital, but he was afflicted with a stammer that made public speaking torturous and conversation difficult. Indeed, there is evidence that Maugham began *Of Human Bondage* in 1911 after the American playwright Edward Sheldon suggested that it might help him overcome the sense of inferiority caused by his stammer. This theory gains strength when one remembers that the protagonist of the earlier draft, "The Artistic Temperament of Stephen Carey," has no such disability.

An English writer and friend of Maugham, Francis King, argues that Philip's clubfoot was "a metaphor for a graver disability than the stammer that most critics have assumed it to have been": that is, his homosexuality. Referring to his sexual nature late in his life, Maugham once told his nephew that his great mistake was that he "tried to persuade myself that I was three-quarters normal and that only a quarter of me was queer—whereas really it was the other way round." In this confession can be seen one of the most fundamental and damaging conflicts in Maugham's life: that between his natural impulses and his acceptance of society's definition of normalcy. He had, after all, seen Oscar Wilde destroyed at the peak of his fame for his sexual orientation, and he lived during a period in which British society considered homosexuality abnormal and unacceptable.

Maugham's homosexuality may also explain the extraordinary relationship between Philip and the vulgar cockney waitress Mildred. Readers have always been puzzled by the strength of her attraction since, unlike the conventional femme fatale of novels of adolescence, she does not bind the young man to her with feminine beauty. She is, in fact, described androgynously, with a pale, almost green complexion, flat chest, and thin anemic figure. Philip's enthrallment has little to do with her being female.

Mildred's adrogyny has led a growing number of people to believe that Maugham was recounting a painful and protracted homosexual liaison from his medical student days. The strongest evidence for this is the comment by one of his close friends of the period, Harry Philips, to the French scholar Joseph Dobrinsky that "the real Mildred was a youth." If Maugham did indeed reverse the gender of his antagonist, he would merely have been emulating countless writers of the period who felt compelled by law and public opinion to disguise the homosexual elements in their fiction.

There are, regardless of gender, two significant things to note about the relationship with Mildred. First, it was probably responsible for the inclusion of a highly unusual clause in the original Heinemann contract for *Of Human Bondage*. Into the standard form has been typed the following qualification: "An advance of £500 (five hundred pounds) shall be made on account of royalties, any unearned portion of which shall be returnable by the Author if the free circulation of the book is impeded at the Libraries, by either its being placed in the class 'B' or objection being raised and free access to it is not given to subscribers on account of its contents." This irregular clause, rarely seen in contracts of the period, clearly reveals a fear that something in the novel might offend the private lending libraries, an influential source of income for publishers.

It is now impossible to know what elements in *Of Human Bondage* might have given offence, but the safest assumption is that they involved Mildred's sexual activities. It would not, moreover, be the first time that Maugham's writing had pushed the limits of what, in sexual matters, was acceptable in fiction. His novel *Mrs. Craddock* had been accepted by Heinemann in 1902 only after some passages were excised; even then, a decade before D.H. Lawrence's work, it created a minor sensation. Indeed, throughout his career Maugham presented problems for editors, censors, and other guardians of propriety—whether in the theatre, in print, or in the cinema. Never very innovative in form, he was daring in content, and he deserves more credit than he is often given for extending the boundaries of what can be explored in fiction.

The other important aspect of the relationship with Mildred is that, whether it was with a male or female, Maugham almost certainly had suffered from a very painful liaison with someone. It was so traumatic that it came to dominate his autobiographical novel—so much so that all three film versions focus almost exclusively on it—and variations of its unrequited and tortured emotion recurred in his other works.

Beyond Philip's involvement with Mildred, there is little in the novel's final third that is autobiographical. The Athelny family is probably a fictional creation, and there was certainly no Sally in Maugham's life, though he may have given her some qualities he found attractive in a young actress he knew called Ethelwyn Arthur Jones. As he later admitted, Sally was almost entirely a product of his imagination—the kind of woman he thought he would like to marry—and many readers have found the ending unsatisfactory and inconsistent with the rest of the novel.

In real life, two years after the publication of *Of Human Bondage*, Maugham married a much different woman from Sally. Syrie Barnardo Wellcome was a divorcée, a socialite, and as unsuited to be the wife of a writer as Maugham was to be her husband. After years of unhappiness and separation, they were divorced in 1929.

Despite the many autobiographical elements in *Of Human Bondage*, it is nevertheless, as Maugham reminds us in his foreword, a novel. And, to a remarkable extent, he has cast the details and outline of his own life into a pattern which very closely follows the formula of the conventional novel of adolescence or apprenticeship. In *Wilhelm Meister and His English Kinsmen*, Susanne Howe describes the plot of this genre:

> The adolescent hero of the typical "apprentice" novel sets out on his way through the world, meets with reverses usually due to his own temperament, falls in with various guides and counsellors, makes many false starts choosing his friends, his wife, and his life work, and finally adjusts himself in some way to the demands of his time and environment by finding a sphere of action in which he may work effectively.

The fascination of the apprentice novel lies in the exceptional nature of the apprentice—sensitive, intelligent, and emotional:

> For these heroes are, after all, the elect—a little feeble, impressionable, vacillating, perhaps, but endowed with exceptional powers of mind and spirit, though it takes them a long while to find it out. They are more sensitive and gifted than the average young man; their perceptions are sharper, their failures more heartbreaking, their struggles for adjustment to the world more desperate than those of their fellows, but their ultimate victory is assured.

It is easy to see that, measured against Howe's formula, Philip is both an autobiographical figure and a typical protagonist of the apprentice novel. He is impressionable, vacillating, and a little feeble, and he is more sensitive and perceptive than the average young man. Almost pathologically, his failures hurt him more than others', and his struggle for adjustment is greater than those of his friends.

Philip's progress through the novel is largely that of the conventional apprentice. He encounters many guides and influences—Parsons, Weeks, Hayward, Lawson, Fanny Price, Cronshaw, Griffiths, Mildred, and Athelny—and he must choose the true from the false. His own temperament, so warped by his loneliness and deformity, often brings him unnecessary suffering. Finally, like most of the protagonists of the genre, Philip discovers a philosophy that is tenable in the world he perceives, and he finds his own niche.

In two significant ways, however, Philip is different from the conventional protagonist. Aside from his individualized character, he is hardly endowed with "exceptional powers of mind and spirit"—at least in the sense that Paul Morel, in *Sons and Lovers*, and Stephen Dedalus, in *A Portrait of the Artist as a Young Man*, are both convincing as future artists and adventurers. Philip proves not to have a comparable imagination and creativity, and he is almost unique among such figures in choosing domesticity and a modest occupation over the pursuit of experience, exoticism, and art. In this regard, it is interesting that, while Howe notes that the "ultimate victory" of the apprentice is assured, Maugham calls Philip's choice at the end "a defeat better than many victories."

Philip's decision to live a conventional, unromantic life is actually close to that of Goethe's Wilhelm Meister, who also concluded that "America was here and now." It was not, however, Maugham's own, because by the time that *Of Human Bondage* was published, he was off doing intelligence work during the First World War and beginning fifteen years of wandering through the South Seas and the Far East. The protagonist of his first novel of this period, *The Moon and Sixpence*, published four years after *Of Human Bondage*, in fact abandons family and occupation to pursue art in Tahiti. In 1915 the reviewer of *The Times Literary Supplement* had written that, until the end of the novel, Philip "was so busy yearning for the moon that he never saw the sixpence at his feet." In 1919, Maugham took his title from this comment, and his autobiographical narrator reveals a good deal of admiration for the man who ignores the sixpence in order to pursue the moon.

In the titles of the two novels, however, one can see that, quite apart from indicating any changes in the direction of Maugham's own life, they signal the exploration of quite different themes. While the latter seems to have come easily to him in the form of a reviewer's metaphor, the former went through a surprising number of versions. The original manuscript, now in the Library of Congress, indicates that Maugham's first choice was "Beauty for Ashes," a phrase from Isaiah 61:23, but Lady Henry Somerset's use of it in 1913 forced him to suggest a series of alternatives. The Heinemann contract, signed in October 1914, carries three successive titles: "Of Fleeting Things," "The Pride of Life," and finally, and clearly added later, "Of Human Bondage." Before the final choice, there was yet another: "Life's Thoroughfare," as the work was identified in the American rights contract signed by Heinemann and George Doran in December 1914.

However seriously any of these titles were considered, none is as remotely appropriate as *Of Human Bondage*. Its emphasis on the restrictions—and by implication the freedom—inherent in the human condition underlines the central concern of Maugham's own life and the dominant theme which runs throughout his writing.

Maugham once commented that "the main thing I've always asked from life is freedom. Outer and inner freedom, both in my way of living and my way of writing," and at the age of sixty-two he wrote: "I have sought freedom, material and spiritual, and now on the threshold of old age, I am not disinclined to think that I have at last achieved it." Examined in its entirety, Maugham's very long life was indeed a succession of attempts to discover complete freedom—not merely physical liberty but true independence of spirit. On one level he sought to be free from personal obligations, financial dependence, and the constraints of time and place (which in part explains why he became one of the world's great travellers); on another, he pursued intellectual freedom and emotional detachment. He did in the end achieve a life of considerable independence, but his tragedy is that it did not ultimately ensure happiness.

Maugham's lifelong search for freedom permeated his writing, and though the plots, settings, and characters may vary, the essential theme reiterated throughout is freedom and bondage. Many of the titles—*The Merry-Go-Round, The Circle, The Painted Veil, The Narrow Corner, Cakes and Ale,* and *The Razor's Edge*—suggest that men and women are in various ways confronted with narrowness and restraint on all sides. Liza (*Liza of Lambeth*) is trapped by the slum, Bertha Craddock (*Mrs. Craddock*) is stifled by life among the landed gentry, Charles Strickland (*The Moon and Sixpence*) is driven to paint by a force he cannot control, Rosie Driffield (*Cakes and Ale*) defies puritanical convention, Dr. Saunders (*The Narrow Corner*) is on a voyage of liberation, and Larry Darrell (*The Razor's Edge*), seeking to escape American materialism, finds spiritual liberation in Indian mysticism.

Of Human Bondage, however, remains Maugham's deepest and most comprehensive expression of his concern for the freedom of the individual. Its theme is the development within Philip of a spiritual independence, a liberation from what the author once called the "strange and ruthless forces that are beyond our control." Although it is a very long novel, there is little in it which is not an integral part of the central theme, and it is a serious mistake to focus attention on one episode—the affair with Mildred, for example—and ignore the others. Each section, setting, or character demonstrates the mistakes, falsehoods, and delusions that Philip must face and escape before he can discover a desirable and feasible pattern for his life.

In delineating the many "strange and ruthless forces" in Philip's world, Maugham is very much a realistic novelist of his time, influenced by the French naturalists such as Flaubert, Zola, and de Maupassant, with their emphasis on the power of heredity and environment. In the realistic tradition, he describes the two elements in exhaustive detail, and one of the novel's great strengths is its demonstration of how a relatively simple influence exerted early in one's life can become much more complex and destructive as one grows to adulthood. The constraints of physical disability, pressures to conform, economic hardship, and domestic tyranny are easily recognized and relatively easily combatted. As Maugham demonstrates, the real danger is that these forces create in Philip a host of deeply ingrained psychological handicaps, much less easy to identify and much more difficult to eliminate. As Kingsley Amis says, "the novel shows how one barrier, in the shape of lameness, loneliness, puritanism or stupidity, will set up others: suspicion, over-exclusive affection, vindictiveness, exhibitionism, obstinacy, intolerance, self-torture—the state of what a later generation has learnt to call the injustice collector."

Nowhere is this progression more obviously delineated than in the effect on Philip of his clubfoot, an impediment with which he was born. Hardly an overwhelming handicap—Byron, for example, overcame his—Philip's foot prevents his playing sports but otherwise does little to restrict his movement, and, while it elicits ridicule when he first enters school, the other boys soon treat him as they do anyone else. By this point, however, he has been conditioned to feel that he is different, inferior, and somehow separate from the others. By the time he is a young adult, he has developed a supersensitivity to any suggestion that he is not a whole man, and much of his initial determination to win Mildred comes from his perception that she has treated him as less than normal. Thus an accident of birth, which became a physical impediment, has been transmuted into a complicated and deeply ingrained psychological shackle.

Philip's personality is similarly shaped by a variety of influences in his environment. When, for example, as a young boy he is humiliated by his failure to memorize the collect, he is consoled by a picture book of Middle Eastern scenes, and he begins to discover the joy of reading. But, as the author observes, this escape into the imagination also creates "an unreal world which would make the real world of every day a source of bitter disappointment." Philip does not realize "how wide a country, arid and precipitous, must be crossed before the traveller through life comes to an acceptance of reality."

It is not until the novel's final pages that Philip is able to accept reality, to stop suffering repeated disillusionments as the world fails to meet his idealized and romanticized expectations. He undertakes to seduce Miss Wilkinson, for example, because he thinks that it is what any young man in his position would do, and his reading has led him to believe that love will come in the shape of "great violet eyes," "alabaster skin," and "rippling masses of . . . auburn hair." Miss Wilkinson, though, comes from life rather than literature, and her half-undressed form, in Philip's eyes, is "grotesque."

This highly romantic view of life still dominates the young man years later, when he imagines entering a ballroom, seeing a woman "tall and dark and beautiful, with eyes like the night . . . dressed in white," with diamonds in her hair. Sweeping from the room, they catch the midnight train to Paris, speeding "through the silent, star-lit night into the unknown." Measured against this vision, no woman, least of all Mildred Rogers, can hope to be acceptable.

A similar pattern of illusion and reality underlies Philip's experience with the art colony in Paris. On reading Murger's *La Vie de Bohème*—the novel on which Puccini based his famous romantic opera—Philip succumbs to its "picture of starvation which is so good-humored, of squalor which is so picturesque, of sordid love which is so romantic, of bathos which is so moving." When he arrives in Paris, he views the city through the novelist's eyes, drinking absinthe, seeing men who look like artists with women who look like mistresses, and dressing himself as he believes a painter should.

By the end of his Paris experience, however, Philip has not only discovered that he does not have the talent to paint; he has learned what the bohemian life really entails. He comes to recognize the poseurs, and the formerly colorful patrons of the music halls are now merely petty and sordid. More than anything else, it is the pathetic Fanny Price, who hangs herself after exhausting all her resources in a vain pursuit of an art career, who teaches Philip that starvation is not good-humored and squalor is not picturesque. Maugham always detested the Victorian belief that suffering ennobles, and nowhere does he attack it with more vigor than in his portrayal of what deprivation does to Fanny Price.

Philip comes away from Paris with a heightened aesthetic sense, but he also comes to realize that the artistic temperament is a form of bondage. The genuinely talented painters are driven not by their intellects but by almost autonomous instincts. Clutton, in whom Philip sees a "mysterious force," states that "the only reason that one paints is that one cannot help it." To prove the power of the obsession, he points to a man in Brittany who abandoned wife, family, and income in order to paint in Tahiti. This, of course, became the plot of *The Moon and Sixpence*, Maugham's most thorough examination of the creative impulse.

Fanny Price's tragedy is that her obsession is not matched by any talent, but she is also destroyed by poverty. In this, she is only one of many examples in *Of Human Bondage* and throughout Maugham's writing of the immense power of economics to trap or liberate. The turn-of-the-century realists had grown up in an age of imperialism, industrialism, and material acquisition, and it is hardly surprising that they—Wells, Gissing, Galsworthy, Bennett, Moore, and others—should see money or the lack of it as a powerful determining force. Maugham himself once referred to money as "the string with which a sardonic destiny directs the motions of its puppets" and poverty as "a more exacting master than all the conventions of society put together."

Of Human Bondage vividly shows how economic deprivation imprisons both the body and the spirit. In the hospital, Philip sees tuberculosis patients sentenced to death because they cannot possibly afford to travel to a warm climate or to rest from hard labor. His Paris art teacher, Foinet, in the novel's most often quoted line, tells him that "money is like a sixth sense without which you cannot make complete use of the other five." "There is nothing," he says, "so degrading as the constant anxiety about one's means of livelihood."

Philip himself later demonstrates the degradation that economic hardship can bring. When a foolish gamble on the stock market costs him practically all his capital, he becomes bankrupt and homeless. Forced to abandon his medical studies to work at the humiliating task of floorwalker at a hosiery store, he becomes preoccupied with the possibility of his uncle's death. Studying Mr. Carey with a medical student's eye, he calculates his age, consults his texts about chronic bronchitis, and hopes for cold and rainy weather. Finally, he even contemplates murder, considering how easily he could give his uncle an overdose of drugs. This is the point of the novel where Philip is least attractive, as he is later able to recognize. "He knew," writes Maugham, "that the lack [of money] made a man petty, mean, grasping; it distorted his character and caused him to view the world from a vulgar angle." Only when Mr. Carey's death gives Philip economic security is he free to resume his medical studies, to turn his interests outside himself, and to regain a mastery of his own life.

Philip's deepest and most protracted enslavement is his obsession with Mildred, and it is here that the novel's title is most appropriate. Maugham took it from a chapter of Spinoza's *Ethics*, "Of Human Bondage, or the Strength of the Emotions," where the philosopher writes: "The impotence of man to govern or restrain the [emotions] I call bondage, for a man who is under their control is not his own master, but is mastered by fortune, in whose power he is, so that he is often forced to follow the worse, although he sees the better before him."

Though there are many places in *Of Human Bondage* where Philip's reason is overruled by his emotions, the relationship with Mildred is the most dramatic—and unique among the heroes of apprentice novels. Almost universally, these young men become involved with, and must free themselves from, a destructive woman, but the attractions of these sirens are always romantic or sexual. Mildred, however, is thin, anemic, and has an unattractive complexion. A snob, she is unintelligent, insensitive, and vulgar. Lacking generosity, cold, and completely selfish, she has few redeeming qualities.

Most young men in fiction who suffer at the hands of a woman have their reason so overwhelmed by passion that they do not see her realistically. Philip is unique in that he always sees Mildred precisely as she is, often to the point of repulsion, but he is still powerfully drawn to her. Maugham thus creates a genuine split between reason and emotion, and dramatizes the

Spinozan dilemma of being forced to follow a destructive course even while recognizing a better one.

The split in Philip baffles readers who expect his attraction to Mildred to be conventionally romantic when it is actually driven by complex psychological needs arising from deeply rooted problems. The relationship begins when her indifferent treatment of him in the tea shop makes him feel "strangely humiliated" and he does not feel that he can rest until he regains his dignity. As the relationship develops, Philip is moved by contradictory feelings of affection and hatred, and of self-loathing for being enslaved by a woman he so despises. "He was a prisoner," Maugham writes, "and he longed for his freedom." Later, in one of the novel's most cynical lines, he concludes that love is some sort of force "that passed from a man to a woman, from a woman to a man, and made one of them a slave."

Before Philip can effect any surrender from Mildred, she elopes with Miller, and his desire remains unrequited. When she returns after being abandoned, Philip's emotional bondage reaches its greatest intensity. Not happy in her presence, his desire for her is strongest when she is with another man, and Maugham introduces a strong element of masochism to the self-pity which has always been part of Philip's character.

When Mildred leaves a second time, Philip's enslavement lessens, and though he becomes involved with her twice more before the end, he is never as emotionally troubled. On learning that she has turned to prostitution, he feels nothing but "infinite pity," and ironically it is Mildred who reveals a greater enslavement to her emotions. Philip's indifference to her attempts to seduce him enrage her, and, hoping to strike at his most vulnerable point, she spits out: "Cripple!"

When Philip encounters Mildred for the last time, he feels nothing but horror for the venereal disease she has contracted, but he is not truly free until he can forgive her. This comes when he sees Mildred, Griffiths, and others as puppets in the hands of fate, and he repeats Christ's words: "Forgive them, for they know not what they do." Even so, Maugham shrewdly reminds us that deeply traumatic experiences can never be entirely left behind, and so Philip still feels a quickening of the pulse when he sees a woman in the street who reminds him of Mildred.

Despite the horrified fascination of many readers, the climax of *Of Human Bondage* comes not with Philip's liberation from his obsession with Mildred but with his discovery of a philo-sophical foundation to his life. Coming in Chapter CVI, when he realizes the significance of Cronshaw's reference to a Persian rug, this knowledge frees him from his greatest bondage—that of finding meaning in human existence—and resolves most of the conflicts which have built up in him from the opening pages of the novel.

When Philip loses his religious faith in Heidelberg, his feeling is characteristically one of liberation, of freedom from an "intolerable burden." Believing that he has lost "that burden of responsibility which had made every action of his life a matter of urgent consequence," he confidently assumes that he is at last his own master. Having lost a pattern of belief dictated from without, however, he is driven for the rest of the novel to find one from within. In this he is very much a twentieth-century figure.

Behind Philip's need to see meaning in his life lies a long line of lives he views as futile and wasted. His aunt, he believes, lives a life without significance, faithfully attending an egotistic and selfish husband. Monsieur Ducroz, his French teacher in Germany, seems to have spent his life "in the pursuit of that which was not worth the finding." Miguel Ajuria is passionately devoted to writing, but his mind is trivial and his talent minimal. Having sacrificed everything for artistic success, Fanny Price dies wretchedly after making no impression on the world, as if she had never existed. At Cronshaw's death, Philip is dismayed by "the absolute futility of the life," and when Hayward dies in South Africa, he concludes that things are "just the same now as if he had never lived."

Determined that his own life should have significance, Philip is dismayed by what seems to be people's inability to control their own destinies. They are, in the most common image in the novel, puppets or robots driven by forces much more powerful than their wills. Hayward inexplicably enlists in the Boer War, and even Griffiths and Mildred are "the helpless instruments of blind chance."

The question of how much free will could be exercised in the face of deterministic forces was a central concern of naturalistic writers, and it is explored at length in *Of Human Bondage*. It first arises in Paris in discussions with Cronshaw, who argues for fatalism but a kind of fatalism which permits the illusion of free choice. "I act as though I were a free agent," he says, "but when an action is performed it is clear that all the forces of the universe conspired to cause it, and nothing I could do could have prevented it." Maugham reiterates this position in *The*

Summing Up by using the metaphor of chess, where the player is limited by the particular moves of the pieces provided but can seem to make freely willed choices.

Because modern man is a social animal, many of the rules of the game are determined by society and the state, and here again Cronshaw, reflecting Maugham's reading of Spinoza, describes how a free man is to function. Public opinion and law, the weapons of society and the state, are necessary because they protect the individual from those more powerful and ruthless; or, in Spinoza's words, "a man . . . who is guided by reason desires, in order that he may live more freely, to maintain the common rights of the state." Within the limits of these common rights, says Cronshaw, the free person will do what he wants, which means to "follow one's instincts with due regard to the policeman around the corner."

Cronshaw's Spinozan credo provides Philip with a rule of conduct, but his realization of the meaning of life, as symbolized by the Persian rug, does not come until Chapter CVI, when he seeks solace in the British Museum after the death of Hayward. At his despairing cry about the purpose of life, with all its futility and pettiness, the illumination comes: "The answer was obvious. Life had no meaning. . . . Life was insignificant and death without consequence."

This epiphany, as James Joyce would have called it, is a release, a liberation from the pursuit of the unattainable: a logical and comprehensive design which accounts for the state of the world. No longer will he need to question the origins of cruelty, stupidity, disease, suffering, and death; no longer will he need to explain the waste and futility of so many lives; and no longer will he feel compelled to weigh the appropriateness of his actions against any eternal plan. Once again, Philip experiences a great sense of liberation: "It seemed to him that the last burden of responsibility was taken from him; and for the first time he was utterly free."

According to Graham Greene, Maugham's dismissal of divine meaning diminishes the importance of human activity: "Rob human beings of their heavenly and their infernal importance, and you rob your characters of their individuality." He may be right, but Philip is representative of millions of people in the twentieth century who, confronted by a Godless universe, must find the meaning of their lives within themselves. Recalling Cronshaw's Persian rug, Philip realizes that, just as its weaver created an elaborate and beautiful pattern for no purpose but his own aesthetic pleasure, a man can make his life into a pattern whose significance will be apparent only to himself. "It would," Maugham writes, "be a work of art, and it would be none the less beautiful because he alone knew of its existence, and with his death it would at once cease to be." It is arguable, moreover, that Philip is no less interesting or individual because he has come to this modern, existential position.

Those readers who find the ending of *Of Human Bondage* contrived and inconsistent with the rest of the novel overlook the fundamental change in Philip after this revelation. Though his view of life is, in philosophical terms, pessimistic, his acceptance of its meaninglessness has given him an equanimity and a willingness to settle for more modest goals. Furthermore, Sally is not a romantic ideal nor is her relationship with Philip idyllic; and Phillip's love for her never has the compulsion of his attraction to Mildred. In *The Summing Up,* Maugham distinguishes between two types of love: "love pure and simple, sexual love, namely; and loving-kindness." Sexual love, though bringing excitement, intensity, and exultation, often involves unrequitement and enslavement for one of the lovers. Loving-kindness, on the other hand, is not binding or transitory; more akin to affection and friendship, it is more durable. Above all, it is "the better part of goodness."

In the final chapters of *The Summing Up,* Maugham examines the three values "Truth, Beauty, and Goodness," which he says give "man the illusion that through them he escapes from human bondage." Philip's story is really an exploration of this triad: truth is analyzed in Heidelberg, in discussions with Cronshaw, and in the vision in the British Museum; beauty is introduced in Paris and becomes an essential part of his life; and goodness is the central issue in the latter half of the novel, where the treachery of Mildred and Griffiths is contrasted with the goodness of the Athelny family. Maugham concludes *The Summing Up* by placing the greatest value on goodness; and in choosing marriage to Sally, who is an Athelny, Philip is doing the same.

Of Human Bondage is also a novel about free will and determinism, and Maugham is careful to arrange the elements of Philip's decision so that it is as close to being a free choice as is possible. When it appears that Sally is pregnant, Philip chooses marriage and constraint over Spain and freedom in a gesture of self-sacrifice, rationalizing the decision by considering the pleasures of domesticity. When, however, he discovers that Sally is not pregnant, he can act positively out of free will. Having learned that he is willing to abandon his dreams of travel, he is free from his romantic illusion of exotic exploration and the compulsion to do what he thinks a young man in his position should. Now that he knows that Sally is not pregnant, there is no need to marry her out of honor or convention; if he chooses her, it will be from positive desire, not from a negative force of conscience. Thus Maugham has created what Dean Doner has called the perfect Spinozan situation, "a positive act of will in terms of the entire situation unaffected by prior desire or decision."

Of Human Bondage remains Maugham's most complete statement of the importance of physical and spiritual liberty, a theme that has become one of the most important issues of twentieth-century life. From the latter part of the last century onward, human progress has generally been toward more and more essential freedoms. Economically, socially, morally, intellectually, and spiritually, it has been a period of liberation. *Of Human Bondage* reflects its age in treating the effects of these developments on people. Unlike previous youthful figures such as Tom Jones and David Copperfield, Philip is confronted with many new freedoms, and Maugham shows how each carries with it a corresponding obligation. Whereas the former protagonists could be confident of certain basic assumptions, Philip, the representative of a new age, must find his own truth. His is an era of agnosticism and, while this brings intellectual freedom, it also demands that he seek his own vision of human purpose. Similarly, morality has become complex and ambiguous, and Philip must therefore establish his own set of values. In examining these and many other issues, *Of Human Bondage* explores people's new freedom in the twentieth century.

In the seventy-six years since its publication, *Of Human Bondage* has become one of the most widely read of modern novels, particularly by young people, who still find relevance in Philip's struggle for a free and meaningful life. With a few exceptions, however, the critical response in 1915 was lukewarm, many reviewers objecting to the novel's length, its protagonist's morbid and unpleasant character, and the distasteful affair with Mildred. The American novelist Theodore Dreiser, in a review published in *The New Republic* in December 1915, was almost alone in hailing it as "a novel or biography or autobiography or social transcript of utmost importance" and describing its author as a "genius."

Of Human Bondage found a much better general response from the reading public, and sales were steady enough to warrant seven new editions or reprints in the twenties and numerous more in the thirties. As early as 1931, first editions were becoming scarce collector's items, and in the forties it was one of Modern Library's most popular titles. Though Maugham's reputation underwent the usual decline after his death, *Of Human Bondage* continued—and continues—to be read throughout the world.

Despite the reservations of the initial reviewers, *Of Human Bondage* gradually earned the respect of critics, scholars, and other writers. In the decade after its first appearance, Dreiser's high praise was followed by similar notices by such influential critics as F.P. Adams, Alexander Woollcott, Heywood Broun, Grant Overton, St. John Adcock, S.P.B. Mais, and Carl Van Doren. Then, in a *New York Times* article in 1925, Marcus Aurelius Goodrich pronounced *Of Human Bondage* a "classic." *Of Human Bondage* had, he claimed, "risen in England almost to a place beside *The Way of All Flesh*, and in the United States is on the way to becoming an uncanonical sensation."

By the 1920s *Of Human Bondage* had reached cult status, mandatory reading for those who fancied themselves intellectuals. In 1925, Dorothea Mann wrote: "I should like to see the time come when the well-read person would be as unwilling to admit not having read *Of Human Bondage* as he would be to admit that he had not seen the plays of Shakespeare." That time seems to have long since arrived, if one is to judge by the well-read Gore Vidal's admission in 1990 that "it is very difficult for a writer of my generation, if he is honest, to pretend indifference to the work of Somerset Maugham. He was always so entirely *there*. By seventeen I had read all of Shakespeare; all of Maugham."

At the end of his writing career, Maugham left a substantial body of work, and he was unusual among writers in achieving success in three genres. After *Of Human Bondage,* he wrote another eleven novels, the best being *The Moon and Sixpence* (1919), *The Painted Veil* (1925), *Cakes and Ale* (1930), *The Narrow Corner* (1932), and *The Razor's Edge* (1944). By 1933, when he left the theatre, he had written twenty-five plays, several of which—*The Circle* (1921), *The Constant Wife* (1927), and *For Services Rendered* (1932)—will continue to be produced for many years. His hundred or so short stories—which include such memorable tales as "The Letter," "Rain," and "The Alien Corn"—are as good a collection as can be found in English literature. *The Summing Up,* moreover, has become a classic modern philosophical autobiography.

As well crafted as many of these works are, though, they lack the intensity of *Of Human Bondage,* the willingness of the author to bare his soul that is a mark of the greatest literature. The novel did not in fact provide the catharsis that Maugham was seeking, and in his senile last years the memories came flooding back. On the other hand, because, as Dreiser says, "it bears the imprint of an eager, almost consuming desire to say truly what is in his heart," *Of Human Bondage* will remain not only Maugham's most important work but one of the most widely read of twentieth-century novels.

—Robert Calder

SUGGESTIONS FOR FURTHER READING

Brander, Laurence. *Somerset Maugham: A Guide.* Edinburgh: Oliver and Boyd, 1963.

Burt, Forrest D. *W. Somerset Maugham.* Boston: Twayne, 1985.

Calder, Robert. *Willie: The Life of W. Somerset Maugham.* London: Heinemann, 1989.

Cordell, Richard. *Somerset Maugham: A Biographical and Critical Study.* Bloomington: Indiana University Press, 1969.

Curtis, Anthony. *The Pattern of Maugham.* London: Hamish Hamilton, 1974.

Kuner, Mildred C. "The Human Condition: Bondage," in *The World of Somerset Maugham,* edited by Klaus W. Jonas. Westport, Conn.: Greenwood Press, 1972, pp. 37–95.

Loss, Archie K. *Of Human Bondage: Coming of Age in the Novel.* Boston: Twayne, 1990.

Morgan, Ted. *Maugham: A Biography.* New York: Simon and Schuster, 1980.

Whitehead, John. *Maugham: A Reappraisal.* Totowa, N.J.: Barnes and Noble, 1987.

OF HUMAN BONDAGE

FOREWORD

THIS is a very long novel and I am ashamed to make it longer by writing a preface to it. An author is probably the last person who can write fitly of his own work. In this connexion an instructive story is told by Roger Martin du Gard, a distinguished French novelist, about Marcel Proust. Proust wanted a certain French periodical to publish an important article on his great novel and thinking that no one could write it better than he, sat down and wrote it himself. Then he asked a young friend of his, a man of letters, to put his name to it and take it to the editor. This the young man did, but after a few days the editor sent for him. 'I must refuse your article,' he told him. 'Marcel Proust would never forgive me if I printed a criticism of his work that was so perfunctory and so unsympathetic.' Though authors are touchy about their productions and inclined to resent unfavourable criticism they are seldom self-satisfied. They are conscious how far the work on which they have spent much time and trouble comes short of their conception, and when they consider it are much more vexed with their failure to express this in its completeness than pleased with the passages here and there that they can regard with complacency. Their aim is perfection and they are wretchedly aware that they have not attained it.

I will say nothing then about my book itself, but will content myself with telling the reader of these lines how a novel that has now had a fairly long life, as novels go, came to be written; and if it does not interest him I ask him to forgive me. I wrote it first when, at the age of twenty-three, having taken my medical degrees after five years at St Thomas's Hospital, I went to Seville determined to earn my living as a writer. The manuscript of the book I wrote then still exists, but I have not looked at it since I corrected the typescript, and I have no doubt that it is very immature. I sent it to Fisher Unwin, who had published my first book (while still a medical student I had written a novel called *Liza of Lambeth*, which had had something of a success), but he refused to give me the hundred pounds I wanted for it, and none of the other publishers to whom I afterwards submitted it would have it at any price. This distressed me at the time, but now I know that I was fortunate; for if one of them had taken my book (it was called *The Artistic Temperament of Stephen Carey*) I should have lost a subject which I was too young to make proper use of. I was not far enough away from the events I described to make good use of them, and I had not had a number of experiences which later went to enrich the book I finally wrote. Nor had I learnt that it is easier to write of what you know than of what you don't. For instance, I sent my hero to Rouen (which I knew only as an occasional visitor) to learn French, instead of to Heidelberg (where I had been myself) to learn German.

Thus rebuffed I put the manuscript away. I wrote other novels, which were published, and I wrote plays. I became in due course a very successful playwright and determined to devote the rest of my life to the drama. But I reckoned without a force within me that made my resolutions vain. I was happy, I was prosperous, I was busy. My head was full of the plays I wanted to write. I do not know whether it was that success did not bring me all I had expected or whether it was a natural reaction from it, but I was no sooner firmly established as the most popular dramatist of the day than I began once more to be obsessed by the teeming memories of my past life. They came back to me so pressingly, in my sleep, on my walks, at rehearsals, at parties, they became such a burden to me, that I made up my mind there was only one way to be free of them and that was to write them all down on paper. After submitting myself for some years to the exigencies of the drama I hankered after the wide liberty of the novel. I knew the book I had in mind would be a long one and I wanted to be undisturbed, so I refused the contracts that managers were eagerly offering me and temporarily retired from the stage. I was then thirty-seven.

For long after I became a writer by profession I spent much time on learning how to write and subjected myself to a very tiresome training in the endeavour to improve my style. But these efforts I abandoned when my plays began to be produced, and when I started to write again it was with a different aim. I no longer sought a jewelled prose and a rich texture, on unavailing attempts to achieve which I had formerly wasted much labour; I sought on the contrary plainness and simplicity. With so much that I wanted to say within reasonable limits I felt that I could not afford to waste words and I set out now with the notion of using only such as were necessary to make my meaning clear. I had no space for ornament. My experience in the theatre had taught me the value of succinctness. I worked unremittingly for two years. I did not know what to call my book and after looking about a great deal hit upon *Beauty from Ashes*, a quotation from Isaiah, which seemed to me apposite; but learning that this title had been recently used I was obliged to search for another. I chose finally the name of one of the books in Spinoza's *Ethics* and called my novel *Of Human Bondage*. I have a notion that I was once more lucky in finding that I could not use the first title I had thought of.

Of Human Bondage is not an autobiography, but an autobiographical novel; fact and fiction are inextricably mingled; the emotions are my own, but not all the incidents are related as they happened, and some of them are transferred to my hero not from my own life but from that of persons with whom I was intimate. The book did for me what I wanted, and when it was issued to the world (a world in the throes of a dreadful war and too much concerned with its own sufferings and fears to bother with the adventures of a creature of fiction) I found myself free from the pains and unhappy recollections that had tormented me. It was very well reviewed; Theodore Dreiser wrote for *The New Republic* a long criticism in which he dealt with it with the intelligence and sympathy that distinguish everything he has ever written; but it looked very much as though it would go the way of the vast majority of novels and be forgotten for ever a few months after its appearance. But, I do not know through what accident, it happened after some years that it attracted the attention of a number of distinguished writers in the United States, and the references they continued to make to it in the press gradually brought it to the notice of the public. To these writers is due the new lease of life that the book was thus given and them must I thank for the success it has continued increasingly to have as the years go by.

I

THE day broke grey and dull. The clouds hung heavily, and there was a rawness in the air that suggested snow. A woman servant came into a room in which a child was sleeping and drew the curtains. She glanced mechanically at the house opposite, a stucco house with a portico, and went to the child's bed.

'Wake up, Philip,' she said.

She pulled down the bed-clothes, took him in her arms, and carried him downstairs. He was only half awake.

'Your mother wants you,' she said.

She opened the door of a room on the floor below and took the child over to a bed in which a woman was lying. It was his mother. She stretched out her arms, and the child nestled by her side. He did not ask why he had been awakened. The woman kissed his eyes, and with thin, small hands felt the warm body through his white flannel nightgown. She pressed him closer to herself.

'Are you sleepy, darling?' she said.

Her voice was so weak that it seemed to come already from a great distance. The child did not answer, but smiled comfortably. He was very happy in the large, warm bed, with those soft arms about him. He tried to make himself smaller still as he cuddled against his mother, and he kissed her sleepily. In a moment he closed his eyes and was fast asleep. The doctor came forward and stood by the bedside.

'Oh, don't take him away yet,' she moaned.

The doctor, without answering, looked at her gravely. Knowing she would not be allowed to keep the child much longer, the woman kissed him again; and she passed her hand down his body till she came to his feet; she held the right foot in her hand and felt the five small toes; and then slowly passed her hand over the left one. She gave a sob.

'What's the matter?' said the doctor. 'You're tired.'

She shook her head, unable to speak, and the tears rolled down her cheeks. The doctor bent down.

'Let me take him.'

She was too weak to resist his wish, and she gave the child up. The doctor handed him back to his nurse.

'You'd better put him back in his own bed.'

'Very well, sir.'

9

The little boy, still sleeping, was taken away. His mother sobbed now broken-heartedly.

'What will happen to him, poor child?'

The monthly nurse tried to quiet her, and presently, from exhaustion, the crying ceased. The doctor walked to a table on the other side of the room, upon which, under a towel, lay the body of a still-born child. He lifted the towel and looked. He was hidden from the bed by a screen, but the woman guessed what he was doing.

'Was it a girl or a boy?' she whispered to the nurse.

'Another boy.'

The woman did not answer. In a moment the child's nurse came back. She approached the bed.

'Master Philip never woke up,' she said.

There was a pause. Then the doctor felt his patient's pulse once more.

'I don't think there's anything I can do just now,' he said. 'I'll call again after breakfast.'

'I'll show you out, sir,' said the child's nurse.

They walked downstairs in silence. In the hall the doctor stopped.

'You've sent for Mrs Carey's brother-in-law, haven't you?'

'Yes, sir.'

'D'you know at what time he'll be here?'

'No, sir, I'm expecting a telegram.'

'What about the little boy? I should think he'd be better out of the way.'

'Miss Watkin said she'd take him, sir.'

'Who's she?'

'She's his godmother, sir. D'you think Mrs Carey will get over it, sir?'

The doctor shook his head.

II

It was a week later. Philip was sitting on the floor in the drawing-room at Miss Watkin's house in Onslow Gardens. He was an only child and used to amusing himself. The room was filled with massive furniture, and on each of the sofas were three big cushions. There was a cushion too in each armchair. All these he had taken and, with the help of the gilt rout chairs, light and easy to move, had made an elaborate cave in which he could hide himself from the Red Indians who were lurking behind the curtains. He put his ear to the floor and listened to the herd of buffaloes that raced across the prairie. Presently, hearing the door open, he held his breath so that he might not be discovered; but a violent hand pulled away a chair and the cushions fell down.

'You naughty boy, Miss Watkin *will* be cross with you.'

'Hulloa, Emma!' he said.

The nurse bent down and kissed him, then began to shake out the cushions, and put them back in their places.

'Am I to come home?' he asked.

'Yes, I've come to fetch you.'

'You've got a new dress on.'

It was in 1885, and she wore a bustle. Her gown was of black velvet, with tight sleeves and sloping shoulders, and the skirt had three large flounces. She wore a black bonnet with velvet strings. She hesitated. The question she had expected did not come, and so she could not give the answer she had prepared.

'Aren't you going to ask how your mamma is?' she said at length.

'Oh, I forgot. How is mamma?'

Now she was ready.

'Your mamma is quite well and happy.'

'Oh, I am glad.'

'Your mamma's gone away. You won't ever see her any more.'

Philip did not know what she meant.

'Why not?'

'Your mamma's in heaven.'

She began to cry, and Philip, though he did not quite understand, cried too. Emma was a tall, big-boned woman, with fair hair and large features. She came from Devonshire and, notwithstanding her many years of service in London, had never lost the breadth of her accent. Her tears increased her emotion, and she pressed the little boy to her heart. She felt vaguely the pity of that child deprived of the only love in the world that is quite unselfish. It seemed dreadful that he must be handed over to strangers. But in a little while she pulled herself together.

'Your Uncle William is waiting in to see you,' she said. 'Go and say good-bye to Miss Watkin, and we'll go home.'

'I don't want to say good-bye,' he answered, instinctively anxious to hide his tears.

11

'Very well, run upstairs and get your hat.'

He fetched it, and when he came down Emma was waiting for him in the hall. He heard the sound of voices in the study behind the dining-room. He paused. He knew that Miss Watkin and her sister were talking to friends, and it seemed to him – he was nine years old – that if he went in they would be sorry for him.

'I think I'll go and say good-bye to Miss Watkin.'

'I think you'd better,' said Emma.

'Go in and tell them I'm coming,' he said.

He wished to make the most of his opportunity. Emma knocked at the door and walked in. He heard her speak.

'Master Philip wants to say good-bye to you, miss.'

There was a sudden hush of the conversation, and Philip limped in. Henrietta Watkin was a stout woman, with a red face and dyed hair. In those days to dye the hair excited comment, and Philip had heard much gossip at home when his godmother's changed colour. She lived with an elder sister, who had resigned herself contentedly to old age. Two ladies, whom Philip did not know, were calling, and they looked at him curiously.

'My poor child,' said Miss Watkin, opening her arms.

She began to cry. Philip understood now why she had not been in to luncheon and why she wore a black dress. She could not speak.

'I've got to go home,' said Philip, at last.

He disengaged himself from Miss Watkin's arms, and she kissed him again. Then he went to her sister and bade her good-bye too. One of the strange ladies asked if she might kiss him, and he gravely gave her permission. Though crying, he keenly enjoyed the sensation he was causing; he would have been glad to stay a little longer to be made so much of, but felt they expected him to go, so he said that Emma was waiting for him. He went out of the room. Emma had gone downstairs to speak with a friend in the basement, and he waited for her on the landing. He heard Henrietta Watkin's voice.

'His mother was my greatest friend. I can't bear to think that she's dead.'

'You oughtn't to have gone to the funeral, Henrietta,' said her sister. 'I knew it would upset you.'

Then one of the strangers spoke.

'Poor little boy, it's dreadful to think of him quite alone in the world. I see he limps.'

'Yes, he's got a club-foot. It was such a grief to his mother.'

Then Emma came back. They called a hansom, and she told the driver where to go.

III

WHEN they reached the house Mrs Carey had died in – it was in a dreary, respectable street between Notting Hill Gate and High Street, Kensington – Emma led Philip into the drawing-room. His uncle was writing letters of thanks for the wreaths which had been sent. One of them, which had arrived too late for the funeral, lay in its cardboard box on the hall-table.

'Here's Master Philip,' said Emma.

Mr Carey stood up slowly and shook hands with the little boy. Then on second thoughts he bent down and kissed his forehead. He was a man of somewhat less than average height, inclined to corpulence, with his hair, worn long, arranged over the scalp so as to conceal his baldness. He was clean-shaven. His features were regular, and it was possible to imagine that in his youth he had been good-looking. On his watch-chain he wore a gold cross.

'You're going to live with me now, Philip,' said Mr Carey. 'Shall you like that?'

Two years before Philip had been sent down to stay at the vicarage after an attack of chicken-pox; but there remained with him a recollection of an attic and a large garden rather than of his uncle and aunt.

'Yes.'

'You must look upon me and your Aunt Louisa as your father and mother.'

The child's mouth trembled a little, he reddened, but did not answer.

'Your dear mother left you in my charge.'

Mr Carey had no great ease in expressing himself. When the news came that his sister-in-law was dying, he set off at once for London, but on the way thought of nothing but the disturbance in his life that would be caused if her death forced him to undertake the care of her son. He was well over fifty, and his wife, to whom he had been married for thirty years, was childless; he did not look forward with any pleasure to the presence of a small boy who might be noisy and rough. He had never much liked his sister-in-law.

'I'm going to take you down to Blackstable tomorrow,' he said.

'With Emma?'

The child put his hand in hers, and she pressed it.

'I'm afraid Emma must go away,' said Mr Carey.

'But I want Emma to come with me.'

Philip began to cry, and the nurse could not help crying too. Mr Carey looked at them helplessly.

'I think you'd better leave me alone with Master Philip for a moment.'

'Very good, sir.'

Though Philip clung to her, she released herself gently. Mr Carey took the boy on his knee and put his arm round him.

'You mustn't cry,' he said. 'You're too old to have a nurse now. We must see about sending you to school.'

'I want Emma to come with me,' the child repeated.

'It costs too much money, Philip. Your father didn't leave very much, and I don't know what's become of it. You must look at every penny you spend.'

Mr Carey had called the day before on the family solicitor. Philip's father was a surgeon in good practice, and his hospital appointments suggested an established position; so that it was a surprise on his sudden death from blood-poisoning to find that he had left his widow little more than his life insurance and what could be got from the lease of their house in Bruton Street. This was six months ago; and Mrs Carey, already in delicate health, finding herself with child, had lost her head and accepted for the lease the first offer that was made. She stored her furniture, and, at a rent which the parson thought outrageous, took a furnished house for a year, so that she might suffer from no inconvenience till her child was born. But she had never been used to the management of money, and was unable to adapt her expenditure to her altered circumstances. The little she had slipped through her fingers in one way and another, so that now, when all expenses were paid, not much more than two thousand pounds remained to support the boy till he was able to earn his own living. It was impossible to explain all this to Philip and he was sobbing still.

'You'd better go to Emma,' Mr Carey said, feeling that she could console the child better than anyone.

Without a word Philip slipped off his uncle's knee, but Mr Carey stopped him.

'We must go tomorrow, because on Saturday I've got to prepare my sermon, and you must tell Emma to get your things ready today. You can bring all your toys. And if you want anything to remember your father and mother by you can take one thing for each of them. Everything else is going to be sold.'

The boy slipped out of the room. Mr Carey was unused to work, and he turned to his correspondence with resentment. On one side of the desk was a bundle of bills, and these filled him with irritation. One especially seemed preposterous. Immediately after Mrs Carey's death Emma had ordered from the florist masses of white flowers for the room in which the dead woman lay. It was sheer waste of money. Emma took far too much upon herself. Even if there had been no financial necessity, he would have dismissed her.

But Philip went to her, and hid his face in her bosom, and wept as though his heart would break. And she, feeling that he was almost her own son – she had taken him when he was a month old – consoled him with soft words. She promised that she would come and see him sometimes, and that she would never forget him; and she told him about the country he was going to and about her own home in Devonshire – her father kept a turnpike on the high-road that led to Exeter, and there were pigs in the sty, and there was a cow, and the cow had just had a calf – till Philip forgot his tears and grew excited at the thought of his approaching journey. Presently she put him down, for there was much to be done, and he helped her to lay out his clothes on the bed. She sent him into the nursery to gather up his toys, and in a little while he was playing happily.

But at last he grew tired of being alone and went back to the bedroom, in which Emma was now putting his things into a big tin box; he remembered then that his uncle had said that he might take something to remember his father and mother by. He told Emma and asked her what he should take.

'You'd better go into the drawing-room and see what you fancy.'

'Uncle William's there.'

'Never mind that. They're your own things now.'

Philip went downstairs slowly and found the door open. Mr Carey had left the room. Philip walked slowly round. They had been in the house so short a time that there was little in it that had a particular interest to him. It was a stranger's room, and Philip saw nothing that struck his fancy. But he knew which were his mother's things and which belonged to the landlord, and presently fixed on a little clock that he had once heard his mother say she liked. With this he walked again rather disconsolately upstairs. Outside the door of his mother's bedroom he stopped and listened. Though no one had told him not to go in, he had a feeling that it would be wrong to do so; he was a little frightened, and his heart beat uncomfortably; but at the same time something impelled him to turn the handle. He turned it very gently, as if to prevent anyone within from hearing, and then slowly pushed the door open. He stood on the threshold for a moment before he had the courage to enter. He was not frightened now, but it seemed strange. He closed the door behind him. The blinds were drawn, and the room, in the cold light of a January afternoon, was dark. On the dressing-table were Mrs Carey's brushes and the hand mirror. In a little tray were hairpins. There was a photograph of himself on the chimney-piece and one of his father. He had often been in the room when his mother was not in it, but now it seemed different. There was something curious in the look of the chairs. The bed was made as though someone were going to sleep in it that night, and in a case on the pillow was a night-dress.

Philip opened a large cupboard filled with dresses and, stepping in, took as many of them as he could in his arms and buried his face in them. They smelt of the scent his mother used. Then he pulled open the drawers, filled with his mother's things, and looked at them: there were lavender bags among the linen; and their scent was fresh and pleasant. The strangeness of the room left it, and it seemed to him that his mother had just gone out for a walk. She would be in presently and would come upstairs to have nursery tea with him. And he seemed to feel her kiss on his lips.

It was not true that he would never see her again. It was not true simply because it was impossible. He climbed up on the bed and put his head on the pillow. He lay there quite still.

IV

PHILIP parted from Emma with tears, but the journey to Blackstable amused him, and, when they arrived, he was resigned and cheerful. Blackstable was sixty miles from London. Giving their luggage to a porter, Mr Carey set out to walk with Philip to the vicarage; it took them little more than five minutes, and, when they reached it, Philip suddenly remembered the gate. It was red and five-barred; it swung both ways on easy hinges; and it was possible, though forbidden, to swing backwards and forwards on it. They walked through the garden to the front door. This was only used by visitors and on

Sundays, and on special occasions, as when the Vicar went up to London or came back. The traffic of the house took place through a side door, and there was a back door as well for the gardener and for beggars and tramps. It was a fairly large house of yellow brick, with a red roof, built about five-and-twenty years before in an ecclesiastical style. The front door was like a church porch, and the drawing-room windows were Gothic.

Mrs Carey, knowing by what train they were coming, waited in the drawing-room and listened for the click of the gate. When she heard it she went to the door.

'There's Aunt Louisa,' said Mr Carey, when he saw her. 'Run and give her a kiss.'

Philip started to run, awkwardly, trailing his club-foot, and then stopped. Mrs Carey was a little, shrivelled woman of the same age as her husband, with a face extraordinarily filled with deep wrinkles, and pale blue eyes. Her grey hair was arranged in ringlets according to the fashion of her youth. She wore a black dress, and her only ornament was a gold chain, from which hung a cross. She had a shy manner and a gentle voice.

'Did you walk, William?' she said, almost reproachfully, as she kissed her husband.

'I didn't think of it,' he answered, with a glance at his nephew.

'It didn't hurt you to walk, Philip, did it?' she asked the child.

'No. I always walk.'

He was a little surprised at their conversation. Aunt Louisa told him to come in, and they entered the hall. It was paved with red and yellow tiles, on which alternately were a Greek Cross and the Lamb of God. An imposing staircase led out of the hall. It was of polished pine, with a peculiar smell, and had been put in because fortunately, when the church was reseated, enough wood remained over. The balusters were decorated with emblems of the Four Evangelists.

'I've had the stove lighted as I thought you'd be cold after your journey,' said Mrs Carey.

It was a large black stove that stood in the hall and was only lighted if the weather was very bad and the Vicar had a cold. It was not lighted if Mrs Carey had a cold. Coal was expensive. Besides, Mary Ann, the maid, didn't like fires all over the place. If they wanted all them fires they must keep a second girl. In the winter Mr and Mrs Carey lived in the dining-room so that one fire should do, and in the summer they could not get out of the habit, so the drawing-room was used only by Mr Carey on Sunday afternoons for his nap. But every Saturday he had a fire in the study so that he could write his sermon.

Aunt Louisa took Philip upstairs and showed him into a tiny bedroom that looked out on the drive. Immediately in front of the window was a large tree, which Philip remembered now because the branches were so low that it was possible to climb quite high up it.

'A small room for a small boy,' said Mrs Carey. 'You won't be frightened at sleeping alone?'

'Oh, no.'

On his first visit to the vicarage he had come with his nurse, and Mrs Carey had had little to do with him. She looked at him now with some uncertainty.

'Can you wash your own hands, or shall I wash them for you?'

'I can wash myself,' he answered firmly.

'Well, I shall look at them when you come down to tea,' said Mrs Carey.

She knew nothing about children. After it was settled that Philip should come down to Blackstable, Mrs Carey had thought much how she should treat him; she was anxious to do her duty; but now he was there she found herself just as shy of him as he was of her. She hoped he would not be noisy and rough, because her husband did not like rough and noisy boys. Mrs Carey made an excuse to leave Philip alone, but in a moment came back and knocked at the door; she asked him, without coming in, if he could pour out the water himself. Then she went downstairs and rang the bell for tea.

The dining-room, large and well proportioned, had windows on two sides of it, with heavy curtains of red rep; there was a big table in the middle; and at one end an imposing mahogany sideboard with a looking-glass in it. In one corner stood a harmonium. On each side of the fireplace were chairs covered in stamped leather, each with an antimacassar; one had arms and was called the husband, and the other had none and was called the wife. Mrs Carey never sat in the armchair; she said she preferred a chair that was not too comfortable; there was always a lot to do, and if her chair had had arms she might not be so ready to leave it.

Mr Carey was making up the fire when Philip came in, and he pointed out to his nephew that there were two pokers. One was large and bright and polished and unused, and was called the Vicar; and the other, which was much smaller and had evidently passed through many fires, was called the Curate.

'What are we waiting for?' said Mr Carey.

'I told Mary Ann to make you an egg. I thought you'd be hungry after your journey.'

Mrs Carey thought the journey from London to Blackstable very tiring. She seldom travelled herself, for the living was only three hundred a year, and, when her husband wanted a holiday, since there was not money for two, he went by himself. He was very fond of Church Congresses and usually managed to go up to London once a year; and once he had been to Paris for the exhibition, and two or three times to Switzerland. Mary Ann brought in the egg, and they sat down. The chair was much too low for Philip, and for a moment neither Mr Carey nor his wife knew what to do.

'I'll put some books under him,' said Mary Ann.

She took from the top of the harmonium the large Bible and the prayer-book from which the Vicar was accustomed to read prayers, and put them on Philip's chair.

'Oh, William, he can't sit on the Bible,' said Mrs Carey, in a shocked tone. 'Couldn't you get him some books out of the study?'

Mr Carey considered the question for an instant.

'I don't think it matters this once if you put the prayer-book on the top, Mary Ann,' he said. 'The book of Common Prayer is the composition of men like ourselves. It has no claim to divine authorship.'

'I hadn't thought of that, William,' said Aunt Louisa.

Philip perched himself on the books, and the Vicar, having said grace, cut the top off his egg.

'There,' he said, handing it to Philip, 'you can eat my top if you like.'

Philip would have liked an egg to himself, but he was not offered one, so took what he could.

'How have the chickens been laying since I went away?' asked the Vicar.

'Oh, they've been dreadful, only one or two a day.'

'How did you like that top, Philip?' asked his uncle.

'Very much, thank you.'

'You shall have another one on Sunday afternoon.'

Mr Carey always had a boiled egg at tea on Sunday, so that he might be fortified for the evening service.

V

PHILIP came gradually to know the people he was to live with, and by fragments of conversation, some of it not meant for his ears, learned a good deal both about himself and about his dead parents. Philip's father had been much younger than the Vicar of Blackstable. After a brilliant career at St Luke's Hospital he was put on the staff, and presently began to earn money in considerable sums. He spent it freely. When the parson set about restoring his church and asked his brother for a subscription, he was surprised by receiving a couple of hundred pounds: Mr Carey, thrifty by inclination and economical by necessity, accepted it with mingled feelings; he was envious of his brother because he could afford to give so much, pleased for the sake of his church, and vaguely irritated by a generosity which seemed almost ostentatious. Then Henry Carey married a patient, a beautiful girl but penniless, an orphan with no near relations, but of good family; and there was an array of fine friends at the wedding. The parson, on his visits to her when he came to London, held himself with reserve. He felt shy with her and in his heart he resented her great beauty: she dressed more magnificently than became the wife of a hardworking surgeon; and the charming furniture of her house, the flowers among which she lived even in winter, suggested an extravagance which he deplored. He heard her talk of entertainments she was going to; and, as he told his wife on getting home again, it was impossible to accept hospitality without making some return. He had seen grapes in the dining-room that must have cost at least eight shillings a pound; and at luncheon he had been given asparagus two months before it was ready in the vicarage garden. Now all he had anticipated was come to pass; the Vicar felt the satisfaction of the prophet who saw fire and brimstone consume the city which would not mend its way to his warning. Poor Philip was practically penniless, and what was the good of his mother's fine friends now? He heard that his father's extravagance was really criminal, and it was a mercy that Providence had seen fit to take his dear mother to itself: she had no more idea of money than a child.

When Philip had been a week at Blackstable an incident happened which seemed to irritate his uncle very much. One morning he found on the breakfast table a small packet which had been sent on by post from the late Mrs Carey's house in London. It was addressed to her. When the parson opened it he found a dozen photographs of Mrs Carey. They showed the head and shoulders only, and her hair was more plainly done than usual, low on the forehead, which gave her an unusual look; the face was thin and worn, but no illness could impair the beauty of her features. There was in the large dark eyes a sadness which Philip did not remember. The first sight of the dead woman gave Mr Carey a little shock, but this was quickly followed by perplexity. The photographs seemed quite recent, and he could not imagine who had ordered them.

'D'you know anything about these, Philip?' he asked.

'I remember mamma said she'd been taken,' he answered. 'Miss Watkin scolded her. ... She said: I wanted the boy to have something to remember me by when he grows up.'

Mr Carey looked at Philip for an instant. The child spoke in a clear treble. He recalled the words, but they meant nothing to him.

'You'd better take one of the photographs and keep it in your room,' said Mr Carey. 'I'll put the others away.'

He sent one to Miss Watkin, and she wrote and explained how they came to be taken.

One day Mrs Carey was lying in bed, but she was feeling a little better than usual, and the doctor in the morning had seemed hopeful; Emma had taken the child out, and the maids were downstairs in the basement; suddenly Mrs Carey felt desperately alone in the world. A great fear seized her that she would not recover from the confinement which she was expecting in a fortnight. Her son was nine years old. How could he be expected to remember her? She could not bear to think that he would grow up and forget, forget her utterly; and she had loved him so passionately, because he was weakly and deformed, and because he was her child. She had no photographs of herself taken since her marriage, and that was ten years before. She wanted her son to know what she looked like at the end. He could not forget her then, not forget utterly. She knew that if she called her maid and told her she wanted to get up, the maid would prevent her, and perhaps send for the doctor, and she had not the strength now to struggle or argue. She got out of bed and began to dress herself. She had been on her back so long that her legs gave way beneath her, and then the soles of her feet tingled so that she could hardly bear to put them to the ground. But she went on. She was unused to doing her own hair and, when she raised her arms and began to brush it, she felt faint. She could never do it as her maid did. It was beautiful hair, very fine, and of a deep rich gold. Her eyebrows were straight and dark. She put on a black skirt, but chose the bodice of the evening dress which she liked best: it was of white damask which was fashionable in those days. She looked at herself in the glass. Her face was very pale, but her skin was clear: she had never had much colour, and this had always made the redness of her beautiful mouth emphatic. She could not restrain a sob. But she could not afford to be sorry for herself; she was feeling already desperately tired; and she put on the furs which Henry had given her the Christmas before – she had been so proud of them and so happy then – and slipped downstairs with beating heart. She got safely out of the house and drove to a photographer. She paid for a dozen photographs. She was obliged to ask for a glass of water in the middle of the sitting; and the assistant, seeing she was ill, suggested that she should come another day, but she insisted on staying till the end. At last it was finished, and she drove back again to the dingy little house in Kensington which she hated with all her heart. It was a horrible house to die in.

She found the front door open, and when she drove up the maid and Emma ran down the steps to help her. They had been frightened when they found her room empty. At first they thought she must have gone to Miss Watkin, and the cook was sent round. Miss Watkin came back with her and was waiting anxiously in the drawing-room. She came downstairs now full of anxiety and reproaches; but the exertion had been more than Mrs Carey was fit for, and when the occasion for firmness no longer existed she gave way. She fell heavily into Emma's arms and was carried upstairs. She remained unconscious for a time that seemed incredibly long to those that watched her, and the doctor, hurriedly sent for, did not come. It was next day, when she was a little better, that Miss Watkin got some explanation out of her. Philip was playing on the floor of his mother's bedroom, and neither of the ladies paid attention to him. He only understood vaguely what they were talking about, and he could not have said why those words remained in his memory.

'I wanted the boy to have something to remember me by when he grows up.'

'I can't make out why she ordered a dozen,' said Mr Carey. 'Two would have done.'

22

VI

ONE day was very like another at the vicarage.

Soon after breakfast Mary Ann brought in *The Times*. Mr Carey shared it with two neighbours. He had it from ten till one, when the gardener took it over to Mr Ellis at the Limes, with whom it remained till seven; then it was taken to Miss Brooks at the Manor House, who, since she got it late, had the advantage of keeping it. In summer Mrs Carey, when she was making jam, often asked her for a copy to cover the pots with. When the Vicar settled down to his paper his wife put on her bonnet and went out to do the shopping. Philip accompanied her. Blackstable was a fishing village. It consisted of a high street in which were the shops, the bank, the doctor's house, and the houses of two or three coalship owners; round the little harbour were shabby streets in which lived fishermen and poor people; but since they went to chapel they were of no account. When Mrs Carey passed the dissenting ministers in the street she stepped over to the other side to avoid meeting them, but if there was not time for this fixed her eyes on the pavement. It was a scandal to which the Vicar had never resigned himself that there were three chapels in the High Street: he could not help feeling that the law should have stepped in to prevent their erection. Shopping in Blackstable was not a simple matter; for dissent, helped by the fact that the parish church was two miles from the town, was very common; and it was necessary to deal only with churchgoers; Mrs Carey knew perfectly that the vicarage custom might make all the difference to a tradesman's faith. There were two butchers who went to church, and they would not understand that the Vicar could not deal with both of them at once; nor were they satisfied with his simple plan of going for six months to one and for six months to the other. The butcher who was not sending meat to the vicarage constantly threatened not to come to church, and the Vicar was sometimes obliged to make a threat: it was very wrong of him not to come to church, but if he carried iniquity further and actually went to chapel, then of course, excellent as his meat was, Mr Carey would be forced to leave him for ever. Mrs Carey often stopped at the bank to deliver a message to Josiah Graves, the manager, who was choir-master, treasurer, and churchwarden. He was a tall, thin man with a sallow face and a long nose; his hair was very white, and to Philip he seemed extremely old. He kept the parish accounts, arranged the treats for the choir and the schools; though there was no organ in the parish church, it was generally considered (in Blackstable) that the choir he led was the best in Kent; and when there was any ceremony, such as a visit from the Bishop for confirmation or from the Rural Dean to preach at the Harvest Thanksgiving, he made the necessary preparations. But he had no hesitation in doing all manner of things without more than a perfunctory consultation with the Vicar, and the Vicar, though always ready to be saved trouble, much resented the churchwarden's managing ways. He really seemed to look upon himself as the most important person in the parish. Mr Carey constantly told his wife that if Josiah Graves did not take care he would give him a good rap over the knuckles one day; but Mrs Carey advised him to bear with Josiah Graves: he meant well, and it was not his fault if he was not quite a gentleman. The Vicar, finding his comfort in the practice of a Christian virtue, exercised forbearance; but he revenged himself by calling the churchwarden Bismarck behind his back.

Once there had been a serious quarrel between the pair, and Mrs Carey still thought of that anxious time with dismay. The Conservative candidate had announced his intention of addressing a meeting at Blackstable; and Josiah Graves, having arranged that it should take place in the Mission Hall, went to Mr Carey and told him that he hoped he would say a few words. It appeared that the candidate had asked Josiah Graves to take the chair. This was more than Mr Carey could put up with. He had firm views upon the respect which was due to the cloth, and it was ridiculous for a churchwarden to take the chair at a meeting when the Vicar was there. He reminded Josiah Graves that parson meant person, that is, the vicar was the person of the parish. Josiah Graves answered that he was the first to recognize the dignity of the church, but this was a matter of politics, and in his turn he reminded the Vicar that their Blessed Saviour had enjoined upon them to render unto Caesar the things that were Caesar's. To this Mr Carey replied that the devil could quote scripture to his purpose, himself had sole authority over the Mission Hall, and if he were not asked to be chairman he would refuse the use of it for a political meeting. Josiah Graves told Mr Carey that he might do as he chose, and for his part he thought the Wesleyan Chapel would be an equally suitable place. Then Mr Carey said that if Josiah Graves set foot in what was little better than a heathen temple he was not fit to be churchwarden in a Christian parish. Josiah Graves thereupon resigned all his offices, and that very evening sent to the church for his cassock and surplice. His sister, Miss Graves, who kept house for him, gave up her secretaryship of the Maternity Club, which provided the pregnant poor with flannel, baby linen, coals, and five shillings. Mr Carey said he was at last master in his own house. But soon he found that he was obliged to see to all sorts of things that he knew nothing about; and Josiah Graves, after the first moment of irritation, discovered that he had lost his chief interest in life. Mrs Carey and Miss Graves were much distressed by the quarrel; they met after a discreet exchange of letters, and made up their minds to put the matter right: they talked, one to her husband, the other to her brother, from morning till night; and since they were persuading these gentlemen to do what in their hearts they wanted, after three weeks of anxiety a reconciliation was effected. It was to both their interests, but they ascribed it to a common love for their Redeemer. The meeting was held at the Mission Hall, and the doctor was asked to be chairman. Mr Carey and Josiah Graves both made speeches.

When Mrs Carey had finished her business with the banker, she generally went upstairs to have a little chat with his sister; and while the ladies talked of parish matters, the curate, or the new bonnet of Mrs Wilson – Mr Wilson was the richest man in Blackstable, he was thought to have at least five hundred a year, and he had married his cook – Philip sat demurely in the stiff parlour, used only to receive visitors, and busied himself with the restless movements of goldfish in a bowl. The windows were never opened except to air the room for a few minutes in the morning, and it had a stuffy smell which seemed to Philip to have a mysterious connexion with banking.

Then Mrs Carey remembered that she had to go to the grocer, and they continued on their way. When the shopping was done they often went down a side street of little houses, mostly of wood, in which fishermen dwelt (and here and there a fisherman sat on his doorstep mending his nets, and nets hung to dry upon the doors), till they came to a small beach, shut in on each side by warehouses, but with a view of the sea. Mrs Carey stood for a few minutes and looked at it, it was turbid and yellow (and who knows what thoughts passed through her mind?), while Philip searched for flat stones to play ducks and drakes. Then they walked slowly back. They looked into the post office to get the right time, nodded to

Mrs Wigram the doctor's wife, who sat at her window sewing, and so got home.

Dinner was at one o'clock; and on Monday, Tuesday, and Wednesday it consisted of beef, roast, hashed, and minced, and on Thursday, Friday, and Saturday of mutton. On Sunday they ate one of their own chickens. In the afternoon Philip did his lessons. He was taught Latin and mathematics by his uncle who knew neither, and French and the piano by his aunt. Of French she was ignorant, but she knew the piano well enough to accompany the old-fashioned songs she had sung for thirty years. Uncle William used to tell Philip that when he was a curate his wife had known twelve songs by heart, which she could sing at a moment's notice whenever she was asked. She often sang still when there was a tea-party at the vicarage. There were few people whom the Careys cared to ask there, and their parties consisted always of the curate, Josiah Graves with his sister, Dr Wigram and his wife. After tea Miss Graves played one or two of Mendelssohn's *Songs without Words*, and Mrs Carey sang *When the Swallows Homeward Fly*, or *Trot, Trot, My Pony*.

But the Careys did not give tea-parties often; the preparations upset them, and when their guests were gone they felt themselves exhausted. They preferred to have tea by themselves, and after tea they played backgammon. Mrs Carey arranged that her husband should win, because he did not like losing. They had cold supper at eight. It was a scrappy meal because Mary Ann resented getting anything ready after tea, and Mrs Carey helped to clear away. Mrs Carey seldom ate more than bread and butter, with a little stewed fruit to follow, but the Vicar had a slice of cold meat. Immediately after supper Mrs Carey rang the bell for prayers, and then Philip went to bed. He rebelled against being undressed by Mary Ann and after a while succeeded in establishing his right to dress and undress himself. At nine o'clock Mary Ann brought in the eggs and the plate. Mrs Carey wrote the date on each egg and put the number down in a book. She then took the plate-basket on her arm and went upstairs. Mr Carey continued to read one of his old books, but as the clock struck ten he got up, put out the lamps, and followed his wife to bed.

When Philip arrived there was some difficulty in deciding on which evening he should have his bath. It was never easy to get plenty of hot water, since the kitchen boiler did not work, and it was impossible for two persons to have a bath on the same day. The only man who had a bathroom in Blackstable was Mr Wilson, and it was thought ostentatious of him. Mary Ann had her bath in the kitchen on Monday night, because she liked to begin the week clean. Uncle William could not have his on Saturday, because he had a heavy day before him and he was always a little tired after a bath, so he had it on Friday. Mrs Carey had hers on Thursday for the same reason. It looked as though Saturday were naturally indicated for Philip, but Mary Ann said she couldn't keep the fire up on Saturday night: what with all the cooking on Sunday, having to make pastry and she didn't know what all, she did not feel up to giving the boy his bath on Saturday night; and it was quite clear that he could not bath himself. Mrs Carey was shy about bathing a boy, and of course the Vicar had his sermon. But the Vicar insisted that Philip should be clean and sweet for the Lord's Day. Mary Ann said she would rather go than be put upon – and after eighteen years she didn't expect to have more work given her, and they might show some consideration – and Philip said he didn't want anyone to bath him, but could very well bath himself. This settled it. Mary Ann said she was quite sure he wouldn't bath himself properly, and rather than he should go dirty – and not because he was going into the presence of the Lord, but because she couldn't abide a boy who wasn't properly washed – she'd work herself to the bone even if it was Saturday night.

VII

SUNDAY was a day crowded with incident. Mr Carey was accustomed to say that he was the only man in his parish who worked seven days a week.

The household got up half an hour earlier than usual. No lying abed for a poor parson on the day of rest, Mr Carey remarked as Mary Ann knocked at the door punctually at eight. It took Mrs Carey longer to dress, and she got down to breakfast at nine, a little breathless, only just before her husband. Mr Carey's boots stood in front of the fire to warm. Prayers were longer than usual, and the breakfast more substantial. After breakfast the Vicar cut thin slices of bread for the communion, and Philip was privileged to cut off the crust. He was sent to the study to fetch a marble paperweight, with which Mr Carey pressed the bread till it was thin and pulpy, and then it was cut into small squares. The amount was regulated by the weather. On a very bad day few people came to church, and on a very fine one, though many came, few stayed for communion. There were most when it was dry enough to make the walk to church pleasant, but not so fine that people wanted to hurry away.

Then Mrs Carey brought the communion plate out of the safe, which stood in the pantry, and the Vicar polished it with a chamois leather. At ten the fly drove up, and Mr Carey got into his boots. Mrs Carey took several minutes to put on her bonnet, during which the Vicar, in a voluminous cloak, stood in the hall with just such an expression on his face as would have become an early Christian about to be led into the arena. It was extraordinary that after thirty years of marriage his wife could not be ready in time on Sunday morning. At last she came, in black satin; the Vicar did not like colours in a clergyman's wife at any time, but on Sundays he was determined that she should wear black; now and then, in conspiracy with Miss Graves, she ventured a white feather or a pink rose in her bonnet, but the Vicar insisted that it should disappear; he said he would not go to church with the scarlet woman: Mrs Carey sighed as a woman but obeyed as a wife. They were about to step into the carriage when the Vicar remembered that no one had given him his egg. They knew that he must have an egg for his voice, there were two women in the house, and no one had the least regard for his comfort. Mrs Carey scolded Mary Ann, and Mary Ann answered that she could not think of everything. She hurried away to fetch an egg, and Mrs Carey beat it up in a glass of sherry. The Vicar swallowed it at a gulp. The communion plate was stowed in the carriage, and they set off.

The fly came from *The Red Lion* and had a peculiar smell of stale straw. They drove with both windows closed so that the Vicar should not catch cold. The sexton was waiting at the porch to take the communion plate, and while the Vicar went to the vestry Mrs Carey and Philip settled themselves in the vicarage pew. Mrs Carey placed in front of her the sixpenny bit she was accustomed to put in the plate, and gave Philip threepence for the same purpose. The church filled up gradually and the service began.

Philip grew bored during the sermon, but if he fidgeted Mrs Carey put a gentle hand on his arm and looked at him reproachfully. He regained interest when the final hymn was sung and Mr Graves passed round with the plate.

When everyone had gone Mrs Carey went into Miss Graves's pew to have a few words with her while they were waiting for the gentlemen, and Philip went to the vestry. His uncle, the curate, and Mr Graves were still in their surplices. Mr Carey gave him the remains of the consecrated bread and told him he might eat it. He had been accustomed to eat it himself, as it seemed blasphemous to throw it away, but Philip's keen appetite relieved him from the duty. Then they counted the money. It consisted of pennies, sixpences, and threepenny bits. There were always two single shillings, one put in the plate by the Vicar and the other by Mr Graves; and sometimes there was a florin. Mr Graves told the Vicar who had given this. It was always a stranger to Blackstable, and Mr Carey wondered who he was. But Miss Graves had observed the rash act and was able to tell Mrs Carey that the stranger came from London, was married, and had children. During the drive home Mrs Carey passed the information on, and the Vicar made up his mind to call on him and ask for a subscription to the Additional Curates Society. Mr Carey asked if Philip had behaved properly; and Mrs Carey remarked that Mrs Wigram had a new mantle, Mr Cox was not in church, and somebody thought that Miss Phillips was engaged. When they reached the vicarage they all felt that they deserved a substantial dinner.

When this was over Mrs Carey went to her room to rest, and Mr Carey lay down on the sofa in the drawing-room for forty winks.

They had tea at five, and the Vicar ate an egg to support himself for evensong. Mrs Carey did not go to this so that Mary Ann might, but she read the service through and the hymns. Mr Carey walked to church in the evening, and Philip limped along by his side. The walk through the darkness along the country road strangely impressed him, and the church with all its lights in the distance, coming gradually nearer, seemed very friendly. At first he was shy with his uncle, but little by little grew used to him, and he would slip his hand in his uncle's and walk more easily for the feeling of protection.

They had supper when they got home. Mr Carey's slippers were waiting for him on a footstool in front of the fire, and by their side Philip's, one the shoe of a small boy, the other misshapen and odd. He was dreadfully tired when he went up to bed, and he did not resist when Mary Ann undressed him. She kissed him after she tucked him up, and he began to love her.

VIII

PHILIP had led always the solitary life of an only child, and his loneliness at the vicarage was no greater than it had been when his mother lived. He made friends with Mary Ann. She was a chubby little person of thirty-five, the daughter of a fisherman, and had come to the vicarage at eighteen; it was her first place and she had no intention of leaving it; but she held a possible marriage as a rod over the timid heads of her master and mistress. Her father and mother lived in a little house off Harbour Street, and she went to see them on her evenings out. Her stories of the sea touched Philip's imagination, and the narrow alleys round the harbour grew rich with the romance which his young fancy lent them. One evening he asked whether he might go home with her; but his aunt was afraid that he might catch something, and his uncle said that evil communications corrupted good manners. He disliked the fisher folk, who were rough, uncouth, and went to chapel. But Philip was more comfortable in the kitchen than in the dining-room, and, whenever he could, he took his toys and played there. His aunt was not sorry. She did not like disorder, and though she recognized that boys must be expected to be untidy she preferred that he should make a mess in the kitchen. If he fidgeted his uncle was apt to grow restless and say it was high time he went to school. Mrs Carey thought Philip very young for this, and her heart went out to the motherless child; but her attempts to gain his affection were awkward, and the boy, feeling shy, received her demonstrations with so much sullenness that she was mortified. Sometimes she heard his shrill voice raised in laughter in the kitchen, but when she went in, he grew suddenly silent, and he flushed darkly when Mary Ann explained the joke. Mrs Carey could not see anything amusing in what she heard, and she smiled with constraint.

'He seems happier with Mary Ann than with us, William,' she said, when she returned to her sewing.

'One can see he's been very badly brought up. He wants licking into shape.'

On the second Sunday after Philip arrived an unlucky incident occurred. Mr Carey had retired as usual after dinner for a little snooze in the drawing-room, but he was in an irritable mood and could not sleep. Josiah Graves that morning had objected strongly to some candlesticks with which the Vicar had

adorned the altar. He had bought them second-hand in Tercanbury, and he thought they looked very well. But Josiah Graves
said they were popish. This was a taunt that always aroused the
Vicar. He had been at Oxford during the movement which
ended in the secession from the Established Church of Edward
Manning, and he felt a certain sympathy for the Church of
Rome. He would willingly have made the service more ornate
than had been usual in the low-church parish of Blackstable,
and in his secret soul he yearned for processions and lighted
candles. He drew the line at incense. He hated the word protestant. He called himself a Catholic. He was accustomed to say
that Papists required an epithet, they were Roman Catholic;
but the Church of England was Catholic in the best, the fullest,
and the noblest sense of the term. He was pleased to think that
his shaven face gave him the look of a priest, and in his youth
he had possessed an ascetic air which added to the impression.
He often related that on one of his holidays in Boulogne, one
of those holidays upon which his wife for economy's sake did
not accompany him, when he was sitting in a church, the *curé*
had come up to him and invited him to preach a sermon. He
dismissed his curates when they married, having decided views
on the celibacy of the unbeneficed clergy. But when at an election the Liberals had written on his garden fence in large blue
letters: *This way to Rome,* he had been very angry, and threatened to prosecute the leaders of the Liberal party in Blackstable.
He made up his mind now that nothing Josiah Graves said
would induce him to remove the candlesticks from the altar,
and he muttered Bismarck to himself once or twice irritably.

Suddenly he heard an unexpected noise. He pulled the handkerchief off his face, got up from the sofa on which he was
lying, and went into the dining-room. Philip was seated on the
table with all his bricks around him. He had built a monstrous
castle, and some defect in the foundation had just brought the
structure down in noisy ruin.

'What are you doing with those bricks, Philip? You know
you're not allowed to play games on Sunday.'

Philip stared at him for a moment with frightened eyes, and,
as his habit was, flushed deeply.

'I always used to play at home,' he answered.

'I'm sure your dear mamma never allowed you to do such
a wicked thing as that.'

Philip did not know it was wicked; but if it was, he did not
wish it to be supposed that his mother had consented to it.
He hung his head and did not answer.

'Don't you know it's very, very wicked to play on Sunday? What d'you suppose it's called the day of rest for? You're going to church tonight, and how can you face your Maker when you've been breaking one of His laws in the afternoon?'

Mr Carey told him to put the bricks away at once, and stood over him while Philip did so.

'You're a very naughty boy,' he repeated. 'Think of the grief you're causing your poor mother in heaven.'

Philip felt inclined to cry, but he had an instinctive disinclination to letting other people see his tears, and he clenched his teeth to prevent the sobs from escaping. Mr Carey sat down in his armchair and began to turn over the pages of a book. Philip stood at the window. The vicarage was set back from the high road to Tercanbury, and from the dining-room one saw a semi-circular strip of lawn and then as far as the horizon green fields. Sheep were grazing in them. The sky was forlorn and grey. Philip felt infinitely unhappy.

Presently Mary Ann came in to lay the tea, and Aunt Louisa descended the stairs.

'Have you had a nice little nap, William?' she asked.

'No,' he answered. 'Philip made so much noise that I couldn't sleep a wink.'

This was not quite accurate, for he had been kept awake by his own thoughts; and Philip, listening sullenly, reflected that he had only made a noise once, and there was no reason why his uncle should not have slept before or after. When Mrs Carey asked for an explanation the Vicar narrated the facts.

'He hasn't even said he was sorry,' he finished.

'Oh, Philip, I'm sure you're sorry,' said Mrs Carey, anxious that the child should not seem wickeder to his uncle than need be.

Philip did not reply. He went on munching his bread and butter. He did not know what power it was in him that prevented him from making any expression of regret. He felt his ears tingling, he was a little inclined to cry, but no word would issue from his lips.

'You needn't make it worse by sulking,' said Mr Carey.

Tea was finished in silence. Mrs Carey looked at Philip surreptitiously now and then, but the Vicar elaborately ignored him. When Philip saw his uncle go upstairs to get ready for church he went into the hall and got his hat and coat, but when the Vicar came downstairs and saw him, he said:

'I don't wish you to go to church tonight, Philip. I don't think you're in a proper frame of mind to enter the House of God.'

Philip did not say a word. He felt it was a deep humiliation that was placed upon him, and his cheeks reddened. He stood silently watching his uncle put on his broad hat and his voluminous cloak. Mrs Carey as usual went to the door to see him off. Then she turned to Philip.

'Never mind, Philip, you won't be a naughty boy next Sunday, will you, and then your uncle will take you to church with him in the evening.'

She took off his hat and coat, and led him into the dining-room.

'Shall you and I read the service together, Philip, and we'll sing the hymns at the harmonium. Would you like that?'

Philip shook his head decidedly. Mrs Carey was taken aback. If he would not read the evening service with her, she did not know what to do with him.

'Then what would you like to do until your uncle comes back?' she asked helplessly.

Philip broke his silence at last.

'I want to be left alone,' he said.

'Philip, how can you say anything so unkind? Don't you know that your uncle and I only want your good? Don't you love me at all?'

'I hate you. I wish you was dead.'

Mrs Carey gasped. He said the words so savagely that it gave her quite a start. She had nothing to say. She sat down in her husband's chair; and as she thought of her desire to love the friendless, crippled boy and her eager wish that he should love her – she was a barren woman and, even though it was clearly God's will that she should be childless, she could scarcely bear to look at little children sometimes, her heart ached so – the tears rose to her eyes and one by one, slowly, rolled down her cheeks. Philip watched her in amazement. She took out her handkerchief, and now she cried without restraint. Suddenly Philip realized that she was crying because of what he had said, and he was sorry. He went up to her silently and kissed her. It was the first kiss he had ever given her without being asked. And the poor lady, so small in her black satin, shrivelled up and sallow, with her funny corkscrew curls, took the little boy on her lap and put her arms around him and wept as though her heart would break. But her tears were partly tears of happiness, for she felt that the strangeness between them was gone. She loved him now with a new love because he had made her suffer.

IX

ON the following Sunday, when the Vicar was making his preparations to go into the drawing-room for his nap – all the actions of his life were conducted with ceremony – and Mrs Carey was about to go upstairs, Philip asked:

'What shall I do if I'm not allowed to play?'

'Can't you sit still for once and be quiet?'

'I can't sit still till tea-time.'

Mr Carey looked out of the window, but it was cold and raw, and he could not suggest that Philip should go into the garden.

'I know what you can do. You can learn by heart the collect for the day.'

He took the prayer-book which was used for prayers from the harmonium, and turned the pages till he came to the place he wanted.

'It's not a long one. If you can say it without a mistake when I come in to tea you shall have the top of my egg.'

Mrs Carey drew up Philip's chair to the dining-room table – they had bought him a high chair by now – and placed the book in front of him.

'The devil finds work for idle hands to do,' said Mr Carey.

He put some more coals on the fire so that there should be a cheerful blaze when he came in to tea, and went into the drawing-room. He loosened his collar, arranged the cushions, and settled himself comfortably on the sofa. But thinking the drawing-room a little chilly, Mrs Carey brought him a rug from the hall; she put it over his legs and tucked it round his feet. She drew the blinds so that the light should not offend his eyes, and since he had closed them already went out of the room on tiptoe. The Vicar was at peace with himself today, and in ten minutes he was asleep. He snored softly.

It was the Sixth Sunday after Epiphany, and the collect began with the words: *O God, whose blessed Son was manifested that he might destroy the works of the devil, and make us the sons of God, and heirs of Eternal life.* Philip read it through. He could make no sense of it. He began saying the words aloud to himself, but many of them were unknown to him, and the construction of the sentences was strange. He could not get more than two lines in his head. And his attention was constantly wandering: there were fruit trees trained on the walls of the vicarage, and a long twig beat now and then against the windowpane; sheep grazed stolidly in the field beyond the garden. It seemed as though there were knots inside his brain. Then panic seized him that he would not know the words by tea-time, and he kept on whispering them to himself quickly; he did not try to understand, but merely to get them parrot-like into his memory.

Mrs Carey could not sleep that afternoon, and by four o'clock she was so wide awake that she came downstairs. She thought she would hear Philip say his collect so that he should make no mistakes when he said it to his uncle. His uncle then would be pleased; he would see that the boy's heart was in the right place. But when Mrs Carey came to the dining-room and was about to go in, she heard a sound that made her stop suddenly. Her heart gave a little jump. She turned away and quietly slipped out of the front door. She walked round the house till she came to the dining-room window and then cautiously looked in. Philip was still sitting on the chair she had put him in, but his head was on the table buried in his arms, and he was sobbing desperately. She saw the convulsive movement of his shoulders. Mrs Carey was frightened. A thing that had always struck her about the child was that he seemed so collected. She had never seen him cry. And now she realized that his calmness was some instinctive shame of showing his feelings: he hid himself to weep.

Without thinking that her husband disliked being wakened suddenly, she burst into the drawing-room.

'William, William,' she said. 'The boy's crying as though his heart would break.'

Mr Carey sat up and disentangled himself from the rug about his legs.

'What's he got to cry about?'

'I don't know. ... Oh, William, we can't let the boy be unhappy. D'you think it's our fault? If we'd had children we'd have known what to do.'

Mr Carey looked at her in perplexity. He felt extraordinarily helpless.

'He can't be crying because I gave him the collect to learn. It's not more than ten lines.'

'Don't you think I might take him some picture books to look at, William? There are some of the Holy Land. There couldn't be anything wrong in that.'

'Very well, I don't mind.'

Mrs Carey went into the study. To collect books was Mr Carey's only passion, and he never went into Tercanbury without spending an hour or two in the second-hand shop; he always brought back four or five musty volumes. He never read them, for he had long lost the habit of reading, but he liked to turn the pages, look at the illustrations if they were illustrated, and mend the bindings. He welcomed wet days because on them he could stay at home without pangs of conscience and spend the afternoon with white of egg and a glue-pot, patching up the Russia leather of some battered quarto. He had many volumes of old travels, with steel-engravings, and Mrs Carey quickly found two which described Palestine. She coughed elaborately at the door so that Philip should have time to compose himself; she felt that he would be humiliated if she came upon him in the midst of his tears; then she rattled the door handle. When she went in Philip was poring over the prayer-book, hiding his eyes with his hands so that she might not see he had been crying.

'Do you know the collect yet?' she said.

He did not answer for a moment, and she felt that he did not trust his voice. She was oddly embarrassed.

'I can't learn it by heart,' he said at last, with a gasp.

'Oh, well, never mind,' she said. 'You needn't. I've got some picture books for you to look at. Come and sit on my lap, and we'll look at them together.'

Philip slipped off his chair and limped over to her. He looked down so that she should not see his eyes. She put her arms round him.

'Look,' she said, 'that's the place where our Blessed Lord was born.'

She showed him an Eastern town with flat roofs and cupolas and minarets. In the foreground was a group of palm-trees, and under them were resting two Arabs and some camels. Philip passed his hand over the picture as if he wanted to feel the houses and the loose habiliments of the nomads.

'Read what it says,' he asked.

Mrs Carey in her even voice read the opposite page. It was a romantic narrative of some Eastern traveller of the thirties, pompous maybe, but fragrant with the emotion with which the East came to the generation that followed Byron and Chateaubriand. In a moment or two Philip interrupted her.

'I want to see another picture.'

When Mary Ann came in and Mrs Carey rose to help her

lay the cloth, Philip took the book in his hands and hurried through the illustrations. It was with difficulty that his aunt induced him to put the book down for tea. He had forgotten his horrible struggle to get the collect by heart; he had forgotten his tears. Next day it was raining, and he asked for the book again. Mrs Carey gave it him joyfully. Talking over his future with her husband she had found that both desired him to take orders, and this eagerness for the book which described places hallowed by the presence of Jesus seemed a good sign. It looked as though the boy's mind addressed itself naturally to holy things. But in a day or two he asked for more books. Mr Carey took him into his study, showed him the shelf in which he kept illustrated works, and chose for him one that dealt with Rome. Philip took it greedily. The pictures led him to a new amusement. He began to read the page before and the page after each engraving to find out what it was about, and soon he lost all interest in his toys.

Then, when no one was near, he took out books for himself; and perhaps because the first impression on his mind was made by an Eastern town, he found his chief amusement in those which described the Levant. His heart beat with excitement at the pictures of mosques and rich palaces; but there was one, in a book on Constantinople, which peculiarly stirred his imagination. It was called the Hall of the Thousand Columns. It was a Byzantine cistern, which the popular fancy had endowed with fantastic vastness; and the legend which he read told that a boat was always moored at the entrance to tempt the unwary, but no traveller venturing into the darkness had ever been seen again. And Philip wondered whether the boat went on for ever through one pillared alley after another or came at last to some strange mansion.

One day a good fortune befell him, for he hit upon Lane's translation of *The Thousand Nights and a Night*. He was captured first by the illustrations, and then he began to read, to start with, the stories that dealt with magic, and then the others; and those he liked he read again and again. He could think of nothing else. He forgot the life about him. He had to be called two or three times before he would come to his dinner. Insensibly he formed the most delightful habit in the world, the habit of reading: he did not know that thus he was providing himself with a refuge from all the distress of life; he did not know either that he was creating for himself an unreal world which would make the real world of every day a source of bitter disappointment. Presently he began to read other things. His brain was precocious. His uncle and aunt, seeing that he occupied himself and neither worried nor made a noise, ceased to trouble themselves about him. Mr Carey had so many books that he did not know them, and as he read little he forgot the odd lots he had bought at one time and another because they were cheap. Haphazard among the sermons and homilies, the travels, the lives of the Saints, the Fathers, the histories of the church, were old-fashioned novels; and these Philip at last discovered. He chose them by their titles, and the first he read was *The Lancashire Witches*, and then he read *The Admirable Crichton*, and then many more. Whenever he started a book with two solitary travellers riding along the brink of a desperate ravine he knew he was safe.

The summer was come now, and the gardener, an old sailor, made him a hammock and fixed it up for him in the branches of a weeping willow. And here for long hours he lay, hidden from anyone who might come to the vicarage, reading, reading passionately. Time passed and it was July; August came: on Sundays the church was crowded with strangers, and the collection at the offertory often amounted to two pounds. Neither the Vicar nor Mrs Carey went out of the garden much during this period; for they disliked strange faces, and they looked upon the visitors from London with aversion. The house opposite was taken for six weeks by a gentleman who had two little boys, and he sent in to ask if Philip would like to go and play with them; but Mrs Carey returned a polite refusal. She was afraid that Philip would be corrupted by little boys from London. He was going to be a clergyman, and it was necessary that he should be preserved from contamination. She liked to see in him an infant Samuel.

X

THE Careys made up their minds to send Philip to King's School at Tercanbury. The neighbouring clergy sent their sons there. It was united by long tradition to the Cathedral: its headmaster was an honorary Canon, and a past headmaster was the Archdeacon. Boys were encouraged there to aspire to Holy Orders, and the education was such as might prepare an honest lad to spend his life in God's service. A preparatory school was attached to it, and to this it was arranged that Philip should go. Mr Carey took him into Tercanbury one Thursday afternoon towards the end of September. All day

Philip had been excited and rather frightened. He knew little of school life but what he had read in the stories of *The Boy's Own Paper*. He had also read *Eric, or Little by Little*.

When they got out of the train at Tercanbury, Philip felt sick with apprehension, and during the drive in to the town sat pale and silent. The high brick wall in front of the school gave it the look of a prison. There was a little door in it, which opened on their ringing; and a clumsy, untidy man came out and fetched Philip's tin trunk and his play-box. They were shown into the drawing-room; it was filled with massive, ugly furniture, and the chairs of the suite were placed round the walls with a forbidding rigidity. They waited for the head-master.

'What's Mr Watson like?' asked Philip, after a while.

'You'll see for yourself.'

There was another pause. Mr Carey wondered why the headmaster did not come. Presently Philip made an effort and spoke again.

'Tell him I've got a club-foot,' he said.

Before Mr Carey could speak the door burst open and Mr Watson swept into the room. To Philip he seemed gigantic. He was a man of over six feet high, and broad, with enormous hands and a great red beard; he talked loudly in a jovial manner; but his aggressive cheerfulness struck terror in Philip's heart. He shook hands with Mr Carey, and then took Philip's small hand in his.

'Well, young fellow, are you glad to come to school?' he shouted.

Philip reddened and found no word to answer.

'How old are you?'

'Nine,' said Philip.

'You must say sir,' said his uncle.

'I expect you've got a good lot to learn,' the headmaster bellowed cheerily.

To give the boy confidence he began to tickle him with rough fingers. Philip, feeling shy and uncomfortable, squirmed under his touch.

'I've put him in the small dormitory for the present. ... You'll like that, won't you?' he added to Philip. 'Only eight of you in there. You won't feel so strange.'

Then the door opened, and Mrs Watson came in. She was a dark woman with black hair, neatly parted in the middle. She had curiously thick lips and a small round nose. Her eyes were large and black. There was a singular coldness in her appearance. She seldom spoke and smiled more seldom still. Her husband introduced Mr Carey to her, and then gave Philip a friendly push towards her.

'This is a new boy, Helen. His name's Carey.'

Without a word she shook hands with Philip and then sat down, not speaking, while the headmaster asked Mr Carey how much Philip knew and what books he had been working with. The Vicar of Blackstable was a little embarrassed by Mr Watson's boisterous heartiness, and in a moment or two got up.

'I think I'd better leave Philip with you now.'

'That's all right,' said Mr Watson. 'He'll be safe with me. He'll get on like a house on fire. Won't you, young fellow?'

Without waiting for an answer from Philip the big man burst into a great bellow of laughter. Mr Carey kissed Philip on the forehead and went away.

'Come along, young fellow,' shouted Mr Watson. 'I'll show you the schoolroom.'

He swept out of the drawing-room with giant strides, and Philip hurriedly limped behind him. He was taken into a long, bare room with two tables that ran along its whole length; on each side of them were wooden forms.

'Nobody much here yet,' said Mr Watson. 'I'll just show you the playground, and then I'll leave you to shift for yourself.'

Mr Watson led the way. Philip found himself in a large playground with high brick walls on three sides of it. On the fourth side was an iron railing through which you saw a vast lawn and beyond this some of the buildings of King's School. One small boy was wandering disconsolately, kicking up the gravel as he walked.

'Hullo, Venning,' shouted Mr Watson. 'When did you turn up?'

The small boy came forward and shook hands.

'Here's a new boy. He's older and bigger than you, so don't you bully him.'

The headmaster glared amicably at the two children, filling them with fear by the roar of his voice, and then with a guffaw left them.

'What's your name?'

'Carey.'

'What's your father?'

'He's dead.'

'Oh! Does your mother wash?'

'My mother's dead, too.'

Philip thought this answer would cause the boy a certain

awkwardness, but Venning was not to be turned from his facetiousness for so little.

'Well, did she wash?' he went on.

'Yes,' said Philip indignantly.

'She was a washerwoman then?'

'No, she wasn't.'

'Then she didn't wash.'

The little boy crowed with delight at the success of his dialectic. Then he caught sight of Philip's feet.

'What's the matter with your foot?'

Philip instinctively tried to withdraw it from sight. He hid it behind the one which was whole.

'I've got a club-foot,' he answered

'How did you get it?'

'I've always had it.'

'Let's have a look.'

'No.'

'Don't then.'

The little boy accompanied the words with a sharp kick on Philip's shin, which Philip did not expect and thus could not guard against. The pain was so great that it made him gasp, but greater than the pain was the surprise. He did not know why Venning kicked him. He had not the presence of mind to give him a black eye. Besides, the boy was smaller than he, and he had read in *The Boy's Own Paper* that it was a mean thing to hit anyone smaller than yourself. While Philip was nursing his shin a third boy appeared, and his tormentor left him. In a little while he noticed that the pair were talking about him, and he felt they were looking at his feet. He grew hot and uncomfortable.

But others arrived, a dozen together, and then more, and they began to talk about their doings during the holidays, where they had been, and what wonderful cricket they had played. A few new boys appeared, and with these presently Philip found himself talking. He was shy and nervous. He was anxious to make himself pleasant, but he could not think of anything to say. He was asked a great many questions and answered them all quite willingly. One boy asked him whether he could play cricket.

'No,' answered Philip. 'I've got a club-foot.'

The boy looked down quickly and reddened. Philip saw that he felt he had asked an unseemly question. He was too shy to apologize and looked at Philip awkwardly.

XI

NEXT morning when the clanging of a bell awoke Philip he looked round his cubicle in astonishment. Then a voice sang out, and he remembered where he was.

'Are you awake, Singer?'

The partitions of the cubicle were of polished pitch-pine, and there was a green curtain in front. In those days there was little thought of ventilation, and the windows were closed except when the dormitory was aired in the morning.

Philip got up and knelt down to say his prayers. It was a cold morning, and he shivered a little; but he had been taught by his uncle that his prayers were more acceptable to God if he said them in his nightshirt than if he waited till he was dressed. This did not surprise him, for he was beginning to realize that he was the creature of a God who appreciated the discomfort of his worshippers. Then he washed. There were two baths for the fifty boarders, and each boy had a bath once a week. The rest of his washing was done in a small basin on a washstand, which, with the bed and a chair, made up the furniture of each cubicle. The boys chatted gaily while they dressed. Philip was all ears. Then another bell sounded, and they ran downstairs. They took their seats on the forms on each side of the two long tables in the schoolroom; and Mr Watson, followed by his wife and the servants, came in and sat down. Mr Watson read prayers in an impressive manner, and the supplications thundered out in his loud voice as though they were threats personally addressed to each boy. Philip listened with anxiety. Then Mr Watson read a chapter from the Bible, and the servants trooped out. In a moment the untidy youth brought in two large pots of tea and on a second journey immense dishes of bread and butter.

Philip had a squeamish appetite, and the thick slabs of poor butter on the bread turned his stomach, but he saw other boys scraping it off and followed their example. They all had potted meats and such like, which they had brought in their play-boxes; and some had 'extras', eggs or bacon, upon which Mr Watson made a profit. When he had asked Mr Carey whether Philip was to have these, Mr Carey replied that he did not think boys should be spoilt. Mr Watson quite agreed with him – he considered nothing was better than bread and butter for growing lads – but some parents, unduly pampering their off-spring, insisted on it.

Philip noticed that 'extras' gave boys a certain consideration and made up his mind, when he wrote to Aunt Louisa, to ask for them.

After breakfast the boys wandered out into the playground. Here the day-boys were gradually assembling. They were sons of the local clergy, of the officers at the Depot, and of such manufacturers or men of business as the old town possessed. Presently a bell rang, and they all trooped into school. This consisted of a large, long room at opposite ends of which two under-masters conducted the second and third forms, and of a smaller one, leading out of it, used by Mr Watson, who taught the first form. To attach the preparatory to the senior school these three classes were known officially, on speech days and in reports, as upper, middle, and lower second. Philip was put in the last. The master, a red-faced man with a pleasant voice, was called Rice; he had a jolly manner with boys, and the time passed quickly. Philip was surprised when it was a quarter to eleven and they were let out for ten minutes' rest.

The whole school rushed noisily into the playground. The new boys were told to go into the middle, while the others stationed themselves along opposite walls. They began to play *Pig in the Middle*. The old boys ran from wall to wall while the new boys tried to catch them: when one was seized and the mystic words said – one, two, three, and a pig for me – he became a prisoner and, turning sides, helped to catch those who were still free. Philip saw a boy running past and tried to catch him, but his limp gave him no chance; and the runners, taking their opportunity, made straight for the ground he covered. Then one of them had the brilliant idea of imitating Philip's clumsy run. Other boys saw it and began to laugh; then they all copied the first; and they ran round Philip, limping grotesquely, screaming in their treble voices with shrill laughter. They lost their heads with the delight of their new amusement, and choked with helpless merriment. One of them tripped Philip up and he fell, heavily as he always fell, and cut his knee. They laughed all the louder when he got up. A boy pushed him from behind, and he would have fallen again if another had not caught him. The game was forgotten in the entertainment of Philip's deformity. One of them invented an odd, rolling limp that struck the rest as supremely ridiculous, and several of the boys lay down on the ground and rolled about in laughter: Philip was completely scared. He could not make out why they were laughing at him. His heart beat so

43

that he could hardly breathe, and he was more frightened than he had ever been in his life. He stood still stupidly while the boys ran round him, mimicking and laughing; they shouted to him to try and catch them; but he did not move. He did not want them to see him run any more. He was using all his strength to prevent himself from crying.

Suddenly the bell rang, and they all trooped back to school. Philip's knee was bleeding, and he was dusty and dishevelled. For some minutes Mr Rice could not control his form. They were excited still by the strange novelty, and Philip saw one or two of them furtively looking down at his feet. He tucked them under the bench.

In the afternoon they went up to play football, but Mr Watson stopped Philip on the way out after dinner.

'I suppose you can't play football, Carey?' he asked him.

Philip blushed self-consciously.

'No, sir.'

'Very well. You'd better go up to the field. You can walk as far as that, can't you?'

Philip had no idea where the field was, but he answered all the same.

'Yes, sir.'

The boys went in charge of Mr Rice, who glanced at Philip and, seeing he had not changed, asked why he was not going to play.

'Mr Watson said I needn't, sir,' said Philip.

'Why?'

There were boys all round him, looking at him curiously, and a feeling of shame came over Philip. He looked down without answering. Others gave the reply.

'He's got a club-foot, sir.'

'Oh, I see.'

Mr Rice was quite young; he had only taken his degree a year before; and he was suddenly embarrassed. His instinct was to beg the boy's pardon, but he was too shy to do so. He made his voice gruff and loud.

'Now then, you boys, what are you waiting about for? Get on with you.'

Some of them had already started and those that were left now set off, in groups of two or three.

'You'd better come along with me, Carey,' said the master. 'You don't know the way, do you?'

Philip guessed the kindness, and a sob came to his throat.

'I can't go very fast, sir.'

44

'Then I'll go very slow,' said the master, with a smile.

Philip's heart went out to the red-faced, commonplace young man who said a gentle word to him. He suddenly felt less unhappy.

But at night when they went up to bed and were undressing, the boy who was called Singer came out of his cubicle and put his head in Philip's.

'I say, let's look at your foot,' he said.

'No,' answered Philip.

He jumped into bed quickly.

'Don't say no to me,' said Singer. 'Come on, Mason.'

The boy in the next cubicle was looking round the corner, and at the words he slipped in. They made for Philip and tried to tear the bed-clothes off him, but he held them tightly.

'Why can't you leave me alone?' he cried.

Singer seized a brush and with the back of it beat Philip's hands clenched on the blanket. Philip cried out.

'Why don't you show us your foot quietly?'

'I won't.'

In desperation Philip clenched his fist and hit the boy who tormented him, but he was at a disadvantage, and the boy seized his arm. He began to turn it.

'Oh, don't, don't,' said Philip. 'You'll break my arm.'

'Stop still then and put out your foot.'

Philip gave a sob and a gasp. The boy gave the arm another wrench. The pain was unendurable.

'All right. I'll do it,' said Philip.

He put out his foot. Singer still kept his hand on Philip's wrist. He looked curiously at the deformity.

'Isn't it beastly?' said Mason.

Another came in and looked too.

'Ugh,' he said, in disgust.

'My word, it is rum,' said Singer, making a face. 'Is it hard?'

He touched it with the tip of his forefinger, cautiously, as though it were something that had a life of its own. Suddenly they heard Mr Watson's heavy tread on the stairs. They threw the clothes back on Philip and dashed like rabbits into their cubicles. Mr Watson came into the dormitory. Raising himself on tiptoe he could see over the rod that bore the green curtain, and he looked into two or three of the cubicles. The little boys were safely in bed. He put out the light and went out.

Singer called out to Philip, but he did not answer. He had got his teeth in the pillow so that his sobbing should be inaudible. He was not crying for the pain they had caused him, nor for the humiliation he had suffered when they looked at his foot, but with rage at himself because, unable to stand the torture, he had put out his foot of his own accord.

And then he felt the misery of his life. It seemed to his childish mind that this unhappiness must go on for ever. For no particular reason he remembered that cold morning when Emma had taken him out of bed and put him beside his mother. He had not thought of it once since it happened, but now he seemed to feel the warmth of his mother's body against his and her arms around him. Suddenly, it seemed to him that his life was a dream, his mother's death, and the life at the vicarage, and these two wretched days at school, and he would awake in the morning and be back again at home. His tears dried as he thought of it. He was too unhappy, it must be nothing but a dream, and his mother was alive, and Emma would come up presently and go to bed. He fell asleep.

But when he awoke next morning it was to the clanging of a bell, and the first thing his eyes saw was the green curtain of his cubicle.

XII

As time went on Philip's deformity ceased to interest. It was accepted like one boy's red hair and another's unreasonable corpulence. But meanwhile he had grown horribly sensitive. He never ran if he could help it, because he knew it made his limp more conspicuous, and he adopted a peculiar walk. He stood still as much as he could, with his club-foot behind the other, so that it should not attract notice, and he was constantly on the look out for any reference to it. Because he could not join in the games which other boys played, their life remained strange to him; he only interested himself from the outside in their doings; and it seemed to him that there was a barrier between them and him. Sometimes they seemed to think that it was his fault if he could not play football, and he was unable to make them understand. He was left a good deal to himself. He had been inclined to talkativeness, but gradually he became silent. He began to think of the difference between himself and others.

The biggest boy in his dormitory, Singer, took a dislike to him, and Philip, small for his age, had to put up with a good deal of hard treatment. About half-way through the term a mania ran through the school for a game called Nibs. It was a

game for two, played on a table or a form with steel pens. You
had to push your nib with the finger-nail so as to get the point
of it over your opponent's, while he manoeuvred to prevent
this and to get the point of his nib over the back of yours;
when this result was achieved you breathed on the ball of your
thumb, pressed it hard on the two nibs, and if you were able
then to lift them without dropping either, both nibs became
yours. Soon nothing was seen but boys playing this game, and
the more skilful acquired vast stores of nibs. But in a little
while Mr Watson made up his mind that it was a form of
gambling, forbade the game, and confiscated all the nibs in
the boys' possession. Philip had been very adroit, and it was
with a heavy heart that he gave up his winnings; but his fingers
itched to play still, and a few days later, on his way to the football field, he went into a shop and bought a pennyworth of J
pens. He carried them loose in his pocket and enjoyed feeling
them. Presently Singer found out that he had them. Singer had
given up his nibs too, but he had kept back a very large one,
called a Jumbo, which was almost unconquerable, and he
could not resist the opportunity of getting Philip's Js out of
him. Though Philip knew that he was at a disadvantage with
his small nibs, he had an adventurous disposition and was
willing to take the risk; besides, he was aware that Singer would
not allow him to refuse. He had not played for a week and sat
down to the game now with a thrill of excitement. He lost two
of his small nibs quickly, and Singer was jubilant, but the third
time by some chance the Jumbo slipped round and Philip was
able to push his J across it. He crowed with triumph. At that
moment Mr Watson came in.

'What are you doing?' he asked.

He looked from Singer to Philip, but neither answered.

'Don't you know that I've forbidden you to play that idiotic
game?'

Philip's heart beat fast. He knew what was coming and was
dreadfully frightened, but in his fright there was a certain
exultation. He had never been swished. Of course it would
hurt, but it was something to boast about afterwards.

'Come into my study.'

The headmaster turned, and they followed him side by side.
Singer whispered to Philip:

'We're in for it.'

Mr Watson pointed to Singer.

'Bend over,' he said.

Philip, very white, saw the boy quiver at each stroke, and

after the third he heard him cry out. Three more followed.

'That'll do. Get up.'

Singer stood up. The tears were streaming down his face. Philip stepped forward. Mr Watson looked at him for a moment.

'I'm not going to cane you. You're a new boy. And I can't hit a cripple. Go away, both of you, and don't be naughty again.'

When they got back into the schoolroom a group of boys, who had learned in some mysterious way what was happening, were waiting for them. They set upon Singer at once with eager questions. Singer faced them, his face red with the pain and marks of tears still on his cheeks. He pointed with his head at Philip, who was standing a little behind him.

'He got off because he's a cripple,' he said angrily.

Philip stood silent and flushed. He felt that they looked at him with contempt.

'How many did you get?' one boy asked Singer.

But he did not answer. He was angry because he had been hurt.

'Don't ask me to play Nibs with you again,' he said to Philip. 'It's jolly nice for you. You don't risk anything.'

'I didn't ask you.'

'Didn't you?'

He quickly put out his foot and tripped Philip up. Philip was always rather unsteady on his feet, and he fell heavily to the ground.

'Cripple,' said Singer.

For the rest of the term he tormented Philip cruelly, and though Philip tried to keep out of his way, the school was so small that it was impossible; he tried being friendly and jolly with him; he abased himself so far as to buy him a knife; but though Singer took the knife he was not placated. Once or twice, driven beyond endurance, he hit and kicked the bigger boy, but Singer was so much stronger that Philip was helpless, and he was always forced after more or less torture to beg his pardon. It was that which rankled with Philip: he could not bear the humiliation of apologies, which were wrung from him by pain greater than he could bear. And what made it worse was that there seemed no end to his wretchedness; Singer was only eleven and would not go to the upper school till he was thirteen. Philip realized that he must live two years with a tormentor from whom there was no escape. He was only happy while he was working and when he got into bed. And often there recurred to him then that queer feeling that his life with all its misery was nothing but a dream, and that he would awake in the morning in his own little bed in London.

XIII

Two years passed, and Philip was nearly twelve. He was in the first form, within two or three places of the top, and after Christmas when several boys would be leaving for the senior school he would be head boy. He had already quite a collection of prizes, worthless books on bad paper, but in gorgeous bindings decorated with the arms of the school: his position had freed him from bullying, and he was not unhappy. His fellows forgave him his success because of his deformity.

'After all, it's jolly easy for him to get prizes,' they said, 'there's nothing he *can* do but swot.'

He had lost his early terror of Mr Watson. He had grown used to the loud voice, and when the headmaster's heavy hand was laid on his shoulder Philip discerned vaguely the intention of a caress. He had the good memory which is more useful for scholastic achievements than mental power, and he knew Mr Watson expected him to leave the preparatory school with a scholarship.

But he had grown very self-conscious. The new-born child does not realize that his body is more a part of himself than surrounding objects, and will play with his toes without any feeling that they belong to him more than the rattle by his side; and it is only by degrees, through pain, that he understands the fact of the body. And experiences of the same kind are necessary for the individual to become conscious of himself; but here there is the difference that, although everyone becomes equally conscious of his body as a separate and complete organism, everyone does not become equally conscious of himself as a complete and separate personality. The feeling of apartness from others comes to most with puberty, but it is not always developed to such a degree as to make the difference between the individual and his fellows noticeable to the individual. It is such as he, as little conscious of himself as the bee in a hive, who are the lucky in life, for they have the best chance of happiness: their activities are shared by all, and their pleasures are only pleasures because they are enjoyed in common; you will see them on Whit-Monday dancing on Hampstead Heath, shouting at a football match, or from club windows in Pall Mall cheering a royal procession. It is because of them that man has been called a social animal.

Philip passed from the innocence of childhood to bitter consciousness of himself by the ridicule which his club-foot had excited. The circumstances of his case were so peculiar that he could not apply to them the ready-made rules which acted well enough in ordinary affairs, and he was forced to think for himself. The many books he had read filled his mind with ideas which, because he only half understood them, gave more scope to his imagination. Beneath his painful shyness something was growing up within him, and obscurely he realized his personality. But at times it gave him odd surprises; he did things, he knew not why, and afterwards when he thought of them found himself all at sea.

There was a boy called Luard between whom and Philip a friendship had arisen, and one day, when they were playing together in the schoolroom, Luard began to perform some trick with an ebony pen-holder of Philip's.

'Don't play the giddy ox,' said Philip. 'You'll only break it.'

'I shan't.'

But no sooner were the words out of the boy's mouth than the pen-holder snapped in two. Luard looked at Philip with dismay.

'Oh, I say, I'm awfully sorry.'

The tears rolled down Philip's cheeks, but he did not answer.

'I say, what's the matter?' said Luard, with surprise. 'I'll get you another one exactly the same.'

'It's not about the pen-holder I care,' said Philip, in a trembling voice, 'only it was given me by my mater just before she died.'

'I say, I'm awfully sorry, Carey.'

'It doesn't matter. It wasn't your fault.'

Philip took the two pieces of the pen-holder and looked at them. He tried to restrain his sobs. He felt utterly miserable. And yet he could not tell why, for he knew quite well that he had bought the pen-holder during his last holidays at Blackstable for one and twopence. He did not know in the least what had made him invent that pathetic story, but he was quite as unhappy as though it had been true. The pious atmosphere of the vicarage and the religious tone of the school had made Philip's conscience very sensitive; he absorbed insensibly the feeling about him that the Tempter was ever on the watch to gain his immortal soul; and though he was not more truthful than most boys he never told a lie without suffering from remorse. When he thought over this incident he was very much distressed, and made up his mind that he must go to Luard and tell him that the story was an invention. Though he dreaded humiliation more than anything in the world, he hugged himself for two or three days at the thought of the agonizing joy of humiliating himself to the Glory of God. But he never got any further. He satisfied his conscience by the more comfortable method of expressing his repentance only to the Almighty. But he could not understand why he should have been so genuinely affected by the story he was making up. The tears that flowed down his grubby cheeks were real tears. Then by some accident of association there occurred to him that scene when Emma had told him of his mother's death, and, though he could not speak for crying, he had insisted on going in to say good-bye to the Misses Watkin so that they might see his grief and pity him.

XIV

THEN a wave of religiosity passed through the school. Bad language was no longer heard, and the little nastinesses of small boys were looked upon with hostility; the bigger boys, like the lords temporal of the Middle Ages, used the strength of their arms to persuade those weaker than themselves to virtuous courses.

Philip, his restless mind avid for new things, became very devout. He heard soon that it was possible to join a Bible League, and wrote to London for particulars. These consisted in a form to be filled up with the applicant's name, age, and school; a solemn declaration to be signed that he would read a set portion of Holy Scripture every night for a year; and a request for half a crown; this, it was explained, was demanded partly to prove the earnestness of the applicant's desire to become a member of the League, and partly to cover clerical expenses. Philip duly sent the papers and the money, and in return received a calendar worth about a penny, on which was set down the appointed passage to be read each day, and a sheet of paper on one side of which was a picture of the Good Shepherd and a lamb, and on the other, decoratively framed in red lines, a short prayer which had to be said before beginning to read.

Every evening he undressed as quickly as possible in order to have time for his task before the gas was put out. He read industriously, as he read always, without criticism, stories of cruelty, deceit, ingratitude, dishonesty, and low cunning. Actions which would have excited his horror in the life about him, in the reading passed through his mind without comment, because they were committed under the direct inspiration of God. The method of the League was to alternate a book of the Old Testament with a book of the New, and one night Philip came across these words of Jesus Christ:

If ye have faith, and doubt not, ye shall not only do this which is done to the fig-tree, but also if ye shall say unto this mountain, Be thou removed, and be thou cast into the sea: it shall be done.

And all this, whatsoever ye shall ask in prayer, believing, ye shall receive.

They made no particular impression on him, but it happened that two or three days later, being Sunday, the Canon in residence chose them for the text of his sermon. Even if Philip had wanted to hear this it would have been impossible, for the boys of King's School sit in the choir, and the pulpit stands at the corner of the transept so that the preacher's back is almost turned to them. The distance also is so great that it needs a man with a fine voice and a knowledge of elocution to make himself heard in the choir; and according to long usage the Canons of Tercanbury are chosen for their learning rather than for any qualities which might be of use in a cathedral church. But the words of the text, perhaps because he had read them so short a while before, came clearly enough to Philip's ears, and they seemed on a sudden to have a personal application. He thought about them through most of the sermon, and that night, on getting into bed, he turned over the pages of the gospel and found once more the passage. Though he believed implicitly everything he saw in print, he had learned already that in the Bible things that said one thing quite clearly often mysteriously meant another. There was no one he liked to ask at school, so he kept the question he had in mind till the Christmas holidays, and then one day he made an opportunity. It was after supper and prayers were just finished. Mrs Carey was counting the eggs that Mary Ann had brought in as usual and writing on each one the date. Philip stood at the table and pretended to turn listlessly the pages of the Bible.

'I say, Uncle William, this passage here, does it really mean that?'

He put his finger against it as though he had come across it accidentally.

Mr Carey looked up over his spectacles. He was holding *The Blackstable Times* in front of the fire. It had come in that evening damp from the press, and the Vicar always aired it for ten minutes before he began to read.

'What passage is that?' he askéd.

'Why, this about if you have faith you can remove mountains.'

'If it says so in the Bible it is so, Philip,' said Mrs Carey gently, taking up the plate-basket.

Philip looked at his uncle for an answer.

'It's a matter of faith.'

'D'you mean to say that if you really believed you could move mountains you could?'

'By the grace of God,' said the Vicar.

'Now, say good-night to your uncle, Philip,' said Aunt Louisa. 'You're not wanting to move a mountain tonight, are you?'

Philip allowed himself to be kissed on the forehead by his uncle and preceded Mrs Carey upstairs. He had got the information he wanted. His little room was icy, and he shivered when he put on his nightgown. But he always felt that his prayers were more pleasing to God when he said them under conditions of discomfort. The coldness of his hands and feet was an offering to the Almighty. And tonight he sank on his knees, buried his face in his hands, and prayed to God with all his might that He would make his club-foot whole. It was a very small thing beside the moving of mountains. He knew that God could do it if He wished, and his own faith was complete. Next morning, finishing his prayers with the same request, he fixed a date for the miracle.

'Oh, God, in Thy loving mercy and goodness, if it be Thy will, please make my foot all right on the night before I go back to school.'

He was glad to get his petition into a formula, and he repeated it later in the dining-room during the short pause which the Vicar always made after prayers, before he rose from his knees. He said it again in the evening and again, shivering in his nightshirt, before he got into bed. And he believed. For once he looked forward with eagerness to the end of the holidays. He laughed to himself as he thought of his uncle's astonishment when he ran down the stairs three at a time; and after breakfast he and Aunt Louisa would have to hurry out and buy a new pair of boots. At school they would be astounded.

'Hullo, Carey, what have you done with your foot?'

'Oh, it's all right now,' he would answer casually, as though it were the most natural thing in the world.

He would be able to play football. His heart leaped as he saw himself running, running, faster than any of the other boys. At the end of the Easter term there were the sports, and he would be able to go in for the races; he rather fancied himself over the hurdles. It would be splendid to be like everyone else, not to be stared at curiously by new boys who did not know about his deformity, nor at the baths in summer to need incredible precautions, while he was undressing, before he could hide his foot in the water.

He prayed with all the power of his soul. No doubts assailed him. He was confident in the word of God. And the night before he was to go back to school he went up to bed tremulous with excitement. There was snow on the ground, and Aunt Louisa had allowed herself the unaccustomed luxury of a fire in her bedroom; but in Philip's little room it was so cold that his fingers were numb, and he had great difficulty in undoing his collar. His teeth chattered. The idea came to him that he must do something more than usual to attract the attention of God, and he turned back the rug which was in front of his bed so that he could kneel on the bare boards; and then it struck him that his nightshirt was a softness that might displease his Maker, so he took it off and said his prayers naked. When he got into bed he was so cold that for some time he could not sleep, but when he did, it was so soundly that Mary Ann had to shake him when she brought in his hot water next morning. She talked to him while she drew the curtains, but he did not answer; he had remembered at once that this was the morning for the miracle. His heart was filled with joy and gratitude. His first instinct was to put down his hand and feel the foot which was whole now, but to do this seemed to doubt the goodness of God. He knew that his foot was well. But at last he made up his mind, and with the toes of his right foot he just touched the ground. Then he passed his hand over it.

He limped downstairs just as Mary Ann was going into the dining-room for prayers, and then he sat down to breakfast.

'You're very quiet this morning, Philip,' said Aunt Louisa presently.

'He's thinking of the good breakfast he'll have at school tomorrow,' said the Vicar.

When Philip answered, it was in a way that always irritated his uncle, with something that had nothing to do with the matter in hand. He called it a bad habit of wool-gathering.

'Supposing you'd asked God to do something,' said Philip, 'and really believed it was going to happen, like moving a mountain, I mean, and you had faith, and it didn't happen, what would it mean?'

'What a funny boy you are!' said Aunt Louisa. 'You asked about moving mountains two or three weeks ago.'

'It would just mean that you hadn't got faith,' answered Uncle William.

Philip accepted the explanation. If God had not cured him, it was because he did not really believe. And yet he did not see how he could believe more than he did. But perhaps he had not given God enough time. He had only asked Him for nineteen days. In a day or two he began his prayer again, and this time he fixed upon Easter. That was the day of His Son's glorious resurrection, and God in His happiness might be mercifully inclined. But now Philip added other means of attaining his desire: he began to wish, when he saw a new moon or a dappled horse, and he looked out for shooting stars; during exeat they had a chicken at the vicarage, and he broke the lucky bone with Aunt Louisa and wished again, each time that his foot might be made whole. He was appealing unconsciously to gods older to his race than the God of Israel. And he bombarded the Almighty with his prayer, at odd times of the day, whenever it occurred to him, in identical words always, for it seemed to him important to make his request in the same terms. But presently the feeling came to him that this time also his faith would not be great enough. He could not resist the doubt that assailed him. He made his own experience into a general rule.

'I suppose no one ever has faith enough,' he said.

It was like the salt which his nurse used to tell him about: you could catch any bird by putting salt on his tail; and once he had taken a little bag of it into Kensington Gardens. But he could never get near enough to put the salt on the bird's tail. Before Easter he had given up the struggle. He felt a dull resentment against his uncle for taking him in. The text which spoke of the moving of mountains was just one of those that said one thing and meant another. He thought his uncle had been playing a practical joke on him.

XV

THE King's School at Tercanbury, to which Philip went when
he was thirteen, prided itself on its antiquity. It traced its
origin to an abbey school, founded before the Conquest, where
the rudiments of learning were taught by Augustine monks;
and, like many another establishment of this sort, on the
destruction of the monasteries it had been reorganized by the
officers of King Henry VIII and thus acquired its name. Since
then, pursuing its modest course, it had given to the sons of
the local gentry and of the professional people of Kent an
education sufficient to their needs. One or two men of letters,
beginning with a poet, than whom only Shakespeare had a
more splendid genius, and ending with a writer of prose whose
view of life has affected profoundly the generation of which
Philip was a member, had gone forth from its gates to achieve
fame; it had produced one or two eminent lawyers, but
eminent lawyers are common, and one or two soldiers of
distinction; but during the three centuries since its separation
from the monastic order it had trained especially men of the
church, bishops, deans, canons, and above all country clergymen: there were boys in the school whose fathers, grand-
fathers, great-grandfathers, had been educated there and had
all been rectors of parishes in the diocese of Tercanbury; and
they came to it with their minds made up already to be ordained. But there were signs notwithstanding that even there
changes were coming; for a few, repeating what they had
heard at home, said that the Church was no longer what it
used to be. It wasn't so much the money; but the class of
people who went in for it weren't the same; and two or three
boys knew curates whose fathers were tradesmen; they'd rather
go out to the Colonies (in those days the Colonies were still the
last hope of those who could get nothing to do in England)
than be a curate under some chap who wasn't a gentleman. At
King's School, as at Blackstable Vicarage, a tradesman was
anyone who was not lucky enough to own land (and here a
fine distinction was made between the gentleman farmer and
the landowner), or did not follow one of the four professions
to which it was possible for a gentleman to belong. Among
the day-boys, of whom there were about a hundred and fifty,
sons of the local gentry and of the men stationed at the depot,
those whose fathers were engaged in business were made to feel
the degradation of their state.

The masters had no patience with modern ideas of education, which they read of sometimes in *The Times* or *The Guardian*, and hoped fervently that King's School would remain true to its old traditions. The dead languages were taught with such thoroughness that an old boy seldom thought of Homer or Virgil in after life without a qualm of boredom; and though in the common room at dinner one or two bolder spirits suggested that mathematics were of increasing importance, the general feeling was that they were a less noble study than the classics. Neither German nor chemistry was taught, and French only by the form-masters; they could keep order better than a foreigner, and, since they knew the grammar as well as any Frenchman, it seemed unimportant that none of them could have got a cup of coffee in the restaurant at Boulogne unless the waiter had known a little English. Geography was taught chiefly by making boys draw maps, and this was a favourite occupation, especially when the country dealt with was mountainous: it was possible to waste a great deal of time in drawing the Andes or the Apennines. The masters, graduates of Oxford or Cambridge, were ordained and unmarried; if by chance they wished to marry they could only do so by accepting one of the smaller livings at the disposal of the Chapter; but for many years none of them had cared to leave the refined society of Tercanbury, which owing to the cavalry depot had a martial as well as an ecclesiastical tone, for the monotony of life in a country rectory; and they were now all men of middle age.

The headmaster, on the other hand, was obliged to be married, and he conducted the school till age began to tell upon him. When he retired he was rewarded with a much better living than any of the under-masters could hope for, and an honorary Canonry.

But a year before Philip entered the school a great change had come over it. It had been obvious for some time that Dr Fleming, who had been headmaster for a quarter of a century, was become too deaf to continue his work to the greater glory of God; and when one of the livings on the outskirts of the city fell vacant, with a stipend of six hundred a year, the Chapter offered it to him in such a manner as to imply that they thought it high time for him to retire. He could nurse his ailments comfortably on such an income. Two or three curates who had hoped for preferment told their wives it was scandalous to give a parish that needed a young, strong, and energetic man to an old fellow who knew nothing of parochial work, and had feathered his nest already; but the mutterings of the unbeneficed clergy do not reach the ears of a cathedral Chapter. And as for the parishioners, they had nothing to say in the matter, and therefore nobody asked for their opinion. The Wesleyans and the Baptists both had chapels in the village.

When Dr Fleming was thus disposed of it became necessary to find a successor. It was contrary to the traditions of the school that one of the lower-masters should be chosen. The common-room was unanimous in desiring the election of Mr Watson, headmaster of the preparatory school; he could hardly be described as already a master of King's School, they had all known him for twenty years, and there was no danger that he would make a nuisance of himself. But the Chapter sprang a surprise on them. It chose a man called Perkins. At first nobody knew who Perkins was, and the name favourably impressed no one; but before the shock of it had passed away, it was realized that Perkins was the son of Perkins the linen-draper. Dr Fleming informed the masters just before dinner, and his manner showed his consternation. Such of them as were dining in ate their meal almost in silence, and no reference was made to the matter till the servants had left the room. Then they set to. The names of those present on this occasion are unimportant, but they had been known to generations of schoolboys as Sighs, Tar, Winks, Squirts, and Pat.

They all knew Tom Perkins. The first thing about him was that he was not a gentleman. They remembered him quite well. He was a small, dark boy, with untidy black hair and large eyes. He looked like a gipsy. He had come to the school as a day-boy, with the best scholarship on their endowment, so that his education had cost him nothing. Of course he was brilliant. At every Speech-Day he was loaded with prizes. He was their show-boy, and they remembered now bitterly their fear that he would try to get some scholarship at one of the larger public schools and so pass out of their hands. Dr Fleming had gone to the linen-draper his father – they all remembered the shop, Perkins and Cooper, in St Catherine's Street – and said he hoped Tom would remain with them till he went to Oxford. The school was Perkins and Cooper's best customer, and Mr Perkins was only too glad to give the required assurance. Tom Perkins continued to triumph, he was the finest classical scholar that Dr Fleming remembered, and on leaving the school took with him the most valuable scholarship they had to offer. He got another at Magdalen and settled down to a brilliant career at the University. The school magazine recorded the distinctions he achieved year after year, and when he got his double first Dr Fleming himself wrote a few words of eulogy on the front page. It was with greater satisfaction that they welcomed his success, since Perkins and Cooper had fallen upon evil days: Cooper drank like a fish, and just before Tom Perkins took his degree the linen-drapers filed their petition in bankruptcy.

In due course Tom Perkins took Holy Orders and entered upon the profession for which he was so admirably suited. He had been an assistant master at Wellington and then at Rugby.

But there was quite a difference between welcoming his success at other schools and serving under his leadership in their own. Tar had frequently given him lines, and Squirts had boxed his ears. They could not imagine how the Chapter had made such a mistake. No one could be expected to forget that he was the son of a bankrupt linen-draper, and the alcoholism of Cooper seemed to increase the disgrace. It was understood that the Dean had supported his candidature with zeal, so the Dean would probably ask him to dinner; but would the pleasant little dinners in the precincts ever be the same when Tom Perkins sat at the table? And what about the depot? He really could not expect officers and gentlemen to receive him as one of themselves. It would do the school incalculable harm. Parents would be dissatisfied, and no one could be surprised if there were wholesale withdrawals. And then the indignity of calling him Mr Perkins! The masters thought by way of protest of sending in their resignations in a body, but the uneasy fear that they would be accepted with equanimity restrained them.

'The only thing is to prepare ourselves for changes,' said Sighs, who had conducted the fifth form for five-and-twenty years with unparalleled incompetence.

And when they saw him they were not reassured. Dr Fleming invited them to meet him at luncheon. He was now a man of thirty-two, tall and lean, but with the same wild and unkempt look they remembered on him as a boy. His clothes, ill-made and shabby, were put on untidily. His hair was as black and as long as ever, and he had plainly never learned to brush it; it fell over his forehead with every gesture, and he had a quick movement of the hand with which he pushed it back from his eyes. He had a black moustache and a beard which came high up on his face almost to the cheek-bones. He talked to the masters quite easily, as though he had parted from them a week or two before; he was evidently delighted to see them.

59

He seemed unconscious of the strangeness of the position and appeared not to notice any oddness in being addressed as Mr Perkins.

When he bade them good-bye, one of the masters, for something to say, remarked that he was allowing himself plenty of time to catch his train.

'I want to go round and have a look at the shop,' he answered cheerfully.

There was a distinct embarrassment. They wondered that he could be so tactless, and to make it worse Dr Fleming had not heard what he said. His wife shouted it in his ear.

'He wants to go round and look at his father's old shop.'

Only Tom Perkins was unconscious of the humiliation which the whole party felt. He turned to Mrs Fleming.

'Who's got it now, d'you know?'

She could hardly answer. She was very angry.

'It's still a linen-draper's,' she said bitterly. 'Grove is the name. We don't deal there any more.'

'I wonder if he'd let me go over the house.'

'I expect he would if you explain who you are.'

It was not till the end of dinner that evening that any reference was made in the common-room to the subject that was in all their minds. Then it was Sighs who asked:

'Well, what did you think of our new head?'

They thought of the conversation at luncheon. It was hardly a conversation; it was a monologue. Perkins had talked incessantly. He talked very quickly, with a flow of easy words and in a deep, resonant voice. He had a short, odd little laugh which showed his white teeth. They had followed him with difficulty, for his mind darted from subject to subject with a connexion they did not always catch. He talked of pedagogics, and this was natural enough; but he had much to say of modern theories in Germany which they had never heard of and received with misgiving. He talked of the classics, but he had been to Greece, and he discoursed of archaeology; he had once spent a winter digging; they could not see how that helped a man to teach boys to pass examinations. He talked of politics. It sounded odd to them to hear him compare Lord Beaconsfield with Alcibiades. He talked of Mr Gladstone and Home Rule. They realized that he was a Liberal. Their hearts sank. He talked of German philosophy and of French fiction. They could not think a man profound whose interests were so diverse.

It was Winks who summed up the general impression and

put it into a form they all felt conclusively damning. Winks was the master of the upper third, a weak-kneed man with drooping eyelids. He was too tall for his strength, and his movements were slow and languid. He gave an impression of lassitude, and his nickname was eminently appropriate.

'He's very enthusiastic,' said Winks.

Enthusiasm was ill-bred. Enthusiasm was ungentlemanly. They thought of the Salvation Army with its braying trumpets and its drums. Enthusiasm meant change. They had goose-flesh when they thought of all the pleasant old habits which stood in imminent danger. They hardly dared to look forward to the future.

'He looks more of a gipsy than ever,' said one, after a pause.

'I wonder if the Dean and Chapter knew that he was a Radical when they elected him,' another observed bitterly.

But conversation halted. They were too much disturbed for words.

When Tar and Sighs were walking together to the Chapter House on Speech-Day a week later, Tar, who had a bitter tongue, remarked to his colleague:

'Well, we've seen a good many Speech-Days here, haven't we? I wonder if we shall see another.'

Sighs was more melancholy even than usual.

'If anything worth having comes along in the way of a living I don't mind when I retire.'

XVI

A YEAR passed, and when Philip came to the school the old masters were all in their places; but a good many changes had taken place notwithstanding their stubborn resistance, none the less formidable because it was concealed under an apparent desire to fall in with the new head's ideas. Though the form-masters still taught French to the lower school, another master had come, with a degree of doctor of philology from the University of Heidelberg and a record of three years spent in a French *lycée*, to teach French to the upper forms and German to anyone who cared to take it up instead of Greek. Another master was engaged to teach mathematics more systematically than had been found necessary hitherto. Neither of these was ordained. This was a real revolution, and when the pair arrived the older masters received them with distrust. A laboratory had been fitted up, army classes were instituted; they all said the character of the school was changing. And heaven only knew what further projects Mr Perkins turned in that untidy head of his. The school was small as public schools go, there were not more than two hundred boarders; and it was difficult for it to grow larger, for it was huddled up against the cathedral; the precincts, with the exception of a house in which some of the masters lodged, were occupied by the cathedral clergy; and there was no more room for building. But Mr Perkins devised an elaborate scheme by which he might obtain sufficient space to make the school double its present size. He wanted to attract boys from London. He thought it would be good for them to be thrown in contact with the Kentish lads, and it would sharpen the country wits of these.

'It's against all our traditions,' said Sighs, when Mr Perkins made the suggestion to him. 'We've rather gone out of our way to avoid the contamination of boys from London.'

'Oh, what nonsense!' said Mr Perkins.

No one had ever told the form-master before that he talked nonsense, and he was meditating an acid reply, in which perhaps he might insert a veiled reference to hosiery, when Mr Perkins in his impetuous way attacked him outrageously.

'That house in the Precincts – if you'd only marry I'd get the Chapter to put another couple of storeys on, and we'd make dormitories and studies, and your wife could help you.'

The elderly clergyman gasped. Why should he marry? He was fifty-seven, a man couldn't marry at fifty-seven. He couldn't start looking after a house at his time of life. He didn't want to marry. If the choice lay between that and the country living he would much sooner resign. All he wanted now was peace and quietness.

'I'm not thinking of marrying,' he said.

Mr Perkins looked at him with his dark, bright eyes, and if there was a twinkle in them poor Sighs never saw it.

'What a pity! Couldn't you marry to oblige me? It would help me a great deal with the Dean and Chapter when I suggest rebuilding your house.'

But Mr Perkins's most unpopular innovation was his system of taking occasionally another man's form. He asked it as a favour, but after all it was a favour which could not be refused, and as Tar, otherwise Mr Turner, said, it was undignified for all parties. He gave no warning, but after morning prayers would say to one of the masters:

'I wonder if you'd mind taking the Sixth today at eleven. We'll change over, shall we?'

They did not know whether this was usual at other schools, but certainly it had never been done at Tercanbury. The results were curious. Mr Turner, who was the first victim, broke the news to his form that the headmaster would take them for Latin that day, and on the pretence that they might like to ask him a question or two so that they should not make perfect fools of themselves, spent the last quarter of an hour of the history lesson in construing for them the passage of Livy which had been set for the day; but when he rejoined his class and looked at the paper on which Mr Perkins had written the marks, a surprise awaited him; for the two boys at the top of the form seemed to have done very ill, while others who had never distinguished themselves before were given full marks. When he asked Eldridge, his cleverest boy, what was the meaning of this the answer came sullenly:

'Mr Perkins never gave us any construing to do. He asked me what I knew about General Gordon.'

Mr Turner looked at him in astonishment. The boys evidently felt they had been hardly used, and he could not help agreeing with their silent dissatisfaction. He could not see either what General Gordon had to do with Livy. He hazarded an inquiry afterwards.

'Eldridge was dreadfully put out because you asked him what he knew about General Gordon,' he said to the headmaster, with an attempt at a chuckle.

Mr Perkins laughed.

'I saw they'd got to the agrarian laws of Caius Gracchus, and I wondered if they knew anything about the agrarian troubles in Ireland. But all they knew about Ireland was that Dublin was on the Liffey. So I wondered if they'd ever heard of General Gordon.'

Then the horrid fact was disclosed that the new head had a mania for general information. He had doubts about the utility of examinations on subjects which had been crammed for the occasion. He wanted common sense.

Sighs grew more worried every month; he could not get the thought out of his head that Mr Perkins would ask him to fix a day for his marriage; and he hated the attitude the head adopted towards classical literature. There was no doubt that he was a fine scholar, and he was engaged on a work which was in the right tradition: he was writing a treatise on the trees in Latin literature, but he talked of it flippantly, as though it were a pastime of no great importance, like billiards, which engaged his leisure but was not to be considered with seriousness. And Squirts, the master of the middle-third, grew more ill-tempered every day.

It was in his form that Philip was put on entering the school. The Rev. B. B. Gordon was a man by nature ill-suited to be a schoolmaster: he was impatient and choleric. With no one to call him to account, with only small boys to face him, he had long lost all power of self-control. He began his work in a rage and ended it in a passion. He was a man of middle height and of a corpulent figure; he had sandy hair, worn very short and now growing grey, and a small bristly moustache. His large face, with indistinct and small blue eyes, was naturally red, but during his frequent attacks of anger it grew dark and purple. His nails were bitten to the quick, for while some trembling boy was construing he would sit at his desk shaking with the fury that consumed him, and gnaw his fingers. Stories, perhaps exaggerated, were told of his violence, and two years before there had been some excitement in the school when it was heard that one father was threatening a prosecution: he had boxed the ears of a boy named Walters with a book so violently that his hearing was affected and the boy had to be taken away from the school. The boy's father lived in Tercanbury, and there had been much indignation in the city, the local paper had referred to the matter; but Mr Walters was only a brewer, so the sympathy was divided. The rest of the boys, for reasons best known to themselves, though they loathed the master, took his side in the affair, and, to show their indignation that the school's business had been dealt with outside, made things as uncomfortable as they could for Walters's younger brother, who still remained. But Mr Gordon had only escaped the country living by the skin of his teeth, and he had never hit a boy since. The right the masters possessed to cane boys on the hand was taken away from them, and Squirts could no longer emphasize his anger by beating his desk with his cane. He never did more now than take a boy by the shoulders and shake him. He still made a naughty or refractory lad stand with one arm stretched out for anything from ten minutes to half an hour, and he was as violent as before with his tongue.

No master could have been more unfitted to teach things to so shy a boy as Philip. He had come to the school with fewer terrors than he had when he first went to Mr Watson's. He knew a good many boys who had been with him at the preparatory school. He felt more grown-up, and instinctively realized that among the larger numbers his deformity would be less noticeable. But from the first day Mr Gordon struck terror in his heart; and the master, quick to discern the boys who were frightened of him, seemed on that account to take a peculiar dislike to them. Philip had enjoyed his work, but now he began to look upon the hours passed in school with horror. Rather than risk an answer which might be wrong and excite a storm of abuse from the master, he would sit stupidly silent, and when it came towards his turn to stand up and construe he became sick with apprehension. His happy moments were those when Mr Perkins took the form. He was able to gratify the passion for general knowledge which beset the headmaster; he had read all sorts of strange books beyond his years, and often Mr Perkins, when a question was going round the room, would stop at Philip with a smile that filled the boy with rapture, and say:

'Now, Carey, you tell them.'

The good marks he got on these occasions increased Mr Gordon's indignation. One day it came to Philip's turn to translate, and the master sat there glaring at him and furiously biting his thumb. He was in a ferocious mood. Philip began to speak in a low voice.

'Don't mumble,' shouted the master.

Something seemed to stick in Philip's throat.

'Go on. Go on. Go on.'

Each time the words were screamed more loudly. The effect was to drive all he knew out of Philip's head, and he looked at the printed page vacantly. Mr Gordon began to breathe heavily.

'If you don't know why don't you say so? Do you know it or not? Did you hear all this construed last time or not? Why don't you speak? Speak, you blockhead, speak!'

The master seized the arms of his chair and grasped them as though to prevent himself from falling upon Philip. They knew that in past days he often used to seize boys by the throat till they almost choked. The veins in his forehead stood out and his face grew dark and threatening. He was a man insane.

Philip had known the passage perfectly the day before, but now he could remember nothing.

'I don't know it,' he gasped.

'Why don't you know it? Let's take the words one by one. We'll soon see if you don't know it.'

Philip stood silent, very white, trembling a little, with his head bent down on the book. The master's breathing grew almost stertorious.

'The headmaster says you're clever. I don't know how he sees it. General information.' He laughed savagely. 'I don't know what they put you in this form for. Blockhead.'

He was pleased with the word and he repeated it at the top of his voice.

'Blockhead! Blockhead! Club-footed blockhead!'

That relieved him a little. He saw Philip redden suddenly. He told him to fetch the Black Book. Philip put down his Caesar and went silently out. The Black Book was a sombre volume in which the names of boys were written with their misdeeds, and when a name was down three times it meant a caning. Philip went to the headmaster's house and knocked at his study-door. Mr Perkins was seated at his table.

'May I have the Black Book, please, sir?'

'There it is,' answered Mr Perkins, indicating its place by a nod of his head. 'What have you been doing that you shouldn't?'

'I don't know, sir.'

Mr Perkins gave him a quick look, but without answering went on with his work. Philip took the book and went out. When the hour was up, a few minutes later, he brought it back.

'Let me have a look at it,' said the headmaster. 'I see Mr Gordon has black-booked you for "gross impertinence". What was it?'

'I don't know, sir. Mr Gordon said I was a club-footed blockhead.'

Mr Perkins looked at him again. He wondered whether there was sarcasm behind the boy's reply, but he was still much too shaken. His face was white and his eyes had a look of terrified distress. Mr Perkins got up and put the book down. As he did so he took up some photographs.

'A friend of mine sent me some pictures of Athens this morning,' he said casually. 'Look here, there's the Acropolis.'

He began explaining to Philip what he saw The ruin grew vivid with his words. He showed him the theatre of Dionysus and explained in what order the people sat, and how beyond they could see the blue Aegean. And then suddenly he said:

'I remember Mr Gordon used to call me a gipsy counter-jumper when I was in his form.'

And before Philip, his mind fixed on the photographs, had time to gather the meaning of the remark, Mr Perkins was showing him a picture of Salamis, and with his finger, a finger of which the nail had a little black edge to it, was pointing out how the Greek ships were placed and how the Persian.

XVII

PHILIP passed the next two years with comfortable monotony. He was not bullied more than other boys of his size; and his deformity, withdrawing him from games, acquired for him an insignificance for which he was grateful. He was not popular, and he was very lonely. He spent a couple of terms with Winks in the Upper Third. Winks, with his weary manner and his drooping eyelids, looked infinitely bored. He did his duty, but he did it with an abstracted mind. He was kind, gentle, and foolish. He had a great belief in the honour of boys; he felt that the first thing to make them truthful was not to let it enter your head for a moment that it was possible for them to lie. 'Ask much,' he quoted, 'and much shall be given to you.' Life was easy in the Upper Third. You knew exactly what lines would come to your turn to construe, and with the crib that passed from hand to hand you could find out all you wanted in two minutes; you could hold a Latin Grammar open on your knees while questions were passing round; and Winks never noticed anything odd in the fact that the same incredible mistake was to be found in a dozen different exercises. He had no great faith in examinations, for he noticed that boys never did so well in them as in form: it was disappointing, but not significant. In due course they were moved up, having learned little but a cheerful effrontery in the distortion of truth, which was possibly of greater service to them in after life than an ability to read Latin at sight.

Then they fell into the hands of Tar. His name was Turner; he was the most vivacious of the old masters, a short man with an immense belly, a black beard turning now to grey, and a swarthy skin. In his clerical dress there was indeed something in him to suggest the tar-barrel; and though on principle he gave five hundred lines to any boy on whose lips he overheard his nickname, at dinner-parties in the precincts he often made little jokes about it. He was the most worldly of the masters; he dined out more frequently than any of the others, and the society he kept was not so exclusively clerical. The boys looked upon him as rather a dog. He left off his clerical attire during the holidays and had been seen in Switzerland in gay tweeds. He liked a bottle of wine and a good dinner, and having once been seen at the Café Royal with a lady who was very probably a near relation, was thenceforward supposed by generations of schoolboys to indulge in orgies the circumstantial details of which pointed to an unbounded belief in human depravity.

Mr Turner reckoned that it took him a term to lick boys into shape after they had been in the Upper Third; and now and then he let fall a sly hint, which showed that he knew perfectly what went on in his colleague's form. He took it good-humouredly. He looked upon boys as young ruffians who were more apt to be truthful if it was quite certain a lie would be found out, whose sense of honour was peculiar to themselves and did not apply to dealings with masters, and who were least likely to be troublesome when they learned that it did not pay. He was proud of his form and as eager at fifty-five that it should do better in examinations than any of the others as he had been when he first came to the school. He had the choler of the obese, easily roused and as easily calmed, and his boys soon discovered that there was much kindness beneath the invective with which he constantly assailed them. He had no patience with fools, but was willing to take much trouble with boys whom he suspected of concealing intelligence behind their wilfulness. He was fond of inviting them to tea; and, though vowing they never got a look in with him at the cakes and muffins, for it was the fashion to believe that his corpulence pointed to a voracious appetite, and his voracious appetite to tape-worms, they accepted his invitations with real pleasure.

Philip was now more comfortable, for space was so limited that there were only studies for boys in the upper school, and till then he had lived in the great hall in which they all ate and in which the lower forms did preparation in a promiscuity which was vaguely distasteful to him. Now and then it made him restless to be with people and he wanted urgently to be alone. He set out for solitary walks into the country. There was a little stream, with pollards on both sides of it, that ran through green fields, and it made him happy, he knew not why, to wander along its banks. When he was tired he lay face-downward on the grass and watched the eager scurrying of minnows and of tadpoles. It gave him a peculiar satisfaction to saunter round the precincts. On the green in the middle they practised at nets in the summer, but during the rest of the year it was quiet: boys used to wander round sometimes arm in arm, or a studious fellow with abstracted gaze walked slowly, repeating to himself something he had to learn by heart. There was a colony of rooks in the great elms, and they filled the air with melancholy cries. Along one side lay the Cathedral with its great central tower, and Philip, who knew as yet nothing of beauty, felt when he looked at it a troubling delight which he could not understand. When he had a study (it was a little square room looking on a slum, and four boys shared it), he bought a photograph of that view of the Cathedral, and pinned it up over his desk. And he found himself taking a new interest in what he saw from the window of the Fourth Form room. It looked on to old lawns, carefully tended, and fine trees with foliage dense and rich. It gave him an odd feeling in his heart, and he did not know if it was pain or pleasure. It was the first dawn of the aesthetic emotion. It accompanied other changes. His voice broke. It was no longer quite under his control, and queer sounds issued from his throat.

Then he began to go to the classes which were held in the headmaster's study, immediately after tea, to prepare boys for confirmation. Philip's piety had not stood the test of time, and he had long since given up his nightly reading of the Bible; but now, under the influence of Mr Perkins, with this new condition of the body which made him so restless, his old feelings revived, and he reproached himself bitterly for his backsliding. The fires of Hell burned fiercely before his mind's eye. If he had died during that time when he was little better than an infidel he would have been lost: he believed implicitly in pain everlasting, he believed in it much more than in eternal happiness; and he shuddered at the dangers he had run.

Since the day on which Mr Perkins had spoken kindly to him, when he was smarting under the particular form of abuse which he could least bear, Philip had conceived for his headmaster a dog-like adoration. He racked his brains vainly for some way to please him. He treasured the smallest word of commendation which by chance fell from his lips. And when he came to the quiet little meetings in his house he was prepared to surrender himself entirely. He kept his eyes fixed on Mr Perkins's shining eyes, and sat with mouth half open, his head a little thrown forward so as to miss no word. The ordinariness of the surroundings made the matters they dealt with extraordinarily moving. And often the master, seized himself by the wonder of his subject, would push back the book in front of him, and with his hands clasped together over his heart, as though to still the beating, would talk of the mysteries of their religion. Sometimes Philip did not understand, but he did not want to understand, he felt vaguely that it was enough to feel. It seemed to him then that the headmaster, with his

69

black, straggling hair and his pale face, was like those prophets of Israel who feared not to take kings to task; and when he thought of the Redeemer he saw Him only with the same dark eyes and those wan cheeks.

Mr Perkins took this part of his work with great seriousness. There was never here any of that flashing humour which made the other masters suspect him of flippancy. Finding time for everything in his busy day, he was able at certain intervals to take separately for a quarter of an hour or twenty minutes the boys whom he was preparing for confirmation. He wanted to make them feel that this was the first consciously serious step in their lives; he tried to grope into the depths of their souls; he wanted to instil in them his own vehement devotion. In Philip, notwithstanding his shyness, he felt the possibility of a passion equal to his own. The boy's temperament seemed to him essentially religious. One day he broke off suddenly from the subject on which he had been talking.

'Have you thought at all what you're going to be when you grow up?' he asked.

'My uncle wants me to be ordained,' said Philip.

'And you?'

Philip looked away. He was ashamed to answer that he felt himself unworthy.

'I don't know any life that's so full of happiness as ours. I wish I could make you feel what a wonderful privilege it is. One can serve God in every walk, but we stand nearer to Him. I don't want to influence you, but if you made up your mind – oh, at once – you couldn't help feeling that joy and relief which never desert one again.'

Philip did not answer, but the headmaster read in his eyes that he realized already something of what he tried to indicate.

'If you go on as you are now you'll find yourself head of the school one of these days, and you ought to be pretty safe for a scholarship when you leave. Have you got anything of your own?'

'My uncle says I shall have a hundred a year when I'm twenty-one.'

'You'll be rich. I had nothing.'

The headmaster hesitated a moment, and then, idly drawing lines with a pencil on the blotting paper in front of him, went on.

'I'm afraid your choice of profession will be rather limited. You naturally couldn't go in for anything that required physical activity.'

Philip reddened to the roots of his hair, as he always did when any reference was made to his club-foot. Mr Perkins looked at him gravely.

'I wonder if you're not over-sensitive about your misfortune. Has it ever struck you to thank God for it?'

Philip looked up quickly. His lips tightened. He remembered how for months, trusting in what they told him, he had implored God to heal him as He had healed the Leper and made the Blind to see.

'As long as you accept it rebelliously it can only cause you shame. But if you looked upon it as a cross that was given you to bear only because your shoulders were strong enough to bear it, a sign of God's favour, then it would be a source of happiness to you instead of misery.'

He saw that the boy hated to discuss the matter and he let him go.

But Philip thought over all that the headmaster had said, and presently, his mind taken up entirely with the ceremony that was before him, a mystical rapture seized him. His spirit seemed to free itself from the bonds of the flesh and he seemed to be living a new life. He aspired to perfection with all the passion that was in him. He wanted to surrender himself entirely to the service of God, and he made up his mind definitely that he would be ordained. When the great day arrived, his soul deeply moved by all the preparation, by the books he had studied, and above all by the overwhelming influence of the head, he could hardly contain himself for fear and joy. One thought had tormented him. He knew that he would have to walk alone through the chancel, and he dreaded showing his limp thus obviously, not only to the whole school, who were attending the service, but also to the strangers, people from the city or parents who had come to see their sons confirmed. But when the time came he felt suddenly that he could accept the humiliation joyfully; and as he limped up the chancel, very small and insignificant beneath the lofty vaulting of the Cathedral, he offered consciously his deformity as a sacrifice to the God who loved him.

XVIII

BUT Philip could not live long in the rarefied air of the hilltops. What had happened to him when first he was seized by the religious emotion happened to him now. Because he felt

71

so keenly the beauty of faith, because the desire for self-sacrifice burned in his heart with such a gem-like glow, his strength seemed inadequate to his ambition. He was tired out by the violence of his passion. His soul was filled on a sudden with a singular aridity. He began to forget the presence of God which had seemed so surrounding; and his religious exercises, still very punctually performed, grew merely formal. At first he blamed himself for this falling away, and the fear of hell-fire urged him to renewed vehemence; but the passion was dead, and gradually other interests distracted his thoughts.

Philip had few friends. His habit of reading isolated him: it became such a need that after being in company for some time he grew tired and restless; he was vain of the wider knowledge he had acquired from the perusal of so many books, his mind was alert, and he had not the skill to hide his contempt for his companions' stupidity. They complained that he was conceited; and, since he excelled only in matters which to them were unimportant, they asked satirically what he had to be conceited about. He was developing a sense of humour, and found that he had a knack of saying bitter things, which caught people on the raw; he said them because they amused him, hardly realizing how much they hurt, and was much offended when he found that his victims regarded him with active dislike. The humiliations he suffered when first he went to school had caused in him a shrinking from his fellows which he could never entirely overcome; he remained shy and silent. But though he did everything to alienate the sympathy of other boys he longed with all his heart for the popularity which to some was so easily accorded. These from his distance he admired extravagantly; and though he was inclined to be more sarcastic with them than with others, though he made little jokes at their expense, he would have given anything to change places with them. Indeed he would gladly have changed places with the dullest boy in the school who was whole of limb. He took to a singular habit. He would imagine that he was some boy whom he had a particular fancy for; he would throw his soul, as it were, into the other's body, talk with his voice and laugh with his laugh; he would imagine himself doing all the things the other did. It was so vivid that he seemed for a moment really to be no longer himself. In this way he enjoyed many intervals of fantastic happiness.

At the beginning of the Christmas term which followed on

his confirmation Philip found himself moved into another study. One of the boys who shared it was called Rose. He was in the same form as Philip, and Philip had always looked upon him with envious admiration. He was not good-looking; though his large hands and big bones suggested that he would be a tall man, he was clumsily made; but his eyes were charming, and when he laughed (he was constantly laughing) his face wrinkled all round them in a jolly way. He was neither clever nor stupid, but good enough at his work and better at games. He was a favourite with masters and boys, and he in his turn liked everyone.

When Philip was put in the study he could not help seeing that the others, who had been together for three terms, welcomed him coldly. It made him nervous to feel himself an intruder; but he had learned to hide his feelings, and they found him quiet and unobtrusive. With Rose, because he was as little able as anyone else to resist his charm, Philip was even more than usually shy and abrupt; and whether on account of this, unconsciously bent upon exerting the fascination he knew was his only by the results, or whether from sheer kindness of heart, it was Rose who first took Philip into the circle. One day, quite suddenly, he asked Philip if he would walk to the football field with him. Philip flushed.

'I can't walk fast enough for you,' he said.

'Rot. Come on.'

And just before they were setting out some boy put his head in the study-door and asked Rose to go with him.

'I can't,' he answered. 'I've already promised Carey.'

'Don't bother about me,' said Philip quickly. 'I shan't mind.'

'Rot,' said Rose.

He looked at Philip with those good-natured eyes of his and laughed. Philip felt a curious tremor in his heart.

In a little while, their friendship growing with boyish rapidity, the pair were inseparable. Other fellows wondered at the sudden intimacy, and Rose was asked what he saw in Philip.

'Oh, I don't know,' he answered. 'He's not half a bad chap, really.'

Soon they grew accustomed to the two walking into chapel arm in arm or strolling round the precincts in conversation; wherever one was the other could be found also, and, as though acknowledging his proprietorship, boys who wanted Rose would leave messages with Carey. Philip at first was reserved. He would not let himself yield entirely to the proud joy that filled him; but presently his distrust of the fates gave way before a wild happiness. He thought Rose the most wonderful fellow he had ever seen. His books now were insignificant; he could not bother about them when there was something infinitely more important to occupy him. Rose's friends used to come in to tea in the study sometimes or sit about when there was nothing better to do – Rose liked a crowd and the chance of a rag – and they found that Philip was quite a decent fellow. Philip was happy.

When the last day of term came he and Rose arranged by which train they should come back, so that they might meet at the station and have tea in the town before returning to school. Philip went home with a heavy heart. He thought of Rose all through the holidays, and his fancy was active with the things they would do together next term. He was bored at the vicarage, and when on the last day his uncle put him the usual question in the usual facetious tone:

'Well, are you glad to be going back to school?'

Philip answered joyfully:

'Rather.'

In order to be sure of meeting Rose at the station he took an earlier train than he usually did, and he waited about the platform for an hour. When the train came in from Faversham, where he knew Rose had to change, he ran along it excitedly. But Rose was not there. He got a porter to tell him when another train was due, and he waited; but again he was disappointed; and he was cold and hungry, so he walked, through side-streets and slums, by a short cut to the school. He found Rose in the study, with his feet on the chimneypiece, talking eighteen to the dozen with half a dozen boys who were sitting on whatever there was to sit on. He shook hands with Philip enthusiastically, but Philip's face fell, for he realized that Rose had forgotten all about their appointment.

'I say, why are you so late?' said Rose. 'I thought you were never coming.'

'You were at the station at half-past four,' said another boy. 'I saw you when I came.'

Philip blushed a little. He did not want Rose to know that he had been such a fool as to wait for him.

'I had to see about a friend of my people's,' he invented readily. 'I was asked to see her off.'

But his disappointment made him a little sulky. He sat in silence, and when spoken to answered in monosyllables. He

74

was making up his mind to have it out with Rose when they were alone. But when the others had gone Rose at once came over and sat on the arm of the chair in which Philip was lounging.

'I say, I'm jolly glad we're in the same study this term. Ripping, isn't it?'

He seemed so genuinely pleased to see Philip that Philip's annoyance vanished. They began as if they had not been separated for five minutes to talk eagerly of the thousand things that interested them.

XIX

AT first Philip had been too grateful for Rose's friendship to make any demands on him. He took things as they came and enjoyed life. But presently he began to resent Rose's universal amiability; he wanted a more exclusive attachment, and he claimed as a right what before he had accepted as a favour. He watched jealously Rose's companionship with others; and though he knew it was unreasonable could not help sometimes saying bitter things to him. If Rose spent an hour playing the fool in another study, Philip would receive him when he returned to his own with a sullen frown. He would sulk for a day, and he suffered more because Rose either did not notice his ill-humour or deliberately ignored it. Not seldom Philip, knowing all the time how stupid he was, would force a quarrel, and they would not speak to one another for a couple of days. But Philip could not bear to be angry with him long, and even when convinced that he was in the right, would apologize humbly. Then for a week they would be as great friends as ever. But the best was over, and Philip could see that Rose often walked with him merely from old habit or from fear of his anger; they had not so much to say to one another as at first, and Rose was often bored. Philip felt that his lameness began to irritate him.

Towards the end of the term two or three boys caught scarlet fever, and there was much talk of sending them all home in order to escape an epidemic; but the sufferers were isolated, and since no more were attacked it was supposed that the outbreak was stopped. One of the stricken was Philip. He remained in hospital through the Easter holidays, and at the beginning of the summer term was sent home to the vicarage to get a little fresh air. The Vicar, notwithstanding medical assurance that the boy was no longer infectious, received him with suspicion; he thought it very inconsiderate of the doctor to suggest that his nephew's convalescence should be spent by the seaside, and consented to have him in the house only because there was nowhere else he could go.

Philip went back to school at half-term. He had forgotten the quarrels he had had with Rose, but remembered only that he was his greatest friend. He knew that he had been silly. He made up his mind to be more reasonable. During his illness Rose had sent him in a couple of little notes, and he had ended each with the words: 'Hurry up and come back.' Philip thought Rose must be looking forward as much to his return as he was himself to seeing Rose.

He found that owing to the death from scarlet fever of one of the boys in the Sixth there had been some shifting in the studies and Rose was no longer in his. It was a bitter disappointment. But as soon as he arrived he burst into Rose's study. Rose was sitting at his desk, working with a boy called Hunter, and turned round crossly as Philip came in.

'Who the devil's that?' he cried. And then, seeing Philip: 'Oh, it's you.'

Philip stopped in embarrassment.

'I thought I'd come in and see how you were.'

'We were just working.'

Hunter broke into the conversation.

'When did you get back?'

'Five minutes ago.'

They sat and looked at him as though he was disturbing them. They evidently expected him to go quickly. Philip reddened.

'I'll be off. You might look in when you've done,' he said to Rose.

'All right.'

Philip closed the door behind him and limped back to his own study. He felt frightfully hurt. Rose, far from seeming glad to see him, had looked almost put out. They might never have been more than acquaintances. Though he waited in his study, not leaving it for a moment in case just then Rose should come, his friend never appeared; and next morning when he went into prayers he saw Rose and Hunter swinging along arm in arm. What he could not see for himself others told him. He had forgotten that three months is a long time in a schoolboy's life, and though he had passed them in solitude Rose had lived in the world. Hunter had stepped into the vacant place. Philip found that Rose was quietly avoiding him. But he was not the boy to accept a situation without putting it into words; he waited till he was sure Rose was alone in his study and went in.

'May I come in?' he asked.

Rose looked at him with an embarrassment that made him angry with Philip.

'Yes, if you want to.'

'It's very kind of you,' said Philip sarcastically.

'What d'you want?'

'I say, why have you been so rotten since I came back?'

'Oh, don't be an ass,' said Rose.

'I don't know what you see in Hunter.'

'That's my business.'

Philip looked down. He could not bring himself to say what was in his heart. He was afraid of humiliating himself. Rose got up.

'I've got to go to the Gym,' he said.

When he was at the door Philip forced himself to speak.

'I say, Rose, don't be a perfect beast.'

'Oh, go to hell.'

Rose slammed the door behind him and left Philip alone. Philip shivered with rage. He went back to his study and turned the conversation over in his mind. He hated Rose now, he wanted to hurt him, he thought of biting things he might have said to him. He brooded over the end to their friendship and fancied that others were talking of it. In his sensitiveness he saw sneers and wonderings in other fellows' manner when they were not bothering their heads with him at all. He imagined to himself what they were saying.

'After all, it wasn't likely to last long. I wonder he ever stuck Carey at all. Blighter!'

To show his indifference he struck up a violent friendship with a boy called Sharp whom he hated and despised. He was a London boy, with a loutish air, a heavy fellow with the beginnings of a moustache on his lip and bushy eyebrows that joined one another across the bridge of his nose. He had soft hands and manners too suave for his years. He spoke with the suspicion of a cockney accent. He was one of those boys who are too slack to play games, and he exercised great ingenuity in making excuses to avoid such as were compulsory. He was regarded by boys and masters with a vague dislike, and it was from arrogance that Philip now sought his society. Sharp in a couple of terms was going to Germany for a year.

77

He hated school, which he looked upon as an indignity to be endured till he was old enough to go out into the world. London was all he cared for, and he had many stories to tell of his doings there during the holidays. From his conversation – he spoke in a soft, deep-toned voice – there emerged the vague rumour of the London streets by night. Philip listened to him at once fascinated and repelled. With his vivid fancy he seemed to see the surging throng round the pit-door of theatres, and the glitter of cheap restaurants, bars where men, half drunk, sat on high stools talking with barmaids; and under the street lamps the mysterious passing of dark crowds bent upon pleasure. Sharp lent him cheap novels from Holywell Street, which Philip read in his cubicle with a sort of wonderful fear.

Once Rose tried to effect a reconciliation. He was a good-natured fellow, who did not like having enemies.

'I say, Carey, why are you being such a silly ass? It doesn't do you any good cutting me and all that.'

'I don't know what you mean,' answered Philip.

'Well, I don't see why we shouldn't talk.'

'You bore me,' said Philip.

'Please yourself.'

Rose shrugged his shoulders and left him. Philip was very white, as he always became when he was moved, and his heart beat violently. When Rose went away he felt suddenly sick with misery. He did not know why he had answered in that fashion. He would have given anything to be friends with Rose. He hated to have quarrelled with him, and now that he saw he had given him pain he was very sorry. But at the moment he had not been master of himself. It seemed that some devil had seized him, forcing him to say bitter things against his will, even though at the time he wanted to shake hands with Rose and meet him more than half-way. The desire to wound had been too strong for him. He had wanted to revenge himself for the pain and the humiliation he had endured. It was pride: it was folly too, for he knew that Rose would not care at all, while he would suffer bitterly. The thought came to him that he would go to Rose, and say:

'I say, I'm sorry I was such a beast. I couldn't help it. Let's make it up.'

But he knew he would never be able to do it. He was afraid that Rose would sneer at him. He was angry with himself, and when Sharp came in a little while afterwards he seized upon the first opportunity to quarrel with him. Philip had a fiendish instinct for discovering other people's raw spots, and was able to say things that rankled because they were true. But Sharp had the last word.

'I heard Rose talking about you to Mellor just now,' he said. 'Mellor said: why didn't you kick him? It would teach him manners. And Rose said: I didn't like to. Damned cripple.'

Philip suddenly became scarlet. He could not answer, for there was a lump in his throat that almost choked him.

XX

PHILIP was moved into the Sixth, but he hated school now with all his heart, and, having lost his ambition, cared nothing whether he did ill or well. He awoke in the morning with a sinking heart because he must go through another day of drudgery. He was tired of having to do things because he was told; and the restrictions irked him, not because they were unreasonable, but because they were restrictions. He yearned for freedom. He was weary of repeating things that he knew already and of the hammering away, for the sake of a thick-witted fellow, at something that he understood from the beginning.

With Mr Perkins you could work or not as you chose. He was at once eager and abstracted. The Sixth Form room was in a part of the old abbey which had been restored, and it had a Gothic window: Philip tried to cheat his boredom by drawing this over and over again; and sometimes out of his head he drew the great tower of the Cathedral or the gateway that led into the precincts. He had a knack for drawing. Aunt Louisa during her youth had painted in water colours, and she had several albums filled with sketches of churches, old bridges, and picturesque cottages. They were often shown at the vicarage tea-parties. She had once given Philip a paint-box as a Christmas present, and he had started by copying her pictures. He copied them better than anyone could have expected, and presently he did little pictures of his own. Mrs Carey encouraged him. It was a good way to keep him out of mischief, and later on his sketches would be useful for bazaars. Two or three of them had been framed and hung in his bedroom.

But one day, at the end of the morning's work, Mr Perkins stopped him as he was lounging out of the form-room.

'I want to speak to you, Carey.'

Philip waited. Mr Perkins ran his lean fingers through his beard and looked at Philip. He seemed to be thinking over what he wanted to say.

'What's the matter with you, Carey?' he said abruptly.

Philip, flushing, looked at him quickly. But knowing him well by now, without answering, he waited for him to go on.

'I've been dissatisfied with you lately. You've been slack and inattentive. You seem to take no interest in your work. It's been slovenly and bad.'

'I'm very sorry, sir,' said Philip.

'Is that all you have to say for yourself?'

Philip looked down sulkily. How could he answer that he was bored to death?

'You know, this term you'll go down instead of up. I shan't give you a very good report.'

Philip wondered what he would say if he knew how the report was treated. It arrived at breakfast, Mr Carey glanced at it indifferently, and passed it over to Philip.

'There's your report. You'd better see what it says,' he remarked, as he ran his fingers through the wrapper of a catalogue of second-hand books.

Philip read it.

'Is it good?' asked Aunt Louisa.

'Not so good as I deserve,' answered Philip, with a smile, giving it to her.

'I'll read it afterwards when I've got my spectacles,' she said.

But after breakfast Mary Ann came in to say the butcher was there, and she generally forgot.

Mr Perkins went on.

'I'm disappointed with you. And I can't understand. I know you *can* do things if you want to, but you don't seem to want. to any more. I was going to make you a monitor next term, but I think I'd better wait a bit.'

Philip flushed. He did not like the thought of being passed over. He tightened his lips.

'And there's something else. You must begin thinking of your scholarship now. You won't get anything unless you start working very seriously.'

Philip was irritated by the lecture. He was angry with the headmaster, and angry with himself.

'I don't think I'm going up to Oxford,' he said.

'Why not? I thought your idea was to be ordained.'

'I've changed my mind.'

'Why?'

Philip did not answer. Mr Perkins, holding himself oddly as he always did, like a figure in one of Perugino's pictures, drew his fingers thoughtfully through his beard. He looked at Philip as though he were trying to understand and then abruptly told him he might go.

Apparently he was not satisfied, for one evening, a week later, when Philip had to go into his study with some papers, he resumed the conversation; but this time he adopted a different method: he spoke to Philip not as a schoolmaster with a boy but as one human being with another. He did not seem to care now that Philip's work was poor, that he ran small chance against keen rivals of carrying off the scholarship necessary for him to go to Oxford: the important matter was his changed intention about his life afterwards. Mr Perkins set himself to revive his eagerness to be ordained. With infinite skill he worked on his feelings, and this was easier since he was himself genuinely moved. Philip's change of mind caused him bitter distress, and he really thought he was throwing away his chance of happiness in life for he knew not what. His voice was very persuasive. And Philip, easily moved by the emotion of others, very emotional himself notwithstanding a placid exterior – his face, partly by nature but also from the habit of all these years at school, seldom except by his quick flushing showed what he felt – Philip was deeply touched by what the master said. He was very grateful to him for the interest he showed, and he was conscience-stricken by the grief which he felt his behaviour caused him. It was subtly flattering to know that with the whole school to think about Mr Perkins should trouble with him, but at the same time something else in him, like another person standing at his elbow, clung desperately to two words.

'I won't. I won't. I won't.'

He felt himself slipping. He was powerless against the weakness that seemed to well up in him; it was like the water that rises up in an empty bottle held over a full basin; and he set his teeth, saying the words over and over to himself.

'I won't. I won't. I won't.'

At last Mr Perkins put his hand on Philip's shoulder.

'I don't want to influence you,' he said. 'You must decide for yourself. Pray to Almighty God for help and guidance.'

When Philip came out of the headmaster's house there was a light rain falling. He went under the archway that led to the precincts, there was not a soul there, and the rooks were silent in the elms. He walked round slowly. He felt hot, and the rain did him good. He thought over all that Mr Perkins had said, calmly now that he was withdrawn from the fervour of his personality, and he was thankful he had not given way.

In the darkness he could but vaguely see the great mass of the Cathedral: he hated it now because of the irksomeness of the long services which he was forced to attend. The anthem was interminable, and you had to stand drearily while it was being sung; you could not hear the droning sermon, and your body twitched because you had to sit still when you wanted to move about. Then Philip thought of the two services every Sunday at Blackstable. The church was bare and cold, and there was a smell all about one of pomade and starched clothes. The curate preached once and his uncle preached once. As he grew up he had learned to know his uncle; Philip was downright and intolerant, and he could not understand that a man might sincerely say things as a clergyman which he never acted up to as a man. The deception outraged him. His uncle was a weak and selfish man, whose chief desire it was to be saved trouble.

Mr Perkins had spoken to him of the beauty of a life dedicated to the service of God. Philip knew what sort of lives the clergy led in the corner of East Anglia which was his home. There was the Vicar of Whitestone, a parish a little way from Blackstable: he was a bachelor and to give himself something to do had lately taken up farming: the local paper constantly reported the cases he had in the county court against this one and that, labourers he would not pay their wages to or tradesmen whom he accused of cheating him; scandal said he starved his cows, and there was much talk about some general action which should be taken against him. Then there was the Vicar of Ferne, a bearded, fine figure of a man: his wife had been forced to leave him because of his cruelty, and she had filled the neighbourhood with stories of his immorality. The Vicar of Surle, a tiny hamlet by the sea, was to be seen every evening in the public house a stone's throw from his vicarage; and the churchwardens had been to Mr Carey to ask his advice. There was not a soul for any of them to talk to except small farmers or fishermen; there were long winter evenings when the wind blew, whistling drearily through the leafless teees, and all around they saw nothing but the bare monotony of ploughed fields; and there was poverty, and there was lack of any work that seemed to matter; every kink in their characters had free play; there was nothing to restrain them; they grew narrow and eccentric: Philip knew all this, but in his young intolerance he did not offer it as an excuse. He shivered at the thought of leading such a life; he wanted to get out into the world.

XXI

MR PERKINS soon saw that his words had had no effect on Philip, and for the rest of the term ignored him. He wrote a report which was vitriolic. When it arrived and Aunt Louisa asked Philip what it was like, he answered cheerfully:

'Rotten.'

'Is it?' said the Vicar. 'I must look at it again.'

'Do you think there's any use in my staying on at Tercanbury? I should have thought it would be better if I went to Germany for a bit.'

'What has put that in your head?' said Aunt Louisa.

'Don't you think it's rather a good idea?'

Sharp had already left King's School and had written to Philip from Hanover. He was really starting life, and it made Philip more restless to think of it. He felt he could not bear another year of restraint.

'But then you wouldn't get a scholarship.'

'I haven't got a chance of getting one anyhow. And besides, I don't know that I particularly want to go to Oxford.'

'But if you're going to be ordained, Philip?' Aunt Louisa exclaimed in dismay.

'I've given up that idea long ago.'

Mrs Carey looked at him with startled eyes, and then, used to self-restraint, she poured out another cup of tea for his uncle. They did not speak. In a moment Philip saw tears slowly falling down her cheeks. His heart was suddenly wrung because he caused her pain. In her tight black dress, made by the dressmaker down the street, with her wrinkled face and pale tired eyes, her grey hair still done in the frivolous ringlets of her youth, she was a ridiculous but strangely pathetic figure. Philip saw it for the first time.

Afterwards, when the Vicar was shut up in his study with the curate, he put his arm round her waist.

'I say, I'm sorry you're upset, Aunt Louisa,' he said. 'But it's no good my being ordained if I haven't a real vocation, is it?'

'I'm so disappointed, Philip,' she moaned. 'I'd set my heart on it. I thought you could be your uncle's curate, and then

when our time came – after all, we can't last for ever, can we?
– you might have taken his place.'

Philip shivered. He was seized with panic. His heart beat
like a pigeon in a trap beating with its wings. His aunt wept
softly, her head upon his shoulder.

'I wish you'd persuade Uncle William to let me leave Tercanbury. I'm so sick of it.'

But the Vicar of Blackstable did not easily alter any arrangements he had made, and it had always been intended that
Philip should stay at King's School till he was eighteen, and
should then go to Oxford. At all events he would not hear of
Philip leaving then, for no notice had been given and the term's
fee would have to be paid in any case.

'Then will you give notice for me to leave at Christmas?'
said Philip, at the end of a long and often bitter conversation.

'I'll write to Mr Perkins about it and see what he says.'

'Oh, I wish to goodness I were twenty-one. It is awful to be
at somebody else's beck and call.'

'Philip, you shouldn't speak to your uncle like that,' said
Mrs Carey gently.

'But don't you see that Perkins will want me to stay? He gets
so much a head for every chap in the school.'

'Why don't you want to go to Oxford?'

'What's the good if I'm not going into the Church?'

'You can't go into the Church: you're in the Church already,' said the Vicar.

'Ordained then,' replied Philip impatiently.

'What are you going to be, Philip?' asked Mrs Carey.

'I don't know. I've not made up my mind. But whatever I
am, it'll be useful to know foreign languages. I shall get far
more out of a year in Germany than by staying on at that
hole.'

He would not say that he felt Oxford would be little better
than a continuation of his life at school. He wished immensely
to be his own master. Besides he would be known to a certain
extent among old school-fellows, and he wanted to get away
from them all. He felt that his life at school had been a failure.
He wanted to start afresh.

It happened that his desire to go to Germany fell in with
certain ideas which had been of late discussed at Blackstable.
Sometimes friends came to stay with the doctor and brought
news of the world outside; and the visitors spending August by
the sea had their own way of looking at things. The Vicar had
heard that there were people who did not think the old-fash-

ioned education so useful nowadays as it had been in the past, and modern languages were gaining an importance which they had not had in his own youth. His own mind was divided, for a younger brother of his had been sent to Germany when he failed in some examination, thus creating a precedent, but since he had there died of typhoid it was impossible to look upon the experiment as other than dangerous. The result of innumerable conversations was that Philip should go back to Tercanbury for another term and then should leave. With this agreement Philip was not dissatisfied. But when he had been back a few days the headmaster spoke to him.

'I've had a letter from your uncle. It appears you want to go to Germany, and he asks me what I think about it.'

Philip was astounded. He was furious with his guardian for going back on his word.

'I thought it was settled, sir,' he said.

'Far from it. I've written to say I think it the greatest mistake to take you away.'

Philip immediately sat down and wrote a violent letter to his uncle. He did not measure his language. He was so angry that he could not get to sleep till quite late that night, and he awoke in the early morning and began brooding over the way they had treated him. He waited impatiently for an answer. In two or three days it came. It was a mild, pained letter from Aunt Louisa, saying that he should not write such things to his uncle, who was very much distressed. He was unkind and unchristian. He must know they were only trying to do their best for him, and they were so much older than he that they must be better judges of what was good for him. Philip clenched his hands. He had heard that statement so often, and he could not see why it was true; they did not know the conditions as he did, why should they accept it as self-evident that their greater age gave them greater wisdom? The letter ended with the information that Mr Carey had withdrawn the notice he had given.

Philip nursed his wrath till the next half-holiday. They had them on Tuesdays and Thursdays, since on Saturday afternoons they had to go to a service in the Cathedral. He stopped behind when the rest of the Sixth went out.

'May I go to Blackstable this afternoon, please, sir?' he asked.

'No,' said the headmaster briefly.

'I wanted to see my uncle about something very important.'

'Didn't you hear me say no?'

Philip did not answer. He went out. He felt almost sick with humiliation, the humiliation of having to ask and the humiliation of the curt refusal. He hated the headmaster now. Philip writhed under that despotism which never vouchsafed a reason for the most tyrannous act. He was too angry to care what he did, and after dinner walked down to the station, by the back ways he knew so well, just in time to catch the train to Blackstable. He walked into the vicarage and found his uncle and aunt sitting in the dining-room.

'Hullo, where have you sprung from?' said the Vicar.

It was very clear that he was not pleased to see him. He looked a little uneasy.

'I thought I'd come and see you about my leaving. I want to know what you mean by promising me one thing when I was here, and doing something different a week after.'

He was a little frightened at his own boldness, but he had made up his mind exactly what words to use, and, though his heart beat violently, he forced himself to say them.

'Have you got leave to come here this afternoon?'

'No. I asked Perkins and he refused. If you like to write and tell him I've been here you can get me into a really fine old row.'

Mrs Carey sat knitting with trembling hands. She was unused to scenes and they agitated her extremely.

'It would serve you right if I told him,' said Mr Carey.

'If you like to be a perfect sneak you can. After writing to Perkins as you did you're quite capable of it.'

It was foolish of Philip to say that, because it gave the Vicar exactly the opportunity he wanted.

'I'm not going to sit still while you say impertinent things to me,' he said with dignity.

He got up and walked quickly out of the room into his study. Philip heard him shut the door and lock it.

'Oh, I wish to God I were twenty-one. It is awful to be tied down like this.'

Aunt Louisa began to cry quietly.

'Oh, Philip, you oughtn't to have spoken to your uncle like that. Do please go and tell him you're sorry.'

'I'm not in the least sorry. He's taking a mean advantage. Of course it's just waste of money keeping me on at school, but what does he care? It's not his money. It was cruel to put me under the guardianship of people who know nothing about things.'

'Philip.'

Philip in his voluble anger stopped suddenly at the sound of her voice. It was heart-broken. He had not realized what bitter things he was saying.

'Philip, how can you be so unkind? You know we are only trying to do our best for you, and we know that we have no experience; it isn't as if we'd had any children of our own: that's why we consulted Mr Perkins.' Her voice broke. 'I've tried to be like a mother to you. I've loved you as if you were my own son.'

She was so small and frail, there was something so pathetic in her old-maidish air, that Philip was touched. A great lump came suddenly in his throat and his eyes filled with tears.

'I'm so sorry,' he said. 'I didn't mean to be beastly.'

He knelt down beside her and took her in his arms, and kissed her wet, withered cheeks. She sobbed bitterly, and he seemed to feel on a sudden the pity of that wasted life. She had never surrendered herself before to such a display of emotion.

'I know I've not been what I wanted to be to you, Philip, but I didn't know how. It's been just as dreadful for me to have no children as for you to have no mother.'

Philip forgot his anger and his own concerns, but thought only of consoling her, with broken words and clumsy little caresses. Then the clock struck, and he had to bolt off at once to catch the only train that would get him back to Tercanbury in time for call-over. As he sat in the corner of the railway carriage he saw that he had done nothing. He was angry with himself for his weakness. It was despicable to have allowed himself to be turned from his purpose by the pompous airs of the Vicar and the tears of his aunt. But as the result of he knew not what conversations between the couple another letter was written to the headmaster. Mr Perkins read it with an impatient shrug of the shoulders. He showed it to Philip. It ran:

Dear Mr Perkins –

Forgive me for troubling you again about my ward, but both his Aunt and I have been uneasy about him. He seems very anxious to leave school, and his Aunt thinks he is unhappy. It is very difficult for us to know what to do as we are not his parents. He does not seem to think he is doing very well and he feels it is wasting his money to stay on. I should be very much obliged if you would have a talk to him, and if he is still of the same mind perhaps it would be better if he left at Christmas as I originally intended.

Yours very truly,

William Carey

Philip gave him back the letter. He felt a thrill of pride in his triumph. He had got his own way, and he was satisfied. His will had gained a victory over the wills of others.

'It's not much good my spending half an hour writing to your uncle if he changes his mind the next letter he gets from you,' said the headmaster irritably.

Philip said nothing, and his face was perfectly placid; but he could not prevent the twinkle in his eyes. Mr Perkins noticed it and broke into a little laugh.

'You've rather scored, haven't you?' he said.

Then Philip smiled outright. He could not conceal his exultation.

'Is it true that you're very anxious to leave?'

'Yes, sir.'

'Are you unhappy here?'

Philip blushed. He hated instinctively any attempt to get into the depths of his feelings.

'Oh, I don't know, sir.'

Mr Perkins, slowly dragging his fingers through his beard, looked at him thoughtfully. He seemed to speak almost to himself.

'Of course schools are made for the average. The holes are all round, and whatever shape the pegs are they must wedge in somehow. One hasn't time to bother about anything but the average.' Then suddenly he addressed himself to Philip: 'Look here, I've got a suggestion to make to you. It's getting on to-wards the end of the term now. Another term won't kill you, and if you want to go to Germany you'd better go after Easter than after Christmas. It'll be much pleasanter in the spring than in midwinter. If at the end of next term you still want to go I'll make no objection. What d'you say to that?'

'Thank you very much, sir.'

Philip was so glad to have gained the last three months that he did not mind the extra term. The school seemed less of a prison when he knew that before Easter he would be free from it for ever. His heart danced within him. That evening in chapel he looked round at the boys, standing according to their forms, each in his due place, and he chuckled with satisfaction at the thought that soon he would never see them again. It made him regard them almost with a friendly feeling. His eyes rested on Rose. Rose took his position as a monitor very seriously: he had quite an idea of being a good influence in the school; it was his turn to read the lesson that evening, and he read it very well. Philip smiled when he thought that he would be rid of him for ever, and it would not matter in six months whether Rose was tall and straight-limbed; and where would the importance be that he was a monitor and captain of the eleven? Philip looked at the masters in their gowns. Gordon was dead, he had died of apoplexy two years before, but all the rest were there. Philip knew now what a poor lot they were, except Turner perhaps, there was something of a man in him; and he writhed at the thought of the subjection in which they had held him. In six months they would not matter either. Their praise would mean nothing to him, and he would shrug his shoulders at their censure.

Philip had learned not to express his emotions by outward signs, and shyness still tormented him, but he had often very high spirits; and then, though he limped about demurely, silent and reserved, it seemed to be hallooing in his heart. He seemed to himself to walk more lightly. All sorts of ideas danced through his head, fancies chased one another so furiously that he could not catch them; but their coming and their going filled him with exhilaration. Now, being happy, he was able to work, and during the remaining weeks of the term set himself to make up for his long neglect. His brain worked easily, and he took a keen pleasure in the activity of his intellect. He did very well in the examinations that closed the term. Mr Perkins made only one remark: he was talking to him about an essay he had written, and, after the usual criticisms, said:

'So you've made up your mind to stop playing the fool for a bit, have you?'

He smiled at him with his shining teeth, and Philip, looking down, gave an embarrassed smile.

The half dozen boys who expected to divide between them the various prizes which were given at the end of the summer term had ceased to look upon Philip as a serious rival, but now they began to regard him with some uneasiness. He told no one that he was leaving at Easter and so was in no sense a competitor, but left them to their anxieties. He knew that Rose flattered himself on his French, for he had spent two or three holidays in France; and he expected to get the Dean's Prize for English essay; Philip got a good deal of satisfaction in watching his dismay when he saw how much better Philip was doing in these subjects than himself. Another fellow, Norton, could not go to Oxford unless he got one of the scholarships at the disposal of the school. He asked Philip if he was going in for them.

'Have you any objection?' asked Philip.

It entertained him to think that he held someone else's future in his hand. There was something romantic in getting these various rewards actually in his grasp, and then leaving them to others because he disdained them. At last the breaking-up day came, and he went to Mr Perkins to bid him goodbye.

'You don't mean to say you really want to leave?'

Philip's face fell at the headmaster's evident surprise.

'You said you wouldn't put any objection in the way, sir,' he answered.

'I thought it was only a whim that I'd better humour. I know you're obstinate and headstrong. What on earth d'you want to leave for now? You've only got another term in any case. You can get the Magdalen scholarship easily; you'll get half the prizes we've got to give.'

Philip looked at him sullenly. He felt that he had been tricked; but he had the promise, and Perkins would have to stand by it.

'You'll have a very pleasant time at Oxford. You needn't decide at once what you're going to do afterwards. I wonder if you realize how delightful the life is up there for anyone who has brains.'

'I've made all my arrangements now to go to Germany, sir,' said Philip.

'Are they arrangements that couldn't possibly be altered?' asked Mr Perkins, with his quizzical smile. 'I shall be very sorry to lose you. In schools the rather stupid boys who work always do better than the clever boy who's idle, but when the clever boy works – why then, he does what you've done this term.'

Philip flushed darkly. He was unused to compliments, and no one had ever told him he was clever. The headmaster put his hand on Philip's shoulder.

'You know, driving things into the heads of thick-witted boys is dull work, but when now and then you have the chance of teaching a boy who comes half-way towards you, who understands almost before you've got the words out of your mouth, why, then teaching is the most exhilarating thing in the world.'

Philip was melted by kindness; it had never occurred to him that it mattered really to Mr Perkins whether he went or stayed. He was touched and immensely flattered. It would be pleasant to end up his school-days with glory and then go to Oxford: in a flash there appeared before him the life which he had heard described from boys who came back to play in the O.K.S. match or in letters from the University read out in one of the studies. But he was ashamed; he would look such a fool in his own eyes if he gave in now; his uncle would chuckle at the success of the headmaster's ruse. It was rather a come-down from the dramatic surrender of all these prizes which were in his reach, because he disdained to take them, to the plain, ordinary winning of them. It only required a little more persuasion, just enough to save his self-respect, and Philip would have done anything that Mr Perkins wished; but his face showed nothing of his conflicting emotions. It was placid and sullen.

'I think I'd rather go, sir,' he said.

Mr Perkins, like many men who manage things by their personal influence, grew a little impatient when his power was not immediately manifest. He had a great deal of work to do, and could not waste more time on a boy who seemed to him insanely obstinate.

'Very well, I promised to let you if you really wanted it, and I keep my promise. When do you go to Germany?'

Philip's heart beat violently. The battle was won, and he did not know whether he had not rather lost it.

'At the beginning of May, sir,' he answered.

'Well, you must come and see us when you get back.'

He held out his hand. If he had given him one more chance Philip would have changed his mind, but he seemed to look upon the matter as settled. Philip walked out of the house. His school-days were over, and he was free; but the wild exultation to which he had looked forward at that moment was not there. He walked round the precincts slowly, and a profound depression seized him. He wished now that he had not been foolish. He did not want to go, but he knew he could never bring himself to go to the headmaster and tell him he would stay. That was a humiliation he could never put upon himself. He wondered whether he had done right. He was dissatisfied with himself and with all his circumstances. He asked himself dully whether whenever you got your way you wished afterwards that you hadn't.

XXII

PHILIP's uncle had an old friend, called Miss Wilkinson, who lived in Berlin. She was the daughter of a clergyman, and it was with her father, the rector of a village in Lincolnshire, that Mr Carey had spent his last curacy; on his death, forced to earn her living, she had taken various situations as a governess in France and Germany. She had kept up a correspondence with Mrs Carey, and two or three times had spent her holidays at Blackstable Vicarage, paying as was usual with the Careys' unfrequent guests a small sum for her keep. When it became clear that it was less trouble to yield to Philip's wishes than to resist them, Mrs Carey wrote to ask her for advice. Miss Wilkinson recommended Heidelberg as an excellent place to learn German in and the house of Frau Professor Erlin as a comfortable home. Philip might live there for thirty marks a week, and the Professor himself, a teacher at the local high school, would instruct him.

Philip arrived in Heidelberg one morning in May. His things were put on a barrow and he followed the porter out of the station. The sky was bright blue, and the trees in the avenue through which they passed were thick with leaves; there was something in the air fresh to Philip, and mingled with the timidity he felt at entering on a new life, among strangers, was a great exhilaration. He was a little disconsolate that no one had come to meet him, and felt very shy when the porter left him at the front door of a big white house. An untidy lad let him in and took him into a drawing-room. It was filled with a large suite covered in green velvet, and in the middle was a round table. On this in water stood a bouquet of flowers tightly packed together in a paper frill like the bone of a mutton chop, and carefully spaced round it were books in leather bindings. There was a musty smell.

Presently, with an odour of cooking, the Frau Professor came in, a short, very stout woman, with tightly dressed hair and a red face; she had little eyes, sparkling like beads, and an effusive manner. She took both Philip's hands and asked him about Miss Wilkinson, who had twice spent a few weeks with her. She spoke in German and in broken English. Philip could not make her understand that he did not know Miss Wilkinson. Then her two daughters appeared. They seemed hardly young to Philip, but perhaps they were not more than twenty-five: the elder, Thekla, was as short as her mother, with the same rather shifty air, but with a pretty face and abundant dark hair; Anna, her younger sister, was tall and plain, but since she had a pleasant smile Philip immediately preferred her. After a few minutes of polite conversation the Frau Professor took Philip to his room and left him. It was in a turret, looking over the tops of the trees in the *Anlage*; and

the bed was in an alcove, so that when you sat at the desk it
had not the look of a bedroom at all. Philip unpacked his
things and set out all his books. He was his own master at
last.

A bell summoned him to dinner at one o'clock, and he
found the Frau Professor's guests assembled in the drawing-
room. He was introduced to her husband, a tall man of middle
age with a large fair head, turning now to grey, and mild blue
eyes. He spoke to Philip in correct, rather archaic English,
having learned it from a study of the English classics, not from
conversation; and it was odd to hear him use words colloqui-
ally which Philip had only met in the plays of Shakespeare.
Frau Professor Erlin called her establishment a family and not
a pension; but it would have required the subtlety of a meta-
physician to find out exactly where the difference lay. When
they sat down to dinner in a long dark apartment that led out
of the drawing-room, Philip, feeling very shy, saw that there
were sixteen people. The Frau Professor sat at one end and
carved. The service was conducted, with a great clattering of
plates, by the same clumsy lout who had opened the door for
him; and though he was quick, it happened that the first
persons to be served had finished before the last had received
their appointed portions. The Frau Professor insisted that
nothing but German should be spoken, so that Philip, even if
his bashfulness had permitted him to be talkative, was forced
to hold his tongue. He looked at the people among whom he
was to live. By the Frau Professor sat several old ladies, but
Philip did not give them much of his attention. There were
two young girls, both fair and one of them very pretty, whom
Philip heard addressed as Fräulein Hedwig and Fräulein
Cäcilie. Fräulein Cäcilie had a long pig-tail hanging down her
back. They sat side by side and chattered to one another, with
smothered laughter: now and then they glanced at Philip
and one of them said something in an undertone; they both
giggled, and Philip blushed awkwardly, feeling that they were
making fun of him. Near them sat a Chinaman, with a yellow
face and an expansive smile, who was studying Western conditions at the University. He spoke so quickly, with a queer
accent, that the girls could not always understand him, and
then they burst out laughing. He laughed too, good-
humouredly, and his almond eyes almost closed as he did so.
There were two or three American men, in black coats, rather
yellow and dry of skin: they were theological students; Philip
heard the twang of their New England accent through their

bad German, and he glanced at them with suspicion; for he had been taught to look upon Americans as wild and desperate barbarians.

Afterwards, when they had sat for a little on the stiff green velvet chairs of the drawing-room, Fräulein Anna asked Philip if he would like to go for a walk with them.

Philip accepted the invitation. They were quite a party. There were the two daughters of the Frau Professor, the two other girls, one of the American students, and Philip. Philip walked by the side of Anna and Fräulein Hedwig. He was a little fluttered. He had never known any girls. At Blackstable there were only the farmers' daughters and the girls of the local tradesmen. He knew them by name and by sight, but he was timid, and he thought they laughed at his deformity. He accepted willingly the difference which the Vicar and Mrs Carey put between their own exalted rank and that of the farmers. The doctor had two daughters, but they were both much older than Philip and had been married to successive assistants while Philip was still a small boy. At school there had been two or three girls of more boldness than modesty whom some of the boys knew; and desperate stories, due in all probability to the masculine imagination, were told of intrigues with them; but Philip had always concealed under a lofty contempt the terror with which they filled him. His imagination and the books he had read had inspired in him a desire for the Byronic attitude; and he was torn between a morbid self-consciousness and a conviction that he owed it to himself to be gallant. He felt now that he should be bright and amusing, but his brain seemed empty and he could not for the life of him think of anything to say. Fräulein Anna, the Frau Professor's daughter, addressed herself to him frequently from a sense of duty, but the other said little: she looked at him now and then with sparkling eyes, and sometimes to his confusion laughed outright. Philip felt that she thought him perfectly ridiculous. They walked along the side of a hill among pine-trees, and their pleasant odour caused Philip a keen delight. The day was warm and cloudless. At last they came to an eminence from which they saw the valley of the Rhine spread out before them under the sun. It was a vast stretch of country, sparkling with golden light, with cities in the distance; and through it meandered the silver ribband of the river. Wide spaces are rare in the corner of Kent which Philip knew, the sea offers the only broad horizon, and the immense distance he saw now gave him a peculiar, an indescribable thrill. He felt suddenly elated. Though he did not know it, it was the first time that he had experienced, quite undiluted with foreign emotions, the sense of beauty. They sat on a bench, the three of them, for the others had gone on, and while the girls talked in rapid German, Philip, indifferent to their proximity, feasted his eyes.

'By jove, I am happy,' he said to himself, unconsciously.

XXIII

PHILIP thought occasionally of the King's School at Tercanbury, and laughed to himself as he remembered what at some particular moment of the day they were doing. Now and then he dreamed that he was there still, and it gave him an extraordinary satisfaction, on awaking, to realize that he was in his little room in the turret. From his bed he could see the great cumulus clouds that hung in the blue sky. He revelled in his freedom. He could go to bed when he chose and get up when the fancy took him. There was no one to order him about. It struck him that he need not tell any more lies.

It had been arranged that Professor Erlin should teach him Latin and German; a Frenchman came every day to give him lessons in French; and the Frau Professor had recommended for mathematics an Englishman who was taking a philological degree at the University. This was a man named Wharton. Philip went to him every morning. He lived in one room on the top floor of a shabby house. It was dirty and untidy, and it was filled with a pungent odour made up of many different stinks. He was generally in bed when Philip arrived at ten o'clock, and he jumped out, put on a filthy dressing-gown and felt slippers, and, while he gave instruction, ate his simple breakfast. He was a short man, stout from excessive beer-drinking, with a heavy moustache and long, unkempt hair. He had been in Germany for five years and was become very Teutonic. He spoke with scorn of Cambridge where he had taken his degree and with horror of the life which awaited him when, having taken his doctorate in Heidelberg, he must return to England and a pedagogic career. He adored the life of the German University with its happy freedom and its jolly companionships. He was a member of a *Burschenschaft*, and promised to take Philip to a *Kneipe*. He was very poor and made no secret that the lessons he was giving Philip meant the difference between meat for his dinner and bread and cheese. Sometimes after a heavy night he had such a headache that he could not drink his coffee, and he gave his lesson with heaviness of spirit. For these occasions he kept a few bottles of beer under the bed, and one of these and a pipe would help him to bear the burden of life.

'A hair of the dog that bit him,' he would say as he poured out the beer, carefully, so that the foam should not make him wait too long to drink.

Then he would talk to Philip of the University, the quarrels between the rival corps, the duels, and the merits of this and that professor. Philip learnt more of life from him than of mathematics. Sometimes Wharton would sit back with a laugh and say:

'Look here, we've not done anything today. You needn't pay me for the lesson.'

'Oh, it doesn't matter,' said Philip.

This was something new and very interesting, and he felt that it was of greater import than trigonometry, which he never could understand. It was like a window on life that he had a chance of peeping through, and he looked with a wildly beating heart.

'No, you can keep your dirty money,' said Wharton.

'But how about your dinner?' said Philip, with a smile, for he knew exactly how his master's finances stood.

Wharton had even asked him to pay him the two shillings which the lesson cost once a week rather than once a month, since it made things less complicated.

'Oh, never mind my dinner. It won't be the first time I've dined off a bottle of beer, and my mind's never clearer than when I do.'

He dived under the bed (the sheets were grey with want of washing), and fished out another bottle. Philip, who was young and did not know the good things of life, refused to share it with him, so he drank alone.

'How long are you going to stay here?' asked Wharton.

Both he and Philip had given up with relief the pretence of mathematics.

'Oh, I don't know. I suppose about a year. Then my people want me to go to Oxford.'

Wharton gave a contemptuous shrug of the shoulders. It was a new experience for Philip to learn that there were persons who did not look upon that seat of learning with awe.

'What d'you want to go there for? You'll only be a glorified schoolboy. Why don't you matriculate here? A year's no good. Spend five years here. You know, there are two good things in life, freedom of thought and freedom of action. In France you get freedom of action: you can do what you like and nobody bothers, but you must think like everybody else. In Germany you must do what everybody else does, but you may think as you choose. They're both very good things. I personally prefer freedom of thought. But in England you get neither: you're ground down by convention. You can't think as you like and you can't act as you like. That's because it's a democratic nation. I expect America's worse.'

He leaned back cautiously, for the chair on which he sat had a rickety leg, and it was disconcerting when a rhetorical flourish was interrupted by a sudden fall to the floor.

'I ought to go back to England this year, but if I can scrape together enough to keep body and soul on speaking terms I shall stay another twelve months. But then I shall have to go. And I must leave all this' – he waved his arm round the dirty garret, with its unmade bed, the clothes lying on the floor, a row of empty beer bottles against the wall, piles of unbound, ragged books in every corner – 'for some provincial university where I shall try and get a chair of philology. And I shall play tennis and go to tea-parties.' He interrupted himself and gave Philip, very neatly dressed, with a clean collar on and his hair well brushed, a quizzical look. 'And, my God! I shall have to wash.'

Philip reddened, feeling his own spruceness an intolerable reproach; for of late he had begun to pay some attention to his toilet, and he had come out from England with a pretty selection of ties.

The summer came upon the country like a conqueror. Each day was beautiful. The sky had an arrogant blue which goaded the nerves like a spur. The green of the trees in the *Anlage* was violent and crude; and the houses, when the sun caught them, had a dazzling white which stimulated till it hurt. Sometimes on his way back from Wharton Philip would sit in the shade on one of the benches in the *Anlage*, enjoying the coolness and watching the patterns of light which the sun, shining through the leaves, made on the ground. His soul danced with delight as gaily as the sunbeams. He revelled in those moments of idleness stolen from his work. Sometimes he sauntered through the streets of the old town. He looked with awe at the students of the corps, their cheeks gashed and red, who swaggered about in their coloured caps. In the afternoons he wandered about the hills with the girls in the Frau Professor's house, and sometimes they went up the river and had tea in a leafy beer-garden. In the evenings they walked round and round the *Stadtgarten*, listening to the band.

Philip soon learned the various interests of the household. Fräulein Thekla, the professor's elder daughter, was engaged to a man in England who had spent twelve months in the house to learn German, and their marriage was to take place at the end of the year. But the young man wrote that his father, an india-rubber merchant who lived in Slough, did not approve of the union, and Fräulein Thekla was often in tears. Sometimes she and her mother might be seen, with stern eyes and determined mouths, looking over the letters of the reluctant lover. Thekla painted in water colour, and occasionally she and Philip, with another of the girls to keep them company, would go out and paint little pictures. The pretty Fräulein Hedwig had amorous troubles too. She was the daughter of a merchant in Berlin and a dashing hussar had fallen in love with her, a *von* if you please; but his parents opposed a marriage with a person of her condition, and she had been sent to Heidelberg to forget him. She could never, never do this, and corresponded with him continually, and he was making every effort to induce an exasperating father to change his mind. She told all this to Philip with pretty sighs and becoming blushes, and showed him the photograph of the gay lieutenant. Philip liked her best of all the girls at the Frau Professor's, and on their walks always tried to get by her side. He blushed a great deal when the others chaffed him for his obvious preference. He made the first declaration in his life to Fräulein Hedwig, but unfortunately it was an accident, and it happened in this manner. In the evenings when they did not go out, the young women sang little songs in the green velvet drawing-room, while Fräulein Anna, who always made herself useful, industriously accompanied. Fräulein Hedwig's favourite song was called *Ich liebe dich* (I love you); and one evening after she had sung this, when Philip was standing with her on the balcony, looking at the stars, it occurred to him to make some remark about it. He began ·

'*Ich liebe dich.*'

His German was halting, and he looked about for the word he wanted. The pause was infinitesimal, but before he could go on Fräulein Hedwig said:

'*Ach, Herr Carey, Sie müssen mir nicht "du" sagen* – you mustn't talk to me in the second person singular.'

Philip felt himself grow hot all over, for he would never have dared to do anything so familiar, and he could think of

nothing on earth to say. It would be ungallant to explain that
he was not making an observation, but merely mentioning the
title of a song.

'*Entschuldigen Sie*,' he said. 'I beg your pardon.'

'It does not matter,' she whispered.

She smiled pleasantly, quietly took his hand and pressed it,
then turned back into the drawing-room.

Next day he was so embarrassed that he could not speak to
her, and in his shyness did all that was possible to avoid her.
When he was asked to go for the usual walk he refused because, he said, he had work to do. But Fräulein Hedwig seized
an opportunity to speak to him alone.

'Why are you behaving in this way?' she said kindly. 'You
know, I'm not angry with you for what you said last night.
You can't help it if you love me. I'm flattered. But although
I'm not exactly engaged to Hermann I can never love anyone
else, and I look upon myself as his bride.'

Philip blushed again, but he put on quite the expression of
a rejected lover.

'I hope you'll be very happy,' he said.

XXIV

PROFESSOR ERLIN gave Philip a lesson every day. He made
out a list of books which Philip was to read till he was ready
for the final achievement of *Faust*, and meanwhile, ingeniously
enough, started him on a German translation of one of the
plays by Shakespeare which Philip had studied at school. It was
the period in Germany of Goethe's highest fame. Notwithstanding his rather condescending attitude towards patriotism
he had been adopted as the national poet, and seemed since
the war of seventy to be one of the most significant glories of
national unity. The enthusiastic seemed in the wildness of the
Walpurgisnacht to hear the rattle of artillery at Gravelotte.
But one mark of a writer's greatness is that different minds can
find in him different inspirations; and Professor Erlin, who
hated the Prussians, gave his enthusiastic admiration to Goethe
because his works, Olympian and sedate, offered the only
refuge for a sane mind against the onslaughts of the present
generation. There was a dramatist whose name of late had
been much heard at Heidelberg, and the winter before one of
his plays had been given at the theatre amid the cheers of
adherents and the hisses of decent people. Philip heard dis-

cussions about it at the Frau Professor's long table, and at these Professor Erlin lost his wonted calm: he beat the table with his fist, and drowned all opposition with the roar of his fine deep voice. It was nonsense and obscene nonsense. He forced himself to sit the play out, but he did not know whether he was more bored or nauseated. If that was what the theatre was coming to, then it was high time the police stepped in and closed the playhouses. He was no prude and could laugh as well as anyone at the witty immorality of a farce at the Palais Royal, but here was nothing but filth. With an emphatic gesture he held his nose and whistled through his teeth. It was the ruin of the family, the uprooting of morals, the destruction of Germany.

'*Aber, Adolf,*' said the Frau Professor from the other end of the table. 'Calm yourself.'

He shook his fist at her. He was the mildest of creatures and ventured upon no action in his life without consulting her.

'No, Helene, I tell you this,' he shouted. 'I would sooner my daughters were lying dead at my feet than see them listening to the garbage of that shameless fellow.'

The play was *A Doll's House* and the author was Henrik Ibsen.

Professor Erlin classed him with Richard Wagner, but of him he spoke not with anger but with good-humoured laughter. He was a charlatan but a successful charlatan, and in that was always something for the comic spirit to rejoice in.

'*Verrückter Kerl!* A madman!' he said.

He had seen *Lohengrin* and that passed muster. It was dull, but no worse. But *Siegfried*! When he mentioned it Professor Erlin leaned his head on his hand and bellowed with laughter. Not a melody in it from beginning to end! He could imagine Richard Wagner sitting in his box and laughing till his sides ached at the sight of all the people who were taking it seriously. It was the greatest hoax of the nineteenth century. He lifted his glass of beer to his lips, threw back his head, and drank till the glass was empty. Then wiping his mouth with the back of his hand, he said:

'I tell you young people that before the nineteenth century is out Wagner will be as dead as mutton. Wagner! I would give all his works for one opera by Donizetti.'

XXV

THE oddest of Philip's masters was his teacher of French. Monsieur Ducroz was a citizen of Geneva. He was a tall old man, with a sallow skin and hollow cheeks; his grey hair was thin and long. He wore shabby black clothes, with holes at the elbows of his coat and frayed trousers. His linen was very dirty. Philip had never seen him in a clean collar. He was a man of few words, who gave his lesson conscientiously but without enthusiasm, arriving as the clock struck and leaving on the minute. His charges were very small. He was taciturn, and what Philip learnt about him he learnt from others: it appeared that he had fought with Garibaldi against the Pope, but had left Italy in disgust when it was clear that all his efforts for freedom, by which he meant the establishment of a republic, tended to no more than an exchange of yokes; he had been expelled from Geneva for it was not known what political offences. Philip looked upon him with puzzled surprise; for he was very unlike his idea of the revolutionary: he spoke in a low voice and was extraordinarily polite; he never sat down till he was asked to; and when on rare occasions he met Philip in the street took off his hat with an elaborate gesture; he never laughed, he never even smiled. A more complete imagination than Philip's might have pictured a youth of splendid hope, for he must have been entering upon manhood in 1848 when kings, remembering their brother of France, went about with an uneasy crick in their necks; and perhaps that passion for liberty which passed through Europe, sweeping before it what of absolutism and tyranny had reared its head during the reaction from the revolution of 1789, filled no breast with a hotter fire. One might fancy him, passionate with theories of human equality and human rights, discussing, arguing, fighting behind barricades in Paris, flying before the Austrian cavalry in Milan, imprisoned here, exiled from there, hoping on and upborne ever with the word which seemed so magical, the word Liberty; till at last, broken with disease and starvation, old, without means to keep body and soul together but such lessons as he could pick up from poor students, he found himself in that neat little town under the heel of a personal tyranny greater than any in Europe. Perhaps his taciturnity hid a contempt for the human race which had abandoned the great dreams of his youth and now wallowed in sluggish ease; or perhaps these thirty years of revolution had taught him that men are unfit for liberty, and he thought that he had spent his life in the pursuit of that which was not worth the finding. Or maybe he was tired out and waited only with indifference for the release of death.

One day Philip, with the bluntness of his age, asked him if it was true he had been with Garibaldi. The old man did not seem to attach any importance to the question. He answered quite quietly in as low a voice as usual:

'*Oui, monsieur.*'

'They say you were in the Commune?'

'Do they? Shall we get on with our work?'

He held the book open and Philip, intimidated, began to translate the passage he had prepared.

One day Monsieur Ducroz seemed to be in great pain. He had been scarcely able to drag himself up the many stairs to Philip's room; and when he arrived sat down heavily, his sallow face drawn, with beads of sweat on his forehead, trying to recover himself.

'I'm afraid you're ill,' said Philip.

'It's of no consequence.'

But Philip saw that he was suffering, and at the end of the hour asked whether he would not prefer to give no more lessons till he was better.

'No,' said the old man, in his even low voice. 'I prefer to go on while I am able.'

Philip, morbidly nervous when he had to make any reference to money, reddened.

'But it won't make any difference to you,' he said. 'I'll pay for the lessons just the same. If you wouldn't mind I'd like to give you the money for next week in advance.'

Monsieur Ducroz charged eighteenpence an hour. Philip took a ten-mark piece out of his pocket and shyly put it on the table. He could not bring himself to offer it as if the old man were a beggar.

'In that case I think I won't come again till I'm better.' He took the coin and, without anything more than the elaborate bow with which he always took his leave, went out.

'*Bonjour, monsieur.*'

Philip was vaguely disappointed. Thinking he had done a generous thing, he had expected that Monsieur Ducroz would overwhelm him with expressions of gratitude. He was taken aback to find that the old teacher accepted the present as though it were his due. He was so young, he did not realize how much less is the sense of obligation in those who receive favours than in those who grant them. Monsieur Ducroz appeared again five or six days later. He tottered a little more and was very weak, but seemed to have overcome the severity of the attack. He was no more communicative than he had been before. He remained mysterious, aloof, and dirty. He made no reference to his illness till after the lesson; and then, just as he was leaving, at the door, which he held open, he paused. He hesitated, as though to speak were difficult.

'If it hadn't been for the money you gave me I should have starved. It was all I had to live on.'

He made his solemn, obsequious bow, and went out. Philip felt a little lump in his throat. He seemed to realize in a fashion the hopeless bitterness of the old man's struggle, and how hard life was for him when to himself it was so pleasant.

XXVI

PHILIP had spent three months in Heidelberg when one morning the Frau Professor told him that an Englishman named Hayward was coming to stay in the house, and the same evening at supper he saw a new face. For some days the family had lived in a state of excitement. First, as the result of heaven knows what scheming, by dint of humble prayers and veiled threats, the parents of the young Englishman to whom Fräulein Thekla was engaged had invited her to visit them in England, and she had set off with an album of water colours to show how accomplished she was and a bundle of letters to prove how deeply the young man had compromised himself. A week later Fräulein Hedwig with radiant smiles announced that the lieutenant of her affections was coming to Heidelberg with his father and mother. Exhausted by the importunity of their son and touched by the dowry which Fräulein Hedwig's father offered, the lieutenant's parents had consented to pass through Heidelberg to make the young woman's acquaintance. The interview was satisfactory and Fräulein Hedwig had the satisfaction of showing her lover in the *Stadtgarten* to the whole of Frau Professor Erlin's household. The silent old ladies who sat at the top of the table near the Frau Professor were in a flutter, and when Fräulein Hedwig said she was to go home at once for the formal engagement to take place, the Frau Professor, regardless of expense, said she would give a *Maibowle*. Professor Erlin prided himself on his skill in preparing this mild intoxicant, and after supper the large bowl of hock and soda, with scented herbs floating in it, and wild strawberries, was placed with solemnity on the round table in the drawing-room. Fräulein Anna teased Philip about the departure of his lady-love, and he felt very uncomfortable and rather melancholy. Fräulein Hedwig sang several songs. Fräulein Anna played the Wedding March, and the Professor sang *Die Wacht am Rhein*. Amid all this jollification Philip paid little attention to the new arrival. They had sat opposite one another at supper, but Philip was chattering busily with Fräulein Hedwig, and the stranger, knowing no German, had eaten his food in silence. Philip, observing that he wore a pale blue tie, had on that account taken a sudden dislike to him. He was a man of twenty-six, very fair, with long, wavy hair through which he passed his hand frequently with a careless gesture. His eyes were large and blue, but the blue was very pale, and they looked rather tired already. He was clean-shaven, and his mouth, notwithstanding its thin lips, was well shaped. Fräulein Anna took an interest in physiognomy, and she made Philip nótice afterwards how finely shaped was his skull, and how weak was the lower part of his face. The head, she remarked, was the head of a thinker, but the jaw lacked character. Fräulein Anna, foredoomed to a spinster's life, with her high cheekbones and large misshapen nose, laid great stress upon character. While they talked of him he stood a little apart from the others, watching the noisy party with a good-humoured but faintly supercilious expression. He was tall and slim. He held himself with a deliberate grace. Weeks, one of the American students, seeing him alone, went up and began to talk to him. The pair were oddly contrasted: the American very neat in his black coat and pepper-and-salt trousers, thin and dried-up, with something of ecclesiastical unction already in his manner; and the Englishman in his loose tweed suit, large-limbed and slow of gesture.

Philip did not speak to the new-comer till next day. They found themselves alone on the balcony of the drawing-room before dinner. Hayward addressed him.

'You're English, aren't you?'

'Yes.'

'Is the food always as bad as it was last night?'

'It's always about the same.'

'Beastly, isn't it?'

'Beastly.'

Philip had found nothing wrong with the food at all, and

104

in fact had eaten it in large quantities with appetite and enjoyment, but he did not want to show himself a person of so little discrimination as to think a dinner good which another thought execrable.

Fräulein Thekla's visit to England made it necessary for her sister to do more in the house, and she could not often spare the time for long walks; and Fräulein Cäcilie, with her long plait of fair hair and her little snub-nosed face, had of late shown a certain disinclination for society. Fräulein Hedwig was gone, and Weeks, the American who generally accompanied them on their rambles, had set out for a tour of South Germany. Philip was left a good deal to himself. Hayward sought his acquaintance; but Philip had an unfortunate trait: from shyness or from some atavistic inheritance of the cave-dweller, he always disliked people on first acquaintance; and it was not till he became used to them that he got over his first impression. It made him difficult of access. He received Hayward's advances very shyly, and when Hayward asked him one day to go for a walk he accepted only because he could not think of a civil excuse. He made his usual apology, angry with himself for the flushing cheeks he could not control, and trying to carry it off with a laugh.

'I'm afraid I can't walk very fast.'

'Good heavens, I don't walk for a wager. I prefer to stroll. Don't you remember the chapter in *Marius* where Peter talks of the gentle exercise of walking as the best incentive to conversation?'

Philip was a good listener; though he often thought of clever things to say, it was seldom till after the opportunity to say them had passed; but Hayward was communicative; anyone more experienced than Philip might have thought he liked to hear himself talk. His supercilious attitude impressed Philip. He could not help admiring, and yet being awed by, a man who faintly despised so many things which Philip had looked upon as almost sacred. He cast down the fetish of exercise, damning with the contemptuous word pot-hunters all those who devoted themselves to its various forms; and Philip did not realize that he was merely putting up in its stead the other fetish of culture.

They wandered up to the castle, and sat on the terrace that overlooked the town. It nestled in the valley along the pleasant Neckar with a comfortable friendliness. The smoke from the chimneys hung over it, a pale blue haze; and the tall roofs, the spires of the churches, gave it a pleasantly medieval air.

There was a homeliness in it which warmed the heart. Hayward talked of *Richard Feverel* and *Madame Bovary*, of Verlaine, Dante, and Matthew Arnold. In those days Fitzgerald's translation of Omar Khayyám was known only to the elect, and Hayward repeated it to Philip. He was very fond of reciting poetry, his own and that of others, which he did in a monotonous sing-song. By the time they reached home Philip's distrust of Hayward was changed to enthusiastic admiration.

They made a practice of walking together every afternoon, and Philip learned presently something of Hayward's circumstances. He was the son of a country judge, on whose death some time before he had inherited three hundred a year. His record at Charterhouse was so brilliant that when he went to Cambridge the Master of Trinity Hall went out of his way to express his satisfaction that he was going to that college. He prepared himself for a distinguished career. He moved in the most intellectual circles; he read Browning with enthusiasm and turned up his well-shaped nose at Tennyson; he knew all the details of Shelley's treatment of Harriet; he dabbled in the history of art (on the walls of his rooms were reproductions of pictures by G. F. Watts, Burne-Jones, and Botticelli); and he wrote not without distinction verses of a pessimistic character. His friends told one another that he was a man of excellent gifts, and he listened to them willingly when they prophesied his future eminence. In course of time he became an authority on art and literature. He came under the influence of Newman's *Apologia*; the picturesqueness of the Roman Catholic faith appealed to his aesthetic sensibility; and it was only the fear of his father's wrath (a plain, blunt man of narrow ideas, who read Macauley) which prevented him from 'going over'. When he only got a pass degree his friends were astonished; but he shrugged his shoulders and delicately insinuated that he was not the dupe of examiners. He made one feel that a first class was ever so slightly vulgar. He described one of the vivas with tolerant humour; some fellow in an outrageous collar was asking him questions in logic; it was infinitely tedious, and suddenly he noticed that he wore elastic-sided boots: it was grotesque and ridiculous; so he withdrew his mind and thought of the Gothic beauty of the Chapel at King's. But he had spent some delightful days at Cambridge; he had given better dinners than anyone he knew; and the conversation in his rooms had been often memorable. He quoted to Philip the exquisite epigram:

'They told me, Herakleitus, they told me you were dead.'

And now, when he related again the picturesque little anecdote about the examiner and his boots, he laughed.

'Of course, it was folly,' he said, 'but it was a folly in which there was something fine.'

Philip, with a little thrill, thought it magnificent.

Then Hayward went to London to read for the bar. He had charming rooms in Clement's Inn, with panelled walls, and he tried to make them look like his old rooms at the Hall. He had ambitions that were vaguely political, he described himself as a Whig, and he was put up for a club which was of Liberal but gentlemanly flavour. His idea was to practise at the Bar (he chose the Chancery side as less brutal), and get a seat for some pleasant constituency as soon as the various promises made him were carried out; meanwhile he went a great deal to the opera, and made acquaintance with a small number of charming people who admired the things that he admired. He joined a dining-club of which the motto was, The Whole, The Good, and The Beautiful. He formed a platonic friendship with a lady some years older than himself, who lived in Kensington Square; and nearly every afternoon he drank tea with her by the light of shaded candles, and talked of George Meredith and Walter Pater. It was notorious that any fool could pass the examinations of the Bar Council, and he pursued his studies in a dilatory fashion. When he was ploughed for his final he looked upon it as a personal affront. At the same time the lady in Kensington Square told him that her husband was coming home from India on leave, and was a man, though worthy in every way, of a common-place mind, who would not understand a young man's frequent visits. Hayward felt that life was full of ugliness, his soul revolted from the thought of affronting again the cynicism of examiners, and he saw something rather splendid in kicking away the ball which lay at his feet. He was also a good deal in debt: it was difficult to live in London like a gentleman on three hundred a year; and his heart yearned for the Venice and Florence which John Ruskin had so magically described. He felt that he was unsuited to the vulgar bustle of the Bar, for he had discovered that it was not sufficient to put your name on a door to get briefs; and modern politics seemed to lack nobility. He felt himself a poet. He disposed of his rooms in Clement's Inn and went to Italy. He had spent a winter in Florence and a winter in Rome, and now was passing his second summer abroad in Germany, so that he might read Goethe in the original.

Hayward had one gift which was very precious. He had a real feeling for literature, and he could impart his own passion with an admirable fluency. He could throw himself into sympathy with a writer and see all that was best in him, and then he could talk about him with understanding. Philip had read a great deal, but he had read without discrimination everything that he happened to come across, and it was very good for him now to meet someone who could guide his taste. He borrowed books from the small lending library which the town possessed and began reading all the wonderful things that Hayward spoke of. He did not read always with enjoyment but invariably with perseverance. He was eager for self-improvement. He felt himself very ignorant and very humble. By the end of August, when Weeks returned from South Germany, Philip was completely under Hayward's influence. Hayward did not like Weeks. He deplored the American's black coat and pepper-and-salt trousers, and spoke with a scornful shrug of his New England conscience. Philip listened complacently to the abuse of a man who had gone out of his way to be kind to him, but when Weeks in his turn made disagreeable remarks about Hayward he lost his temper.

'Your new friend looks like a poet,' said Weeks, with a thin smile on his careworn, bitter mouth.

'He is a poet.'

'Did he tell you so? In America we should call him a pretty fair specimen of a waster.'

'Well, we're not in America,' said Philip frigidly.

'How old is he? Twenty-five? And he does nothing but stay in pensions and write poetry.'

'You don't know him,' said Philip hotly.

'Oh yes, I do: I've met a hundred and forty-seven of him.'

Weeks's eyes twinkled, but Philip, who did not understand American humour, pursed his lips and looked severe. Weeks to Philip seemed a man of middle age, but he was in point of fact little more than thirty. He had a long, thin body and the scholar's stoop; his head was large and ugly; he had pale scanty hair and an earthy skin; his thin mouth and thin, long nose, and the great protuberance of his frontal bones, gave him an uncouth look. He was cold and precise in his manner, a bloodless man, without passion; but he had a curious vein of frivolity which disconcerted the serious-minded among whom his instincts naturally threw him. He was studying theology in Heidelberg, but the other theological students of his own nationality looked upon him with suspicion. He was very unorthodox, which frightened them; and his freakish humour excited their disapproval.

'How can you have known a hundred and forty-seven of him?' asked Philip seriously.

'I've met him in the Latin Quarter in Paris, and I've met him in pensions in Berlin and Munich. He lives in small hotels in Perugia and Assisi. He stands by the dozen before the Botticellis in Florence, and he sits on all the benches of the Sistine Chapel in Rome. In Italy he drinks a little too much wine, and in Germany he drinks a great deal too much beer. He always admires the right thing, whatever the right thing is, and one of these days he's going to write a great work. Think of it, there are a hundred and forty-seven great works reposing in the bosoms of a hundred and forty-seven great men, and the tragic thing is that not one of those hundred and forty-seven great works will ever be written. And yet the world goes on.'

Weeks spoke seriously, but his grey eyes twinkled a little at the end of his long speech, and Philip flushed when he saw that the American was making fun of him.

'You do talk rot,' he said crossly.

XXVII

WEEKS had two little rooms at the back of Frau Erlin's house, and one of them, arranged as a parlour, was comfortable enough for him to invite people to sit in. After supper, urged perhaps by the impish humour which was the despair of his friends in Cambridge, Mass., he often asked Philip and Hayward to come in for a chat. He received them with elaborate courtesy and insisted on their sitting in the only two comfortable chairs in the room. Though he did not drink himself, with a politeness of which Philip recognized the irony, he put a couple of bottles of beer at Hayward's elbow, and he insisted on lighting matches whenever in the heat of argument Hayward's pipe went out. At the beginning of their acquaintance Hayward, as a member of so celebrated a university, had adopted a patronizing attitude towards Weeks, who was a graduate of Harvard; and when by chance the conversation turned upon the Greek tragedians, a subject upon which Hayward felt he spoke with authority, he had assumed the air that it was his part to give information rather than to exchange ideas. Weeks had listened politely, with smiling modesty, till Hayward finished; then he asked one or two insidious questions, so innocent in appearance that Hayward, not seeing into what a quandary they led him, answered blandly; Weeks made a courteous objection, then a correction of fact, after that a quotation from some little known Latin commentator, then a reference to a German authority; and the fact was disclosed that he was a scholar. With smiling ease, apologetically, Weeks tore to pieces all that Hayward had said; with elaborate civility he displayed the superficiality of his attainments. He mocked him with gentle irony. Philip could not help seeing that Hayward looked a perfect fool, and Hayward had not the sense to hold his tongue; in his irritation, his self-assurance undaunted, he attempted to argue: he made wild statements and Weeks amicably corrected them; he reasoned falsely and Weeks proved that he was absurd: Weeks confessed that he had taught Greek Literature at Harvard. Hayward gave a laugh of scorn.

'I might have known it. Of course you read Greek like a schoolmaster,' he said. 'I read it like a poet.'

'And do you find it more poetic when you don't quite know what it means? I thought it was only in revealed religion that a mistranslation improved the sense.'

At last, having finished the beer, Hayward left Weeks's room hot and dishevelled; with an angry gesture he said to Philip:

'Of course the man's a pedant. He has no real feeling for beauty. Accuracy is the virtue of clerks. It's the spirit of the Greeks that we aim at. Weeks is like that fellow who went to hear Rubinstein and complained that he played false notes. False notes! What did they matter when he played divinely?'

Philip, not knowing how many incompetent people have found solace in these false notes, was much impressed.

Hayward could never resist the opportunity which Weeks offered him of regaining ground lost on a previous occasion, and Weeks was able with the greatest ease to draw him into a discussion. Though he could not help seeing how small his attainments were beside the American's, his British pertinacity, his wounded vanity (perhaps they are the same thing), would not allow him to give up the struggle. Hayward seemed to take a delight in displaying his ignorance, self-satisfaction, and wrongheadedness. Whenever Hayward said something which was illogical, Weeks in a few words would show the falseness of his reasoning, pause for a moment to enjoy his triumph, and then hurry on to another subject as though Christian charity impelled him to spare the vanquished foe. Philip tried sometimes to put in something to help his friend, and Weeks gently crushed him, but so kindly, differently from the way in which he answered Hayward, that even Philip, outrageously sensitive, could not feel hurt. Now and then, losing his calm as he felt himself more and more foolish, Hayward became abusive, and only the American's smiling politeness prevented the argument from degenerating into a quarrel. On these occasions when Hayward left Weeks's room he muttered angrily:

'Damned Yankee!'

That settled it. It was a perfect answer to an argument which had seemed unanswerable.

Though they began by discussing all manner of subjects in Weeks's little room eventually the conversation always turned to religion: the theological student took a professional interest in it, and Hayward welcomed a subject in which hard facts need not disconcert him; when feeling is the gauge you can snap your fingers at logic, and when your logic is weak that is very agreeable. Hayward found it difficult to explain his beliefs to Philip without a great flow of words; but it was clear (and this fell in with Philip's idea of the natural order of things) that he had been brought up in the church by law established. Though he had now given up all idea of becoming a Roman Catholic, he still looked upon that communion with sympathy. He had much to say in its praise, and he compared favourably its gorgeous ceremonies with the simple services of the Church of England. He gave Philip Newman's *Apologia* to read, and Philip, finding it very dull, nevertheless read it to the end.

'Read it for its style, not for its matter,' said Hayward.

He talked enthusiastically of the music at the Oratory, and said charming things about the connexion between incense and the devotional spirit. Weeks listened to him with his frigid smile.

'You think it proves the truth of Roman Catholicism that John Henry Newman wrote good English and that Cardinal Manning has a picturesque appearance?'

Hayward hinted that he had gone through much trouble with his soul. For a year he had swum in a sea of darkness. He passed his fingers through his fair, waving hair and told them that he would not for five hundred pounds endure again those agonies of mind. Fortunately he had reached calm waters at last.

'But what *do* you believe?' asked Philip, who was never satisfied with vague statements.

'I believe in the Whole, the Good, and the Beautiful.'

Hayward with his loose large limbs and the fine carriage of his head looked very handsome when he said this, and he said it with an air.

'Is that how you would describe your religion in a census paper?' asked Weeks, in mild tones.

'I hate the rigid definition: it's so ugly, so obvious. If you like I will say that I believe in the church of the Duke of Wellington and Mr Gladstone.'

'That's the Church of England,' said Philip.

'Oh, wise young man!' retorted Hayward, with a smile which made Philip blush, for he felt that in putting into plain words what the other had expressed in a paraphrase he had been guilty of vulgarity. 'I belong to the Church of England. But I love the gold and the silk which clothe the priest of Rome, and his celibacy, and the confessional, and purgatory; and in the darkness of an Italian cathedral, incense-laden and mysterious, I believe with all my heart in the miracle of the Mass. In Venice I have seen a fisherwoman come in, barefoot, throw down her basket of fish by her side, fall on her knees, and pray to the Madonna; and that I felt was the real faith, and I prayed and believed with her. But I believe also in Aphrodite and Apollo and the Great God Pan.'

He had a charming voice, and he chose his words as he spoke; he uttered them almost rhythmically. He would have gone on, but Weeks opened a second bottle of beer.

'Let me give you something to drink.'

Hayward turned to Philip with the slightly condescending gesture which so impressed the youth.

'Now are you satisfied?' he asked.

Philip somewhat bewildered, confessed that he was.

'I'm disappointed that you didn't add a little Buddhism,' said Weeks. 'And I confess I have a sort of sympathy for Mahomet; I regret that you should have left him out in the cold.'

Hayward laughed, for he was in a good humour with himself that evening, and the ring of his sentences still sounded pleasant in his ears. He emptied his glass.

'I didn't expect you to understand me,' he answered. 'With your cold American intelligence you can only adopt the critical attitude. Emerson and all that sort of thing. But what is criticism? Criticism is purely destructive; anyone can destroy, but not everyone can build up. You are a pedant, my dear fellow. The important thing is to construct: I am constructive; I am a poet.'

Weeks looked at him with eyes which seemed at the same time to be quite grave and yet to be smiling brightly.

'I think, if you don't mind my saying so, you're a little drunk.'

'Nothing to speak of,' answered Hayward cheerfully. 'And not enough for me to be unable to overwhelm you in argument. But come, I have unbosomed my soul; now tell us what your religion is.'

Weeks put his head on one side so that he looked like a sparrow on a perch.

'I've been trying to find that out for years. I think I'm a Unitarian.'

'But that's a dissenter,' said Philip.

He could not imagine why they both burst into laughter, Hayward uproariously, and Weeks with a funny chuckle.

'And in England dissenters aren't gentlemen, are they?' asked Weeks.

'Well, if you ask me point-blank, they're not,' replied Philip rather crossly.

He hated being laughed at, and they laughed again.

'And will you tell me what a gentleman is?' asked Weeks.

'Oh, I don't know; everyone knows what it is.'

'Are you a gentleman?'

No doubt had ever crossed Philip's mind on the subject, but he knew it was not a thing to state of oneself.

'If a man tells you he's a gentleman you can bet your boots he isn't,' he retorted.

'Am I a gentleman?'

Philip's truthfulness made it difficult for him to answer, but he was naturally polite.

'Oh, well, you're different,' he said. 'You're American, aren't you?'

'I suppose we may take it that only Englishmen are gentlemen,' said Weeks gravely.

Philip did not contradict him.

'Couldn't you give me a few more particulars?' asked Weeks.

Philip reddened, but, growing angry, did not care if he made himself ridiculous.

'I can give you plenty.' He remembered his uncle's saying that it took three generations to make a gentleman: it was a companion proverb to the silk purse and the sow's ear. 'First of all he's the son of a gentleman, and he's been to a public school and to Oxford or Cambridge.'

'Edinburgh wouldn't do, I suppose?' asked Weeks.

'And he talks English like a gentleman, and he wears the right sort of things, and if he's a gentleman he can always tell if another chap's a gentleman.'

It seemed rather lame to Philip as he went on, but there it was: that was what he meant by the word, and everyone he had ever known meant that too.

'It is evident to me that I am not a gentleman,' said Weeks. 'I don't see why you should have been so surprised because I was a dissenter.'

'I don't quite know what a Unitarian is,' said Philip.

Weeks in his odd way again put his head on one side: you almost expected him to twitter.

'A Unitarian very earnestly believes in almost everything that anybody else believes, and he has a very lively-sustaining faith in he doesn't quite know what.'

'I don't see why you should make fun of me,' said Philip. 'I really want to know.'

'My friend, I'm not making fun of you. I have arrived at that definition after years of great labour and the most anxious, nerve-racking study.'

When Philip and Hayward got up to go, Weeks handed Philip a little book in a paper cover.

'I suppose you can read French pretty well by now. I wonder if this would amuse you.'

Philip thanked him and, taking the book, looked at the title. It was Renan's *Vie de Jésus*.

XXVIII

IT occurred neither to Hayward nor to Weeks that the conversations which helped them to pass an idle evening were being turned over afterwards in Philip's active brain. It had never struck him before that religion was a matter upon which discussion was possible. To him it meant the Church of England, and not to believe in its tenets was a sign of wilfulness which could not fail of punishment here or hereafter. There was some doubt in his mind about the chastisement of unbelievers. It was possible that a merciful judge, reserving the flames of hell for the heathen – Mahommedans, Buddhists, and the rest – would spare Dissenters and Roman Catholics (though at the cost of how much humiliation when they were made to realize their error!), and it was also possible that He would be pitiful to those who had had no chance of learning the truth – this was reasonable enough, though such were the activities of the Missionary Society there could not be many in this condition – but if the chance had been theirs and they had neglected it (in which category were obviously Roman Catholics and Dissenters), the punishment was sure and merited. It was clear that the miscreant was in a parlous state. Perhaps Philip had not been taught it in so many words, but certainly the impression had been given him that only members of the Church of England had any real hope of eternal happiness.

One of the things that Philip had heard definitely stated was that the unbeliever was a wicked and a vicious man; but Weeks, though he believed in hardly anything that Philip believed, led a life of Christian purity. Philip had received little kindness in his life, and he was touched by the American's desire to help him: once when a cold kept him in bed for three days, Weeks nursed him like a mother. There was neither vice nor wickedness in him, but only sincerity and loving-kindness. It was evidently possible to be virtuous and unbelieving.

Also Philip had been given to understand that people adhered to other faiths only from obstinacy or self-interest: in their hearts they knew they were false; they deliberately sought to deceive others. Now, for the sake of his German he had been accustomed on Sunday mornings to attend the Lutheran service, but when Hayward arrived he began instead to go with him to Mass. He noticed that, whereas the protestant church was nearly empty and the congregation had a listless air, the Jesuit on the other hand was crowded and the worshippers seemed to pray with all their hearts. They had not the look of hypocrites. He was surprised at the contrast; for he knew of course that the Lutherans, whose faith was closer to that of the Church of England, on that account were nearer to the truth than the Roman Catholics. Most of the men – it was largely a masculine congregation – were South Germans; and he could not help saying to himself that if he had been born in South Germany he would certainly have been a Roman Catholic. He might just as well have been born in a Roman Catholic country as in England; and in England as well in a Wesleyan, Baptist, or Methodist family as in one that fortunately belonged to the church by law established. He was a little breathless at the danger he had run. Philip was on friendly terms with the little Chinaman who sat at table with him twice each day. His name was Sung. He was always smiling, affable, and polite. It seemed strange that he should frizzle in hell merely because he was a Chinaman; but if salvation was possible whatever a man's faith was, there did not seem to be any particular advantage in belonging to the Church of England.

Philip, more puzzled than he had ever been in his life, sounded Weeks. He had to be careful, for he was very sensitive to ridicule; and the acidulous humour with which the American treated the Church of England disconcerted him. Weeks only puzzled him more. He made Philip acknowledge that those South Germans whom he saw in the Jesuit church were every bit as firmly convinced of the truth of Roman Catholicism as he was of that of the Church of England, and from that he led him to admit that the Mahommedan and the Buddhist were convinced also of the truth of their respective religions. It looked as though knowing that you were right meant nothing; they all knew they were right. Weeks had no intention of undermining the boy's faith, but he was deeply interested in religion, and found it an absorbing topic of conversation. He had described his own views accurately when he said that he very earnestly disbelieved in almost everything that other people believed. Once Philip asked him a question, which he had heard his uncle put when the conversation at the vicarage had fallen upon some mildly rationalistic work which was then exciting discussion in the newspapers.

'But why should you be right and all those fellows like St Anselm and St Augustine be wrong?'

'You mean that they were very clever and learned men, while you have grave doubts whether I am either?' asked Weeks.

'Yes,' answered Philip uncertainly, for put in that way his question seemed impertinent.

'St Augustine believed that the earth was flat and that the sun turned round it.'

'I don't know what that proves.'

'Why, it proves that you believe with your generation. Your saints lived in an age of faith, when it was practically impossible to disbelieve what to us is positively incredible.'

'Then how d'you know that we have the truth now?'

'I don't.'

Philip thought this over for a moment, then he said:

'I don't see why the things we believe absolutely now shouldn't be just as wrong as what they believed in the past.'

'Neither do I.'

'Then how can you believe anything at all?'

'I don't know.'

Philip asked Weeks what he thought of Hayward's religion.

'Men have always formed gods in their own image,' said Weeks. 'He believes in the picturesque.'

Philip paused for a little while, then he said:

'I don't see why one should believe in God at all.'

The words were no sooner out of his mouth than he realized that he had ceased to do so. It took his breath away like a plunge into cold water. He looked at Weeks with startled eyes. Suddenly he felt afraid. He left Weeks as quickly as he could. He wanted to be alone. It was the most startling experience that he had ever had. He tried to think it all out; it was very exciting, since his whole life seemed concerned (he thought his decision on this matter must profoundly affect its course) and a mistake might lead to eternal damnation; but the more he reflected the more convinced he was; and though during the next few weeks he read books, aids to scepticism, with eager interest it was only to confirm him in what he felt instinctively. The fact was that he had ceased to believe not for this reason or the other, but because he had not the religious temperament. Faith had been forced upon him from the outside. It was a matter of environment and example. A new environment and a new example gave him the opportunity to find himself. He put off the faith of his childhood quite simply, like a cloak that he no longer needed. At first life seemed strange and lonely without the belief which, though he never realized it, had been an unfailing support. He felt like a man who has leaned on a stick and finds himself forced suddenly to walk without assistance. It really seemed as though the days were colder and the nights more solitary. But he was upheld by the excitement; it seemed to make life a more thrilling adventure; and in a little while the stick which he had thrown aside, the cloak which had fallen from his shoulders, seemed an intolerable burden of which he had been eased. The religious exercises which for so many years had been forced upon him were part and parcel of religion to him. He thought of the collects and epistles which he had been made to learn by heart, and the long services in the Cathedral through which he had sat when every limb itched with the desire for movement; and he remembered those walks at night through muddy roads to the parish church at Blackstable, and the coldness of that bleak building; he sat with his feet like ice, his fingers numb and heavy, and all

117

around was the sickly smell of pomatum. Oh, he had been so bored! His heart leaped when he saw he was free from all that.

He was surprised at himself because he ceased to believe so easily, and, not knowing that he felt as he did on account of the subtle workings of his inmost nature, he ascribed the certainty he had reached to his own cleverness. He was unduly pleased with himself. With youth's lack of sympathy for an attitude other than its own he despised not a little Weeks and Hayward because they were content with the vague emotion which they called God and would not take the further step which to himself seemed so obvious. One day he went alone up a certain hill so that he might see a view which, he knew not why, filled him always with wild exhilaration. It was autumn now, but often the days were cloudless still, and then the sky seemed to glow with a more splendid light: it was as though nature consciously sought to put a fuller vehemence into the remaining days of fair weather. He looked down upon the plain, a-quiver with the sun, stretching vastly before him: in the distance were the roofs of Mannheim and ever so far away the dimness of Worms. Here and there a more piercing glitter was the Rhine. The tremendous spaciousness of it was glowing with rich gold. Philip, as he stood there, his heart beating with sheer joy, thought how the tempter had stood with Jesus on a high mountain and shown him the kingdoms of the earth. To Philip, intoxicated with the beauty of the scene, it seemed that it was the whole world which was spread before him, and he was eager to step down and enjoy it. He was free from degrading fears and free from prejudice. He could go his way without the intolerable dread of hell-fire. Suddenly he realized that he had lost also that burden of responsibility which made every action of his life a matter of urgent consequence. He could breathe more freely in a lighter air. He was responsible only to himself for the things he did. Freedom! He was his own master at last. From old habit, unconsciously he thanked God that he no longer believed in Him.

Drunk with pride in his intelligence and in his fearlessness, Philip entered deliberately upon a new life. But his loss of faith made less difference in his behaviour than he expected. Though he had thrown on one side the Christian dogmas it never occurred to him to criticize the Christian ethics; he accepted the Christian virtues, and indeed thought it fine to practise them for their own sake, without a thought of reward or punishment. There was small occasion for heroism in the Frau Professor's house, but he was a little more exactly truthful than he had been, and he forced himself to be more than commonly attentive to the dull, elderly ladies who sometimes engaged him in conversation. The gentle oath, the violent adjective, which are typical of our language and which he had cultivated before as a sign of manliness, he now elaborately eschewed.

Having settled the whole matter to his satisfaction he sought to put it out of his mind, but that was morely easily said than done; and he could not prevent the regrets nor stifle the misgivings which sometimes tormented him. He was so young and had so few friends that immortality had no particular attractions for him, and he was able without trouble to give up belief in it; but there was one thing which made him wretched; he told himself that he was unreasonable, he tried to laugh himself out of such pathos; but the tears really came to his eyes when he thought that he would never see again the beautiful mother whose love for him had grown more precious as the years since her death passed on. And sometimes, as though the influence of innumerable ancestors, God-fearing and devout, were working in him unconsciously, there seized him a panic fear that perhaps after all it was all true, and there was, up there behind the blue sky, a jealous God who would punish in everlasting flames the atheist. At these times his reason could offer him no help, he imagined the anguish of a physical torment which would last endlessly, he felt quite sick with fear and burst into a violent sweat. At last he would say to himself desperately:

'After all, it's not my fault. I can't force myself to believe. If there is a God after all and He punishes me because I honestly don't believe in Him I can't help it.'

XXIX

WINTER set in. Weeks went to Berlin to attend the lectures of Paulssen, and Hayward began to think of going South. The local theatre opened its doors. Philip and Hayward went to it two or three times a week with the praiseworthy intention of improving their German, and Philip found it a more diverting manner of perfecting himself in the language than listening to sermons. They found themselves in the midst of a revival of the drama. Several of Ibsen's plays were on the repertory for the winter; Sudermann's *Die Ehre* was then a new play, and on its production in the quiet university town caused the greatest excitement; it was extravagantly praised and bitterly attacked; other dramatists followed with plays written under the modern influence and Philip witnessed a series of works in which the vileness of mankind was displayed before him. He had never been to a play in his life till then (poor touring companies sometimes came to the Assembly Rooms at Blackstable, but the Vicar, partly on account of his profession, partly because he thought it would be vulgar, never went to see them) and the passion of the stage seized him. He felt a thrill the moment he got into the little, shabby, ill-lit theatre. Soon he came to know the peculiarities of the small company, and by the casting could tell at once what were the characteristics of the persons in the drama; but this made no difference to him. To him it was real life. It was a strange life, dark and tortured, in which men and women showed to remorseless eyes the evil that was in their hearts; a fair face concealed a depraved mind; the virtuous used virtue as a mask to hide their secret vice, the seeming-strong fainted within with their weakness; the honest were corrupt, the chaste were lewd. You seemed to dwell in a room where the night before an orgy had taken place: the windows had not been opened in the morning; the air was foul with the dregs of beer, and stale smoke, and flaring gas. There was no laughter. At most you sniggered at the hypocrite or the fool: the characters expressed themselves in cruel words that seemed wrung out of their hearts by shame and anguish.

Philip was carried away by the sordid intensity of it. He seemed to see the world again in another fashion, and this world too he was anxious to know. After the play was over he went to a tavern and sat in the bright warmth with Hayward to eat a sandwich and drink a glass of beer. All round were little groups of students, talking and laughing; and here and there was a family, father and mother, a couple of sons and a girl; and sometimes the girl said a sharp thing, and the father leaned back in his chair and laughed, laughed heartily. It was very friendly and innocent. There was a pleasant homeliness in the scene, but for this Philip had no eyes. His thoughts ran on the play he had just come from.

'You do feel it's life, don't you?' he said excitedly. 'You know, I don't think I can stay here much longer. I want to get to London so that I can really begin. I want to have experiences. I'm so tired of preparing for life: I want to live it now.'

Sometimes Hayward left Philip to go home by himself. He would never exactly reply to Philip's eager questioning, but with a merry, rather stupid laugh, hinted at a romantic amour; he quoted a few lines of Rossetti, and once showed Philip a sonnet in which passion and purple, pessimism and pathos, were packed together on the subject of a young lady called Trude. Hayward surrounded his sordid and vulgar little adventures with a glow of poetry, and thought he touched hands with Pericles and Pheidias because to describe the object of his attentions he used the word *hetaira* instead of one of those, more blunt and apt, provided by the English language. Philip in the daytime had been led by curiosity to pass through the little street near the old bridge, with its neat white houses and green shutters, in which according to Hayward the Fräulein Trude lived; but the women, with brutal faces and painted cheeks, who came out of their doors and cried out to him, filled him with fear; and he fled in horror from the rough hands that sought to detain him. He yearned above all things for experience and felt himself ridiculous because at his age he had not enjoyed that which all fiction taught him was the most important thing in life; but he had the unfortunate gift of seeing things as they were, and the reality which was offered him differed too terribly from the ideal of his dreams.

He did not know how wide a country, arid and precipitous, must be crossed before the traveller through life comes to an acceptance of reality. It is an illusion that youth is happy, an illusion of those who have lost it; but the young know they are wretched, for they are full of the truthless ideals which have been instilled into them, and each time they come in contact with the real they are bruised and wounded. It looks as if they were victims of a conspiracy; for the books they read, ideal by the necessity of selection, and the conversation of their elders, who look back upon the past through a rosy haze of forgetfulness, prepare them for an unreal life. They must discover for themselves that all they have read and all they have been told are lies, lies, lies; and each discovery is another nail driven into the body on the cross of life. The strange thing is that each one who has gone through that bitter disillusionment adds to it in his turn, unconsciously, by the power within him which is stronger than himself. The companionship of Hayward was the worst possible thing for Philip. He was a man who saw nothing for himself, but only through a literary atmosphere, and he was dangerous because he had deceived himself into sincerity. He honestly mistook his sensuality for romantic emotion, his vacillation for the artistic temperament, and his idleness for philosophic calm. His mind, vulgar in its effort at refinement, saw everything a little larger than life size, with the outlines blurred, in a golden mist of sentimentality. He lied and never knew that he lied, and when it was pointed out to him said that lies were beautiful. He was an idealist.

XXX

PHILIP was restless and dissatisfied. Hayward's poetic allusions troubled his imagination, and his soul yearned for romance. At least that was how he put it to himself.

And it happened that an incident was taking place in Frau Erlin's house which increased Philip's preoccupation with the matter of sex. Two or three times on his walks among the hills he had met Fräulein Cäcilie wandering by herself. He had passed her with a bow, and a few yards further on had seen the Chinaman. He thought nothing of it; but one evening on his way home, when night had already fallen, he passed two people walking very close together. Hearing his footsteps, they separated quickly, and though he could not see well in the darkness he was almost certain they were Cäcilie and Herr Sung. Their rapid movement apart suggested that they had been walking arm in arm. Philip was puzzled and surprised. He had never paid much attention to Fräulein Cäcilie. She was a plain girl, with a square face and blunt features. She could not have been more than sixteen, since she still wore her long fair hair in a plait. That evening at supper he looked at her curiously; and, though of late she had talked little at meals, she addressed him.

'Where did you go for your walk today, Herr Carey?' she asked.

'Oh, I walked up towards the Königsstuhl.'

'I didn't go out,' she volunteered. 'I had a headache.'

The Chinaman, who sat next to her, turned round.

'I'm so sorry,' he said. 'I hope it's better now.'

Fräulein Cäcilie was evidently uneasy, for she spoke again to Philip.

'Did you meet many people on the way?'

Philip could not help reddening when he told a downright lie.

'No. I don't think I saw a living soul.'

He fancied that a look of relief passed across her eyes.

Soon, however, there could be no doubt that there was something between the pair, and other people in the Frau Professor's house saw them lurking in dark places. The elderly ladies who sat at the head of the table began to discuss what was now a scandal. The Frau Professor was angry and harassed. She had done her best to see nothing. The winter was at hand, and it was not as easy a matter then as in the summer to keep her house full. Herr Sung was a good customer: he had two rooms on the ground floor, and he drank a bottle of Moselle at each meal. The Frau Professor charged him three marks a bottle and made a good profit. None of her other guests drank wine, and some of them did not even drink beer. Neither did she wish to lose Fräulein Cäcilie, whose parents were in business in South America and paid well for the Frau Professor's motherly care, and she knew that if she wrote to the girl's uncle, who lived in Berlin, he would immediately take her away. The Frau Professor contented herself with giving them both severe looks at table and, though she dared not be rude to the Chinaman, got a certain satisfaction out of incivility to Cäcilie. But the three elderly ladies were not content. Two were widows, and one, a Dutchwoman, was a spinster of masculine appearance; they paid the smallest possible sum for their pension, and gave a good deal of trouble, but they were permanent and therefore had to be put up with. They went to the Frau Professor and said that something must be done; it was disgraceful, and the house was ceasing to be respectable. The Frau Professor tried obstinacy, anger, tears, but the three old ladies routed her, and with a sudden assumption of virtuous indignation she said that she would put a stop to the whole thing.

After luncheon she took Cäcilie into her bedroom and began to talk very seriously to her; but to her amazement the girl adopted a brazen attitude; she proposed to go about as she liked; and if she chose to walk with the Chinaman she could not see it was anybody's business but her own. The Frau Professor threatened to write to her uncle.

'Then Onkel Heinrich will put me in a family in Berlin for the winter, and that will be much nicer for me. And Herr Sung will come to Berlin too.'

The Frau Professor began to cry. The tears rolled down her coarse, red, fat cheeks; and Cäcilie laughed at her.

'That will mean three rooms empty all through the winter,' she said.

Then the Frau Professor tried another plan. She appealed to Fräulein Cäcilie's better nature: she was kind, sensible, tolerant; she treated her no longer as a child, but as a grown woman. She said that it wouldn't be so dreadful, but a Chinaman, with his yellow skin and flat nose, and his little pig's eyes! That's what made it so horrible. It filled one with disgust to think of it.

'*Bitte, bitte,*' said Cäcilie, with a rapid intake of the breath, 'I won't listen to anything against him.'

'But it's not serious?' gasped Frau Erlin.

'I love him. I love him. I love him.'

'*Gott im Himmel!*'

The Frau Professor stared at her with horrified surprise; she had thought it was no more than naughtiness on the child's part, and innocent folly; but the passion in her voice revealed everything. Cäcilie looked at her for a moment with flaming eyes, and then with a shrug of her shoulders went out of the room.

Frau Erlin kept the details of the interview to herself, and a day or two later altered the arrangement of the table. She asked Herr Sung if he would not come and sit at her end, and he with his unfailing politeness accepted with alacrity. Cäcilie took the change indifferently. But as if the discovery that the relations between them were known to the whole household made them more shameless, they made no secret now of their walks together, and every afternoon quite openly set out to wander about the hills. It was plain that they did not care what was said of them. At last even the placidity of Professor Erlin was moved, and he insisted that his wife should speak to the China-man. She took him aside in his turn and expostulated; he was ruining the girl's reputation, he was doing harm to the house, he must see how wrong and wicked his conduct was; but she was met with smiling denials; Herr Sung did not know what she was talking about, he was not paying any attention to Fräulein Cäcilie, he never walked with her; it was all untrue, every word of it.

'*Ach*, Herr Sung, how can you say such things? You've been seen again and again.'

'No, you're mistaken. It's untrue.'

He looked at her with an unceasing smile, which showed his even, little white teeth. He was quite calm. He denied everything. He denied with bland effrontery. At last the Frau Professor lost her temper and said the girl had confessed she loved him. He was not moved. He continued to smile.

'Nonsense! Nonsense! It's all untrue.'

She could get nothing out of him. The weather grew very bad; there was snow and frost, and then a thaw with a long succession of cheerless days, on which walking was a poor amusement. One evening when Philip had just finished his

German lesson with the Herr Professor and was standing for a moment in the drawing-room, talking to Frau Erlin, Anna came quickly in.

'Mamma, where is Cäcilie?' she said.

'I suppose she's in her room.'

'There's no light in it.'

The Frau Professor gave an exclamation, and she looked at her daughter in dismay. The thought which was in Anna's head had flashed across hers.

'Ring for Emil,' she said hoarsely.

This was the stupid lout who waited at table and did most of the housework. He came in.

'Emil, go down to Herr Sung's room and enter without knocking. If anyone is there say you came in to see about the stove.'

No sign of astonishment appeared on Emil's phlegmatic face. He went slowly downstairs. The Frau Professor and Anna left the door open and listened. Presently they heard Emil come up again, and they called him.

'Was any one there?' asked the Frau Professor.

'Yes, Herr Sung was there.'

'Was he alone?'

The beginning of a cunning smile narrowed his mouth.

'No, Fräulein Cäcilie was there.'

'Oh, it's disgraceful,' cried the Frau Professor.

Now he smiled broadly.

'Fräulein Cäcilie is there every evening. She spends hours at a time there.'

Frau Professor began to wring her hands.

'Oh, how abominable! But why didn't you tell me?'

'It was no business of mine,' he answered, slowly shrugging his shoulders.

'I suppose they paid you well. Go away. Go.'

He lurched clumsily to the door.

'They must go away, mamma,' said Anna.

'And who is going to pay the rent? And the taxes are falling due. It's all very well for you to say they must go away. If they go away I can't pay the bills.' She turned to Philip, with tears streaming down her face. '*Ach*, Herr Carey, you will not say what you have heard. If Fräulein Förster –' this was the Dutch spinster – 'if Fräulein Förster knew she would leave at once. And if they all go we must close the house. I cannot afford to keep it.'

'Of course I won't say anything.'

'If she stays, I will not speak to her,' said Anna.

That evening at supper Fräulein Cäcilie, redder than usual, with a look of obstinacy on her face, took her place punctually; but Herr Sung did not appear, and for a while Philip thought he was going to shirk the ordeal. At last he came, very smiling, his eyes dancing with the apologies he made for his late arrival. He insisted as usual on pouring out the Frau Professor a glass of his Moselle, and he offered a glass to Fräulein Förster. The room was very hot, for the stove had been alight all day and the windows were seldom opened. Emil blundered about, but succeeded somehow in serving everyone quickly and with order. The three old ladies sat in silence, visibly disapproving: the Frau Professor had scarcely recovered from her tears; her husband was silent and oppressed. Conversation languished. It seemed to Philip that there was something dreadful in that gathering which he had sat with so often; they looked different under the light of the two hanging lamps from what they had ever looked before; he was vaguely uneasy. Once he caught Cäcilie's eye, and he thought she looked at him with hatred and contempt. The room was stifling. It was as though the beastly passion of that pair troubled them all; there was a feeling of Oriental depravity; a faint savour of joss-sticks, a mystery of hidden vices, seemed to make their breath heavy. Philip could feel the beating of the arteries in his forehead. He could not understand what strange emotion distracted him; he seemed to feel something infinitely attractive, and yet he was repelled and horrified.

For several days things went on. The air was sickly with the unnatural passion which all felt about them, and the nerves of the little household seemed to grow exasperated. Only Herr Sung remained unaffected; he was no less smiling, affable, and polite than he had been before: one could not tell whether his manner was a triumph of civilization or an expression of contempt on the part of the Oriental for the vanquished West. Cäcilie was flaunting and cynical. At last even the Frau Professor could bear the position no longer. Suddenly panic seized her; for Professor Erlin with brutal frankness had suggested the possible consequences of an intrigue which was now manifest to everyone, and she saw her good name in Heidelberg and the repute of her house ruined by a scandal which could not possibly be hidden. For some reason, blinded perhaps by her interests, this possibility had never occurred to her; and now, her wits muddled by a terrible fear, she could hardly be prevented from turning the girl out of the house at once. It was

126

due to Anna's good sense that a cautious letter was written to the uncle in Berlin suggesting that Cäcilie should be taken away.

But having made up her mind to lose the two lodgers, the Frau Professor could not resist the satisfaction of giving rein to the ill-temper she had curbed so long. She was free now to say anything she liked to Cäcilie.

'I have written to your uncle, Cäcilie, to take you away. I cannot have you in my house any longer.'

Her little round eyes sparkled when she noticed the sudden whiteness of the girl's face.

'You're shameless. Shameless,' she went on.

She called her foul names.

'What did you say to my uncle Heinrich, Frau Professor?' the girl asked, suddenly falling from her attitude of flaunting independence.

'Oh, he'll tell you himself. I expect to get a letter from him tomorrow.'

Next day, in order to make the humiliation more public, at supper she called down the table to Cäcilie.

'I have had a letter from your uncle, Cäcilie. You are to pack your things tonight, and we will put you in the train tomorrow morning. He will meet you himself in Berlin at the Central Bahnhof.'

'Very good, Frau Professor.'

Herr Sung smiled in the Frau Professor's eyes, and notwithstanding her protests insisted on pouring out a glass of wine for her. The Frau Professor ate her supper with a good appetite. But she had triumphed unwisely. Just before going to bed she called the servant.

'Emil, if Fräulein Cäcilie's box is ready you had better take it downstairs tonight. The porter will fetch it before breakfast.'

The servant went away and in a moment came back.

'Fräulein Cäcilie is not in her room, and her bag has gone.'

With a cry the Frau Professor hurried along: the box was on the floor, strapped and locked; but there was no bag, and neither hat nor cloak. The dressing-table was empty. Breathing heavily, the Frau Professor ran downstairs to the Chinaman's rooms, she had not moved so quickly for twenty years, and Emil called out after her to beware she did not fall; she did not trouble to knock, but burst in. The rooms were empty. The luggage had gone, and the door into the garden, still open, showed how it had been got away. In an envelope on the table were notes for the money due on the month's board and an

127

approximate sum for extras. Groaning, suddenly overcome by her haste, the Frau Professor sank obesely on to a sofa. There could be no doubt. The pair had gone off together. Emil remained stolid and unmoved.

XXXI

HAYWARD, after saying for a month that he was going South next day and delaying from week to week out of inability to make up his mind to the bother of packing and the tedium of a journey, had at last been driven off just before Christmas by the preparations for that festival. He could not support the thought of a Teutonic merry-making. It gave him goose-flesh to think of the season's aggressive cheerfulness, and in his desire to avoid the obvious he determined to travel on Christmas Eve.

Philip was not sorry to see him off, for he was a downright person and it irritated him that anybody should not know his own mind. Though much under Hayward's influence, he would not grant that indecision pointed to a charming sensitiveness; and he resented the shadow of a sneer with which Hayward looked upon his straight ways. They corresponded. Hayward was an admirable letter-writer, and knowing his talent took pains with his letters. His temperament was receptive to the beautiful influences with which he came in contact, and he was able in his letters from Rome to put a subtle fragrance of Italy. He thought the city of the ancient Romans a little vulgar, finding distinction only in the decadence of the Empire; but the Rome of the Popes appealed to his sympathy, and in his chosen words, quite exquisitely, there appeared a Rococo beauty. He wrote of old church music and the Alban Hills, and of the languor of incense and the charm of the streets by night, in the rain, when the pavements shone and the light of the street lamps was mysterious. Perhaps he repeated these admirable letters to various friends. He did not know what a troubling effect they had upon Philip; they seemed to make his life very humdrum. With the spring Hayward grew dithyrambic. He proposed that Philip should come down to Italy. He was wasting his time at Heidelberg. The Germans were gross and life there was common: how could the soul come to her own in that prim landscape? In Tuscany the spring was scattering flowers through the land, and Philip was nineteen; let him come and they could wander through the mountain towns of

Umbria. Their names sank in Philip's heart. And Cäcilie too, with her lover, had gone to Italy. When he thought of them Philip was seized with a restlessness he could not account for. He cursed his fate because he had no money to travel, and he knew his uncle would not send him more than the fifteen pounds a month which had been agreed upon. He had not managed his allowance very well. His pension and the price of his lessons left him very little over, and he had found going about with Hayward expensive. Hayward had often suggested excursions, a visit to the play, or a bottle of wine, when Philip had come to the end of his month's money; and with the folly of his age he had been unwilling to confess he could not afford an extravagance.

Luckily Hayward's letters came seldom, and in the intervals Philip settled down again to his industrious life. He had matriculated at the university and attended one or two courses of lectures. Kuno Fischer was then at the height of his fame and during the winter had been lecturing brilliantly on Schopenhauer. It was Philip's introduction to philosophy. He had a practical mind and moved uneasily amid the abstract; but he found an unexpected fascination in listening to metaphysical disquisitions; they made him breathless; it was a little like watching a tight-rope dancer doing perilous feats over an abyss; but it was very exciting. The pessimism of the subject attracted his youth; and he believed that the world he was about to enter was a place of pitiless woe and of darkness. That made him none the less eager to enter it; and when, in due course, Mrs Carey, acting as the correspondent for his guardian's views, suggested that it was time for him to come back to England, he agreed with enthusiasm. He must make up his mind now what he meant to do. If he left Heidelberg at the end of July they could talk things over during August, and it would be a good time to make arrangements.

The date of his departure was settled, and Mrs Carey wrote to him again. She reminded him of Miss Wilkinson, through whose kindness he had gone to Frau Erlin's house at Heidelberg, and told him that she had arranged to spend a few weeks with them at Blackstable. She would be crossing from Flushing on such and such a day, and if he travelled at the same time he could look after her and come on to Blackstable in her company. Philip's shyness immediately made him write to say that he could not leave till a day or two afterwards. He pictured himself looking out for Miss Wilkinson, the embarrassment of going up to her and asking if it were she (and he might so

129

easily address the wrong person and be snubbed), and then the difficulty of knowing whether in the train he ought to talk to her or whether he could ignore her and read his book.

At last he left Heidelberg. For three months he had been thinking of nothing but the future; and he went without regret. He never knew that he had been happy there. Fräulein Anna gave him a copy of *Der Trompeter von Säckingen* and in return he presented her with a volume of William Morris. Very wisely neither of them ever read the other's present.

XXXII

PHILIP was surprised when he saw his uncle and aunt. He had never noticed before that they were quite old people. The Vicar received him with his usual, not unamiable, indifference. He was a little stouter, a little balder, a little greyer. Philip saw how insignificant he was. His face was weak and self-indulgent. Aunt Louisa took him in her arms and kissed him; and tears of happiness flowed down her cheeks. Philip was touched and embarrassed; he had not known with what a hungry love she cared for him.

'Oh, the time has seemed long since you've been away, Philip,' she cried.

She stroked his hands and looked into his face with glad eyes.

'You've grown. You're quite a man now.'

There was a very small moustache on his upper lip. He had bought a razor and now and then with infinite care shaved the down off his smooth chin.

'We've been so lonely without you.' And then shyly, with a little break in her voice, she asked: 'You are glad to come back to your home, aren't you?'

'Yes, rather.'

She was so thin that she seemed almost transparent, the arms she put round his neck were frail bones that reminded you of chicken bones, and her faded face was oh! so wrinkled. The grey curls which she still wore in the fashion of her youth gave her a queer, pathetic look; and her little withered body was like an autumn leaf, you felt it might be blown away by the first sharp wind. Philip realized that they had done with life, these two quiet little people: they belonged to a past generation, and they were waiting there patiently, rather stupidly, for death; and he, in his vigour and his youth, thirsting for excitement and adventure, was appalled at the waste. They had done nothing, and when they went it would be just as if they had never been. He felt a great pity for Aunt Louisa, and he loved her suddenly because she loved him.

Then Miss Wilkinson, who had kept discreetly out of the way till the Careys had had a chance of welcoming their nephew, came into the room.

'This is Miss Wilkinson, Philip,' said Mrs Carey.

'The prodigal has returned,' she said, holding out her hand. 'I have brought a rose for the prodigal's buttonhole.'

With a gay smile she pinned to Philip's coat the flower she had just picked in the garden. He blushed and felt foolish. He knew that Miss Wilkinson was the daughter of his Uncle William's last rector, and he had a wide acquaintance with the daughters of clergymen. They wore ill-cut clothes and stout boots. They were generally dressed in black, for in Philip's early years at Blackstable homespuns had not reached East Anglia, and the ladies of the clergy did not favour colours. Their hair was done very untidily, and they smelt aggressively of starched linen. They considered the feminine graces unbecoming and looked the same whether they were old or young. They bore their religion arrogantly. The closeness of their connexion with the church made them adopt a slightly dictatorial attitude to the rest of mankind.

Miss Wilkinson was very different. She wore a white muslin gown stamped with gay little bunches of flowers, and pointed, high-heeled shoes, with open-work stockings. To Philip's inexperience it seemed that she was wonderfully dressed; he did not see that her frock was cheap and showy. Her hair was elaborately dressed, with a neat curl in the middle of the forehead: it was very black, shiny, and hard, and it looked as though it could never be in the least disarranged. She had large black eyes and her nose was slightly aquiline; in profile she had somewhat the look of a bird of prey, but full face she was prepossessing. She smiled a great deal, but her mouth was large and when she smiled she tried to hide her teeth, which were big and rather yellow. But what embarrassed Philip most was that she was heavily powdered; he had very strict views on feminine behaviour and did not think a lady ever powdered; but of course Miss Wilkinson was a lady because she was a clergyman's daughter, and a clergyman was a gentleman.

Philip made up his mind to dislike her thoroughly. She spoke with a slight French accent; and he did not know why she should, since she had been born and bred in the heart of

England. He thought her smile affected, and the coy sprightliness of her manner irritated him. For two or three days he remained silent and hostile, but Miss Wilkinson apparently did not notice it. She was very affable. She addressed her conversation almost exclusively to him, and there was something flattering in the way she appealed constantly to his sane judgement. She made him laugh too, and Philip could never resist people who amused him: he had a gift now and then of saying neat things; and it was pleasant to have an appreciative listener. Neither the Vicar nor Mrs Carey had a sense of humour, and they never laughed at anything he said. As he grew used to Miss Wilkinson, and his shyness left him, he began to like her better; he found the French accent picturesque; and at a garden party which the doctor gave she was very much better dressed than anyone else. She wore a blue foulard with large white spots, and Philip was tickled at the sensation it caused.

'I'm certain they think you're no better than you should be,' he told her, laughing.

'It's the dream of my life to be taken for an abandoned hussy,' she answered.

One day when Miss Wilkinson was in her room he asked Aunt Louisa how old she was.

'Oh, my dear, you should never ask a lady's age; but she's certainly too old for you to marry.'

The Vicar gave his slow, obese smile.

'She's no chicken, Louisa,' he said. 'She was nearly grown up when we were in Lincolnshire, and that was twenty years ago. She wore a pigtail hanging down her back.'

'She may not have been more than ten,' said Philip.

'She was older than that,' said Aunt Louisa.

'I think she was nearer twenty,' said the Vicar.

'Oh, no, William. Sixteen or seventeen at the outside.'

'That would make her well over thirty,' said Philip.

At that moment Miss Wilkinson tripped downstairs, singing a song by Benjamin Goddard. She had put her hat on, for she and Philip were going for a walk, and she held out her hand for him to button her glove. He did it awkwardly. He felt embarrassed but gallant. Conversation went easily between them now, and as they strolled along they talked of all manner of things. She told Philip about Berlin, and he told her of his year in Heidelberg. As he spoke, things which had appeared of no importance gained a new interest: he described the people at Frau Erlin's house; and to the conversations between Hayward and Weeks, which at the time seemed so significant, he gave a little twist, so that they looked absurd. He was flattered at Miss Wilkinson's laughter.

'I'm quite frightened of you,' she said. 'You're so sarcastic.'

Then she asked him playfully whether he had not had any love affairs at Heidelberg. Without thinking, he frankly answered that he had not; but she refused to believe him.

'How secretive you are!' she said. 'At your age is it likely?'

He blushed and laughed.

'You want to know too much,' he said.

'Ah, I thought so,' she laughed triumphantly. 'Look at him blushing.'

He was pleased that she should think he had been a sad dog, and he changed the conversation so as to make her believe he had all sorts of romantic things to conceal. He was angry with himself that he had not. There had been no opportunity.

Miss Wilkinson was dissatisfied with her lot. She resented having to earn her living and told Philip a long story of an uncle of her mother's, who had been expected to leave her a fortune but had married his cook and changed his will. She hinted at the luxury of her home and compared her life in Lincolnshire, with horses to ride and carriages to drive in, with the mean dependence of her present state. Philip was a little puzzled when he mentioned this afterwards to Aunt Louisa, and she told him that when she knew the Wilkinsons they had never had anything more than a pony and a dog-cart; Aunt Louisa had heard of the rich uncle, but as he was married and had children before Emily was born she could never have had much hope of inheriting his fortune. Miss Wilkinson had little good to say of Berlin, where she was now in a situation. She complained of the vulgarity of German life, and compared it bitterly with the brilliance of Paris, where she had spent a number of years. She did not say how many. She had been governess in the family of a fashionable portrait-painter, who had married a Jewish wife of means, and in their house she had met many distinguished people. She dazzled Philip with their names. Actors from the Comédie Française had come to the house frequently, and Coquelin, sitting next her at dinner, had told her he had never met a foreigner who spoke such perfect French. Alphonse Daudet had come also, and he had given her a copy of *Sapho*: he had promised to write her name in it, but she had forgotten to remind him. She treasured the volume none the less and she would lend it to Philip. Then there was Maupassant. Miss Wilkinson with a rippling laugh looked at Philip knowingly. What a man, but what a writer!

Hayward had talked of Maupassant, and his reputation was not unknown to Philip.

'Did he make love to you?' he asked.

The words seemed to stick funnily in his throat, but he asked them nevertheless. He liked Miss Wilkinson very much now, and was thrilled by her conversation, but he could not imagine anyone making love to her.

'What a question!' she cried. 'Poor Guy, he made love to every woman he met. It was a habit that he could not break himself of.'

She sighed a little, and seemed to look back tenderly on the past.

'He was a charming man,' she murmured.

A greater experience than Philip's would have guessed from these words the probabilities of the encounter: the distinguished writer invited to luncheon *en famille*, the governess coming in sedately with the two tall girls she was teaching; the introduction:

'*Notre Miss Anglaise.*'

'*Mademoiselle.*'

And the luncheon during which the *Miss Anglaise* sat silent while the distinguished writer talked to his host and hostess.

But to Philip her words called up much more romantic fancies.

'Do tell me all about him,' he said excitedly.

'There's nothing to tell,' she said truthfully, but in such a manner as to convey that three volumes would scarcely have contained the lurid facts. 'You mustn't be curious.'

She began to talk of Paris. She loved the boulevards and the Bois. There was grace in every street, and the trees in the Champs-Élysées had a distinction which trees had not elsewhere. They were sitting on a stile now by the high-road, and Miss Wilkinson looked with disdain upon the stately elms in front of them. And the theatres: the plays were brilliant, and the acting was incomparable. She often went with Madame Foyot, the mother of the girls she was educating, when she was trying on clothes.

'Oh, what a misery to be poor!' she cried. 'These beautiful things, it's only in Paris they know how to dress, and not to be able to afford them! Poor Madame Foyot, she had no figure. Sometimes the dressmaker used to whisper to me: "Ah, Mademoiselle, if she only had your figure."'

Philip noticed then that Miss Wilkinson had a robust form, and was proud of it.

'Men are so stupid in England. They only think of the face. The French, who are a nation of lovers, know how much more important the figure is.'

Philip had never thought of such things before, but he observed now that Miss Wilkinson's ankles were thick and ungainly. He withdrew his eyes quickly.

'You should go to France. Why don't you go to Paris for a year. You would learn French, and it would – *déniaiser* you.'

'What is that?' asked Philip.

She laughed slyly.

'You must look it out in the dictionary. Englishmen do not know how to treat women. They are so shy. Shyness is ridiculous in a man. They don't know how to make love. They can't even tell a woman she is charming without looking foolish.'

Philip felt himself absurd. Miss Wilkinson evidently expected him to behave very differently; and he would have been delighted to say gallant and witty things, but they never occurred to him; and when they did he was much to afraid of making a fool of himself to say them.

'Oh, I loved Paris,' sighed Miss Wilkinson. 'But I had to go to Berlin. I was with the Foyots girls till the girls married, and then I could get nothing to do, and I had the chance of this post in Berlin. They're relations of Madame Foyot, and I accepted. I had a tiny apartment in the Rue Bréda, on the *cinquième*: it wasn't at all respectable. You know about the Rue Bréda – *ces dames*, you know.'

Philip nodded, not knowing at all what she meant, but vaguely suspecting, and anxious she should not think him too ignorant.

'But I didn't care. *Je suis libre, n'est-ce pas?*' She was very fond of speaking French, which indeed she spoke well. 'Once I had such a curious adventure there.'

She paused a little and Philip pressed her to tell it.

'You wouldn't tell me yours in Heidelberg,' she said.

'They were so unadventurous,' he retorted.

'I don't know what Mrs Carey would say if she knew the sort of things we talk about together.'

'You don't imagine I shall tell her.'

'Will you promise?'

When he had done this, she told him how an art-student who had a room on the floor above her – but she interrupted herself.

'Why don't you go in for art? You paint so prettily.'

'Not well enough for that.'

'That is for others to judge. *Je m'y connais*, and I believe you have the making of a great artist.'

'Can't you see Uncle William's face if I suddenly told him I wanted to go to Paris and study art?'

'You're your own master, aren't you?'

'You're trying to put me off. Please go on with the story.'

Miss Wilkinson, with a little laugh, went on. The art-student had passed her several times on the stairs, and she had paid no particular attention. She saw that he had fine eyes, and he took off his hat very politely. And one day she found a letter slipped under her door. It was from him. He told her that he had adored her for months, and that he waited about the stairs for her to pass. Oh, it was a charming letter! Of course she did not reply, but what woman could help being flattered? And next day there was another letter! It was wonderful, passionate, and touching. When next she met him on the stairs she did not know which way to look. And every day the letters came, and now he begged her to see him. He said he would come in the evening, *vers neuf heures*, and she did not know what to do. Of course it was impossible, and he might ring and ring, but she would never open the door; and then while she was waiting for the tinkling of the bell, all nerves, suddenly he stood before her. She had forgotten to shut the door when she came in.

'*C'était une fatalité.*'

'And what happened then?' asked Philip.

'That is the end of the story,' she replied, with a ripple of laughter.

Philip was silent for a moment. His heart beat quickly, and strange emotions seemed to be hustling one another in his heart. He saw the dark staircase and the chance meetings, and he admired the boldness of the letters – oh, he would never have dared to do that – and then the silent, almost mysterious entrance. It seemed to him the very soul of romance.

'What was he like?'

'Oh, he was handsome. *Charmant garçon.*'

'Do you know him still?'

Philip felt a slight feeling of irritation as he asked this.

'He treated me abominably. Men are always the same. You're heartless, all of you.'

'I don't know about that,' said Philip, not without embarrassment.

'Let us go home,' said Miss Wilkinson.

XXXIII

PHILIP could not get Miss Wilkinson's story out of his head. It was clear enough what she meant, even though she cut it short, and he was a little shocked. That sort of thing was all very well for married women, he had read enough French novels to know that in France it was indeed the rule, but Miss Wilkinson was English and unmarried; her father was a clergyman. Then it struck him that the art-student probably was neither the first nor the last of her lovers, and he gasped: he had never looked upon Miss Wilkinson like that; it seemed incredible that anyone should make love to her. In his ingenuousness he doubted her story as little as he doubted what he read in books, and he was angry that such wonderful things never happened to him. It was humiliating that if Miss Wilkinson insisted upon his telling her of his adventures in Heidelberg he would have nothing to tell. It was true that he had some power of invention, but he was not sure whether he could persuade her that he was steeped in vice; women were full of intuition, he had read that, and she might easily discover that he was fibbing. He blushed scarlet as he thought of her laughing up her sleeve.

Miss Wilkinson played the piano and sang in a rather tired voice; but her songs, Massenet, Benjamin Goddard and Augusta Holmes, were new to Philip; and together they spent many hours at the piano. One day she wondered if he had a voice and insisted on trying it. She told him he had a pleasant baritone and offered to give him lessons. At first with his usual bashfulness he refused, but she insisted, and then every morning at a convenient time after breakfast she gave him an hour's lesson. She had a natural gift for teaching, and it was clear that she was an excellent governess. She had method and firmness. Though her French accent was so much part of her that it remained, all the mellifluousness of her manner left her when she was engaged in teaching. She put up with no nonsense. Her voice became a little peremptory, and instinctively she suppressed inattention and corrected slovenliness. She knew what she was about and put Philip to scales and exercises.

When the lesson was over she resumed without effort her seductive smiles, her voice became again soft and winning, but Philip could not so easily put away the pupil as she the peda-

gogue; and this impression conflicted with the feelings her
stories had aroused in him. He looked at her more narrowly.
He liked her much better in the evening than in the morning.
In the morning she was rather lined and the skin of her neck
was just a little rough. He wished she would hide it, but the
weather was very warm just then and she wore blouses which
were cut low. She was very fond of white; in the morning it
did not suit her. At night she often looked very attractive, she
put on a gown which was almost a dinner dress, and she wore
a chain of garnets round her neck; the lace about her bosom
and at her elbows gave her a pleasant softness, and the
scent she wore (at Blackstable no one used anything but *eau-
de-Cologne*, and that only on Sundays or when suffering from
a sick headache) was troubling and exotic. She really looked
very young then.

Philip was much exercised over her age. He added twenty
and seventeen together, and could not bring them to a satisfactory total. He asked Aunt Louisa more than once why she
thought Miss Wilkinson was thirty-seven: she didn't look
more than thirty, and everyone knew that foreigners aged more
rapidly than English women; Miss Wilkinson had lived so long
abroad that she might almost be called a foreigner. He personally wouldn't have thought her more than twenty-six.

'She's more than that,' said Aunt Louisa.

Philip did not believe in the accuracy of the Careys' statements. All they distinctly remembered was that Miss Wilkinson
had not got her hair up the last time they saw her in Lincolnshire. Well, she might have been twelve then: it was so long
ago and the Vicar was always so unreliable. They said it was
twenty years ago, but people used round figures, and it was just
as likely to be eighteen years, or seventeen. Seventeen and
twelve were only twenty-nine, and hang it all, that wasn't old,
was it? Cleopatra was forty-eight when Antony threw away
the world for her sake.

It was a fine summer. Day after day was hot and cloudless; but the heat was tempered by the neighbourhood of the
sea, and there was a pleasant exhilaration in the air, so that
one was excited and not oppressed by the August sunshine.
There was a pond in the garden in which a fountain played;
water-lilies grew in it and goldfish sunned themselves on the
surface. Philip and Miss Wilkinson used to take rugs and
cushions there after dinner and lie on the lawn in the shade of a
tall hedge of roses. They talked and read all the afternoon.
They smoked cigarettes, which the Vicar would not allow in the

house; he thought smoking a disgusting habit, and used frequently to say that it was disgraceful for anyone to grow a slave to a habit. He forgot that he was himself a slave to afternoon tea.

One day Miss Wilkinson gave Philip *La Vie de Bohème*. She had found it by accident when she was rummaging among the books in the Vicar's study. It had been bought in a lot with something Mr Carey wanted and had remained undiscovered for ten years.

Philip began to read Murger's fascinating, ill-written, absurd masterpiece, and fell at once under its spell. His soul danced with joy at that picture of starvation which is so good-humoured, of squalor which is so picturesque, of sordid love which is so romantic, of bathos which is so moving. Rodolphe and Mimi, Musette and Schaunard! They wander through the grey streets of the Latin Quarter, finding refuge now in one attic, now in another, in their quaint costumes of Louis Philippe, with their tears and their smiles, happy-go-lucky and reckless. Who can resist them? It is only when you return to the book with a sounder judgement that you find how gross their pleasures were, how vulgar their minds; and you feel the utter worthlessness, as artists and as human beings, of that gay procession. Philip was enraptured.

'Don't you wish you were going to Paris instead of London?' asked Miss Wilkinson, smiling at his enthusiasm.

'It's too late now even if I did,' he answered.

During the fortnight he had been back from Germany there had been much discussion between himself and his uncle about his future. He had refused definitely to go to Oxford, and now that there was no chance of his getting scholarships even Mr Carey came to the conclusion that he could not afford it. His entire fortune had consisted of only two thousand pounds, and though it had been invested in mortgages at five per cent he had not been able to live on the interest. It was now a little reduced. It would be absurd to spend two hundred a year, the least he could live on at a university, for three years at Oxford which would lead him no nearer to earning his living. He was anxious to go straight to London. Mrs Carey thought there were only four professions for a gentleman, the Army, the Navy, the Law, and the Church. She had added medicine because her brother-in-law practised it, but did not forget that in her young days no one ever considered the doctor a gentleman. The first two were out of the question, and Philip was firm in his refusal to be ordained. Only the law remained. The local doctor had suggested that many gentlemen now went in for engineering, but Mrs Carey opposed the idea at once.

'I shouldn't like Philip to go into trade,' she said.

'No, he must have a profession,' answered the Vicar.

'Why not make him a doctor like his father?'

'I should hate it,' said Philip.

Mrs Carey was not sorry. The Bar seemed out of the question, since he was not going to Oxford, for the Careys were under the impression that a degree was still necessary for success in that calling; and finally it was suggested that he should become articled to a solicitor. They wrote to the family lawyer, Albert Nixon, who was co-executor with the Vicar of Blackstable for the late Henry Carey's estate, and asked him whether he would take Philip. In a day or two the answer came back that he had not a vacancy, and was very much opposed to the whole scheme; the profession was greatly overcrowded, and without capital or connexions a man had small chance of becoming more than a managing clerk; he suggested, however, that Philip should become a chartered accountant. Neither the Vicar nor his wife knew in the least what this was, and Philip had never heard of anyone being a chartered accountant; but another letter from the solicitor explained that the growth of modern business and the increase of companies had led to the formation of many firms of accountants to examine the books and put into the financial affairs of their clients an order which old-fashioned methods had lacked. Some years before a Royal Charter had been obtained, and the profession was becoming every year more respectable, lucrative, and important. The chartered accountants whom Albert Nixon had employed for thirty years happened to have a vacancy for an articled pupil, and would take Philip for a fee of three hundred pounds. Half of this would be returned during the five years the articles lasted in the form of salary. The prospect was not exciting, but Philip felt that he must decide on something, and the thought of living in London overbalanced the slight shrinking he felt. The Vicar of Blackstable wrote to ask Mr Nixon whether it was a profession suited to a gentleman; and Mr Nixon replied that, since the Charter, men were going into it who had been to public schools and a university; moreover, if Philip disliked the work and after a year wished to leave, Herbert Carter, for that was the accountant's name, would return half the money paid for the articles. This settled it, and it was arranged that Philip should start work on the fifteenth of September.

'I have a full month before me,' said Philip.

'And then you go to freedom and I to bondage,' returned Miss Wilkinson.

Her holidays were to last six weeks, and she would be leaving Blackstable only a day or two before Philip.

'I wonder if we shall ever meet again,' she said.

'I don't know why not.'

'Oh, don't speak in that practical way. I never knew anyone so unsentimental.'

Philip reddened. He was afraid that Miss Wilkinson would think him a milksop: after all she was a young woman, sometimes quite pretty, and he was getting on for twenty; it was absurd that they should talk of nothing but art and literature. He ought to make love to her. They had talked a good deal of love. There was the art-student in the Rue Bréda, and then there was the painter in whose family she had lived so long in Paris: he had asked her to sit for him, and started to make love to her so violently that she was forced to invent excuses not to sit to him again. It was clear enough that Miss Wilkinson was used to attentions of that sort. She looked very nice now in a large straw hat: it was hot that afternoon, the hottest day they had had, and beads of sweat stood in a line on her upper lip. He called to mind Fräulein Cäcilie and Herr Sung. He had never thought of Cäcilie in an amorous way, she was exceedingly plain; but now, looking back, the affair seemed very romantic. He had a chance of romance too. Miss Wilkinson was practically French, and that added zest to a possible adventure. When he thought of it at night in bed, or when he sat by himself in the garden reading a book, he was thrilled by it; but when he saw Miss Wilkinson it seemed less picturesque.

At all events, after what she had told him, she would not be surprised if he made love to her. He had a feeling that she must think it odd of him to make no sign: perhaps it was only his fancy, but once or twice in the last day or two he had imagined that there was a suspicion of contempt in her eyes.

'A penny for your thoughts,' said Miss Wilkinson, looking at him with a smile.

'I'm not going to tell you,' he answered.

He was thinking that he ought to kiss her there and then. He wondered if she expected him to do it; but after all he didn't see how he could without any preliminary business at all. She would just think him mad, or she might slap his face; and perhaps she would complain to his uncle. He wondered how Herr Sung had started with Fräulein Cäcilie. It would be beastly if she told his uncle: he knew what his uncle was, he would tell the doctor and Josiah Graves; and he would look a perfect fool. Aunt Louisa kept on saying that Miss Wilkinson was thirty-seven if she was a day; he shuddered at the thought of the ridicule he would be exposed to; they would say she was old enough to be his mother.

'Twopence for your thoughts,' smiled Miss Wilkinson.

'I was thinking about you,' he answered boldly.

That at all events committed him to nothing.

'What were you thinking?'

'Ah, now you want to know too much.'

'Naughty boy!' said Miss Wilkinson.

There it was again! Whenever he had succeeded in working himself up she said something which reminded him of the governess. She called him playfully a naughty boy when he did not sing his exercises to her satisfaction. This time he grew quite sulky.

'I wish you wouldn't treat me as if I were a child.'

'Are you cross?'

'Very.'

'I didn't mean to.'

She put out her hand and he took it. Once or twice lately when they shook hands at night he had fancied she slightly pressed his hand, but this time there was no doubt about it.

He did not quite know what he ought to say next. Here at last was his chance of an adventure, and he would be a fool not to take it; but it was a little ordinary, and he had expected more glamour. He had read many descriptions of love, and he felt in himself none of that uprush of emotion which novelists described; he was not carried off his feet in wave upon wave of passion; nor was Miss Wilkinson the ideal: he had often pictured to himself the great violet eyes and the alabaster skin of some lovely girl, and he had thought of himself burying his face in the rippling masses of her auburn hair. He could not imagine himself burying his face in Miss Wilkinson's hair, it always struck him as a little sticky. All the same it would be very satisfactory to have an intrigue, and he thrilled with the legitimate pride he would enjoy in his conquest. He owed it to himself to seduce her. He made up his mind to kiss Miss Wilkinson; not then, but in the evening; it would be easier in the dark, and after he had kissed her the rest would follow. He would kiss her that very evening. He swore an oath to that effect.

He laid his plans. After supper he suggested that they should take a stroll in the garden. Miss Wilkinson accepted, and they sauntered side by side. Philip was very nervous. He did not know why, but the conversation would not lead in the right direction; he had decided that the first thing to do was to put his arm round her waist; but he could not suddenly put his arm round her waist when she was talking of the regatta which was to be held next week. He led her artfully into the darkest parts of the garden, but having arrived there his courage failed him. They sat on a bench, and he had really made up his mind that here was his opportunity when Miss Wilkinson said she was sure there were earwigs and insisted on moving. They walked round the garden once more, and Philip promised himself he would take the plunge before they arrived at that bench again; but as they passed the house, they saw Mrs Carey standing at the door.

'Hadn't you young people better come in? I'm sure the night air isn't good for you.'

'Perhaps we had better go in,' said Philip. 'I don't want you to catch cold.'

He said it with a sigh of relief. He could attempt nothing more that night. But afterwards, when he was alone in his room, he was furious with himself. He had been a perfect fool. He was certain that Miss Wilkinson expected him to kiss her, otherwise she wouldn't have come into the garden. She was always saying that only Frenchmen knew how to treat women. Philip had read French novels. If he had been a Frenchman he would have seized her in his arms and told her passionately that he adored her; he would have pressed his lips on her *nuque*. He did not know why Frenchmen always kissed ladies on the *nuque*. He did not himself see anything so very attractive in the nape of the neck. Of course it was much easier for Frenchmen to do these things; the language was such an aid; Philip could never help feeling that to say passionate things in English sounded a little absurd. He wished now that he had never undertaken the siege of Miss Wilkinson's virtue; the first fortnight had been so jolly, and now he was wretched; but he was determined not to give in, he would never respect himself again if he did, and he made up his mind irrevocably that the next night he would kiss her without fail.

Next day when he got up he saw it was raining, and his first thought was that they would not be able to go into the garden that evening. He was in high spirits at breakfast. Miss Wilkinson sent Mary in to say that she had a headache and would remain in bed. She did not come down till tea-time, when she appeared in a becoming wrapper and a pale face; but she was quite recovered by supper, and the meal was very cheerful. After prayers she said she would go straight to bed, and she kissed Mrs Carey. Then she turned to Philip.

'Good gracious!' she cried. 'I was just going to kiss you too.'

'Why don't you?' he said.

She laughed and held out her hand. She distinctly pressed his.

The following day there was not a cloud in the sky, and the garden was sweet and fresh after the rain. Philip went down to the beach to bathe and when he came home ate a magnificent dinner. They were having a tennis party at the vicarage in the afternoon and Miss Wilkinson put on her best dress. She certainly knew how to wear her clothes, and Philip could not help noticing how elegant she looked beside the curate's wife and the doctor's married daughter. There were two roses in her waistband. She sat in a garden chair by the side of the lawn, holding a red parasol over herself, and the light on her face was very becoming. Philip was fond of tennis. He served well and as he ran clumsily played close to the net: notwithstanding his club-foot he was quick, and it was difficult to get a ball past him. He was pleased because he won all his sets. At tea he lay down at Miss Wilkinson's feet, hot and panting.

'Flannels suit you,' she said. 'You look very nice this afternoon.'

He blushed with delight.

'I can honestly return the compliment. You look perfectly ravishing.'

She smiled and gave him a long look with her black eyes.

After supper he insisted that she should come out.

'Haven't you had enough exercise for one day?'

'It'll be lovely in the garden tonight. The stars are all out.'

He was in high spirits.

'D'you know, Mrs Carey has been scolding me on your account?' said Miss Wilkinson, when they were sauntering through the kitchen-garden. 'She says I mustn't flirt with you.'

'Have you been flirting with me? I hadn't noticed it.'

'She was only joking.'

'It was very unkind of you to refuse to kiss me last night.'

'If you saw the look your uncle gave me when I said what I did!'

'Was that all that prevented you?'

'I prefer to kiss people without witnesses.'

'There are no witnesses now.'

Philip put his arm round her waist and kissed her lips. She

144

only laughed a little and made no attempt to withdraw. It had
come quite naturally. Philip was very proud of himself. He
said he would, and he had. It was the easiest thing in the
world. He wished he had done it before. He did it again.

'Oh, you mustn't,' she said.

'Why not?'

'Because I liked it,' she laughed.

XXXIV

NEXT day after dinner they took their rugs and cushions to
the fountain, and their books; but they did not read. Miss
Wilkinson made herself comfortable and she opened the red
sun-shade. Philip was not at all shy now, but at first she would
not let him kiss her.

'It was very wrong of me last night,' she said. 'I couldn't
sleep, I felt I'd done so wrong.'

'What nonsense!' he cried. 'I'm sure you slept like a top.'

'What do you think your uncle would say if he knew?'

'There's no reason why he should know.'

He leaned over her, and his heart went pit-a-pat.

'Why d'you want to kiss me?'

He knew he ought to reply: 'Because I love you.' But he
could not bring himself to say it.

'Why do you think?' he asked instead.

She looked at him with smiling eyes and touched his face
with the tips of her fingers.

'How smooth your face is,' she murmured.

'I want shaving awfully,' he said.

It was astonishing how difficult he found it to make romantic
speeches. He found that silence helped him much more than
words. He could look inexpressible things. Miss Wilkinson
sighed.

'Do you like me at all?'

'Yes, awfully.'

When he tried to kiss her again she did not resist. He pretended to be much more passionate than he really was, and he
succeeded in playing a part which looked very well in his own
eyes.

'I'm beginning to be rather frightened of you,' said Miss
Wilkinson.

'You'll come out after supper, won't you?' he begged.

'Not unless you promise to behave yourself.'

145

'I'll promise anything.'

He was catching fire from the flame he was partly simu-
lating, and at tea-time he was obstreperously merry. Miss
Wilkinson looked at him nervously.

'You mustn't have those shining eyes,' she said to him
afterwards. 'What will your Aunt Louisa think?'

'I don't care what she thinks.'

Miss Wilkinson gave a little laugh of pleasure. They had no
sooner finished supper than he said to her:

'Are you going to keep me company while I smoke a cigarette?'

'Why don't you let Miss Wilkinson rest?' said Mrs Carey.
'You must remember she's not as young as you.'

'Oh, I'd like to go out, Mrs Carey,' she said, rather acidly.

'After dinner walk a mile, after supper rest a while,' said
the Vicar.

'Your aunt is very nice, but she gets on my nerves sometimes,' said Miss Wilkinson, as soon as they closed the side-
door behind them.

Philip threw away the cigarette he had just lighted, and flung
his arms round her. She tried to push him away.

'You promised you'd be good, Philip.'

'You didn't think I was going to keep a promise like that?'

'Not so near the house, Philip,' she said. 'Supposing someone should come out suddenly?'

He led her to the kitchen garden where no one was likely
to come, and this time Miss Wilkinson did not think of earwigs. He kissed her passionately. It was one of the things that
puzzled him that he did not like her at all in the morning,
and only moderately in the afternoon, but at night the touch
of her hand thrilled him. He said things that he would never
have thought himself capable of saying; he could certainly
never have said them in the broad light of day; and he listened
to himself with wonder and satisfaction.

'How beautifully you make love,' she said.

That was what he thought himself.

'Oh, if I could only say all the things that burn my heart!'
he murmured passionately.

It was splendid. It was the most thrilling game he had ever
played; and the wonderful thing was that he felt almost all he
said. It was only that he exaggerated a little. He was tremendously interested and excited in the effect he could see it had
on her. It was obviously with an effort that at last she suggested
going in.

'Oh, don't go yet,' he cried.

'I must,' she muttered. 'I'm frightened.'

He had a sudden intuition what was the right thing to do then.

'I can't go in yet. I shall stay here and think. My cheeks are burning. I want the night-air. Good night.'

He held out his hand seriously, and she took it in silence. He thought she stifled a sob. Oh, it was magnificent! When, after a decent interval during which he had been rather bored in the dark garden by himself, he went in he found that Miss Wilkinson had already gone to bed.

After that things were different between them. The next day and the day after Philip showed himself an eager lover. He was deliciously flattered to discover that Miss Wilkinson was in love with him: she told him so in English, and she told him so in French. She paid him compliments. No one had ever informed him before that his eyes were charming and that he had a sensual mouth. He had never bothered much about his personal appearance, but now, when occasion presented, he looked at himself in the glass with satisfaction. When he kissed her it was wonderful to feel the passion that seemed to thrill her soul. He kissed her a good deal, for he found it easier to do that than to say the things he instinctively felt she expected of him. It still made him feel a fool to say he worshipped her. He wished there were someone to whom he could boast a little, and he would willingly have discussed minute points of his conduct. Sometimes she said things that were enigmatic, and he was puzzled. He wished Hayward had been there so that he could ask him what he thought she meant, and what he had better do next. He could not make up his mind whether he ought to rush things or let them take their time. There were only three weeks more.

'I can't bear to think of that,' she said. 'It breaks my heart. And then perhaps we shall never see one another again.'

'If you cared for me at all, you wouldn't be so unkind to me,' he whispered.

'Oh, why can't you be content to let it go on as it is? Men are always the same. They're never satisfied.'

And when he pressed her, she said:

'But don't you see it's impossible. How can we here?'

He proposed all sorts of schemes, but she would not have anything to do with them.

'I daren't take the risk. It would be too dreadful if your aunt found out.'

147

A day or two later he had an idea which seemed brilliant.

'Look here, if you had a headache on Sunday evening and offered to stay at home and look after the house, Aunt Louisa would go to church.'

Generally Mrs Carey remained in on Sunday evening in order to allow Mary Ann to go to church, but she would welcome the opportunity of attending evensong.

Philip had not found it necessary to impart to his relations the change in his views on Christianity which had occurred in Germany; they could not be expected to understand; and it seemed less trouble to go to church quietly. But he only went in the morning. He regarded this as a graceful concession to the prejudices of society and his refusal to go a second time as an adequate assertion of free thought.

When he made the suggestion, Miss Wilkinson did not speak for a moment, then shook her head.

'No, I won't,' she said.

But on Sunday at tea-time she surprised Philip.

'I don't think I'll come to church this evening,' she said suddenly. 'I've really got a dreadful headache.'

Mrs Carey, much concerned, insisted on giving her some 'drops' which she was herself in the habit of using. Miss Wilkinson thanked her, and immediately after tea announced that she would go to her room and lie down.

'Are you sure there's nothing you'll want?' asked Mrs Carey anxiously.

'Quite sure, thank you.'

'Because, if there isn't, I think I'll go to church. I don't often have the chance of going in the evening.'

'Oh yes, do go.'

'I shall be in,' said Philip. 'If Miss Wilkinson wants anything, she can always call me.'

'You'd better leave the drawing-room door open, Philip, so that if Miss Wilkinson rings, you'll hear.'

'Certainly,' said Philip.

So after six o'clock Philip was left alone in the house with Miss Wilkinson. He felt sick with apprehension. He wished with all his heart that he had not suggested the plan; but it was too late now; he must take the opportunity which he had made. What would Miss Wilkinson think of him if he did not! He went into the hall and listened. There was not a sound. He wondered if Miss Wilkinson really had a headache. Perhaps she had forgotten his suggestion. His heart beat painfully. He crept up the stairs as softly as he could, and he stopped with a start when they creaked. He stood outside Miss Wilkinson's room and listened; he put his hand on the knob of the door-handle. He waited. It seemed to him that he waited for at least five minutes, trying to make up his mind; and his hand trembled. He would willingly have bolted, but he was afraid of the remorse which he knew would seize him. It was like getting on the highest diving-board in a swimming-bath; it looked nothing from below, but when you got up there and stared down at the water your heart sank; and the only thing that forced you to dive was the shame of coming down meekly by the steps you had climbed up. Philip screwed up his courage. He turned the handle softly and walked in. He seemed to himself to be trembling like a leaf.

Miss Wilkinson was standing at the dressing-table with her back to the door, and she turned round quickly when she heard it open.

'Oh, it's you. What d'you want?'

She had taken off her skirt and blouse, and was standing in her petticoat. It was short and only came down to the top of her boots; the upper part of it was black, of some shiny material, and there was a red flounce. She wore a camisole of white calico with short arms. She looked grotesque. Philip's heart sank as he stared at her; she had never seemed so unattractive; but it was too late now. He closed the door behind him and locked it.

XXXV

PHILIP woke early next morning. His sleep had been restless; but when he stretched his legs and looked at the sunshine that slid through the Venetian blinds, making patterns on the floor, he sighed with satisfaction. He was delighted with himself. He began to think of Miss Wilkinson. She had asked him to call her Emily, but, he knew not why, he could not; he always thought of her as Miss Wilkinson. Since she chid him for so addressing her, he avoided using her name at all. During his childhood he had often heard a sister of Aunt Louisa, the widow of a naval officer, spoken of as Aunt Emily. It made him uncomfortable to call Miss Wilkinson by that name, nor could he think of any that would have suited her better. She had begun as Miss Wilkinson, and it seemed inseparable from his impression of her. He frowned a little: somehow or other he saw her now at her worst; he could not forget his dismay when she turned round and he saw her in her camisole and the short petticoat; he remembered the slight roughness of her skin and the sharp, long lines on the side of her neck. His triumph was short-lived. He reckoned out her age again, and he did not see how she could be less than forty. It made the affair ridiculous. She was plain and old. His quick fancy showed her to him, wrinkled, haggard, made-up, in those frocks which were too showy for her position and too young for her years. He shuddered; he felt suddenly that he never wanted to see her again; he could not bear the thought of kissing her. He was horrified with himself. Was that love?

He took as long as he could over dressing in order to put back the moment of seeing her, and when at last he went into the dining-room it was with a sinking heart. Prayers were over, and they were sitting down at breakfast.

'Lazy bones,' Miss Wilkinson cried gaily.

He looked at her and gave a little gasp of relief. She was sitting with her back to the window. She was really quite nice. He wondered why he had thought such things about her. His self-satisfaction returned to him.

He was taken aback by the change in her. She told him in a voice thrilling with emotion immediately after breakfast that she loved him; and when a little later they went into the drawing-room for his singing lesson and she sat down on the music-stool she put up her face in the middle of a scale and said:

'*Embrasse-moi.*'

When he bent down she flung her arms round his neck. It was slightly uncomfortable, for she held him in such a position that he felt rather choked.

'*Ah, je t'aime. Je t'aime. Je t'aime,*' she cried, with her extravagantly French accent.

Philip wished she would speak English.

'I say, I don't know if it's struck you that the gardener's quite likely to pass the window any minute.'

'*Ah, je m'en fiche du jardinier. Je m'en refiche, et je m'en contrefiche.*'

Philip thought it was very like a French novel, and he did not know why it slightly irritated him.

At last he said:

'Well, I think I'll tootle along to the beach and have a dip.'

'Oh, you're not going to leave me this morning – of all mornings?'

Philip did not quite know why he should not, but it did not matter.

150

'Would you like me to stay?' he smiled.

'Oh, you darling! But no, go. Go. I want to think of you mastering the salt sea waves, bathing your limbs in the broad ocean.'

He got his hat and sauntered off.

'What rot women talk!' he thought to himself.

But he was pleased and happy and flattered. She was evidently frightfully gone on him. As he limped along the high street of Blackstable he looked with a tinge of super-ciliousness at the people he passed. He knew a good many to nod to, and as he gave them a smile of recognition he thought to himself, if they only knew! He did want someone to know very badly. He thought he would write to Hayward, and in his mind composed the letter. He would talk of the garden and the roses, and the little French governess, like an exotic flower amongst them, scented and perverse: he would say she was French, because – well, she had lived in France so long that she almost was, and besides it would be shabby to give the whole thing away too exactly, don't you know; and he would tell Hayward how he had seen her first in her pretty muslin dress and of the flower she had given him. He made a delicate idyll of it: the sunshine and the sea gave it passion and magic, and the stars added poetry, and the old vicarage garden was a fit and exquisite setting. There was something Meredithian about it: it was not quite Lucy Feveral and not quite Clara Middleton; but it was inexpressibly charming. Philip's heart beat quickly. He was so delighted with his fancies that he began thinking of them again as soon as he crawled back, drip-ping and cold, into his bathing-machine. He thought of the object of his affections. She had the most adorable little nose and large brown eyes – he would describe her to Hayward – and masses of soft brown hair, the sort of hair it was delicious to bury your face in, and a skin which was like ivory and sun-shine, and her cheek was like a red, red rose. How old was she? Eighteen perhaps, and he called her Musette. Her laughter was like a rippling brook, and her voice was so soft, so low, it was the sweetest music he had ever heard.

'What *are* you thinking about?'

Philip stopped suddenly. He was walking slowly home.

'I've been waving at you for the last quarter of a mile. You *are* absent-minded.'

Miss Wilkinson was standing in front of him, laughing at his surprise.

'I thought I'd come and meet you.'

'That's awfully nice of you,' he said.

'Did I startle you?'

'You did a bit,' he admitted.

He wrote his letter to Hayward all the same. There were eight pages of it.

The fortnight that remained passed quickly, and though each evening, when they went into the garden after supper, Miss Wilkinson remarked that one day more had gone, Philip was in too cheerful spirits to let the thought depress him. One night Miss Wilkinson suggested that it would be delightful if she could exchange her situation in Berlin for one in London. Then they could see one another constantly. Philip said it would be very jolly, but the prospect aroused no enthusiasm in him; he was looking forward to a wonderful life in London, and he preferred not to be hampered. He spoke a little too freely of all he meant to do, and allowed Miss Wilkinson to see that already he was longing to be off.

'You wouldn't talk like that if you loved me,' she cried.

He was taken aback and remained silent.

'What a fool I've been,' she muttered.

To his surprise he saw that she was crying. He had a tender heart, and hated to see anyone miserable.

'Oh, I'm awfully sorry. What have I done? Don't cry.'

'Oh, Philip, don't leave me. You don't know what you mean to me. I have such a wretched life, and you've made me so happy.'

He kissed her silently. There really was anguish in her tone, and he was frightened. It had never occurred to him that she meant what she said quite, quite seriously.

'I'm awfully sorry. You know I'm frightfully fond of you. I wish you would come to London.'

'You know I can't. Places are almost impossible to get, and I hate English life.'

Almost unconscious that he was acting a part, moved by her distress, he pressed her more and more. Her tears vaguely flattered him, and he kissed her with real passion.

But a day or two later she made a real scene. There was a tennis-party at the vicarage, and two girls came, daughters of a retired major in an Indian regiment who had lately settled in Blackstable. They were very pretty, one was Philip's age and the other was a year or two younger. Being used to the society of young men (they were full of stories of hill-stations in India, and at that time the stories of Rudyard Kipling were in every hand) they began to chaff Philip gaily; and he, pleased with the novelty – the young ladies at Blackstable treated the Vicar's nephew with a certain seriousness – was gay and jolly. Some devil within him prompted him to start a violent flirtation with them both, and as he was the only young man there, they were quite willing to meet him half-way. It happened that they played tennis quite well and Philip was tired of pat-ball with Miss Wilkinson (she had only begun to play when she came to Blackstable), so when he arranged the sets after tea he suggested that Miss Wilkinson should play against the curate's wife, with the curate as her partner; and he would play later with the newcomers. He sat down by the elder Miss O'Connor and said to her in an undertone:

'We'll get the duffers out of the way first, and then we'll have a jolly set afterwards.'

Apparently Miss Wilkinson overheard him, for she threw down her racket, and, saying she had a headache, went away. It was plain to everyone that she was offended. Philip was annoyed that she should make the fact public. The set was arranged without her, but presently Mrs Carey called him.

'Philip, you've hurt Emily's feelings. She's gone to her room and she's crying.'

'What about?'

'Oh, something about a duffer's set. Do go to her, and say you didn't mean to be unkind, there's a good boy.'

'All right.'

He knocked at Miss Wilkinson's door, but receiving no answer went in. He found her lying face downwards on her bed, weeping. He touched her on the shoulder.

'I say, what on earth's the matter?'

'Leave me alone. I never want to speak to you again.'

'What have I done? I'm awfully sorry if I've hurt your feelings. I didn't mean to. I say, do get up.'

'Oh, I'm so unhappy. How could you be cruel to me? You know I hate that stupid game. I only play because I want to play with you.'

She got up and walked towards the dressing-table, but after a quick look in the glass sank into a chair. She made her handkerchief into a ball and dabbed her eyes with it.

'I've given you the greatest thing a woman can give a man – oh, what a fool I was! – and you have no gratitude. You must be quite heartless. How could you be so cruel as to torment me by flirting with those vulgar girls. We've only got just over a week. Can't you even give me that?'

Philip stood over her rather sulkily. He thought her behaviour childish. He was vexed with her for having shown her ill-temper before strangers.

'But you know I don't care twopence about either of the O'Connors. Why on earth should you think I do?'

Miss Wilkinson put away her handkerchief. Her tears had made marks on her powdered face, and her hair was somewhat disarranged. Her white dress did not suit her very well just then. She looked at Philip with hungry, passionate eyes.

'Because you're twenty and so's she,' she said hoarsely. 'And I'm old.'

Philip reddened and looked away. The anguish of her tone made him feel strangely uneasy. He wished with all his heart that he had never had anything to do with Miss Wilkinson.

'I don't want to make you unhappy,' he said awkwardly. 'You'd better go down and look after your friends. They'll wonder what has become of you.'

'All right.'

He was glad to leave her.

The quarrel was quickly followed by a reconciliation, but the few days that remained were sometimes irksome to Philip. He wanted to talk of nothing but the future, and the future invariably reduced Miss Wilkinson to tears. At first her weeping affected him, and feeling himself a beast he redoubled his protestations of undying passion; but now it irritated him: it would have been all very well if she had been a girl, but it was silly of a grown-up woman to cry so much. She never ceased reminding him that he was under a debt of gratitude to her which he could never repay. He was willing to acknowledge this, since she made a point of it, but he did not really know why he should be any more grateful to her than she to him. He was expected to show his sense of obligation in ways which were rather a nuisance: he had been a good deal used to solitude, and it was a necessity to him sometimes; but Miss Wilkinson looked upon it as an unkindness if he was not always at her beck and call. The Miss O'Connors asked them both to tea, and Philip would have liked to go, but Miss Wilkinson said she only had five days more and wanted him entirely to herself. It was flattering, but a bore. Miss Wilkinson told him stories of the exquisite delicacy of Frenchmen when they stood in the same relation to fair ladies as he to Miss Wilkinson. She praised their courtesy, their passion for self-sacrifice, their perfect tact. Miss Wilkinson seemed to want a great deal.

Philip listened to her enumeration of the qualities which

must be possessed by the perfect lover, and he could not help feeling a certain satisfaction that she lived in Berlin.

'You will write to me, won't you? Write to me every day. I want to know everything you're doing. You must keep nothing from me.'

'I shall be awfully busy,' he said. 'I'll write as often as I can.'

She flung her arms passionately round his neck. He was embarrassed sometimes by the demonstrations of her affection. He would have preferred her to be more passive. It shocked him a little that she should give him so marked a lead: it did not tally altogether with his prepossessions about the modesty of the feminine temperament.

At length the day came on which Miss Wilkinson was to go, and she came down to breakfast, pale and subdued, in a serviceable travelling dress of black and white check. She looked a very competent governess. Philip was silent too, for he did not quite know what to say that would fit the circumstance; and he was terribly afraid that, if he said something flippant, Miss Wilkinson would break down before his uncle and make a scene. They had said their last good-bye to one another in the garden the night before, and Philip was relieved that there was now no opportunity for them to be alone. He remained in the dining-room after breakfast in case Miss Wilkinson should insist on kissing him on the stairs. He did not want Mary Ann, now a woman hard upon middle age with a sharp tongue, to catch them in a compromising position. Mary Ann did not like Miss Wilkinson and called her an old cat. Aunt Louisa was not very well and could not come to the station, but the Vicar and Philip saw her off. Just as the train was leaving she leaned out and kissed Mr Carey.

'I must kiss you too, Philip,' she said.

'All right,' he said, blushing.

He stood up on the step and she kissed him quickly. The train started, and Miss Wilkinson sank into the corner of her carriage and wept disconsolately. Philip as he walked back to the vicarage felt a distinct sensation of relief.

'Well, did you see her safely off?' asked Aunt Louisa, when they got in.

'Yes, she seemed rather weepy. She insisted on kissing me and Philip.'

'Oh, well, at her age it's not dangerous.' Mrs Carey pointed to the sideboard. 'There's a letter for you, Philip. It came by the second post.'

It was from Hayward and ran as follows:

My dear boy –

I answer your letter at once. I ventured to read it to a great friend of mine, a charming woman whose help and sympathy have been very precious to me, a woman withal with a real feeling for art and literature; and we agreed that it was charming. You wrote from your heart and you do not know the delightful naïveté which is in every line. And because you love you write like a poet. Ah, dear boy, that is the real thing: I felt the glow of your young passion, and your prose was musical from the sincerity of your emotion. You must be happy! I wish I could have been present unseen in that enchanted garden while you wandered hand in hand, like Daphnis and Chloe, amid the flowers. I can see you, my Daphnis, with the light of young love in your eyes, tender, enraptured, and ardent; while Chloe in your arms, so young and soft and fresh, vowing she would ne'er consent – consented. Roses and violets and honeysuckle! Oh, my friend, I envy you. It is so good to think that your first love should have been pure poetry. Treasure the moments; for the immortal gods have given you the Greatest Gift of All, and it will be a sweet, sad memory till your dying day. You will never again enjoy that careless rapture. First love is best love; and she is beautiful and you are young, and all the world is yours. I felt my pulse go faster when with your adorable simplicity you told me that you buried your face in her long hair. I am sure that it is that exquisite chestnut which seems just touched with gold. I would have you sit under a leafy tree side by side, and read together *Romeo and Juliet*; and then I would have you fall on your knees and on my behalf kiss the ground on which her foot has left its imprint; then tell her it is the homage of a poet to her radiant youth and to your love for her.

Yours always,
G. Etheridge Hayward

'What damned rot!' said Philip, when he finished the letter.

Miss Wilkinson, oddly enough, had suggested that they should read *Romeo and Juliet* together; but Philip had firmly declined. Then, as he put the letter in his pocket, he felt a queer little pang of bitterness because reality seemed so different from the ideal.

XXXVI

A FEW days later Philip went to London. The curate had recommended rooms in Barnes, and these Philip engaged by letter at fourteen shillings a week. He reached them in the evening; and the landlady, a funny little old woman with a shrivelled body and a deeply wrinkled face, had prepared high tea for him. Most of the sitting-room was taken up by the side-board and a square table; against one wall was a sofa covered with horsehair, and by the fireplace an armchair to match; there was a white antimacassar over the back of it, and on the seat, because the springs were broken, a hard cushion.

After having his tea he unpacked and arranged his books, then he sat down and tried to read; but he was depressed. The silence in the street made him slightly uncomfortable, and he felt very much alone.

Next day he got up early. He put on his tail-coat and the tall hat which he had worn at school; but it was very shabby, and he made up his mind to stop at the Stores on his way to the office and buy a new one. When he had done this he found himself in plenty of time and so walked along the Strand. The office of Messrs Herbert Carter & Co. was in a little street off Chancery Lane, and he had to ask his way two or three times. He felt that people were staring at him a great deal, and once he took off his hat to see whether by chance the label had been left on. When he arrived he knocked at the door; but no one answered, and looking at his watch he found it was barely half past nine; he supposed he was too early He went away and ten minutes later returned to find an office-boy, with a long nose, pimply face, and a Scotch accent, opening the door. Philip asked for Mr Herbert Carter. He had not come yet.

'When will he be here?'

'Between ten and half past.'

'I'd better wait,' said Philip.

'What are you wanting?' asked the office-boy.

Philip was nervous, but tried to hide the fact by a jocose manner.

'Well, I'm going to work here if you have no objection.'

'Oh, you're the new articled clerk? You'd better come in. Mr Goodworthy'll be here in a while.'

Philip walked in, and as he did so saw the office-boy – he was about the same age as Philip and called himself a junior clerk – look at his foot. He flushed and, sitting down, hid it behind the other. He looked round the room. It was dark and very dingy. It was lit by a skylight. There were three rows of desks in it and against them high stools. Over the chimney-piece was a dirty engraving of a prize-fight. Presently a clerk came in and then another; they glanced at Philip and in an undertone asked the office-boy (Philip found his name was Macdougal) who he was. A whistle blew, and Macdougal got up.

'Mr Goodworthy's come. He's the managing clerk. Shall I tell him you're here?'

'Yes, please,' said Philip.

The office-boy went out and in a moment returned.

'Will you come this way?'

Philip followed him across the passage and was shown into a room, small and barely furnished, in which a little, thin man was standing with his back to the fireplace. He was much below the middle height, but his large head, which seemed to hang loosely on his body, gave him an odd ungainliness. His features were wide and flattened, and he had prominent, pale eyes; his thin hair was sandy; he wore whiskers that grew unevenly on his face, and in places where you would have expected the hair to grow thickly there was no hair at all. His skin was pasty and yellow. He held out his hand to Philip, and when he smiled showed badly decayed teeth. He spoke with a patronizing and at the same time a timid air, as though he sought to assume an importance which he did not feel. He said he hoped Philip would like the work; there was a good deal of drudgery about it, but when you got used to it, it was interesting; and one made money, that was the chief thing, wasn't it? He laughed with his odd mixture of superiority and shyness.

'Mr Carter will be here presently,' he said. 'He's a little late on Monday mornings sometimes. I'll call you when he comes. In the meantime I must give you something to do. Do you know anything about book-keeping or accounts?'

'I'm afraid not,' answered Philip.

'I didn't suppose you would. They don't teach you things at school that are much use in business, I'm afraid.' He considered for a moment. 'I think I can find you something to do.'

He went into the next room and after a little while came out with a large cardboard box. It contained a vast number of letters in great disorder, and he told Philip to sort them out and arrange them alphabetically according to the names of the writers.

'I'll take you to the room in which the articled clerk generally sits. There's a very nice fellow in it. His name is Watson. He's a son of Watson, Crag, and Thompson – you know – the brewers. He's spending a year with us to learn business.'

Mr Goodworthy led Philip through the dingy office, where now six or eight clerks were working, into a narrow room behind. It had been made into a separate apartment by a glass partition, and here they found Watson sitting back in a chair, reading *The Sportsman*. He was a large, stout young man, elegantly dressed, and he looked up as Mr Goodworthy entered. He asserted his position by calling the managing clerk Goodworthy. The managing clerk objected to the familiarity, and pointedly called him Mr Watson, but Watson, instead of seeing that it was a rebuke, accepted the title as a tribute to his gentlemanliness.

'I see they've scratched Rigoletto,' he said to Philip, as soon as they were left alone.

'Have they?' said Philip, who knew nothing about horseracing.

He looked with awe upon Watson's beautiful clothes. His tail-coat fitted him perfectly, and there was a valuable pin artfully stuck in the middle of an enormous tie. On the chimneypiece rested his tall hat; it was saucy and bell-shaped and shiny. Philip felt himself very shabby. Watson began to talk of hunting – it was such an infernal bore having to waste one's time in an infernal office, he would only be able to hunt on Saturdays – and shooting: he had ripping invitations all over the country and of course he had to refuse them. It was infernal luck, but he wasn't going to put up with it long; he was only in this infernal hole for a year, and then he was going into the business, and he would hunt four days a week and get all the shooting there was.

'You've got five years of it, haven't you?' he said, waving his arm round the tiny room.

'I suppose so,' said Philip.

'I daresay I shall see something of you. Carter does our accounts, you know.'

Philip was somewhat overpowered by the young gentleman's condescension. At Blackstable they had always looked upon brewing with civil contempt, the Vicar made little jokes about the beerage, and it was a surprising experience for Philip to discover that Watson was such an important and magnificent fellow. He had been to Winchester and to Oxford, and his conversation impressed the fact upon one with frequency. When he discovered the details of Philip's education his manner became more patronizing still.

'Of course, if one doesn't go to a public school those sort of schools are the next best thing, aren't they?'

Philip asked about the other men in the office.

'Oh, I don't bother about them much, you know,' said Watson. 'Carter's not a bad sort. We have him to dine now and then. All the rest are awful bounders.'

Presently Watson applied himself to some work he had in

hand, and Philip set about sorting his letters. Then Mr Goodworthy came in to say that Mr Carter had arrived. He took Philip into a large room next door to his own. There was a big desk in it, and a couple of big armchairs; a Turkey carpet adorned the floor, and the walls were decorated with sporting prints. Mr Carter was sitting at the desk and got up to shake hands with Philip. He was dressed in a long frock-coat. He looked like a military man; his moustache was waxed, his grey hair was short and neat, he held himself upright, he talked in a breezy way, he lived at Enfield. He was very keen on games and the good of the country. He was an officer in the Hertfordshire Yeomanry and chairman of the Conservative Association. When he was told that a local magnate had said no one would take him for a City man, he felt that he had not lived in vain. He talked to Philip in a pleasant, off-hand fashion. Mr Goodworthy would look after him. Watson was a nice fellow, perfect gentleman, good sportsman – did Philip hunt? Pity, *the* sport for gentlemen. Didn't have much chance of hunting now, had to leave that to his son. His son was at Cambridge, he'd sent him to Rugby, fine school Rugby, nice class of boys there, in a couple of years his son would be articled, that would be nice for Philip, he'd like his son, thorough sportsman. He hoped Philip would get on well and like the work, he mustn't miss his lectures, they were getting up the tone of the profession, they wanted gentlemen in it. Well, well, Mr Goodworthy was there. If he wanted to know anything Mr Goodworthy would tell him. What was his handwriting like? Ah, well, Mr Goodworthy would see about that.

Philip was overwhelmed by so much gentlemanliness: in East Anglia they knew who were gentlemen and who weren't, but the gentlemen didn't talk about it.

XXXVII

AT first the novelty of the work kept Philip interested. Mr Carter dictated letters to him, and he had to make fair copies of statements of accounts.

Mr Carter preferred to conduct the office on gentlemanly lines; he would have nothing to do with typewriting and looked upon shorthand with disfavour: the office-boy knew shorthand, but it was only Mr Goodworthy who made use of his accomplishment. Now and then Philip with one of the more experienced clerks went out to audit the accounts of some firm: he came to know which of the clients must be treated with respect and which were in low water. Now and then long lists of figures were given him to add up. He attended lectures for his first examination. Mr Goodworthy repeated to him that the work was dull at first, but he would grow used to it. Philip left the office at six and walked across the river to Waterloo. His supper was waiting for him when he reached his lodgings and he spent the evening reading. On Saturday afternoons he went to the National Gallery. Hayward had recommended to him a guide which had been compiled out of Ruskin's works, and with this in hand he went industriously through room after room: he read carefully what the critic had said about a picture and then in a determined fashion set himself to see the same things in it. His Sundays were difficult to get through. He knew no one in London and spent them by himself. Mr Nixon, the solicitor, asked him to spend a Sunday at Hampstead, and Philip passed a happy day with a set of exuberant strangers; he ate and drank a great deal, took a walk on the heath, and came away with a general invitation to come again whenever he liked; but he was morbidly afraid of being in the way, so waited for a formal invitation. Naturally enough it never came, for with numbers of friends of their own the Nixons did not think of the lonely, silent boy whose claim upon their hospitality was so small. So on Sundays he got up late and took a walk along the tow-path. At Barnes the river is muddy, dingy, and tidal; it has neither the graceful charm of the Thames above the locks nor the romance of the crowded stream below London Bridge. In the afternoon he walked about the common; and that is grey and dingy too; it is neither country nor town; the gorse is stunted; and all about is the litter of civilization. He went to a play every Saturday night and stood cheerfully for an hour or more at the gallery-door. It was not worth while to go back to Barnes for the interval between the closing of the Museum and his meal in an A.B.C. shop, and the time hung heavily on his hands. He strolled up Bond Street or through the Burlington Arcade, and when he was tired went and sat down in the Park or in wet weather in the public library in St Martin's Lane. He looked at the people walking about and envied them because they had friends; sometimes his envy turned to hatred because they were happy and he was miserable. He had never imagined that it was possible to be so lonely in a great city. Sometimes when he was standing at the gallery-door the man next to him would attempt a conversation; but Philip had the country boy's suspicion of strangers and answered in such a way as to prevent any further acquaintance. After the play was over, obliged to keep to himself all he thought about it, he hurried across the bridge to Waterloo. When he got back to his rooms, in which for economy no fire had been lit, his heart sank. It was horribly cheerless. He began to loathe his lodgings and the long solitary evenings he spent in them. Sometimes he felt so lonely that he could not read, and then he sat looking into the fire hour after hour in bitter wretchedness.

He had spent three months in London now, and except for that one Sunday at Hampstead had never talked to any-one but his fellow-clerks. One evening Watson asked him to dinner at a restaurant and they went to a music-hall to-gether; but he felt shy and uncomfortable. Watson talked all the time of things he did not care about, and while he looked upon Watson as a Philistine he could not help admiring him. He was angry because Watson obviously set no store on his culture, and with his way of taking himself at the estimate at which he saw others held him he began to despise the acquire-ments which till then had seemed to him not unimportant. He felt for the first time the humiliation of poverty. His uncle sent him fourteen pounds a month and he had had to buy a good many clothes. His evening suit cost him five guineas. He had not dared tell Watson that it was bought in the Strand. Watson said there was only one tailor in London.

'I suppose you don't dance,' said Watson, one day, with a glance at Philip's club-foot.

'No,' said Philip.

'Pity. I've been asked to bring some dancing men to a ball. I could have introduced you to some jolly girls.'

Once or twice, hating the thought of going back to Barnes, Philip had remained in town, and late in the evening wandered through the West End till he found some house at which there was a party. He stood among the little group of shabby people, behind the footmen, watching the guests arrive, and he listened to the music that floated through the window. Sometimes, not-withstanding the cold, a couple came on to the balcony and stood for a moment to get some fresh air, and Philip, imagin-ing that they were in love with one another, turned away and limped along the street with a heavy heart. He would never be able to stand in that man's place. He felt that no woman could ever really look upon him without distaste for his deformity.

That reminded him of Miss Wilkinson. He thought of her without satisfaction. Before parting they had made an arrangement that she should write to Charing Cross Post Office till he was able to send her an address, and when he went there he found three letters from her. She wrote on blue paper with violet ink, and she wrote in French. Philip wondered why she could not write in English like a sensible woman, and her passionate expressions, because they reminded him of a French novel, left him cold. She upbraided him for not having written, and when he answered he excused himself by saying that he had been busy. He did not quite know how to start the letter. He could not bring himself to use *dearest* or *darling*, and he hated to address her as Emily, so finally he began with the word *dear*. It looked odd, standing by itself, and rather silly, but he made it do. It was the first love-letter he had ever written, and he was conscious of its tameness; he felt that he should say all sorts of vehement things, how he thought of her every minute of the day and how he longed to kiss her beautiful hands and how he trembled at the thought of her red lips, but some inexplicable modesty prevented him; and instead he told her of his new rooms and his office. The answer came by return of post, angry, heart-broken, reproachful: how could he be so cold? Did he not know that she hung on his letters? She had given him all that a woman could give, and this was her reward. Was he tired of her already? Then, because he did not reply for several days, Miss Wilkinson bombarded him with letters. She could not bear his unkindness, she waited for the post, and it never brought her his letter, she cried herself to sleep night after night, she was looking so ill that everyone remarked on it: if he did not love her why did he not say so? She added that she could not live without him, and the only thing was for her to commit suicide. She told him he was cold and selfish and ungrateful. It was all in French, and Philip knew that she wrote in that language to show off, but he was worried all the same. He did not want to make her unhappy. In a little while she wrote that she could not bear the separation any longer, she would arrange to come over to London for Christmas. Philip wrote back that he would like nothing better, only he had already an engagement to spend Christmas with friends in the country, and he did not see how he could break it. She answered that she did not wish to force herself on him, it was quite evident that he did not wish to see her; she was deeply hurt, and she never thought he would repay with such cruelty all her kindness. Her letter was touching, and Philip thought he saw marks of her tears on the paper; he wrote an impulsive reply saying that he was dreadfully sorry and imploring her to come; but it was with relief that he received her answer in which she said that she found it would be impossible for her to get away. Presently when her letters came his heart sank: he delayed opening them, for he knew what they would contain, angry reproaches and pathetic appeals; they would make him feel a perfect beast, and yet he did not see with what he had to blame himself. He put off his answer from day to day, and then another letter would come, saying she was ill and lonely and miserable.

'I wish to God I'd never had anything to do with her,' he said.

He admired Watson because he arranged these things so easily. The young man had been engaged in an intrigue with a girl who played in touring companies, and his account of the affair filled Philip with envious amazement. But after a time Watson's young affections changed, and one day he described the rupture to Philip.

'I thought it was no good making any bones about it, so I just told her I'd had enough of her,' he said.

'Didn't she make an awful scene?' asked Philip.

'The usual thing, you know, but I told her it was no good trying on that sort of thing with me.'

'Did she cry?'

'She began to, but I can't stand women when they cry, so I said she'd better hook it.'

Philip's sense of humour was growing keener with advancing years.

'And did she hook it?' he asked, smiling.

'Well, there wasn't anything else for her to do, was there?'

Meanwhile the Christmas holidays approached. Mrs Carey had been ill all through November, and the doctor suggested that she and the Vicar should go to Cornwall for a couple of weeks round Christmas so that she should get back her strength. The result was that Philip had nowhere to go, and he spent Christmas Day in his lodgings. Under Hayward's influence he had persuaded himself that the festivities that attend this season were vulgar and barbaric, and he made up his mind that he would take no notice of the day; but when it came, the jollity of all around affected him strangely. His landlady and her husband were spending the day with a married daughter, and to save trouble Philip announced that he would take his meals out. He went up to London towards mid-day and ate a slice of turkey and some Christmas pudding by himself at Gatti's, and since he had nothing to do afterwards went to

Westminster Abbey for the afternoon service. The streets were almost empty, and the people who went along had a preoccupied look; they did not saunter but walked with some definite goal in view, and hardly anyone was alone. To Philip they all seemed happy. He felt himself more solitary than he had ever done in his life. His intention had been to kill the day somehow in the streets and then dine at a restaurant, but he could not face again the sight of cheerful people, talking, laughing, and making merry; so he went back to Waterloo, and on his way through the Westminster Bridge Road bought some ham and a couple of mince pies and went back to Barnes. He ate his food in his lonely little room and spent the evening with a book. His depression was almost intolerable.

When he was back at the office it made him very sore to listen to Watson's account of the short holiday. They had had some jolly girls staying with them, and after dinner they had cleared out the drawing-room and had a dance.

'I didn't get to bed till three and I don't know how I got there then. By George, I was squiffy.'

At last Philip asked desperately:

'How does one get to know people in London?'

Watson looked at him with surprise and with a slightly contemptuous amusement.

'Oh, I don't know, one just knows them. If you go to dances you soon get to know as many people as you can do with.'

Philip hated Watson, and yet he would have given anything to change places with him. The old feeling that he had had at school came back to him, and he tried to throw himself into the other's skin, imagining what life would be if he were Watson.

XXXVIII

AT the end of the year there was a great deal to do. Philip went to various places with a clerk named Thompson and spent the day monotonously calling out items of expenditure, which the other checked; and sometimes he was given long pages of figures to add up. He had never had a head for figures, and he could only do this slowly. Thompson grew irritated at his mistakes. His fellow-clerk was a long, lean man of forty, sallow, with black hair and a ragged moustache; he had hollow cheeks and deep lines on each side of his nose. He took a dislike to Philip because he was an articled clerk. Because he could put down three hundred guineas and keep

himself for five years Philip had the chance of a career; while
he, with his experience and ability, had no possibility of ever
being more than a clerk at thirty-five shillings a week. He was
a cross-grained man, oppressed by a large family, and he resented the superciliousness which he fancied he saw in Philip.
He sneered at Philip because he was better educated than
himself, and he mocked at Philip's pronunciation; he could
not forgive him because he spoke without a cockney accent,
and when he talked to him sarcastically exaggerated his aitches.
At first his manner was merely gruff and repellent, but as he
discovered that Philip had no gift for accountancy he took
pleasure in humiliating him; his attacks were gross and silly,
but they wounded Philip, and in self-defence he assumed an
attitude of superiority which he did not feel.

'Had a bath this morning?' Thompson said when Philip
came to the office late, for his early punctuality had not lasted.

'Yes, haven't you?'

'No, I'm not a gentleman, I'm only a clerk. I have a bath
on Saturday night.'

'I suppose that's why you're more than usually disagreeable
on Monday.'

'Will you condescend to do a few sums in simple addition
today? I'm afraid it's asking a great deal from a gentleman
who knows Latin and Greek.'

'Your attempts at sarcasm are not very happy.'

But Philip could not conceal from himself that the other
clerks, ill-paid and uncouth, were more useful than himself.
Once or twice Mr Goodworthy grew impatient with him.

'You really ought to be able to do better than this by now,'
he said. 'You're not even as smart as the office-boy.'

Philip listened sulkily. He did not like being blamed, and it
humiliated him, when, having been given accounts to make
fair copies of, Mr Goodworthy was not satisfied and gave them
to another clerk to do. At first the work had been tolerable
from its novelty, but now it grew irksome; and when he discovered that he had no aptitude for it, he began to hate it.
Often, when he should have been doing something that was
given him, he wasted his time drawing little pictures on the
office note-paper. He made sketches of Watson in every con-
ceivable attitude, and Watson was impressed by his talent. It
occurred to him to take the drawings home, and he came back
next day with the praises of his family.

'I wonder you didn't become a painter,' he said. 'Only of
course there's no money in it.'

It chanced that Mr Carter two or three days later was dining with the Watsons, and the sketches were shown him. The following morning he sent for Philip. Philip saw him seldom and stood in some awe of him.

'Look here, young fellow, I don't care what you do out of office hours, but I've seen those sketches of yours and they're on office paper, and Mr Goodworthy tells me you're slack. You won't do any good as a chartered accountant unless you look alive. It's a fine profession, and we're getting a very good class of men in it, but it's a profession in which you have to ...' he looked for the termination of his phrase, but could not find exactly what he wanted, so finished rather tamely, 'in which you have to look alive.'

Perhaps Philip would have settled down but for the agreement that if he did not like the work he could leave after a year, and get back half the money paid for his articles. He felt that he was fit for something better than to add up accounts, and it was humiliating that he did so ill something which seemed contemptible. The vulgar scenes with Thompson got on his nerves. In March Watson ended his year at the office and Philip, though he did not care for him, saw him go with regret. The fact that the other clerks disliked them equally, because they belonged to a class a little higher than their own, was a bond of union. When Philip thought that he must spend over four years more with that dreary set of fellows his heart sank. He had expected wonderful things from London and it had given him nothing. He hated it now. He did not know a soul, and he had no idea how he was to get to know anyone. He was tired of going everywhere by himself. He began to feel that he could not stand much more of such a life. He would lie in bed at night and think of the joy of never seeing again that dingy office or any of the men in it, and of getting away from those drab lodgings.

A great disappointment befell him in the spring. Hayward had announced his intention of coming to London for the season, and Philip had looked forward very much to seeing him again. He had read so much lately and thought so much that his mind was full of ideas which he wanted to discuss, and he knew nobody who was willing to interest himself in abstract things. He was quite excited at the thought of talking his fill with someone, and he was wretched when Hayward wrote to say that the spring was lovelier than ever he had known it in Italy, and he could not bear to tear himself away. He went on to ask why Philip did not come. What was the use of squandering the days of his youth in an office when the world was beautiful? The letter proceeded.

I wonder you can bear it. I think of Fleet Street and Lincoln's Inn now with a shudder of disgust. There are only two things in the world that make life worth living, love and art. I cannot imagine you sitting in an office over a ledger, and do you wear a tall hat and an umbrella and a little black bag? My feeling is that one should look upon life as an adventure, one should burn with the hard, gem-like flame, and one should take risks, one should expose oneself to danger. Why do you not go to Paris and study art? I always thought you had talent.

The suggestion fell in with the possibility that Philip for some time had been vaguely turning over in his mind. It startled him at first, but he could not help thinking of it, and in the constant rumination over it he found his only escape from the wretchedness of his present state. They all thought he had talent; at Heidelberg they had admired his water colours, Miss Wilkinson had told him over and over again that they were charming, even strangers like the Watsons had been struck by his sketches. *La Vie de Bohème* had made a deep impression on him. He had brought it to London and when he was most depressed he had only to read a few pages to be transported into those charming attics where Rodolphe and the rest of them danced and loved and sang. He began to think of Paris as before he had thought of London, but he had no fear of a second disillusion; he yearned for romance and beauty and love, and Paris seemed to offer them all. He had a passion for pictures, and why should he not be able to paint as well as anybody else? He wrote to Miss Wilkinson and asked her how much she thought he could live on in Paris. She told him that he could manage easily on eighty pounds a year, and she enthusiastically approved of his project. She told him he was too good to be wasted in an office. Who would be a clerk when he might be a great artist, she asked dramatically, and she besought Philip to believe in himself: that was the great thing. But Philip had a cautious nature. It was all very well for Hayward to talk of taking risks, he had three hundred a year in gilt-edged securities; Philip's entire fortune amounted to no more than eighteen hundred pounds. He hesitated.

Then it chanced that one day Mr Goodworthy asked him suddenly if he would like to go to Paris. The firm did the accounts for a hotel in the Faubourg St Honoré, which was owned by an English company, and twice a year Mr Good-worthy and a clerk went over. The clerk who generally went happened to be ill, and a press of work prevented any of the others from getting away. Mr Goodworthy thought of Philip because he could best be spared, and his articles gave him some claim upon a job which was one of the pleasures of the business. Philip was delighted.

'You'll 'ave to work all day,' said Mr Goodworthy, 'but we get our evenings to ourselves, and Paris is Paris.' He smiled in a knowing way. 'They do us very well at the hotel, and they give us all our meals, so it don't cost one anything. That's the way I like going to Paris, at other people's expense.'

When they arrived at Calais and Philip saw the crowd of gesticulating porters his heart leaped.

'This is the real thing,' he said to himself.

He was all eyes as the train sped through the country; he adored the sand dunes, their colour seemed to him more lovely than anything he had ever seen; and he was enchanted with the canals and the long lines of poplars. When they got out of the Gare du Nord, and trundled along the cobbled streets in a ramshackle, noisy cab, it seemed to him that he was breathing a new air so intoxicating that he could hardly restrain himself from shouting aloud. They were met at the door of the hotel by the manager, a stout, pleasant man, who spoke tolerable English; Mr Goodworthy was an old friend and he greeted them effusively; they dined in his private room with his wife, and to Philip it seemed that he had never eaten anything so delicious as the *beefsteak aux pommes*, nor drunk such nectar as the *vin ordinaire*, which were set before them.

To Mr Goodworthy, a respectable householder with excellent principles, the capital of France was a paradise of the joyously obscene. He asked the manager next morning what there was to be seen that was 'thick'. He thoroughly enjoyed these visits of his to Paris; he said they kept you from growing rusty. In the evenings, after their work was over and they had dined, he took Philip to the Moulin Rouge and the Folies Bergères. His little eyes twinkled and his face wore a sly, sensual smile as he sought out the pornographic. He went into all the haunts which were specially arranged for the foreigner, and afterwards said that a nation could come to no good which permitted that sort of thing. He nudged Philip when at some revue a woman appeared with practically nothing on, and pointed out to him the most strapping of the courtesans who walked about the hall. It was a vulgar Paris that he showed Philip, but Philip saw it with eyes blinded with illusion. In the early morning he would rush out of the hotel and go to the

169

Champs-Élysées, and stand at the Place de la Concorde. It was June, and Paris was silvery with the delicacy of the air. Philip felt his heart go out to the people. Here he thought at last was romance.

They spent the inside of a week there, leaving on Sunday, and when Philip late at night reached his dingy rooms in Barnes his mind was made up; he would surrender his articles, and go to Paris to study art; but so that no one should think him unreasonable he determined to stay at the office till his year was up. He was to have his holiday during the last fortnight in August, and when he went away he would tell Herbert Carter that he had no intention of returning. But though Philip could force himself to go to the office every day he could not even pretend to show any interest in the work. His mind was occupied with the future. In the middle of July there was nothing much to do and he escaped a good deal by pretending he had to go to lectures for his first examination. The time he got in this way he spent in the National Gallery. He read books about Paris and books about painting. He was steeped in Ruskin. He read many of Vasari's lives of the painters. He liked that story of Correggio, and he fancied himself standing before some great masterpiece and crying: *Anch'io son' pittore.* His hesitation had left him now, and he was convinced that he had in him the makings of a great painter.

'After all, I can only try,' he said to himself. 'The great thing in life is to take risks.'

At last came the middle of August. Mr Carter was spending a month in Scotland, and the managing clerk was in charge of the office. Mr Goodworthy had seemed pleasantly disposed to Philip since their trip to Paris, and now that Philip knew he was so soon to be free, he could look upon the funny little man with tolerance.

'You're going for your holiday tomorrow, Carey?' he said to him in the evening.

All day Philip had been telling himself that this was the last time he would ever sit in that hateful office.

'Yes, this is the end of my year.'

'I'm afraid you've not done very well. Mr Carter's very dissatisfied with you.'

'Not nearly so dissatisfied as I am with Mr Carter,' returned Philip cheerfully.

'I don't think you should speak like that, Carey.'

'I'm not coming back. I made the arrangement that if I didn't like accountancy Mr Carter would return me half the money I paid for my articles and I could chuck it at the end of a year.'

'You shouldn't come to such a decision hastily.'

'For ten months I've loathed it all, I've loathed the work, I've loathed the office, I loathe London. I'd rather sweep a crossing than spend my days here.'

'Well, I must say, I don't think you're very fitted for accountancy.'

'Good-bye,' said Philip, holding out his hand. 'I want to thank you for your kindness to me. I'm sorry if I've been troublesome. I knew almost from the beginning I was no good.'

'Well, if you really do make up your mind it is good-bye. I don't know what you're going to do, but if you're in the neighbourhood at any time come in and see us.'

Philip gave a little laugh.

'I'm afraid it sounds very rude, but I hope from the bottom of my heart that I shall never set eyes on any of you again.'

XXXIX

THE Vicar of Blackstable would have nothing to do with the scheme which Philip laid before him. He had a great idea that one should stick to whatever one had begun. Like all weak men he laid an exaggerated stress on not changing one's mind.

'You chose to be an accountant of your own free will,' he said.

'I just took that because it was the only chance I saw of getting up to town. I hate London, I hate the work, and nothing will induce me to go back to it.'

Mr and Mrs Carey were frankly shocked at Philip's idea of being an artist. He should not forget, they said, that his father and mother were gentlefolk, and painting wasn't a serious profession; it was Bohemian, disreputable, immoral. And then Paris!

'So long as I have anything to say in the matter, I shall not allow you to live in Paris,' said the Vicar firmly.

It was a sink of iniquity. The scarlet woman and she of Babylon flaunted their vileness there; the cities of the plain were not more wicked.

'You've been brought up like a gentleman and a Christian, and I should be false to the trust laid upon me by your dead father and mother if I allowed you to expose yourself to such temptation.'

'Well, I know I'm not a Christian and I'm beginning to doubt whether I'm a gentleman,' said Philip.

The dispute grew more violent. There was another year before Philip took possession of his small inheritance, and during that time Mr Carey proposed only to give him an allowance if he remained at the office. It was clear to Philip that if he meant not to continue with accountancy he must leave it while he could still get back half the money that had been paid for his articles. The Vicar would not listen. Philip, losing all reserve, said things to wound and irritate.

'You've got no right to waste my money,' he said at last. 'After all it's my money, isn't it? I'm not a child. You can't prevent me from going to Paris if I make up my mind to. You can't force me to go back to London.'

'All I can do is to refuse you money unless you do what I think fit.'

'Well, I don't care, I've made up my mind to go to Paris. I shall sell my clothes, and my books, and my father's jewellery.'

Aunt Louisa sat by in silence anxious and unhappy: she saw that Philip was beside himself, and anything she said then would but increase his anger. Finally the Vicar announced that he wished to hear nothing more about it and with dignity left the room. For the next three days neither Philip nor he spoke to one another. Philip wrote to Hayward for information about Paris, and made up his mind to set out as soon as he got a reply. Mrs Carey turned the matter over in her mind incessantly; she felt that Philip included her in the hatred he bore her husband, and the thought tortured her. She loved him with all her heart. At length she spoke to him; she listened attentively while he poured out all his disillusionment of London and his eager ambition for the future.

'I may be no good, but at least let me have a try. I can't be a worse failure than I was in that beastly office. And I feel that I *can* paint. I know I've got it in me.'

She was not so sure as her husband that they did right in thwarting so strong an inclination. She had read of great painters whose parents had opposed their wish to study, the event had shown with what folly; and after all it was just as possible for a painter to lead a virtuous life to the glory of God as for a chartered accountant.

'I'm so afraid of your going to Paris,' she said piteously. 'It wouldn't be so bad if you studied in London.'

'If I'm going in for painting I must do it thoroughly, and it's only in Paris that you can get the real thing.'

At his suggestion Mrs Carey wrote to the solicitor, saying that Philip was discontented with his work in London, and asking what he thought of a change. Mr Nixon answered as follows:

Dear Mrs Carey –

I have seen Mr Herbert Carter, and I am afraid I must tell you that Philip has not done so well as one could have wished. If he is very strongly set against the work, perhaps it is better that he should take the opportunity there is now to break his articles. I am naturally very disappointed, but as you know you can take a horse to the water, but you can't make him drink.

Yours very sincerely,
Albert Nixon

The letter was shown to the Vicar, but served only to increase his obstinacy. He was willing enough that Philip should take up some other profession, he suggested his father's calling, medicine, but nothing would induce him to pay an allowance if Philip went to Paris.

'It's a mere excuse for self-indulgence and sensuality,' he said.

'I'm interested to hear you blame self-indulgence in others,' retorted Philip acidly.

But by this time an answer had come from Hayward, giving the name of a hotel where Philip could get a room for thirty francs a month and enclosing a note of introduction to the *massière* of a school. Philip read the letter to Mrs Carey and told her he proposed to start on the first of September.

'But you haven't got any money?' she said.

'I'm going into Tercanbury this afternoon to sell the jewellery.'

He had inherited from his father a gold watch and chain, two or three rings, some links, and two pins. One of them was a pearl and might fetch a considerable sum.

'It's a very different thing, what a thing's worth and what it'll fetch,' said Aunt Louisa.

Philip smiled, for this was one of his uncle's stock phrases.

'I know, but at the worst I think I can get a hundred pounds on the lot, and that'll keep me till I'm twenty-one.'

Mrs Carey did not answer, but she went upstairs, put on her little black bonnet, and went to the bank. In an hour she came back. She went to Philip, who was reading in the drawing-room, and handed him an envelope.

'What's this?' he asked.

'It's a little present for you,' she answered, smiling shyly.

He opened it and found eleven five-pound notes and a little paper sack bulging with sovereigns.

'I couldn't bear to let you sell your father's jewellery. It's the money I had in the bank. It comes to very nearly a hundred pounds.'

Philip blushed, and, he knew not why, tears suddenly filled his eyes.

'Oh, my dear, I can't take it,' he said. 'It's most awfully good of you, but I couldn't bear to take it.'

When Mrs Carey was married she had three hundred pounds, and this money, carefully watched, had been used by her to meet any unforeseen expense, any urgent charity, or to buy Christmas and birthday presents for her husband and for Philip. In the course of years it had diminished sadly, but it was still with the Vicar a subject for jesting. He talked of his wife as a rich woman and he constantly spoke of the 'nest-egg'.

'Oh, please take it, Philip. I'm so sorry I've been extravagant, and there's only that left. But it'll make me so happy if you'll accept it.'

'But you'll want it,' said Philip.

'No, I don't think I shall. I was keeping it in case your uncle died before me. I thought it would be useful to have a little something I could get at immediately if I wanted it, but I don't think I shall live very much longer now.'

'Oh, my dear, don't say that. Why, of course you're going to live for ever. I can't possibly spare you.'

'Oh, I'm not sorry.' Her voice broke and she hid her eyes, but in a moment, drying them, she smiled bravely. 'At first, I used to pray to God that He might not take me first, because I didn't want your uncle to be left alone, I didn't want him to have all the suffering, but now I know that it wouldn't mean so much to your uncle as it would mean to me. He wants to live more than I do, I've never been the wife he wanted, and I daresay he'd marry again if anything happened to me. So I should like to go first. You don't think it's selfish of me, Philip, do you? But I couldn't bear it if he went.'

Philip kissed her wrinkled, thin cheek. He did not know why the sight he had of that overwhelming love made him feel strangely ashamed. It was incomprehensible that she should care so much for a man who was so indifferent, so selfish, so grossly self-indulgent; and he divined dimly that in her heart she knew his indifference and his selfishness, knew them and loved him humbly all the same.

'You will take the money, Philip?' she said, gently stroking his hand. 'I know you can do without it, but it'll give me so much happiness. I've always wanted to do something for you. You see, I never had a child of my own, and I've loved you as if you were my son. When you were a little boy, though I knew it was wicked, I used to wish almost that you might be ill, so that I could nurse you day and night. But you were only ill once and then it was at school. I should so like to help you. It's the only chance I shall ever have. And perhaps some day when you're a great artist you won't forget me, but you'll remember that I gave you your start.'

'It's very good of you,' said Philip. 'I'm very grateful.'

A smile came into her tired eyes, a smile of pure happiness. 'Oh, I'm so glad.'

XL

A FEW days later Mrs Carey went to the station to see Philip off. She stood at the door of the carriage, trying to keep back her tears. Philip was restless and eager. He wanted to be gone.

'Kiss me once more,' she said.

He leaned out of the window and kissed her. The train started, and she stood on the wooden platform of the little station, waving her handkerchief till it was out of sight. Her heart was dreadfully heavy, and the few hundred yards to the vicarage seemed very, very long. It was natural enough that he should be eager to go, she thought, he was a boy and the future beckoned to him; but she – she clenched her teeth so that she should not cry. She uttered a little inward prayer that God would guard him, and keep him out of temptation, and give him happiness and good fortune.

But Philip ceased to think of her a moment after he had settled down in his carriage. He thought only of the future. He had written to Mrs Otter, the *massière* to whom Hayward had given him an introduction, and had in his pocket an invitation to tea on the following day. When he arrived in Paris he had his luggage put on a cab and trundled off slowly through the gay streets, over the bridge, and along the narrow ways of the Latin Quarter. He had taken a room at the Hôtel des Deux Écoles, which was in a shabby street off the Boulevard du Montparnasse; it was convenient for Amitrano's School, at which he was going to work. A waiter took his box up five flights of stairs, and Philip was shown into a tiny room, fusty from unopened windows, the greater part of which was taken up by a large wooden bed with a canopy over it of red rep; there were heavy curtains on the windows of the same dingy material; the chest of drawers served also as a washing-stand; and there was a massive wardrobe of the style which is connected with the good King Louis Philippe. The wallpaper was discoloured with age; it was dark grey, and there could be vaguely seen on it garlands of brown leaves. To Philip the room seemed quaint and charming.

Though it was late he felt too excited to sleep and, going out, made his way into the boulevard and walked towards the light. This led him to the station; and the square in front of it, vivid with arc-lamps, noisy with the yellow trams that seemed to cross it in all directions, made him laugh aloud with joy. There were cafés all round, and by chance, thirsty and eager to get a nearer sight of the crowd, Philip installed himself at a little table outside the Café de Versailles. Every other table was taken, for it was a fine night; and Philip looked curiously at the people, here little family groups, there a knot of men with odd-shaped hats and beards talking loudly and gesticulating; next to him were two men who looked like painters with women who Philip hoped were not their lawful wives; behind him he heard Americans loudly arguing on art. His soul was thrilled. He sat till very late, tired out but too happy to move, and when at last he went to bed he was wide awake; he listened to the manifold noise of Paris.

Next day about tea-time he made his way to the Lion de Belfort, and in a new street that led out of the Boulevard Raspail found Mrs Otter. She was an insignificant woman of thirty, with a provincial air and a deliberately ladylike manner; she introduced him to her mother. He discovered presently that she had been studying in Paris for three years and later that she was separated from her husband. She had in her small drawing-room one or two portraits which she had painted, and to Philip's inexperience they seemed extremely accomplished.

'I wonder if I shall ever be able to paint as well as that,' he said to her.

'Oh, I expect so,' she replied, not without self-satisfaction. 'You can't expect to do everything all at once, of course.'

She was very kind. She gave him the address of a shop where he could get a portfolio, drawing-paper, and charcoal.

'I shall be going to Amitrano's about nine tomorrow, and if you'll be there then I'll see that you get a good place and all that sort of thing.'

She asked him what he wanted to do, and Philip felt that he

176

should not let her see how vague he was about the whole matter.

'Well, first I want to learn to draw,' he said.

'I'm glad to hear you say that. People always want to do things in such a hurry. I never touched oils till I'd been here for two years, and look at the result.'

She gave a glance at the portrait of her mother, a sticky piece of painting that hung over the piano.

'And if I were you, I would be very careful about the people you get to know. I wouldn't mix myself up with any foreigners. I'm very careful myself.'

Philip thanked her for the suggestion, but it seemed to him odd. He did not know that he particularly wanted to be careful.

'We live just as we would if we were in England,' said Mrs Otter's mother, who till then had spoken little. 'When we came here we brought all our own furniture over.'

Philip looked round the room. It was filled with a massive suite, and at the window were the same sort of white lace curtains which Aunt Louisa put up at the vicarage in summer. The piano was draped in Liberty silk and so was the chimney-piece. Mrs Otter followed his wandering eye.

'In the evening when we close the shutters one might really feel one was in England.'

'And we have our meals just as if we were at home,' added her mother. 'A meat breakfast in the morning and dinner in the middle of the day.'

When he left Mrs Otter Philip went to buy drawing materials; and next morning at the stroke of nine, trying to seem self-assured, he presented himself at the school. Mrs Otter was already there, and she came forward with a friendly smile. He had been anxious about the reception he would have as a *nouveau*, for he had read a good deal of the rough joking to which a newcomer was exposed at some of the studios; but Mrs Otter had reassured him.

'Oh, there's nothing like that here,' she said. 'You see, about half our students are ladies, and they set a tone to the place.'

The studio was large and bare, with grey walls, on which were pinned the studies that had received prizes. A model was sitting in a chair with a loose wrap thrown over her, and about a dozen men and women were standing about, some talking and others still working on their sketch. It was the first rest of the model.

'You'd better not try anything too difficult at first,' said Mrs Otter. 'Put your easel here. You'll find that's the easiest pose.'

Philip placed an easel where she indicated, and Mrs Otter introduced him to a young woman who sat next to him.

'Mr Carey – Miss Price. Mr Carey's never studied before, you won't mind helping him a little just at first, will you?' Then she turned to the model. '*La Pose.*'

The model threw aside the paper she had been reading, *La Petite République*, and sulkily throwing off her gown, got on to the stand. She stood, squarely on both feet, with her hands clasped behind her head.

'It's a stupid pose,' said Miss Price. 'I can't imagine why they chose it.'

When Philip entered, the people in the studio looked at him curiously, and the model gave him an indifferent glance, but now they ceased to pay any attention to him. Philip, with his beautiful sheet of paper in front of him, stared awkwardly at the model. He did not know how to begin. He had never seen a naked woman before. She was not young and her breasts were shrivelled. She had colourless, fair hair that fell over her forehead untidily, and her face was covered with large freckles. He glanced at Miss Price's work. She had only been working on it two days, and it looked as though she had had trouble; her paper was in a mess from constant rubbing out, and to Philip's eyes the figure looked strangely distorted.

'I should have thought I could do as well as that,' he said to himself.

He began on the head, thinking that he would work slowly downwards, but, he could not understand why, he found it infinitely more difficult to draw a head from the model than to draw one from his imagination. He got into difficulties. He glanced at Miss Price. She was working with vehement gravity. Her brow was wrinkled with eagerness, and there was an anxious look in her eyes. It was hot in the studio, and drops of sweat stood on her forehead. She was a girl of twenty-six, with a great deal of dull gold hair; it was handsome hair, but it was carelessly done, dragged back from her forehead and tied in a hurried knot. She had a large face, with broad, flat features and small eyes; her skin was pasty, with a singular unhealthiness of tone, and there was no colour in the cheeks. She had an unwashed tone, and you could not help wondering if she slept in her clothes. She was serious and silent. When the next pause came, she stepped back to look at her work.

'I don't know why I'm having so much bother,' she said. 'But I mean to get it right.' She turned to Philip. 'How are you getting on?'

'Not at all,' he answered, with a rueful smile.

She looked at what he had done.

'You can't expect to do anything that way. You must take measurements. And you must square out your paper.'

She showed him rapidly how to set about the business. Philip was impressed by her earnestness, but repelled by her want of charm. He was grateful for the hints she gave him and set to work again. Meanwhile other people had come in, mostly men, for the women always arrived first, and the studio for the time of year (it was early yet) was fairly full. Presently there came in a young man with thin, black hair, an enormous nose, and a face so long that it reminded you of a horse. He sat down next to Philip and nodded across him to Miss Price.

'You're very late,' she said. 'Are you only just up?'

'It was such a splendid day, I thought I'd lie in bed and think how beautiful it was out.'

Philip smiled, but Miss Price took the remark seriously.

'That seems a funny thing to do, I should have thought it would be more to the point to get up and enjoy it.'

'The way of the humorist is very hard,' said the young man gravely.

He did not seem inclined to work. He looked at his canvas; he was working in colour, and had sketched in the day before the model who was posing. He turned to Philip.

'Have you just come out from England?'

'Yes.'

'How did you find your way to Amitrano's?'

'It was the only school I knew of.'

'I hope you haven't come with the idea that you will learn anything here which will be of the smallest use to you.'

'It's the best school in Paris,' said Miss Price. 'It's the only one where they take art seriously.'

'Should art be taken seriously?' the young man asked; and since Miss Price replied only with a scornful shrug, he added: 'But the point is, all schools are bad. They are academical, obviously. Why this is less injurious than most is that the teaching is more incompetent than elsewhere. Because you learn nothing . . .'

'But why d'you come here then?' interrupted Philip.

'I see the better course, but do not follow it. Miss Price, who is cultured, will remember the Latin of that.'

'I wish you would leave me out of your conversation, Mr Clutton,' said Miss Price brusquely.

'The only way to learn to paint,' he went on, imperturbable, 'is to take a studio, hire a model, and just fight it out for yourself.'

'That seems a simple thing to do,' said Philip.

'It only needs money,' replied Clutton.

He began to paint, and Philip looked at him from the corner of his eye. He was long and desperately thin; his huge bones seemed to protrude from his body; his elbows were so sharp that they appeared to jut out through the arms of his shabby coat. His trousers were frayed at the bottom, and on each of his boots was a clumsy patch. Miss Price got up and went over to Philip's easel.

'If Mr Clutton will hold his tongue for a moment, I'll just help you a little,' she said.

'Miss Price dislikes me because I have humour,' said Clutton, looking meditatively at his canvas, 'but she detests me because I have genius.'

He spoke with solemnity, and his colossal, misshaped nose made what he said very quaint. Philip was obliged to laugh, but Miss Price grew darkly red with anger.

'You're the only person who has ever accused you of genius.'

'Also I am the only person whose opinion is of the least value to me.'

Miss Price began to criticize what Philip had done. She talked glibly of anatomy and construction, planes and lines, and of much else which Philip did not understand. She had been at the studio a long time and knew the main points which the masters insisted upon, but though she could show what was wrong with Philip's work she could not tell him how to put it right.

'It's awfully kind of you to take so much trouble with me,' said Philip.

'Oh, it's nothing,' she answered, flushing awkwardly. 'People did the same for me when I first came, I'd do it for anyone.'

'Miss Price wants to indicate that she is giving you the advantage of her knowledge from a sense of duty rather than on account of any charms of your person,' said Clutton.

Miss Price gave him a furious look, and went back to her own drawing. The clock struck twelve, and the model with a cry of relief stepped down from the stand.

Miss Price gathered up her things.

'Some of us go to Gravier's for lunch,' she said to Philip, with a look at Clutton. 'I always go home myself.'

'I'll take you to Gravier's if you like,' said Clutton.

Philip thanked him and made ready to go. On his way out Mrs Otter asked him how he had been getting on.

'Did Fanny Price help you?' she asked. 'I put you there because I know she can do it if she likes. She's a disagreeable, ill-natured girl, and she can't draw herself at all, but she knows the ropes, and she can be useful to a newcomer if she cares to take the trouble.'

On their way down the street Clutton said to him:

'You've made an impression on Fanny Price. You'd better look out.'

Philip laughed. He had never seen anyone on whom he wished less to make an impression. They came to the cheap little restaurant at which several of the students ate, and Clutton sat down at a table at which three or four men were already seated. For a franc, they got an egg, a plate of meat, cheese, and a small bottle of wine. Coffee was extra. They sat on the pavement, and yellow trams passed up and down the boulevard with a ceaseless ringing of bells.

'By the way, what's your name?' said Clutton, as they took their seats.

'Carey.'

'Allow me to introduce an old and trusted friend, Carey by name,' said Clutton gravely. 'Mr Flanagan, Mr Lawson.'

They laughed and went on with their conversation. They talked of a thousand things, and they all talked at once. No one paid the smallest attention to anyone else. They talked of the places they had been to in the summer, of studios, of the various schools; they mentioned names which were unfamiliar to Philip: Monet, Manet, Renoir, Pizarro, Degas. Philip listened with all his ears, and though he felt a little out of it, his heart leaped with exultation. The time flew. When Clutton got up he said:

'I expect you'll find me here this evening if you care to come. You'll find this about the best place for getting dyspepsia at the lowest cost in the Quarter.'

XLI

PHILIP walked down the Boulevard du Montparnasse. It was not at all like the Paris he had seen in the spring during his visit to do the accounts of the Hôtel St Georges – he thought already of that part of his life with a shudder – but reminded him of what he thought a provincial town must be. There was an easy-going air about it, and a sunny spaciousness which invited the mind to day-dreaming. The trimness of the trees, the vivid whiteness of the houses, the breadth, were very agreeable; and he felt himself already thoroughly at home. He sauntered along, staring at the people; there seemed an elegance about the most ordinary, workmen with their broad red sashes and their wide trousers, little soldiers in dingy, charming uniforms. He came presently to the Avenue de l'Observatoire, and he gave a sigh of pleasure at the magnificent, yet so graceful, vista. He came to the gardens of the Luxembourg: children were playing, nurses with long ribbons walked slowly two by two, busy men passed through with satchels under their arms, youths strangely dressed. The scene was formal and dainty; nature was arranged and ordered, but so exquisitely, that nature unordered and unarranged seemed barbaric. Philip was enchanted. It excited him to stand on that spot of which he had read so much; it was classic ground to him; and he felt the awe and the delight which some old don might feel when for the first time he looked on the smiling plain of Sparta.

As he wandered he chanced to see Miss Price sitting by herself on a bench. He hesitated, for he did not at that moment want to see anyone, and her uncouth way seemed out of place amid the happiness he felt around him; but he had divined her sensitiveness to affront, and since she had seen him thought it would be polite to speak to her.

'What are you doing here?' she said, as he came up.

'Enjoying myself. Aren't you?'

'Oh, I come here every day from four to five. I don't think one does any good if one works straight through.'

'May I sit down for a minute?' he said.

'If you want to.'

'That doesn't sound very cordial,' he laughed.

'I'm not much of a one for saying pretty things.'

Philip, a little disconcerted, was silent as he lit a cigarette.

'Did Clutton say anything about my work?' she asked suddenly.

'No, I don't think he did,' said Philip.

'He's no good, you know. He thinks he's a genius, but he isn't. He's too lazy, for one thing. Genius is an infinite capacity for taking pains. The only thing is to peg away. If one only makes up one's mind badly enough to do a thing one can't help doing it.'

She spoke with a passionate strenuousness which was rather striking. She wore a sailor hat of black straw, a white blouse which was not quite clean, and a brown skirt. She had no gloves on, and her hands wanted washing. She was so unattractive that Philip wished he had not begun to talk to her. He could not make out whether she wanted him to stay or go.

'I'll do anything I can for you,' she said all at once, without reference to anything that had gone before. 'I know how hard it is.'

'Thank you very much,' said Philip, then in a moment: 'Won't you come and have tea with me somewhere?'

She looked at him quickly and flushed. When she reddened her pasty skin acquired a curiously mottled look, like strawberries and cream that had gone bad.

'No, thanks. What do you think I want tea for? I've only just had lunch.'

'I thought it would pass the time,' said Philip.

'If you find it long you needn't bother about me, you know. I don't mind being left alone.'

At that moment two men passed, in brown velveteens, enormous trousers, and basque caps. They were young, but both wore beards.

'I say, are those art-students?' said Philip. 'They might have stepped out of the *Vie de Bohème*.'

'They're Americans,' said Miss Price scornfully. 'Frenchmen haven't worn things like that for thirty years, but the Americans from the Far West buy those clothes and have themselves photographed the day after they arrive in Paris. That's about as near to art as they ever get. But it doesn't matter to them, they've all got money.'

Philip liked the daring picturesqueness of the Americans' costume; he thought it showed the romantic spirit. Miss Price asked him the time.

'I must be getting along to the studio,' she said. 'Are you going to the sketch classes?'

Philip did not know anything about them, and she told him that from five to six every evening a model sat, from whom anyone who liked could go and draw at the cost of fifty centimes. They had a different model every day, and it was very good practice.

'I don't suppose you're good enough yet for that. You'd better wait a bit.'

'I don't see why I shouldn't try. I haven't got anything else to do.'

They got up and walked to the studio. Philip could not tell from her manner whether Miss Price wished him to walk with her or preferred to walk alone. He remained from sheer embarrassment, not knowing how to leave her; but she would not talk : she answered his questions in an ungracious manner.

A man was standing at the studio door with a large dish into which each person as he went in dropped his half franc. The studio was much fuller than it had been in the morning, and there was not the preponderance of English and Americans; nor were women there in so large a proportion. Philip felt the assemblage was more the sort of thing he had expected. It was very warm, and the air quickly grew fetid. It was an old man who sat this time, with a vast grey beard, and Philip tried to put into practice the little he had learned in the morning; but he made a poor job of it; he realized that he could not draw nearly as well as he thought. He glanced enviously at one or two sketches of men who sat near him, and wondered whether he would ever be able to use the charcoal with that mastery. The hour passed quickly. Not wishing to press himself upon Miss Price he sat down at some distance from her, and at the end, as he passed her on his way out, she asked brusquely how he had got on.

'Not very well,' he smiled.

'If you'd condescended to come and sit near me I could have given you some hints. I suppose you thought yourself too grand.'

'No, it wasn't that. I was afraid you'd think me a nuisance.'

'When I do that I'll tell you sharp enough.'

Philip saw that in her uncouth way she was offering him help.

'Well, tomorrow I'll just force myself upon you.'

'I don't mind,' she answered.

Philip went out and wondered what he should do with himself till dinner. He was eager to do something characteristic. *Absinthe!* Of course it was indicated, and so, sauntering towards the station, he seated himself outside a café and ordered it. He drank with nausea and satisfaction. He found the taste disgusting, but the moral effect magnificent; he felt every inch an art-student; and since he drank on an empty stomach his spirits presently grew very high. He watched the crowds, and felt all men were his brothers. He was happy. When he reached Gravier's the table at which Clutton sat was full, but as soon as he saw Philip limping along he called out to him. They made room. The dinner was frugal : a plate of soup, a dish of meat, fruit, cheese, and half a bottle of wine; but Philip paid no attention to what he ate. He took note of the men at the table. Flanagan was there again : he was an American, a short snub-

nosed youth with a jolly face and a laughing mouth. He wore
a Norfolk jacket of bold pattern, a blue stock round his neck,
and a tweed cap of fantastic shape. At that time Impressionism
reigned in the Latin Quarter, but its victory over the older
schools was still recent; and Carolus-Duran, Bouguereau, and
their like were set up against Manet, Monet, and Degas. To appreciate these was still a sign of grace. Whistler was an influence
strong with the English and his compatriots, and the discern-
ing collected Japanese prints. The old masters were tested by
new standards. The esteem in which Raphael had been for
centuries held was a matter of derision to wise young men.
They offered to give all his works for Velasquez' head of
Philip IV in the National Gallery. Philip found that a discussion on art was raging. Lawson, whom he had met at luncheon,
sat opposite to him. He was a thin youth with a freckled face
and red hair. He had very bright green eyes. As Philip sat down
he fixed them on him and remarked suddenly:

'Raphael was only tolerable when he painted other people's
pictures. When he painted Peruginos or Pinturicchios he was
charming; when he painted Raphaels he was,' with a scornful
shrug, 'Raphael.'

Lawson spoke so aggressively that Philip was taken aback,
but he was not obliged to answer because Flanagan broke in
impatiently.

'Oh, to hell with art!' he cried. 'Let's get ginny.'

'You were ginny last night, Flanagan,' said Lawson.

'Nothing to what I mean to be tonight,' he answered. 'Fancy
being in Pa-ris and thinking of nothing but art all the time.'
He spoke with a broad Western accent. 'My, it is good to be
alive.' He gathered himself together and then banged his fist
on the table. 'To hell with art, I say.'

'You not only say it, but you say it with tiresome iteration,'
said Clutton severely.

There was another American at the table. He was dressed
like those fine fellows whom Philip had seen that afternoon in
the Luxembourg. He had a handsome face, thin, ascetic, with
dark eyes; he wore his fantastic garb with the dashing air of a
buccaneer. He had a vast quantity of dark hair which fell constantly over his eyes, and his most frequent gesture was to
throw back his head dramatically to get some long wisp out of
the way. He began to talk of the *Olympia* by Manet, which
then hung in the Luxembourg.

'I stood in front of it for an hour today, and I tell you it's
not a good picture.'

Lawson put down his knife and fork. His green eyes flashed fire, he gasped with rage; but he could be seen imposing calm upon himself.

'It's very interesting to hear the mind of the untutored savage,' he said. 'Will you tell us why it isn't a good picture?'

Before the American could answer someone else broke in vehemently.

'D'you mean to say you can look at the painting of that flesh and say it's not good?'

'I don't say that. I think the right breast is very well painted.'

'The right breast be damned,' shouted Lawson. 'The whole thing's a miracle of painting.'

He began to describe in detail the beauties of the picture, but at this table at Gravier's they who spoke at length spoke for their own edification. No one listened to him. The American interrupted angrily.

'You don't mean to say you think the head's good?'

Lawson, white with passion now, began to defend the head; but Clutton, who had been sitting in silence with a look on his face of good-humoured scorn, broke in.

'Give him the head. We don't want the head. It doesn't affect the picture.'

'All right, I'll give you the head,' cried Lawson. 'Take the head and be damned to you.'

'What about the black line?' cried the American, triumphantly pushing back a wisp of hair which nearly fell in his soup. 'You don't see a black line round objects in nature.'

'Oh, God, send down fire from heaven to consume the blasphemer,' said Lawson. 'What has nature got to do with it? No one knows what's in nature and what isn't! The world sees nature through the eyes of the artist. Why, for centuries it saw horses jumping a fence with all their legs extended, and by Heaven, sir, they were extended. It saw shadows black until Monet discovered they were coloured, and by Heaven, sir, they were black. If we choose to surround objects with a black line, the world will see the black line, and there will be a black line; and if we paint grass red and cows blue, it'll see them red and blue, and, by Heaven, they will be red and blue.'

'To hell with art,' murmured Flanagan. 'I want to get ginny.'

Lawson took no notice of the interruption.

'Now look here, when *Olympia* was shown at the Salon, Zola – amid the jeers of the philistines and the hisses of the *pompiers*, the academicians, and the public – Zola said: "I look forward to the day when Manet's picture will hang in the Louvre

186

opposite the *Odalisque* of Ingres, and it will not be the *Odalisque* which will gain by comparison." It'll be there. Every day I see the time grow nearer. In ten years the *Olympia* will be in the Louvre.'

'Never,' shouted the American, using both hands now with a sudden desperate attempt to get his hair once for all out of the way. 'In ten years that picture will be dead. It's only a fashion of the moment. No picture can live that hasn't got something which that picture misses by a million miles.'

'And what is that?'

'Great art can't exist without a moral element.'

'Oh God!' cried Lawson furiously. 'I knew it was that. He wants morality.' He joined his hands and held them towards heaven in supplication. 'Oh, Christopher Columbus, Christopher Columbus, what did you do when you discovered America?'

'Ruskin says...'

But before he could add another word, Clutton rapped with the handle of his knife imperiously on the table.

'Gentlemen,' he said in a stern voice, and his huge nose positively wrinkled with passion, 'a name has been mentioned which I never thought to hear again in decent society. Freedom of speech is all very well, but we must observe the limits of common propriety. You may talk of Bouguereau if you will: there is a cheerful disgustingness in the sound which excites laughter; but let us not sully our chaste lips with the names of J. Ruskin, G. F. Watts, or E. B. Jones.'

'Who was Ruskin, anyway?' asked Flanagan.

'He was one of the Great Victorians. He was a master of English style.'

'Ruskin's style – a thing of shreds and purple patches,' said Lawson. 'Besides, damn the Great Victorians. Whenever I open a paper and see Death of a Great Victorian, I thank Heaven there's one more of them gone. Their only talent was longevity, and no artist should be allowed to live after he's forty; by then a man has done his best work, all he does after that is repetition. Don't you think it was the greatest luck in the world for them that Keats, Shelley, Bonnington, and Byron died early? What a genius we should think Swinburne if he had perished on the day the first series of *Poems and Ballads* was published!'

The suggestion pleased, for no one at the table was more than twenty-four, and they threw themselves upon it with gusto. They were unanimous for once. They elaborated. Someone proposed a vast bonfire made out of the works of the Forty

Academicians into which the Great Victorians might be hurled on their fortieth birthday. The idea was received with acclamation. Carlyle and Ruskin, Tennyson, Browning, G. F. Watts, E. B. Jones, Dickens, Thackeray, they were hurried into the flames; Mr Gladstone, John Bright, and Cobden; there was a moment's discussion about George Meredith, but Matthew Arnold and Emerson were given up cheerfully. At last came Walter Pater.

'Not Walter Pater,' murmured Philip.

Lawson stared at him for a moment with his green eyes and then nodded.

'You're quite right, Walter Pater is the only justification for *Mona Lisa*. D'you know Cronshaw? He used to know Pater.'

'Who's Cronshaw?' asked Philip.

'Cronshaw's a poet. He lives here. Let's go to the Lilas.'

La Closerie des Lilas was a café to which they often went in the evening after dinner, and here Cronshaw was invariably to be found between the hours of nine at night and two in the morning. But Flanagan had had enough of intellectual conversation for one evening, and when Lawson made his suggestion, turned to Philip.

'Oh gee, let's go where there are girls,' he said. 'Come to the Gaîté Montparnasse, and we'll get ginny.'

'I'd rather go and see Cronshaw and keep sober,' laughed Philip.

XLII

THERE was a general disturbance. Flanagan and two or three more went on to the music-hall, while Philip walked slowly with Clutton and Lawson to the Closerie des Lilas.

'You must go to the Gaîté Montparnasse,' said Lawson to him. 'It's one of the loveliest things in Paris. I'm going to paint it one of these days.'

Philip, influenced by Hayward, looked upon music-halls with scornful eyes, but he had reached Paris at a time when their artistic possibilities were just discovered. The peculiarities of lighting, the masses of dingy red and tarnished gold, the heaviness of the shadows and the decorative lines, offered a new theme; and half the studios in the Quarter contained sketches made in one or other of the local theatres. Men of letters, following in the painters' wake, conspired suddenly to find artistic value in the turns; and red-nosed comedians were lauded to the skies for their sense of character; fat female singers, who had bawled obscurely for twenty years, were discovered to possess inimitable drollery; there were those who found an aesthetic delight in performing dogs; while others exhausted their vocabulary to extol the distinction of conjurers and trick cyclists. The crowd too, under another influence, was become an object of sympathetic interest. With Hayward, Philip had disdained humanity in the mass; he adopted the attitude of one who wraps himself in solitariness and watches with disgust the antics of the vulgar; but Clutton and Lawson talked of the multitude with enthusiasm. They described the seething throng that filled the various fairs of Paris, the sea of faces, half seen in the glare of acetylene, half hidden in the darkness, and the blare of trumpets, the hooting of whistles, the hum of voices. What they said was new and strange to Philip. They told him about Cronshaw.

'Have you ever read any of his work?'

'No,' said Philip.

'It came out in *The Yellow Book*.'

They looked upon him, as painters often do writers, with contempt because he was a layman, with tolerance because he practised an art, and with awe because he used a medium in which themselves felt ill at ease.

'He's an extraordinary fellow. You'll find him a bit disappointing at first, he only comes out at his best when he's drunk.'

'And the nuisance is,' added Clutton, 'that it takes him a devil of a time to get drunk.'

When they arrived at the café Lawson told Philip that they would have to go in. There was hardly a bite in the autumn air, but Cronshaw had a morbid fear of draughts and even in the warmest weather sat inside.

'He knows everyone worth knowing,' Lawson explained. 'He knew Pater and Oscar Wilde, and he knows Mallarmé and all those fellows.'

The object of their search sat in the most sheltered corner of the café, with his coat on and the collar turned up. He wore his hat pressed well down on his forehead so that he should avoid cold air. He was a big man, stout but not obese, with a round face, a small moustache, and little, rather stupid eyes. His head did not seem quite big enough for his body. It looked like a pea uneasily poised on an egg. He was playing dominoes with   Frenchman, and greeted the newcomers with a quiet smile; he did not speak, but as if to make room for them pushed away the little pile of saucers on the table which indicated the number of drinks he had already consumed. He nodded to Philip when he was introduced to him, and went on with the game. Philip's knowledge of the language was small, but he knew enough to tell that Cronshaw, although he had lived in Paris for several years, spoke French execrably.

At last he leaned back with a smile of triumph.

'*Je vous ai battu,*' he said, with an abominable accent. '*Garçon!*'

He called the waiter and turned to Philip.

'Just out from England? See any cricket?'

Philip was a little confused at the unexpected question.

'Cronshaw knows the averages of every first-class cricketer for the last twenty years,' said Lawson, smiling.

The Frenchman left them for friends at another table, and Cronshaw, with the lazy enunciation which was one of his peculiarities, began to discourse on the relative merits of Kent and Lancashire. He told them of the last test match he had seen and described the course of the game wicket by wicket.

'That's the only thing I miss in Paris,' he said, as he finished the *bock* which the waiter had brought. 'You don't get any cricket.'

Philip was disappointed, and Lawson, pardonably anxious to show off one of the celebrities of the Quarter, grew impatient. Cronshaw was taking his time to wake up that evening, though the saucers at his side indicated that he had at least made an honest attempt to get drunk. Clutton watched the scene with amusement. He fancied there was something of affectation in Cronshaw's minute knowledge of cricket; he liked to tantalize people by talking to them of things that obviously bored them; Clutton threw in a question.

'Have you seen Mallarmé lately?'

Cronshaw looked at him slowly, as if he were turning the inquiry over in his mind, and before he answered rapped on the marble table with one of the saucers.

'Bring my bottle of whisky,' he called out. He turned again to Philip. 'I keep my own bottle of whisky. I can't afford to pay fifty centimes for every thimbleful.'

The waiter brought the bottle, and Cronshaw held it up to the light.

'They've been drinking it. Waiter, who's been helping himself to my whisky?'

'*Mais personne, Monsieur Cronshaw.*'

'I made a mark on it last night, and look at it.'

'Monsieur made a mark, but he kept on drinking after that. At that rate Monsieur wastes his time in making marks.'

The waiter was a jovial fellow and knew Cronshaw intimately. Cronshaw gazed at him.

'If you give me your word of honour as a nobleman and a gentleman that nobody but I has been drinking my whisky, I'll accept your statement.'

This remark, translated literally into the crudest French, sounded very funny, and the lady at the *comptoir* could not help laughing.

'*Il est impayable,*' she murmured.

Cronshaw, hearing her, turned a sheepish eye upon her – she was stout, matronly, and middle-aged – and solemnly kissed his hand to her. She shrugged her shoulders.

'Fear not, madam,' he said heavily. 'I have passed the age when I am tempted by forty-five and gratitude.'

He poured himself out some whisky and water, and slowly drank it. He wiped his mouth with the back of his hand.

'He talked very well.'

Lawson and Clutton knew that Cronshaw's remark was an answer to the question about Mallarmé. Cronshaw often went to the gatherings on Tuesday evenings when the poet received men of letters and painters, and discoursed with subtle oratory on any subject that was suggested to him. Cronshaw had evidently been there lately.

'He talked very well, but he talked nonsense. He talked about art as though it were the most important thing in the world.'

'If it isn't, what are we here for?' asked Philip.

'What you're here for I don't know. It is no business of mine. But art is a luxury. Men attach importance only to self-preservation and the propagation of their species. It is only when these instincts are satisfied that they consent to occupy themselves with the entertainment which is provided for them by writers, painters, and poets.'

Cronshaw stopped for a moment to drink. He had pondered for twenty years the problem whether he loved liquor because it made him talk or whether he loved conversation because it made him thirsty.

Then he said: 'I wrote a poem yesterday.'

Without being asked he began to recite it, very slowly, marking the rhythm with an extended forefinger. It was possibly a very fine poem, but at that moment a young woman came in. She had scarlet lips, and it was plain that the vivid colour of her

191

cheeks was not due to the vulgarity of nature; she had blackened her eyelashes and eyebrows, and painted both eyelids a bold blue, which was continued to a triangle at the corner of the eyes. It was fantastic and amusing. Her dark hair was done over her ears in the fashion made popular by Mlle Cléo de Merode. Philip's eyes wandered to her, and Cronshaw having finished the recitation of his verses, smiled upon him indulgently.

'You were not listening,' he said.

'Oh yes, I was.'

'I do not blame you, for you have given an apt illustration of the statement I just made. What is art beside love? I respect and applaud your indifference to fine poetry when you can contemplate the meretricious charms of this young person.'

She passed by the table at which they were sitting, and he took her arm.

'Come and sit by my side, dear child, and let us play the divine comedy of love.'

'*Fichez-moi la paix*,' she said, and pushing him on one side continued her perambulation.

'Art,' he continued, with a wave of the hand, 'is merely the refuge which the ingenious have invented, when they were supplied with food and women, to escape the tediousness of life.'

Cronshaw filled his glass again, and began to talk at length. He spoke with rotund delivery. He chose his words carefully. He mingled wisdom and nonsense in the most astounding manner, gravely making fun of his hearers at one moment, and at the next playfully giving them sound advice. He talked of art, and literature, and life. He was by turns devout and obscene, merry and lachrymose. He grew remarkably drunk, and then he began to recite poetry, his own and Milton's, his own and Shelley's, his own and Kit Marlowe's.

At last Lawson, exhausted, got up to go home.

'I shall go too,' said Philip.

Clutton, the most silent of them all, remained behind listening, with a sardonic smile on his lips, to Cronshaw's maunderings. Lawson accompanied Philip to his hotel and then bade him good night. But when Philip got to bed he could not sleep. All these new ideas that had been flung before him carelessly seethed in his brain. He was tremendously excited. He felt in himself great powers. He had never before been so self-confident.

'I know I shall be a great artist,' he said to himself. 'I feel it in me.'

A thrill passed through him as another thought came, but even to himself he would not put it into words:

'By George, I believe I've got genius.'

He was in fact very drunk, but as he had not taken more than one glass of beer, it could have been due only to a more dangerous intoxicant than alcohol.

XLIII

ON Tuesdays and Fridays masters spent the morning at Amitrano's, criticizing the work done. In France the painter earns little unless he paints portraits and is patronized by rich Americans; and men of reputation are glad to increase their incomes by spending two or three hours once a week at one of the numerous studios where art is taught. Tuesday was the day upon which Michel Rollin came to Amitrano's. He was an elderly man, with a white beard and a florid complexion, who had painted a number of decorations for the State, but these were an object of derision to the students he instructed: he was a disciple of Ingres, impervious to the progress of art and angrily impatient with that *tas de farceurs* whose names were Manet, Degas, Monet, and Sisley; but he was an excellent teacher, helpful, polite, and encouraging. Foinet, on the other hand, who visited the studio on Fridays, was a difficult man to get on with. He was a small, shrivelled person, with bad teeth and a bilious air, an untidy grey beard, and savage eyes; his voice was high and his tone sarcastic. He had had pictures bought by the Luxembourg, and at twenty-five looked forward to a great career; but his talent was due to youth rather than to personality, and for twenty years he had done nothing but repeat the landscape which had brought him his early success. When he was reproached with monotony, he answered:

'Corot only painted one thing. Why shouldn't I?'

He was envious of everyone else's success, and had a peculiar, personal loathing of the impressionists; for he looked upon his own failure as due to the mad fashion which had attracted the public, *sale bête*, to their works. The genial disdain of Michel Rollin, who called them impostors, was answered by him with vituperation, of which *crapule* and *canaille* were the least violent items; he amused himself with abuse of their private lives and with sardonic humour, with blasphemous and obscene detail, attacked the legitimacy of their births and the purity of

193

their conjugal relations: he used an Oriental imagery and an Oriental emphasis to accentuate his ribald scorn. Nor did he conceal his contempt for the students whose work he examined. By them he was hated and feared; the women by his brutal sarcasm he reduced often to tears, which again aroused his ridicule; and he remained at the studio, notwithstanding the protests of those who suffered too bitterly from his attacks, because there could be no doubt that he was one of the best masters in Paris. Sometimes the old model who kept the school ventured to remonstrate with him, but his expostulations quickly gave way before the violent insolence of the painter to abject apologies.

It was Foinet with whom Philip first came in contact. He was already in the studio when Philip arrived. He went round from easel to easel, with Mrs Otter, the *massière*, by his side to interpret his remarks for the benefit of those who could not understand French. Fanny Price, sitting next to Philip, was working feverishly. Her face was sallow with nervousness, and every now and then she stopped to wipe her hands on her blouse, for they were hot with anxiety. Suddenly she turned to Philip with an anxious look, which she tried to hide by a sullen frown.

'D'you think it's good?' she asked, nodding at her drawing.

Philip got up and looked at it. He was astounded; he felt she must have no eye at all; the thing was hopelessly out of drawing.

'I wish I could draw half as well as myself,' he answered.

'You can't expect to, you've only just come. It's a bit too much to expect that you should draw as well as I do. I've been here two years.'

Fanny Price puzzled Philip. Her conceit was stupendous. Philip had already discovered that everyone in the studio cordially disliked her; and it was no wonder, for she seemed to go out of her way to wound people.

'I complained to Mrs Otter about Foinet,' she said now. 'The last two weeks he hasn't looked at my drawing. He spends about half an hour on Mrs Otter because she's the *massière*. After all I pay as much as anybody else, and I suppose my money's as good as theirs. I don't see why I shouldn't get as much attention as anybody else.'

She took up her charcoal again, but in a moment put it down with a groan.

'I can't do any more now. I'm so frightfully nervous.'

She looked at Foinet, who was coming towards them with Mrs Otter. Mrs Otter, meek, mediocre, and self-satisfied, wore an air of importance. Foinet sat down at the easel of an untidy little Englishwoman called Ruth Chalice. She had the fine black eyes, languid but passionate, the thin face, ascetic but sensual, the skin like old ivory, which under the influence of Burne-Jones were cultivated at that time by young ladies in Chelsea. Foinet seemed in a pleasant mood; he did not say much to her, but with quick, determined strokes of her charcoal pointed out her errors. Miss Chalice beamed with pleasure when he rose. He came to Clutton, and by this time Philip was nervous too, but Mrs Otter had promised to make things easy for him. Foinet stood for a moment in front of Clutton's work, biting his thumb silently, then absent-mindedly spat out upon the canvas the little piece of skin which he had bitten off.

'That's a fine line,' he said at last, indicating with his thumb what pleased him. 'You're beginning to learn to draw.'

Clutton did not answer, but looked at the master with his usual air of sardonic indifference to the world's opinion.

'I'm beginning to think you have at least a trace of talent.'

Mrs Otter, who did not like Clutton, pursed her lips. She did not see anything out of the way in his work. Foinet sat down and went into technical details. Mrs Otter grew rather tired of standing. Clutton did not say anything, but nodded now and then, and Foinet felt with satisfaction that he grasped what he said and the reasons of it; most of them listened to him, but it was clear they never understood. Then Foinet got up and came to Philip.

'He only arrived two days ago,' Mrs Otter hurried to explain. 'He's a beginner. He's never studied before.'

'*Ça se voit*,' the master said. 'One sees that.'

He passed on, and Mrs Otter murmured to him:

'This is the young lady I told you about.'

He looked at her as though she were some repulsive animal, and his voice grew more rasping.

'It appears that you do not think I pay enough attention to you. You have been complaining to the *massière*. Well, show me this work to which you wish me to give attention.'

Fanny Price coloured. The blood under her unhealthy skin seemed to be of a strange purple. Without answering she pointed to the drawing on which she had been at work since the beginning of the week. Foinet sat down.

'Well, what do you wish me to say to you? Do you wish me to tell you it is good? It isn't. Do you wish me to tell you it is well drawn? It isn't. Do you wish me to say it has merit? It hasn't. Do you wish me to show you what is wrong with it? It is all wrong. Do you wish me to tell you what to do with it? Tear it up. Are you satisfied now?'

Miss Price became very white. She was furious because he had said all this before Mrs Otter. Though she had been in France so long and could understand French well enough, she could hardly speak two words.

'He's got no right to treat me like that. My money's as good as anyone else's. I pay him to teach me. That's not teaching me.'

'What does she say? What does she say?' asked Foinet.

Mrs Otter hesitated to translate, and Miss Price repeated in execrable French:

'Je vous paye pour m'apprendre.'

His eyes flashed with rage, he raised his voice and shook his fist.

'Mais, nom de Dieu, I can't teach you. I could more easily teach a camel.' He turned to Mrs Otter. 'Ask her, does she do this for amusement, or does she expect to earn money by it?'

'I'm going to earn my living as an artist,' Miss Price answered.

'Then it is my duty to tell you that you are wasting your time. It would not matter that you have no talent, talent does not run about the streets in these days, but you have not the beginning of an aptitude. How long have you been here? A child of five after two lessons would draw better than you do. I only say one thing to you, give up this hopeless attempt. You're more likely to earn your living as a *bonne à tout faire* than as a painter. Look.'

He seized a piece of charcoal and it broke as he applied it to the paper. He cursed, and with the stump drew great firm lines. He drew rapidly and spoke at the same time, spitting out the words with venom.

'Look, those arms are not the same length. That knee, it's grotesque. I tell you a child of five. You see, she's not standing on her legs. That foot!'

With each word the angry pencil made a mark, and in a moment the drawing upon which Fanny Price had spent so much time and eager trouble was unrecognizable, a confusion of lines and smudges. At last he flung down the charcoal and stood up.

'Take my advice, Mademoiselle, try dressmaking.' He looked at his watch. 'It's twelve. *À la semaine prochaine, messieurs.'*

Miss Price gathered up her things slowly. Philip waited behind after the others to say to her something consolatory. He could think of nothing but:

196

'I say, I'm awfully sorry. What a beast that man is!'

She turned on him savagely.

'Is that what you're waiting about for? When I want your sympathy I'll ask for it. Please get out of my way.'

She walked past him, out of the studio, and Philip, with a shrug of the shoulders, limped along to Gravier's for luncheon.

'It served her right,' said Lawson, when Philip told him what had happened. 'Ill-tempered slut.'

Lawson was very sensitive to criticism and, in order to avoid it, never went to the studio when Foinet was coming.

'I don't want other people's opinion of my work,' he said. 'I know myself if it's good or bad.'

'You mean you don't want other ·people's bad opinion of your work,' answered Clutton dryly.

In the afternoon Philip thought he would go to the Luxembourg to see the pictures, and walking through the garden he saw Fanny Price sitting in her accustomed seat. He was sore at the rudeness with which she had met his well-meant attempt to say something pleasant, and passed as though he had not caught sight of her. But she got up at once and came towards him.

'Are you trying to cut me?' she said.

'No, of course not. I thought perhaps you didn't want to be spoken to.'

'Where are you going?'

'I wanted to have a look at the Manet, I've heard so much about it.'

'Would you like me to come with you? I know the Luxembourg rather well. I could show you one or two good things.'

He understood that, unable to bring herself to apologize directly, she made this offer as amends.

'It's awfully kind of you. I should like it very much.'

'You needn't say yes if you'd rather go alone,' she said suspiciously.

'I wouldn't.'

They walked towards the gallery. Caillebotte's collection had lately been placed on view, and the student for the first time had the opportunity to examine at his ease the works of the impressionists. Till then it had been possible to see them only at Durand-Ruel's shop in the Rue Lafitte (and the dealer, unlike his fellows in England, who adopt towards the painter an attitude of superiority, was always pleased to show the shabbiest student whatever he wanted to see), or at his private house, to which it was not difficult to get a card of admission on Tuesdays, and where you might see pictures of world-wide reputation. Miss Price led Philip straight up to Manet's *Olympia*. He looked at it in astonished silence.

'Do you like it?' asked Miss Price.

'I don't know,' he answered helplessly.

'You can take it from me that it's the best thing in the gallery except perhaps Whistler's portrait of his mother.'

She gave him a certain time to contemplate the masterpiece and then took him to a picture representing a railway station.

'Look, here's a Monet,' she said. 'It's the Gare St Lazare.'

'But the railway lines aren't parallel,' said Philip.

'What does that matter?' she asked, with a haughty air.

Philip felt ashamed of himself. Fanny Price had picked up the glib chatter of the studios and had no difficulty in impressing Philip with the extent of her knowledge. She proceeded to explain the pictures to him, superciliously but not without insight, and showed him what the painters had attempted and what he must look for. She talked with much gesticulation of the thumb, and Philip, to whom all she said was new, listened with profound but bewildered interest. Till now he had worshipped Watts and Burne-Jones. The pretty colour of the first, the affected drawing of the second, had entirely satisfied his aesthetic sensibilities. Their vague idealism, the suspicion of a philosophical idea which underlay the titles they gave their pictures, accorded very well with the functions of art as from his diligent perusal of Ruskin he understood it; but here was something quite different: here was no moral appeal; and the contemplation of these works could help no one to lead a purer and a higher life. He was puzzled.

At last he said: 'You know, I'm simply dead. I don't think I can absorb anything more profitably. Let's go and sit down on one of the benches.'

'It's better not to take too much art at a time,' Miss Price answered.

When they got outside he thanked her warmly for the trouble she had taken.

'Oh, that's all right,' she said, a little ungraciously. 'I do it because I enjoy it. We'll go to the Louvre tomorrow if you like, and then I'll take you to Durand-Ruel's.'

'You're really awfully good to me.'

'You don't think me such a beast as the most of them do.'

'I don't,' he smiled.

'They think they'll drive me away from the studio; but they won't; I shall stay there just exactly as long as it suits me. All that this morning, it was Lucy Otter's doing, I know it was. She always has hated me. She thought after that I'd take myself off. I daresay she'd like me to go. She's afraid I know too much about her.'

Miss Price told him a long, involved story, which made out that Mrs Otter, a humdrum and respectable little person, had scabrous intrigues. Then she talked of Ruth Chalice, the girl whom Foinet had praised that morning.

'She's been with every one of the fellows at the studio. She's nothing better than a street-walker. And she's dirty. She hasn't had a bath for a month, I know it for a fact.'

Philip listened uncomfortably. He had heard already that various rumours were in circulation about Miss Chalice; but it was ridiculous to suppose that Mrs Otter, living with her mother, was anything but rigidly virtuous. The woman walking by his side with her malignant lying positively horrified him.

'I don't care what they say. I shall go on just the same. I know I've got it in me. I feel I'm an artist. I'd sooner kill myself than give it up. Oh, I shan't be the first they've all laughed at in the schools and then he's turned out the only genius of the lot. Art's the only thing I care for, I'm willing to give my whole life to it. It's only a question of sticking to it and pegging away.'

She found discreditable motives for everyone who would not take her at her own estimate of herself. She detested Clutton. She told Philip that his friend had no talent really; it was just flashy and superficial; he couldn't compose a figure to save his life. And Lawson:

'Little beast, with his red hair and his freckles. He's so afraid of Foinet that he won't let him see his work. After all, I don't funk it, do I? I don't care what Foinet says to me, I know I'm a real artist.'

They reached the street in which she lived, and with a sigh of relief Philip left her.

XLIV

BUT notwithstanding when Miss Price on the following Sunday offered to take him to the Louvre Philip accepted. She showed him *Mona Lisa*. He looked at it with a slight feeling of disappointment, but he had read till he knew by heart the jewelled words with which Walter Pater has added beauty to the most

199

famous picture in the world; and these now he repeated to Miss Price.

'That's all literature,' she said, a little contemptuously. 'You must get away from that.'

She showed him the Rembrandts, and she said many appropriate things about them. She stood in front of the *Disciples at Emmaus*.

'When you feel the beauty of that,' she said, 'you'll know something about painting.'

She showed him the *Odalisque* and *La Source* of Ingres. Fanny Price was a peremptory guide, she would not let him look at the things he wished, and attempted to force his admiration for all she admired. She was desperately in earnest with her study of art, and when Philip, passing in the Long Gallery a window that looked out on the Tuileries, gay, sunny, and urbane, like a picture by Raffaëlli, exclaimed:

'I say, how jolly! Do let's stop here a minute,' she said, indifferently: 'Yes, it's all right. But we've come here to look at pictures.'

The autumn air, blithe and vivacious, elated Philip; and when towards midday they stood in the great courtyard of the Louvre, he felt inclined to cry like Flanagan: To Hell with art.

'I say, do let's go to one of those restaurants in the Boul' Mich' and have a snack together, shall we?' he suggested.

Miss Price gave him a suspicious look.

'I've got my lunch waiting for me at home,' she answered.

'That doesn't matter. You can eat it tomorrow. Do let me stand you a lunch.'

'I don't know why you want to.'

'It would give me pleasure,' he replied, smiling.

They crossed the river, and at the corner of the Boulevard St Michel there was a restaurant.

'Let's go in here.'

'No, I won't go there, it looks too expensive.'

She walked on firmly, and Philip was obliged to follow. A few steps brought them to a smaller restaurant, where a dozen people were already lunching on the pavement under an awning; on the window was announced in large white letters: *Déjeuner 1·25, vin compris*.

'We couldn't have anything cheaper than this, and it looks quite all right.'

They sat down at a vacant table and waited for the omelette which was the first article on the bill of fare. Philip gazed with delight upon the passers-by. His heart went out to them. He was tired but very happy.

'I say, look at that man in the blouse. Isn't he ripping!'

He glanced at Miss Price, and to his astonishment saw that she was looking down at her plate, regardless of the passing spectacle, and two heavy tears were rolling down her cheeks.

'What on earth's the matter?' he exclaimed.

'If you say anything to me I shall get up and go at once,' she answered.

He was entirely puzzled, but fortunately at that moment the omelette came. He divided it in half and they began to eat. Philip did his best to talk of indifferent things, and it seemed as though Miss Price were making an effort on her side to be agreeable; but the luncheon was not altogether a success. Philip was squeamish, and the way in which Miss Price ate took his appetite away. She ate noisily, greedily, a little like a wild beast in a menagerie, and after she had finished each course rubbed the plate with pieces of bread till it was white and shining, as if she did not wish to lose a single drop of gravy. They had Camembert cheese, and it disgusted Philip to see that she ate rind and all of the portion that was given her. She could not have eaten more ravenously if she were starving.

Miss Price was unaccountable, and having parted from her on one day with friendliness he could never tell whether on the next she would not be sulky and uncivil; but he learned a good deal from her: though she could not draw well herself, she knew all that could be taught, and her constant suggestions helped his progress. Mrs Otter was useful to him too, and sometimes Miss Chalice criticized his work; he learned from the glib loquacity of Lawson and from the example of Clutton. But Fanny Price hated him to take suggestions from anyone but herself, and when he asked her help after someone else had been talking to him she would refuse with brutal rudeness. The other fellows, Lawson, Clutton, Flanagan, chaffed him about her.

'You be careful, my lad,' they said, 'she's in love with you.'

'Oh, what nonsense,' he laughed.

The thought that Miss Price could be in love with anyone was preposterous. It made him shudder when he thought of her uncomeliness, the bedraggled hair and the dirty hands, the brown dress she always wore, stained and ragged at the hem: he supposed she was hard up, they were all hard up, but she might at least be clean; and it was surely possible with a needle and thread to make her skirt tidy.

Philip began to sort his impressions of the people he was

thrown in contact with. He was not so ingenuous as in those days which now seemed so long ago at Heidelberg, and, beginning to take a more deliberate interest in humanity, he was inclined to examine and to criticize. He found it difficult to know Clutton any better after seeing him every day for three months than on the first day of their acquaintance. The general impression at the studio was that he was able; it was supposed that he would do great things, and he shared the general opinion; but what exactly he was going to do neither he nor anybody else quite knew. He had worked at several studios before Amitrano's, at Julians, the Beaux-Arts, and MacPherson's, and was remaining longer at Amitrano's than anywhere because he found himself more left alone. He was not fond of showing his work, and unlike most of the young men who were studying art neither sought nor gave advice. It was said that in the little studio in the Rue Campagne Première, which served him for workroom and bedroom, he had wonderful pictures which would make his reputation if only he could be induced to exhibit them. He could not afford a model but painted still life, and Lawson constantly talked of a plate of apples which he declared was a masterpiece. He was fastidious, and aiming at something he did not quite fully grasp, was constantly dissatisfied with his work as a whole: perhaps a part would please him, the forearm or the leg and foot of a figure, a glass or a cup in a still-life; and he would cut this out and keep it, destroying the rest of the canvas; so that when people invited themselves to see his work he could truthfully answer that he had not a single picture to show. In Brittany he had come across a painter whom nobody else had heard of, a queer fellow who had been a stockbroker and taken up painting at middle age, and he was greatly influenced by his work. He was turning his back on the impressionists and working out for himself painfully an individual way not only of painting but of seeing. Philip felt in him something strangely original.

At Gravier's where they ate, and in the evening at the Versailles or at the Closerie des Lilas, Clutton was inclined to taciturnity. He sat quietly, with a sardonic expression on his gaunt face, and spoke only when the opportunity occurred to throw in a witticism. He liked a butt and was most cheerful when someone was there on whom he could exercise his sarcasm. He seldom talked of anything but painting, and then only with the one or two persons whom he thought worth while. Philip wondered whether there was in him really anything: his reticence, the haggard look of him, the pungent humour, seemed to suggest personality, but might be no more than an effective mask which covered nothing.

With Lawson, on the other hand, Philip soon grew intimate. He had a variety of interests which made him an agreeable companion. He read more than most of the students, and though his income was small, loved to buy books. He lent them willingly; and Philip became acquainted with Flaubert and Balzac, with Verlaine, Heredia, and Villiers de L'Isle-Adam. They went to plays together and sometimes to the gallery of the Opéra Comique. There was the Odéon quite near them, and Philip soon shared his friend's passion for the tragedians of Louis XIV and the sonorous Alexandrine. In the Rue Taitbout were the Concerts Rouge, where for seventy-five centimes they could hear excellent music and get into the bargain something which it was quite possible to drink: the seats were uncomfortable, the place was crowded, the air thick with caporal horrible to breathe, but in their young enthusiasm they were indifferent. Sometimes they went to the Bal Bullier. On these occasions Flanagan accompanied them. His excitability and his roisterous enthusiasm made them laugh. He was an excellent dancer, and before they had been ten minutes in the room he was prancing round with some little shop-girl whose acquaintance he had just made.

The desire of all of them was to have a mistress. It was part of the paraphernalia of the art-student in Paris. It gave consideration in the eyes of one's fellows. It was something to boast about. But the difficulty was that they had scarcely enough money to keep themselves, and though they argued that Frenchwomen were so clever it cost no more to keep two than one, they found it difficult to meet young women who were willing to take that view of the circumstances. They had to content themselves for the most part with envying and abusing the ladies who received protection from painters of more settled respectability than their own. It was extraordinary how difficult these things were in Paris. Lawson would become acquainted with some young thing and make an appointment; for twenty-four hours he would be all in a flutter and describe the charmer at length to everyone he met; but she never by any chance turned up at the time fixed. He would come to Gravier's very late, ill-tempered, and exclaim:

'Confound it, another rabbit! I don't know why it is they don't like me. I suppose it's because I don't speak French well, or my red hair. It's too sickening to have spent over a year in Paris without getting hold of anyone.'

'You don't go the right way to work,' said Flanagan.

He had a long and enviable list of triumphs to narrate, and though they took leave not to believe all he said, evidence forced them to acknowledge that he did not altogether lie. But he sought no permanent arrangement. He only had two years in Paris: he had persuaded his people to let him come and study art instead of going to college; but at the end of that period he was to return to Seattle and go into his father's business. He had made up his mind to get as much fun as possible into the time, and demanded variety rather than duration in his love affairs.

'I don't know how you get hold of them,' said Lawson furiously.

'There's no difficulty about that, sonny,' answered Flanagan. 'You just go right in. The difficulty is to get rid of them. That's where you want tact.'

Philip was too much occupied with his work, the books he was reading, the plays he saw, the conversation he listened to, to trouble himself with the desire for female society. He thought there would be plenty of time for that when he could speak French more glibly.

It was more than a year now since he had seen Miss Wilkinson, and during his first weeks in Paris he had been too busy to answer a letter she had written to him just before he left Blackstable. When another came, knowing it would be full of reproaches and not being just then in the mood for them, he put it aside, intending to open it later; but he forgot and did not run across it till a month afterwards, when he was turning out a drawer to find some socks that had no holes in them. He looked at the unopened letter with dismay. He was afraid that Miss Wilkinson had suffered a good deal, and it made him feel a brute; but she had probably got over the suffering by now, at all events the worst of it. It suggested itself to him that women were often very emphatic in their expressions. These did not mean so much as when men used them. He had quite made up his mind that nothing would induce him ever to see her again. He had not written for so long that it seemed hardly worth while to write now. He made up his mind not to read the letter.

'I daresay she won't write again,' he said to himself. 'She can't help seeing the thing's over. After all, she was old enough to be my mother; she ought to have known better.'

For an hour or two he felt a little uncomfortable. His attitude was obviously the right one, but he could not help a feeling of dissatisfaction with the whole business. Miss Wilkinson, however, did not write again; nor did she, as he absurdly feared, suddenly appear in Paris to make him ridiculous before his friends. In a little while he clean forgot her.

Meanwhile he definitely forsook his old gods. The amazement with which at first he had looked upon the works of the impressionists changed to admiration; and presently he found himself talking as emphatically as the rest on the merits of Manet, Monet, and Degas. He bought a photograph of a drawing by Ingres of the *Odalisque* and a photograph of the *Olympia*. They were pinned side by side over his washing-stand so that he could contemplate their beauty while he shaved. He knew now quite positively that there had been no painting of landscape before Monet; and he felt a real thrill when he stood in front of Rembrandt's *Disciples at Emmaus* or Velasquez' *Lady with the Flea-bitten Nose*. That was not her real name, but by that she was distinguished at Gravier's to emphasize the picture's beauty notwithstanding the somewhat revolting peculiarity of the sitter's appearance. With Ruskin, Burne-Jones, and Watts, he had put aside his bowler hat and the neat blue tie with white spots which he had worn on coming to Paris; and now disported himself in a soft, broad-brimmed hat, a flowing black cravat, and a cape of romantic cut. He walked along the Boulevard du Montparnasse as though he had known it all his life, and by virtuous perseverance he had learnt to drink absinthe without distaste. He was letting his hair grow, and it was only because Nature is unkind and had no regard for the immortal longings of youth that he did not attempt a beard.

XLV

PHILIP soon realized that the spirit which informed his friends was Cronshaw's. It was from him that Lawson got his paradoxes; and even Clutton, who strained after individuality, expressed himself in the terms he had insensibly acquired from the older man. It was his ideas that they bandied about at table, and on his authority they formed their judgements. They made up for the respect with which unconsciously they treated him by laughing at his foibles and lamenting his vices.

'Of course, poor old Cronshaw will never do any good,' they said. 'He's quite hopeless.'

They prided themselves on being alone in appreciating his genius; and though, with the contempt of youth for the follies of middle age, they patronized him among themselves, they did not fail to look upon it as a feather in their caps if he had chosen a time when only one was there to be particularly wonderful. Cronshaw never came to Gravier's. For the last four years he had lived in squalid conditions with a woman whom only Lawson had once seen, in a tiny apartment on the sixth floor of one of the most dilapidated houses on the Quai des Grands Augustins: Lawson described with gusto the filth, the untidiness, the litter.

'And the stink nearly blew your head off.'

'Not at dinner, Lawson,' expostulated one of the others.

But he would not deny himself the pleasure of giving picturesque details of the odours which met his nostril. With a fierce delight in his own realism he described the woman who had opened the door for him. She was dark, small, and fat, quite young, with black hair that seemed always on the point of coming down. She worn a slatternly blouse and no corsets. With her red cheeks, large sensual mouth, and shining, lewd eyes, she reminded you of the *Bohémienne* in the Louvre by Franz Hals. She had a flaunting vulgarity which amused and yet horrified. A scrubby, unwashed baby was playing on the floor. It was known that the slut deceived Cronshaw with the most worthless ragamuffins of the Quarter, and it was a mystery to the ingenuous youths who absorbed his wisdom over a café table that Cronshaw with his keen intellect and his passion for beauty could ally himself to such a creature. But he seemed to revel in the coarseness of her language and would often report some phrase which reeked of the gutter. He referred to her ironically as *la fille de mon concierge*. Cronshaw was very poor. He earned a bare subsistence by writing on the exhibitions of pictures for one or two English papers, and he did a certain amount of translating. He had been on the staff of an English paper in Paris, but had been dismissed for drunkenness; he still, however, did odd jobs for it, describing the sales at the Hôtel Drouot or the revues at music-halls. The life of Paris had got into his bones, and he would not change it, notwithstanding its squalor, drudgery, and hardship, for any other in the world. He remained there all through the year, even in summer when everyone he knew was away, and felt himself only at ease within a mile of the Boulevard St Michel. But the curious thing was that he had never learnt to speak French passably, and he kept, in his shabby clothes bought at *La Belle Jardinière*, an ineradicably English appearance.

He was a man who would have made a success of life a century and a half ago when conversation was a passport to good company and inebriety no bar.

'I ought to have lived in the eighteen hundreds,' he said himself. 'What I want is a patron. I should have published my poems by subscription and dedicated them to a nobleman. I long to compose rhymed couplets upon the poodle of a countess. My soul yearns for the love of chambermaids and the conversation of bishops.'

He quoted the romantic Rolla:

'Je suis venu trop tard dans un monde trop vieux'.

He liked new faces, and he took a fancy to Philip, who seemed to achieve the difficult feat of talking just enough to suggest conversation and not too much to prevent monologue. Philip was captivated. He did not realize that little that Cronshaw said was new. His personality in conversation had a curious power. He had a beautiful and a sonorous voice, and a manner of putting things which was irresistible to youth. All he said seemed to excite thought, and often on the way home Lawson and Philip would walk to and from one another's hotels, discussing some point which a chance word of Cronshaw had suggested. It was disconcerting to Philip, who had a youthful eagerness for results, that Cronshaw's poetry hardly came up to expectation. It had never been published in a volume, but most of it had appeared in periodicals; and after a good deal of persuasion Cronshaw brought down a bundle of pages torn out of *The Yellow Book*, *The Saturday Review*, and other journals, on each of which was a poem. Philip was taken aback to find that most of them reminded him either of Henley or of Swinburne. It needed the splendour of Cronshaw's delivery to make them personal. He expressed his disappointment to Lawson, who carelessly repeated his words; and next time Philip went to the Closerie des Lilas the poet turned to him with his sleek smile:

'I hear you don't think much of my verses.'

Philip was embarrassed.

'I don't know about that,' he answered. 'I enjoyed reading them very much.'

'Do not attempt to spare my feelings,' returned Cronshaw, with a wave of his fat hand. 'I do not attach any exaggerated importance to my poetical works. Life is there to be lived rather than to be written about. My aim is to search out the manifold experience that it offers, wringing from each moment what of emotion it presents. I look upon my writing as a graceful accomplishment which does not absorb but rather adds pleasure to existence. As for posterity – damn posterity.'

Philip smiled, for it leaped to one's eyes that the artist in life produced no more than a wretched daub. Cronshaw looked at him meditatively and filled his glass. He sent the waiter for a packet of cigarettes.

'You are amused because I talk in this fashion and you know that I am poor and live in an attic with a vulgar trollop who deceives me with hairdressers and *garçons de café*; I translate wretched books for the British public, and write articles upon contemptible pictures which deserve not even to be abused. But pray tell me what is the meaning of life?'

'I say, that's rather a difficult question. Won't you give the answer yourself?'

'No, because it's worthless unless you yourself discover it. But what do you suppose you are in the world for?'

Philip had never asked himself, and he thought for a moment before replying:

'Oh, I don't know: I suppose to do one's duty, and make the best possible use of one's faculties, and avoid hurting other people.'

'In short, to do unto others as you would they should do unto you?'

'I suppose so.'

'Christianity.'

'No, it isn't,' said Philip indignantly. 'It has nothing to do with Christianity. It's just abstract morality.'

'But there's no such thing as abstract morality.'

'In that case, supposing under the influence of liquor you left your purse behind when you leave here and I picked it up, why do you imagine that I should return it to you? It's not the fear of the police.'

'It's the dread of hell if you sin and the hope of Heaven if you are virtuous.'

'But I believe in neither.'

'That may be. Neither did Kant when he devised the Categorical Imperative. You have thrown aside a creed, but you have preserved the ethic which was based upon it. To all intents you are a Christian still, and if there is a God in Heaven you will undoubtedly receive your reward. The Almighty can hardly be such a fool as the churches make out. If you keep His laws I don't think He can care a packet of pins whether you believe in Him or not.'

'But if I left my purse behind you would certainly return it to me,' said Philip.

'Not from motives of abstract morality, but only from fear of the police.'

'It's a thousand to one that the police would never find out.'

'My ancestors have lived in a civilized state so long that the fear of the police has eaten into my bones. The daughter of my *concierge* would not hesitate for a moment. You answer that she belongs to the criminal classes; not at all, she is merely devoid of vulgar prejudice.'

'But then that does away with honour and virtue and goodness and decency and everything,' said Philip.

'Have you ever committed a sin?'

'I don't know, I suppose so,' answered Philip.

'You speak with the lips of a dissenting minister. I have never committed a sin.'

Cronshaw in his shabby great-coat, with the collar turned up, and his hat well down on his head, with his red fat face and his little gleaming eyes, looked extraordinarily comic; but Philip was too much in earnest to laugh.

'Have you never done anything you regret.'

'How can I regret when what I did was inevitable?' asked Cronshaw in return.

'But that's fatalism.'

'The illusion which man has that his will is free is so deeply rooted that I am ready to accept it. I act as though I were a free agent. But when an action is performed it is clear that all the forces of the universe from all eternity conspired to cause it, and nothing I could do could have prevented it. It was inevitable. If it was good I can claim no merit; if it was bad I can accept no censure.'

'My brain reels,' said Philip.

'Have some whisky,' returned Cronshaw, passing over the bottle. 'There's nothing like it for clearing the head. You must expect to be thick-witted if you insist upon drinking beer.'

Philip shook his head, and Cronshaw proceeded:

'You're not a bad fellow, but you won't drink. Sobriety disturbs conversation. But when I speak of good and bad . . .' Philip saw he was taking up the thread of his discourse, 'I speak conventionally. I attach no meaning to those words. I refuse to make a hierarchy of human actions and ascribe worthiness to some and ill-repute to others. The terms vice and virtue have no significance for me. I do not confer praise or blame: I accept. I am the measure of all things. I am the centre of the world.'

'But there are one or two other people in the world,' objected Philip.

'I speak only for myself. I know them only as they limit my activities. Round each of them too the world turns, and each one for himself is the centre of the universe. My right over them extends only as far as my power. What I can do is the only limit of what I may do. Because we are gregarious we live in society, and society holds together by means of force, force of arms (that is the policeman) and force of public opinion (that is Mrs Grundy). You have society on one hand and the individual on the other: each is an organism striving for self-preservation. It is might against might. I stand alone, bound to accept society and not unwilling, since in return for the taxes I pay it protects me, a weakling, against the tyranny of another stronger than I am; but I submit to its laws because I must; I do not acknowledge their justice; I do not know justice, I only know power. And when I have paid for the policeman who protects me and, if I live in a country where conscription is in force, served in the army which guards my house and land from the invader, I am quits with society: for the rest I counter its might with my wiliness. It makes laws for its self-preservation, and if I break them it imprisons or kills me: it has the might to do so and therefore the right. If I break the laws I will accept the vengeance of the state, but I will not regard it as punishment nor shall I feel myself convicted of wrong-doing. Society tempts me to its service by honours and riches and the good opinion of my fellows; but I am indifferent to their opinion, I despise honours and I can do very well without riches.'

'But if everyone thought like you things would go to pieces at once.'

'I have nothing to do with others, I am only concerned with myself. I take advantage of the fact that the majority of mankind are led by certain rewards to do things which directly or indirectly tend to my convenience.'

'It seems to me an awfully selfish way of looking at things,' said Philip.

'But are you under the impression that men ever do anything except for selfish reasons?'

'Yes.'

'It is impossible that they should. You will find as you grow older that the first thing needful to make the world a tolerable place to live in is to recognize the inevitable selfishness of humanity. You demand unselfishness from others, which is a preposterous claim that they should sacrifice their desires to yours. Why should they? When you are reconciled to the fact that each is for himself in the world you will ask less from your fellows. They will not disappoint you, and you will look upon them more charitably. Men seek but one thing in life – their pleasure.'

'No, no, no!' cried Philip.

Cronshaw chuckled.

'You rear like a frightened colt, because I use a word to which your Christianity ascribes a deprecatory meaning. You have a hierarchy of values; pleasure is at the bottom of the ladder, and you speak with a little thrill of self-satisfaction of duty, charity, and truthfulness. You think pleasure is only of the senses; the wretched slaves who manufactured your morality despised a satisfaction which they had small means of enjoying. You would not be so frightened if I had spoken of happiness instead of pleasure: it sounds less shocking, and your mind wanders from the sty of Epicurus to his garden. But I will speak of pleasure, for I see that men aim at that, and I do not know that they aim at happiness. It is pleasure that lurks in the practice of every one of your virtues. Man performs actions because they are good for him, and when they are good for other people as well they are thought virtuous: if he finds pleasure in giving alms he is charitable; if he finds pleasure in helping others he is benevolent; if he finds pleasure in working for society he is public-spirited; but it is for your private pleasure that you give twopence to a beggar as much as it is for my private pleasure that I drink another whisky and soda. I, less of a humbug than you, neither applaud myself for my pleasure nor demand your admiration.'

'But have you never known people do things they didn't want to instead of things they did?'

'No. You put your question foolishly. What you mean is that people accept an immediate pain rather than an immediate pleasure. The objection is as foolish as your manner of putting it. It is clear that men accept an immediate pain rather than an immediate pleasure, but only because they expect a greater pleasure in the future. Often the pleasure is illusory, but their error in calculation is no refutation of the rule. You are puzzled because you cannot get over the idea that pleasures are only of the senses; but, child, a man who dies for his country dies because he likes it as surely as a man eats pickled cabbage because he likes it. It is a law of creation. If it were possible for men to prefer pain to pleure the human race would have long since become extinct.'

'But if all that is true,' cried Philip, 'what is the use of any-

211

thing? If you take away duty and goodness and beauty, why are we brought into the world?'

'Here comes the gorgeous East to suggest an answer,' smiled Cronshaw.

He pointed to two persons who at that moment opened the door of the café, and, with a blast of cold air, entered. They were Levantines, itinerant vendors of cheap rugs, and each bore on his arm a bundle. It was Sunday evening, and the café was very full. They passed among the tables, and in that atmosphere heavy and discoloured with tobacco smoke, rank with humanity, they seemed to bring an air of mystery. They were clad in European, shabby clothes, their thin great-coats were threadbare, but each wore a tarboosh. Their faces were grey with cold. One was of middle age, with a black beard, but the other was a youth of eighteen, with a face deeply scarred by smallpox and with one eye only. They passed by Cronshaw and Philip.

'Allah is great, and Mahomet is his prophet,' said Cronshaw impressively.

The elder advanced with a cringing smile, like a mongrel used to blows. With a sidelong glance at the door and a quick surreptitious movement he showed a pornographic picture.

'Are you Masr-ed-Deen, the merchant of Alexandria, or is it from far Bagdad that you bring your goods, O, my uncle; and yonder one-eyed youth, do I see in him one of the three kings of whom Scheherazade told stories to her lord?'

The pedlar's smile grew more ingratiating, though he understood no word of what Cronshaw said, and like a conjurer he produced a sandal-wood box.

'Nay, show us the priceless web of Eastern looms,' quoth Cronshaw. 'For I would point a moral and adorn a tale.'

The Levantine unfolded a tablecloth, red and yellow, vulgar, hideous and grotesque.

'Thirty-five francs,' he said.

'O, my uncle, this cloth knew not the weavers of Samarkand, and those colours were never made in the vasts of Bokhara.'

'Twenty-five francs,' smiled the pedlar obsequiously.

'Ultima Thule was the place of its manufacture, even Birmingham, the place of my birth.'

'Fifteen francs,' cringed the bearded man.

'Get thee gone, fellow,' said Cronshaw. 'May wild asses defile the grave of thy maternal grandmother.'

Imperturbably, but smiling no more, the Levantine passed with his wares to another table. Cronshaw turned to Philip.

212

'Have you ever been to the Cluny, the museum? There you will see Persian carpets of the most exquisite hue and of a pattern the beautiful intricacy of which delights and amazes the eye. In them you will see the mystery and the sensual beauty of the East, the roses of Hafiz and the wine-cup of Omar; but presently you will see more. You were asking just now what was the meaning of life. Go and look at those Persian carpets, and one of these days the answer will come to you.'

'You are cryptic,' said Philip.

'I am drunk,' answered Cronshaw.

XLVI

PHILIP did not find living in Paris as cheap as he had been led to believe and by February had spent most of the money with which he started. He was too proud to appeal to his guardian, nor did he wish Aunt Louisa to know that his circumstances were straitened, since he was certain she would make an effort to send him something from her own pocket, and he knew how little she could afford to. In three months he would attain his majority and come into possession of his small fortune. He tided over the interval by selling the few trinkets which he had inherited from his father.

At about this time Lawson suggested that they should take a small studio which was vacant in one of the streets that led out of the Boulevard Raspail. It was very cheap. It had a room attached, which they could use as a bedroom; and since Philip was at the school every morning Lawson could have the undisturbed use of the studio then; Lawson, after wandering from school to school, had come to the conclusion that he could work best alone, and proposed to get a model in three or four days a week. At first Philip hesitated on account of the expense, but they reckoned it out; and it seemed (they were so anxious to have a studio of their own that they calculated pragmatically) that the cost would not be much greater than that of living in a hotel. Though the rent and the cleaning by the *concierge* would come to a little more, they would save on the *petit déjeuner*, which they could make themselves. A year or two earlier Philip would have refused to share a room with anyone, since he was so sensitive about his deformed foot, but his morbid way of looking at it was growing less marked: in Paris it did not seem to matter so much, and though he never

213

by any chance forgot it himself, he ceased to feel that other people were constantly noticing it.

They moved in, bought a couple of beds, a washing-stand, a few chairs, and felt for the first time the thrill of possession. They were so excited that the first night they went to bed in what they could call a home they lay awake talking till three in the morning; and next day found lighting the fire and making their own coffee, which they had in pyjamas, such a jolly business that Philip did not get to Amitrano's till nearly eleven. He was in excellent spirits. He nodded to Fanny Price.

'How are you getting on?' he asked cheerily.

'What does that matter to you?' she asked in reply.

Philip could not help laughing.

'Don't jump down my throat. I was only trying to make myself polite.'

'I don't want your politeness.'

'D'you think it's worth while quarrelling with me too?' asked Philip mildly. 'There are so few people you're on speaking terms with, as it is.'

'That's my business, isn't it?'

'Quite.'

He began to work, vaguely wondering why Fanny Price made herself so disagreeable. He had come to the conclusion that he thoroughly disliked her. Everyone did. People were only civil to her at all from fear of the malice of her tongue; for to their faces and behind their backs she said abominable things. But Philip was feeling so happy that he did not want even Miss Price to bear ill-feeling towards him. He used the artifice which had often before succeeded in banishing her ill-humour.

'I say, I wish you'd come and look at my drawing. I've got in an awful mess.'

'Thank you very much, but I've got something better to do with my time.'

Philip stared at her in surprise, for the one thing she could be counted upon to do with alacrity was to give advice. She went on quickly in a low voice, savage with fury:

'Now that Lawson's gone you think you'll put up with me. Thank you very much. Go and find somebody else to help you. I don't want anybody else's leavings.'

Lawson had the pedagogic instinct; whenever he found anything out he was eager to impart it; and because he taught with delight he taught with profit. Philip, without thinking anything about it, had got into the habit of sitting by his side; it never occurred to him that Fanny Price was consumed with jealousy, and watched his acceptance of someone else's tuition with ever-increasing anger.

'You were very glad to put up with me when you knew nobody here,' she said bitterly, 'and as soon as you made friends with other people you threw me aside, like an old glove' – she repeated the stale metaphor with satisfaction – 'like an old glove. All right, I don't care, but I'm not going to be made a fool of another time.'

There was a suspicion of truth in what she said, and it made Philip angry enough to answer what first came into his head.

'Hang it all, I only asked your advice because I saw it pleased you.'

She gave a gasp and threw him a sudden look of anguish. Then two tears rolled down her cheeks. She looked frowsy and grotesque. Philip, not knowing what on earth this new attitude implied, went back to his work. He was uneasy and conscience-stricken; but he would not go to her and say he was sorry if he had caused her pain, because he was afraid she would take the opportunity to snub him. For two or three weeks she did not speak to him, and after Philip had got over the discomfort of being cut by her, he was somewhat relieved to be free from so difficult a friendship. He had been a little disconcerted by the air of proprietorship she assumed over him. She was an extraordinary woman. She came every day to the studio at eight o'clock, and was ready to start working when the model was in position; she worked steadily, talking to no one, struggling hour after hour with difficulties she could not overcome, and remained till the clock struck twelve. Her work was hopeless. There was not in it the smallest approach even to the mediocre achievement at which most of the young persons were able after some months to arrive. She wore every day the same ugly brown dress, with the mud of the last wet day still caked on the hem and with the raggedness, which Philip had noticed the first time he saw her, still unmended.

But one day she came up to him, and with a scarlet face asked whether she might speak to him afterwards.

'Of course, as much as you like,' smiled Philip. 'I'll wait behind at twelve.'

He went to her when the day's work was over.

'Will you walk a little bit with me?' she said, looking away from him with embarrassment.

'Certainly.'

They walked for two or three minutes in silence.

'D'you remember what you said to me the other day?' she asked then on a sudden.

'Oh, I say, don't let's quarrel,' said Philip. 'It really isn't worth while.'

She gave a quick, painful inspiration.

'I don't want to quarrel with you. You're the only friend I had in Paris. I thought you rather liked me. I felt there was something between us. I was drawn towards you – you know what I mean, your club-foot.'

Philip reddened and instinctively tried to walk without a limp. He did not like anyone to mention the deformity. He knew what Fanny Price meant. She was ugly and uncouth, and because he was deformed there was between them a certain sympathy. He was very angry with her, but he forced himself not to speak.

'You said you only asked my advice to please me. Don't you think my work's any good?'

'I've only seen your drawing at Amitrano's. It's awfully hard to judge from that.'

'I was wondering if you'd come and look at my other work. I've never asked anyone else to look at it. I should like to show it to you.'

'It's awfully kind of you. I'd like to see it very much.'

'I live quite near here,' she said apologetically. 'It'll only take you ten minutes.'

'Oh, that's all right,' he said.

They were walking along the boulevard, and she turned down a side street, then led him into another, poorer still, with cheap shops on the ground floor, and at last stopped. They climbed flight after flight of stairs. She unlocked a door, and they went into a tiny attic with a sloping roof and a small window. This was closed and the room had a musty smell. Though it was very cold there was no fire and no sign that there had been one. The bed was unmade. A chair, a chest of drawers which served also as a wash-stand, and a cheap easel, were all the furniture. The place would have been squalid enough in any case, but the litter, the untidiness, made the impression revolting. On the chimney-piece, scattered over with paints and brushes, were a cup, a dirty plate, and a tea-pot.

'If you'll stand over there I'll put them on the chair so that you can see them better.'

She showed him twenty small canvases, about eighteen by twelve. She placed them on the chair, one after the other, watching his face; he nodded as he looked at each one.

'You do like them, don't you?' she said anxiously, after a bit.

'I just want to look at them all first,' he answered. 'I'll talk afterwards.'

He was collecting himself. He was panic-stricken. He did not know what to say. It was not only that they were ill-drawn, or that the colour was put on amateurishly by someone who had no eye for it; but there was no attempt at getting the values, and the perspective was grotesque. It looked like the work of a child of five, but a child would have had some *naïveté* and might at least have made an attempt to put down what he saw; but here was the work of a vulgar mind chock-full of recollections of vulgar pictures. Philip remembered that she had talked enthusiastically about Monet and the impressionists, but here were only the worst traditions of the Royal Academy.

'There,' she said at last, 'that's the lot.'

Philip was no more truthful than anybody else, but he had a great difficulty in telling a thundering, deliberate lie, and he blushed furiously when he answered :

'I think they're most awfully good.'

A faint colour came into her unhealthy cheeks, and she smiled a little.

'You needn't say so if you don't think so, you know. I want the truth.'

'But I do think so.'

'Haven't you got any criticism to offer? There must be some you don't like as well as others.'

Philip looked round helplessly. He saw a landscape, the typical picturesque 'bit' of the amateur, an old bridge, a creeper-clad cottage, and a leafy bank.

'Of course I don't pretend to know anything about it,' he said. 'But I wasn't quite sure about the values of that.'

She flushed darkly and taking up the picture quickly turned its back to him.

'I don't know why you should have chosen that one to sneer at. It's the best thing I've ever done. I'm sure my values are all right. That's a thing you can't teach anyone, you either understand values or you don't.'

'I think they're all most awfully good,' repeated Philip.

She looked at them with an air of self-satisfaction.

'I don't think they're anything to be ashamed of.'

Philip looked at his watch.

'I say, it's getting late. Won't you let me give you a little lunch?'

'I've got my lunch waiting for me here.'

Philip saw no sign of it, but supposed perhaps the *concierge* would bring it up when he was gone. He was in a hurry to get away. The mustiness of the room made his head ache.

XLVII

In March there was all the excitement of sending in to the Salon. Clutton, characteristically, had nothing ready, and he was very scornful of the two heads that Lawson sent; they were obviously the work of a student, straightforward portraits of models, but they had a certain force; Clutton, aiming at perfection, had no patience with efforts which betrayed hesitancy, and with a shrug of the shoulders told Lawson it was an impertinence to exhibit stuff which should never have been allowed out of his studio; he was not less contemptuous when the two heads were accepted. Flanagan tried his luck too, but his picture was refused. Mrs Otter sent a blameless *Portrait de ma Mère*, accomplished and second-rate; and was hung in a very good place.

Hayward, whom Philip had not seen since he left Heidelberg, arrived in Paris to spend a few days in time to come to the party which Lawson and Philip were giving in their studio to celebrate the hanging of Lawson's pictures. Philip had been eager to see Hayward again, but when at last they met, he experienced some disappointment. Hayward had altered a little in appearance: his fine hair was thinner, and with the rapid wilting of the very fair, he was becoming wizened and colourless; his blue eyes were paler than they had been, and there was a muzziness about his features. On the other hand, in mind he did not seem to have changed at all, and the culture which had impressed Philip at eighteen aroused somewhat the contempt of Philip at twenty-one. He had altered a good deal himself, and regarding with scorn all his old opinions of art, life, and letters, had no patience with anyone who still held them. He was scarcely conscious of the fact that he wanted to show off before Hayward, but when he took him round the galleries he poured out to him all the revolutionary opinions which himself had so recently adopted. He took him to Manet's *Olympia* and said dramatically:

'I would give all the old masters except Velasquez, Rembrandt, and Vermeer for that one picture.'

'Who was Vermeer?' asked Hayward.

'Oh, my dear fellow, don't you know Vermeer? You're not civilized. You mustn't live a moment longer without making his acquaintance. He's the one old master who painted like a modern.'

He dragged Hayward out of the Luxembourg and hurried him off to the Louvre.

'But aren't there any more pictures here?' asked Hayward, with the tourist's passion for thoroughness.

'Nothing of the least consequence. You can come and look at them by yourself with your Baedeker.'

When they arrived at the Louvre Philip led his friend down the Long Gallery.

'I should like to see *La Gioconda*,' said Hayward.

'Oh, my dear fellow, it's only literature,' answered Philip.

At last, in a small room, Philip stopped before *The Lace-maker* of Vermeer van Delft.

'There, that's the best picture in the Louvre. It's exactly like a Manet.'

With an expressive, eloquent thumb Philip expatiated on the charming work. He used the jargon of the studios with overpowering effect.

'I don't know that I see anything so wonderful as all that in it,' said Hayward.

'Of course it's a painter's picture,' said Philip. 'I can quite believe the layman would see nothing much in it.'

'The what?' said Hayward.

'The layman.'

Like most people who cultivate an interest in the arts, Hayward was extremely anxious to be right. He was dogmatic with those who did not venture to assert themselves, but with the self-assertive he was very modest. He was impressed by Philip's assurance, and accepted meekly Philip's implied suggestion that the painter's arrogant claim to be the sole possible judge of painting has anything but its impertinence to recommend it.

A day or two later Philip and Lawson gave their party. Cronshaw, making an exception in their favour, agreed to eat their food; and Miss Chalice offered to come and cook for them. She took no interest in her own sex and declined the suggestion that other girls should be asked for her sake. Clutton, Flanagan, Potter, and two others made up the party. Furniture was scarce, so the model stand was used as a table, and the guests were to sit on portmanteaux if they liked, and if they didn't on the floor. The feast consisted of a *pot-au-feu*, which

Miss Chalice had made, of a leg of mutton roasted round the corner and brought round hot and savoury (Miss Chalice had cooked the potatoes, and the studio was redolent of the carrots she had fried; fried carrots were her speciality); and this was to be followed by *poires flambées*, pears with burning brandy, which Cronshaw had volunteered to make. The meal was to finish with an enormous *fromage de Brie*, which stood near the window and added fragrant odours to all the others which filled the studio. Cronshaw sat in the place of honour on a Gladstone bag, with his legs curled under him like a Turkish bashaw, beaming good-naturedly on the young people who surrounded him. From force of habit, though the small studio with the stove lit was very hot, he kept on his great-coat, with the collar turned up, and his bowler hat: he looked with satisfaction on the four large *fiaschi* of Chianti which stood in front of him in a' row, two on each side of a bottle of whisky; he said it reminded him of a slim fair Circassian guarded by four corpulent eunuchs. Hayward in order to put the rest of them at their ease had clothed himself in a tweed suit and a Trinity Hall tie. He looked grotesquely British. The others were elaborately polite to him, and during the soup they talked of the weather and the political situation. There was a pause while they waited for the leg of mutton, and Miss Chalice lit a cigarette.

'Rampunzel, Rampunzel, let down your hair,' she said suddenly.

With an elegant gesture she untied a ribbon so that her tresses fell over her shoulders. She shook her head.

'I always feel more comfortable with my hair down.'

With her large brown eyes, thin, ascetic face, her pale skin, and broad forehead, she might have stepped out of a picture by Burne-Jones. She had long, beautiful hands, with fingers deeply stained by nicotine. She wore sweeping draperies, mauve and green. There was about her the romantic air of High Street, Kensington. She was wantonly aesthetic; but she was an excellent creature, kind and good-natured; and her affectations were but skin-deep. There was a knock at the door, and they all gave a shout of exultation. Miss Chalice rose and opened. She took the leg of mutton and held it high above her, as though it were the head of John the Baptist on a platter; and, the cigarette still in her mouth, advanced with solemn, hieratic steps.

'Hail, daughter of Herodias,' cried Cronshaw.

The mutton was eaten with gusto, and it did one good to see what a hearty appetite the pale-faced lady had. Clutton and

Potter sat on each side of her, and everyone knew that neither had found her unduly coy. She grew tired of most people in six weeks, but she knew exactly how to treat afterwards the gentlemen who had laid their young hearts at her feet. She bore them no ill-will, though having loved them she had ceased to do so, and treated them with friendliness but without familiarity. Now and then she looked at Lawson with melancholy eyes. The *poires flambées* were a great success, partly because of the brandy and partly because Miss Chalice insisted that they should be eaten with the cheese.

'I don't know whether it's perfectly delicious or whether I'm just going to vomit,' she said, after she had thoroughly tried the mixture.

Coffee and cognac followed with sufficient speed to prevent any untoward consequence, and they settled down to smoke in comfort. Ruth Chalice, who could do nothing that was not deliberately artistic, arranged herself in a graceful attitude by Cronshaw and just rested her exquisite head on his shoulder. She looked into the dark abyss of time with brooding eyes, and now and then with a long meditative glance at Lawson she sighed deeply.

Then came the summer, and restlessness seized these young people. The blue skies lured them to the sea, and the pleasant breeze sighing through the leaves of the plane-trees on the boulevard drew them towards the country. Everyone made plans for leaving Paris; they discussed what was the most suitable size for the canvases they meant to take; they laid in stores of panels for sketching; they argued about the merits of various places in Brittany. Flanagan and Potter went to Concarneau; Mrs Otter and her mother, with a natural instinct for the obvious, went to Pont-Aven; Philip and Lawson made up their minds to go to the forest of Fontainebleau, and Miss Chalice knew of a very good hotel at Moret where there were lots of stuff to paint; it was near Paris, and neither Philip nor Lawson was indifferent to the railway fare. Ruth Chalice would be there, and Lawson had an idea for a portrait of her in the open air. Just then the Salon was full of portraits of people in gardens, in sunlight, with blinking eyes and green reflections of sunlit leaves on their faces. They asked Clutton to go with them, but he preferred spending the summer by himself. He had just discovered Cézanne, and was eager to go to Provence; he wanted heavy skies from which the hot blue seemed to drip like beads of sweat, and broad white dusty roads, and pale roofs out of which the sun had burnt the colour, and olive trees grey with heat.

The day before they were to start, after the morning class, Philip, putting his things together, spoke to Fanny Price.

'I'm off tomorrow,' he said cheerfully.

'Off where?' she said quickly. 'You're not going away?' Her face fell.

'I'm going away for the summer. Aren't you?'

'No, I'm staying in Paris. I thought you were going to stay too. I was looking forward . . .'

She stopped and shrugged her shoulders.

'But won't it be frightfully hot here? It's awfully bad for you.'

'Much you care if it's bad for me. Where are you going?'

'Moret.'

'Chalice is going there. You're not going with her?'

'Lawson and I are going. And she's going there too. I don't know that we're actually going together.'

She gave a low guttural sound, and her large face grew dark and red.

'How filthy! I thought you were a decent fellow. You were about the only one here. She's been with Clutton and Potter and Flanagan, even with old Foinet – that's why he takes so much trouble about her – and now two of you, you and Lawson. It makes me sick.'

'Oh, what nonsense! She's a very decent sort. One treats her just as if she were a man.'

'Oh, don't speak to me, don't speak to me.'

'But what can it matter to you?' asked Philip. 'It's really no business of yours where I spend my summer.'

'I was looking forward to it so much,' she gasped, speaking it seemed almost to herself. 'I didn't think you had the money to go away, and there wouldn't have been anyone else here, and we could have worked together, and we'd have gone to see things.' Then her thoughts flung back to Ruth Chalice. 'The filthy beast,' she cried. 'She isn't fit to speak to.'

Philip looked at her with a sinking heart. He was not a man to think girls were in love with him; he was too conscious of his deformity, and he felt awkward and clumsy with women; but he did not know what else this outburst could mean. Fanny Price, in the dirty brown dress, with her hair falling over her face, sloppy, untidy, stood before him; and tears of anger rolled down her cheeks. She was repellent. Philip glanced at the door, instinctively hoping that someone would come in and put an end to the scene.

'I'm awfully sorry,' he said.

'You're just the same as all of them. You take all you can get, and you don't even say thank you. I've taught you everything you know. No one else would take any trouble with you. Has Foinet ever bothered about you? And I can tell you this – you can work here for a thousand years and you'll never do any good. You haven't got any talent. You haven't got any originality. And it's not only me – they all say it. You'll never be a painter as long as you live.'

'That is no business of yours either, is it?' said Philip, flushing.

'Oh, you think it's only my temper. Ask Clutton, ask Lawson, ask Chalice. Never, never, never. You haven't got it in you.'

Philip shrugged his shoulders and walked out. She shouted after him:

'Never, never, never.'

Moret was in those days an old-fashioned town of one street at the edge of the Forest of Fontainebleau, and the Écu d'Or was a hotel which still had about it the decrepit air of the *Ancien Régime*. It faced the winding river, the Loing; and Miss Chalice had a room with a little terrace overlooking it, with a charming view of the old bridge and its fortified gateway. They sat here in the evenings after dinner, drinking coffee, smoking, and discussing art. There ran into the river, a little way off, a narrow canal bordered by poplars, and along the banks of this after their day's work they often wandered. They spent all day painting. Like most of their generation they were obsessed by the fear of the picturesque, and they turned their backs on the obvious beauty of the town to seek subjects which were devoid of a prettiness they despised. Sisley and Monet had painted the canal with its poplars, and they felt a desire to try their hands at what was so typical of France; but they were frightened of its formal beauty, and set themselves deliberately to avoid it. Miss Chalice, who had a clever dexterity which impressed Lawson notwithstanding his contempt for feminine art, started a picture in which she tried to circumvent the commonplace by leaving out the tops of the trees; and Lawson had the brilliant idea of putting in his foreground a large blue advertisement of *chocolat Menier* in order to emphasize his abhorrence of the chocolate box.

Philip began now to paint in oils. He experienced a thrill of delight when first he used that grateful medium. He went out with Lawson in the morning with his little box and sat by him painting a panel; it gave him so much satisfaction that he did not realize he was doing no more than copy; he was so much under his friend's influence that he saw only with his eyes. Lawson painted very low in tone, and they both saw the emerald of the grass like dark velvet, while the brilliance of the sky turned in their hands to a brooding ultramarine. Through July they had one fine day after another; it was very hot; and the heat, searing Philip's heart, filled him with languor; he could not work; his mind was eager with a thousand thoughts. Often he spent the mornings by the side of the canal in the shade of the poplars, reading a few lines and then dreaming for half an hour. Sometimes he hired a rickety bicycle and rode along the dusty road that led to the forest, and then lay down in a clearing. His head was full of romantic fancies. The ladies of Watteau, gay and insouciant, seemed to wander with their cavaliers among the great trees, whispering to one another careless, charming things, and yet somehow oppressed by a nameless fear.

They were alone in the hotel but for a fat Frenchwoman of middle age, a Rabelaisian figure with a broad, obscene laugh. She spent the day by the river patiently fishing for fish she never caught, and Philip sometimes went down and talked to her. He found out that she had belonged to a profession whose most notorious member for our generation was Mrs Warren, and having made a competence she now lived the quiet life of the *bourgeoise*. She told Philip lewd stories.

'You must go to Seville,' she said – she spoke a little broken English. 'The most beautiful women in the world.'

She leered and nodded her head. Her triple chin, her large belly, shook with inward laughter.

It grew so hot that it was almost impossible to sleep at night. The heat seemed to linger under the trees as though it were a material thing. They did not wish to leave the starlit night, and the three of them would sit on the terrace of Ruth Chalice's room, silent, hour after hour, too tired to talk any more, but in voluptuous enjoyment of the stillness. They listened to the murmur of the river. The church clock struck one and two and sometimes three before they could drag themselves to bed. Suddenly Philip became aware that Ruth Chalice and Lawson were lovers. He divined it in the way the girl looked at the young painter, and in his air of possession; and as Philip sat with them he felt a kind of effluence surrounding them, as though the air were heavy with something strange. The revelation was a shock. He had looked upon Miss Chalice as a very good fellow and he liked to talk to her, but it had never seemed to him possible to enter into a closer relationship. One Sunday they had all gone with a tea-basket into the forest, and when they came to a glade which was suitably sylvan, Miss Chalice, because it was idyllic, insisted on taking off her shoes and stockings. It would have been very charming only her feet were rather large and she had on both a large corn on the third toe. Philip felt it made her proceeding a little ridiculous. But now he looked upon her quite differently; there was something softly feminine in her large eyes and her olive skin; he felt himself a fool not to have seen that she was attractive. He thought he detected in her a touch of contempt for him, because he had not had the sense to see that she was there, in his way, and in Lawson a suspicion of superiority. He was envious of Lawson, and he was jealous, not of the individual concerned, but of his love. He wished that he was standing in his shoes and feeling with his heart. He was troubled, and the fear seized him that love would pass him by. He wanted a passion to seize him, he wanted to be swept off his feet and borne powerless in a mighty rush he cared not whither. Miss Chalice and Lawson seemed to him now somehow different, and the constant companionship with them made him restless. He was dissatisfied with himself. Life was not giving him what he wanted, and he had an uneasy feeling that he was losing his time.

The stout Frenchwoman soon guessed what the relations were between the couple, and talked of the matter to Philip with the utmost frankness.

'And you,' she said, with the tolerant smile of one who had fattened on the lust of her fellows, 'have you got a *petite amie*?'

'No,' said Philip, blushing.

'And why not? *C'est de votre âge.*'

He shrugged his shoulders. He had a volume of Verlaine in his hands, and he wandered off. He tried to read, but his passion was too strong. He thought of the stray amours to which he had been introduced by Flanagan, the sly visits to houses in a *cul-de-sac*, with the drawing-room in Utrecht velvet, and the mercenary graces of painted women. He shuddered. He threw himself on the grass, stretching his limbs like a young animal freshly awaked from sleep; and the rippling water, the poplars gently tremulous in the faint breeze, the blue sky, were almost more than he could bear. He was in love with love. In his fancy he felt the kiss of warm lips on his, and around his neck the touch of soft hands. He imagined himself in the arms of Ruth Chalice, he thought of her dark eyes and the wonderful texture of her skin; he was mad to have let such a wonderful adventure slip through his fingers. And if Lawson had done it why should not he? But this was only when he did not see her, when he lay awake at night or dreamed idly by the side of the canal; when he saw her he felt suddenly quite different; he had no desire to take her in his arms, and he could not imagine himself kissing her. It was very curious. Away from her he thought her beautiful, remembering only her magnificent eyes and the creamy pallor of her face; but when he was with her he saw only that she was flat-chested and that her teeth were slightly decayed; he could not forget the corns on her toes. He could not understand himself. Would he always love only in absence and be prevented from enjoying anything when he had the chance by that deformity of vision which seemed to exaggerate the revolting?

He was not sorry when a change in the weather, announcing the definite end of the long summer, drove them all back to Paris.

XLVIII

When Philip returned to Amitrano's he found that Fanny Price was no longer working there. She had given up the key of her locker. He asked Mrs Otter whether she knew what had become of her; and Mrs Otter, with a shrug of the shoulders, answered that she had probably gone back to England. Philip was relieved. He was profoundly bored by her ill-temper. Moreover, she insisted on advising him about his work, looked upon it as a slight when he did not follow her precepts, and would not understand that he felt himself no longer the duffer he had been at first. Soon he forgot all about her. He was working in oils now and he was full of enthusiasm. He hoped to have something done of sufficient importance to send to the following year's Salon. Lawson was painting a portrait of Miss Chalice. She was very paintable, and all the young men who had fallen victims to her charm had made portraits of her. A natural indolence, joined with a passion for picturesque attitudes, made her an excellent sitter; and she had enough technical knowledge to offer useful criticisms. Since her passion for art was chiefly a passion to live the life of artists, she was quite content to neglect her own work. She liked the warmth of the studio, and the opportunity to smoke innumerable cigarettes; and she spoke in a low, pleasant voice of the love of art and the art of love. She made no clear distinction between the two.

Lawson was painting with infinite labour, working till he could hardly stand for days and then scraping out all he had done. He would have exhausted the patience of anyone but Ruth Chalice. At last he got into a hopeless muddle.

'The only thing is to take a new canvas and start afresh,' he said. 'I know exactly what I want now, and it won't take me long.'

Philip was present at the time, and Miss Chalice said to him:

'Why don't you paint me too? You'll be able to learn a lot by watching Mr Lawson.'

It was one of Miss Chalice's delicacies that she always addressed her lovers by their surnames.

'I should like it awfully if Lawson wouldn't mind.'

'I don't care a damn,' said Lawson.

It was the first time that Philip set about a portrait, and he began with trepidation but also with pride. He sat by Lawson and painted as he saw him paint. He profited by the example and by the advice which both Lawson and Miss Chalice freely gave him. At last Lawson finished and invited Clutton in to criticize. Clutton had only just come back to Paris. From Provence he had drifted down to Spain, eager to see Velasquez at Madrid, and thence he had gone to Toledo. He stayed there three months, and he was returned with a name new to the young men: he had wonderful things to say of a painter called El Greco, who it appeared could only be studied in Toledo.

'Oh, yes, I know about him,' said Lawson, 'he's the old master whose distinction it is that he painted as badly as the moderns.'

Clutton, more taciturn than ever, did not answer, but he looked at Lawson with a sardonic air.

'Are you going to show us the stuff you've brought back from Spain?' asked Philip.

'I didn't paint in Spain, I was too busy.'

'What did you do then?'

'I thought things out. I believe I'm through with the impressionists; I've got an idea they'll seem very thin and superficial in a few years. I want to make a clean sweep of everything I've learnt and start afresh. When I came back I destroyed every-

227

thing I'd painted. I've got nothing in my studio now but an easel, my paints, and some clean canvases.'

'What are you going to do?'

'I don't know yet. I've only got an inkling of what I want.'

He spoke slowly, in a curious manner, as though he were straining to hear something which was only just audible. There seemed to be a mysterious force in him which he himself did not understand, but which was struggling obscurely to find an outlet. His strength impressed you. Lawson dreaded the criticism he asked for and had discounted the blame he thought he might get by affecting a contempt for any opinion of Clutton's; but Philip knew there was nothing which would give him more pleasure than Clutton's praise. Clutton loked at the portrait for some time in silence, then glanced at Philip's picture, which was standing on an easel.

'What's that?' he asked.

'Oh, I had a shot at a portrait too.'

'The sedulous ape,' he murmured.

He turned away again to Lawson's canvas. Philip reddened but did not speak.

'Well, what d'you think of it?' asked Lawson at length.

'The modelling's jolly good,' said Clutton. 'And I think it's very well drawn.'

'D'you think the values are all right?'

'Quite.'

Lawson smiled with delight. He shook himself in his clothes like a wet dog.

'I say, I'm jolly glad you like it.'

'I don't. I don't think it's of the smallest importance.'

Lawson's face fell, and he stared at Clutton with astonishment : he had no notion what he meant. Clutton had no gift of expression in words, and he spoke as though it were an effort. What he had to say was confused, halting, and verbose; but Philip knew the words which served as the text of his rambling discourse. Clutton, who never read, had heard them first from Cronshaw; and though they had made small impression, they had remained in his memory; and lately, emerging on a sudden, had acquired the character of a revelation : a good painter had two chief objects to paint, namely, man and the intention of his soul. The impressionists had been occupied with other problems, they had painted man admirably, but they had troubled themselves as little as the English portrait painters of the eighteenth century with the intention of his soul.

'But when you try to get that you become literary,' said

Lawson, interrupting. 'Let me paint the man like Manet, and the intention of his soul can go to the devil.'

'That would be all very well if you could beat Manet at his own game, but you can't get anywhere near him. You can't feed yourself on the day before yesterday; it's ground which has been swept dry. You must go back. It's when I saw the Grecos that I felt one could get something more out of portraits than we knew before.'

'It's just going back to Ruskin,' cried Lawson.

'No – you see, he went for morality : I don't care a damn for morality : teaching doesn't come in, ethics and all that, but passion and emotion. The greatest portrait painters have painted both, man and the intention of his soul; Rembrandt and El Greco; it's only the second-raters who've only painted man. A lily of the valley would be lovely even if it didn't smell, but its more lovely because it has perfume. That picture' – he pointed to Lawson's portrait – 'Well, the drawing's all right and so's the modelling all right, but just conventional; it ought to be drawn and modelled so that you know the girl's a lousy slut. Correctness is all very well : El Greco made his people eight feet high because he wanted to express something he couldn't get any other way.'

'Damn El Greco,' said Lawson, 'what's the good of jawing about a man when we haven't a chance of seeing any of his work?'

Clutton shrugged his shoulders, smoked a cigarette in silence, and went away. Philip and Lawson looked at one another.

'There's something in what he says,' said Philip.

Lawson stared ill-temperedly at his picture.

'How the devil is one to get the intention of the soul except by painting exactly what one sees?'

About this time Philip made a new friend. On Monday morning models assembled at the school in order that one might be chosen for the week, and one day a young man was taken who was plainly not a model by profession. Philip's attention was attracted by the manner in which he held himself : when he got on to the stand he stood firmly on both feet, square, with clenched hands, and with his head defiantly thrown forward; the attitude emphasized his fine figure; there was no fat on him, and his muscles stood out as though they were of iron. His head, close-cropped, was well-shaped, and he wore a short beard; he had large, dark eyes and heavy eyebrows. He held the pose hour after hour without appearance of fatigue.

229

There was in his mien a mixture of shame and of determination. His air of passionate energy excited Philip's romantic imagination, and when, the sitting ended, he saw him in his clothes, it seemed to him that he wore them as though he were a king in rags. He was uncommunicative, but in a day or two Mrs Otter told Philip that the model was a Spaniard and that he had never sat before.

'I suppose he was starving,' said Philip.

'Have you noticed his clothes? They're quite neat and decent, aren't they?'

It chanced that Potter, one of the Americans who worked at Amitrano's, was going to Italy for a couple of months, and offered his studio to Philip. Philip was pleased. He was growing a little impatient of Lawson's peremptory advice and wanted to be by himself. At the end of the week he went up to the model and on the pretence that his drawing was not finished asked whether he would come and sit to him one day.

'I'm not a model,' the Spaniard answered. 'I have other things to do next week.'

'Come and have luncheon with me now, and we'll talk about it,' said Philip, and as the other hesitated, he added with a smile: 'It won't hurt you to lunch with me.'

With a shrug of the shoulders the model consented, and they went off to a *crémerie*. The Spaniard spoke broken French, fluent but difficult to follow, and Philip managed to get on well enough with him. He found out that he was a writer. He had come to Paris to write novels and kept himself meanwhile by all the expedients possible to a penniless man: he gave lessons, he did any translations he could get hold of, chiefly business documents, and at last had been driven to make money by his fine figure. Sitting was well paid, and what he had earned during the last week was enough to keep him for two more; he told Philip, amazed, that he could live easily on two francs a day; but it filled him with shame that he was obliged to show his body for money, and he looked upon sitting as a degradation which only hunger could excuse. Philip explained that he did not want him to sit for the figure, but only for the head; he wished to do a portrait of him which he might send to the next Salon.

'But why should you want to paint me?' asked the Spaniard.

Philip answered that the head interested him, he thought he could do a good portrait.

'I can't afford the time. I grudge every minute that I have to rob from my writing.'

'But it would only be in the afternoon. I work at the school in the morning. After all, it's better to sit to me than to do translations of legal documents.'

There were legends in the Latin Quarter of a time when students of different countries lived together intimately, but this was long since passed, and now the various nations were almost as much separated as in an Oriental city. At Julian's and at the Beaux-Arts a French student was looked upon with disfavour by his fellow countrymen when he consorted with foreigners, and it was difficult for an Englishman to know more than quite superficially any native inhabitants of the city in which he dwelt. Indeed, many of the students after living in Paris for five years knew no more French than served them in shops and lived as English a life as though they were working in South Kensington.

Philip, with his passion for the romantic, welcomed the opportunity to get in touch with a Spaniard; he used all his persuasiveness to overcome the man's reluctance.

'I'll tell you what I'll do,' said the Spaniard at last. 'I'll sit to you, but not for money, for my own pleasure.'

Philip expostulated, but the other was firm, and at length they arranged that he should come on the following Monday at one o'clock. He gave Philip a card on which was printed his name: Miguel Ajuria.

Miguel sat regularly, and though he refused to accept payment he borrowed fifty francs from Philip every now and then: it was a little more expensive than if Philip had paid for the sittings in the usual way; but gave the Spaniard a satisfactory feeling that he was not earning his living in a degrading manner. His nationality made Philip regard him as a representative of romance, and he asked him about Seville and Granada, Velasquez and Calderón. But Miguel had no patience with the grandeur of his country. For him, as for so many of his compatriots, France was the only country for a man of intelligence and Paris the centre of the world.

'Spain is dead,' he cried. 'It has no writers, it has no art, it has nothing.'

Little by little, with the exuberant rhetoric of his race, he revealed his ambitions. He was writing a novel which he hoped would make his name. He was under the influence of Zola, and he had set his scene in Paris. He told Philip the story at length. To Philip it seemed crude and stupid; the naïve obscenity – *c'est la vie, mon cher, c'est la vie*, he cried – the naïve obscenity served only to emphasize the conventionality of the

231

anecdote. He had written for two years, amid incredible hardships, denying himself all the pleasures of life which had attracted him to Paris, fighting with starvation for art's sake, determined that nothing should hinder his great achievement. The effort was heroic.

'But why don't you write about Spain?' cried Philip. 'It would be so much more interesting. You know the life.'

'But Paris is the only place worth writing about. Paris is life.'

One day he brought part of the manuscript, and in his bad French, translating excitedly as he went along so that Philip could scarcely understand, he read passages. It was lamentable. Philip, puzled, looked at the picture he was painting: the mind behind that broad brow was trivial; and the flashing, passionate eyes saw nothing in life but the obvious. Philip was not satisfied with his portrait, and at the end of a sitting he nearly always scraped out what he had done. It was all very well to aim at the intention of the soul: who could tell what that was when people seemed a mass of contradictions? He liked Miguel, and it distressed him to realize that his magnificent struggle was futile: he had everything to make a good writer but talent. Philip looked at his own work. How could you tell whether there was anything in it or whether you were wasting your time? It was clear that the will to achieve could not help you and confidence in yourself meant nothing. Philip thought of Fanny Price; she had a vehement belief in her talent; her strength of will was extraordinary.

'If I thought I wasn't going to be really good, I'd rather give up painting,' said Philip. 'I don't see any use in being a second-rate painter.'

Then one morning when he was going out, the *concierge* called out to him that there was a letter. Nobody wrote to him but his Aunt Louisa and sometimes Hayward, and this was a handwriting he did not know. The letter was as follows:

Please come at once when you get this. I couldn't put up with it any more. Please come yourself. I can't bear the thought that anyone else should touch me. I want you to have everything.

F. Price

I have not had anything to eat for three days.

Philip felt on a sudden sick with fear. He hurried to the house in which she lived. He was astonished that she was in Paris at all. He had not seen her for months and imagined she had long since returned to England. When he arrived he asked the *concierge* whether she was in.

'Yes, I've not seen her go out for two days.'

Philip ran upstairs and knocked at the door. There was no reply. He called her name. The door was locked, and on bending down he found the key was in the lock.

'Oh, my God, I hope she hasn't done something awful,' he cried aloud.

He ran down and told the porter that she was certainly in the room. He had had a letter from her and feared a terrible accident. He suggested breaking open the door. The porter, who had been sullen and disinclined to listen, became alarmed; he could not take the responsibility of breaking into the room; they must go for the *commissaire de police*. They walked together to the *bureau*, and then they fetched a locksmith. Philip found that Miss Price had not paid the last quarter's rent: on New Year's Day she had not given the *concierge* the present which old-established custom led him to regard as a right. The four of them went upstairs, and they knocked again at the door. There was no reply. The locksmith set to work, and at last they entered the room. Philip gave a cry and instinctively covered his eyes with his hands. The wretched woman was hanging with a rope round her neck, which she had tied to a hook in the ceiling fixed by some previous tenant to hold up the curtains of the bed. She had moved her own little bed out of the way and had stood on a chair, which had been kicked away. It was lying on its side on the floor. They cut her down. The body was quite cold.

XLIX

THE story which Philip made out in one way and another was terrible. One of the grievances of the women-students was that Fanny Price would never share their gay meals in restaurants, and the reason was obvious: she had been oppressed by dire poverty. He remembered the luncheon they had eaten together when first he came to Paris and the ghoulish appetite which had disgusted him: he realized now that she ate in that manner because she was ravenous. The *concierge* told him what her food had consisted of. A bottle of milk was left for her every day and she brought in her own loaf of bread; she ate half the loaf and drank half the milk at midday when she came back from the school, and consumed the rest in the evening. It was the same day after day. Philip thought with anguish of what she must have endured. She had never given anyone to understand that she was poorer than the rest, but it was clear that her money had been coming to an end, and at last she could not afford to come any more to the studio. The little room was almost bare of furniture, and there were no other clothes than the shabby brown dress she had always worn. Philip searched among her things for the address of some friend with whom he could communicate. He found a piece of paper on which his own name was written a score of times. It gave him a peculiar shock. He supposed it was true that she had loved him; he thought of the emaciated body, in the brown dress, hanging from the nail in the ceiling; and he shuddered. But if she had cared for him, why did she not let him help her? He would so gladly have done all he could. He felt remorseful because he had refused to see that she looked upon him with any particular feeling, and now these words in her letter were infinitely pathetic: *I can't bear the thought that anyone else should touch me.* She had died of starvation.

Philip found at length a letter signed: *your loving brother, Albert.* It was two or three weeks old, dated from some road in Surbiton, and refused a loan of five pounds. The writer had his wife and family to think of, he didn't feel justified in lending money, and his advice was that Fanny should come back to London and try to get a situation. Philip telegraphed to Albert Price, and in a little while an answer came:

Deeply distressed. Very awkward to leave my business. Is presence essential? Price

Philip wired a succinct affirmative, and next morning a stranger presented himself at the studio.

'My name's Price,' he said, when Philip opened the door.

He was a commonish man in black with a band round his bowler hat; he had something of Fanny's clumsy look; he wore a stubbly moustache, and had a Cockney accent. Philip asked him to come in. He cast sidelong glances round the studio while Philip gave him details of the accident and told him what he had done.

'I needn't see her, need I?' asked Albert Price. 'My nerves aren't very strong, and it takes very little to upset me.'

He began to talk freely. He was a rubber-merchant, and he had a wife and three children. Fanny was a governess, and he couldn't make out why she hadn't stuck to that instead of coming to Paris.

'Me and Mrs Price told her Paris was no place for a girl. And there's no money in art – never 'as been.'

It was plain enough that he had not been on friendly terms with his sister, and he resented her suicide as a last injury that she had done him. He did not like the idea that she had been forced to it by poverty; that seemed to reflect on the family. The idea struck him that possibly there was a more respectable reason for her act.

'I suppose she 'adn't any trouble with a man, 'ad she? You know what I mean, Paris and all that. She might 'ave done it so as not to disgrace herself.'

Philip felt himself reddening and cursed his weakness. Price's keen little eyes seemed to suspect him of an intrigue.

'I believe your sister to have been perfectly virtuous,' he answered acidly. 'She killed herself because she was starving.'

'Well, it's very 'ard on her family, Mr Carey. She only 'ad to write to me. I wouldn't have let my sister want.'

Philip had found the brother's address only by reading the letter in which he refused a loan; but he shrugged his shoulders: there was no use in recrimination. He hated the little man and wanted to have done with him as soon as possible. Albert Price also wished to get through the necessary business quickly so that he could get back to London. They went to the tiny room in which poor Fanny had lived. Albert Price looked at the pictures and the furniture.

'I don't pretend to know much about art,' he said. 'I suppose these pictures would fetch something, would they?'

'Nothing,' said Philip.

'The furniture's not worth ten shillings.'

Albert Price knew no French and Philip had to do everything. It seemed that it was an interminable process to get the poor body safely hidden away under ground: papers had to be obtained in one place and signed in another; officials had to be seen. For three days Philip was occupied from morning till night. At last he and Albert Price followed the hearse to the cemetery at Montparnasse.

'I want to do the thing decent,' said Albert Price, 'but there's no use wasting money.'

The short ceremony was infinitely dreadful in the cold grey morning. Half a dozen people who had worked with Fanny Price at the studio came to the funeral, Mrs Otter because she was *massière* and thought it her duty, Ruth Chalice because she had a kind heart, Lawson, Clutton, and Flanagan. They had all disliked her during her life. Philip, looking across the cemetery crowded on all sides with monuments, some poor and simple, others vulgar, pretentious, and ugly, shuddered. It was horribly sordid. When they came out Albert Price asked Philip to lunch with him. Philip loathed him now and he was tired; he had not been sleeping well, for he dreamed constantly of Fanny Price in the torn brown dress, hanging from the nail in the ceiling; but he could not think of an excuse.

'You take me somewhere where we can get a regular slap-up lunch. All this is the very worst thing for my nerves.'

'Lavenue's is about the best place round here,' answered Philip.

Albert Price settled himself on a velvet seat with a sigh of relief. He ordered a substantial luncheon and a bottle of wine.

'Well, I'm glad that's over,' he said.

He threw out a few artful questions, and Philip discovered that he was eager to hear about the painter's life in Paris. He represented it to himself as deplorable, but he was anxious for details of the orgies which his fancy suggested to him. With sly winks and discreet sniggering he conveyed that he knew very well that there was a great deal more than Philip confessed. He was a man of the world, and he knew a thing or two. He asked Philip whether he had ever been to any of those places in Montmartre which are celebrated from Temple Bar to the Royal Exchange. He would like to say he had been to the Moulin Rouge. The luncheon was very good and the wine excellent. Albert Price expanded as the processes of digestion went satisfactorily forwards.

'Let's 'ave a little brandy,' he said when the coffee was brought, 'and blow the expense.'

He rubbed his hands.

'You know, I've got 'alf a mind to stay over tonight and go back tomorrow. What d'you say to spending the evening together?'

'If you mean you want me to take you round Montmartre tonight, I'll see you damned,' said Philip.

'I suppose it wouldn't be quite the thing.'

The answer was made so seriously that Philip was tickled.

'Besides it would be rotten for your nerves,' he said gravely.

Albert Price concluded that he had better go back to London by the four o'clock train, and presently he took leave of Philip.

'Well, good-bye, old man,' he said. 'I tell you what, I'll try and come over to Paris again one of these days and I'll look you up. And then we won't 'alf go on the razzle.'

Philip was too restless to work that afternoon, so he jumped on a bus and crossed the river to see whether there were any pictures on view at Durand-Ruel's. After that he strolled along the boulevard. It was cold and wind-swept. People hurried by wrapped up in their coats, shrunk together in an effort to keep out of the cold, and their faces were pinched and careworn. It was icy underground in the cemetery at Montparnasse among all those white tombstones. Philip felt lonely in the world and strangely home-sick. He wanted company. At that hour Cronshaw would be working, and Clutton never welcomed visitors; Lawson was painting another portrait of Ruth Chalice and would not care to be disturbed. He made up his mind to go and see Flanagan. He found him painting, but delighted to throw up his work and talk. The studio was comfortable, for the American had more money than most of them, and warm; Flanagan set about making tea. Philip looked at the two heads that he was sending to the Salon.

'It's awful cheek my sending anything,' said Flanagan, 'but I don't care, I'm going to send. D'you think they're rotten?'

'Not so rotten as I should have expected,' said Philip.

They showed in fact an astounding cleverness. The difficulties had been avoided with skill, and there was a dash about the way in which the paint was put on which was surprising and even attractive. Flanagan, without knowledge or technique, painted with the loose brush of a man who has spent a lifetime in the practice of the art.

'If one were forbidden to look at any picture for more than thirty seconds you'd be a great master, Flanagan,' smiled Philip.

These young people were not in the habit of spoiling one another with excessive flattery.

'We haven't got time in America to spend more than thirty seconds in looking at any picture,' laughed the other.

Flanagan, though he was the most scatter-brained person in the world, had a tenderness of heart which was unexpected and charming. Whenever anyone was ill he installed himself as sick-nurse. His gaiety was better than any medicine. Like many of his countrymen he had not the English dread of sentimentality which keeps so tight a hold on emotion; and, finding nothing absurd in the show of feeling, could offer an exuberant sympathy which was often grateful to his friends in distress. He saw that Philip was depressed by what he had gone through and with unaffected kindliness set himself boisterously to cheer him up. He exaggerated the Americanisms which he knew always made the Englishmen laugh and poured out a breathless stream of conversation, whimsical, high-spirited, and jolly. In due course they went out to dinner and afterwards to the

237

Gaîté Montparnasse, which was Flanagan's favourite place of amusement. By the end of the evening he was in his most extravagant humour. He had drunk a good deal, but any inebriety from which he suffered was due much more to his own vivacity than to alcohol. He proposed that they should go to the Bal Bullier, and Philip, feeling too tired to go to bed, willingly enough consented. They sat down at a table on the platform at the side, raised a little from the level of the floor so that they could watch the dancing, and drank a *bock*. Presently Flanagan saw a friend and with a wild shout leaped over the barrier on to the space where they were dancing. Philip watched the people. Bullier was not the resort of fashion. It was Thursday night and the place was crowded. There were a number of students of the various faculties, but most of the men were clerks or assistants in shops; they wore their everyday clothes, ready-made tweeds or queer tail-coats, and their hats, for they had brought them in with them, and when they danced there was no place to put them but their heads. Some of the women looked like servant-girls, and some were painted hussies, but for the most part they were shop-girls. They were poorly dressed in cheap imitation of the fashions on the other side of the river. The hussies were got up to resemble the music-hall artiste or the dancer who enjoyed notoriety at the moment; their eyes were heavy with black and their cheeks impudently scarlet. The hall was lit with great white lights, low down, which emphasized the shadows on the faces; all the lines seemed to harden under it, and the colours were most crude. It was a sordid scene. Philip leaned over the rail, staring down, and he ceased to hear the music. They danced furiously. They danced round the room, slowly, talking very little, with all their attention given to the dance. The room was hot, and their faces shone with sweat. It seemed to Philip that they had thrown off the guard which people wear on their expression, the homage to convention, and he saw them now as they really were. In that moment of abandon they were strangely animal: some were foxy and some were wolflike; and others had the long, foolish face of sheep. Their skins were sallow from the unhealthy life they led and the poor food they ate. Their features were blunted by mean interests, and their little eyes were shifty and cunning. There was nothing of nobility in their bearing, and you felt that for all of them life was a long succession of petty concerns and sordid thoughts. The air was heavy with the musty smell of humanity. But they danced furiously as though impelled by some strange power within them, and it seemed to Philip that they were driven forward by a rage for enjoyment. They were seeking desperately to escape from a world of horror. The desire for pleasure which Cronshaw said was the only motive of human action urged them blindly on, and the very vehemence of the desire seemed to rob it of all pleasure. They were hurried on by a great wind, helplessly, they knew not why and they knew not whither. Fate seemed to tower above them, and they danced as though everlasting darkness were beneath their feet. Their silence was vaguely alarming. It was as if life terrified them and robbed them of power of speech so that the shriek which was in their hearts died at their throats. Their eyes were haggard and grim; and notwithstanding the beastly lust that disfigured them, and the meanness of their faces, and the cruelty, notwithstanding the stupidness which was worst of all, the anguish of those fixed eyes made all that crowd terrible and pathetic. Philip loathed them, and yet his heart ached with the infinite pity which filled him.

He took his coat from the cloak-room and went out into the bitter coldness of the night.

L

PHILIP could not get the unhappy event out of his head. What troubled him most was the uselessness of Fanny's effort. No one could have worked harder than she, nor with more sincerity; she believed in herself with all her heart; but it was plain that self-confidence meant very little, all his friends had it, Miguel Ajuria among the rest; and Philip was shocked by the contrast between the Spaniard's heroic endeavour and the triviality of the thing he attempted. The unhappiness of Philip's life at school had called up in him the power of self-analysis; and this vice, as subtle as drug-taking, had taken possession of him so that he had now a peculiar keenness in the dissection of his feelings. He could not help seeing that art affected him differently from others. A fine picture gave Lawson an immediate thrill. His appreciation was instinctive. Even Flanagan felt certain things which Philip was obliged to think out. His own appreciation was intellectual. He could not help thinking that if he had in him the artistic temperament (he hated the phrase, but could discover no other) he would feel beauty in the emotional, unreasoning way in which they did. He began to wonder whether he had anything more than a superficial cleverness of the hand which enabled him to copy objects with accuracy. That was nothing. He had learned to despise technical dexterity. The important thing was to feel in terms of paint. Lawson painted in a certain way because it was his nature to, and through the imitativeness of a student sensitive to every influence, there pierced individuality. Philip looked at his own portrait of Ruth Chalice, and now that three months had passed he realized that it was no more than a servile copy of Lawson. He felt himself barren. He painted with the brain, and he could not help knowing that the only painting worth anything was done with the heart.

He had very little money, barely sixteen hundred pounds, and it would be necessary for him to practise the severest economy. He could not count on earning anything for ten years. The history of painting was full of artists who had earned nothing at all. He must resign himself to penury; and it was worth while if he produced work which was immortal; but he had a terrible fear that he would never be more than secondrate. Was it worth while for that to give up one's youth, and the gaiety of life, and the manifold chances of being? He knew the existence of foreign painters in Paris enough to see that the lives they led were narrowly provincial. He knew some who had dragged along for twenty years in the pursuit of a fame which always escaped them till they sank into sordidness and alcoholism. Fanny's suicide had aroused memories, and Philip heard ghastly stories of the way in which one person or another had escaped from despair. He remembered the scornful advice which the master had given poor Fanny: it would have been well for her if she had taken it and given up an attempt which was hopeless.

Philip finished his portrait of Miguel Ajuria and made up his mind to send it to the Salon. Flanagan was sending two pictures, and he thought he could paint as well as Flanagan. He had worked so hard on the portrait that he could not help feeling it must have merit. It was true that when he looked at it he felt that there was something wrong, though he could not tell what; but when he was away from it his spirits went up and he was not dissatisfied. He sent it to the Salon and it was refused. He did not mind much, since he had done all he could to persuade himself that there was little chance that it would be taken, till Flanagan a few days later rushed in to tell Lawson and Philip that one of his pictures was accepted. With a blank face Philip offered his congratulations, and Flanagan was so busy congratulating himself that he did not catch the note of irony which Philip could not prevent from coming into his voice. Lawson, quicker-witted, observed it and looked at Philip curiously. His own picture was all right, he knew that a day or two before, and he was vaguely resentful of Philip's attitude. But he was surprised at the sudden question which Philip put to him as soon as the American was gone.

'If you were in my place would you chuck the whole thing?'

'What *do* you mean?'

'I wonder if it's worth while being a second-rate painter. You see, in other things, if you're a doctor or if you're in business, it doesn't matter so much if you're mediocre. You make a living and you get along. But what is the good of turning out second-rate pictures?'

Lawson was fond of Philip, and, as soon as he thought he was seriously distressed by the refusal of his picture, he set himself to console him. It was notorious that the Salon had refused pictures which were afterwards famous; it was the first time Philip had sent, and he must expect a rebuff; Flanagan's success was explicable, his picture was showy and superficial: it was just the sort of thing a languid jury would see merit in. Philip grew impatient; it was humiliating that Lawson should think him capable of being seriously disturbed by so trivial a calamity and would not realize that his dejection was due to a deep-seated distrust of his powers.

Of late Clutton had withdrawn himself somewhat from the group who took their meals at Gravier's, and lived very much by himself. Flanagan said he was in love with a girl, but Clutton's austere countenance did not suggest passion; and Philip thought it more probable that he separated himself from his friends so that he might grow clear with the new ideas which were in him. But that evening, when the others had left the restaurant to go to a play and Philip was sitting alone, Clutton came in and ordered dinner. They began to talk, and finding Clutton more loquacious and less sardonic than usual, Philip determined to take advantage of his good humour.

'I say, I wish you'd come and look at my picture,' he said. 'I'd like to know what you think of it.'

'No, I won't do that.'

'Why not?' asked Philip, reddening.

The request was one which they all made of one another, and no one ever thought of refusing. Clutton shrugged his shoulders.

'People ask you for criticism, but they only want praise. Besides, what's the good of criticism? What does it matter if your picture is good or bad?'

'It matters to me.'

'No. The only reason that one paints is that one can't help it. It's a function like any of the other functions of the body, only comparatively few people have got it. One paints for one-self: otherwise one would commit suicide. Just think of it, you spend God knows how long trying to get something on to canvas, putting the sweat of your soul into it, and what is the result? Ten to one it will be refused at the Salon; if it's ac-cepted, people glance at it for ten seconds as they pass; if you're lucky some ignorant fool will buy it and put it on his walls and look at it as little as he looks at his dining-room table. Criticism has nothing to do with the artist. It judges objectively, but the objective doesn't concern the artist.'

Clutton put his hands over his eyes so that he might concen-trate his mind on what he wanted to say.

'The artist gets a peculiar sensation from something he sees, and is impelled to express it and, he doesn't know why, he can only express his feeling by lines and colours. It's like a musician; he'll read a line or two, and a certain combination of notes presents itself to him: he doesn't know why such and such words call forth in him such and such notes; they just do. And I'll tell you another reason why criticism is meaningless: a great painter forces the world to see nature as he sees it; but in the next generation another painter sees the world in an-other way, and then the public judges him not by himself but by his predecessor. So the Barbizon people taught our fathers to look at trees in a certain manner, and when Monet came along and painted differently, people said: But trees aren't like that. It never struck them that trees are exactly how a painter chooses to see them. We paint from within outwards – if we force our vision on the world it calls us great painters; if we don't it ignores us; but *we* are the same. We don't attach any meaning to greatness or to smallness. What happens to our work afterwards is unimportant; we have got all we could out of it while we were doing it.'

There was a pause while Clutton with voracious appetite de-voured the food that was set before him. Philip, smoking a cheap cigar, observed him closely. The ruggedness of the head, which looked as though it were carved from a stone refractory to the sculptor's chisel, the rough mane of dark hair, the great nose, and the massive bones of the jaw, suggested a man of strength; and yet Philip wondered whether perhaps the mask concealed a strange weakness. Clutton's refusal to show his work might be sheer vanity: he could not bear the thought of anyone's criticism, and he would not expose himself to the chance of a refusal from the Salon; he wanted to be received as a master and would not risk comparisons with other work which might force him to diminish his own opinion of himself. During the eighteen months Philip had known him Clutton had grown more harsh and bitter; though he would not come out into the open and compete with his fellows, he was indignant with the facile success of those who did. He had no patience with Lawson, and the pair were no longer on the intimate terms upon which they had been when Philip first knew them.

'Lawson's all right,' he said contemptuously, 'he'll go back to England, become a fashionable portrait painter, earn ten thousand a year and be an A.R.A. before he's forty. Portraits done by hand for the nobility and gentry!'

Philip, too, looked into the future, and he saw Clutton in twenty years, bitter, lonely, savage, and unknown; still in Paris, for the life there had got into his bones, ruling a small *cénacle* with a savage tongue, at war with himself and the world, producing little in his increasing passion for a perfection he could not reach; and perhaps sinking at last into drunkenness. Of late Philip had been captivated by an idea that since one had only one life it was important to make a success of it, but he did not count success by the acquiring of money or the achieving of fame; he did not quite know yet what he meant by it, perhaps variety of experience and the making the most of his abilities. It was plain anyway that the life which Clutton seemed destined to was failure. Its only justification would be the painting of imperishable masterpieces. He recollected Cronshaw's whimsical metaphor of the Persian carpet; he had thought of it often; but Cronshaw with his faun-like humour had refused to make his meaning clear: he repeated that it had none unless one discovered it for oneself. It was this desire to make a success of life which was at the bottom of Philip's uncertainty about continuing his artistic career. But Clutton began to talk again.

'D'you remember my telling you about that chap I met in Brittany? I saw him the other day here. He's just off to Tahiti. He was broke to the world. He was a *brasseur d'affaires*, a stockbroker I suppose you call it in English; and he had a wife and family, and he was earning a large income. He chucked it all to become a painter. He just went off and settled down in Brittany and began to paint. He hadn't got any money and did the next best thing to starving.'

'And what about his wife and family?' asked Philip.

'Oh, he dropped them. He left them to starve on their own account.'

'It sounds a pretty low-down thing to do.'

'Oh, my dear fellow, if you want to be a gentleman you must give up being an artist. They've got nothing to do with one another. You hear of men painting pot-boilers to keep an aged mother – well, it shows they're excellent sons, but it's no excuse for bad work. They're only tradesmen. An artist would let his mother go to the workhouse. There's a writer I know over here who told me that his wife died in childbirth. He was in love with her and he was mad with grief, but as he sat at the bedside watching her die he found himself making mental notes of how she looked and what she said and the things he was feeling. Gentlemanly, wasn't it?'

'But is your friend a good painter?' asked Philip.

'No, not yet, he paints just like Pissarro. He hasn't found himself, but he's got a sense of colour and a sense of decoration. But that isn't the question. It's the feeling, and that he's got. He's behaved like a perfect cad to his wife and children, he's always behaving like a perfect cad; the way he treats the people who've helped him – and sometimes he's been saved from starvation merely by the kindness of his friends – is simply beastly. He just happens to be a great artist.'

Philip pondered over the man who was willing to sacrifice everything, comfort, home, money, love, honour, duty, for the sake of getting on to canvas with paint the emotion which the world gave him. It was magnificent, and yet his courage failed him.

Thinking of Cronshaw recalled to him the fact that he had not seen him for a week, and so, when Clutton left him, he wandered along to the café in which he was certain to find the writer. During the first few months of his stay in Paris Philip had accepted as gospel all that Cronshaw said, but Philip had a practical outlook and he grew impatient with the theories which resulted in no action. Cronshaw's slim bundle of poetry did not seem a substantial result for a life which was sordid. Philip could not wrench out of his nature the instincts of the middle-class from which he came; and the penury, the hack work which Cronshaw did to keep body and soul together, the monotony of existence between the slovenly attic and the café table, jarred with his respectability. Cronshaw was astute enough to know that the young man disapproved of him, and he attacked his philistinism with an irony which was sometimes playful but often very keen.

'You're a tradesman,' he told Philip, 'you want to invest life in consols so that it shall bring you in a safe three per cent. I'm a spendthrift, I run through my capital. I shall spend my last penny with my last heartbeat.'

The metaphor irritated Philip, because it assumed for the speaker a romantic attitude and cast a slur upon the position which Philip instinctively felt had more to say for it than he could think of at the moment.

But this evening Philip, undecided, wanted to talk about himself. Fortunately it was late already and Cronshaw's pile of saucers on the table, each indicating a drink, suggested that he was prepared to take an independent view of things in general.

'I wonder if you'd give me some advice,' said Philip suddenly.

'You won't take it, will you?'

Philip shrugged his shoulders impatiently.

'I don't believe I shall ever do much good as a painter. I don't see any use in being second-rate. I'm thinking of chucking it.'

'Why shouldn't you?'

Philip hesitated for an instant.

'I suppose I like the life.'

A change came over Cronshaw's placid, round face. The corners of the mouth were suddenly depressed, the eyes sunk dully in their orbits; he seemed to become strangely bowed and old.

'This?' he cried, looking round the café in which they sat. His voice really trembled a little.

'If you can get out of it, do while there's time.'

Philip stared at him with astonishment, but the sight of emotion always made him feel shy, and he dropped his eyes. He knew that he was looking upon the tragedy of failure. There was silence. Philip thought that Cronshaw was looking upon his own life; and perhaps he considered his youth with its bright hopes and the disappointments which wore out the radiancy; the wretched monotony of pleasure, and the black future. Philip's eyes rested on the little pile of saucers, and he knew that Cronshaw's were on them too.

LI

Two months passed.

It seemed to Philip, brooding over these matters, that in the true painters, writers, musicians there was a power which drove them to such complete absorption in their work as to make it inevitable for them to subordinate life to art. Succumbing to an influence they never realized, they were merely dupes of the instinct that possessed them, and life slipped through their fingers unlived. But he had a feeling that life was to be lived rather than portrayed, and he wanted to search out the various experiences of it and wring from each moment all the emotion that it offered. He made up his mind at length to take a certain step and abide by the result, and, having made up his mind, he determined to take the step at once. Luckily enough the next morning was one of Foinet's days, and he resolved to ask him point-blank whether it was worth his while to go on with the study of art. He had never forgotten the master's brutal advice to Fanny Price. It had been sound. Philip could never get Fanny entirely out of his head. The studio seemed strange without her, and now and then the gesture of one of the women working there or the tone of a voice would give him a sudden start, reminding him of her; her presence was more noticeable now she was dead than it had ever been during her life; and he often dreamed of her at night, waking with a cry of terror. It was horrible to think of all the suffering she must have endured.

Philip knew that on the days Foinet came to the studio he lunched at a little restaurant in the Rue d'Odessa, and he hurried his own meal so that he could go and wait outside till the painter came out. Philip walked up and down the crowded street and at last saw Monsieur Foinet walking, with bent head, towards him; Philip was very nervous, but he forced himself to go up to him.

'Pardon, monsieur, I should like to speak to you for one moment.'

Foinet gave him a rapid glance, recognized him, but did not smile a greeting.

'Speak,' he said.

'I've been working here nearly two years now under you. I wanted to ask you to tell me frankly if you think it worth while for me to continue.'

Philip's voice was trembling a little. Foinet walked on without looking up. Philip, watching his face, saw no trace of expression upon it.

'I don't understand.'

'I'm very poor. If I have no talent I would sooner do something else.'

'Don't you know if you have talent?'

'All my friends know they have talent, but I am aware some of them are mistaken.'

Foinet's bitter mouth outlined the shadow of a smile, and he asked:

'Do you live near here?'

Philip told him where his studio was. Foinet turned round.

'Let us go there. You shall show me your work.'

'Now?' cried Philip.

'Why not?'

Philip had nothing to say. He walked silently by the master's side. He felt horribly sick. It had never struck him that Foinet would wish to see his things there and then; he meant, so that he might have time to prepare himself, to ask him if he would mind coming at some future date or whether he might bring them to Foinet's studio. He was trembling with anxiety. In his heart he hoped that Foinet would look at his picture, and that rare smile would come into his face, and he would shake Philip's hand and say: *'Pas mal.* Go on, my lad. You have talent, real talent.' Philip's heart swelled at the thought. It was such a relief, such a joy! Now he could go on with courage; and what did hardship matter, privation, and disappointment, if he arrived at last? He had worked very hard, it would be too cruel if all that industry were futile. And then with a start he remembered that he had heard Fanny Price say just that. They arrived at the house, and Philip was seized with fear. If he had dared he would have asked Foinet to go away. He did not want to know the truth. They went in and the *concierge* handed him a letter as they passed. He glanced at the envelope and recognized his uncle's handwriting. Foinet followed him up the stairs. Philip could think of nothing to say; Foinet was mute, and the silence got on his nerves. The professor sat down; and Philip without a word placed before him the picture which the Salon had rejected; Foinet nodded but did not speak; then Philip showed him the two portraits he had made of Ruth Chalice, two or three landscapes which he had painted at Moret, and a number of sketches.

'That's all,' he said presently, with a nervous laugh.

Monsieur Foinet rolled himself a cigarette and lit it.

'You have very little private means?' he asked at last.

'Very little,' answered Philip, with a sudden feeling of cold at his heart. 'Not enough to live on.'

'There is nothing so degrading as the constant anxiety about one's means of livelihood. I have nothing but contempt for the people who despise money. They are hypocrites or fools. Money is like a sixth sense without which you cannot make a complete use of the other five. Without an adequate income half the possibilities of life are shut off. The only thing to be careful about is that you do not pay more than a shilling for the shilling you earn. You will hear people say that poverty is the best spur to the artist. They have never felt the iron of it in their flesh. They do not know how mean it makes you. It exposes you to endless humiliation, it cuts your wings, it eats into your soul like a cancer. It is not wealth one asks for, but just enough to preserve one's dignity, to work unhampered, to be generous, frank, and independent. I pity with all my heart the artist, whether he writes or paints, who is entirely dependent for subsistence upon his art.'

Philip quietly put away the various things which he had shown.

'I'm afraid that sounds as if you didn't think I had much chance.'

Monsieur Foinet slightly shrugged his shoulders.

'You have a certain manual dexterity. With hard work and perseverance there is no reason why you should not become a careful, not incompetent painter. You would find hundreds who painted worse than you, hundreds who painted as well. I see no talent in anything you have shown me. I see industry and intelligence. You will never be anything but mediocre.'

Philip obliged himself to answer quite steadily.

'I'm very grateful to you for having taken so much trouble. I can't thank you enough.'

Monsieur Foinet got up and made as if to go, but he changed his mind and, stopping, put his hand on Philip's shoulder.

'But if you were to ask my advice, I should say: take your courage in both hands and try your luck at something else. It sounds very hard, but let me tell you this: I would give all I have in the world if someone had given me that advice when I was your age and I had taken it.'

Philip looked up at him with surprise. The master forced his lips into a smile, but his eyes remained grave and sad.

'It is cruel to discover one's mediocrity only when it is too late. It does not improve the temper.'

He gave a little laugh as he said the last words and quickly walked out of the room.

Philip mechanically took up the letter from his uncle. The sight of his handwriting made him anxious, for it was his aunt who always wrote to him. She had been ill for the last three months, and he had offered to go over to England and see her; but she, fearing it would interfere with his work, had refused. She did not want him to put himself to inconvenience; she said she would wait till August and then she hoped he would come and stay at the vicarage for two or three weeks. If by any chance she grew worse she would let him know, since she did not wish to die without seeing him again. If his uncle wrote to him it must be because she was too ill to hold a pen. Philip opened the letter. It ran as follows:

My dear Philip –

I regret to inform you that your dear Aunt departed this life early this morning. She died very suddenly, but quite peacefully. The change for the worse was so rapid that we had no time to send for you. She was fully prepared for the end and entered into rest with the complete assurance of a blessed resurrection and with resignation to the divine will of our blessed Lord Jesus Christ. Your Aunt would have liked you to be present at the funeral so I trust you will come as soon as you can. There is naturally a great deal of work thrown upon my shoulders and I am very much upset. I trust that you will be able to do everything for me.

Your affectionate uncle,
William Carey

LII

NEXT day Philip arrived at Blackstable. Since the death of his mother he had never lost anyone closely connected with him; his aunt's death shocked him and filled him also with a curious fear; he felt for the first time his own mortality. He could not realize what life would be for his uncle without the constant companionship of the woman who had loved and tended him for forty years. He expected to find him broken down with hopeless grief. He dread the first meeting; he knew that he could say nothing which would be of use. He rehearsed to himself a number of apposite speeches.

He entered the vicarage by the side-door and went into the dining-room. Uncle William was reading the paper.

'Your train was late,' he said, looking up.

Philip was prepared to give way to his emotion, but the matter-of-fact reception startled him. His uncle, subdued but calm, handed him the paper.

'There's a very nice little paragraph about her in *The Blackstable Times*,' he said.

Philip read it mechanically.

'Would you like to come up and see her?'

Philip nodded and together they walked upstairs. Aunt Louisa was lying in the middle of the large bed, with flowers all round her.

'Would you like to say a short prayer?' said the Vicar.

He sank on his knees, and because it was expected of him Philip followed his example. He looked at the little shrivelled face. He was only conscious of one emotion: what a wasted life! In a minute Mr Carey gave a cough, and stood up. He pointed to a wreath at the foot of the bed.

'That's from the Squire,' he said. He spoke in a low voice as though he were in church, but one felt that, as a clergyman, he found himself quite at home. 'I expect tea is ready'

They went down again to the dining-room. The drawn blinds gave a lugubrious aspect. The Vicar sat at the end of the table at which his wife had always sat and poured out the tea with ceremony. Philip could not help feeling that neither of them should have been able to eat anything, but when he saw that his uncle's appetite was unimpaired he fell to with his usual heartiness. They did not speak for a while. Philip set himself to eat an excellent cake with the air of grief which he felt was decent.

'Things have changed a great deal since I was a curate,' said the Vicar presently. 'In my young days the mourners used always to be given a pair of black gloves and a piece of black silk for their hats. Poor Louisa used to make the silk into dresses. She always said that twelve funerals gave her a new dress.'

Then he told Philip who had sent wreaths; there were twenty-four of them already; when Mrs Rawlingson, wife of the Vicar at Ferne, had died she had had thirty-two; but probably a good many more would come the next day; the funeral would start at eleven o'clock from the vicarage, and they should beat Mrs Rawlingson easily. Louisa never liked Mrs Rawlingson.

'I shall take the funeral myself. I promised Louisa I would never let anyone else bury her.'

Philip looked at his uncle with disapproval when he took a

second piece of cake. Under the circumstances he could not help thinking it greedy.

'Mary Ann certainly makes capital cakes. I'm afraid no one else will make such good ones.'

'She's not going?' cried Philip, with astonishment.

Mary Ann had been at the vicarage ever since he could remember. She never forgot his birthday, but made a point always of sending him a trifle, absurd but touching. He had a real affection for her.

'Yes,' answered Mr Carey. 'I didn't think it would do to have a single woman in the house.'

'But, good heavens, she must be over forty.'

'Yes, I think she is. But she's been rather troublesome lately, she's been inclined to take too much on herself, and I thought this was a very good opportunity to give her notice.'

'It's certainly one which isn't likely to recur,' said Philip.

He took out a cigarette, but his uncle prevented him from lighting it.

'Not till after the funeral, Philip,' he said gently.

'All right,' said Philip.

'It wouldn't be respectful to smoke in the house so long as your poor Aunt Louisa is upstairs.'

Josiah Graves, churchwarden and manager of the bank, came back to dinner at the vicarage after the funeral. The blinds had been drawn up, and Philip, against his will, felt a curious sensation of relief. The body in the house had made him uncomfortable: in life the poor woman had been all that was kind and gentle; and yet, when she lay upstairs in her bedroom, cold and stark, it seemed as though she cast upon the survivors a baleful influence. The thought horrified Philip.

He found himself alone for a minute or two in the dining-room with the churchwarden.

'I hope you'll be able to stay with your uncle a while,' he said. 'I don't think he ought to be left alone just yet.'

'I haven't made any plans,' answered Philip. 'If he wants me I shall be very pleased to stay.'

By way of cheering the bereaved husband the churchwarden during dinner talked of a recent fire at Blackstable which had partly destroyed the Wesleyan chapel.

'I hear they weren't insured,' he said, with a little smile.

'That won't make any difference,' said the Vicar. 'They'll get as much money as they want to rebuild. Chapel people are always ready to give money.'

'I see that Holden sent a wreath.'

Holden was the dissenting minister, and though for Christ's sake, who died for both of them, Mr Carey nodded to him in the street, he did not speak to him.

'I think it was very pushing,' he remarked. 'There were forty-one wreaths. Yours was beautiful. Philip and I admired it very much.'

'Don't mention it,' said the banker.

He had noticed with satisfaction that it was larger than anyone else's. It had looked very well. They began to discuss the people who attended the funeral. Shops had been closed for it, and the churchwarden took out of his pocket the notice which had been printed: *Owing to the funeral of Mrs Carey this establishment will not be opened till one o'clock.*

'It was my idea,' he said.

'I think it was very nice of them to close,' said the Vicar. 'Poor Louisa would have appreciated that.'

Philip ate his dinner. Mary Ann had treated the day as Sunday, and they had roast chicken and a gooseberry tart.

'I suppose you haven't thought about a tombstone yet?' said the churchwarden.

'Yes, I have. I thought of a plain stone cross. Louisa was always against ostentation.'

'I don't think one can do much better than a cross. If you're thinking of a text, what do you say to: *With Christ, which is far better?*'

The Vicar pursed his lips. It was just like Bismarck to try and settle everything himself. He did not like that text; it seemed to cast an aspersion on himself.

'I don't think I should put that. I much prefer: *The Lord has given and the Lord has taken away.*'

'Oh, do you? That always seems to be a little indifferent.'

The Vicar answered with some acidity, and Mr Graves replied in a tone which the widower thought too authoritative for the occasion. Things were going rather far if he could not choose his own text for his own wife's tombstone. There was a pause, and then the conversation drifted to parish matters. Philip went into the garden to smoke his pipe. He sat on a bench, and suddenly began to laugh hysterically.

A few days later his uncle expressed the hope that he would spend the next few weeks at Blackstable.

'Yes, that will suit me very well,' said Philip.

'I suppose it'll do if you go back to Paris in September.'

Philip did not reply. He had thought much of what Foinet said to him, but he was still so undecided that he did not wish to speak of the future. There would be something fine in giving up art because he was convinced that he could not excel; but unfortunately it would seem so only to himself: to others it would be an admission of defeat, and he did not want to confess that he was beaten. He was an obstinate fellow, and the suspicion that his talent did not lie in one direction made him inclined to force circumstances and aim notwithstanding precisely in that direction. He could not bear that his friends should laugh at him. This might have prevented him from ever taking the definite step of abandoning the study of painting, but the different environment made him on a sudden see things differently. Like many another he discovered that crossing the Channel makes things which had seemed important singularly futile. The life which had been so charming that he could not bear to leave it now seemed inept; he was seized with a distaste for the cafés, the restaurants with their ill-cooked food, the shabby way in which they all lived. He did not care any more what his friends thought about him: Cronshaw with his rhetoric, Mrs Otter with her respectability, Ruth Chalice with her affectations. Lawson and Clutton with their quarrels; he felt a revulsion from them all. He wrote to Lawson and asked him to send over all his belongings. A week later they arrived. When he unpacked his canvases he found himself able to examine his work without emotion. He noticed the fact with interest. His uncle was anxious to see his pictures. Though he had so greatly disapproved of Philip's desire to go to Paris, he accepted the situation now with equanimity. He was interested in the life of students and constantly put Philip questions about it. He was in fact a little proud of him because he was a painter, and when people were present made attempts to draw him out. He looked eagerly at the studies of models which Philip showed him. Philip set before him his portrait of Miguel Ajuria.

'Why did you paint him?' asked Mr Carey.

'Oh, I wanted a model, and his head interested me.'

'As you haven't got anything to do here I wonder you don't paint me.'

'It would bore you to sit.'

'I think I should like it.'

'We must see about it.'

Philip was amused at his uncle's vanity. It was clear that he was dying to have his portrait painted. To get something for

253

nothing was a chance not to be missed. For two or three days he threw out little hints. He reproached Philip for laziness, asked him when he was going to start work, and finally began telling everyone he met that Philip was going to paint him. At last there came a rainy day, and after breakfast Mr Carey said to Philip:

'Now, what d'you say to starting on my portrait this morning?' Philip put down the book he was reading and leaned back in his chair.

'I've given up painting,' he said.

'Why?' asked his uncle in astonishment.

'I don't think there's much object in being a second-rate painter, and I came to the conclusion that I should never be anything else.'

'You surprise me. Before you went to Paris you were quite certain that you were a genius.'

'I was mistaken,' said Philip.

'I should have thought now you'd taken up a profession you'd have the pride to stick to it. It seems to me that what you lack is perseverance.'

Philip was a little annoyed that his uncle did not even see how truly heroic his determination was.

'"A rolling stone gathers no moss,"' proceeded the clergyman. Philip hated that proverb above all, and it seemed to him perfectly meaningless. His uncle had repeated it often during the arguments which had preceded his departure from business. Apparently it recalled that occasion to his guardian.

'You're no longer a boy, you know; you must begin to think of settling down. First you insist on becoming a chartered accountant, and then you get tired of that and you want to become a painter. And now, if you please, you change your mind again. It points to ...'

He hesitated for a moment to consider what defects of character exactly it indicated, and Philip finished the sentence.

'Irresolution, incompetence, want of foresight, and lack of determination.'

The Vicar looked up at his nephew quickly to see whether he was laughing at him. Philip's face was serious, but there was a twinkle in his eyes which irritated him. Philip should really be getting more serious. He felt it right to give him a rap over the knuckles.

'Your money matters have nothing to do with me now. You're your own master; but I think you should remember that your money won't last for ever, and the unlucky deformity

254

you have doesn't exactly make it easier for you to earn your living.'

Philip knew by now that whenever anyone was angry with him his first thought was to say something about his club-foot. His estimate of the human race was determined by the fact that scarcely anyone failed to resist the temptation. But he had trained himself not to show any sign that the reminder wounded him. He had even acquired control over the blushing which in his boyhood had been one of his torments.

'As you justly remarked,' he answered, 'my money matters have nothing to do with you and I am my own master.'

'At all events you will do me the justice to acknowledge that I was justified in my opposition when you made up your mind to become an art-student.'

'I don't know so much about that. I daresay one profits more by the mistakes one makes off one's own bat than by doing the right thing on somebody else's advice. I've had my fling, and I don't mind settling down now.'

'What at?'

Philip was not prepared for the question, since in fact he had not made up his mind. He had thought of a dozen callings.

'The most suitable thing you could do is to enter your father's profession and become a doctor.'

'Oddly enough, that is precisely what I intend.'

He had thought of doctoring among other things, chiefly because it was an occupation which seemed to give a good deal of personal freedom, and his experience of life in an office had made him determine never to have anything more to do with one; his answer to the Vicar slipped out almost unawares, because it was in the nature of a repartee. It amused him to make up his mind in that accidental way, and he resolved then and there to enter his father's old hospital in the autumn.

'Then your two years in Paris may be regarded as so much wasted time?'

'I don't know about that. I had a very jolly two years, and I learned one or two useful things.'

'What?'

Philip reflected for an instant, and his answer was not devoid of a gentle desire to annoy.

'I learned to look at hands, which I'd never looked at before. And instead of just looking at houses and trees I learned to look at houses and trees against the sky. And I learned also that shadows are not black but coloured.'

'I suppose you think you're very clever. I think your flippancy is quite inane.'

LIII

TAKING the paper with him Mr Carey retired to his study. Philip changed his chair for that in which his uncle had been sitting (it was the only comfortable one in the room), and looked out of the window at the pouring rain. Even in that sad weather there was something restful about the green fields that stretched to the horizon. There was an intimate charm in the landscape which he did not remember ever to have noticed before. Two years in France had opened his eyes to the beauty of his own countryside.

He thought with a smile of his uncle's remark. It was lucky that the turn of his mind tended to flippancy. He had begun to realize what a great loss he had sustained in the death of his father and mother. That was one of the differences in his life which prevented him from seeing things in the same way as other people. The love of parents for their children is the only emotion which is quite disinterested. Among strangers he had grown up as best he could, but he had seldom been used with patience or forbearance. He prided himself on his self-control. It had been whipped into him by the mockery of his fellows. Then they called him cynical and callous. He had acquired calmness of demeanour and under most circumstances an unruffled exterior, so that now he could not show his feelings. People told him he was unemotional; but he knew that he was at the mercy of his emotions: an accidental kindness touched him so much that sometimes he did not venture to speak in order not to betray the unsteadiness of his voice. He remembered the bitterness of his life at school, the humiliation which he had endured, the banter which had made him morbidly afraid of making himself ridiculous; and he remembered the loneliness he had felt since, faced with the world, the disillusion and the disappointment caused by the difference between what it promised to his active imagination and what it gave. But notwithstanding he was able to look at himself from the outside and smile with amusement.

'By Jove, if I weren't flippant, I should hang myself,' he thought cheerfully.

His mind went back to the answer he had given his uncle when he asked him what he had learnt in Paris. He had learnt a good deal more than he told him. A conversation with Cronshaw had stuck in his memory, and one phrase he had used, a commonplace one enough, had set his brain working.

'My dear fellow,' Cronshaw said, 'there's no such thing as abstract morality.'

When Philip ceased to believe in Christianity he felt that a great weight was taken from his shoulders; casting off the responsibility which weighed down every action, when every action was infinitely important for the welfare of his immortal soul, he experienced a vivid sense of liberty. But he knew now that this was an illusion. When he put away the religion in which he had been brought up, he had kept unimpaired the morality which was part and parcel of it. He made up his mind therefore to think things out for himself. He determined to be swayed by no prejudices. He swept away the virtues and the vices, the established laws of good and evil, with the idea of finding out the rules of life for himself. He did not know whether rules were necessary at all. That was one of the things he wanted to discover. Clearly much that seemed valid seemed so only because he had been taught it from his earliest youth. He had read a number of books, but they did not help him much, for they were based on the morality of Christianity; and even the writers who emphasized the fact that they did not believe in it were never satisfied till they had framed a system of ethics in accordance with that of the Sermon on the Mount. It seemed hardly worth while to read a long volume in order to learn that you ought to behave exactly like everybody else. Philip wanted to find out how he ought to behave, and he thought he could prevent himself from being influenced by the opinions that surrounded him. But meanwhile he had to go on living, and, until he formed a theory of conduct, he made himself a provisional rule.

'Follow your inclinations with due regard to the policeman round the corner.'

He thought the best thing he had gained in Paris was a complete liberty of spirit, and he felt himself at last absolutely free. In a desultory way he had read a good deal of philosophy, and he looked forward with delight to the leisure of the next few months. He began to read at haphazard. He entered upon each system with a little thrill of excitement, expecting to find in each some guide by which he could rule his conduct; he felt himself like a traveller in unknown countries and as he pushed forward the enterprise fascinated him; he read emotionally, as other men read pure literature, and his heart leaped as he discovered in noble words what himself had obscurely felt. His mind was concrete and moved with difficulty in regions of the abstract; but, even when he could not follow the reasoning, it gave him a curious pleasure to follow the tortuosities of thoughts that threaded their nimble way on the edge of the incomprehensible. Sometimes great philosophers seemed to have nothing to say to him, but at others he recognized a mind with which he felt himself at home. He was like the explorer in Central Africa who comes suddenly upon wide uplands, with great trees in them and stretches of meadow, so that he might fancy himself in an English park. He delighted in the robust common sense of Thomas Hobbes; Spinoza filled him with awe, he had never before come in contact with a mind so noble, so unapproachable and austere; it reminded him of that statue by Rodin, *L'Âge d'Airain*, which he passionately admired; and then there was Hume: the scepticism of that charming philosopher touched a kindred note in Philip; and, revelling in the lucid style which seemed able to put complicated thought into simple words, musical and measured, he read as he might have read a novel, a smile of pleasure on his lips. But in none could he find exactly what he wanted. He had read somewhere that every man was born a Platonist, an Aristotelian, a Stoic, or an Epicurean; and the history of George Henry Lewes (besides telling you that philosophy was all moonshine) was there to show that the thought of each philosopher was inseparably connected with the man he was. When you knew that, you could guess to a great extent the philosophy he wrote. It looked as though you did not act in a certain way because you thought in a certain way, but rather that you thought in a certain way because you were made in a certain way. Truth had nothing to do with it. There was no such thing as truth. Each man was his own philosopher, and the elaborate systems which the great men of the past had composed were only valid for the writers.

The thing then was to discover what one was and one's system of philosophy would devise itself. It seemed to Philip that there were three things to find out: man's relation to the world he lives in, man's relation with the men among whom he lives, and finally man's relation to himself. He made an elaborate plan of study.

The advantage of living abroad is that, coming in contact with the manners and customs of the people among whom you live, you observe them from the outside and see that they have not the necessity which those who practise them believe. You cannot fail to discover that the beliefs which to you are self-evident to the foreigner are absurd. The year in Germany, the long stay in Paris, had prepared Philip to receive the sceptical teaching which came to him now with such a feeling of relief. He saw that nothing was good and nothing was evil: things were merely adapted to an end. He read *The Origin of Species*. It seemed to offer an explanation of much that troubled him. He was like an explorer now who has reasoned that certain natural features must present themselves, and, beating up a broad river, finds here the tributary that he expected, there the fertile, populated plains, and further on the mountains. When some great discovery is made the world is surprised afterwards that it was not accepted at once, and even on those who acknowledged its truth the effect is unimportant. The first readers of *The Origin of Species* accepted it with their reason; but their emotions, which are the ground of conduct, were untouched. Philip was born a generation after this great book was published, and much that horrified its contemporaries had passed into the feeling of the time, so that he was able to accept it with a joyful heart. He was intensely moved by the grandeur of the struggle for life, and the ethical rule which it suggested seemed to fit in with his predispositions. He said to himself that might was right. Society stood on one side, an organism with its own laws of growth and self-preservation, while the individual stood on the other. The actions which were to the advantage of society it termed virtuous and those which were not it called vicious. Good and evil meant nothing more than that. Sin was a prejudice from which the free man should rid himself. Society had three arms in its contest with the individual, laws, public opinion, and conscience: the first two could be met by guile, guile is the only weapon of the weak against the strong: common opinion put the matter well when it stated that sin consisted in being found out; but conscience was the traitor within the gates; it fought in each heart the battle of society, and caused the individual to throw himself, a wanton sacrifice, to the prosperity of his enemy. For it was clear that the two were irreconcilable, the state and the individual concious of himself. *That* uses the individual for its own ends, trampling upon him if he thwarts it, rewarding him with medals, pensions, honours, when he serves it faithfully; *this*, strong only in his independence, threads his way through the state, for convenience' sake, paying in money or service for certain benefits, but with no sense of obligation; and, indifferent to the rewards, asks only to be left alone. He is the independent traveller, who uses Cook's tickets because they save trouble,

but looks with good-humoured contempt on the personally conducted parties. The free man can do no wrong. He does everything he likes – if he can. His power is the only measure of his
morality. He recognizes the laws of the state and he can break
them without sense of sin, but if he is punished he accepts the
punishment without rancour. Society has the power.

But if for the individual there was no right and no wrong,
then it seemed to Philip that conscience lost its power. It was
with a cry of triumph that he seized the knave and flung him
from his breast. But he was no nearer to the meaning of life
than he had been before. Why the world was there and what
men had come into existence for at all was as inexplicable as
ever. Surely there must be some reason. He thought of Cronshaw's parable of the Persian Carpet. He offered it as a solution of the riddle, and mysteriously he stated that it was no
answer at all unless you found it out for yourself.

'I wonder what the devil he meant,' Philip smiled.

And so, on the last day of September, eager to put into practice all these new theories of life, Philip, with sixteen hundred
pounds and his club-foot, set out for the second time to London
to make his third start in life.

LIV

THE examination Philip had passed before he was articled to
a chartered accountant was sufficient qualification for him to
enter a medical school. He chose St Luke's because his father
had been a student there, and before the end of the summer
session had gone up to London for a day in order to see the
secretary. He got a list of rooms from him, and took lodgings
in a dingy house which had the advantage of being within two
minutes' walk of the hospital.

'You'll have to arrange about a part to dissect,' the secretary
told him. 'You'd better start on a leg; they generally do; they
seem to think it easier.'

Philip found that his first lecture was in anatomy, at eleven,
and about half past ten he limped across the road, and a little
nervously made his way to the Medical School. Just inside the
door a number of notices were pinned up, lists of lectures,
football fixtures, and the like; and these he looked at idly, trying to seem at his ease. Young men and boys dribbled in and
looked for letters in the rack, chatted with one another, and
passed downstairs to the basement, in which was the students'

reading-room. Philip saw several fellows with a desultory, timid look dawdling around, and surmised that, like himself, they were there for the first time. When he had exhausted the notices he saw a glass door which led into what was apparently a museum, and having still twenty minutes to spare he walked in. It was a collection of pathological specimens. Presently a boy of about eighteen came up to him.

'I say, are you first year?' he said.

'Yes,' answered Philip.

'Where's the lecture room, d'you know? It's getting on for eleven.'

'We'd better try and find it.'

They walked out of the museum into a long, dark corridor, with the walls painted in two shades of red, and other youths walking along suggested the way to them. They came to a door marked Anatomy Theatre. Philip found that there were a good many people already there. The seats were arranged in tiers, and just as Philip entered an attendant came in, put a glass of water on the table in the well of the lecture-room, and then brought in a pelvis and two thigh-bones, right and left. More men entered and took their seats, and by eleven the theatre was fairly full. There were about sixty students. For the most part they were a good deal younger than Philip, smooth-faced boys of eighteen, but there were a few who were older than he; he noticed one tall man, with a fierce red moustache, who might have been thirty; another little fellow with black hair, only a year or two younger; and there was one man with spectacles and a beard which was quite grey.

The lecturer came in, Mr Cameron, a handsome man with white hair and clean-cut features. He called out the long list of names. Then he made a little speech. He spoke in a pleasant voice, with well-chosen words, and he seemed to take a discreet pleasure in their careful arrangement. He suggested one or two books which they might buy and advised the purchase of a skeleton. He spoke of anatomy with enthusiasm: it was essential to the study of Surgery; a knowledge of it added to the appreciation of art. Philip pricked up his ears. He heard later that Mr Cameron lectured also to the students at the Royal Academy. He had lived many years in Japan, with a post at the University of Tokio, and he flattered himself on his appreciation of the beautiful.

'You will have to learn many tedious things,' he finished, with an indulgent smile, 'which you will forget the moment you have passed your final examination, but in anatomy it is better to have learned and lost than never to have learned at all.'

He took up the pelvis which was lying on the table and began to describe it. He spoke well and clearly.

At the end of the lecture the boy who had spoken to Philip in the pathological museum and sat next to him in the theatre suggested that they should go to the dissecting-room. Philip and he walked along the corridor again, and an attendant told them where it was. As soon as they entered Philip understood what the acrid smell was which he had noticed in the passage. He lit a pipe. The attendant gave a short laugh.

'You'll soon get used to the smell. I don't notice it myself.'

He asked Philip's name and looked at a list on the board.

'You've got a leg – number four.'

Philip saw that another name was bracketed with his own.

'What's the meaning of that?' he asked.

'We've very short of bodies just now. We've had to put two on each part.'

The dissecting-room was a large apartment painted like the corridors, the upper part a rich salmon and the dado a dark terracotta. At regular intervals down the long sides of the room, at right angles with the wall, were iron slabs, grooved like meat-dishes; and on each lay a body. Most of them were men. They were very dark from the preservative in which they had been kept, and the skin had almost the look of leather. They were extremely emaciated. The attendant took Philip up to one of the slabs. A youth was standing by it.

'Is your name Carey?' he asked.

'Yes.'

'Oh, then we've got this leg together. It's lucky it's a man, isn't it?'

'Why?' asked Philip.

'They generally always like a male better,' said the attendant. 'A female's liable to have a lot of fat about her.'

Philip looked at the body. The arms and legs were so thin that there was no shape in them, and the ribs stood out so that the skin over them was tense. A man of about forty-five with a thin, grey beard, and on his skull scanty, colourless hair: the eyes were closed and the lower jaw sunken. Philip could not feel that this had ever been a man, and yet in the row of them there was something terrible and ghastly.

'I thought I'd start at two,' said the young man who was dissecting with Philip.

'All right, I'll be here then.'

He had bought the day before the case of instruments which

was needful, and now he was given a locker. He looked at the boy who had accompanied him into the dissecting-room and saw that he was white.

'Make you feel rotten?' Philip asked him.

'I've never seen anyone dead before.'

They walked along the corridor till they came to the entrance of the school. Philip remembered Fanny Price. She was the first dead person he had ever seen, and he remembered how strangely it affected him. There was an immeasurable distance between the quick and the dead; they did not seem to belong to the same species; and it was strange to think that but a little while before they had spoken and moved and eaten and laughed. There was something horrible about the dead, and you could imagine that they might cast an evil influence on the living.

'What d'you say to having something to eat?' said his new friend to Philip.

They went down into the basement, where there was a dark room fitted up as a restaurant, and here the students were able to get the same sort of fare as they might have at an aerated bread shop. While they ate (Philip had a scone and butter and a cup of chocolate), he discovered that his companion was called Dunsford. He was a fresh-complexioned lad, with pleasant blue eyes and curly, dark hair, large-limbed, slow of speech and movement. He had just come from Clifton.

'Are you taking the Conjoint?' he asked Philip.

'Yes, I want to get qualified as soon as I can.'

'I'm taking it too, but I shall take the F.R.C.S. afterwards. I'm going in for surgery.'

Most of the students took the curriculum of the Conjoint Board of the College of Surgeons and the College of Physicians; but the more ambitious or the more industrious added to this the longer studies which led to a degree from the University of London. When Philip went to St Luke's changes had recently been made in the regulations, and the course took five years instead of four as it had done for those who registered before the autumn of 1892. Dunsford was well up in his plans and told Philip the usual course of events. The 'first conjoint' examination consisted of Biology, Anatomy, and Chemistry; but it could be taken in sections, and most fellows took their biology three months after entering the school. This science had been recently added to the list of subjects upon which the student was obliged to inform himself, but the amount of knowledge required was very small.

When Philip went back to the dissecting-room, he was a few minutes late, since he had forgotten to buy the loose sleeves which they wore to protect their shirts, and he found a number of men already working. His partner had started on the minute and was busy dissecting out cutaneous nerves. Two others were engaged on the second leg, and more were occupied with the arms.

'You don't mind my having started?'

'That's all right, fire away,' said Philip.

He took the book, open at a diagram of the dissected part, and looked at what they had to find.

'You're rather a dab at this,' said Philip.

'Oh, I've done a good deal of dissecting before, animals, you know, for the Pre Sci.'

There was a certain amount of conversation over the dissecting-table, partly about the work, partly about the prospects of the football season, the demonstrators, and the lectures. Philip felt himself a great deal older than the others. They were raw schoolboys. But age is a matter of knowledge rather than of years; and Newson, the active young man who was dissecting with him, was very much at home with his subject. He was perhaps not sorry to show off, and he explained very fully to Philip what he was about. Philip, notwithstanding his hidden stores of wisdom, listened meekly. Then Philip took up the scalpel and the tweezers and began working while the other looked on.

'Ripping to have him so thin,' said Newson, wiping his hands. 'The blighter can't have had anything to eat for a month.'

'I wonder what he died of,' murmured Philip.

'Oh, I don't know, any old thing, starvation chiefly, I suppose. . . . I say, look out, don't cut that artery.'

'It's all very fine to say, "don't cut that artery",' remarked one of the men working on the opposite leg. 'Silly old fool's got an artery in the wrong place.'

'Arteries always are in the wrong place,' said Newson. 'The normal's the one thing you practically never get. That's why it's called the normal.'

'Don't say things like that,' said Philip, 'or I shall cut myself.'

'If you cut yourself,' answered Newson, full of information, 'wash it at once with antiseptic. It's the one thing you've got to be careful about. There was a chap here last year who gave himself only a prick, and he didn't bother about it, and he got septicaemia.'

'Did he get all right?'

'Oh no, he died in a week. I went and had a look at him in the P.M. room.'

Philip's back ached by the time it was proper to have tea, and his luncheon had been so light that he was quite ready for it. His hands smelt of that peculiar odour which he had first noticed that morning in the corridor. He thought his muffin tasted of it too.

'Oh, you'll get used to that,' said Newson. 'When you don't have the good old dissecting-room stink about, you feel quite lonely.'

'I'm not going to let it spoil my appetite,' said Philip, as he followed up the muffin with a piece of cake.

LV

PHILIP'S ideas of the life of medical students, like those of the public at large, were founded on the pictures which Charles Dickens drew in the middle of the nineteenth century. He soon discovered that Bob Sawyer, if he ever existed, was no longer at all like the medical student of the present.

It is a mixed lot which enters upon the medical profession, and naturally there are some who are lazy and reckless. They think it is an easy life, idle away a couple of years; and then, because their funds come to an end or because angry parents refuse any longer to support them, drift away from the hospital. Others find the examinations too hard for them: one failure after another robs them of their nerve; and, panic-stricken, they forget as soon as they come into the forbidding buildings of the Conjoint Board the knowledge which before they had so pat. They remain year after year, objects of good-humoured scorn to younger men: some of them crawl through the examination of the Apothecaries' Hall; others become non-qualified assistants, a precarious position in which they are at the mercy of their employer; their lot is poverty, drunkenness, and Heaven only knows their end. But for the most part medical students are industrious young men of the middle-class with a sufficient allowance to live in the respectable fashion they have been used to; many are the sons of doctors who have already something of the professional manner; their career is mapped out: as soon as they are qualified they propose to apply for a hospital appointment, after holding which (and perhaps a trip to the Far East as a ship's doctor), they will join their father and spend the rest of their days in a country practice. One or two are marked out as exceptionally brilliant; they will take the various prizes and scholarships which are open each year to the deserving, get one appointment after another at the hospital, go on the staff, take a consulting-room in Harley Street and, specializing in one subject or another, become prosperous, eminent, and titled.

The medical profession is the only one which a man may enter at any age with some chance of making a living. Among the men of Philip's year were three or four who were past their first youth: one had been in the Navy, from which according to report he had been dismissed for drunkenness; he was a man of thirty, with a red face, a brusque manner, and a loud voice. Another was a married man with two children, who had lost money through a defaulting solicitor; he had a bowed look as if the world were too much for him; he went about his work silently, and it was plain that he found it difficult at his age to commit facts to memory. His mind worked slowly. His effort at application was painful to see.

Philip made himself at home in his tiny rooms. He arranged his books and hung on the walls such pictures and sketches as he possessed. Above him, on the drawing-room floor, lived a fifth-year man called Griffiths; but Philip saw little of him, partly because he was occupied chiefly in the wards and partly because he had been to Oxford. Such of the students as had been to a university kept a good deal together: they used a variety of means natural to the young in order to impress upon the less fortunate a proper sense of inferiority; the rest of the students found their Olympian serenity rather hard to bear. Griffiths was a tall fellow, with a quantity of curly red hair and blue eyes, a white skin, and a very red mouth; he was one of those fortunate people whom everybody liked, for he had high spirits and a constant gaiety. He strummed a little on the piano and sang comic songs with gusto; and evening after evening, while Philip was reading in his solitary room, he heard the shouts and the uproarious laughter of Griffiths' friends above him. He thought of those delightful evenings in Paris when they would sit in the studio, Lawson and he, Flanagan and Clutton, and talk of art and morals, the love-affairs of the present, and the fame of the future. He felt sick at heart. He found that it was easy to make a heroic gesture, but hard to abide by its results. The worst of it was that the work seemed to him very tedious. He had got out of the habit of being asked questions by demonstrators. His attention wandered at lectures.

Anatomy was a dreary science, a mere matter of learning by heart an enormous number of facts; dissection bored him; he did not see the use of dissecting out laboriously nerves and arteries when with much less trouble you could see in the diagrams of a book or in the specimens of the pathological museum exactly where they were.

He made friends by chance, but not intimate friends, for he seemed to have nothing in particular to say to his companions. When he tried to interest himself in their concerns, he felt that they found him patronizing. He was not of those who can talk of what moves them without caring whether it bores or not the people they talk to. One man, hearing that he had studied art in Paris, and fancying himself on his taste, tried to discuss art with him; but Philip was impatient of views which did not agree with his own; and, finding quickly that the other's ideas were conventional, grew monosyllabic. Philip desired popularity but could bring himself to make no advances to others. A fear of rebuff prevented him from affability, and he concealed his shyness, which was still intense, under a frigid taciturnity. He was going through the same experience as he had done at school, but here the freedom of the medical students' life made it possible for him to live a good deal by himself.

It was through no effort of his that he became friendly with Dunsford, the fresh-complexioned, heavy lad whose acquaintance he had made at the beginning of the session. Dunsford attached himself to Philip merely because he was the first person he had known at St Luke's. He had no friends in London, and on Saturday night he and Philip got into the habit of going together to the pit of a music-hall or the gallery of a theatre. He was stupid, but he was good-humoured and never took offence; he always said the obvious thing, but when Philip laughed at him merely smiled. He had a very sweet smile. Though Philip made him his butt, he liked him; he was amused by his candour and delighted with his agreeable nature: Dunsford had the charm which himself was acutely conscious of not possessing.

They often went to have tea at a shop in Parliament Street, because Dunsford admired one of the young women who waited. Philip did not find anything attractive in her. She was tall and thin, with narrow hips and the chest of a boy.

'No one would look at her in Paris,' said Philip scornfully.

'She's got a ripping face,' said Dunsford.

'What *does* the face matter?'

She had the small regular features, the blue eyes, and the

broad low brow which the Victorian painters, Lord Leighton, Alma Tadema, and a hundred others, induced the world they lived in to accept as a type of Greek beauty. She seemed to have a great deal of hair: it was arranged with peculiar elaboration and done over the forehead in what she called an Alexandra fringe. She was very anaemic. Her thin lips were pale, and her skin was delicate, of a faint green colour, without a touch of red even in the cheeks. She had very good teeth. She took great pains to prevent her work from spoiling her hands, and they were small, thin, and white. She went about her duties with a bored look.

Dunsford, very shy with women, had never succeeded in getting into conversation with her; and he urged Philip to help him.

'All I want is a lead,' he said, 'and then I can manage for myself.'

Philip, to please him, made one or two remarks, but she answered with monosyllables. She had taken their measure. They were boys, and she surmised they were students. She had no use for them. Dunsford noticed that a man with sandy hair and a bristly moustache, who looked like a German, was favoured with her attention whenever he came into the shop; and then it was only by calling her two or three times that they could induce her to take their order. She used the clients whom she did not know with frigid insolence, and when she was talking to a friend was perfectly indifferent to the calls of the hurried. She had the art of treating women who desired refreshment with just that degree of impertinence which irritated them without affording them an opportunity of complaining to the management. One day Dunsford told him her name was Mildred. He had heard one of the other girls in the shop address her.

'What an odious name,' said Philip.

'Why?' asked Dunsford. 'I like it.'

'It's so pretentious.'

It chanced that on this day the German was not there, and, when she brought the tea, Philip, smiling, remarked:

'Your friend's not here today.'

'I don't know what you mean,' she said coldly.

'I was referring to the nobleman with the sandy moustache. Has he left you for another?'

'Some people would do better to mind their own business,' she retorted.

She left them, and, since for a minute or two there was no one to attend to, sat down and looked at the evening paper which a customer had left behind him.

'You are a fool to put her back up,' said Dunsford.

'I'm really quite indifferent to the attitude of her vertebrae,' replied Philip.

But he was piqued. It irritated him that when he tried to be agreeable with a woman she should take offence. When he asked for the bill, he hazarded a remark which he meant to lead further.

'Are we no longer on speaking terms?' he smiled.

'I'm here to take orders and to wait on customers. I've got nothing to say to them, and I don't want them to say anything to me.'

She put down the slip of paper on which she had marked the sum they had to pay, and walked back to the table at which she had been sitting. Philip flushed with anger.

'That's one in the eye for you, Carey,' said Dunsford, when they got outside.

'Ill-mannered slut,' said Philip. 'I shan't go there again.'

His influence with Dunsford was strong enough to get him to take tea elsewhere, and Dunsford soon found another young woman to flirt with. But the snub which the waitress had inflicted on him rankled. If she had treated him with civility he would have been perfectly indifferent to her; but it was obvious that she disliked him rather than otherwise, and his pride was wounded. He could not suppress a desire to be even with her. He was impatient with himself because he had so petty a feeling, but three or four days' firmness, during which he would not go to the shop, did not help him to surmount it; and he came to the conclusion that it would be least trouble to see her. Having done so he would certainly cease to think of her. Pretexting an appointment one afternoon, for he was not a little ashamed of his weakness, he left Dunsford and went straight to the shop which he had vowed never again to enter. He saw the waitress the moment he came in and sat down at one of her tables. He expected her to make some reference to the fact that he had not been there for a week, but when she came up for his order she said nothing. He had heard her say to other customers:

'You're quite a stranger.'

She gave no sign that she had ever seen him before. In order to see whether she had really forgotten him, when she brought his tea, he asked:

'Have you seen my friend tonight?'

269

'No, he's not been in here for some days.'

He wanted to use this as the beginning of a conversation, but he was strangly nervous and could think of nothing to say. She gave him no opportunity, but at once went away. He had no chance of saying anything till he asked for his bill.

'Filthy weather, isn't it?' he said.

It was mortifying that he had been forced to prepare such a phrase as that. He could not make out why she filled him with such embarrassment.

'It don't make much difference to me what the weather is, having to be in here all day.'

There was an insolence in her tone that peculiarly irritated him. A sarcasm rose to his lips, but he forced himself to be silent.

'I wish to God she'd say something really cheeky,' he raged to himself, 'so that I could report her and get her sacked. It would serve her damned well right.'

LVI

HE could not get her out of his mind. He laughed angrily at his own foolishness: it was absurd to care what an anaemic little waitress said to him; but he was strangely humiliated. Though no one knew of the humiliation but Dunsford, and he had certainly forgotten, Philip felt that he could have no peace till he had wiped it out. He thought over what he had better do. He made up his mind that he would go to the shop every day; it was obvious that he had made a disagreeable impression on her, but he thought he had the wits to eradicate it; he would take care not to say anything at which the most susceptible person could be offended. All this he did, but it had no effect. When he went in and said good evening she answered with the same words, but when once he omitted to say it in order to see whether she would say it first, she said nothing at all. He murmured in his heart an expression which though frequently applicable to members of the female sex is not often used by them in polite society; but with an unmoved face he ordered his tea. He made up his mind not to speak a word, and left the shop without his usual good night. He promised himself that he would not go any more, but the next day at tea-time he grew restless. He tried to think of other things, but he had no command over his thoughts. At last he said desperately:

'After all there's no reason why I shouldn't go if I want to.'

The struggle with himself had taken a long time, and it was getting on for seven when he entered the shop.

'I thought you weren't coming,' the girl said to him, when he sat down.

His heart leaped in his bosom and he felt himself reddening. 'I was detained. I couldn't come before.'

'Cutting up people, I suppose?'

'Not so bad as that.'

'You are a stoodent, aren't you?'

'Yes.'

But that seemed to satisfy her curiosity. She went away and, since at that late hour there was nobody else at her tables, she immersed herself in a novelette. This was before the time of the sixpenny reprints. There was a regular supply of inexpensive fiction written to order by poor hacks for the consumption of the illiterate. Philip was elated; she had addressed him of her own accord; he saw the time approaching when his turn would come and he would tell her exactly what he thought of her. It would be a great comfort to express the immensity of his contempt. He looked at her. It was true that her profile was beautiful; it was extraordinary how English girls of that class had so often a perfection of outline which took your breath away, but it was as cold as marble; and the faint green of her delicate skin gave an impression of unhealthiness. All the waitresses were dressed alike, in plain black dresses, with a white apron, cuffs, and a small cap. On a half sheet of paper that he had in his pocket Philip made a sketch of her as she sat leaning over her book (she outlined the words with her lips as she read), and left it on the table when he went away. It was an inspiration, for next day, when he came in, she smiled at him.

'I didn't know you could draw,' she said.

'I was an art student in Paris for two years.'

'I showed that drawing you left be'ind you last night to the manageress and she *was* struck by it. Was it meant to be me?'

'It was,' said Philip.

When she went for his tea, one of the other girls came up to him.

'I saw that picture you done of Miss Rogers. It was the very image of her,' she said.

That was the first time he had heard her name, and when he wanted his bill he called her by it.

'I see you know my name,' she said, when she came.

'Your friend mentioned it when she said something to me about that drawing.'

271

'She wants you to do one of her. Don't you do it. If you once begin you'll have to go on, and they'll all be wanting you to do them.' Then without a pause, with peculiar inconsequence, she said: 'Where's that young fellow that used to come with you? Has he gone away.'

'Fancy you remembering him,' said Philip.

'He was a nice-looking young fellow.'

Philip felt quite a peculiar sensation in his heart. He did not know what it was. Dunsford had jolly curling hair, a fresh complexion, and a beautiful smile. Philip thought of these advantages with envy.

'Oh, he's in love,' said he, with a little laugh.

Philip repeated every word of the conversation to himself as he limped home. She was quite friendly with him now. When opportunity arose he would offer to make a more finished sketch of her, he was sure she would like that; her face was interesting, the profile was lovely, and there was something curiously fascinating about the chlorotic colour. He tried to think what it was like; at first he thought of pea soup; but, driving away that idea angrily, he thought of the petals of a yellow rosebud when you tore it to pieces before it had burst. He had no ill-feeling towards her now.

'She's not a bad sort,' he murmured.

It was silly of him to take offence at what she had said; it was doubtless his own fault; she had not meant to make herself disagreeable: he ought to be accustomed by now to making at first sight a bad impression on people. He was flattered at the success of his drawing; she looked upon him with more interest now that she was aware of this small talent. He was restless next day. He thought of going to lunch at the tea-shop, but he was certain there would be many people there then, and Mildred would not be able to talk to him. He had managed before this to get out of having tea with Dunsford, and, punctually at half past four (he had looked at his watch a dozen times), he went into the shop.

Mildred had her back turned to him. She was sitting down, talking to the German whom Philip had seen there every day till a fortnight ago and since then had not seen at all. She was laughing at what he said. Philip thought she had a common laugh, and it made him shudder. He called her, but she took no notice; he called her again; then, growing angry, for he was impatient, he rapped the table loudly with his stick. She approached sulkily.

'How d'you do?' he said.

272

'You seem to be in a great hurry.'

She looked down at him with the insolent manner which he knew so well.

'I say, what's the matter with you?' he asked.

'If you'll kindly give your order I'll get what you want. I can't stand talking all night.'

'Tea and toasted bun, please,' Philip answered briefly.

He was furious with her. He had *The Star* with him and read it elaborately when she brought the tea.

'If you'll give me my bill now I needn't trouble you again,' he said icily.

She wrote out the slip, placed it on the table, and went back to the German. Soon she was talking to him with animation. He was a man of middle height, with the round head of his nation and a sallow face; his moustache was large and bristling; he had on a tail-coat and grey trousers, and he wore a massive gold watch-chain. Philip thought the other girls looked from him to the pair at the table and exchanged significant glances. He felt certain they were laughing at him, and his blood boiled. He detested Mildred now with all his heart. He knew that the best thing he could do was to cease coming to the tea-shop, but he could not bear to think that he had been worsted in the affair, and he devised a plan to show her that he despised her. Next day he sat down at another table and ordered his tea from another waitress. Mildred's friend was there again and she was talking to him. She paid no attention to Philip, and so when he went out he chose a moment when she had to cross his path: as she passed he looked at her as though he had never seen her before. He repeated this for three or four days. He expected that presently she would take the opportunity to say something to him; he thought she would ask why he never came to one of her tables now, and he had prepared an answer charged with all the loathing he felt for her. He knew it was absurd to trouble, but he could not help himself. She had beaten him again. The German suddenly disappeared, but Philip still sat at other tables. She paid no attention to him. Suddenly he realized that what he did was a matter of complete indifference to her; he could go on in that way till doomsday, and it would have no effect.

'I've not finished yet,' he said to himself.

The day after he sat down in his old seat, and when she came up said good evening as though he had not ignored her for a week. His face was placid, but he could not prevent the mad beating of his heart. At that time the musical comedy had

lately leaped into public f
would be delighted to go to one.

'I say,' he said suddenly, 'I wonder if you'd dine with me one
night and come to *The Belle of New York*. I'll get a couple of
stalls.'

He added that last sentence in order to tempt her. He knew
that when girls went to the play it was either in the pit, or, if
some man took them, seldom to more expensive seats than the
upper circle. Mildred's pale face showed no change of expression.

'I don't mind,' she said.

'When will you come?'

'I get off early on Thursdays.'

They made arrangements. Mildred lived with an aunt at
Herne Hill. The play began at eight, so they must dine at seven.
She proposed that he should meet her in the second-class wait-
ing-room at Victoria Station. She showed no pleasure, but
accepted the invitation as though she conferred a favour.
Philip was vaguely irritated.

LVII

PHILIP arrived at Victoria Station nearly half an hour before
the time which Mildred had appointed, and sat down in the
second-class waiting-room. He waited and she did not come.
He began to grow anxious, and walked into the station to watch
the incoming suburban trains; the hour which she had fixed
passed, and still there was no sign of her. Philip was impatient.
He went into the other waiting-rooms and looked at the people
in them. Suddenly his heart gave a great thud.

'There you are. I thought you were never coming.'

'I like that after keeping me waiting all this time. I had half
a mind to go back home again.'

'But you said you'd come to the second-class waiting-room.'

'I didn't say any such thing. It isn't exactly likely I'd sit in
the second-class room when I could sit in the first, is it?'

Though Philip was sure he had not make a mistake, he said
nothing, and they got into a cab.

'Where are we dining?' she asked.

'I thought of the Adelphi Restaurant. Will that suit you?'

'I don't mind where we dine.'

She spoke ungraciously. She was put out by being kept
waiting and answered Philip's attempt at conversation with

monosyllables. She wore a long cloak of some rough, dark material and a crochet shawl over her head. They reached the restaurant and sat down at a table. She looked round with satisfaction. The red shades to the candles on the tables, the gold of the decorations, the looking-glasses, lent the room a sumptuous air.

'I've never been here before.'

She gave Philip a smile. She had taken off her cloak; and he saw that she wore a pale blue dress, cut square at the neck; and her hair was more elaborately arranged than ever. He had ordered champagne and when it came her eyes sparkled.

'You are going it,' she said.

'Because I've ordered fizz?' he asked carelessly, as though he never drank anything else.

'I *was* surprised when you asked me to do a theatre with you.'

Conversation did not go very easily, for she did not seem to have much to say; and Philip was nervously conscious that he was not amusing her. She listened carelessly to his remarks, with her eyes on other diners, and made no pretence that she was interested in him. He made one or two little jokes, but she took them quite seriously. The only sign of vivacity he got was when he spoke of the other girls in the shop; she could not bear the manageress and told him all her misdeeds at length.

'I can't stick her at any price and all the airs she gives herself. Sometimes I've got more than half a mind to tell her something she doesn't even think I know about.'

'What is that?' asked Philip.

'Well, I happen to know that she's not above going to Eastbourne with a man for the week-end now and again. One of the girls has a married sister who goes there with her husband, and she's seen her. She was staying at the same boarding-house, and she 'ad a wedding-ring on, and I know for one she's not married.'

Philip filled her glass, hoping that champagne would make her more affable; he was anxious that his little jaunt should be a success. He noticed that she held her knife as though it were a penholder, and when she drank protruded her little finger. He started several topics of conversation, but he could get little out of her, and he remembered with irritation that he had seen her talking nineteen to the dozen and laughing with the German. They finished dinner and went to the play. Philip was a very cultured young man, and he looked upon musical comedy with scorn. He thought the jokes vulgar and the melodies obvious;

275

it seemed to him that they did these things much better in France; but Mildred enjoyed herself thoroughly; she laughed till her sides ached, looking at Philip now and then when something tickled her to exchange a glance of pleasure; and she applauded rapturously.

'This is the seventh time I've been,' she said, after the first act, 'and I don't mind if I come seven times more.'

She was much interested in the women who surrounded them in the stalls. She pointed out to Philip those who were painted and those who wore false hair.

'It is horrible, these West-end people,' she said. 'I don't know how they can do it. She put her hand to her hair. 'Mine's all my own, every bit of it.'

She found no one to admire, and whenever she spoke of anyone it was to say something disagreeable. It made Philip uneasy. He supposed that next day she would tell the girls in the shop that he had taken her out and that he bored her to death. He disliked her, and yet, he knew not why, he wanted to be with her. On the way home he asked:

'I hope you've enjoyed yourself?'

'Rather.'

'Will you come out with me again one evening?'

'I don't mind.'

He could never get beyond such expressions as that. Her indifference maddened him.

'That sounds as if you didn't much care if you came or not.'

'Oh, if you don't take me out some other fellow will. I need never want for men who'll take me to the theatre.'

Philip was silent. They came to the station, and he went to the booking-office.

'I've got my season,' she said.

'I thought I'd take you home as it's rather late, if you don't mind.'

'Oh, I don't mind if it gives you any pleasure.'

He took a single first for her and a return for himself.

'Well, you're not mean, I will say that for you,' she said, when he opened the carriage door.

Philip did not know whether he was pleased or sorry when other people entered and it was impossible to speak. They got out at Herne Hill, and he accompanied her to the corner of the road in which she lived.

'I'll say good night to you here,' she said, holding out her hand. 'You'd better not come up to the door. I know what people are, and I don't want to have anybody talking.'

She said good night and walked quickly away. He could see the white shawl in the darkness. He thought she might turn round, but she did not. Philip saw which house she went into, and in a moment he walked along to look at it. It was a trim, common little house of yellow brick, exactly like all the other little houses in the street. He stood outside for a few minutes, and presently the window on the top floor was darkened. Philip strolled slowly back to the station. The evening had been unsatisfactory. He felt irritated, restless, and miserable.

When he lay in bed he seemed still to see her sitting in the corner of the railway carriage, with the white crochet shawl over her head. He did not know how he was to get through the hours that must pass before his eyes rested on her again. He thought drowsily of her thin face, with its delicate features, and the greenish pallor of her skin. He was not happy with her, but he was unhappy away from her. He wanted to sit by her side and look at her, he wanted to touch her, he wanted . . . the thought came to him and he did not finish it, suddenly he grew wide awake . . . he wanted to kiss the thin, pale mouth with its narrow lips. The truth came to him at last. He was in love with her. It was incredible.

He had often thought of falling in love, and there was one scene which he had pictured to himself over and over again. He saw himself coming into a ballroom; his eyes fell on a little group of men and women talking; and one of the women turned round. Her eyes fell upon him, and he knew that the gasp in his throat was in her throat too. He stood quite still. She was tall and dark and beautiful, with eyes like the night; she was dressed in white, and in her black hair shone diamonds; they stared at one another, forgetting that people surrounded them. He went straight up to her, and she moved a little towards him. Both felt that the formality of introduction was out of place. He spoke to her.

'I've been looking for you all my life,' he said.

'You've come at last,' she murmured.

'Will you dance with me?'

She surrendered herself to his outstretched hands and they danced. (Philip always pretended that he was not lame.) She danced divinely.

'I've never danced with anyone who danced like you,' she said.

She tore up her programme, and they danced together the whole evening.

'I'm so thankful that I waited for you,' he said to her. 'I knew that in the end I must meet you.'

People in the ballroom stared. They did not care. They did not wish to hide their passion. At last they went into the garden. He flung a light cloak over her shoulders and put her in a waiting cab. They caught the midnight train to Paris; and they sped through the silent, star-lit night into the unknown.

He thought of this old fancy of his, and it seemed impossible that he should be in love with Mildred Rogers. Her name was grotesque. He did not think her pretty; he hated the thinness of her, only that evening he had noticed how the bones of her chest stood out in evening dress; he went over her features one by one; he did not like her mouth, and the unhealthiness of her colour vaguely repelled him. She was common. Her phrases, so bald and few, constantly repeated, showed the emptiness of her mind; he recalled her vulgar little laugh at the jokes of the musical comedy; and he remembered the little finger carefully extended when she held her glass to her mouth; her manners, like her conversation, were odiously genteel. He remembered her insolence; sometimes he had felt inclined to box her ears; and suddenly, he knew not why, perhaps it was the thought of hitting her or the recollection of her tiny, beautiful ears, he was seized by an uprush of emotion. He yearned for her. He thought of taking her in his arms, the thin, fragile body, and kissing her pale mouth; he wanted to pass his fingers down the slightly greenish cheeks. He wanted her.

He had thought of love as a rapture which seized one so that all the world seemed spring-like, he had looked forward to an ecstatic happiness; but this was not happiness; it was a hunger of the soul, it was a painful yearning, it was a bitter anguish, he had never known before. He tried to think when it had first come to him. He did not know. He only remembered that each time he had gone into the shop, after the first two or three times, it had been with a little feeling in the heart that was pain; and he remembered that when she spoke to him he felt curiously breathless. When she left him it was wretchedness, and when she came to him again it was despair.

He stretched himself in his bed as a dog stretches himself. He wondered how he was going to endure that ceaseless aching of his soul.

LVIII

PHILIP woke early next morning, and his first thought was of
Mildred. It struck him that he might meet her at Victoria
Station and walk with her to the shop. He shaved quickly,
scrambled into his clothes, and took a bus to the station. He
was there by twenty to eight and watched the incoming trains.
Crowds poured out of them, clerks and shop-people at that
early hour, and thronged up the platform: they hurried along,
sometimes in pairs, here and there a group of girls, but more
often alone. They were white, most of them, ugly in the early
morning, and they had an abstracted look; the younger ones
walked lightly, as though the cement of the platform were
pleasant to tread, but the others went as though impelled by a
machine: their faces were set in an anxious frown.

At last Philip saw Mildred, and he went up to her eagerly.

'Good morning,' he said. 'I thought I'd come and see how
you were after last night.'

She wore an old brown ulster and a sailor hat. It was very
clear that she was not pleased to see him.

'Oh, I'm all right. I haven't got much time to waste.'

'D'you mind if I walk down Victoria Street with you?'

'I'm none too early. I shall have to walk fast,' she answered,
looking down at Philip's club-foot.

He turned scarlet.

'I beg your pardon. I won't detain you.'

'You can please yourself.'

She went on, and he with a sinking heart made his way home
to breakfast. He hated her. He knew he was a fool to bother
about her; she was not the sort of woman who would ever care
two straws for him, and she must look upon his deformity
with distaste. He made up his mind that he would not go in to
tea that afternoon, but, hating himself, he went. She nodded
to him as he came in and smiled.

'I expect I was rather short with you this morning,' she said.
'You see, I didn't expect you, and it came like a surprise.'

'Oh, it doesn't matter at all.'

He felt that a great weight had suddenly been lifted from
him. He was infinitely grateful for one word of kindness.

'Why don't you sit down?' he asked. 'Nobody's wanting you
just now.'

'I don't mind if I do.'

He looked at her, but could think of nothing to say; he racked his brains anxiously, seeking for a remark which should keep her by him; he wanted to tell her how much she meant to him; but he did not know how to make love now that he loved in earnest.

'Where's your friend with the fair moustache? I haven't seen him lately.'

'Oh, he's gone back to Birmingham. He's in business there. He only comes up to London every now and again.'

'Is he in love with you?'

'You'd better ask him,' she said, with a laugh. 'I don't know what it's got to do with you if he is.'

A bitter answer leaped to his tongue, but he was learning self-restraint.

'I wonder why you say things like that,' was all he permitted himself to say.

She looked at him with those indifferent eyes of hers.

'It looks as if you didn't set much store on me,' he added.

'Why should I?'

'No reason at all.'

He reached over for his paper.

'You are quick-tempered,' she said, when she saw the gesture. 'You do take offence easily.'

He smiled and looked at her appealingly.

'Will you do something for me?' he asked.

'That depends what it is.'

'Let me walk back to the station with you tonight.'

'I don't mind.'

He went out after tea and went back to his rooms, but at eight o'clock, when the shop closed, he was waiting outside.

'You are a caution,' she said, when she came out. 'I don't understand you.'

'I shouldn't have thought it was very difficult,' he answered bitterly.

'Did any of the girls see you waiting for me?'

'I don't know and I don't care.'

'They all laugh at you, you know. They say you're spoony on me.'

'Much you care,' he muttered.

'Now then, quarrelsome.'

At the station he took a ticket and said he was going to accompany her home.

'You don't seem to have much to do with your time,' she said.

'I suppose I can waste it in my own way.'

They seemed to be always on the verge of a quarrel. The fact was that he hated himself for loving her. She seemed to be constantly humiliating him, and for each snub that he endured he owed her a grudge. But she was in a friendly mood that evening, and talkative: she told him that her parents were dead; she gave him to understand that she did not have to earn her living, but worked for amusement.

'My aunt doesn't like my going to business. I can have the best of everything at home. I don't want you to think I work because I need to.'

Philip knew that she was not speaking the truth. The gentility of her class made her use this pretence to avoid the stigma attached to earning her living.

'My family's very well-connected,' she said.

Philip smiled faintly, and she noticed it.

'What are you laughing at?' she said quickly. 'Don't you believe I'm telling you the truth?'

'Of course I do,' he answered.

She looked at him suspiciously, but in a moment could not resist the temptation to impress him with the splendour of her early days.

'My father always kept a dog-cart, and we had three servants. We had a cook and a housemaid and an odd man. We used to grow beautiful roses. People used to stop at the gate and ask who the house belonged to, the roses were so beautiful. Of course it isn't very nice for me having to mix with them girls in the shop, it's not the class of person I've been used to, and sometimes I really think I'll give up business on that account. It's not the work I mind, don't think that; but it's the class of people I have to mix with.'

They were sitting opposite one another in the train, and Philip, listening sympathetically to what she said, was quite happy. He was amused at her *naïveté* and slightly touched. There was a very faint colour in her cheeks. He was thinking that it would be delightful to kiss the tip of her chin.

'The moment you come into the shop I saw you was a gentleman in every sense of the word. Was your father a professional man?'

'He was a doctor.'

'You can always tell a professional man. There's something about them. I don't know what it is, but I know at once.'

They walked along from the station together.

'I say, I want you to come and see another play with me,'
he said.

'I don't mind,' she said.

'You might go so far as to say you'd like to.'

'Why?'

'It doesn't matter. Let's fix a day. Would Saturday night
suit you?'

'Yes, that'll do.'

They made further arrangements, and then found themselves at the corner of the road in which she lived. She gave
him her hand, and he held it.

'I say, I do so awfully want to call you Mildred.'

'You may if you like, I don't care.'

'And you'll call me Philip, won't you?'

'I will if I can think of it. It seems more natural to call you
Mr Carey.'

He drew her slightly towards him, but she leaned back.

'What are you doing?'

'Won't you kiss me good night?' he whispered.

'Impudence!' she said.

She snatched away her hand and hurried towards her house.

Philip bought tickets for Saturday night. It was not one of
the days on which she got off early and therefore she would
have no time to go home and change; but she meant to bring
a frock up with her in the morning and hurry into her clothes
at the shop. If the manageress was in a good temper she would
let her go at seven. Philip had agreed to wait outside from a
quarter past seven onwards. He looked forward to the occasion with painful eagerness, for in the cab on the way from the
theatre to the station he thought she would let him kiss her.
The vehicle gave every facility for a man to put his arm round
a girl's waist (an advantage which the hansom had over the
taxi of the present day), and the delight of that was worth the
cost of the evening's entertainment.

But on Saturday afternoon when he went in to have tea, in
order to confirm the arrangements, he met the man with the
fair moustache coming out of the shop. He knew by now that
he was called Miller. He was a naturalized German, who had
anglicized his name, and he had lived many years in England.
Philip had heard him speak, and, though his English was
fluent and natural, it had not quite the intonation of the native.
Philip knew that he was flirting with Mildred, and he was horribly jealous of him; but he took comfort in the coldness of her

282

temperament, which otherwise distressed him; and, thinking her incapable of passion, he looked upon his rival as no better off than himself. But his heart sank now, for his first thought was that Miller's sudden appearance might interfere with the jaunt which he had so looked forward to. He entered, sick with apprehension. The waitress came up to him, took his order for tea, and presently brought it.

'I'm awfully sorry,' she said, with an expression on her face of real distress. 'I shan't be able to come tonight after all.'

'Why?' said Philip.

'Don't look so stern about it,' she laughed. 'It's not my fault. My aunt was taken ill last night, and it's the girl's night out so I must go and sit with her. She can't be left alone, can she?'

'It doesn't matter. I'll see you home instead.'

'But you've got the tickets. It would be a pity to waste them.'

He took them out of his pocket and deliberately tore them up.

'What are you doing that for?'

'You don't suppose I want to go and see a rotten musical comedy by myself, do you? I only took seats there for your sake.'

'You can't see me home if that's what you mean?'

'You've made other arrangements.'

'I don't know what you mean by that. You're just as selfish as all the rest of them. You only think of yourself. It's not my fault if my aunt's queer.'

She quickly wrote out his bill and left him. Philip knew very little about women, or he would have been aware that one should accept their most transparent lies. He made up his mind that he would watch the shop and see for certain whether Mildred went out with the German. He had an unhappy passion for certainty. At seven he stationed himself on the opposite pavement. He looked about for Miller, but did not see him. In ten minutes she came out, she had on the cloak and shawl which she had worn when he took her to the Shaftesbury Theatre. It was obvious that she was not going home. She saw him before he had time to move away, started a little, and then came straight up to him.

'What are you doing here?' she said.

'Taking the air,' he answered.

'You're spying on me, you dirty little cad. I thought you was a gentleman.'

'Did you think a gentleman would be likely to take any interest in you?' he murmured.

There was a devil within him which forced him to make matters worse. He wanted to hurt her as much as she was hurting him.

'I suppose I can change my mind if I like. I'm not obliged to come out with you. I tell you I'm going home, and I won't be followed or spied upon.'

'Have you seen Miller today?'

'That's no business of yours. In point of fact I haven't, so you're wrong again.'

'I saw him this afternoon. He'd just come out of the shop when I went in.'

'Well, what if he did? I can go out with him if I want to, can't I? I don't know what you've got to say to it.'

'He's keeping you waiting, isn't he?'

'Well, I'd rather wait for him than have you wait for me. Put that in your pipe and smoke it. And now p'raps you'll go off home and mind your own business in future.'

His mood changed suddenly from anger to despair, and his voice trembled when he spoke.

'I say, don't be beastly with me, Mildred. You know I'm awfully fond of you. I think I love you with all my heart. Won't you change your mind? I was looking forward to this evening so awfully. You see, he hasn't come, and he can't care twopence about you really. Won't you dine with me? I'll get some more tickets, and we'll go anywhere you like.'

'I tell you I won't. It's no good you talking. I've made up my mind, and when I make up my mind I keep to it.'

He looked at her for a moment. His heart was torn with anguish. People were hurrying past them on the pavement, and cabs and omnibuses rolled by noisily. He saw that Mildred's eyes were wandering. She was afraid of missing Miller in the crowd.

'I can't go on like this,' groaned Philip. 'It's too degrading. If I go now I go for good. Unless you'll come with me tonight you'll never see me again.'

'You seem to think that'll be an awful thing for me. All I say is, good riddance to bad rubbish.'

'Then, good-bye.'

He nodded and limped away slowly, for he hoped with all his heart that she would call him back. At the next lamp-post he stopped and looked over his shoulder. He thought she might beckon to him – he was willing to forget everything, he was ready for any humiliation – but she had turned away, and apparently had ceased to trouble about him. He realized that she was glad to be quit of him.

LIX

PHILIP passed the evening wretchedly. He had told his land-lady that he would not be in, so there was nothing for him to eat, and he had to go to Gatti's for dinner. Afterwards he went back to his rooms, but Griffiths on the floor above him was having a party, and the noisy merriment made his own misery more hard to bear. He went to a music-hall, but it was Satur-day night and there was standing-room only: after half an hour of boredom his legs grew tired and he went home. He tried to read, but he could not fix his attention; and yet it was necessary that he should work hard. His examination in biology was in little more than a fortnight, and, though it was easy, he had neglected his lectures of late and was con-scious that he knew nothing. It was only a *viva*, however, and he felt sure that in a fortnight he could find out enough about the subject to scrape through. He had confidence in his intelli-gence. He threw aside his book and gave himself up to think-ing deliberately of the matter which was in his mind all the time.

He reproached himself bitterly for his behaviour that even-ing. Why had he given her the alternative that she must dine with him or else never see him again? Of course she refused. He should have allowed for her pride. He had burnt his ships behind him. It would not be so hard to bear if he thought that she was suffering now, but he knew her too well: she was perfectly indifferent to him. If he hadn't been a fool he would have pretended to believe her story; he ought to have had the strength to conceal his disappointment and the self-control to master his temper. He could not tell why he loved her. He had read of the idealization that takes place in love, but he saw her exactly as she was. She was not amusing or clever, her mind was common; she had a vulgar shrewdness which revolted him, she had no gentleness nor softness. As she would have put it herself, she was 'on the make'. What aroused her admiration was a clever trick played on an unsus-pecting person; to 'do' somebody always gave her satisfaction. Philip laughed savagely as he thought of her gentility and the refinement with which she ate her food; she could not bear a coarse word, so far as her limited vocabulary reached she had a passion for euphemisms, and she scented indecency everywhere; she never spoke of trousers but referred to them as nether garments; she thought it slightly indelicate to blow her nose and did it in a deprecating way. She was dreadfully anaemic and suffered from the dyspepsia which accompanies that ailing. Philip was repelled by her flat breast and narrow hips, and he hated the vulgar way in which she did her hair. He loathed and despised himself for loving her.

The fact remained that he was helpless. He felt just as he had felt sometimes in the hands of a bigger boy at school. He had struggled against the superior strength till his own strength was gone, and he was rendered quite powerless – he remembered the peculiar languor he had felt in his limbs, almost as though he were paralysed – so that he could not help himself at all. He might have been dead. He felt just that same weakness now. He loved the woman so that he knew he had never loved before. He did not mind her faults of person or of character, he thought he loved them too: at all events they meant nothing to him. It did not seem himself that was concerned; he felt that he had been seized by some strange force that moved him against his will, contrary to his interests; and because he had a passion for freedom he hated the chains which bound him. He laughed at himself when he thought how often he had longed to experience the overwhelming passion. He cursed himself because he had given way to it. He thought of the beginnings; nothing of all this would have happened if he had not gone into the shop with Dunsford. The whole thing was his own fault. Except for his ridiculous vanity he would never have troubled himself with the ill-mannered slut.

At all events the occurrences of that evening had finished the whole affair. Unless he was lost to all sense of shame he could not go back. He wanted passionately to get rid of the love that obsessed him; it was degrading and hateful. He must prevent himself from thinking of her. In a little while the anguish he suffered must grow less. His mind went back to the past. He wondered whether Emily Wilkinson and Fanny Price had endured on his account anything like the torment that he suffered now. He felt a pang of remorse.

'I didn't know then what it was like,' he said to himself.

He slept very badly. The next day was Sunday, and he worked at his biology. He sat with the book in front of him, forming the words with his lips in order to fix his attention, but he could remember nothing. He found his thoughts going back to Mildred every minute, and he repeated to himself the exact words of the quarrel they had had. He had to force himself back to his book. He went out for a walk. The streets on the south side of the river were dingy enough on weekdays, but there was an energy, a coming and going, which gave them a sordid vivacity; but on Sundays, with no shops open, no carts in the roadway, silent and depressed, they were indescribably dreary. Philip thought that day would never end. But he was so tired that he slept heavily, and when Monday came he entered upon life with determination. Christmas was approaching, and a good many of the students had gone into the country for the short holiday between the two parts of the winter session; but Philip had refused his uncle's invitation to go down to Blackstable. He had given the approaching examination as his excuse, but in point of fact he had been unwilling to leave London and Mildred. He had neglected his work so much that now he had only a fortnight to learn what the curriculum allowed three months for. He set to work seriously. He found it easier each day not to think of Mildred. He congratulated himself on his force of character. The pain he suffered was no longer anguish, but a sort of soreness, like what one might be expected to feel if one had been thrown off a horse and, though no bones were broken, were bruised all over and shaken. Philip found that he was able to observe with curiosity the condition he had been in during the last few weeks. He analysed his feelings with interest. He was a little amused at himself. One thing that struck him was how little under those circumstances it mattered what one thought; the system of personal philosophy, which had given him great satisfaction to devise, had not served him. He was puzzled by this.

But sometimes in the street he would see a girl who looked so like Mildred that his heart seemed to stop beating. Then he could not help himself, he hurried on to catch her up, eager and anxious, only to find that it was a total stranger. Men came back from the country, and he went with Dunsford to have tea at an A.B.C. shop. The well-known uniform made him so miserable that he could not speak. The thought came to him that perhaps she had been transferred to another establishment of the firm for which she worked, and he might suddenly find himself face to face with her. The idea filled him with panic, so that he feared Dunsford would see that something was the matter with him: he could not think of anything to say; he pretended to listen to what Dunsford was talking about; the conversation maddened him; and it was all he could do to prevent himself from crying out to Dunsford for Heaven's sake to hold his tongue.

Then came the day of his examination. Philip, when his turn arrived, went forward to the examiner's table with the utmost confidence. He answered three or four questions. Then they showed him various specimens; he had been to very few lectures and, as soon as he was asked about things which he could not learn from books, he was floored. He did what he could to hide his ignorance, the examiner did not insist, and soon his ten minutes were over. He felt certain he had passed; but next day, when he went up to the examination buildings to see the result posted on the door, he was astounded not to find his number among those who had satisfied the examiners. In amazement he read the list three times. Dunsford was with him.

'I say, I'm awfully sorry you're ploughed,' he said.

He had just inquired Philip's number. Philip turned and saw by his radiant face that Dunsford had passed.

'Oh, it doesn't matter a bit,' said Philip. 'I'm jolly glad you're all right. I shall go up again in July.'

He was very anxious to pretend he did not mind, and on their way back along the Embankment insisted on talking of indifferent things. Dunsford good naturedly wanted to discuss the causes of Philip's failure, but Philip was obstinately casual. He was horribly mortified; and the fact the Dunsford, whom he looked upon as a very pleasant but quite stupid fellow, had passed made his own rebuff harder to bear. He had always been proud of his intelligence, and now he asked himself desperately whether he was not mistaken in the opinion he held of himself. In the three months of the winter session the students who had joined in October had already shaken down into groups, and it was clear which were brilliant, which were clever or industrious, and which were 'rotters'. Philip was conscious that his failure was a surprise to no one but himself. It was tea-time, and he knew that a lot of men would be having tea in the basement of the Medical School: those who had passed the examination would be exultant, those who disliked him would look at him with satisfaction, and the poor devils who had failed would sympathize with him in order to receive sympathy. His instinct was not to go near the hospital for a week, when the affair would be no more thought of, but, because he hated so much to go just then, he went: he wanted to inflict suffering upon himself. He forgot for the moment his maxim of life to follow his inclinations with due regard for the policeman round the corner; or, if he acted in accordance with it, there must have been some strange morbidity in his nature which made him take a grim pleasure in self-torture.

But later on, when he had endured the ordeal to which he forced himself, going out into the night after the noisy conversation in the smoking-room, he was seized with a feeling of utter loneliness. He seemed to himself absurd and futile. He had an urgent need of consolation, and the temptation to see Mildred was irresistible. He though bitterly that there was small chance of consolation from her; but he wanted to see her even if he did not speak to her; after all, she was a waitress and would be obliged to serve him. She was the only person in the world he cared for. There was no use in hiding that fact from himself. Of course it would be humiliating to go back to the shop as though nothing had happened, but he had not much self-respect left. Though he would not confess it to himself, he had hoped each day that she would write to him; she knew that a letter addressed to the hospital would find him; but she had not written: it was evident that she cared nothing if she saw him again or not. And he kept on repeating to himself:

'I must see her. I must see her.'

The desire was so great that he could not give the time necessary to walk, but jumped in a cab. He was too thrifty to use one when it could possibly be avoided. He stood outside the shop for a minute or two. The thought came to him that perhaps she had left, and in terror he walked in quickly. He saw her at once. He sat down and she came up to him.

'Cup of tea and a muffin, please,' he ordered.

He could hardly speak. He was afraid for a moment that he was going to cry.

'I almost thought you was dead,' she said.

She was smiling. Smiling! She seemed to have forgotten completely that last scene which Philip had repeated to himself a hundred times.

'I thought if you'd wanted to see me you'd write,' he answered.

'I've got too much to do to think about writing letters.'

It seemed impossible for her to say a gracious thing. Philip cursed the fate which chained him to such a woman. She went away to fetch his tea.

'Would you like me to sit down for a minute or two?' she said, when she brought it.

'Yes.'

'Where have you been all this time?'

'I've been in London.'

'I thought you'd gone away for the holidays. Why haven't you been in then?'

Philip looked at her with haggard, passionate eyes.

'Don't you remember that I said I'd never see you again?'

'What are you doing now then?'

She seemed anxious to make him drink up the cup of his humiliation; but he knew her well enough to know that she spoke at random; she hurt him frightfully, and never even tried to. He did not answer.

'It was a nasty trick you played on me, spying on me like that. I always thought you was a gentleman in every sense of the word.'

'Don't be beastly to me, Mildred. I can't bear it.'

'You are a funny feller. I can't make you out.'

'It's very simple. I'm such a blasted fool as to love you with all my heart and soul, and I know that you don't care two-pence for me.'

'If you had been a gentleman I think you'd have come next day and begged my pardon.'

She had no mercy. He looked at her neck and thought how he would like to jab it with the knife he had for his muffin. He knew enough anatomy to make pretty certain of getting the carotid artery. And at the same time he wanted to cover her pale, thin face with kisses.

'If I could only make you understand how frightfully I'm in love with you.'

'You haven't begged my pardon yet.'

He grew very white. She felt that she had done nothing wrong on that occasion. She wanted him now to humble himself. He was very proud. For one instant he felt inclined to tell her to go to hell, but he dared not. His passion made him abject. He was willing to submit to anything rather than not see her.

'I'm very sorry, Mildred. I beg your pardon.'

He had to force the words out. It was a horrible effort.

'Now you've said that I don't mind telling you that I wish I had come out with you that evening. I thought Miller was a gentleman, but I've discovered my mistake now. I soon sent him about his business.'

Philip gave a little gasp.

'Mildred, won't you come out with me tonight? Let's go and dine somewhere.'

'Oh, I can't. My aunt'll be expecting me home.'

'I'll send her a wire. You can say you've been detained in the shop; she won't know any better. Oh, do come, for God's sake. I haven't seen you for so long, and I want to talk to you.'

She looked down at her clothes.

'Never mind about that. We'll go somewhere where it doesn't matter how you're dressed. And we'll go to a music-hall afterwards. Please say yes. It would give me so much pleasure.'

She hesitated a moment; he looked at her with pitifully appealing eyes.

'Well, I don't mind if I do. I haven't been out anywhere since I don't know how long.'

It was with the greatest difficulty he could prevent himself from seizing her hand there and then to cover it with kisses.

LX

THEY dined in Soho, Philip was tremulous with joy. It was not one of the more crowded of those cheap restaurants where the respectable and needy dine in the belief that it is bohemian and the assurance that it is economical. It was a humble establishment, kept by a good man from Rouen and his wife, that Philip had discovered by accident. He had been attracted by the Gallic look of the window, in which was generally an uncooked steak on one plate and on each side two dishes of raw vegetables. There was one seedy French waiter, who was to learn English in a house where he never heard anything but French; and the customers were a few ladies of easy virtue, a *ménage* or two, who had their own napkins reserved for them, and a few queer men who came in for hurried, scanty meals.

Here Mildred and Philip were able to get a table to themselves. Philip sent the waiter for a bottle of Burgundy from the neighbouring tavern, and they had a *potage aux herbes*, a steak from the window *aux pommes*, and an *omelette au kirsch*. There was really an air of romance in the meal and in the place. Mildred, at first a little reserved in her appreciation – 'I never quite trust these foreign places, you never know what there is in these messed-up dishes' – was insensibly moved by it.

291

'I like this place, Philip,' she said. 'You feel you can put your elbows on the table, don't you?'

A tall fellow came in, with a mane of grey hair and a ragged thin beard. He wore a dilapidated cloak and a wide-awake hat. He nodded to Philip, who had met him there before.

'He looks like an anarchist,' said Mildred.

'He is, one of the most dangerous in Europe. He's been in every prison on the Continent and has assassinated more persons than any gentleman unhung. He always goes about with a bomb in his pocket, and of course it makes conversation a little difficult because if you don't agree with him he lays it on the table in a marked manner.'

She looked at the man with horror and surprise, and then glanced suspiciously at Philip. She saw that his eyes were laughing. She frowned a little.

'You're getting at me.'

He gave a little shout of joy. He was so happy. But Mildred didn't like being laughed at.

'I don't see anything funny in telling lies.'

'Don't be cross.'

He took her hand, which was lying on the table, and pressed it gently.

'You are lovely, and I could kiss the ground you walk on,' he said.

The greenish pallor of her skin intoxicated him, and her thin white lips had an extraordinary fascination. Her anaemia made her rather short of breath, and she held her mouth slightly open. It seemed to add somehow to the attractiveness of her face.

'You do like me a bit, don't you?' he asked.

'Well, if I didn't I suppose I shouldn't be here, should I? You're a gentleman in every sense of the word, I will say that for you.'

They had finished their dinner and were drinking coffee. Philip, throwing economy to the winds, smoked a threepenny cigar.

'You can't imagine what a pleasure it is to me just to sit opposite and look at you. I've yearned for you. I was sick for a sight of you.'

Mildred smiled a little and faintly flushed. She was not then suffering from the dyspepsia which generally attacked her immediately after a meal. She felt more kindly disposed to Philip than ever before, and the unaccustomed tenderness in her eyes filled him with joy. He knew instinctively that it was madness to give himself into her hands; his only chance was to treat her casually and never allow her to see the untamed passions that seethed in his breast; she would only take advantage of his weakness; but he could not be prudent now: he told her all the agony he had endured during the separation from her; he told her of his struggles with himself, how he had tried to get over his passion, thought he had succeeded, and how he found out that is was as strong as ever. He knew that he had never really wanted to get over it. He loved her so much that he did not mind suffering. He bared his heart to her. He showed her proudly all his weakness.

Nothing would have pleased him more than to sit on in the cosy, shabby restaurant, but he knew that Mildred wanted entertainment. She was restless and, wherever she was, wanted after a while to go somewhere else. He dared not bore her.

'I say, how about going to a music-hall?' he said.

He thought rapidly that if she cared for him at all she would say she preferred to stay there.

'I was just thinking we ought to be going if we are going,' she answered.

'Come on then.'

Philip waited impatiently for the end of the performance. He had made up his mind exactly what to do, and when they got into the cab he passed his arm, as though almost by accident, round her waist. But he drew it back quickly with a little cry. He had pricked himself. She laughed.

'There, that comes of putting your arm where it's got no business to be,' she said. 'I always know when men try and put their arm round my waist. That pin always catches them.'

'I'll be more careful.'

He put his arm round again. She made no objection.

'I'm so comfortable,' he sighed blissfully.

'So long as you're happy,' she retorted.

They drove down St James's Street into the Park, and Philip quickly kissed her. He was strangely afraid of her, and it required all his courage. She turned her lips to him without speaking. She neither seemed to mind nor to like it.

'If you only knew how long I've wanted to do that,' he murmured.

He tried to kiss her again, but she turned her head away.

'Once is enough,' she said.

On the chance of kissing her a second time he travelled down to Herne Hill with her, and at the end of the road in which she lived he asked her:

'Won't you give me another kiss?'

She looked at him indifferently and then glanced up the road to see that no one was in sight.

'I don't mind.'

He seized her in his arms and kissed her passionately, but she pushed him away.

'Mind my hat, silly. You are clumsy,' she said.

LXI

HE saw her then every day. He began going to lunch at the shop, but Mildred stopped him: she said it made the girls talk; so he had to content himself with tea; but he always waited about to walk with her to the station; and once or twice a week they dined together. He gave her little presents, a gold bangle, gloves, handkerchiefs, and the like. He was spending more than he could afford, but he could not help it: it was only when he gave her anything that she showed any affection. She knew the price of everything, and her gratitude was in exact proportion with the value of his gift. He did not care. He was too happy when she volunteered to kiss him to mind by what means he got her demonstrativeness. He discovered that she found Sundays at home tedious, so he went down to Herne Hill in the morning, met her at the end of the road, and went to church with her.

'I always like to go to church once,' she said. 'It looks well, doesn't it?'

Then she went back to dinner, he got a scrappy meal at a hotel, and in the afternoon they took a walk in Brockwell Park. They had nothing much to say to one another, and Philip, desperately afraid she was bored (she was very easily bored), racked his brain for topics of conversation. He realized that these walks amused neither of them, but he could not bear to leave her, and did all he could to lengthen them till she became tired and out of temper. He knew that she did not care for him, and he tried to force a love which his reason told him was not in her nature: she was cold. He had no claim on her, but he could not help being exacting. Now that they were more intimate he found it less easy to control his temper; he was often irritable and could not help saying bitter things. Often they quarrelled, and she would not speak to him for a while; but this always reduced him to subjection, and he crawled before her. He was angry with himself for showing so little dignity. He grew furiously jealous if he saw her speaking to any other man in the shop, and when he was jealous he seemed to be beside himself. He would deliberately insult her, leave the shop, and spend afterwards a sleepless night tossing on his bed, by turns angry and remorseful. Next day he would go to the shop and appeal for forgiveness.

'Don't be angry with me,' he said. 'I'm so awfully fond of you that I can't help myself.'

'One of these days you'll go too far,' she answered.

He was anxious to come to her home in order that the greater intimacy should give him an advantage over the stray acquaintances she made during her working hours; but she would not let him.

'My aunt would think it so funny,' she said.

He suspected that her refusal was due only to a disinclination to let him see her aunt. Mildred had represented her as the widow of a professional man (that was her formula of distinction), and was uneasily conscious that the good woman could hardly be called distinguished. Philip imagined that she was in point of fact the widow of a small tradesman. He knew that Mildred was a snob. But he found no means by which he could indicate to her that he did not mind how common the aunt was.

Their worst quarrel took place one evening at dinner when she told him that a man had asked her to go to a play with him. Philip turned pale, and his face grew hard and stern.

'You're not going?' he said.

'Why shouldn't I? He's a very nice gentlemanly fellow.'

'I'll take you anywhere you like.'

'But that isn't the same thing. I can't always go about with you. Besides he's asked me to fix my own day, and I'll just go one evening when I'm not going out with you. It won't make any difference to you.'

'If you had any sense of decency, if you had any gratitude, you wouldn't dream of going.'

'I don't know what you mean by gratitude. If you're referring to the things you've given me you can have them back. I don't want them.'

Her voice had the shrewish tone it sometimes got.

'It's not very lively, always going about with you. It's always "do you love me? do you love me?" till I just get about sick of it.'

(He knew it was madness to go on asking her that, but he could not help himself.

'Oh, I like you all right,' she would answer.

'Is that all? I love you with all my heart.'

'I'm not that sort, I'm not one to say much.'

'If you knew how happy just one word would make me!'

'Well, what I always say is, people must take me as they find me, and if they don't like it they can lump it.'

But sometimes she expressed herself more plainly still, and, when he asked the question, answered:

'Oh, don't go on at that again.'

Then he became sulky and silent. He hated her.)

And now he said:

'Oh, well, if you feel like that about it I wonder you condescend to come out with me at all.'

'It's not my seeking, you can be very sure of that, you just force me to.'

His pride was bitterly hurt, and he answered madly:

'You think I'm just good enough to stand you dinners and theatres when there's no one else to do it, and when someone else turns up I can go to hell. Thank you, I'm about sick of being made a convenience.'

'I'm not going to be talked to like that by anyone. I'll just show you how much I want your dirty dinner.'

She got up, put on her jacket, and walked quickly out of the restaurant. Philip sat on. He determined he would not move, but ten minutes afterwards he jumped in a cab and followed her. He guessed that she would take a bus to Victoria, so that they would arrive about the same time. He saw her on the platform, escaped her notice, and went down to Herne Hill in the same train. He did not want to speak to her till she was on the way home and could not escape him.

As soon as she had turned out of the main street, brightly lit and noisy with traffic, he caught her up.

'Mildred,' he called.

She walked on and would neither look at him nor answer. He repeated her name. Then she stopped and faced him.

'What d'you want? I saw you hanging about Victoria. Why don't you leave me alone?'

'I'm awfully sorry. Won't you make it up?

'No. I'm sick of your temper and your jealousy. I don't care for you, I never have cared for you, and I never shall care for you. I don't want to have anything more to do with you.'

She walked on quickly, and he had to hurry to keep up with her.

'You never make allowances for me,' he said. 'It's all very well to be jolly and amiable when you're indifferent to anyone. It's very hard when you're as much in love as I am. Have mercy on me. I don't mind that you don't care for me. After all you can't help it. I only want you to let me love you.'

She walked on, refusing to speak, and Philip saw with agony that they had only a few hundred yards to go before they reached her house. He abased himself. He poured out an incoherent story of love and penitence.

'If you'll only forgive me this time I promise you you'll never have to complain of me in future. You can go out with whoever you choose. I'll be only too glad if you'll come with me when you've got nothing better to do.'

She stopped again, for they had reached the corner at which he always left her.

'Now you can take yourself off. I won't have you coming up to the door.'

'I won't go till you say you forgive me.'

'I'm sick and tired of the whole thing.'

He hesitated a moment, for he had an instinct that he could say something that would move her. It made him feel almost sick to utter the words.

'It is cruel, I have so much to put up with. You don't know what it is to be a cripple. Of course you don't like me. I can't expect you to.'

'Philip, I didn't mean that,' she answered quickly, with a sudden break of pity in her voice. 'You know it's not true.'

He was beginning to act now, and his voice was husky and low.

'Oh, I've felt it,' he said.

She took his hand and looked at him, her own eyes were filled with tears.

'I promise you it never made any difference to me. I never thought about it after the first day or two.'

He kept a gloomy, tragic silence. He wanted her to think he was overcome with emotion.

'You know I like you awfully, Philip. Only you are so trying sometimes. Let's make it up.'

She put up her lips to his, and with a sigh of relief he kissed her.

'Now are you happy again?' she asked.

'Madly.'

She bade him good night and hurried down the road. Next day he took her in a little watch with a brooch to pin on her dress. She had been hankering for it.

But three or four days later, when she brought him his tea, Mildred said to him:

297

'You remember what you promised the other night? You mean to keep that, don't you?'

'Yes.'

He knew exactly what she meant and was prepared for her next words.

'Because I'm going out with that gentleman I told you about tonight.'

'All right. I hope you'll enjoy yourself.'

'You don't mind, do you?'

He had himself now under excellent control.

'I don't like it,' he smiled, 'but I'm not going to make myself more disagreeable than I can help.'

She was excited over the outing and talked about it willingly. Philip wondered whether she did so in order to pain him or merely because she was callous. He was in the habit of condoning her cruelty by the thought of her stupidity. She had not the brains to see when she was wounding him.

'It's not much fun to be in love with a girl who has no imagination and no sense of humour,' he thought, as he listened.

But the want of these things excused her. He felt that if he had not realized this he could never forgive her for the pain she caused him.

'He's got seats for the Tivoli,' she said. 'He gave me my choice and I chose that. And we're going to dine at the Café Royal. He says it's the most expensive place in London.'

'He's a gentleman in every sense of the word,' thought Philip, but he clenched his teeth to prevent himself from uttering a syllable.

Philip went to the Tivoli and saw Mildred with her companion, a smooth-faced young man with sleek hair and the spruce look of a commercial traveller, sitting in the second row of the stalls. Mildred wore a black picture hat with ostrich feathers in it, which became her well. She was listening to her host with that quiet smile which Philip knew; she had no vivacity of expression, and it required broad farce to excite her laughter; but Philip could see that she was interested and amused. He thought to himself bitterly that her companion, flashy and jovial, exactly suited her. Her sluggish temperament made her appreciate noisy people. Philip had a passion for discussion, but no talent for small-talk. He admired the easy drollery of which some of his friends were masters, Lawson for instance, and his sense of inferiority made him shy and awkward. The things which interested him bored Mildred. She expected men to talk about football and racing, and he knew nothing of either. He did not know the catchwords which only need be said to excite a laugh.

Printed matter had always been a fetish to Philip, and now, in order to make himself more interesting, he read industriously *The Sporting Times*.

LXII

PHILIP did not surrender himself willingly to the passion that consumed him. He knew that all things human are transitory and therefore that it must cease one day or another. He looked forward to that day with eager longing. Love was like a parasite in his heart, nourishing a hateful existence on his life's blood; it absorbed his existence so intensely that he could take pleasure in nothing else. He had been used to delight in the grace of St James's Park, and often he sat and looked at the branches of a tree silhouetted against the sky, it was like a Japanese print; and he found a continual magic in the beautiful Thames with its barges and its wharves; the changing sky of London had filled his soul with pleasant fancies. But now beauty meant nothing to him. He was bored and restless when he was not with Mildred. Sometimes he thought he would console his sorrow by looking at pictures, but he walked through the National Gallery like a sightseer; and no picture called in him a thrill of emotion. He wondered if he could ever care again for all the things he had loved. He had been devoted to reading, but now books were meaningless; and he spent his spare hours in the smoking-room of the hospital club, turning over innumerable periodicals. This love was a torment, and he resented bitterly the subjugation in which it held him; he was a prisoner and he longed for freedom.

Sometimes he awoke in the morning and felt nothing; his soul leaped, for he thought he was free; he loved no longer; but in a little while, as he grew wide awake, the pain settled in his heart, and he knew that he was not cured yet. Though he yearned for Mildred so madly he despised her. He thought to himself that there could be no greater torture in the world than at the same time to love and to contemn.

Philip, burrowing as was his habit into the state of his feelings, discussing with himself continually his condition, came to the conclusion that he could only cure himself of his degrading passion by making Mildred his mistress. It was sexual hunger that he suffered from, and if he could satisfy this he might free himself from the intolerable chains that bound him. He knew that Mildred did not care for him at all in that way. When he kissed her passionately she withdrew herself from him with instinctive distaste. She had no sensuality. Sometimes he had tried to make her jealous by talking of adventures in Paris, but they did not interest her; once or twice he had sat at other tables in the tea-shop and affected to flirt with the waitress who attended them, but she was entirely indifferent. He could see that it was no pretence on her part.

'You didn't mind my not sitting at one of your tables this afternoon?' he asked once, when he was walking to the station with her. 'Yours seemed to be all full.'

This was not a fact, but she did not contradict him. Even if his desertion meant nothing to her, he would have been grateful if she had pretended it did. A reproach would have been balm to his soul.

'I think it's silly of you to sit at the same table every day. You ought to give the other girls a turn now and again.'

But the more he thought of it the more he was convinced that complete surrender on her part was his only way to freedom. He was like a knight of old, metamorphosed by magic spells, who sought the potions which should restore him to his fair and proper form. Philip had only one hope. Mildred greatly desired to go to Paris. To her, as to most English people, it was the centre of gaiety and fashion: she had heard of the Magasin du Louvre, where you could get the very latest thing for about half the price you had to pay in London; a friend of hers had passed her honeymoon in Paris and had spent all day at the Louvre; and she and her husband, my dear, they never went to bed till six in the morning all the time they were there; the Moulin Rouge and I don't know what all. Philip did not care that if she yielded to his desires it would only be the unwilling price she paid for the gratification of her wish. He did not care upon what terms he satisfied his passion. He had even had a mad, melodramatic idea to drug her. He had plied her with liquor in the hope of exciting her, but she had no taste for wine; and though she liked him to order champagne because it looked well, she never drank more than half a glass. She liked to leave untouched a large glass filled to the brim.

'It shows the waiters who you are,' she said.

Philip chose an opportunity when she seemed more than usually friendly. He had an examination in anatomy at the end of March. Easter, which came a week later, would give Mildred three whole days' holiday.

'I say, why don't you come over to Paris then?' he suggested. 'We'd have such a ripping time.'

'How could you? It would cost no end of money.'

Philip had thought of that. It would cost at least five-and-twenty-pounds. It was a large sum to him. He was willing to spend his last penny on her.

'What does that matter? Say you'll come, darling?'

'What next, I should like to know. I can't see myself going away with a man that I wasn't married to. You oughtn't to suggest such a thing.'

'What does it matter?'

He enlarged on the glories of the Rue de la Paix and the garish splendour of the Folies Bergère. He described the Louvre and the Bon Marché. He told her about the Cabaret du Néant, the Abbaye, and the various haunts to which foreigners go. He painted in glowing colours the side of Paris which he despised. He pressed her to come with him.

'You know, you say you love me, but if you really loved me you'd want to marry me. You've never asked me to marry you.'

'You know I can't afford it. After all, I'm in my first year, I shan't earn a penny for six years.'

.'Oh, I'm not blaming you. I wouldn't marry you if you went down on your bended knees to me.'

He had thought of marriage more than once, but it was a step from which he shrank. In Paris he had come by the opinion that marriage was a ridiculous institution of the philistines. He knew also that a permanent tie would ruin him. He had middle-class instincts, and it seemed a dreadful thing to him to marry a waitress. A common wife would prevent him from getting a decent practice. Besides, he had only just enough money to last him till he was qualified; he could not keep a wife even if they arranged not to have children. He thought of Cronshaw bound to a vulgar slattern, and he shuddered with dismay. He foresaw what Mildred, with her genteel ideas and her mean mind, would become: it was impossible for him to marry her. But he decided only with his reason; he felt that he must have her whatever happened; and if he could not get her without marrying her he would do that; the future could look after itself. It might end in disaster; he did not care. When he got hold of an idea it obsessed him, he could think of nothing else, and he had a more than common power to persuade himself of the reasonableness of what he wished to do. He found himself overthrowing all the sensible arguments which had occurred to him against marriage. Each day he found that he was more passionately devoted to her; and his unsatisfied love became angry and resentful.

'By George, if I marry her I'll make her pay for all the suffering I've endured,' he said to himself.

At last he could bear the agony no longer. After dinner one evening in the little restaurant in Soho, to which now they often went, he spoke to her.

'I say, did you mean it the other day that you wouldn't marry me if I asked you?'

'Yes, why not?'

'Because I can't live without you. I want you with me always. I've tried to get over it and I can't. I never shall now. I want you to marry me.'

She had read too many novelettes not to know how to take such an offer.

'I'm sure I'm very grateful to you, Philip. I'm very much flattered at your proposal.'

'Oh, don't talk rot. You will marry me, won't you?'

'D'you think we should be happy?'

'No. But what does that matter.'

The words were wrung out of him almost against his will. They surprised her.

'Well, you are a funny chap. Why d'you want to marry me then? The other day you said you couldn't afford it.'

'I think I've got about fourteen hundred pounds left. Two can live just as cheaply as one. That'll keep us till I'm qualified and have got through with my hospital appointments, and then I can get an assistantship.'

'It means you wouldn't be able to earn anything for six years. We should have about four pounds a week to live on till then, shouldn't we?'

'Not much more than three. There are all my fees to pay.'

'And what would you get as an assistant?'

'Three pounds a week.'

'D'you mean to say you have to work all that time and spend a small fortune just to earn three pounds a week at the end of it? I don't see that I should be any better off than I am now.'

He was silent for a moment.

'D'you mean to say you won't marry me?' he asked hoarsely. 'Does my great love mean nothing to you at all?'

'One has to think of oneself in those things, don't one? I shouldn't mind marrying, but I don't want to marry if I'm

302

going to be no better off than what I am now. I don't see the use of it.'

'If you cared for me you wouldn't think of all that.'

'P'raps not.'

He was silent. He drank a glass of wine in order to get rid of the choking in his throat.

'Look at that girl who's just going out,' said Mildred. 'She got them furs at the Bon Marché at Brixton. I saw them in the window last time I went down there.'

Philip smiled grimly.

'What are you laughing at?' she asked. 'It's true. And I said to my aunt at the time, I wouldn't buy anything that had been in the window like that, for everyone to know how much you paid for it.'

'I can't understand you. You make me frightfully unhappy, and in the next breath you talk rot that has nothing to do with what we're speaking about.'

'You are nasty to me,' she answered, aggrieved. 'I can't help noticing those furs, because I said to my aunt . . .'

'I don't care a damn what you said to your aunt,' he interrupted impatiently.

'I wish you wouldn't use bad language when you speak to to me, Philip. You know I don't like it.'

Philip smiled a little, but his eyes were wild. He was silent for a while. He looked at her sullenly. He hated, despised and loved her.

'If I had an ounce of sense I'd never see you again,' he said at last. 'If you only knew how heartily I despise myself for loving you!'

'That's not a very nice thing to say to me,' she replied sulkily.

'It isn't,' he laughed. 'Let's go to the Pavilion.'

'That's what's so funny in you, you start laughing just when one doesn't expect you to. And if I make you that unhappy why d'you want to take me to the Pavilion? I'm quite ready to go home.'

'Merely because I'm less unhappy with you than away from you.'

'I should like to know what you really think of me.'

He laughed outright.

'My dear, if you did you'd never speak to me again.'

LXIII

PHILIP did not pass the examination in anatomy at the end of March. He and Dunsford had worked at the subject together on Philip's skeleton, asking each other questions till both knew by heart every attachment and the meaning of every nodule and groove on the human bones; but in the examination room Philip was seized with panic, and failed to give right answers to questions from a sudden fear that they might be wrong. He knew he was ploughed and did not even trouble to go up to the building next day to see whether his number was up. The second failure put him definitely among the incompetent and idle men of his year.

He did not care much. He had other things to think of. He told himself that Mildred must have senses like anybody else, it was only a question of awakening them; he had theories about woman, the rip at heart, and thought that there must come a time with everyone when she would yield to persistence. It was a question of watching for the opportunity, keeping his temper, wearing her down with small attentions, taking advantage of the physical exhaustion which opened the heart to tenderness, making himself a refuge from the petty vexations of her work. He talked to her of the relations between his friends in Paris and the fair ladies they admired. The life he described had a charm, an easy gaiety, in which was no grossness. Weaving into his own recollections the adventures of Mimi and Rodolphe, of Musette and the rest of them, he poured into Mildred's ears a story of poverty made picturesque by song and laughter, of lawless love made romantic by beauty and youth. He never attacked her prejudices directly, but sought to combat them by the suggestion that they were suburban. He never let himself be disturbed by her inattention, nor irritated by her indifference. He thought he had bored her. By an effort he made himself affable and entertaining; he never let himself be angry, he never asked for anything, he never complained, he never scolded. When she made engagements and broke them, he met her next day with a smiling face; when she excused herself, he said it did not matter. He never let her see that she pained him. He understood that his passionate grief had wearied her, and he took care to hide every sentiment which could be in the least degree troublesome. He was heroic.

Though she never mentioned the change, for she did not take

any conscious notice of it, it affected her nevertheless; she became more confidential with him; she took her little grievances to him, and she always had some grievance against the manageress of the shop, one of her fellow-waitresses, or her aunt; she was talkative enough now, and though she never said anything that was not trivial Philip was never tired of listening to her.

'I like you when you don't want to make love to me,' she told him once.

'That's flattering for me,' he laughed.

She did not realize how her words made his heart sink nor what an effort it needed for him to answer so lightly.

'Oh, I don't mind your kissing me now and then. It doesn't hurt me and it gives you pleasure.'

Occasionally she went so far as to ask him to take her out to dinner, and the offer, coming from her, filled him with rapture.

'I wouldn't do it to anyone else,' she said, by way of apology. 'But I know I can with you.'

'You couldn't give me greater pleasure,' he smiled.

She asked him to give her something to eat one evening towards the end of April.

'All right,' he said. 'Where would you like to go afterwards?'

'Oh, don't let's go anywhere. Let's just sit and talk. You don't mind, do you?'

'Rather not.'

He thought she must be beginning to care for him. Three months before the thought of an evening spent in conversation would have bored her to death. It was a fine day, and the spring added to Philip's high spirits. He was content with very little now.

'I say, won't it be ripping when the summer comes along,' he said, as they drove along on the top of a bus to Soho – she had herself suggested that they should not be so extravagant as to go by cab. 'We shall be able to spend every Sunday on the River. We'll take our luncheon in a basket.'

She smiled slightly, and he was encouraged to take her hand. She did not withdraw it.

'I really think you're beginning to like me a bit,' he smiled.

'You *are* silly, you know I like you, or else I shouldn't be here, should I?'

They were old customers at the little restaurant in Soho by now, and the *patronne* gave them a smile as they came in. The waiter was obsequious.

305

'Let me order the dinner tonight,' said Mildred.

Philip, thinking her more enchanting than ever, gave her the menu, and she chose her favourite dishes. The range was small, and they had eaten many times all that the restaurant could provide. Philip was gay. He looked into her eyes, and he dwelt on every perfection of her pale cheeks. When they had finished Mildred by way of exception took a cigarette. She smoked very seldom.

'I don't like to see a lady smoking,' she said.

She hesitated a moment and then spoke.

'Were you surprised, my asking you to take me out and give me a bit of dinner tonight?'

'I was delighted.'

'I've got something to say to you, Philip.'

He looked at her quickly, his heart sank, but he had trained himself well.

'Well, fire away,' he said, smiling.

'You're not going to be silly about it, are you? The fact is I'm going to get married.'

'Are you?' said Philip.

He could think of nothing else to say. He had considered the possibility often and had imagined to himself what he would do and say. He had suffered agonies when he thought of the despair he would suffer, he had thought of suicide, of the mad passion of anger that would seize him; but perhaps he had too completely anticipated the emotion he would experience, so that now he felt merely exhausted. He felt as one does in a serious illness when the vitality is so low that one is indifferent to the issue and wants only to be left alone.

'You see, I'm getting on,' she said. 'I'm twenty-four and it's time I settled down.'

He was silent. He looked at the *patronne* sitting behind the counter, and his eye dwelt on a red feather one of the diners wore in her hat. Mildred was nettled.

'You might congratulate me,' she said.

'I might, mightn't I? I can hardly believe it's true. I've dreamt it so often. It rather tickles me that I should have been so jolly glad that you asked me to take you out to dinner. Whom are you going to marry?'

'Miller,' she answered, with a slight blush.

'Miller?' cried Philip, astounded. 'But you've not seen him for months?'

'He came in to lunch one day last week and asked me then. He's earning very good money. He makes seven pounds a week now and he's got prospects.'

Philip was silent again. He remembered that she had always liked Miller; he amused her; there was in his foreign birth an exotic charm which she felt unconsciously.

'I suppose it was inevitable,' he said at last. 'You were bound to accept the highest bidder. When are you going to marry?'

'On Saturday next. I have given notice.'

Philip felt a sudden pang.

'As soon as that?'

'We're going to be married at a registry office, Emil prefers it.'

Philip felt dreadfully tired. He wanted to get away from her. He thought he would go straight to bed. He called for the bill.

'I'll put you in a cab and send you down to Victoria. I daresay you won't have to wait long for a train.'

'Won't you come with me?'

'I think I'd rather not, if you don't mind.'

'It's just as you please,' she answered haughtily. 'I suppose I shall see you at tea-time tomorrow?'

'No, I think we'd better make a full-stop now. I don't see why I should go on making myself unhappy. I've paid the cab.'

He nodded to her and forced a smile on his lips, then jumped on a bus and made his way home. He smoked a pipe before he went to bed, but he could hardly keep his eyes open. He suffered no pain. He fell into a heavy sleep almost as soon as his head touched the pillow.

LXIV

BUT about three in the morning Philip awoke and could not sleep again. He began to think of Mildred. He tried not to, but could not help himself. He repeated to himself the same thing time after time till his brain reeled. It was inevitable that she should marry: life was hard for a girl who had to earn her own living; and if she found someone who could give her a comfortable home she should not be blamed if she accepted. Philip acknowledged that from her point of view it would have been madness to marry him: only love could have made such poverty bearable, and she did not love him. It was no fault of hers; it was a fact that must be accepted like any other. Philip tried to reason with himself. He told himself that deep down in his heart was mortified pride;

his passion had begun in wounded vanity, and it was this at bottom which caused now great part of his wretchedness. He despised himself as much as he despised her. Then he made plans for the future, the same plans over and over again, interrupted by recollections of kisses on her soft pale cheek and by the sound of her voice with its trailing accent; he had a great deal of work to do, since in the summer he was taking Chemistry as well as the two examinations he had failed in. He had separated himself from his friends at the hospital, but now he wanted companionship. There was one happy occurrence: Hayward a fortnight before had written to say that he was passing through London and had asked him to dinner; but Philip, unwilling to be bothered, had refused. He was coming back for the season, and Philip made up his mind to write to him.

He was thankful when eight o'clock struck and he could get up. He was pale and weary. But when he had bathed, dressed, and had breakfast, he felt himself joined up again with the world at large; and his pain was a little easier to bear. He did not feel like going to lectures that morning, but went instead to the Army and Navy Stores to buy Mildred a wedding present. After much wavering he settled on a dressing-bag. It cost twenty pounds, which was much more than he could afford, but it was showy and vulgar: he knew she would be aware exactly how much it cost; he got a melancholy satisfaction in choosing a gift which would give her pleasure and at the same time indicate for himself the contempt he had for her.

Philip had looked forward with apprehension to the day on which Mildred was to be married; he was expecting an intolerable anguish; and it was with relief that he got a letter from Hayward on Saturday morning to say that he was coming up early on that very day and would fetch Philip to help him to find rooms. Philip, anxious to be distracted, looked up a time-table and discovered the only train Hayward was likely to come by; he went to meet him, and the reunion of the friends was enthusiastic. They left the luggage at the station, and set off gaily. Hayward characteristically proposed that first of all they should go for an hour to the National Gallery; he had not seen pictures for some time, and he stated that it needed a glimpse to set him in tune with life. Philip for months had had no one with whom he could talk of art and books. Since the Paris days Hayward had immersed himself in the modern French versifiers, and, such a plethora of poets is there in France, he had several new geniuses to tell Philip about. They walked through the gallery pointing out to one another their favourite pictures; one subject led to another; they talked excitedly. The sun was shining and the air was warm.

'Let's go and sit in the Park,' said Hayward. 'We'll look for rooms after luncheon.'

The spring was pleasant there. It was a day upon which one felt it good merely to live. The young green of the trees was exquisite against the sky; and the sky, pale and blue, was dappled with little white clouds. At the end of the ornamental water was the grey mass of the Horse Guards. The ordered elegance of the scene had the charm of an eighteenth century picture. It reminded you not of Watteau, whose landscapes are so idyllic that they recall only the woodland glens seen in dreams, but of the more prosaic Jean-Baptiste Pater. Philip's heart was filled with lightness. He realized, what he had only read before, that art (for there was art in the manner in which he looked upon nature) might liberate the soul from pain.

They went to an Italian restaurant for luncheon and ordered themselves a *fiaschetto* of Chianti. Lingering over the meal they talked on. They reminded one another of the people they had known at Heidelberg, they spoke of Philip's friends in Paris, they talked of books, pictures, morals, life; and suddenly Philip heard a clock strike three. He remembered that by this time Mildred was married. He felt a sort of stitch in his heart, and for a minute or two he could not hear what Hayward was saying. But he filled his glass with Chianti. He was unaccustomed to alcohol and it had gone to his head. For the time at all events he was free from care. His quick brain had lain idle for so many months that he was intoxicated now with conversation. He was thankful to have someone to talk to who would interest himself in the things that interested him.

'I say, don't let's waste this beautiful day in looking for rooms. I'll put you up tonight. You can look for rooms tomorrow or Monday.'

'All right. What shall we do?' answered Hayward.

'Let's get on a penny steamboat and go down to Greenwich.'

The idea appealed to Hayward, and they jumped into a cab which took them to Westminster Bridge. They got on the steamboat just as she was starting. Presently Philip, a smile on his lips, spoke.

'I remember when first I went to Paris, Clutton, I think it was, gave a long discourse on the subject that beauty is put into things by painters and poets. They create beauty. In themselves there is nothing to choose between the Campanile of Giotto and a factory chimney. And then beautiful things grow rich with the emotion that they have aroused in succeeding generations. That is why old things are more beautiful than modern. The *Ode to a Grecian Urn* is more lovely now than when it was written, because for a hundred years lovers have read it and the sick at heart take comfort in its lines.'

Philip left Hayward to infer what in the passing scene had suggested these words to him, and it was a delight to know that he could safely leave the inference. It was in sudden reaction from the life he had been leading for so long that he was now deeply affected. The delicate iridescence of the London air gave the softness of a pastel to the grey stone of the buildings; and in the wharves and storehouses there was the severity of grace of a Japanese print. They went further down, and the splendid channel, a symbol of the great empire, broadened, and it was crowded with traffic; Philip thought of the painters and the poets who had made all these things so beautiful, and his heart was filled with gratitude. They came to the Pool of London, and who can describe its majesty? The imagination thrills, and Heaven knows what figures people still its broad stream, Doctor Johnson with Boswell by his side, and old Pepys going on board a man-o'-war: the pagent of English history, and romance and high adventure. Philip turned to Hayward with shining eyes.

'Dear Charles Dickens,' he murmured, smiling a little at his own emotion.

'Aren't you rather sorry you chucked painting?' asked Hayward.

'No.'

'I suppose you like doctoring?'

'No, I hate it; but there was nothing else to do. The drudgery of the first two years is awful, and unfortunately I haven't got the scientific temperament.'

'Well, you can't go on changing professions.'

'Oh, no. I'm going to stick to this. I think I shall like it better when I get into the wards. I have an idea that I'm more interested in people than in anything else in the world. And as far as I can see, it's the only profession in which you have your freedom. You carry your knowledge in your head; with a box of instruments and a few drugs you can make your living anywhere.'

'Aren't you going to take a practice then?'

'Not for a good long time at any rate,' Philip answered. 'As soon as I've got through my hospital appointments I shall get a ship; I want to go to the East – the Malay Archipelago, Siam, China, and all that sort of thing – and then I shall take odd jobs. Something always comes along – cholera duty in India and things like that. I want to go from place to place. I want to see the world. The only way a poor man can do that is by going in for the medical.'

They came to Greenwich then. The noble building of Inigo Jones faced the river grandly.

'I say, look, that must be the place where Poor Jack dived into the mud for pennies,' said Philip.

They wandered in the Park. Ragged children were playing in it, and it was noisy with their cries: here and there old seamen were basking in the sun. There was an air of a hundred years ago.

'It seems a pity you wasted two years in Paris,' said Hayward.

'Waste? Look at the movement of that child, look at the pattern which the sun makes on the ground, shining through the trees, look at that sky – why, I should never have seen that sky if I hadn't been to Paris.'

Hayward thought that Philip choked a sob, and he looked at him with astonishment.

'What's the matter with you?'

'Nothing. I'm sorry to be so damned emotional, but for six months I've been starved for beauty.'

'You used to be so matter-of-fact. It's very interesting to hear you say that.'

'Damn it all, I don't want to be interesting,' laughed Philip. 'Let's go and have a stodgy tea.'

LXV

HAYWARD'S visit did Philip a great deal of good. Each day his thoughts dwelt less on Mildred. He looked back upon the past with disgust. He could not understand how he had submitted to the dishonour of such a love; and when he thought of Mildred it was with angry hatred, because she had submitted him to so much humiliation. His imagination presented her to him now with her defects of person and manner exaggerated, so that he shuddered at the thought of having been connected with her.

'It just shows how damned weak I am,' he said to himself. The adventure was like a blunder that one had committed at a party so horrible that one felt nothing could be done to excuse it: the only remedy was to forget. His horror at the degradation he had suffered helped him. He was like a snake casting its skin and he looked upon the old covering with nausea. He exulted in the possession of himself once more; he realized how much of the delight of the world he had lost when he was absorbed in that madness which they called love; he had had enough of it; he did not want to be in love any more if love was that. Philip told Hayward something of what he had gone through.

'Wasn't it Sophocles,' he asked, 'who prayed for the time when he would be delivered from the wild beast of passion that devoured his heart-strings?'

Philip seemed really to be born again. He breathed the circumambient air as though he had never breathed it before, and he took a child's pleasure in all the facts of the world. He called his period of insanity six months' hard labour.

Hayward had only been settled in London a few days when Philip received from Backstable, where it had been sent, a card for a private view at some picture gallery. He took Hayward, and, on looking at the catalogue, saw that Lawson had a picture in it.

'I suppose he sent the card,' said Philip. 'Let's go and find him, he's sure to be in front of his picture.'

This, a profile of Ruth Chalice, was tucked away in a corner, and Lawson was not far from it. He looked a little lost, in his large soft hat and loose, pale clothes, amongst the fashionable throng that had gathered for the private view. He greeted Philip with enthusiasm, and with his usual volubility told him that he had come to live in London, Ruth Chalice was a hussy, he had taken a studio, Paris was played out, he had a commission for a portrait, and they'd better dine together and have a good old talk. Philip reminded him of his acquaintance with Hayward, and was entertained to see that Lawson was slightly awed by Hayward's elegant clothes and grand manner. They sat upon him better than they had done in the shabby little studio which Lawson and Philip had shared.

At dinner Lawson went on with his news. Flanagan had

gone back to America. Clutton had disappeared. He had come to the conclusion that a man had no chance of doing anything so long as he was in contact with art and artists: the only thing was to get right away. To make the step easier he had quarrelled with all his friends in Paris. He developed a talent for telling them home truths, which made them bear with fortitude his declaration that he had done with that city and was settling in Gerona, a little town in the north of Spain which had attracted him when he saw it from the train on his way to Barcelona. He was living there now alone.

'I wonder if he'll ever do any good,' said Philip.

He was interested in the human side of that struggle to express something which was so obscure in the man's mind that he was become morbid and querulous. Philip felt vaguely that he was himself in the same case, but with him it was the conduct of his life as a whole that perplexed him. That was his means of self-expression, and what he must do with it was not clear. But he had no time to continue with this train of thought, for Lawson poured out a frank recital of his affair with Ruth Chalice. She had left him for a young student who had just come from England, and was behaving in a scandalous fashion. Lawson really thought someone ought to step in and save the young man. She would ruin him. Philip gathered that Lawson's chief grievance was that the rupture had come in the middle of a portait he was painting.

'Women have no feeling for art,' he said. 'They only pretend they have.' But he finished philosophically enough: 'However, I got four portraits out of her, and I'm not sure if the last I was working on would ever have been a success.'

Philip envied the easy way in which the painter managed his love affairs. He had passed eighteen months pleasantly enough, had got an excellent model for nothing, and had parted from her at the end with no great pang.

'And what about Cronshaw?' asked Philip.

'Oh, he's done for,' answered Lawson, with the cheerful callousness of his youth. 'He'll be dead in six months. He got pneumonia last winter. He was in the English hospital for seven weeks, and when he came out they told him his only chance was to give up liquor.'

'Poor devil,' smiled the abstemious Philip.

'He kept off for a bit. He used to go to the Lilas all the same, he couldn't keep away from that, but he used to drink hot milk, *avec de la fleur d'oranger*, and he was damned dull.'

'I take it you did not conceal the fact from him.'

'Oh, he knew it himself. A little while ago he started on whisky again. He said he was too old to turn over any new leaves. He would rather be happy for six months and die at the end of it than linger on for five years. And then I think he's been awfully hard up lately. You see, he didn't earn anything while he was ill, and the slut he lives with has been giving him a rotten time.'

'I remember, the first time I saw him I admired him awfully,' said Philip. 'I thought he was wonderful. It is sickening that vulgar, middle-class virtue should pay.'

'Of course he was a rotter. He was bound to end in the gutter sooner or later,' said Lawson.

Philip was hurt because Lawson would not see the pity of it. Of course it was cause and effect, but in the necessity with which one follows the other lay all the tragedy of life.

'Oh, I'd forgotten,' said Lawson. 'Just after you left he sent round a present for you. I thought you'd be coming back and I didn't bother about it, and then I didn't think it worth sending on; but it'll come over to London with the rest of my things, and you can come to my studio one day and fetch it away if you want it.'

'You haven't told me what it is yet.'

'Oh, it's only a ragged little bit of carpet. I shouldn't think it's worth anything. I asked him one day what the devil he'd sent the filthy thing for. He told me he'd seen it in a shop in the Rue de Rennes and bought it for fifteen francs. It appears to be a Persian rug. He said you'd asked him the meaning of life and that was the answer. But he was very drunk.'

Philip laughed.

'Oh yes, I know. I'll take it. It was a favourite wheeze of his. He said I must find out for myself, or else the answer meant nothing.'

LXVI

PHILIP worked well and easily; he had a good deal to do, since he was taking in July the three parts of the First Conjoint examination, two of which he had failed in before; but he found life pleasant. He made a new friend. Lawson, on the look-out for models, had discovered a girl who was understudying at one of the theatres, and in order to induce her to sit to him arranged a little luncheon party one Sunday. She brought a chaperon with her; and to her Philip, asked to

314

make a fourth, was instructed to confine his attentions. He found this easy, since she turned out to be an agreeable chatterbox with an amusing tongue. She asked Philip to go and see her; she had rooms in Vincent Square, and was always in to tea at five o'clock; he went, was delighted with his welcome, and went again. Mrs Nesbit was not more than twenty-five, very small, with a pleasant, ugly face; she had very bright eyes, high cheek-bones, and a large mouth: the excessive contrasts of her colouring reminded one of a portrait by one of the modern French painters; her skin was very white, her cheeks were very red, her thick eyebrows, her hair, were very black. The effect was odd, a little unnatural, but far from unpleasing. She was separated from her husband and earned her living and her child's by writing penny novelettes. There were one or two publishers who made a speciality of that sort of thing, and she had as much work as she could do. It was ill-paid, she received fifteen pounds for a story of thirty thousand words; but she was satisfied.

'After all it only costs the reader twopence,' she said, 'and they like the same thing over and over again. I just change the names and that's all. When I'm bored I think of the washing and the rent and clothes for baby, and I go on again.'

Besides, she walked on at various theatres where they wanted supers and earned by this when in work from sixteen shillings to a guinea a week. At the end of her day she was so tired that she slept like a top. She made the best of her difficult lot. Her keen sense of humour enabled her to get amusement out of every vexatious circumstance. Sometimes things went wrong, and she found herself with no money at all; then her trifling possessions found their way to a pawnshop in the Vauxhall Bridge Road, and she ate bread and butter till things grew brighter. She never lost her cheerfulness.

Philip was interested in her shiftless life, and she made him laugh with the fantastic narration of her struggles. He asked her why she did not try her hand at literary work of a better sort, but she knew that she had no talent, and the abominable stuff she turned out by the thousand words was not only tolerably paid, but was the best she could do. She had nothing to look forward to but a continuation of the life she led. She seemed to have no relations, and her friends were as poor as herself.

'I don't think of the future,' she said. 'As long as I have enough money for three weeks' rent and a pound or two over for food I never bother. Life wouldn't be worth living if I worried over the future as well as the present. When things are at their worst I find something always happens.'

Soon Philip grew in the habit of going in to tea with her every day, and so that his visits might not embarrass her he took in a cake or a pound of butter or some tea. They started to call one another by their Christian names. Feminine sympathy was new to him, and he delighted in someone who gave a willing ear to all his troubles. The hours went quickly. He did not hide his admiration for her. She was a delightful companion. He could not help comparing her with Mildred; and he contrasted with the one's obstinate stupidity, which refused interest to everything she did not know, the other's quick appreciation and ready intelligence. His heart sank when he thought that he might have been tied for life to such a woman as Mildred. One evening he told Norah the whole story of his love. It was not one to give him much reason for self-esteem, and it was very pleasant to receive such charming sympathy.

'I think you're well out of it,' she said, when he had finished.

She had a funny way at times of holding her head on one side like an Aberdeen puppy. She was sitting in an upright chair, sewing, for she had no time for doing nothing, and Philip had made himself comfortable at her feet.

'I can't tell you how heartily thankful I am it's all over,' he sighed.

'Poor thing, you must have had a rotten time,' she murmured, and by way of showing her sympathy put her hand on his shoulder.

He took it and kissed it, but she withdrew it quickly.

'Why did you do that?' she asked, with a blush.

'Have you any objection?'

She looked at him for a moment with twinkling eyes, and she smiled.

'No,' she said.

He got up on his knees and faced her. She looked into his eyes steadily, and her large mouth trembled with a smile.

'Well?' she said.

'You know, you are a ripper. I'm so grateful to you for being nice to me. I like you so much.'

'Don't be idiotic,' she said.

Philip took hold of her elbows and drew her towards him. She made no resistance, but bent forward a little, and he kissed her red lips.

'Why did you do that?' she asked again.

316

'Because it's comfortable.'

She did not answer, but a tender look came into her eyes, and she passed her hand softly over his hair.

'You know, it's awfully silly of you to behave like this. We were such good friends. It would be so jolly to leave it at that.'

'If you really want to appeal to my better nature,' replied Philip, 'you'll do well not to stroke my cheek while you're doing it.'

She gave a little chuckle, but she did not stop.

'It's very wrong of me, isn't it?' she said.

Philip, surprised and a little amused, looked into her eyes, and as he looked he saw them soften and grow liquid, and there was an expression in them that enchanted him. His heart was suddenly stirred, and tears came to his eyes.

'Norah, you're not fond of me, are you?' he asked, incredulously.

'You clever boy, you ask such stupid questions.'

'Oh, my dear, it never struck me that you could be.'

He flung his arms round her and kissed her, while she, laughing, blushing, and crying, surrendered herself willingly to his embrace.

Presently he released her and sitting back on his heels looked at her curiously.

'Well, I'm blowed!' he said.

'Why?'

'I'm so surprised.'

'And pleased?'

'Delighted,' he cried with all his heart, 'and so proud and so happy and so grateful.'

He took her hands and covered them with kisses. This was the beginning for Philip of a happiness which seemed both solid and durable. They became lovers but remained friends. There was in Norah a maternal instinct which received satisfaction in her love for Philip; she wanted someone to pet, and scold, and make a fuss of; she had a domestic temperament and found pleasure in looking after his health and his linen. She pitied his deformity, over which he was so sensitive, and her pity expressed itself instinctively in tenderness. She was young, strong, and healthy, and it seemed quite natural to her to give her love. She had high spirits and a merry soul. She liked Philip because he laughed with her at all the amusing things in life that caught her fancy, and above all she liked him because he was he.

When she told him this he answered gaily:

'Nonsense. You like me because I'm a silent person and never want to get a word in.'

Philip did not love her at all. He was extremely fond of her, glad to be with her, amused and interested by her conversation. She restored his belief in himself and put healing ointments, as it were, on all the bruises of his soul. He was immensely flattered that she cared for him. He admired her courage, her optimism, her impudent defiance of fate; she had a little philosophy of her own, ingenuous and practical.

'You know, I don't believe in churches and parsons and all that,' she said, 'but I believe in God, and I don't believe He minds much about what you do as long as you keep your end up and help a lame dog over a stile when you can. And I think people on the whole are very nice, and I'm sorry for those who aren't.'

'And what about afterwards?' asked Philip.

'Oh, well, I don't know for certain, you know,' she smiled, 'but I hope for the best. And anyhow there'll be no rent to pay and no novelettes to write.'

She had a feminine gift for delicate flattery. She thought that Philip did a brave thing when he left Paris because he was conscious he could not be a great artist; and he was enchanted when she expressed enthusiastic admiration for him. He had never been quite certain whether this action indicated courage or infirmity of purpose. It was delightful to realize that she considered it heroic. She ventured to tackle him on a subject which his friends instinctively avoided.

'It's very silly of you to be so sensitive about your club-foot,' she said. She saw him flush darkly, but went on. 'You know, people don't think about it nearly as much as you do. They notice it the first time they see you, and then they forget about it.'

He would not answer.

'You're not angry with me, are you?'

'No.'

She put her arm round his neck.

'You know, I only speak about it because I love you. I don't want it to make you unhappy.'

'I think you can say anything you choose to me,' he answered, smiling. 'I wish I could do something to show you how grateful I am to you.'

She took him in hand in other ways. She would not let him be bearish and laughed at him when he was out of temper. She made him more urbane.

'You can make me do anything you like,' he said to her once.

318

'D'you mind?'

'No, I want to do what you like.'

He had the sense to realize his happiness. It seemed to him that she gave him all that a wife could, and he preserved his freedom; she was the most charming friend he had ever had, with a sympathy that he had never found in a man. The sexual relationship was no more than the strongest link in their friendship. It completed it, but was not essential. And because Philip's appetites were satisfied, he became more equable and easier to live with. He felt in complete possession of himself. He thought sometimes of the winter, during which he had been obsessed by a hideous passion, and he was filled with loathing for Mildred and with horror of himself.

His examinations were approaching, and Norah was as interested in them as he. He was flattered and touched by her eagerness. She made him promise to come at once and tell her the result. He passed the three parts this time without mishap, and when he went to tell her she burst into tears.

'Oh, I'm so glad, I was so anxious.'

'You silly little thing,' he laughed, but he was choking.

No one could help being pleased with the way she took it.

'And what are you going to do now?' she asked.

'I can take a holiday with a clear conscience. I have no work to do till the winter session begins in October.'

'I suppose you'll go down to your uncle's at Blackstable?'

'You suppose quite wrong. I'm going to stay in London and play with you.'

'I'd rather you went away.'

'Why? Are you tired of me?'

She laughed and put her hands on his shoulders.

'Because you've been working hard, and you look utterly washed out. You want some fresh air and a rest. Please go.'

He did not answer for a moment. He looked at her with loving eyes.

'You know, I'd never believe it of anyone but you. You're only thinking of my good. I wonder what you see in me.'

'Will you give me a good character with my month's notice?' she laughed gaily.

'I'll say that you're thoughtful and kind, and you're not exacting; you never worry, you're not troublesome, and you're easy to please.'

'All that's nonsense,' she said, 'but I'll tell you one thing: I'm one of the few persons I ever met who are able to learn from experience.'

LXVII

PHILIP looked forward to his return to London with impatience. During the two months he spent at Blackstable Norah wrote to him frequently, long letters in a bold, large hand, in which with cheerful humour she described the little events of the daily round, the domestic troubles of her landlady, rich food for laughter, the comic vexations of her rehearsals – she was walking on in an important spectacle at one of the London theatres – and her odd adventures with the publishers of novelettes. Philip read a great deal, bathed, played tennis, and sailed. At the beginning of October he settled down in London to work for the Second Conjoint examination. He was eager to pass it, since that ended the drudgery of the curriculum; after it was done with the student became an out-patients' clerk, and was brought in contact with men and women as well as with textbooks. Philip saw Norah every day.

Lawson had been spending the summer at Poole, and had a number of sketches to show of the harbour and of the beach. He had a couple of commissions for portraits and proposed to stay in London till the bad light drove him away. Hayward, in London too, intended to spend the winter abroad, but remained week after week from sheer inability to make up his mind to go. Hayward had run to fat during the last two or three years – it was five years since Philip first met him in Heidelberg – and he was prematurely bald. He was very sensistive about it and wore his hair long to conceal the unsightly patch on the crown of his head. His only consolation was that his brow was now very noble. His blue eyes had lost their colour; they had a listless droop; and his mouth, losing the fullness of youth, was weak and pale. He still talked vaguely of the things he was going to do in the future, but with less conviction; and he was conscious that his friends no longer believed in him: when he had drunk two or three glasses of whisky he was inclined to be elegiac.

'I'm a failure,' he murmured, 'I'm unfit for the brutality of the struggle of life. All I can do is to stand aside and let the vulgar throng bustle by in their pursuit of the good things.'

He gave you the impression that to fail was a more delicate, a more exquisite thing than to succeed. He insinuated that his aloofness was due to distaste for all that was common and low. He talked beautifully of Plato.

'I should have thought you'd got through with Plato by now,' said Philip impatiently.

'Would you?' he asked, raising his eyebrows.

He was not inclined to pursue the subject. He had discovered of late the effective dignity of silence.

'I don't see the use of reading the same thing over and over again,' said Philip. 'That's only a laborious form of idleness.'

'But are you under the impression that you have so great a mind that you can understand the most profound writer at a first reading?'

'I don't want to understand him, I'm not a critic. I'm not interested in him for his sake but for mine.'

'Why d'you read then?'

'Partly for pleasure, because it's a habit and I'm just as uncomfortable if I don't read as if I don't smoke, and partly to know myself. When I read a book I seem to read it with my eyes only, but now and then I come across a passage, perhaps only a phrase, which has a meaning for *me*, and it becomes part of me; I've got out of the book all that's any use to me, and I can't get anything more if I read it a dozen times. You see, it seems to me, one's like a closed bud, and most of what one reads and does has no effect at all; but there are certain things that have a peculiar significance for one, and they open a petal; and the petals open one by one; and at last the flower is there.'

Philip was not satisfied with his metaphor, but he did not know how else to explain a thing which he felt and yet was not clear about.

'You want to do things, you want to become things,' said Hayward, with a shrug of the shoulders. 'It's so vulgar.'

Philip knew Hayward very well by now. He was weak and vain, so vain that you had to be on the watch constantly not to hurt his feelings; he mingled idleness and idealism so that he could not separate them. At Lawson's studio one day he met a journalist, who was charmed by his conversation, and a week later the editor of a paper wrote to suggest that he should do some criticism for him. For forty-eight hours Hayward lived in an agony of indecision. He had talked of getting occupation of this sort so long that he had not the face to refuse outright, but the thought of doing anything filled him with panic. At last he declined the offer and breathed freely.

'It would have interfered with my work,' he told Philip.

'What work?' asked Philip brutally.

'My inner life,' he answered.

Then he went on to say beautiful things about Amiel, the

professor of Geneva, whose brilliancy promised achievement which was never fulfilled; till at his death the reason of his failure and the excuse were at once manifest in the minute, wonderful journal which was found among his papers. Hayward smiled enigmatically.

But Hayward could still talk delightfully about books; his taste was exquisite and his discrimination elegant; and he had a constant interest in ideas, which made him an entertaining companion. They meant nothing to him really, since they never had any effect on him; but he treated them as he might have pieces of china in an auction-room, handling them with pleasure in their shape and their glaze, pricing them in his mind; and then, putting them back into their case, thought of them no more.

And it was Hayward who made a momentous discovery. One evening, after due preparation, he took Philip and Lawson to a tavern situated in Beak Street, remarkable not only in itself and for its history – it had memories of eighteenth-century glories which excited the romantic imagination – but for its snuff, which was the best in London, and above all for its punch. Hayward led them into a large, long room, dingily magnificent, with huge pictures on the walls of nude women: they were vast allegories of the school of Haydon; but smoke, gas, and the London atmosphere had given them a richness which made them look like old masters. The dark panelling, the massive, tarnished gold of the cornice, the mahogany tables, gave the room an air of sumptuous comfort, and the leather-covered seats along the wall were soft and easy. There was a ram's head on a table opposite the door, and this contained the celebrated snuff. They ordered punch. They drank it. It was hot rum punch. The pen falters when it attempts to treat of the excellence thereof; the sober vocabulary, the sparse epithet of this narrative, are inadequate to the task; and pompous terms, jewelled, exotic phrases rise to the excited fancy. It warmed the blood and cleared the head; it filled the soul with well-being; it disposed the mind at once to utter wit, and to appreciate the wit of others; it had the vagueness of music and the precision of mathematics. Only one of its qualities was comparable to anything else; it had the warmth of a good heart; but its taste, its smell, its feel, were not to be described in words. Charles Lamb, with his infinite tact, attempting to, might have drawn charming pictures of the life of his day; Lord Byron in a stanza of Don Juan, aiming at the impossible, might have achieved the sublime; Oscar Wilde, heaping jewels of Ispahan upon brocades

322

of Byzantium, might have created a troubling beauty. Considering it, the mind reeled under visions of the feasts of Elagabalus; and the subtle harmonies of Debussy mingled with the musty, fragrant romance of chests in which have been kept old clothes, ruffs, hose, doublets, of a forgotten generation, and the wan odour of lilies of the valley and the savour of Cheddar cheese.

Hayward discovered the tavern at which this priceless beverage was to be obtained, by meeting in the street a man called Macalister who had been at Cambridge with him. He was a stockbroker and a philosopher. He was accustomed to go to the tavern once a week; and soon Philip, Lawson, and Hayward got into the habit of meeting there every Tuesday evening: change of manners made it now little frequented, which was an advantage to persons who took pleasure in conversation. Macalister was a big-boned fellow, much too short for his width, with a large, fleshy face and a soft voice. He was a student of Kant and judged everything from the standpoint of pure reason. He was fond of expounding his doctrines. Philip listened with excited interest. He had long come to the conclusion that nothing amused him more than metaphysics, but he was not so sure of their efficacy in the affairs of life. The neat little system which he had formed as the result of his meditations at Blackstable had not been of conspicuous use during his infatuation for Mildred. He could not be positive that reason was much help in the conduct of life. It seemed to him that life lived itself. He remembered very vividly the violence of the emotion which had possessed him and his inability, as if he were tied down to the ground with ropes, to react against it. He read many wise things in books, but he could only judge from his own experience (he did not know whether he was different from other people); he did not calculate the pros and cons of an action, the benefits which must befall him if he did it, the harm which might result from the omission; but his whole being was urged on irresistibly. He did not act with a part of himself but altogether. The power that possessed him seemed to have nothing to do with reason: all that reason did was to point out the methods of obtaining what his whole soul was striving for.

Macalister reminded him of the Categorical Imperative:

'Act so that every action of yours should be capable of becoming a universal rule of action for all men.'

'That seems to me perfect nonsense,' said Philip.

'You're a bold man to say that of anything stated by Immanuel Kant,' retorted Macalister.

'Why? Reverence for what somebody said is a stultifying quality: there's a damned sight too much reverence in the world. Kant thought things, not because they were true, but because he was Kant.'

'Well, what is your objection to the Categorical Imperative?'

(They talked as though the fate of empires were in the balance.)

'It suggests that one can choose one's course by an effort of will. And it suggests that reason is the surest guide. Why should its dictates be any better than those of passion? They're different. That's all.'

'You seem to be a contented slave of your passions.'

'A slave because I can't help myself, but not a contented one,' laughed Philip.

While he spoke he thought of that hot madness which had driven him in pursuit of Mildred. He remembered how he had chafed against it and how he had felt the degradation of it.

'Thank God, I'm free from all that now,' he thought.

And yet even as he said it he was not quite sure whether he spoke sincerely. When he was under the influence of passion he had felt a singular vigour, and his mind had worked with unwonted force. He was more alive, there was an excitement in sheer being, an eager vehemence of soul, which made life now a trifle dull. For all the misery he had endured there was a compensation in that sense of rushing, overwhelming existence.

But Philip's unlucky words engaged him in a discussion on the freedom of the will, and Macalister, with his well-stored memory, brought out argument after argument. He had a mind that delighted in dialectics, and he forced Philip to contradict himself; he pushed him into corners from which he could only escape by damaging concessions; he tripped him up with logic and battered him with authorities.

At last Philip said:

'Well, I can't say anything about other people. I can only speak for myself. The illusion of free will is so strong in my mind that I can't get away from it, but I believe it is only an illusion. But it is an illusion which is one of the strongest motives of my actions. Before I do anything I feel that I have choice, and that influences what I do; but afterwards, when the thing is done, I believe that it was inevitable from all eternity.'

'What do you deduce from that?' asked Hayward.

'Why, merely the futility of regret. It's no good crying over spilt milk, because all the forces of the universe were bent on spilling it.'

LXVIII

ONE morning Phillip on getting up felt his head swim, and going back to bed suddenly discovered he was ill. All his limbs ached and he shivered with cold. When the landlady brought in his breakfast he called to her through the open door that he was not well, and asked for a cup of tea and a piece of toast. A few minutes later there was a knock at his door, and Griffiths came in. They had lived in the same house for over a year, but had never done more than nod to one another in the passage.

'I say, I hear you're seedy,' said Griffiths. 'I thought I'd come in and see what was the matter with you.'

Philip, blushing he knew not why, made light of the whole thing. He would be all right in an hour or two.

'Well, you'd better let me take your temperature,' said Griffiths.

'It's quite unnecessary,' answered Philip irritably.

'Come on.'

Philip put the thermometer in his mouth. Griffiths sat on the bed and chatted brightly for a moment, then he took it out and looked at it.

'Now, look here, old man, you must stay in bed, and I'll bring old Deacon in to have a look at you.'

'Nonsense,' said Philip. 'There's nothing the matter. I wish you wouldn't bother about me.'

'But it isn't any bother. You've got a temperature and you must stay in bed. You will, won't you?'

There was a peculiar charm in his manner, a mingling of gravity and kindliness, which was infinitely attractive.

'You've got a wonderful bedside manner,' Philip murmured, closing his eyes with a smile.

Griffiths shook out his pillow for him, deftly smoothed down the bedclothes, and tucked him up. He went into Philip's sitting-room to look for a siphon, could not find one, and fetched it from his own room. He drew down the blind.

'Now go to sleep and I'll bring the old man round as soon as he's done the wards.'

It seemed hours before anyone came to Philip. His head felt as if it would split, anguish rent his limbs, and he was afraid he was going to cry. Then there was a knock at the door and Griffiths, healthy, strong, and cheerful, came in.

'Here's Doctor Deacon,' he said.

The physician stepped forward, an elderly man with a bland manner, whom Philip knew only by sight. A few questions, a brief examination, and the diagnosis.

'What d'you make of it?' he asked Griffiths, smiling.

'Influenza.'

'Quite right.'

Doctor Deacon looked round the dingy lodging-house room.

'Wouldn't you like to go to the hospital? They'll put you in a private ward, and you can be better looked after than you can here.'

'I'd rather stay where I am,' said Philip.

He did not want to be disturbed, and he was always shy of new surroundings. He did not fancy nurses fussing about him, and the dreary cleanliness of the hospital.

'I can look after him, sir,' said Griffiths at once.

'Oh, very well.'

He wrote a prescription, gave instructions, and left.

'Now you've got to do exactly as I tell you,' said Griffiths. 'I'm day-nurse and night-nurse all in one.'

'It's very kind of you, but I shan't want anything,' said Philip.

Griffiths put his hand on Philip's forehead, a large cool, dry hand, and the touch seemed to him good.

'I'm just going to take this round to the dispensary to have it made up, and then I'll come back.'

In a little while he brought the medicine and gave Philip a dose. Then he went upstairs to fetch his books.

'You won't mind my working in your room this afternoon, will you?' he said, when he came down. 'I'll leave the door open so that you can give me a shout if you want anything.'

Later in the day Philip, awaking from an uneasy doze, heard voices in his sitting-room. A friend had come in to see Griffiths.

'I say, you'd better not come in tonight,' he heard Griffiths say.

And then a minute or two afterwards someone else entered the room and expressed his surprise at finding Griffiths there. Philip heard him explain.

'I'm looking after a second year's man who's got these rooms. The wretched blighter's down with influenza. No whist tonight, old man.'

Presently Griffiths was left alone and Philip called him.

'I say, you're not putting off a party tonight, are you?' he asked.

'Not on your account. I must work at my surgery.'

'Don't put it off. I shall be all right. You needn't bother about me.'

'That's all right.'

Philip grew worse. As the night came on he became slightly delirious, but towards morning he awoke from a restless sleep. He saw Griffiths get out of an armchair, go down on his knees, and with his fingers put piece after piece of coal on the fire. He was in pyjamas and a dressing-gown.

'What are you doing here?' he asked.

'Did I wake you up? I tried to make up the fire without making a row.'

'Why aren't you in bed? What's the time?'

'About five. I thought I'd better sit up with you tonight. I brought an armchair in as I thought if I put a mattress down I should sleep so soundly that I shouldn't hear you if you wanted anything.'

'I wish you wouldn't be so good to me,' groaned Philip. 'Suppose you catch it?'

'Then you shall nurse me, old man,' said Griffiths, with a laugh.

In the morning Griffiths drew up the blind. He looked pale and tired after his night's watch, but was full of spirits.

'Now I'm going to wash you,' he said to Philip cheerfully.

'I can wash myself,' said Philip, ashamed.

'Nonsense. If you were in the small ward a nurse would wash you, and I can do it just as well as a nurse.'

Philip, too weak and wretched to resist, allowed Griffiths to wash his hands and face, his feet, his chest and back. He did it with charming tenderness, carrying on meanwhile a stream of friendly chatter; and he changed the sheet just as they did at the hospital, shook out the pillow, and arranged the bed-clothes.

'I should like Sister Arthur to see me. It would make her sit up. Deacon's coming in to see you early.'

'I can't imagine why you should be so good to me,' said Philip.

'It's good practice for me. It's rather a lark having a patient.'

Griffiths gave him his breakfast and went off to get dressed and have something to eat. A few minutes before ten he came back with a bunch of grapes and a few flowers.

'You are awfully kind,' said Philip.

He was in bed for five days.

Norah and Griffiths nursed him between them. Though Griffiths was the same age as Philip he adopted towards him a humorous, motherly attitude. He was a thoughtful fellow, gentle and encouraging; but his greatest quality was a vitality which seemed to give health to everyone with whom he came in contact. Philip was unused to the petting which most people enjoy from mothers or sisters and he was deeply touched by the feminine tenderness of this strong young man. Philip grew better. Then Griffiths, sitting idly in Philip's room, amused him with gay stories of amorous adventure. He was a flirtatious creature, capable of carrying on three or four affairs at a time; and his account of the devices he was forced to in order to keep out of difficulties made excellent hearing. He had a gift for throwing a romantic glamour over everything that happened to him. He was crippled with debts, everything he had of any value was pawned, but he managed always to be cheerful, extravagant, and generous. He was the adventurer by nature. He loved people of doubtful occupations and shifty purposes; and his acquaintance among the riff-raff that frequents the bars of London was enormous. Loose women, treating him as a friend, told him the troubles, difficulties, and successes of their lives; and card-sharpers, respecting his impecuniosity, stood him dinners and lent him five-pound notes. He was ploughed in his examinations time after time; but he bore this cheerfully, and submitted with such a charming grace to the parental expostulations that his father, a doctor in practice at Leeds, had not the heart to be seriously angry with him.

'I'm an awful fool at books,' he said cheerfully, 'but I *can't* work.'

Life was much too jolly. But it was clear that when he had got through the exuberance of his youth, and was at last qualified, he would be a tremendous success in practice. He would cure people by the sheer charm of his manner.

Philip worshipped him as at school he had worshipped boys who were tall and straight and high of spirits. By the time he was well they were fast friends, and it was a peculiar satisfaction to Philip that Griffiths seemed to enjoy sitting in his little parlour, wasting Philip's time with his amusing chatter and smoking innumerable cigarettes. Philip took him sometimes to the tavern off Regent Street. Hayward found him stupid, but Lawson recognized his charm and was eager to paint him; he was a picturesque figure with his blue eyes, white skin, and curly hair. Often they discussed things he knew nothing about, and then he sat quietly, with a good-natured smile on his handsome face, feeling quite rightly that his presence was sufficient contribution to the entertainment of the company.

When he discovered that Macalister was a stockbroker he was eager for tips; and Macalister, with his grave smile, told him what fortunes he could have made if he had bought certain stock at certain times. It made Philip's mouth water, for in one way and another he was spending more than he had expected, and it would have suited him very well to make a little money by the easy method Macalister suggested.

'Next time I hear of a really good thing I'll let you know,' said the stockbroker. 'They do come along sometimes. It's only a matter of biding one's time.'

Philip could not help thinking how delightful it would be to make fifty pounds, so that he could give Norah the furs she so badly needed for the winter. He looked at the shops in Regent Street and picked out the articles he could buy for the money. She deserved everything. She made his life very happy.

LXIX

ONE afternoon, when he went back to his rooms from the hospital to wash and tidy himself before going to tea as usual with Norah, as he let himself in with his latch-key, his landlady opened the door for him.

'There's a lady waiting to see you,' she said.

'Me?' exclaimed Philip.

He was surprised. It would only be Norah, and he had no idea what had brought her.

'I shouldn't 'ave let her in, only she's been three times, and she seemed that upset at not finding you, so I told her she could wait.'

He pushed past the explaining landlady and burst into the room. His heart turned sick. It was Mildred. She was sitting down, but got up hurriedly as he came in. She did not move towards him nor speak. He was so surprised that he did not know what he was saying.

'What the hell d'you want?' he asked.

She did not answer, but began to cry. She did not put her hands to her eyes, but kept them hanging by the side of her body. She looked like a housemaid applying for a situation. There was a dreadful humility in her bearing. Philip did not know what feelings came over him. He had a sudden impulse to turn round and escape from the room.

'I didn't think I'd ever see you again,' he said at last.

'I wish I was dead,' she moaned.

Philip left her standing where she was. He could only think at the moment of steadying himself. His knees were shaking. He looked at her, and he groaned in despair.

'What's the matter?' he said.

'He's left me – Emil.'

Philip's heart bounded. He knew then that he loved her as passionately as ever. He had never ceased to love her. She was standing before him humble and unresisting. He wished to take her in his arms and cover her tear-stained face with kisses. Oh, how long the separation had been! He did not know how he could have endured it.

'You'd better sit down. Let me give you a drink.'

He drew the chair near the fire and she sat in it. He mixed her whisky and soda, and, sobbing still, she drank it. She looked at him with great, mournful eyes. There were large black lines under them. She was thinner and whiter than when last he had seen her.

'I wish I'd married you when you asked me,' she said.

Philip did not know why the remark seemed to swell his heart. He could not keep the distance from her which he had forced upon himself. He put his hand on her shoulder.

'I'm awfully sorry you're in trouble.'

She leaned her head against his bosom and burst into hysterical crying. Her hat was in the way and she took it off. He had never dreamt that she was capable of crying like that. He kissed her again and again. It seemed to ease her a little.

'You were always good to me, Philip,' she said. 'That's why I knew I could come to you.'

'Tell me what's happened.'

'Oh, I can't, I can't,' she cried out, breaking away from him.

He sank down on his knees beside her and put his cheek against hers.

'Don't you know that there's nothing you can't tell me. I can never blame you for anything.'

She told him the story little by little, and sometimes she sobbed so much that he could hardly understand.

'Last Monday week he went up to Birmingham, and he promised to be back on Thursday, and he never came, and he didn't come on the Friday, so I wrote to ask what was the matter, and he never answered the letter. And I wrote and said that if I didn't hear from him by return I'd go up to Birmingham, and this morning I got a solicitor's letter to say I had no claim on him, and if I molested him he'd seek the protection of the law.'

'But it's absurd,' cried Philip. 'A man can't treat his wife like that. Had you had a row?'

'Oh, yes, we'd had a quarrel on the Sunday, and he said he was sick of me, but he'd said it before, and he'd come back all right. I didn't think he meant it. He was frightened because I told him a baby was coming. I kept it from him as long as I could. Then I had to tell him. He said it was my fault, and I ought to have known better. If you'd only heard the things he said to me! But I found out precious quick that he wasn't a gentleman. He left me without a penny. He hadn't paid the rent, and I hadn't got the money to pay it, and the woman who kept the house said such things to me – well, I might have been a thief the way she talked.'

'I thought you were going to take a flat.'

'That's what he said, but we just took furnished apartments in Highbury. He was that mean. He said I was extravagant; he didn't give me anything to be extravagant with.'

She had an extraordinary way of mixing the trivial with the important. Philip was puzzled. The whole thing was incomprehensible.

'No man could be such a blackguard.'

'You don't know him. I wouldn't go back to him now not if he was to come and ask me on his bended knees. I was a fool ever to think of him. And he wasn't earning the money he said he was. The lies he told me!'

Philip thought for a minute or two. He was so deeply moved by her distress that he could not think of himself.

'Would you like me to go to Birmingham? I could see him and try to make things up.'

'Oh, there's no chance of that. He'll never come back now, I know him.'

'But he must provide for you. He can't get out of that. I don't know anything about these things, you'd better go and see a solicitor.'

'How can I? I haven't got the money.'

'I'll pay all that. I'll write a note to my own solicitor, the sportsman who was my father's executor. Would you like me to come with you now? I expect he'll still be at his office.'

'No, give me a letter to him. I'll go alone.'

She was a little calmer now. He sat down and wrote a note. Then he remembered that she had no money. He had fortunately changed a cheque the day before and was able to give her five pounds.

'You are good to me, Philip,' she said.

331

'I'm so happy to be able to do something for you.'

'Are you fond of me still?'

'Just as fond as ever.'

She put up her lips and he kissed her. There was a surrender in the action which he had never seen in her before. It was worth all the agony he had suffered.

She went away and he found that she had been there for two hours. He was extraordinarily happy.

'Poor thing, poor thing,' he murmured to himself, his heart glowing with a greater love than he had ever felt before.

He never thought of Norah at all till about eight o'clock a telegram came. He knew before opening it that it was from her.

Is anything the matter? Norah.

He did not know what to do nor what to answer. He could fetch her after the play, in which she was walking on, was over and stroll home with her as he sometimes did; but his whole soul revolted against the idea of seeing her that evening. He thought of writing to her, but he could not bring himself to address her as usual, *dearest Norah*. He made up his mind to telegraph.

Sorry. Could not get away. Philip.

He visualized her. He was slightly repelled by the ugly little face, with its high cheek-bones and the crude colour. There was a coarseness in her skin which gave him goose-flesh. He knew that his telegram must be followed by some action on his part, but at all events it postponed it.

Next day he wired again.

Regret, unable to come. Will write.

Mildred had suggested coming at four in the afternoon, and he would not tell her that the hour was inconvenient. After all she came first. He waited for her impatiently. He watched for her at the window and opened the front door himself.

'Well? Did you see Nixon?'

'Yes,' she answered. 'He said it wasn't any good. Nothing's to be done. I must just grin and bear it.'

'But that's impossible,' cried Philip.

She sat down wearily.

'Did he give any reasons?' he asked.

She gave him a crumpled letter.

'There's your letter, Philip. I never took it. I couldn't tell you yesterday, I really couldn't. Emil didn't marry me. He couldn't. He had a wife already and three children.'

Philip felt a sudden pang of jealousy and anguish. It was almost more than he could bear.

'That's why I couldn't go back to my aunt. There's no one I can go to but you.'

'What made you go away with him?' Philip asked, in a low voice which he struggled to make firm.

'I don't know. I didn't know he was a married man at first, and when he told me I gave him a piece of my mind. And then I didn't see him for months, and when he came to the shop again and asked me I don't know what came over me. I felt as if I couldn't help it. I had to go with him.'

'Were you in love with him?'

'I don't know. I couldn't hardly help laughing at the things he said. And there was something about him – he said I'd never regret it, he promised to give me seven pounds a week – he said he was earning fifteen, and it was all a lie, he wasn't. And then I was sick of going to the shop every morning, and I wasn't getting on very well with my aunt; she wanted to treat me as a servant instead of a relation, said I ought to do my own room, and if I didn't do it nobody was going to do it for me. Oh, I wish I hadn't. But when he came to the shop and asked me I felt I couldn't help it.'

Philip moved away from her. He sat down at the table and buried his face in his hands. He felt dreadfully humiliated.

'You're not angry with me, Philip?' she asked piteously.

'No,' he answered, looking up but away from her, 'only I'm awfully hurt.'

'Why?'

'You see, I was so dreadfully in love with you. I did everything I could to make you care for me. I thought you were incapable of loving anyone. It's so horrible to know that you were willing to sacrifice everything for that bounder. I wonder what you saw in him.'

'I'm awfully sorry, Philip. I regretted it bitterly afterwards, I promise you that.'

He thought of Emil Miller, with his pasty, unhealthy look, his shifty blue eyes, and the vulgar smartness of his appearance; he always wore bright red knitted waistcoats. Philip sighed. She got up and went to him. She put her arm round his neck.

'I shall never forget that you offered to marry me, Philip.'

He took her hand and looked up at her. She bent down and kissed him.

'Philip, if you want me still I'll do anything you like now. I know you're a gentleman in every sense of the word.'

333

His heart stood still. Her words made him feel slightly sick.

'It's awfully good of you, but I couldn't.'

'Don't you care for me any more?'

'Yes, I love you with all my heart.'

'Then why shouldn't we have a good time while we've got the chance? You see, it can't matter now.'

He released himself from her.

'You don't understand. I've been sick with love for you ever since I saw you, but now – that man. I've unfortunately got a vivid imagination. The thought of it simply disgusts me.'

'You are funny,' she said.

He took her hand again and smiled at her.

'You mustn't think I'm not grateful. I can never thank you enough, but, you see, it's just stronger than I am.'

'You are a good friend, Philip.'

They went on talking, and soon they had returned to the familiar companionship of old days. It grew late. Philip suggested that they should dine together and go to a music-hall. She wanted some persuasion, for she had an idea of acting up to her situation, and felt instinctively that it did not accord with her distressed condition to go to a place of entertainment. At last Philip asked her to go simply to please him, and when she could look upon it as an act of self-sacrifice she accepted. She had a new thoughtfulness which delighted Philip. She asked him to take her to the little restaurant in Soho to which they had so often been; he was infinitely grateful to her, because her suggestion showed that happy memories were attached to it. She grew much more cheerful as dinner proceeded. The Burgundy from the public-house at the corner warmed her heart, and she forgot that she ought to preserve a dolorous countenance. Philip thought it safe to speak to her of the future.

'I suppose you haven't got a brass farthing, have you?' he asked, when an opportunity presented itself.

'Only what you gave me yesterday, and I had to give the landlady three pounds of that.'

'Well, I'd better give you a tenner to go on with. I'll go and see my solicitor and get him to write to Miller. We can make him pay up something, I'm sure. If we can get a hundred pounds out of him it'll carry you on till after the baby comes.'

'I wouldn't take a penny from him. I'd rather starve.'

'But it's monstrous that he should leave you in the lurch like this.'

'I've got my pride to consider.'

It was a little awkward for Philip. He needed rigid economy to make his own money last till he was qualified, and he must have something over to keep him during the year he intended to spend as house physician and house surgeon either at his own or at some other hospital. But Mildred had told him various stories of Emil's meanness, and he was afraid to remonstrate with her in case she accused him too of want of generosity.

'I wouldn't take a penny piece from him. I'd sooner beg my bread. I'd have seen about getting some work to do long before now, only it wouldn't be good for me in the state I'm in. You have to think of your health, don't you?'

'You needn't bother about the present,' said Philip. 'I can let you have all you want till you're fit to work again.'

'I knew I could depend on you. I told Emil he needn't think I hadn't got somebody to go to. I told him you was a gentleman in every sense of the word.'

By degrees Philip learned how the separation had come about. It appeared that the fellow's wife had discovered the adventure he was engaged in during his periodical visits to London, and had gone to the head of the firm that employed him. She threatened to divorce him, and they announced that they would dismiss him if she did. He was passionately devoted to his children and could not bear the thought of being separated from them. When he had to choose between his wife and his mistress he chose his wife. He had always been anxious that there should be no child to make the entanglement more complicated; and when Mildred, unable longer to conceal its approach, informed him of the fact, he was seized with panic. He picked a quarrel and left her without more ado.

'When d'you expect to be confined?' asked Philip.

'At the beginning of March.'

'Three months.'

It was necessary to discuss plans. Mildred declared she would not remain in the rooms at Highbury, and Philip thought it more convenient too that she should be nearer to him. He promised to look for something next day. She suggested the Vauxhall Bridge Road as a likely neighbourhood.

'And it would be near for afterwards,' she said.

'What do you mean?'

'Well, I should only be able to stay there about two months or a little more, and then I should have to go into a house. I know a very respectable place, where they have a most superior class of people, and they take you for four guineas a week and

335

no extras. Of course the doctor's extra, but that's all. A friend
of mine went there, and the lady who keeps it is a thorough
lady. I mean to tell her that my husband's an officer in India
and I've come to London for my baby, because it's better for
my health.'

It seemed extraordinary to Philip to hear her talking in this
way. With her delicate little features and her pale face she
looked cold and maidenly. When he thought of the passions
that burnt within her, so unexpectedly, his heart was strangely
troubled. His pulse beat quickly.

LXX

PHILIP expected to find a letter from Norah when he got back
to his rooms, but there was nothing; nor did he receive one the
following morning. The silence irritated and at the same time
alarmed him. They had seen one another every day he had been
in London since the previous June, and it must seem odd to
her that he should let two days go by without visiting her or
offering a reason for his absence; he wondered whether by au
unlucky chance she had seen him with Mildred. He could not
bear to think that she was hurt or unhappy, and he made up
his mind to call on her that afternoon. He was almost inclined
to reproach her because he had allowed himself to get on such
intimate terms with her. The thought of continuing them filled
him with disgust.

He found two rooms for Mildred on the second floor of a
house in the Vauxhall Bridge Road. They were noisy, but he
knew that she liked the rattle of traffic under her windows.

'I don't like a dead-and-alive street where you don't see a
soul pass all day,' she said. 'Give me a bit of life.'

Then he forced himself to go to Vincent Square. He was sick
with apprehension when he rang the bell. He had an uneasy
sense that he was treating Norah badly; he dreaded reproaches;
he knew she had a quick temper, and he hated scenes: perhaps
the best way would be to tell her frankly that Mildred had
come back to him and his love for her was as violent as it had
ever been; he was very sorry, but he had nothing to offer Norah
any more. Then he thought of her anguish, for he knew she
loved him; it had flattered him before, and he was immensely
grateful; but now it was horrible. She had not deserved that he
should inflict pain upon her. He asked himself how she would
greet him now, and as he walked up the stairs all possible forms

of behaviour flashed across his mind. He knocked at the door. He felt that he was pale, and wondered how to conceal his nervousness.

She was writing away industriously, but she sprang to her feet as he entered.

'I recognized your step,' she cried. 'Where have you been hiding yourself, you naughty boy?'

She came towards him joyfully and put her arms round his neck. She was delighted to see him. He kissed her, and then, to give himself countenance, said he was dying for tea. She bustled the fire to make the kettle boil.

'I've been awfully busy,' he said lamely.

She began to chatter in her bright way, telling him of a new commission she had to provide a novelette for a firm which had not hitherto employed her. She was to get fifteen guineas for it.

'It's money from the clouds. I'll tell you what we'll do, we'll stand ourselves a little jaunt. Let's go and spend a day at Oxford, shall we? I'd love to see the colleges.'

He looked at her to see whether there was any shadow of reproach in her eyes; but they were as frank and merry as ever; she was overjoyed to see him. His heart sank. He could not tell her the brutal truth. She made some toast for him, and cut it into little pieces, and gave it him as though he were a child.

'Is the brute fed?' she asked.

He nodded, smiling; and she lit a cigarette for him. Then, as she loved to do, she came and sat on his knees. She was very light. She leaned back in his arms with a sigh of delicious happiness.

'Say something nice to me,' she murmured.

'What shall I say?'

'You might by an effort of imagination say that you rather liked me.'

'You know I do that.'

He had not the heart to tell her then. He would give her peace at all events for that day, and perhaps he might write to her. That would be easier. He could not bear to think of her crying. She made him kiss her, and as he kissed her he thought of Mildred and Mildred's pale, thin lips. The recollection of Mildred remained with him all the time, like an incorporeal form, but more substantial than a shadow; and the sight continually distracted his attention.

'You're very quiet today,' Norah said.

Her loquacity was a standing joke between them, and he answered:

'You never let me get a word in, and I've got out of the habit of talking.'

'But you're not listening, and that's bad manners.'

He reddened a little, wondering whether she had some inkling of his secret; he turned away his eyes uneasily. The weight of her irked him this afternoon, and he did not want her to touch him.

'My foot's gone to sleep,' he said.

'I'm so sorry,' she cried, jumping up. 'I shall have to bant if I can't break myself of this habit of sitting on gentlemen's knees.'

He went through an elaborate form of stamping his foot and walking about. Then he stood in front of the fire so that she should not resume her position. While she talked he thought that she was worth ten of Mildred; she amused him much more and was jollier to talk to; she was cleverer, and she had a much nicer nature. She was a good, brave, honest little woman; and Mildred, he thought bitterly, deserved none of these epithets. If he had any sense he would stick to Norah, she would make him much happier than he would ever be with Mildred: after all she loved him, and Mildred was only grateful for his help. But when all was said the important thing was to love rather than to be loved; and he yearned for Mildred with his whole soul. He would sooner have ten minutes with her than a whole afternoon with Norah, he prized one kiss of her cold lips more than all Norah could give him.

'I can't help myself,' he thought. 'I've just got her in my bones.'

He did not care if she was heartless, vicious and vulgar, stupid and grasping, he loved her. He would rather have misery with one than happiness with the other.

When he got up to go Norah said casually:

'Well, I shall see you tomorrow, shan't I?'

'Yes,' he answered.

He knew that he would not be able to come, since he was going to help Mildred with her moving, but he had not the courage to say so. He made up his mind that he would send a wire. Mildred saw the rooms in the morning, was satisfied with them, and after luncheon Philip went up with her to Highbury. She had a trunk for her clothes and another for the various odds and ends, cushions, lamp-shades, photograph frames, with which she had tried to give the apartments a home-like air; she had two or three large cardboard boxes besides, but in all

338

there was no more than could be put on the roof of a four-wheeler. As they drove through Victoria Street Philip sat well back in the cab in case Norah should happen to be passing. He had not had an opportunity to telegraph and could not do so from the post office in the Vauxhall Bridge Road, since she would wonder what he was doing in that neighbourhood; and if he was there he could have no excuse for not going into the neighbouring square where she lived. He made up his mind that he had better go in and see her for half an hour; but the necessity irritated him: he was angry with Norah, because she forced him to vulgar and degrading shifts. But he was happy to be with Mildred. It amused him to help her with the unpacking; and he experienced a charming sense of possession in installing her in these lodgings which he had found and was paying for. He would not let her exert herself. It was a pleasure to do things for her, and she had no desire to do what somebody else seemed desirous to do for her. He unpacked her clothes and put them away. She was not proposing to go out again, so he got her slippers and took off her boots. It delighted him to perform menial offices.

'You do spoil me,' she said, running her fingers affectionately through his hair, while he was on his knees unbuttoning her boots.

He took her hands and kissed them.

'It is ripping to have you here.'

He arranged the cushions and the photograph frames. She had several jars of green earthenware.

'I'll get you some flowers for them,' he said.

He looked round at his work proudly.

'As I'm not going out any more I think I'll get into a tea-gown,' she said. 'Undo me behind, will you?'

She turned round as unconcernedly as though he were a woman. His sex meant nothing to her. But his heart was filled with gratitude for the intimacy her request showed. He undid the hooks and eyes with clumsy fingers.

'That first day I came into the shop I never thought I'd be doing this for you now,' he said, with a laugh which he forced.

'Somebody must do it,' she answered.

She went into the bedroom and slipped into a pale blue tea-gown decorated with a great deal of cheap lace. Then Philip settled her on a sofa and made tea for her.

'I'm afraid I can't stay and have it with you,' he said regretfully. 'I've got a beastly appointment. But I shall be back in half an hour.'

He wondered what he should say if she asked him what the appointment was, but she showed no curiosity. He had ordered dinner for the two of them when he took the rooms, and proposed to spend the evening with her quietly. He was in such a hurry to get back that he took a tram along the Vauxhall Bridge Road. He thought he had better break the fact to Norah at once that he could not stay more than a few minutes.

'I say, I've only just got time to say how d'you do,' he said, as soon as he got into her rooms. 'I'm frightfully busy.'

Her face fell.

'Why, what's the matter?'

It exasperated him that she should force him to tell lies, and he knew that he reddened when he answered that there was a demonstration at the hospital which he was bound to go to. He fancied that she looked as though she did not believe him, and this irritated him all the more.

'Oh, well, it doesn't matter,' she said. 'I shall have you all tomorrow.'

He looked at her blankly. It was Sunday, and he had been looking forward to spending the day with Mildred. He told himself that he must do that in common decency; he could not leave her by herself in a strange house.

'I'm awfully sorry, I'm engaged tomorrow.'

He knew this was the beginning of a scene which he would have given anything to avoid. The colour on Norah's cheeks grew brighter.

'But I've asked the Gordons to lunch' – they were an actor and his wife who were touring the provinces and in London for Sunday – 'I told you about it a week ago.'

'I'm awfully sorry, I forgot.' He hesitated. 'I'm afraid I can't possibly come. Isn't there somebody else you can get?'

'What are you doing tomorrow then?'

'I wish you wouldn't cross-examine me.'

'Don't you want to tell me?'

'I don't in the least mind telling you, but it's rather annoying to be forced to account for all one's movements.'

Norah suddenly changed. With an effort of self-control she got the better of her temper, and going up to him took his hands.

'Don't disappoint me tomorrow, Philip, I've been looking forward so much to spending the day with you. The Gordons want to see you, and we'll have such a jolly time.'

'I'd love to if I could.'

'I'm not very exacting, am I? I don't often ask you to do

340

anything that's a bother. Won't you get out of your horrid engagement – just this once?'

'I'm awfully sorry, I don't see how I can,' he replied sullenly.

'Tell me what it is,' she said coaxingly.

He had had time to invent something.

'Griffiths' two sisters are up for the week-end and we're taking them out.'

'Is that all?' she said joyfully. 'Griffiths can so easily get another man.'

He wished he had thought of something more urgent than that. It was a clumsy lie.

'No, I'm awfully sorry, I can't – I promised and I mean to keep my promise.'

'But you promised me too. Surely I come first.'

'I wish you wouldn't persist,' he said.

She flared up.

'You won't come because you don't want to. I don't know what you've been doing the last few days, you've been quite different.'

He looked at his watch.

'I'm afraid I'll have to be going,' he said.

'You won't come tomorrow?'

'No.'

'In that case you needn't trouble to come again,' she cried losing her temper for good.

'That's just as you like,' he answered.

'Don't let me detain you any longer,' she added ironically.

He shrugged his shoulders and walked out. He was relieved that it had gone no worse. There had been no tears. As he walked along he congratulated himself on getting out of the affair so easily. He went into Victoria Street and bought a few flowers to take in to Mildred.

The little dinner was a great success. Philip had sent in a small pot of caviare, which he knew she was very fond of, and and landlady brought them up some cutlets with vegetables and a sweet. Philip had ordered Burgundy, which was her favourite wine. With the curtains drawn, a bright fire, and one of Mildred's shades on the lamp, the room was cosy.

'It's really just like home,' smiled Philip.

'I might be worse off, mightn't I?' she answered.

When they finished, Philip drew two armchairs in front of the fire, and they sat down. He smoked his pipe comfortably. He felt happy and generous.

341

'What would you like to do tomorrow?' he asked.

'Oh, I'm going to Tulse Hill. You remember the manageress at the shop, well, she's married now, and she's asked me to go and spend the day with her. Of course she thinks I'm married too.'

Philip's heart sank.

'But I refused an invitation so that I might spend Sunday with you.'

He thought that if she loved him she would say that in that case she would stay with him. He knew very well that Norah would not have hesitated.

'Well, you were a silly to do that. I've promised to go for three weeks and more.'

'But how can you go alone?'

'Oh, I shall say that Emil's away on business. Her husband's in the glove trade, and he's a very superior fellow.'

Philip was silent, and bitter feelings passed through his heart. She gave him a sidelong glance.

'You don't grudge me a little pleasure, Philip? You see, it's the last time I shall be able to go anywhere for I don't know how long, and I had promised.'

He took her hand and smiled.

'No, darling, I want you to have the best time you can. I only want you to be happy.'

There was a little book bound in blue paper lying open, face downwards, on the sofa, and Philip idly took it up. It was a twopenny novelette, and the author was Courtenay Paget. That was the name under which Norah wrote.

'I do like his books,' said Mildred. 'I read them all. They're so refined.'

He remembered what Norah had said of herself.

'I have an immense popularity among kitchen-maids. They think me so genteel.'

LXXI

PHILIP, in return for Griffiths' confidences, had told him the details of his own complicated amours, and on Sunday morning, after breakfast, when they sat by the fire in their dressing-gowns and smoked, he recounted the scene of the previous day. Griffiths congratulated him because he had got out of his difficulties so easily.

'It's the simplest thing in the world to have an affair with a woman,' he remarked sententiously, 'but it's a devil of a nuisance to get out of it.'

Philip felt inclined to pat himself on the back for his skill in managing the business. At all events he was immensely relieved. He thought of Mildred enjoying herself in Tulse Hill, and he found in himself a real satisfaction because she was happy. It was an act of self-sacrifice on his part that he did not grudge her pleasure even though paid for by his own disappointment, and it filled his heart with a comfortable glow.

But on Monday morning he found on his table a letter from Norah. She wrote:

Dearest –

I'm sorry I was cross on Saturday. Forgive me and come to tea in the afternoon as usual. I love you.

Your Norah

His heart sank, and he did not know what to do. He took the note to Griffiths and showed it to him.

'You'd better leave it unanswered,' said he.

'Oh, I can't,' cried Philip. 'I should be miserable if I thought of her waiting and waiting. You don't know what it is to be sick for the postman's knock. I do, and I can't expose anybody else to that torture.'

'My dear fellow, one can't break that sort of affair off without somebody suffering. You must just set your teeth to that. One thing is, it doesn't last very long.'

Philip felt that Norah had not deserved that he should make her suffer; and what did Griffiths know about the degrees of anguish she was capable of? He remembered his own pain when Mildred had told him she was going to be married. He did not want anyone to experience what he had experienced then.

'If you're so anxious not to give her pain, go back to her,' said Griffiths.

'I can't do that.'

He got up and walked up and down the room nervously. He was angry with Norah because she had not let the matter rest. She must have seen that he had no more love to give her. They said women were so quick at seeing those things.

'You might help me,' he said to Griffiths.

'My dear fellow, don't make such a fuss about it. People do get over these things, you know. She probably isn't so wrapped up in you as you think, either. One's always rather apt to exaggerate the passion one's inspired other people with.'

343

He paused and looked at Philip with amusement.

'Look here, there's only one thing you can do. Write to her, and tell her the thing's over. Put it so that there can be no mistake about it. It'll hurt her, but it'll hurt her less if you do the thing brutally than if you try half-hearted ways.'

Philip sat down and wrote the following letter:

My dear Norah –

I am sorry to make you unhappy, but I think we had better let things remain where we left them on Saturday. I don't think there's any use in letting these things drag on when they've ceased to be amusing. You told me to go and I went. I do not propose to come back. Good-bye.

Philip Carey

He showed the letter to Griffiths and asked him what he thought of it. Griffiths read it and looked at Philip with twinkling eyes. He did not say what he felt.

'I think that'll do the trick,' he said.

Philip went out and posted it. He passed an uncomfortable morning, for he imagined with great detail what Norah would feel when she received the letter. He tortured himself with the thought of her tears. But at the same time he was relieved. Imagined grief was more easy to bear than grief seen, and he was free now to love Mildred with all his soul. His heart leaped at the thought of going to see her that afternoon, when his day's work at the hospital was over.

When as usual he went back to his rooms to tidy himself, he had no sooner put the latch-key in his door than he heard a voice behind him.

'May I come in? I've been waiting for you for half an hour.'

It was Norah. He felt himself blush to the roots of his hair. She spoke gaily. There was no trace of resentment in her voice and nothing to indicate that there was a rupture between them. He felt himself cornered. He was sick with fear, but he did his best to smile.

'Yes, do,' he said.

He opened the door, and she preceded him into his sitting-room. He was nervous and, to give himself countenance, offered her a cigarette and lit one for himself. She looked at him brightly.

'Why did you write me such a horrid letter, you naughty boy? If I'd taken it seriously it would have made me perfectly wretched.'

'It was meant seriously,' he answered gravely.

'Don't be silly. I lost my temper the other day, and I wrote and apologized. You weren't satisfied, so I've come here to apologize again. After all, you're your own master and I have no claims upon you. I don't want you to do anything you don't want to.'

She got up from the chair in which she was sitting and went towards him impulsively, with outstretched hands.

'Let's make friends again, Philip. I'm so sorry if I offended you.'

He could not prevent her from taking his hands, but he could not look at her.

'I'm afraid it's too late,' he said.

She let herself down on the floor by his side and clasped his knees.

'Philip, don't be silly. I'm quick-tempered too and I can understand that I hurt you, but it's so stupid to sulk over it. What's the good of making us both unhappy? It's been so jolly, our friendship.' She passed her fingers slowly over his hand. 'I love you, Philip.'

He got up, disengaging himself from her, and went to the other side of the room.

'I'm awfully sorry, I can't do anything. The whole thing's over.'

'D'you mean to say you don't love me any more?'

'I'm afraid so.'

'You were just looking for an opportunity to throw me over and you took that one?'

He did not answer. She looked at him steadily for a time which seemed intolerable. She was sitting on the floor where he had left her, leaning against the armchair. She began to cry quite silently, without trying to hide her face, and the large tears rolled down her cheeks one after the other. She did not sob. It was horribly painful to see her. Philip turned away.

'I'm awfully sorry to hurt you. It's not my fault if I don't love you.'

She did not answer. She merely sat there, as though she were overwhelmed, and the tears flowed down her cheeks. It would have been easier to bear if she had reproached him. He had thought her temper would get the better of her, and he was prepared for that. At the back of his mind was a feeling that a real quarrel, in which each said to the other cruel things, would in some way be a justification of his behaviour. The time passed. At last he grew frightened by her silent crying; he went into his bedroom and got a glass of water; he leaned over her.

345

'Won't you drink a little? It'll relieve you.'

She put her lips listlessly to the glass and drank two or three mouthfuls. Then in an exhausted whisper she asked him for a handkerchief. She dried her eyes.

'Of course I knew you never loved me as much as I loved you,' she moaned.

'I'm afraid that's always the case,' he said. 'There's always one who loves and one who lets himself be loved.'

He thought of Mildred, and a bitter pain traversed his heart. Norah did not answer for a long time.

'I'd been so miserably unhappy, and my life was so hateful,' she said at last.

She did not speak to him, but to herself. He had never heard her before complain of the life she had led with her husband or of her poverty. He had always admired the bold front she displayed to the world.

'And then you came along and you were so good to me. And I admired you because you were clever and it was so heavenly to have someone I could put my trust in. I loved you. I never thought it could come to an end. And without any fault of mine at all.'

Her tears began to flow again, but now she was more mistress of herself, and she hid her face in Philip's handkerchief. She tried hard to control herself.

'Give me some more water,' she said.

She wiped her eyes.

'I'm sorry to make such a fool of myself. I was so unprepared.'

'I'm awfully sorry, Norah. I want you to know that I'm very grateful for all you've done for me.'

He wondered what it was she saw in him.

'Oh, it's always the same,' she sighed; 'if you want men to behave well to you, you must be beastly to them; if you treat them decently they make you suffer for it.'

She got up from the floor and said she must go. She gave Philip a long, steady look. Then she sighed.

'It's so inexplicable. What does it all mean?'

Philip took a sudden determination.

'I think I'd better tell you, I don't want you to think too badly of me, I want you to see that I can't help myself. Mildred's come back.'

The colour came to her face.

'Why didn't you tell me at once? I deserved that surely.'

'I was afraid to.'

She looked at herself in the glass and set her hat straight. 'Will you call me a cab?' she said. 'I don't feel I *can* walk.'

He went to the door and stopped a passing hansom; but when she followed him into the street he was startled to see how white she was. There was a heaviness in her movements as though she had suddenly grown older. She looked so ill that he had not the heart to let her go alone.

'I'll drive back with you if you don't mind.'

She did not answer, and he got into the cab. They drove along in silence over the bridge, through shabby streets in which children, with shrill cries, played in the road. When they arrived at her door she did not immediately get out. It seemed as though she could not summon enough strength to her legs to move.

'I hope you'll forgive me, Norah,' he said.

She turned her eyes towards him, and he saw that they were bright again with tears, but she forced a smile to her lips.

'Poor fellow, you're quite worried about me. You mustn't bother. I don't blame you. I shall get over it all right.'

Lightly and quickly she stroked his face to show him that she bore no ill-feeling, the gesture was scarcely more than suggested; then she jumped out of the cab and let herself into her house.

Philip paid the hansom and walked to Mildred's lodgings. There was a curious heaviness in his heart. He was inclined to reproach himself. But why? He did not know what else he could have done. Passing a fruiterer's, he remembered that Mildred was fond of grapes. He was so grateful that he could show his love for her by recollecting every whim she had.

LXXII

FOR the next three months Philip went every day to see Mildred. He took his books with him and after tea worked, while Mildred lay on the sofa reading novels. Sometimes he would look up and watch her for a minute. A happy smile crossed his lips. She would feel his eyes upon her.

'Don't waste your time looking at me, silly. Go on with your work,' she said.

'Tyrant,' he answered gaily.

He put aside his book when the landlady came in to lay the cloth for dinner, and in his high spirits he exchanged chaff with her. She was a little cockney, of middle age, with an amusing humour and a quick tongue. Mildred had become great friends with her and had given her an elaborate but mendacious account of the circumstances which had brought her to the pass she was in. The good-hearted little woman was touched and found no trouble too great to make Mildred comfortable. Mildred's sense of propriety had suggested that Philip should pass himself off as her brother. They dined together, and Philip was delighted when he had ordered something which tempted Mildred's capricious appetite. It enchanted him to see her sitting opposite him, and every now and then from sheer joy he took her hand and pressed it. After dinner she sat in the armchair by the fire, and he settled himself down on the floor beside her, leaning against her knees, and smoked. Often they did not talk at all, and sometimes Philip noticed that she had fallen into a doze. He dared not move then in case he woke her, and he sat very quietly, looking lazily into the fire and enjoying his happiness.

'Had a nice little nap?' he smiled, when she woke.

'I've not been sleeping,' she answered. 'I only just closed my eyes.'

She would never acknowledge that she had been asleep. She had a phlegmatic temperament, and her condition did not seriously inconvenience her. She took a lot of trouble about her health and accepted the advice of anyone who chose to offer it. She went for a 'constitutional' every morning that it was fine and remained out a definite time. When it was not too cold she sat in St James's Park. But the rest of the day she spent quite happily on her sofa, reading one novel after another or chatting with the landlady; she had an inexhaustible interest in gossip, and told Philip with abundant detail the history of the landlady, of the lodgers on the drawing-room floor, and of the people who lived in the next house on either side. Now and then she was seized with panic; she poured out her fears to Philip about the pain of the confinement and was in terror lest she should die; she gave him a full account of the confinements of the landlady and of the lady on the drawing-room floor (Mildred did not know her; 'I'm one to keep myself to myself,' she said; 'I'm not one to go about with anybody'), and she narrated details with a queer mixture of horror and gusto; but for the most part she looked forward to the occurrence with equanimity.

'After all, I'm not the first one to have a baby, am I? And the doctor says I shan't have any trouble. You see, it isn't as if I wasn't well made.'

Mrs Owen, the owner of the house she was going to when her time came, had recommended a doctor, and Mildred saw him once a week. He was to charge fifteen guineas.

'Of course I could have got it done cheaper, but Mrs Owen strongly recommended him, and I thought it wasn't worth while to spoil the ship for a coat of tar.'

'If you feel happy and comfortable I don't mind a bit about the expense,' said Philip.

She accepted all that Philip did for her as if it were the most natural thing in the world, and on his side he loved to spend money on her: each five-pound note he gave her caused him a little thrill of happiness and pride; he gave her a good many, for she was not economical.

'I don't know where the money goes,' she said herself, 'it seems to slip through my fingers like water.'

'It doesn't matter,' said Philip. 'I'm so glad to be able to do anything I can do for you.'

She could not sew well and so did not make the necessary things for the baby; she told Philip it was much cheaper in the end to buy them. Philip had lately sold one of the mortgages in which his money had been put; and now, with five hundred pounds in the bank waiting to be invested in something that could be more easily realized, he felt himself uncommonly well-to-do. They talked often of the future. Philip was anxious that Mildred should keep the child with her, but she refused; she had her living to earn, and it would be more easy to do this if she had not also to look after a baby. Her plan was to get back into one of the shops of the company for which she had worked before, and the child could be put with some decent woman in the country.

'I can find someone who'll look after it well for seven and sixpence a week. It'll be better for the baby and better for me.'

It seemed callous to Philip, but when he tried to reason with her she pretended to think he was concerned with the expense.

'You needn't worry about that,' she said. 'I shan't ask *you* to pay for it.'

'You know I don't care how much I pay.'

At the bottom of her heart was the hope that the child would be still-born. She did no more than hint it, but Philip saw that the thought was there. He was shocked at first; and then, reasoning with himself, he was obliged to confess that for all concerned such an event was to be desired.

'It's all very fine to say this and that,' Mildred remarked

querulously, 'but it's jolly difficult for a girl to earn her living by herself; it doesn't make it any easier when she's got a baby.'

'Fortunately you've got me to fall back on,' smiled Philip, taking her hand.

'You have been good to me, Philip.'

'Oh, what rot!'

'You can't say I didn't offer anything in return for what you've done.'

'Good heavens, I don't want a return. If I've done anything for you, I've done it because I love you. You owe me nothing. I don't want you to do anything unless you love me.'

He was a little horrified by her feeling that her body was a commodity which she could deliver indifferently as an acknowledgement for services rendered.

'But I do want to, Philip. You've been so good to me.'

'Well, it won't hurt for waiting. When you're all right again we'll go for our little honeymoon.'

'You are naughty,' she said, smiling.

Mildred expected to be confined early in March, and as soon as she was well enough she was to go to the seaside for a fort-night: that would give Philip a chance to work without inter-ruption for his examination; after that came the Easter holi-days, and they had arranged to go to Paris together. Philip talked endlessly of the things they would do. Paris was delight-ful then. They would take a room in a little hotel he knew in the Latin Quarter, and they would eat in all sorts of charming little restaurants; they would go to the play, and he would take her to music-halls. It would amuse her to meet his friends. He had talked to her about Cronshaw, she would see him; and there was Lawson, he had gone to Paris for a couple of months; and they would go to the Bal Bullier; there were excursions; they would make trips to Versailles, Chartres, Fontainebleau.

'It'll cost a lot of money,' she said.

'Oh, damn the expense. Think how I've been looking forward to it. Don't you know what it means to me? I've never loved anyone but you. I never shall.'

She listened to his enthusiasm with smiling eyes. He thought he saw in them a new tenderness, and he was grateful to her. She was much gentler than she used to be. There was in her no longer the superciliousness which had irritated him. She was so accustomed to him now that she took no pains to keep up before him any pretences. She no longer troubled to do her hair with the old elaboration, but just tied it in a knot; and she left off the vast fringe which she generally wore: the more careless style suited her. Her face was so thin that it made her eyes seem very large; there were heavy lines under them, and the pallor of her cheeks made their colour more profound. She had a wistful look which was infinitely pathetic. There seemed to Philip to be in her something of the Madonna. He wished they could continue in that same way always. He was happier than he had ever been in his life.

He used to leave her at ten o'clock every night, for she liked to go to bed early, and he was obliged to put in another couple of hours' work to make up for the lost evening. He generally brushed her hair for her before he went. He had made a ritual of the kisses he gave her when he bade her good-night; first he kissed the palms of her hands (how thin the fingers were, the nails were beautiful, for she spent much time manicuring them), then he kissed her closed eyes, first the right one and then the left, and at last he kissed her lips. He went home with a heart overflowing with love. He longed for an opportunity to gratify the desire for self-sacrifice which consumed him.

Presently the time came for her to move to the nursing-home where she was to be confined. Philip was then able to visit her only in the afternoons. Mildred changed her story and represented herself as the wife of a soldier who had gone to India to join his regiment, and Philip was introduced to the mistress of the establishment as her brother-in-law.

'I have to be rather careful what I say,' she told him, 'as there's another lady here whose husband's in the Indian Civil.'

'I wouldn't let that disturb me if I were you,' said Philip. 'I'm convinced that her husband and yours went out on the same boat.'

'What boat?' she asked innocently.

'The Flying Dutchman.'

Mildred was safely delivered of a daughter, and when Philip was allowed to see her the child was lying by her side. Mildred was very weak, but relieved that everything was over. She showed him the baby, and herself looked at it curiously.

'It's a funny-looking little thing, isn't it? I can't believe it's mine.'

It was red and wrinkled and odd. Philip smiled when he looked at it. He did not quite know what to say; and it embarrassed him because the nurse who owned the house was standing by his side; and he felt by the way she was looking at him that, disbelieving Mildred's complicated story, she thought he was the father.

'What are you going to call her?' asked Philip.

'I can't make up my mind if I shall call her Madeleine or Cecilia.'

The nurse left them alone for a few minutes, and Philip bent down and kissed Mildred on the mouth.

'I'm so glad it's all over happily, darling.'

She put her thin arms round his neck.

'You've been a brick to me, Phil dear.'

'Now I feel that you're mine at last. I've waited so long for you, my dear.'

They heard the nurse at the door, and Philip hurriedly got up. The nurse entered. There was a slight smile on her lips.

LXXIII

THREE weeks later Philip saw Mildred and her baby off to Brighton. She had made a quick recovery and looked better than he had ever seen her. She was going to a boarding-house where she had spent a couple of week-ends with Emil Miller, and had written to say that her husband was obliged to go to Germany on business and she was coming down with her baby. She got pleasure out of the stories she invented, and she showed a certain fertility of invention in the working out of the details. Mildred proposed to find in Brighton some woman who would be willing to take charge of the baby. Philip was startled at the callousness with which she insisted on getting rid of it so soon, but she argued with common sense that the poor child had much better be put somewhere before it grew used to her. Philip had expected the maternal instinct to make itself felt when she had had the baby two or three weeks, and had counted on this to help him persuade her to keep it; but nothing of the sort occurred. Mildred was not unkind to her baby, she did all that was necessary; it amused her sometimes, and she talked about it a good deal; but at heart she was indifferent to it. She could not look upon it as part of herself. She fancied it resembled its father already. She was continually wondering how she would manage when it grew older; and she was exasperated with herself for being such a fool as to have it at all.

'If I'd only known then all I do now,' she said.

She laughed at Philip because he was anxious about its welfare.

'You couldn't make more fuss if you was the father,' she said. 'I'd like to see Emil getting into such a stew about it.'

Philip's mind was full of the stories he had heard of baby-farming and the ghouls who ill-treat the wretched children that selfish, cruel parents have put in their charge.

'Don't be so silly,' said Mildred. 'That's when you give a woman a sum down to look after a baby. But when you're going to pay so much a week it's to their interest to look after it well.'

Philip insisted that Mildred should place the child with people who had no children of their own and would promise to take no other.

'Don't haggle about the price,' he said. 'I'd rather pay half a guinea a week than run any risk of the kid being starved or beaten.'

'You're a funny old thing, Philip,' she laughed.

To him there was something very touching in the child's helplessness. It was small, ugly, and querulous. Its birth had been looked forward to with shame and anguish. Nobody wanted it. It was dependent on him, a stranger, for food, shelter, and clothes to cover its nakedness.

As the train started he kissed Mildred. He would have kissed the baby too, but he was afraid she would laugh at him.

'You will write to me, darling, won't you? And I shall look forward to your coming back with, oh! such impatience.'

'Mind you get through your exam.'

He had been working for it industriously, and now with only ten days before him he made a final effort. He was very anxious to pass, first to save himself time and expense, for money had been slipping through his fingers during the last four months with incredible speed; and then because this examination marked the end of the drudgery: after that the student had to do with medicine, midwifery, and surgery, the interest of which was more vivid than the anatomy and physiology with which he had been hitherto concerned. Philip looked forward with interest to the rest of the curriculum. Nor did he want to have to confess to Mildred that he had failed: though the examination was difficult and the majority of candidates were ploughed at the first attempt, he knew that she would think less well of him if he did not succeed; she had a peculiarly humiliating way of showing what she thought.

Mildred sent him a postcard to announce her safe arrival, and he snatched half an hour every day to write a long letter to her. He had always a certain shyness in expressing himself by word of mouth, but he found he could tell her, pen in hand, all sorts of things which it would have made him feel ridiculous to say. Profiting by the discovery, he poured out to her his whole heart. He had never been able to tell her before how his adoration filled every part of him so that all his actions, all his thoughts, were touched with it. He wrote to her of the future, of the happiness that lay before him, and the gratitude which he owed her. He asked himself (he had often asked himself before but had never put it into words) what it was in her that filled him with such extravagant delight; he did not know; he knew only that when she was with him he was happy, and when she was away from him the world was on a sudden cold and grey; he knew only that when he thought of her his heart seemed to grow big in his body so that it was difficult to breathe (as if it pressed against his lungs) and it throbbed, so that the delight of her presence was almost pain; his knees shook, and he felt strangely weak, as though, not having eaten, he were tremulous from want of food. He looked forward eagerly to her answers. He did not expect her to write often, for he knew that letter-writing came difficultly to her; and he was quite content with the clumsy little note that arrived in reply to four of his. She spoke of the boarding-house in which she had taken a room, of the weather and the baby, told him she had been for a walk on the front with a lady friend whom she had met in the boarding-house and who had taken such a fancy to baby, she was going to the theatre on Saturday night, and Brighton was filling up. It touched Philip because it was so matter of fact. The crabbed style, the formality of the matter, gave him a queer desire to laugh and to take her in his arms and kiss her.

He went into the examination with happy confidence. There was nothing in either of the papers that gave him trouble. He knew that he had done well, and though the second part of the examination was *viva voce* and he was more nervous, he managed to answer the questions adequately. He sent a triumphant telegram to Mildred when the result was announced.

When he got back to his rooms Philip found a letter from her, saying that she thought it would be better for her to stay another week in Brighton. She had found a woman who would be glad to take the baby for seven shillings a week, but she wanted to make inquiries about her, and she was herself benefiting so much by the sea-air that she was sure a few days more would do her no end of good. She hated asking Philip for money, but would he send some by return, as she had had to buy herself a new hat, she couldn't go about with her lady friend always in the same hat, and her lady friend was so dressy. Philip had a moment of bitter disappointment. It took away all his pleasure at getting through his examination.

'If she loved me one quarter as much as I love her she couldn't bear to stay away a day longer than necessary.'

He put the thought away from him quickly; it was pure selfishness; of course her health was more important than anything else. But he had nothing to do now; he might spend the week with her in Brighton, and they could be together all day. His heart leaped at the thought. It would be amusing to appear before Mildred suddenly with the information that he had taken a room in the boarding-house. He looked out trains. But he paused. He was not certain that she would be pleased to see him; she had made friends in Brighton; he was quiet, and she liked boisterous joviality; he realized that she amused herself more with other people than with him. It would torture him if he felt for an instant that he was in the way. He was afraid to risk it. He dared not even write and suggest that, with nothing to keep him in town, he would like to spend the week where he could see her every day. She knew he had nothing to do; if she wanted him to come she would have asked him to. He dared not risk the anguish he would suffer if he proposed to come and she made excuses to prevent him.

He wrote to her next day, sent her a five-pound note, and at the end of his letter said that if she were very nice and cared to see him for the week-end he would be glad to run down; but she was by no means to alter any plans she had made. He awaited her answer with impatience. In it she said that if she had only known before she could have arranged it, but she had promised to go to a music-hall on the Saturday night; besides, it would make the people at the boarding-house talk if he stayed there. Why did he not come on Sunday morning and spend the day? They could lunch at the Metropole, and she would take him afterwards to see the very superior lady-like person who was going to take the baby.

Sunday. He blessed the day because it was fine. As the train approached Brighton the sun poured through the carriage window. Mildred was waiting for him on the platform.

'How jolly of you to come and meet me!' he cried, as he seized her hands.

'You expected me, didn't you?'

'I hoped you would. I say, how well you're looking.'

'It's done me a rare lot of good, but I think I'm wise to stay here as long as I can. And there are a very nice class of people at the boarding-house. I wanted cheering up after seeing nobody all these months. It was dull sometimes.'

She looked very smart in her new hat, a large black straw

with a great many inexpensive flowers on it; and round her neck floated a long boa of imitation swansdown. She was still very thin, and she stooped a little when she walked (she had always done that), but her eyes did not seem so large; and though she never had any colour, her skin had lost the earthy look it had. They walked down to the sea. Philip remembering he had not walked with her for months, grew suddenly conscious of his limp and walked stiffly in the attempt to conceal it.

'Are you glad to see me?' he asked, love dancing madly in his heart.

'Of course I am. You needn't ask that.'

'By the way, Griffiths sends you his love.'

'What cheek!'

He had talked to her a great deal of Griffiths. He had told her how flirtatious he was and had amused her often with the narration of some adventure which Griffiths under the seal of secrecy had imparted to him. Mildred had listened, with some pretence of disgust sometimes, but generally with curiosity; and Philip, admiringly, had enlarged upon his friend's good looks and charm.

'I'm sure you'll like him just as much as I do. He's so jolly and amusing, and he's such an awfully good sort.'

Philip told her how, when they were perfect strangers, Griffiths had nursed him through an illness; and in the telling Griffiths' self-sacrifice lost nothing.

'You can't help liking him,' said Philip.

'I don't like good-looking men,' said Mildred. 'They're too conceited for me.'

'He wants to know you. I've talked to him about you an awful lot.'

'What have you said?' asked Mildred.

Philip had no one but Griffiths to talk to of his love for Mildred, and little by little had told him the whole story of his connexion with her. He described her to him fifty times. He dwelt amorously on every detail of her appearance, and Griffiths knew exactly how her thin hands were shaped and how white her face was, and he laughed at Philip when he talked of the charm of her pale, thin lips.

'By jove, I'm glad I don't take things so badly as that,' he said. 'Life wouldn't be worth living.'

Philip smiled. Griffiths did not know the delight of being so madly in love that it was like meat and wine and the air one breathed and whatever else was essential to existence.

Griffiths knew that Philip had looked after the girl while she was having her baby and was now going away with her.

'Well, I must say you've deserved to get something,' he remarked. 'It must have cost you a pretty penny. It's lucky you can afford it.'

'I can't,' said Philip. 'But what do I care!'

Since it was early for luncheon, Philip and Mildred sat in one of the shelters on the parade, sunning themselves, and watched the people pass. There were the Brighton shop-boys who walked in twos and threes swinging their canes, and there were the Brighton shop-girls who tripped along in giggling bunches. They could tell the people who had come down from London for the day; the keen air gave a fillip to their weariness. There were many Jews, stout ladies in tight satin dresses and diamonds, little corpulent men with a gesticulative manner. There were middle-aged gentlemen spending a week-end in one of the hotels, carefully dressed; and they walked industriously after too substantial a breakfast to give themselves an appetite for too substantial a luncheon: they exchanged the time of day with friends and talked of Dr Brighton or London-by-the-Sea. Here and there a well-known actor passed, elaborately unconscious of the attention he excited: sometimes he wore patent leather boots, a coat with an astrakhan collar, and carried a silver-knobbed stick; and sometimes, looking as though he had come from a day's shooting, he strolled in knicker-bockers, an ulster of Harris tweed, and a tweed hat on the back of his head. The sun shone on the blue sea, and the blue sea was trim and neat.

After luncheon they went to Hove to see the woman who was to take charge of the baby. She lived in a small house in a back street, but it was clean and tidy. Her name was Mrs Harding. She was an elderly, stout person, with grey hair and a red, fleshy face. She looked motherly in her cap, and Philip thought she seemed kind.

'Won't you find it an awful nuisance to look after a baby?' he asked her.

She explained that her husband was a curate, a good deal older than herself, who had difficulty in getting permanent work, since vicars wanted young men to assist them; he earned a little now and then by doing locums when someone took a holiday or fell ill, and a charitable institution gave them a small pension; but her life was lonely, it would be something to do to look after a child, and the few shillings a week paid for it

357

would help her to keep things going. She promised that it should be well fed.

'Quite the lady, isn't she?' said Mildred, when they went away.

They went back to have tea at the Metropole. Mildred liked the crowd and the band. Philip was tired of talking, and he watched her face as she looked with keen eyes at the dresses of the women who came in. She had a peculiar sharpness for reckoning up what things cost, and now and then she leaned over to him and whispered the result of her meditations.

'D'you see that aigrette there? That cost every bit of seven guineas.'

Or: 'Look at that ermine, Philip. That's rabbit, that is – that's not ermine.' She laughed triumphantly. 'I'd know it a mile off.'

Philip smiled happily. He was glad to see her pleasure, and the ingenuousness of her conversation amused and touched him. The band played sentimental music.

After dinner they walked down to the station, and Philip took her arm. He told her what arrangements he had made for their journey to France. She was to come up to London at the end of the week, but she told him that she could not go away till the Saturday of the week after that. He had already engaged a room in a hotel in Paris. He was looking forward eagerly to taking the tickets.

'You won't mind going second-class, will you? We mustn't be extravagant, and it'll be all the better if we can do ourselves pretty well when we get there.'

He had talked to her a hundred times of the Quarter. They would wander through its pleasant old streets, and they would sit idly in the charming gardens of the Luxembourg. If the weather was fine perhaps, when they had had enough of Paris, they might go to Fontainebleau. The trees would be just bursting into leaf. The green of the forest in spring was more beautiful than anything he knew; it was like a song, and it was like the happy pain of love. Mildred listened quietly. He turned to her and tried to look deep into her eyes.

'You do want to come, don't you?' he said.

'Of course I do,' she smiled.

'You don't know how I'm looking forward to it. I don't know how I shall get through the next days. I'm so afraid something will happen to prevent it. It maddens me sometimes that I can't tell you how much I love you. And at last, at last . . .'

He broke off. They reached the station, but they had dawdled on the way, and Philip had barely time to say good night. He kissed her quickly and ran towards the wicket as fast as he could. She stood where he left her. He was strangely grotesque when he ran.

LXXIV

THE following Saturday Mildred returned, and that evening Philip kept her to himself. He took seats for the play, and they drank champagne at dinner. It was her first gaiety in London for so long that she enjoyed everything ingenuously. She cuddled up to Philip when they drove from the theatre to the room he had taken for her in Pimlico.

'I really believe you're quite glad to see me,' he said.

She did not answer, but gently pressed his hand. Demonstrations of affection were so rare with her that Philip was enchanted.

'I've asked Griffiths to dine with us tomorrow,' he told her.

'Oh, I'm glad you've done that. I wanted to meet him.'

There was no place of entertainment to take her to on Sunday night, and Philip was afraid she would be bored if she were alone with him all day. Griffiths was amusing; he would help them to get through the evening; and Philip was so fond of them both that he wanted them to know and to like one another. He left Mildred with the words:

'Only six days more.'

They had arranged to dine in the gallery at Romano's on Sunday, because the dinner was excellent and looked as though it cost a good deal more than it did. Philip and Mildred arrived first and had to wait some time for Griffiths.

'He's an unpunctual devil,' said Philip. 'He's probably making love to one of his numerous flames.'

But presently he appeared. He was a handsome creature, tall and thin; his head was placed well on the body, it gave him a conquering air which was attractive; and his curly hair, his bold, friendly blue eyes, his red mouth, were charming. Philip saw Mildred look at him with appreciation, and he felt a curious satisfaction. Griffiths greeted them with a smile.

'I've heard a great deal about you,' he said to Mildred, as he took her hand.

'Not so much as I've heard about you,' she answered.

'Nor so bad,' said Philip.

'Has he been blackening my character?'

Griffiths laughed, and Philip saw that Mildred noticed how white and regular his teeth were and how pleasant his smile.

'You ought to feel like old friends,' said Philip. 'I've talked so much about you to one another.'

Griffiths was in the best possible humour, for, having at length passed his final examination, he was qualified, and he had just been appointed house-surgeon at a hospital in the North of London. He was taking up his duties at the beginning of May and meanwhile was going home for a holiday; this was his last week in town, and he was determined to get as much enjoyment into it as he could. He began to talk the gay nonsense which Philip admired because he could not copy it. There was nothing much in what he said, but his vivacity gave it point. There flowed from him a force of life which affected everyone who knew him; it was almost as sensible as bodily warmth. Mildred was more lively than Philip had ever known her, and he was delighted to see that his little party was a success. She was amusing herself enormously. She laughed louder and louder. She quite forgot the genteel reserve which had become second nature to her.

Presently Griffiths said:

'I say, it's dreadfully difficult for me to call you Mrs Miller. Philip never calls you anything but Mildred.'

'I daresay she won't scratch your eyes out if you call her that too,' laughed Philip.

'Then she must call me Harry.'

Philip sat silent while they chattered away and thought how good it was to see people happy. Now and then Griffiths teased him a little, kindly, because he was always so serious.

'I believe he's quite fond of you, Philip,' smiled Mildred.

'He isn't a bad old thing,' answered Griffiths, and taking Philip's hand he shook it gaily.

It seemed an added charm in Griffiths that he liked Philip. They were all sober people, and the wine they had drunk went to their heads. Griffiths became more talkative and so boisterous that Philip, amused, had to beg him to be quiet. He had a gift for story-telling, and his adventures lost nothing of their romance and their laughter in his narration. He played in all of them a gallant, humorous part. Mildred, her eyes shining with excitement, urged him on. He poured out anecdote after anecdote. When the lights began to be turned out she was astonished.

'My word, the evening has gone quickly. I thought it wasn't more than half past nine.'

They got up to go and when she said good-bye, she added:

'I'm coming to have tea at Philip's room tomorrow. You might look in if you can.'

'All right,' he smiled back.

On the way back to Pimlico Mildred talked of nothing but Griffiths. She was taken with his good looks, his well-cut clothes, his voice, his gaiety.

'I *am* glad you like him,' said Philip. 'D'you remember you were rather sniffy about meeting him?'

'I think it's so nice of him to be so fond of you, Philip. He is a nice friend for you to have.'

She put up her face to Philip for him to kiss her. It was a thing she did rarely.

'I have enjoyed myself this evening, Philip. Thank you so much.'

'Don't be so absurd,' he laughed, touched by her appreciation so that he felt the moisture come to his eyes.

She opened her door and, just before she went in, turned again to Philip.

'Tell Harry I'm madly in love with him,' she said.

'All right,' he laughed. 'Good night.'

Next day, when they were having tea, Griffiths came in. He sank lazily into an armchair. There was something strangely sensual in the slow movements of his large limbs. Philip remained silent, while the others chattered away, but he was enjoying himself. He admired them both so much that it seemed natural enough for them to admire one another. He did not care if Griffiths absorbed Mildred's attention, he would have her to himself during the evening; he had something the attitude of a loving husband, confident in his wife's affection, who looks on with amusement while she flirts harmlessly with a stranger. But at half past seven he looked at his watch and said:

'It's about time we went out to dinner, Mildred.'

There was a moment's pause, and Griffiths seemed to be considering.

'Well, I'll be getting along,' he said at last. 'I didn't know it was so late.'

'Are you doing anything tonight?' asked Mildred.

'No.'

There was another silence. Philip felt slightly irritated.

'I'll just go and have a wash,' he said, and to Mildred he added: 'Would you like to wash your hands?'

She did not answer him.

'Why don't you come and dine with us?' she said to Griffiths.

He looked at Philip and saw him staring at him sombrely.

'I dined with you last night,' he laughed. 'I should be in the way.'

'Oh, that doesn't matter,' insisted Mildred. 'Make him come, Philip. He won't be in the way, will he?'

'Let him come by all means if he'd like to.'

'All right then,' said Griffiths promptly. 'I'll just go upstairs and tidy myself.'

The moment he left the room Philip turned to Mildred angrily.

'Why on earth did you ask him to dine with us?'

'I couldn't help myself. It would have looked so funny to say nothing when he said he wasn't doing anything.'

'Oh, what rot! And why the hell did you ask him if he was doing anything?'

Mildred's pale lips tightened a little.

'I want a little amusement sometimes. I get tired always being alone with you.'

They heard Griffiths coming heavily down the stairs, and Philip went into his bedroom to wash. They dined in the neighbourhood in an Italian restaurant. Philip was cross and silent, but he quickly realized that he was showing to disadvantage in comparison with Griffiths, and he forced himself to hide his annoyance. He drank a good deal of wine to destroy the pain that was gnawing at his heart, and he set himself to talk. Mildred, as though remorseful for what she had said, did all she could to make herself pleasant to him. She was kindly and affectionate. Presently Philip began to think he had been a fool to surrender to a feeling of jealousy. After dinner when they got into a hansom to drive to a music-hall, Mildred, sitting between the two men, of her own accord gave him her hand. His anger vanished. Suddenly, he knew not how, he grew conscious that Griffiths was holding her other hand. The pain seized him again violently, it was a real physical pain, and he asked himself, panic-stricken, what he might have asked himself before, whether Mildred and Griffiths were in love with one another. He could not see anything of the performance on account of the mist of suspicion, anger, dismay, and wretchedness which seemed to be before his eyes; but he forced himself to conceal the fact that anything was the matter; he went on talking and laughing. Then a strange desire to torture himself seized him, and he got up, saying he wanted to go and drink something. Mildred and Griffiths had never been alone together for a moment. He wanted to leave them by themselves.

'I'll come too,' said Griffiths. 'I've got rather a thirst on.'

'Oh, nonsense, you stay and talk to Mildred.'

Philip did not know why he said that. He was throwing them together now to make the pain he suffered more intolerable. He did not go to the bar, but up into the balcony, from where he could watch them and not be seen. They had ceased to look at the stage and were smiling into one another's eyes. Griffiths was talking with his usual happy fluency and Mildred seemed to hang on his lips. Philip's head began to ache frightfully. He stood there motionless. He knew he would be in the way if he went back. They were enjoying themselves without him, and he was suffering, suffering. Time passed, and now he had an extraordinary shyness about rejoining them. He knew they had not thought of him at all, and he reflected bitterly that he had paid for the dinner and their seats in the music-hall. What a fool they were making of him! He was hot with shame. He could see how happy they were without him. His instinct was to leave them to themselves and go home, but he had not his hat and coat, and it would necessitate endless explanations. He went back. He felt a shadow of annoyance in Mildred's eyes when she saw him, and his heart sank.

'You've been a devil of a time,' said Griffiths, with a smile of welcome.

'I met some men I knew. I've been talking to them, and I couldn't get away. I thought you'd be all right together.'

'I've been enjoying myself thoroughly,' said Griffiths. 'I don't know about Mildred.'

She gave a little laugh of happy complacency. There was a vulgar sound in the ring of it that horrified Philip. He suggested that they should go.

'Come on,' said Griffiths, 'we'll both drive you home.'

Philip suspected that she had suggested that arrangement so that she might not be left alone with him. In the cab he did not take her hand nor did she offer it, and he knew all the time that she was holding Griffiths'. His chief thought was that it was all so horribly vulgar. As they drove along he asked himself what plans they had made to meet without his knowledge, he cursed himself for having left them alone, he had actually gone out of his way to enable them to arrange things.

'Let's keep the cab,' said Philip, when they reached the house in which Mildred was lodging. 'I'm too tired to walk home.'

On the way back Griffiths talked gaily and seemed indifferent to the fact that Philip answered in monosyllables. Philip felt he must notice that something was the matter. Philip's silence at last grew too significant to struggle against, and Griffiths, suddenly nervous, ceased talking. Philip wanted to say something, but he was so shy he could hardly bring himself to, and yet the time was passing and the opportunity would be lost. It was best to get at the truth at once. He forced himself to speak.

'Are you in love with Mildred?' he asked suddenly.

'I?' Griffiths laughed. 'Is that what you've been so funny about this evening? Of course not. My dear old man.'

He tried to slip his hand through Philip's arm, but Philip drew himself away. He knew Griffiths was lying. He could not bring himself to force Griffiths to tell him that he had not been holding the girl's hand. He suddenly felt very weak and broken.

'It doesn't matter to you, Harry,' he said. 'You've got so many women – don't take her away from me. It means my whole life. I've been so awfully wretched.'

His voice broke, and he could not prevent the sob that was torn from him. He was horribly ashamed of himself.

'My dear old boy, you know I wouldn't do anything to hurt you. I'm far too fond of you for that. I was only playing the fool. If I'd known you were going to take it like that I'd have been more careful.'

'Is that true?' asked Philip.

'I don't care a twopenny damn for her. I give you my word of honour.'

Philip gave a sigh of relief. The cab stopped at their door.

LXXV

NEXT day Philip was in a good temper. He was very anxious not to bore Mildred with too much of his society, and so had arranged that he should not see her till dinner-time. She was ready when he fetched her, and he chaffed her for her unwonted punctuality. She was wearing a new dress he had given her. He remarked on its smartness.

'It'll have to go back and be altered,' she said. 'The skirt hangs all wrong.'

'You'll have to make the dressmaker hurry up if you want to take it to Paris with you.'

'It'll be ready in time for that.'

'Only three more whole days. We'll go over by the eleven o'clock, shall we?'

'If you like.'

He would have her for nearly a month entirely to himself. His eyes rested on her with hungry adoration. He was able to laugh a little at his own passion.

'I wonder what it is I see in you,' he smiled.

'That's a nice thing to say,' she answered.

Her body was so thin that one could almost see her skeleton. Her chest was as flat as a boy's. Her mouth, with its narrow pale lips, was ugly, and her skin was faintly green.

'I shall give you Blaud's Pills in quantities when we're away,' said Philip laughing. 'I'm going to bring you back fat and rosy.'

'I don't want to get fat,' she said.

She did not speak of Griffiths, and presently while they were dining Philip, half in malice, for he felt sure of himself and his power over her, said:

'It seems to me you were having a great flirtation with Harry last night?'

'I told you I was in love with him,' she laughed.

'I'm glad to know that he's not in love with you.'

'How d'you know?'

'I asked him.'

She hesitated a moment, looking at Philip, and a curious gleam came into her eyes.

'Would you like to read a letter I had from him this morning?'

She handed him an envelope and Philip recognized Griffiths' bold, legible writing. There were eight pages. It was well written, frank and charming; it was the letter of a man who was used to making love to women. He told Mildred that he loved her passionately, he had fallen in love with her the first moment he saw her; he did not want to love her, for he knew how fond Philip was of her, but he could not help himself. Philip was such a dear, and he was very much ashamed of himself, but it was not his fault, he was just carried away. He paid her delightful compliments. Finally he thanked her for consenting to lunch with him next day and said he was dreadfully impatient to see her. Philip noticed that the letter was dated the night before; Griffiths must have written it after leaving Philip, and had taken the trouble to go out and post it when Philip thought he was in bed.

He read it with a sickening palpitation of his heart, but gave no outward sign of surprise. He handed it back to Mildred with a smile, calmly.

'Did you enjoy your lunch?'

'Rather,' she said emphatically.

He felt that his hands were trembling, so he put them under the table.

'You mustn't take Griffiths too seriously. He's just a butterfly, you know.'

She took the letter and looked at it again.

'I can't help it either,' she said, in a voice which she tried to make nonchalant. 'I don't know what's come over me.'

'It's a little awkward for me, isn't it?' said Philip.

She gave him a quick look.

'You're taking it pretty calmly, I must say.'

'What do you expect me to do? Do you want me to tear out my hair in handfuls?'

'I knew you'd be angry with me.'

'The funny thing is, I'm not at all. I ought to have known this would happen. I was a fool to bring you together. I know perfectly well that he's got every advantage over me; he's much jollier, and he's very handsome, he's more amusing, he can talk to you about the things that interest you.'

'I don't know what you mean by that. If I'm not clever I can't help it, but I'm not the fool you think I am, not by a long way, I can tell you. You're a bit too superior for me, my young friend.'

'D'you want to quarrel with me?' he asked mildly.

'No, but I don't see why you should treat me as if I was I don't know what.'

'I'm sorry, I didn't mean to offend you. I just wanted to talk things over quietly. We don't want to make a mess of them if we can help it. I saw you were attracted by him and it seemed to me very natural. The only thing that really hurts me is that he should have encouraged you. He knew how awfully keen I was on you. I think it's rather shabby of him to have written that letter to you five minutes after he told me he didn't care twopence about you.'

'If you think you're going to make me like him any the less by saying nasty things about him, you're mistaken.'

Philip was silent for a moment. He did not know what words he could use to make her see his point of view. He wanted to speak coolly and deliberately, but he was in such a turmoil of emotion that he could not clear his thoughts.

'It's not worth while sacrificing everything for an infatuation that you know can't last. After all, he doesn't care for anyone more than ten days, and you're rather cold; that sort of thing doesn't mean very much to you.'

'That's what you think.'

She made it more difficult for him by adopting a cantankerous tone.

'If you're in love with him you can't help it. I'll just bear it as best I can. We get on very well together, you and I, and I've not behaved badly to you, have I? I've always known that you're not in love with me, but you like me all right, and when we get over to Paris you'll forget about Griffiths. If you make up your mind to put him out of your thoughts you won't find it so hard as all that, and I've deserved that you should do something for me.'

She did not answer, and they went on eating their dinner. When the silence grew oppressive Philip began to talk of different things. He pretended not to notice that Mildred was inattentive. Her answers were perfunctory, and she volunteered no remarks of her own. At last she interrupted abruptly what he was saying.

'Philip, I'm afraid I shan't be able to go away on Saturday. The doctor says I oughtn't to.'

He knew this was not true, but he answered:

'When will you be able to come away?'

She glanced at him, saw that his face was white and rigid, and looked nervously away. She was at that moment a little afraid of him.

'I may as well tell you and have done with it, I can't come away with you at all.'

'I thought you were driving at that. It's too late to change your mind now. I've got the tickets and everything.'

'You said you didn't wish me to go unless I wanted it too, and I don't.'

'I've changed my mind. I'm not going to have any more tricks played with me. You must come.'

'I like you very much, Philip, as a friend. But I can't bear to think of anything else. I don't like you that way. I couldn't, Philip.'

'You were quite willing to a week ago.'

'It was different then.'

'You hadn't met Griffiths?'

'You said yourself I couldn't help it if I'm in love with him.'

Her face was set into a sulky look, and she kept her eyes fixed on her plate. Philip was white with rage. He would have liked to hit her in the face with his clenched fist, and in fancy he saw how she would look with a black eye. There were two lads of eighteen dining at a table near them, and now and then they looked at Mildred; he wondered if they envied him

367

dining with a pretty girl; perhaps they were wishing they stood in his shoes. It was Mildred who broke the silence.

'What's the good of our going away together? I'd be thinking of him all the time. It wouldn't be much fun for you.'

'That's my business,' he answered.

She thought over all his reply indicated, and she reddened.

'But that's just beastly.'

'What of it?'

'I thought you were a gentleman in every sense of the word.'

'You were mistaken.'

His reply entertained him, and he laughed as he said it.

'For God's sake don't laugh,' she cried. 'I can't come away with you, Philip. I'm awfully sorry. I know I haven't behaved well to you, but one can't force themselves.'

'Have you forgotten that when you were in trouble I did everything for you? I planked out the money to keep you till your baby was born, I paid for your doctor and everything, I paid for you to go to Brighton, and I'm paying for the keep of your baby, I'm paying for your clothes, I'm paying for every stitch you've got on now.'

'If you was a gentleman you wouldn't throw what you've done for me in my face.'

'Oh, for goodness' sake, shut up. What d'you suppose I care if I'm a gentleman or not? If I were a gentleman I shouldn't waste my time with a vulgar slut like you. I don't care a damn if you like me or not. I'm sick of being made a blasted fool of. You're jolly well coming to Paris with me on Saturday or you can take the consequences.'

Her cheeks were red with anger, and when she answered her voice had the hard commonness which she concealed generally by a genteel enunciation.

'I never liked you, not from the beginning, but you forced yourself on me, I always hated it when you kissed me. I wouldn't let you touch me now not if I was starving.'

Philip tried to swallow the food on his plate, but the muscles of his throat refused to act. He gulped down something to drink and lit a cigarette. He was trembling in every part. He did not speak. He waited for her to move, but she sat in silence, staring at the white tablecloth. If they had been alone he would have flung his arms round her and kissed her passionately; he fancied the throwing back of her long white throat as he pressed upon her mouth with his lips. They passed an hour without speaking, and at last Philip thought the waiter began to stare at them curiously. He called for the bill.

'Shall we go?' he said then, in an even tone.

She did not reply, but gathered together her bag and her gloves. She put on her coat.

'When are you seeing Griffiths again?'

'Tomorrow,' she answered indifferently.

'You'd better talk it over with him.'

She opened her bag mechanically and saw a piece of paper in it. She took it out.

'Here's the bill for this dress,' she said hesitatingly.

'What of it?'

'I promised I'd give her the money tomorrow.'

'Did you?'

'Does that mean you won't pay for it after having told me I could get it?'

'It does.'

'I'll ask Harry,' she said, flushing quickly.

'He'll be glad to help you. He owes me seven pounds at the moment, and he pawned his microscope last week, because he was so broke.'

'You needn't think you can frighten me by that. I'm quite capable of earning my own living.'

'It's the best thing you can do. I don't propose to give you a farthing more.'

She thought of her rent due on Saturday and the baby's keep, but did not say anything. They left the restaurant, and in the street Philip asked her:

'Shall I call a cab for you? I'm going to take a little stroll.'

'I haven't got any money. I had to pay a bill this afternoon.'

'It won't hurt you to walk. If you want to see me tomorrow I shall be in about tea-time.'

He took off his hat and sauntered away. He looked round in a moment and saw that she was standing helplessly where he had left her, looking at the traffic. He went back and with a laugh pressed a coin into her hand.

'Here's two bob for you to get home with.'

Before she could speak he hurried away.

LXXVI

NEXT day, in the afternoon, Philip sat in his room and wondered whether Mildred would come. He had slept badly. He had spent the morning in the club of the Medical School, reading one newspaper after another. It was the vacation and

369

few students he knew were in London, but he found one or two
people to talk to, he played a game of chess, and so wore out
the tedious hours. After luncheon he felt so tired, his head was
aching so, that he went back to his lodgings and lay down; he
tried to read a novel. He had not seen Griffiths. He was not in
when Philip returned the night before; he heard him come
back, but he did not as usual look into Philip's room to see if
he was asleep; and in the morning Philip heard him go out
early. It was clear that he wanted to avoid him. Suddenly there
was a light tap at his door. Philip sprang to his feet and opened
it. Mildred stood on the threshold. She did not move.

'Come in,' said Philip.

He closed the door after her. She sat down. She hesitated to
begin.

'Thank you for giving me that two shillings last night,' she
said.

'Oh, that's all right.'

She gave him a faint smile. It reminded Philip of the timid,
ingratiating look of a puppy that has been beaten for naughtiness and wants to reconcile himself with his master.

'I've been lunching with Harry,' she said.

'Have you?'

'If you still want me to go away with you on Saturday,
Philip, I'll come.'

A quick thrill of triumph shot through his heart, but it was
a sensation that only lasted an instant; it was followed by a
suspicion.

'Because of the money?' he asked.

'Partly,' she answered simply. 'Harry can't do anything. He
owes five weeks' here, and he owes you seven pounds, and his
tailor's pressing him for money. He'd pawn anything he could,
but he's pawned everything already. I had a job to put the
woman off about my new dress, and on Saturday there's the
book at my lodgings, and I can't get work in five minutes.
It always means waiting some little time till there's a
vacancy.'

She said all this in an even, querulous tone, as though she
were recounting the injustices of fate, which had to be borne
as part of the natural order of things. Philip did not answer.
He knew what she told him well enough.

'You said "partly",' he observed as last.

'Well, Harry says you've been a brick to both of us. You've
been a real good friend to him, he says, and you've done for me
what p'raps no other man would have done. We must do the

straight thing, he says. And he said what you said about him, that he's fickle by nature, he's not like you, and I should be a fool to throw you away for him. He won't last and you will, he says so himself.'

'D'you *want* to come away with me?' asked Philip.

'I don't mind.'

He looked at her, and the corners of his mouth turned down in an expression of misery. He had triumphed indeed, and he was going to have his way. He gave a little laugh of derision at his own humiliation. She looked at him quickly, but did not speak.

'I've looked forward with all my soul to going away with you, and I thought at last, after all that wretchedness, I was going to be happy . . .'

He did not finish what he was going to say. And then on a sudden, without warning, Mildred broke into a storm of tears. She was sitting in the chair in which Norah had sat and wept, and like her she hid her face on the back of it, towards the side where there was a little bump formed by the sagging in the middle, where the head had rested.

'I'm not lucky with women,' thought Philip.

Her thin body was shaken with sobs. Philip had never seen a woman cry with such an utter abandonment. It was horribly painful and his heart was torn. Without realizing what he did, he went up to her and put his arms round her; she did not resist, but in her wretchedness surrendered herself to his comforting. He whispered to her little words of solace. He scarcely knew what he was saying, he bent over her and kissed her repeatedly.

'Are you awfully unhappy?' he said at last.

'I wish I was dead,' she moaned. 'I wish I'd died when the baby come.'

Her hat was in her way, and Philip took it off for her. He placed her head more comfortably in the chair, and then he went and sat down at the table and looked at her.

'It is awful, love, isn't it?' he said. 'Fancy anyone wanting to be in love.'

Presently the violence of her sobbing diminished and she sat in the chair, exhausted, with her head thrown back and her arms hanging by her side. She had the grotesque look of one of those painters' dummies used to hang draperies on.

'I didn't know you loved him so much as all that,' said Philip.

He understood Griffiths' love well enough, for he put him-

371

self in Griffiths' place and saw with his eyes, touched with his hands; he was able to think himself in Griffiths' body, and he kissed her with his lips, smiled at her with his smiling blue eyes. It was her emotion that surprised him. He had never thought her capable of passion, and this was passion : there was no mistaking it. Something seemed to give way in his heart; it really felt to him as though something were breaking, and he felt strangely weak.

'I don't want to make you unhappy. You needn't come away with me if you don't want to. I'll give you the money all the same.'

She shook her head.

'No, I said I'd come, and I'll come.'

'What's the good, if you're sick with love for him?'

'Yes, that's the word. I'm sick with love. I know it won't last, just as well as he does, but just now . . .'

She paused and shut her eyes as though she were going to faint. A strange idea came to Philip, and he spoke it as it came, without stopping to think it out.

'Why don't you go away with him?'

'How can I? You know we haven't got the money.'

'I'll give you the money.'

'You?'

She sat up and looked at him. Her eyes began to shine, and the colour came into her cheeks.

'Perhaps the best thing would be to get it over, and then you'd come back to me.'

Now that he had made the suggestion he was sick with anguish, and yet the torture of it gave him a strange, subtle sensation. She stared at him with open eyes.

'Oh, how could we, on your money? Harry wouldn't think of it.'

'Oh yes, he would, if you persuaded him.'

Her objections made him insist, and yet he wanted her with all his heart to refuse vehemently.

'I'll give you a fiver, and you can go away from Saturday to Monday. You could easily do that. On Monday he's going home till he takes up his appointment at the North London.'

'Oh, Philip, do you mean that?' she cried, clasping her hands. 'If you could only let us go – I would love you so much afterwards, I'll do anything for you. I'm sure I shall get over it if you'll only do that. Would you really give us the money?'

'Yes,' he said.

She was entirely changed now. She began to laugh. He could

372

see that she was insanely happy. She got up and knelt down by
Philip's side, taking his hands.

'You are a brick, Philip. You're the best fellow I've ever
known. Won't you be angry with me afterwards?'

He shook his head, smiling, but with what agony in his
heart!

'May I go and tell Harry now? And can I say to him that
you don't mind? He won't consent unless you promise it
doesn't matter. Oh, you don't know how I love him! And
afterwards I'll do anything you like. I'll come over to Paris
with you or anywhere on Monday.'

She got up and put on her hat.

'Where are you going?'

'I'm going to ask him if he'll take me.'

'Already?'

'D'you want me to stay? I'll stay if you like.'

She sat down, but he gave a little laugh.

'No, it doesn't matter, you'd better go at once. There's only
one thing: I can't bear to see Griffiths just now, it would hurt
me too awfully. Say I have no ill-feeling towards him or anything like that, but ask him to keep out of my way.'

'All right.' She sprang up and put on her gloves. 'I'll let you
know what he says.'

'You'd better dine with me tonight.'

'Very well.'

She put up her face for him to kiss her, and when he pressed
his lips to hers she threw her arms round his neck.

'You are a darling, Philip.'

She sent him a note a couple of hours later to say that she
had a headache and could not dine with him. Philip had almost
expected it. He knew that she was dining with Griffiths. He
was horribly jealous, but the sudden passion which had seized
the pair of them seemed like something that had come from
the outside, as though a god had visited them with it, and he
felt himself helpless. It seemed so natural that they should love
one another. He saw all the advantages that Griffiths had over
himself and confessed that in Mildred's place he would have
done as Mildred did. What hurt him most was Griffiths'
treachery; they had been such good friends, and Griffiths knew
how passionately devoted he was to Mildred: he might have
spared him.

He did not see Mildred again till Friday; he was sick for a
sight of her by then; but when she came and he realized that
he had gone out of her thoughts entirely, for they were en-

grossed in Griffiths, he suddenly hated her. He saw now why she and Griffiths loved one another. Griffiths was stupid, oh, so stupid! he had known that all along, but had shut his eyes to it, stupid and empty-headed: that charm of his concealed an utter selfishness; he was willing to sacrifice anyone to his appetites. And how inane was the life he led, lounging about bars and drinking in music-halls, wandering from one light *amour* to another! He never read a book, he was blind to everything that was not frivolous and vulgar; he had never a thought that was fine: the word most common on his lips was 'smart'; that was his highest praise for man or woman. Smart! It was no wonder he pleased Mildred. They suited one another.

Philip talked to Mildred of things that mattered to neither of them. He knew she wanted to speak of Griffiths, but he gave her no opportunity. He did not refer to the fact that two evenings before she had put off dining with him on a trivial excuse. He was casual with her, trying to make her think he was suddenly grown indifferent; and he exercised peculiar skill in saying little things which he knew would wound her; but which were so indefinite, so delicately cruel, that she could not take exception to them. At last she got up.

'I think I must be going off now,' she said.

'I daresay you've got a lot to do,' he answered.

She held out her hand, he took it, said good-bye, and opened the door for her. He knew what she wanted to speak about, and he knew also that his cold, ironical air intimidated her. Often his shyness made him seem so frigid that unintentionally he frightened people, and, having discovered this, he was able when occasion arose to assume the same manner.

'You haven't forgotten what you promised?' she said at last, as he held open the door.

'What is that?'

'About the money.'

'How much d'you want?'

He spoke with an icy deliberation which made his words peculiarly offensive. Mildred flushed. He knew she hated him at that moment, and he wondered at the self-control by which she prevented herself from flying out at him. He wanted to make her suffer.

'There's the dress and the book tomorrow. That's all. Harry won't come, so we shan't want money for that.'

Philip's heart gave a great thud against his ribs, and he let the door-handle go. The door swung to.

'Why not?'

'He says we couldn't, not on your money.'

A devil seized Philip, a devil of self-torture which was always lurking within him, and, though with all his soul he wished that Griffiths and Mildred should not go away together, he could not help himself; he set himself to persuade Griffiths through her.

'I don't see why not, if I'm willing,' he said.

'That's what I told him.'

'I should have thought if he really wanted to go he wouldn't hesitate.'

'Oh, it's not that, he wants to all right. He'd go at once if he had the money.'

'If he's squeamish about it I'll give *you* the money.'

'I said you'd lend it if he liked, and we'd pay it back as soon as we could.'

'It's rather a change for you going on your knees to get a man to take you away for the week-end.'

'It is rather, isn't it?' she said, with a shameless little laugh. It sent a cold shudder down Philip's spine.

'What are you going to do then?' he asked.

'Nothing. He's going home tomorrow. He must.'

That would be Philip's salvation. With Griffiths out of the way he could get Mildred back. She knew no one in London, she would be thrown on to his society, and when they were alone together he could soon make her forget this infatuation. If he said nothing more he was safe. But he had a fiendish desire to break down their scruples, he wanted to know how abominably they could behave towards him; if he tempted them a little more they would yield, and he took a fierce joy at the thought of their dishonour. Though every word he spoke tortured him, he found in the torture a horrible delight.

'It looks as if it were now or never.'

'That's what I told him,' she said.

There was a passionate note in her voice which struck Philip. He was biting his nails in his nervousness.

'Where are you thinking of going?'

'Oh, to Oxford. He was at the 'Varsity there, you know. He said he'd show me the colleges.'

Philip remembered that once he had suggested going to Oxford for the day, and she had expressed firmly the boredom she felt at the thought of sights.

'And it looks as if you'd have fine weather. It ought to be very jolly there just now.'

'I've done all I could to persuade him.'

'Why don't you have another try?'

'Shall I say you want us to go?'

'I don't think you must go as far as that.' said Philip.

She paused for a minute or two, looking at him. Philip forced himself to look at her in a friendly way. He hated her, he despised her, he loved her with all his heart.

'I'll tell you what I'll do. I'll go and see if he can't arrange it. And then, if he says yes, I'll come and fetch the money to-morrow. When shall you be in?'

'I'll come back here after luncheon and wait.'

'All right.'

'I'll give you the money for your dress and your room now.'

He went to his desk and took out what money he had. The dress was six guineas; there was besides her rent and her food, and the baby's keep for a week. He gave her eight pounds ten.

'Thanks very much,' she said.

She left him.

LXXVII

AFTER lunching in the basement of the Medical School Philip went back to his rooms. It was Saturday afternoon, and the landlady was cleaning the stairs.

'Is Mr Griffiths in?' he asked.

'No, sir. He went away this morning, soon after you went out.'

'Isn't he coming back?'

'I don't think so, sir. He's taken his luggage.'

Philip wondered what this could mean. He took a book and began to read. It was Burton's *Journey to Meccah*, which he had just got out of the Westminster Public Library; and he read the first page, but could make no sense of it, for his mind was elsewhere; he was listening all the time for a ring at the bell. He dared not hope that Griffiths had gone away already, without Mildred, to his home in Cumberland. Mildred would be coming presently for the money. He set his teeth and read on; he tried desperately to concentrate his attention; the sentences etched themselves in his brain by the force of his effort, but they were distorted by the agony he was enduring. He wished with all his heart that he had not made the horrible proposition to give them money; but now that he had made it he lacked the strength to go back on it, not on Mildred's account, but on his own. There was a morbid obstinacy in him

376

which forced him to do the thing he had determined. He discovered that the three pages he had read had made no impression on him at all; and he went back and started from the beginning: he found himself reading one sentence over and over again; and now it weaved itself in with his thoughts, horribly, like some formula in a nightmare. One thing he could do was to go out and keep away till midnight; they could not go then; and he saw them calling at the house every hour to ask if he was in. He enjoyed the thought of their disappointment. He repeated that sentence to himself mechanically. But he could not do that. Let them come and take the money, and he would know then to what depths of infamy it was possible for men to descend. He could not read any more now. He simply could not see the words. He leaned back in his chair, closing his eyes, and, numb with misery, waited for Mildred.

The landlady came in.

'Will you see Mrs Miller, sir?'

'Show her in.'

Philip pulled himself together to receive her without any sign of what he was feeling. He had an impulse to throw himself on his knees and seize her hands and beg her not to go; but he knew there was no way of moving her; she would tell Griffiths what he had said and how he had acted. He was ashamed.

'Well, how about the little jaunt?' he said gaily.

'We're going. Harry's outside. I told him you didn't want to see him, so he's kept out of your way. But he wants to know if he can come in just for a minute to say good-bye to you.'

'No, I won't see him,' said Philip.

He could see she did not care if he saw Griffiths or not. Now that she was there he wanted her to go quickly.

'Look here, here's the fiver. I'd like you to go now.'

She took it and thanked him. She turned to leave the room.

'When are you coming back?' he asked.

'Oh, on Monday. Harry must go home then.'

He knew what he was going to say was humiliating, but he was broken down with jealousy and desire.

'Then I shall see you, shan't I?'

He could not help the note of appeal in his voice.

'Of course. I'll let you know the moment I'm back.'

He shook hands with her. Through the curtains he watched her jump into a four-wheeler that stood at the door. It rolled away. Then he threw himself on his bed and hid his face in his hands. He felt tears coming to his eyes, and he was angry with himself; he clenched his hands and screwed up his body to prevent them; but he could not; and great painful sobs were forced from him.

He got up at last, exhausted and ashamed, and washed his face. He mixed himself a strong whisky and soda. It made him feel a little better. Then he caught sight of the tickets to Paris, which were on the chimney-piece, and, seizing them, with an impulse of rage he flung them in the fire. He knew he could have got the money back on them, but it relieved him to destroy them. Then he went out in search of someone to be with. The club was empty. He felt he would go mad unless he found someone to talk to; but Lawson was abroad; he went on to Hayward's rooms; the maid who opened the door told him that he had gone down to Brighton for the week-end. Then Philip went to a gallery and found it was just closing. He did not know what to do. He was distracted. And he thought of Griffiths and Mildred going to Oxford, sitting opposite one another in the train, happy. He went back to his rooms, but they filled him with horror, he had been so wretched in them; he tried once more to read Burton's book, but, as he read, he told himself again and again what a fool he had been; it was he who had made the suggestion that they should go away, he had offered the money, he had forced it upon them; he might have known what would happen when he introduced Griffiths to Mildred; his own vehement passion was enough to arouse the other's desire. By this time they had reached Oxford. They would put up in one of the lodging-houses in John Street; Philip had never been to Oxford, but Griffiths had talked to him about it so much that he knew exactly where they would go; and they would dine at the Clarendon; Griffiths had been in the habit of dining there when he went on the spree. Philip got himself something to eat in a restaurant near Charing Cross; he had made up his mind to go to a play, and afterwards he fought his way into the pit of a theatre at which one of Oscar Wilde's pieces was being performed. He wondered if Mildred and Griffiths would go to a play that evening: they must kill the evening somehow; they were too stupid, both of them, to content themselves with conversation; he got a fierce delight in reminding himself of the vulgarity of their minds which suited them so exactly to one another. He watched the play with an abstracted mind, trying to give himself gaiety by drinking whisky in each interval; he was unused to alcohol, and it affected him quickly, but his drunkenness was savage and morose. When the play was over he had another drink. He could not go to bed, he knew he would not sleep, and he dreaded the pictures which his vivid imagination would place before him. He tried not to think of them. He knew he had drunk too much. Now he was seized with a desire to do horrible, sordid things; he wanted to roll himself in gutters; his whole being yearned for beastliness; he wanted to grovel.

He walked up Piccadilly, dragging his club-foot, sombrely drunk, with rage and misery clawing at his heart. He was stopped by a painted harlot, who put her hand on his arm; he pushed her violently away with brutal words. He walked on a few steps and then stopped. She would do as well as another. He was sorry he had spoken so roughly to her. He went up to her.

'I say,' he began.

'Go to hell,' she said.

Philip laughed.

'I merely wanted to ask if you'd do me the honour of supping with me tonight.'

She looked at him with amazement, and hesitated for a while. She saw he was drunk.

'I don't mind.'

He was amused that she should use a phrase he had heard so often on Mildred's lips. He took her to one of the restaurants he had been in the habit of going to with Mildred. He noticed as they walked along that she looked down at his limb.

'I've got a club-foot,' he said. 'Have you any objection?'

'You are a cure,' she laughed.

When he got home his bones were aching, and in his head there was a hammering that made him nearly scream. He took another whisky and soda to steady himself, and going to bed sank into a dreamless sleep till midday.

LXXVIII

AT last Monday came, and Philip thought his long torture was over. Looking out the trains he found that the latest by which Griffiths could reach home that night left Oxford soon after one, and he supposed that Mildred would take one which started a few minutes later to bring her to London. His desire was to go and meet it, but he thought Mildred would like to be left alone for a day; perhaps she would drop him a line in the evening to say she was back, and if not he would call at her lodgings next morning: his spirit was cowed. He felt a bitter hatred for Griffiths, but for Mildred, notwithstanding all that had passed, only a heart-rending desire. He was glad now that Hayward was not in London on Saturday afternoon when, distraught, he went in search of human comfort: he could not have prevented himself from telling him everything, and Hayward would have been astonished at his weakness. He would despise him, and perhaps be shocked or disgusted that he could envisage the possibility of making Mildred his mistress after she had given herself to another man. What did he care if it was shocking or disgusting? He was ready for any compromise, prepared for more degrading humiliations still, if he could only gratify his desire.

Towards the evening his steps took him against his will to the house in which she lived, and he looked up at her window. It was dark. He did not venture to ask if she was back. He was confident in her promise. But there was no letter from her in the morning, and, when about midday he called, the maid told him she had not arrived. He could not understand it. He knew that Griffiths would have been obliged to go home the day before, for he was to be best man at a wedding, and Mildred had no money. He turned over in his mind every possible thing that might have happened. He went again in the afternoon and left a note, asking her to dine with him that evening as calmly as though the events of the last fortnight had not happened. He mentioned the place and time at which they were to meet, and hoping against hope kept the appointment: though he waited for an hour she did not come. On Wednesday morning he was ashamed to ask at the house and sent a messenger-boy with a letter and instructions to bring back a reply; but in an hour the boy came back with Philip's letter unopened and the answer that the lady had not returned from the country. Philip was beside himself. The last deception was more than he could bear. He repeated to himself over and over again that he loathed Mildred, and, ascribing to Griffiths this new disappointment, he hated him so much that he knew what was the delight of murder: he walked about considering what a joy it would be to come upon him on a dark night and stick a knife into his throat, just about the carotid artery, and leave him to die in the street like a dog. Philip was out of his senses with grief and rage. He did not like whisky, but he drank to stupefy himself. He went to bed drunk on the Tuesday and on the Wednesday night.

On Thursday morning he got up very late and dragged himself, blear-eyed and sallow, into his sitting-room to see if there were any letters. A curious feeling shot through his heart when he recognized the handwriting of Griffiths.

Dear old man –
    I hardly know how to write to you and yet I feel I must write. I hope you're not awfully angry with me. I know I oughtn't to have gone away with Milly, but I simply couldn't help myself. She simply carried me off my feet and I would have done anything to get her. When she told me you had offered us the money to go I simply couldn't resist. And now it's all over I'm awfully ashamed of myself and I wish I hadn't been such a fool. I wish you'd write and say you're not angry with me, and I want you to let me come and see you. I was awfully hurt at your telling Milly you didn't want to see me. Do write me a line, there's a good chap, and tell me you forgive me. It'll ease my conscience. I thought you wouldn't mind or you wouldn't have offered the money. But I know I oughtn't to have taken it. I came home on Monday and Milly wanted to stay a couple of days at Oxford by herself. She's going back to London on Wednesday, so by the time you receive this letter you will have seen her and I hope everything will go off all right. Do write and say you forgive me. Please write at once.
Yours ever,
Harry

Philip tore up the letter furiously. He did not mean to answer it. He despised Griffiths for his apologies, he had no patience with his prickings of conscience: one, could do a dastardly thing if one chose, but it was contemptible to regret it afterwards. He thought the letter cowardly and hypocritical. He was disgusted at its sentimentality.

'It would be very easy if you could do a beastly thing,' he muttered to himself, 'and then say you were sorry, and that put it all right again.'

He hoped with all his heart he would have the chance one day to do Griffiths a bad turn.

But at all events he knew that Mildred was in town. He dressed hurriedly, not waiting to shave, drank a cup of tea, and took a cab to her rooms. The cab seemed to crawl. He was painfully anxious to see her, and unconsciously he uttered a prayer to the God he did not believe in to make her receive him kindly. He only wanted to forget. With beating heart he rang the bell. He forgot all his suffering in the passionate desire to enfold her once more in his arms.

'Is Mrs Miller in?' he asked joyously.

'She's gone,' the maid answered.

He looked at her blankly.

'She came about an hour ago and took away her things.'

For a moment he did not know what to say.

'Did you give her my letter? Did she say where she was going?'

Then he understood that Mildred had deceived him again. She was not coming back to him. He made an effort to save his face.

'Oh, well, I daresay I shall hear from her. She may have sent a letter to another address.'

He turned away and went back hopeless to his rooms. He might have known that she would do this; she had never cared for him, she had made a fool of him from the beginning; she had no pity, she had no kindness, she had no charity. The only thing was to accept the inevitable. The pain he was suffering was horrible, he would sooner be dead than endure it; and the thought came to him that it would be better to finish with the whole thing: he might throw himself in the river or put his neck on a railway line; but he had no sooner set the thought into words than he rebelled against it. His reason told him that he would get over his unhappiness in time; if he tried with all his might he could forget her; and it would be grotesque to kill himself on account of a vulgar slut. He had only one life, and it was madness to fling it away. He *felt* that he would never overcome his passion, but he *knew* that after all it was only a matter of time.

He would not stay in London. There everything reminded him of his unhappiness. He telegraphed to his uncle that he was coming to Blackstable, and, hurrying to pack, took the first train he could. He wanted to get away from the sordid rooms in which he had endured so much suffering. He wanted to breathe clean air. He was disgusted with himself. He felt that he was a little mad.

Since he was grown up Philip had been given the best spare room at the vicarage. It was a corner-room and in front of one window was an old tree which blocked the view, but from the other you saw, beyond the garden and the vicarage field, broad meadows. Philip remembered the wallpaper from his earliest years. On the walls were quaint water colours of the early Victorian period by a friend of the Vicar's youth. They had a faded charm. The dressing-table was surrounded by stiff muslin. There was an old tallboy to put your clothes in. Philip gave a sigh of pleasure; he had never realized that all those things meant anything to him at all. At the vicarage life went on as it had always done. No piece of furniture had been moved from one place to another; the Vicar ate the same things, said the same things, went for the same walk every day; he had grown a little fatter, a little more silent, a little more narrow. He had become accustomed to living without his wife and missed her very little .He bickered still with Josiah Graves. Philip went to see the churchwarden. He was a little thinner, a little whiter, a little more austere; he was autocratic still and still disapproved of candles on the altar. The shops had still a pleasant quaintness; and Philip stood in front of that in which things useful to seamen were sold, sea-boots and tarpaulins and tackle, and remembered that he had felt there in his childhood the thrill of the sea and the adventurous magic of the unknown.

He could not help his heart beating at each double knock of the postman in case there might be a letter from Mildred sent on by his landlady in London; but he knew that there would be none. Now that he could think it out more calmly he understood that in trying to force Mildred to love him he had been attempting the impossible. He did not know what it was that passed from a man to a woman, from a woman to a man, and made one of them a slave: it was convenient to call it the sexual instinct; but if it was no more than that, he did not understand why it should occasion so vehement an attraction to one person rather than another. It was irresistible: the mind could not battle with it; friendship, gratitude, interest, had no power beside it. Because he had not attracted Mildred sexually, nothing that he did had any effect upon her. The idea revolted him; it made human nature beastly; and he felt suddenly that the hearts of men were full of dark places. Because Mildred was indifferent to him he had thought her sexless; her anaemic appearance and thin lips, the body with its narrow hips and flat chest, the languor of her manner, carried out his supposition; and yet she was capable of sudden passions which made her willing to risk everything to gratify them. He had never understood her adventure with Emil Miller: it had seemed so unlike her, and she had never been able to explain it; but now that he had seen her with Griffiths he knew that just the same thing had happened then: she had been carried off her feet by an ungovernable desire. He tried to think out what those two men had which so strangely attracted her. They both had a vulgar facetiousness which tickled her simple sense of humour, and a certain coarseness of nature; but what took her perhaps was the blatant sexuality which was their most marked characteristic. She had a genteel refinement which shuddered at the facts of life, she looked upon the bodily functions as indecent, she had all sorts of euphemisms for common objects, she always chose an elaborate word as more becoming than a simple one: the brutality of these men was like a whip on her thin white shoulders, and she shuddered with voluptuous pain.

One thing Philip had made up his mind about. He would not go back to the lodgings in which he had suffered. He wrote to his landlady and gave her notice. He wanted to have his own things about him. He determined to take unfurnished rooms: it would be pleasant and cheaper; and this was an urgent consideration, for during the last year and a half he had spent nearly seven hundred pounds. He must make up for it now by the most rigid economy. Now and then he thought of the future with panic; he had been a fool to spend so much money on Mildred; but he knew that if it were to come again he would act in the same way. It amused him sometimes to consider that his friends, because he had a face which did not express his feelings very vividly and a rather slow way of moving, looked upon him as strong-minded, deliberate, and cool. They thought him reasonable and praised his common sense; but he knew that his placid expression was no more than a mask, assumed unconsciously, which acted like the protective colouring of butterflies; and himself was astonished at the weakness of his will. It seemed to him that he was swayed by every light emotion, as though he were a leaf in the wind, and when passion seized him he was powerless. He had no self-control. He merely seemed to possess it because he was indifferent to many of the things which moved other people.

He considered with some irony the philosophy which he had developed for himself, for it had not been of much use to him in the conjuncture he had passed through; and he wondered whether thought really helped a man in any of the critical affairs of life: it seemed to him rather that he was swayed by some power alien to and yet within himself, which urged him like that great wind of Hell which drove Paolo and Francesca ceaselessly on. He thought of what he was going to do and, when the time came to act, he was powerless in the grasp of instincts, emotions, he knew not what. He acted as though he were a machine driven by two forces of his environment and his personality; his reason was someone looking on, observing the facts but powerless to interfere: it was like those gods of

Epicurus, who saw the doings of men from their empyrean heights and had no might to alter one smallest particle of what occurred

LXXIX

PHILIP went up to London a couple of days before the session began in order to find himself rooms. He hunted about the streets that led out of the Westminster Bridge Road, but their dinginess was distasteful to him; and at last he found one in Kennington which had a quiet and old-world air. It reminded one a little of the London which Thackeray knew on that side of the river, and in the Kennington Road, through which the great barouche of the Newcomes must have passed as it drove the family to the West of London, the plane-trees were bursting into leaf. The houses in the street which Philip fixed upon were two-storeyed, and in most of the windows was a notice to state that lodgings were to let. He knocked at one which announced that the lodgings were unfurnished, and was shown by an austere, silent woman four very small rooms, in one of which there was a kitchen range and a sink. The rent was nine shillings a week. Philip did not want so many rooms, but the rent was low and he wished to settle down at once. He asked the landlady if she could keep the place clean for him and cook his breakfast, but she replied that she had enough work to do without that; and he was pleased rather than otherwise because she intimated that she wished to have nothing more to do with him than to receive his rent. She told him that, if he inquired at the grocer's round the corner, which was also a post office, he might hear of a woman who would 'do' for him.

Philip had a little furniture which he had gathered as he went along, an arm-chair that he had bought in Paris, and a table, a few drawings, and the small Persian rug which Cronshaw had given him. His uncle had offered a fold-up bed for which, now that he no longer let his house in August, he had no further use; and by spending another ten pounds Philip bought himself whatever else was essential. He spent ten shillings on putting a corn-coloured paper in the room he was making his parlour; and he hung on the walls a sketch which Lawson had given him of the Quai des Grands Augustins, and the photograph of the *Odalisque* by Ingres and Manet's *Olympia* which in Paris had been the objects of his contemplation while he shaved. To remind himself that he too had once been

engaged in the practice of art, he put up a charcoal drawing of
the young Spaniard Miguel Ajuria: it was the best thing he
had ever done, a nude standing with clenched hands, his feet
gripping the floor with a peculiar force, and on his face that
air of determination which had been so impressive; and though
Philip after the long interval saw very well the defects of his
work its associations made him look upon it with tolerance.
He wondered what had happened to Miguel. There is nothing
so terrible as the pursuit of art by those who have no talent.
Perhaps, worn out by exposure, starvation, disease, he had
found an end in some hospital, or in an access of despair had
sought death in the turbid Seine; but perhaps with his Southern
instability he had given up the struggle of his own accord, and
now, a clerk in some office in Madrid, turned his fervent
rhetoric to politics and bull-fighting.

Philip asked Lawson and Hayward to come and see his new
rooms, and they came, one with a bottle of whisky, the other
with a *pâté de foie gras*; and he was delighted when they praised
his taste. He would have invited the Scotch stockbroker too,
but he had only three chairs, and thus could entertain only a
definite number of guests. Lawson was aware that through him
Philip had become very friendly with Norah Nesbit and now
remarked that he had run across her a few days before.

'She was asking how you were.'

Philip flushed at the mention of her name (he could not get
himself out of the awkward habit of reddening when he was
embarrassed), and Lawson looked at him quizzically. Lawson,
who now spent most of the year in London, had so far surrendered to his environment as to wear his hair short and to
dress himself in a neat serge suit and a bowler hat.

'I gather that all is over between you,' he said.

'I've not seen her for months.'

'She was looking rather nice. She had a very smart hat on
with a lot of white ostrich feathers on it. She must be doing
pretty well.'

Philip changed the conversation, but he kept thinking of
her, and after an interval, when the three of them were talking
of something else, he asked suddenly:

'Did you gather that Norah was angry with me?'

'Not a bit. She talked very nicely of you.'

'I've got half a mind to go and see her.'

'She won't eat you.'

Philip had thought of Norah often. When Mildred left him
his first thought was of her, and he told himself bitterly that

she would never have treated him so. His impulse was to go to her; he could depend on her pity; but he was ashamed; she had been good to him always, and he had treated her abominably.

'If I'd only had the sense to stick to her!' he said to himself, afterwards, when Lawson and Hayward had gone and he was smoking a last pipe before going to bed.

He remembered the pleasant hours they had spent together in the cosy sitting-room in Vincent Square, their visits to galleries and to the play, and the charming evenings of intimate conversation. He recollected her solicitude for his welfare and her interest in all that concerned him. She had loved him with a love that was kind and lasting, there was more than sensuality in it, it was almost maternal; he had always known that it was a precious thing for which with all his soul he should thank the gods. He made up his mind to throw himself on her mercy. She must have suffered horribly, but he felt she had the greatness of heart to forgive him; she was incapable of malice. Should he write to her? No. He would break in on her suddenly and cast himself at her feet – he knew that when the time came he would feel too shy to perform such a dramatic gesture, but that was how he liked to think of it – and tell her that if she would take him back she might rely on him for ever. He was cured of the hateful disease from which he had suffered, he knew her worth, and now she might trust him. His imagination leaped forward to the future. He pictured himself rowing with her on the river on Sundays; he would take her to Greenwich, he had never forgotten that delightful excursion with Hayward, and the beauty of the Port of London remained a permanent treasure in his recollection; and on the warm summer afternoons they would sit in the Park together and talk: he laughed to himself as he remembered her gay chatter, which poured out like a brook bubbling over little stones, amusing, flippant, and full of character. The agony he had suffered would pass from his mind like a bad dream.

But when next day, about tea-time, an hour at which he was pretty certain to find Norah at home, he knocked at her door his courage suddenly failed him. Was it possible for her to forgive him? It would be abominable of him to force himself on her presence. The door was opened by a maid new since he had been in the habit of calling every day, and he inquired if Mrs Nesbit was in.

'Will you ask her if she could see Mr Carey?' he said. 'I'll wait here.'

The maid ran upstairs and in a moment clattered down again.

'Will you step up, please, sir? Second floor front.'

'I know,' said Philip, with a slight smile.

He went with a fluttering heart. He knocked at the door.

'Come in,' said the well-known, cheerful voice.

It seemed to say come in to a new life of peace and happiness. When he entered Norah stepped forward to greet him. She shook hands with him as if they had parted the day before. A man stood up.

'Mr Carey – Mr Kingsford.'

Philip, bitterly disappointed at not finding her alone, sat down and took stock of the stranger. He had never heard her mention his name, but he seemed to Philip to occupy his chair as though he were very much at home. He was a man of forty, clean-shaven, with long fair hair very neatly plastered down, and the reddish skin and pale, tired eyes which fair men get when their youth is passed. He had a large nose, a large mouth; the bones of his face were prominent, and he was heavily made; he was a man of more than average height, and broad-shouldered.

'I was wondering what had become of you,' said Norah, in her sprightly manner. 'I met Mr Lawson the other day – did he tell you? – and I informed him that it was really high time you came to see me again.'

Philip could see no shadow of embarrassment in her countenance, and he admired the ease with which she carried off an encounter of which himself felt the intense awkwardness. She gave him tea. She was about to put sugar in it when he stopped her.

'How stupid of me!' she cried. 'I forgot.'

He did not believe that. She must remember quite well that he never took sugar in his tea. He accepted the incident as a sign that her nonchalance was affected.

The conversation which Philip had interrupted went on, and presently he began to feel a little in the way. Kingsford took no particular notice of him. He talked fluently and well, not without humour, but with a slightly dogmatic manner: he was a journalist, it appeared, and had something amusing to say on every topic that was touched upon; but it exasperated Philip to find himself edged out of the conversation. He was determined to stay the visitor out. He wondered if he admired Norah. In the old days they had often talked of the men who wanted to flirt with her and had laughed at them together.

Philip tried to bring back the conversation to matters which only he and Norah knew about, but each time the journalist broke in and succeeded in drawing it away to a subject upon which Philip was forced to be silent. He grew faintly angry with Norah, for she must see he was being made ridiculous; but perhaps she was inflicting this upon him as a punishment, and with this thought he regained his good humour. At last, however, the clock struck six, and Kingsford got up.

'I must go,' he said.

Norah shook hands with him, and accompanied him to the landing. She shut the door behind her and stood outside for a couple of minutes. Philip wondered what they were talking about.

'Who is Mr Kingsford?' he asked cheerfully, when she returned.

'Oh, he's the editor of one of Harmsworth's magazines. He's been taking a good deal of my work lately.'

'I thought he was never going.'

'I'm glad you stayed. I wanted to have a talk with you.' She curled herself into the large arm-chair, feet and all, in a way her small size made possible, and lit a cigarette. He smiled when he saw her assume the attitude which had always amused him.

'You look just like a cat.'

She gave him a flash of her dark, fine eyes.

'I really ought to break myself of the habit. It's absurd to behave like a child when you're my age, but I'm comfortable with my legs under me.'

'It's awfully jolly to be sitting in this room again,' said Philip happily. 'You don't know how I've missed it.'

'Why on earth didn't you come before?' she asked gaily.

'I was afraid to,' he said, reddening.

She gave him a look full of kindness. Her lips outlined a charming smile.

'You needn't have been.'

He hesitated for a moment. His heart beat quickly.

'D'you remember the last time we met? I treated you awfully badly – I'm dreadfully ashamed of myself.'

She looked at him steadily. She did not answer. He was losing his head; he seemed to have come on an errand of which he was only now realizing the outrageousness. She did not help him, and he could only blurt out bluntly:

'Can you ever forgive me?'

Then impetuously he told her that Mildred had left him

389

and that his unhappiness had been so great that he almost
killed himself. He told her of all that had happened between
them, of the birth of the child, and of the meeting with
Griffiths, of his folly and his trust and his immense deception.
He told her how often he had thought of her kindness and
of her love, and how bitterly he had regretted throwing it
away: he had only been happy when he was with her, and he
knew now how great was her worth. His voice was hoarse with
emotion. Sometimes he was so ashamed of what he was saying
that he spoke with his eyes fixed on the ground. His face was
distorted with pain, and yet he felt it a strange relief to speak.
At last he finished. He flung himself back in his chair, exhausted, and waited. He had concealed nothing, and even, in
his self-abasement, he had striven to make himself more
despicable than he had really been. He was surprised that she
did not speak, and at last he raised his eyes. She was not looking at him. Her face was quite white, and she seemed to be
lost in thought.

'Haven't you got anything to say to me?'

She started and reddened.

'I'm afraid you've had a rotten time,' she said. 'I'm dreadfully sorry.'

She seemed about to go on, but she stopped, and again he
waited. At length she seemed to force herself to speak.

'I'm engaged to be married to Mr Kingsford.'

'Why didn't you tell me at once?' he cried. 'You needn't
have allowed me to humiliate myself before you.'

'I'm sorry, I couldn't stop you ... I met him soon after you'
— she seemed to search for an expression that should not
wound him — 'told me your friend had come back. I was very
wretched for a bit, he was extremely kind to me. He knew
someone had made me suffer, of course he doesn't know it
was you, and I don't know what I should have done without
him. And suddenly I felt I couldn't go on working, working,
working; I was so tired, I felt so ill. I told him about my husband. He offered to give me the money to get my divorce if I
would marry him as soon as I could. He had a very good job,
and it wouldn't be necessary for me to do anything unless I
wanted to. He was so fond of me and so anxious to take care
of me. I was awfully touched. And now I'm very, very fond
of him.'

'Have you got your divorce then?' asked Philip.

'I've got the decree *nisi*. It'll be made absolute in July, and
then we are going to be married at once.'

For some time Philip did not say anything.

'I wish I hadn't made such a fool of myself,' he muttered at length.

He was thinking of his long, humiliating confession. She looked at him curiously.

'You were never really in love with me,' she said.

'It's not very pleasant being in love.'

But he was always able to recover himself quickly, and, getting up now and holding out his hand, he said:

'I hope you'll be very happy. After all, it's the best thing that could have happened to you.'

She looked a little wistfully at him as she took his hand and held it.

'You'll come and see me again, won't you?' she asked.

'No,' he said, shaking his head. 'It would make me too envious to see you happy.'

He walked slowly away from her house. After all she was right when she said he had never loved her. He was disappointed, irritated even, but his vanity was more affected than his heart. He knew that himself. And presently he grew conscious that the gods had played a very good practical joke on him, and he laughed at himself mirthlessly. It was not very comfortable to have the gift of being amused at one's own absurdity.

LXXX

For the next three months Philip worked on subjects which were new to him. The unwieldy crowd which had entered the Medical School nearly two years before had thinned out: some had left the hospital, finding the examinations more difficult to pass than they expected, some had been taken away by parents who had not foreseen the expense of life in London, and some had drifted away to other callings. One youth whom Philip knew had devised an ingenious plan to make money; he had bought things at sales and pawned them, but presently found it more profitable to pawn goods bought on credit; and it had caused a little excitement at the hospital when someone pointed out his name in police-court proceedings. There had been a remand, then assurances on the part of a harassed father, and the young man had gone out to bear the White Man's Burden overseas. The imagination of another, a lad who had never before been in a town at all, fell to the glamour of music-halls and bar parlours; he spent his time among racing-men, tipsters, and trainers, and now was become a bookmaker's clerk. Philip had seen him once in a bar near Piccadilly Circus in a tight-waisted coat and a brown hat with a broad, flat brim. A third, with a gift for singing and mimicry, who had achieved success at the smoking concerts of the Medical School by his imitation of notorious comedians, had abandoned the hospital for the chorus of a musical comedy. Still another, and he interested Philip because his uncouth manner and interjectional speech did not suggest that he was capable of any deep emotion, had felt himself stifle among the houses of London. He grew haggard in shut-in spaces, and the soul he knew not he possessed struggled like a sparrow held in the hand, with little frightened gasps and a quick palpitation of the heart: he yearned for the broad skies and the open, desolate places among which his childhood had been spent; and he walked off one day, without a word to anybody, between one lecture and another; and the next thing his friends heard was that he had thrown up medicine and was working on a farm.

Philip attended now lectures on medicine and on surgery. On certain mornings in the weeks he practised bandaging on out-patients, glad to earn a little money, and he was taught auscultation and how to use the stethoscope. He learned dispensing. He was taking the examination in *Materia Medica* in July, and it amused him to play with various drugs, concocting mixtures, rolling pills, and making ointments. He seized avidly upon anything from which he could extract a suggestion of human interest.

He saw Griffiths once in the distance, but, not to have the pain of cutting him dead, avoided him. Philip had felt a certain self-consciousness with Griffiths' friends, some of whom were now friends of his, when he realized they knew of his quarrel with Griffiths and surmised they were aware of the reason. One of them, a very tall fellow, with a small head and a languid air, a youth called Ramsden, who was one of Griffiths' most faithful admirers, copied his ties, his boots, his manner of talking, and his gestures, told Philip that Griffiths was very much hurt because Philip had not answered his letter. He wanted to be reconciled with him.

'Has he asked you to give me the message?' asked Philip.

'Oh, no, I'm saying this entirely on my own,' said Ramsden. 'He's awfully sorry for what he did, and he says you always behaved like a perfect brick to him. I know he'd be glad to make it up. He doesn't come to the hospital because he's afraid of meeting you, and he thinks you'd cut him.'

'I should.'

'It makes him feel rather wretched, you know.'

'I can bear the trifling inconvenience that he feels with a good deal of fortitude,' said Philip.

'He'll do anything he can to make it up.'

'How childish and hysterical! Why should he care? I'm a very insignificant person, and he can do very well without my company. I'm not interested in him any more.'

Ramsden thought Philip hard and cold. He paused for a moment or two, looking about him in a perplexed way.

'Harry wishes to God he'd never had anything do with the woman.'

'Does he?' asked Philip.

He spoke with an indifference which he was satisfied with. No one could have guessed how violently his heart was beating. He waited impatiently for Ramsden to go on.

'I suppose you've quite got over it now, haven't you?'

'I?' said Philip. 'Quite.'

Little by little he discovered the history of Mildred's relations with Griffiths. He listened with a smile on his lips, feigning an equanimity which quite deceived the dull-witted boy who talked to him. The week-end she spent with Griffiths at Oxford inflamed rather than extinguished her sudden passion; and when Griffiths went home, with a feeling that was unexpected in her, she determined to stay in Oxford by herself for a couple of days, because she had been so happy in it. She felt that nothing could induce her to go back to Philip. He revolted her. Griffiths was taken aback at the fire he had aroused, for he had found his two days with her in the country somewhat tedious; and he had no desire to turn an amusing episode into a tiresome affair. She made him promise to write to her, and, being an honest, decent fellow, with natural politeness and a desire to make himself pleasant to everybody, when he got home he wrote her a long and charming letter. She answered it with reams of passion, clumsy, for she had no gift of expression, ill-written and vulgar; the letter bored him, and when it was followed next day by another, and the day after by a third, he began to think her love no longer flattering but alarming. He did not answer; and she bombarded him with telegrams, asking him if he were ill and had received her letters; she said his silence made her dreadfully anxious. He was forced to write, but he sought to make his reply as casual as was possible without being offensive: he begged her not to wire, since it was difficult to explain telegrams to his mother, an old-fashioned person for whom a telegram was still an event to excite tremor. She answered by return of post that she must see him and announced her intention to pawn things (she had the dressing-case which Philip had given her as a wedding-present and could raise eight pounds on that) in order to come up and stay at the market town four miles from which was the village in which his father practised. This frightened Griffiths; and he, this time, made use of the telegraph wires to tell her that she must do nothing of the kind. He promised to let her know the moment he came up to London, and, when he did, found that she had already been asking for him at the hospital at which he had an appointment. He did not like this, and, on seeing her, told Mildred that she was not to come there on any pretext; and now, after an absence of three weeks, he found that she bored him quite decidedly; he wondered why he had ever troubled about her, and made up his mind to break with her as soon as he could. He was a person who dreaded quarrels, nor did he want to give pain; but at the same time he had other things to do, and he was quite determined not to let Mildred bother him. When he met her he was pleasant, cheerful, amusing, affectionate; he invented convincing excuses for the interval since last he had seen her; but he did everything he could to avoid her. When she forced him to make appointments he sent telegrams to her at the last moment to put himself off; and his landlady (the first three months of his appointment he was spending in rooms) had orders to say he was out when Mildred called. She would waylay him in the street and, knowing she had been waiting about for him to come out of the hospital for a couple of hours, he would give her a few charming, friendly words and bolt off with the excuse that he had a business engagement. He grew very skilful in slipping out of the hospital unseen. Once, when he went back to his lodgings at midnight, he saw a woman standing at the area railings and suspecting who it was went to beg a shake-down in Ramsden's rooms; next day the landlady told him that Mildred had sat crying on the doorstep for hours, and she had been obliged to tell her at last that if she did not go away she would send for a policeman.

'I tell you, my boy,' said Ramsden, 'you're jolly well out of it. Harry says that if he'd suspected for half a second she was going to make such a blooming nuisance of herself he'd have seen himself damned before he had anything to do with her.'

Philip thought of her sitting on that doorstep through the long hours of the night. He saw her face as she looked up dully at the landlady who sent her away.

'I wonder what she's doing now.'

'Oh, she's got a job somewhere, thank God. That keeps her busy all day.'

The last thing he heard, just before the end of the summer session, was that Griffiths' urbanity had given way at length under the exasperation of the constant persecution. He had told Mildred that he was sick of being pestered, and she had better take herself off and not bother him again.

'It was the only thing he could do,' said Ramsden. 'It was getting a bit too thick.'

'Is it all over then?' asked Philip.

'Oh, he hasn't seen her for ten days. You know, Harry's wonderful at dropping people. This is about the toughest nut he's ever had to crack, but he's cracked it all right.'

Then Philip heard nothing more of her at all. She vanished into the vast anonymous mass of the population of London.

LXXXI

AT the beginning of the winter session Philip became an out-patients' clerk. There were three assistant-physicians who took out-patients, two days a week each, and Philip put his name down for Dr Tyrell. He was popular with the students, and there was some competition to be his clerk. Dr Tyrell was a tall, thin man of thirty-five, with a very small head, red hair cut short, and prominent blue eyes: his face was bright scarlet. He talked well in a pleasant voice, was fond of a little joke, and treated the world lightly. He was a successful man, with a large consulting practice and a knighthood in prospect. From commerce with students and poor people he had the patronizing air, and from dealing always with the sick he had the healthy man's jovial condescension, which some consultants achieve as the professional manner. He made the patient feel like a boy confronted by a jolly schoolmaster; his illness was an absurd piece of naughtiness which amused rather than irritated.

The student was supposed to attend in the out-patients' room every day, see cases, and pick up what information he could; but on the days on which he clerked his duties were a little more definite. At that time the out-patients' department at St

Luke's consisted of three rooms, leading into one another, and a large, dark waiting-room with massive pillars of masonry and long benches. Here the patients waited after having been given their 'letters' at midday; and the long rows of them, bottles and gallipots in hand, some tattered and dirty, others decent enough, sitting in the dimness, men and women of all ages, children, gave one an impression which was weird and horrible. They suggested the grim drawings of Daumier. All the rooms were painted alike, in salmon-colour with a high dado of maroon; and there was in them an odour of disinfectants, mingling as the afternoon wore on with the crude stench of humanity. The first room was the largest, and in the middle of it were a table and an office chair for the physician; on each side of this were two smaller tables, a little lower: at one of these sat the house-physician and at the other the clerk who took the 'book' for the day. This was a large volume in which were written down the name, age, sex, profession of the patient, and the diagnosis of his disease.

At half past one the house-physician came in, rang the bell, and told the porter to send in the old patients. There were always a good many of these, and it was necessary to get through as many of them as possible before Dr Tyrell came at two. The H.P. with whom Philip came in contact was a dapper little man, excessively conscious of his importance: he treated the clerks with condescension and patently resented the familiarity of older students who had been his contemporaries and did not use him with the respect he felt his present position demanded. He set about the cases. A clerk helped him. The patients streamed in. The men came first. Chronic bronchitis, 'a nasty 'acking cough', was what they chiefly suffered from; one went to the H.P. and the other to the clerk, handing in their letters: if they were going on well the words *Rep 14* were written on them, and they went to the dispensary with their bottles or gallipots in order to have medicine given them for fourteen days more. Some old stagers held back so that they might be seen by the physician himself, but they seldom succeeded in this; and only three or four, whose condition seemed to demand his attention, were kept.

Dr Tyrell came in with quick movements and a breezy manner. He reminded one slightly of a clown leaping into the arena of a circus with the cry: Here we are again. His air seemed to indicate: What's all this nonsense about being ill? I'll soon put that right. He took his seat, asked if there were any old patients for him to see, rapidly passed them in review, looking at them with shrewd eyes as he discussed their symptoms, cracked a joke (at which all the clerks laughed heartily) with the H.P., who laughed heartily too, but with an air as if he thought it was rather impudent for the clerks to laugh, remarked that it was a fine day or a hot one, and rang the bell for the porter to show in the new patients.

They came in one by one and walked up to the table at which sat Dr Tyrell. They were old men and young men and middle-aged men, mostly of the labouring class, dock labourers, draymen, factory hands, barmen; but some, neatly dressed, were of a station which was obviously superior, shop-assistants, clerks, and the like. Dr Tyrell looked at these with suspicion. Sometimes they put on shabby clothes in order to pretend they were poor; but he had a keen eye to prevent what he regarded as fraud and sometimes refused to see people who, he thought, could well pay for medical attendance. Women were the worst offenders and they managed the thing more clumsily. They would wear a cloak and a skirt which were almost in rags, and neglect to take the rings off their fingers.

'If you can afford to wear jewellery you can afford a doctor. A hospital is a charitable institution,' said Dr Tyrell.

He handed back the letter and called for the next case.

'But I've got my letter.'

'I don't care a hang about your letter; you get out. You've got no business to come and steal the time which is wanted by the really poor.'

The patient retired sulkily, with an angry scowl.

'She'll probably write a letter to the papers on the gross mismanagement of the London hospitals,' said Dr Tyrell, with a smile, as he took the next paper and gave the patient one of his shrewd glances.

Most of them were under the impression that the hospital was an institution of the state, for which they paid out of the rates, and took the attendance they received as a right they could claim. They imagined the physician who gave them his time was heavily paid.

Dr Tyrell gave each of his clerks a case to examine. The clerk took the patient into one of the inner rooms; they were smaller, and each had a couch in it covered with black horsehair: he asked his patient a variety of questions, examined his lungs, his heart, and his liver, made notes of fact on the hospital letter, formed in his own mind some idea of the diagnosis, and then waited for Dr Tyrell to come in. This he did, followed by a small crowd of students, when he had finished the men, and the clerk read out what he had learned. The physician asked him one or two questions, and examined the patient himself. If there was anything interesting to hear students applied their stethoscope: you would see a man with two or three to the chest, and two perhaps to his back, while others waited impatiently to listen. The patient stood among them a little embarrassed, but not altogether displeased to find himself the centre of attention: he listened confusedly while Dr Tyrell discoursed glibly on the case. Two or three students listened again to recognize the murmur or the crepitation which the physician described, and then the man was told to put on his clothes.

When the various cases had been examined Dr Tyrell went back into the large room and sat down again at his desk. He asked any student who happened to be standing near him what he would prescribe for a patient he had just seen. The student mentioned one or two drugs.

'Would you?' said Dr Tyrell. 'Well, that's original at all events. I don't think we'll be rash.'

This always made the students laugh, and with a twinkle of amusement at his own bright humour the physician prescribed some other drug than that which the student had suggested. When there were two cases of exactly the same sort and the student proposed the treatment which the physician had ordered for the first, Dr Tyrell exercised considerable ingenuity in thinking of something else. Sometimes, knowing that in the dispensary they were worked off their legs and preferred to give the medicines which they had all ready, the good hospital mixtures which had been found by the experience of years to answer their purpose so well, he amused himself by writing an elaborate prescription.

'We'll give the dispenser something to do. If we go on prescribing *mist: alb:* he'll lose his cunning.'

The students laughed, and the doctor gave them a circular glance of enjoyment in his joke. Then he touched the bell and, when the porter poked his head in, said:

'Old women, please.'

He leaned back in his chair, chatting with the H.P. while the porter herded along the old patients. They came in, strings of anaemic girls, with large fringes and pallid lips, who could not digest their bad, insufficient food; old ladies, fat and thin, aged prematurely by frequent confinements, with winter coughs; women with this, that, and the other, the matter with them. Dr Tyrell and his house-physician got through them quickly. Time was getting on, and the air in the small room was growing more sickly. The physician looked at his watch.

'Are there many new women today?' he asked.

'A good few, I think,' said the H.P.

'We'd better have them in. You can go on with the old ones.'

They entered. With the men the most common ailments were due to the excessive use of alcohol, but with the women they were due to defective nourishment. By about six o'clock they were finished. Philip, exhausted by standing all the time, by the bad air, and by the attention he had given, strolled over with his fellow-clerks to the Medical School to have tea.

He found the work of absorbing interest. There was humanity there in the rough, the materials the artist worked on; and Philip felt a curious thrill when it occurred to him that he was in the position of the artist and the patients were like clay in his hands. He remembered with an amused shrug of the shoulders his life in Paris, absorbed in colour, tone, values, Heaven knows what, with the aim of producing beautiful things: the directness of contact with men and women gave a thrill of power which he had never known. He found an endless excitement in looking at their faces and hearing them speak; they came in each with his peculiarity, some shuffling uncouthly, some with a little trip, others with heavy, slow tread, some shyly. Often you could guess their trades by the look of them. You learnt in what way to put your questions so that they should be understood, you discovered on what subjects nearly all lied, and by what inquiries you could extort the truth notwithstanding. You saw the different way people took the same things. The diagnosis of dangerous illness would be accepted by one with a laugh and a joke, by another with dumb despair. Philip found that he was less shy with these people than he had ever been with others; he felt not exactly sympathy, for sympathy suggests condescension; but he felt at home with them. He found that he was able to put them at their ease, and, when he had been given a case to find out what he could about it, it seemed to him that the patient delivered himself into his hands with a peculiar confidence.

'Perhaps,' he thought to himself, with a smile, 'perhaps I'm cut out to be a doctor. It would be rather a lark if I'd hit upon the one thing I'm fit for.'

It seemed to Philip that he alone of the clerks saw the dramatic interest of those afternoons. To the others men and women were only cases, good if they were complicated, tiresome if obvious; they heard murmurs and were astonished at abnormal livers; an unexpected sound in the lungs gave them something to talk about. But to Philip there was much more. He found an interest in just looking at them, in the shape of their heads and their hands, in the look of their eyes and the length of their noses. You saw in that room human nature taken by surprise, and often the mask of custom was torn off rudely, showing you the soul all raw. Sometimes you saw an untaught stoicism which was profoundly moving. Once Philip saw a man, rough and illiterate, told his case was hopeless; and, self-controlled himself, he wondered at the splendid instinct which forced the fellow to keep a stiff upper-lip before strangers. But was it possible for him to be brave when he was by himself, face to face with his soul, or would he then surrender to despair? Sometimes there was tragedy. Once a young woman brought her sister to be examined, a girl of eighteen, with delicate features and large blue eyes, fair hair that sparkled with gold when a ray of autumn sunshine touched it for a moment, and a skin of amazing beauty. The students' eyes went to her with little smiles. They did not often see a pretty girl in these dingy rooms. The elder woman gave the family history, father and mother had died of phthisis, a brother and a sister, these two were the only ones left. The girl had been coughing lately and losing weight. She took off her blouse and the skin of her neck was like milk. Dr Tyrell examined her quietly, with his usual rapid method; he told two or three of the clerks to apply their stethoscopes to a place he indicated with his finger; and then she was allowed to dress. The sister was standing a little apart and she spoke to him in a low voice, so that the girl should not hear. Her voice trembled with fear.

'She hasn't got it, doctor, has she?'

'I'm afraid there's no doubt about it.'

'She was the last one. When she goes I shan't have anybody.'

She began to cry, while the doctor looked at her gravely; he thought she too had the type; she would not make old bones either. The girl turned round and saw her sister's tears. She understood what they meant. The colour fled from her lovely face and tears fell down her cheeks. The two stood for a minute or two, crying silently, and then the older, forgetting the indifferent crowd that watched them, went up to her, took her in her arms, and rocked her gently to and fro as if she were a baby.

When they were gone a student asked:

'How long d'you think she'll last, sir?'

Dr Tyrell shrugged his shoulders.

'Her brother and sister died within three months of the first symptoms. She'll do the same. If they were rich one might do something. You can't tell these people to go to St Moritz. Nothing can be done for them.'

Once a man who was strong and in all the power of his manhood came because a persistent aching troubled him and his club-doctor did not seem to do him any good; and the verdict for him too was death, not the inevitable death that horrified and yet was tolerable because science was helpless before it, but the death which was inevitable because the man was a little wheel in the great machine of a complex civilization, and had as little power of changing the circumstances as an automaton. Complete rest was his only chance. The physician did not ask impossibilities.

'You ought to get some very much lighter job.'

'There ain't no light jobs in my business.'

'Well, if you go on like this you'll kill yourself. You've very ill.'

'D'you mean to say I'm going to die?'

'I shouldn't like to say that, but you're certainly unfit for hard work.'

'If I don't work who's to keep the wife and the kids?'

Dr Tyrell shrugged his shoulders. The dilemma had been presented to him a hundred times. Time was pressing and there were many patients to be seen.

'Well, I'll give you some medicine and you can come back in a week and tell me how you're getting on.'

The man took his letter with the useless prescription written upon it and walked out. The doctor might say what he liked. He did not feel so bad that he could not go on working. He had a good job and he could not afford to throw it away.

'I give him a year,' said Dr Tyrell.

Sometimes there was comedy. Now and then came a flash of cockney humour, now and then some old lady, a character such as Charles Dickens might have drawn, would amuse them by her garrulous oddities. Once a woman came who was a member of the ballet at a famous music-hall. She looked fifty, but gave her age as twenty-eight. She was outrageously painted and ogled the students impudently with large black eyes; her smiles were grossly alluring. She had abundant self-confidence and treated Dr Tyrell, vastly amused, with the easy familiarity with which she might have used an intoxicated admirer. She had chronic bronchitis, and told him it hindered her in the exercise of her profession.

'I don't know why I should 'ave such a thing, upon my word I don't. I've never 'ad a day's illness in my life. You've only got to look at me to know that.'

She rolled her eyes round the young men, with a long sweep of her painted eyelashes, and flashed her yellow teeth at them. She spoke with a cockney accent, but with an affectation of refinement which made every word a feast of fun.

'It's what they call a winter cough,' answered Dr Tyrell gravely. 'A great many middle-aged women have it.'

'Well, I never! This is a nice thing to say to a lady. No one ever called me middle-aged before.'

She opened her eyes very wide and cocked her head on one side, looking at him with indescribable archness.

'That is the disadvantage of our profession,' said he. 'It forces us sometimes to be ungallant.'

She took the prescription and gave him one last, luscious smile.

'You will come and see me dance, dearie, won't you?'

'I will indeed.'

He rang the bell for the next case.

'I am glad you gentlemen were here to protect me.'

But·on the whole the impression was neither of tragedy nor of comedy. There was no describing it. It was manifold and various; there were tears and laughter, happiness and woe; it was tedious and interesting and indifferent; it was as you saw it: it was tumultuous and passionate; it was grave; it was sad and comic; it was trivial; it was simple and complex; joy was there and despair; the love of mothers for their children, and of men for women; lust trailed itself through the rooms with leaden feet, punishing the guilty and the innocent, helpless wives and wretched children; drink seized men and women and cost its inevitable price; death sighed in these rooms; and the beginning of life, filling some poor girl with terror and shame, was diagnosed there. There was neither good nor bad there. There were just facts. It was life.

LXXXII

TOWARDS the end of the year, when Philip was bringing to a close his three months as clerk in the out-patients' department, he received a letter from Lawson, who was in Paris.

Dear Philip –

Cronshaw is in London and would be glad to see you. He is living at 43 Hyde Street, Soho. I don't know where it is, but I daresay you will be able to find out. Be a brick and look after him a bit. He is very down on his luck. He will tell you what he is doing. Things are going on here very much as usual. Nothing seems to have changed since you were here. Clutton is back, but he has become quite impossible. He has quarrelled with everybody. As far as I can make out he hasn't got a cent, he lives in a little studio right away beyond the Jardin des Plantes, but he won't let anybody see his work. He doesn't show anywhere, so one doesn't know what he is doing. He may be a genius, but on the other hand he may be off his head. By the way, I ran against Flanagan the other day. He was showing Mrs Flanagan round the Quarter. He has chucked art and is now in popper's business. He seems to be rolling. Mrs Flanagan is very pretty and I'm trying to work a portrait. How much would you ask if you were me? I don't want to frighten them, and then on the other hand I don't want to be such an ass as to ask £150 if they're quite willing to give £300.

Yours ever,
Frederick Lawson

Philip wrote to Cronshaw and received in reply the following letter. It was written on a half-sheet of common note-paper, and the flimsy envelope was dirtier than was justified by its passage through the post.

Dear Carey –

Of course I remember you very well. I have an idea that I had some part in rescuing you from the Slough of Despond in which myself am hopelessly immersed. I shall be glad to see you. I am a stranger in a strange city and I am buffeted by the philistines. It will be pleasant to talk of Paris. I do not ask you to come and see me, since my lodging is not of a magnificence fit for the reception of an eminent member of Monsieur Purgon's profession, but you will find me eating modestly any evening between seven and eight at a restaurant yclept Au Bon Plaisir in Dean Street.

Your sincere
J. Cronshaw

Philip went the day he received this letter. The restaurant, consisting of one small room, was of the poorest class, and Cronshaw seemed to be its only customer. He was sitting in the corner, well away from draughts, wearing the same shabby great-coat which Philip had never seen him without, with his old bowler on his head.

'I eat here because I can be alone,' he said. 'They are not doing well; the only people who come are a few trollops and one or two waiters out of a job; they are giving up business, and the food is execrable. But in the ruin of their fortunes is my advantage.'

Cronshaw had before him a glass of absinthe. It was nearly three years since they had met, and Philip was shocked by the change in his appearance. He had been rather corpulent, but now he had a dried-up, yellow look: the skin of his neck was loose and wrinkled; his clothes hung about him as though they had been bought for someone else; and his collar, three or four sizes too large, added to the slatternliness of his appearance. His hands trembled continually. Philip remembered the handwriting which scrawled over the page with shapeless, haphazard letters. Cronshaw was evidently very ill.

'I eat little these days,' he said. 'I'm very sick in the mornings. I'm just having some soup for my dinner, and then I shall have a bit of cheese.'

Philip's glance unconsciously went to the absinthe, and Cronshaw, seeing it, gave him the quizzical look with which he reproved the admonitions of common sense.

'You have diagnosed my case, and you think it's very wrong of me to drink absinthe.'

'You've evidently got cirrhosis of the liver,' said Philip.

'Evidently.'

He looked at Philip in the way which had formerly had the power of making him feel incredibly narrow. It seemed to point out that what he was thinking was distressingly obvious; and when you have agreed with the obvious what more is there to say? Philip changed the topic.

'When are you going back to Paris?'

'I'm not going back to Paris. I'm going to die.'

The very naturalness with which he said this startled Philip. He thought of half a dozen things to say, but they seemed futile. He knew that Cronshaw was a dying man.

'Are you going to settle in London then?' he asked lamely.

'What is London to me? I am a fish out of water. I walk through the crowded streets, men jostle me, and I seem to walk in a dead city. I felt that I couldn't die in Paris. I wanted to die among my own people. I don't know what hidden instinct drew me back at the last.'

Philip knew of the woman Cronshaw had lived with and the two draggle-tailed children, but Cronshaw had never mentioned them to him, and he did not like to speak of them. He wondered what had happened to them.

'I don't know why you talk of dying,' he said.

'I had pneumonia a couple of winters ago, and they told me then it was a miracle that I came through. It appears I'm extremely liable to it, and another bout will kill me.'

'Oh, what nonsense! You're not so bad as all that. You've only got to take precautions. Why don't you give up drinking?'

'Because I don't choose. It doesn't matter what a man does if he's ready to take the consequences. Well, I'm ready to take the consequences. You talk glibly of giving up drinking, but it's the only thing I've got left now. What do you think life would be to me without it? Can you understand the happiness I get out of my absinthe? I yearn for it; and when I drink it I savour every drop, and afterwards I feel my soul swimming in ineffable happiness. It disgusts you. You are a puritan and in your heart you despise sensual pleasures. Sensual pleasures are the most violent and the most exquisite. I am a man blessed with vivid senses, and I have indulged them with all my soul. I have to pay the penalty now, and I am ready to pay.'

Philip looked at him for a while steadily.

'Aren't you afraid?'

For a moment Cronshaw did not answer. He seemed to consider his reply.

'Sometimes, when I'm alone.' He looked at Philip. 'You think that's a condemnation? You're wrong. I'm not afraid of my fear. It's folly, the Christian argument that you should live always in view of your death. The only way to live is to forget that you're going to die. Death is unimportant. The fear of it should never influence a single action of the wise man. I know that I shall die struggling for breath, and I know that I shall be horribly afraid. I know that I shall not be able to keep myself from regretting bitterly the life that has brought me to such a pass; but I disown that regret. I now, weak, old, diseased, poor, dying, hold still my soul in my hands, and I regret nothing.'

'D'you remember that Persian carpet you gave me?' asked Philip.

Cronshaw smiled his old, slow smile of past days.

'I told you that it would give you an answer to your question when you asked me what was the meaning of life. Well, have you discovered the answer?'

'No,' smiled Philip. 'Won't you tell it me?'

'No, no, I can't do that. The answer is meaningless unless you discover it for yourself.'

LXXXIII

CRONSHAW was publishing his poems. His friends had been urging him to do this for years, but his laziness made it impossible for him to take the necessary steps. He had always answered their exhortations by telling them that the love of poetry was dead in England. You brought out a book which had cost you years of thought and labour; it was given two or three contemptuous lines among a batch of similar volumes, twenty or thirty copies were sold, and the rest of the edition was pulped. He had long since worn out the desire for fame. That was an illusion like all else. But one of his friends had taken the matter into his own hands. This was a man of letters, named Leonard Upjohn, whom Philip had met once or twice with Cronshaw in the cafés of the Quarter. He had a considerable reputation in England as a critic and was the accredited exponent in this country of modern French literature. He had lived a good deal in France among the men who made the *Mercure de France* the liveliest review of the day, and by the simple process of expressing in English their point of view he had acquired in England a reputation for originality. Philip had read some of his articles. He had formed a style for himself by a close imitation of Sir Thomas Browne; he used elaborate sentences, carefully balanced, and obsolete, resplendent words; it gave his writing an appearance of individuality. Leonard Upjohn had induced Cronshaw to give him all his poems and found that there were enough to make a volume of reasonable size. He promised to use his influence with publishers. Cronshaw was in want of money. Since his illness he had found it more difficult than ever to work steadily; he made barely enough to keep himself in liquor; and when Upjohn wrote to him that this publisher and the other, though admiring the poems, thought it not worth while to publish them, Cronshaw began to grow interested. He wrote impressing upon Upjohn his great need and urging him to make more strenuous efforts. Now that he was going to die he wanted to leave behind him a published book, and at the back of his mind was the feeling that he had produced great poetry. He expected to burst upon the world like a new star. There was something fine in keeping to himself these treasures of beauty all his life and giving them to the world disdainfully when, he and the world parting company, he had no further use for them.

His decision to come to England was caused directly by an announcement from Leonard Upjohn that a publisher had consented to print the poems. By a miracle of persuasion Upjohn had persuaded him to give ten pounds in advance of royalties.

'In advance of royalties, mind you,' said Cronshaw to Philip. 'Milton only got ten pounds down.'

Upjohn had promised to write a signed article about them, and he would ask his friends who reviewed to do their best. Cronshaw pretended to treat the matter with detachment, but it was easy to see that he was delighted with the thought of the stir he would make.

One day Philip went to dine by arrangement at the wretched eating-house at which Cronshaw insisted on taking his meals, but Cronshaw did not appear. Philip learned that he had not been there for three days. He got himself something to eat and went round to the address from which Cronshaw had first written to him. He had some difficulty in finding Hyde Street. It was a street of dingy houses huddled together; many of the windows had been broken and were clumsily repaired with strips of French newspaper; the doors had not been painted for years; there were shabby little shops on the ground floor, laundries, cobblers, stationers. Ragged children played in the road, and an old barrel-organ was grinding out a vulgar tune. Philip knocked at the door of Cronshaw's house (there was a shop of cheap sweetstuffs at the bottom), and it was opened by an elderly Frenchwoman in a dirty apron. Philip asked her if Cronshaw was in.

'Ah, yes, there is an Englishman who lives at the top, at the back. I don't know if he's in. If you want him you had better go up and see.'

The staircase was lit by one jet of gas. There was a revolting odour in the house. When Philip was passing up a woman came out of a room on the first floor, looked at him suspiciously, but made no remark. There were three doors on the top landing. Philip knocked at one, and knocked again; there was no reply; he tried the handle, but the door was locked. He knocked at another door, got no answer, and tried the door again. It opened. The room was dark.

'Who's that?'

He recognized Cronshaw's voice.

'Carey. Can I come in?'

He received no answer. He walked in. The window was closed and the stink was overpowering. There was a certain

amount of light from the arc-lamp in the street, and he saw
that it was a small room with two beds in it, end to end; there
was a washing-stand and one chair, but they left little space for
anyone to move in. Cronshaw was in the bed nearest the window. He made no movement. but gave a low chuckle.

'Why don't you light the candle?' he said then.

Philip struck a match and discovered that there was a candle-
stick on the floor beside the bed. He lit it and put it on the
washing-stand. Cronshaw was lying on his back immobile; he
looked very odd in his nightshirt; and his baldness was disconcerting. His face was earthy and deathlike.

'I say, old man, you look awfully ill. Is there anyone to look
after you here?'

'George brings me in a bottle of milk in the morning before
he goes to his work.'

'Who's George?'

'I call him George because his name is Adolphe. He shares
this palatial apartment with me.'

Philip noticed then that the second bed had not been made
since it was slept in. The pillow was black where the head had
rested.

'You don't mean to say you're sharing this room with somebody else?' he cried.

'Why not? Lodging costs money in Soho. George is a waiter.
He goes out at eight in the morning and does not come in till
closing time, so he isn't in my way at all. We neither of us
sleep well, and he helps to pass away the hours of the night by
telling me stories of his life. He's a Swiss, and I've always had
a taste for waiters. They see life from an entertaining angle.'

'How long have you been in bed?'

'Three days.'

'D'you mean to say you've had nothing but a bottle of milk
for the last three days? Why on earth didn't you send me a
line? I can't bear to think of you lying here all day long without a soul to attend to you.'

Cronshaw gave a little laugh.

'Look at your face. Why, dear boy, I really believe you're
distressed. You nice fellow.'

Philip blushed. He had not suspected that his face showed
the dismay he felt at the sight of that horrible room and the
wretched circumstances of the poor poet. Cronshaw, watching
Philip, went on with a gentle smile.

'I've been quite happy. Look, here are my proofs. Remember
that I am indifferent to discomforts which would harass other

folk. What do the circumstances of your life matter if your dreams make you lord paramount of time and space.'

The proofs were lying on his bed, and as he lay in the darkness he had been able to place his hands on them. He showed them to Philip and his eyes glowed. He turned over the pages, rejoicing in the clear type; he read out a stanza.

'They don't look bad, do they?'

Philip had an idea. It would involve him in a little expense and he could not afford even the smallest increase in expenditure; but on the other hand this was a case where it revolted him to think of economy.

'I say, I can't bear the thought of your remaining here. I've got an extra room, it's empty at present, but I can easily get someone to lend me a bed. Won't you come and live with me for a while? It'll save you the rent of this.'

'Oh, my dear boy, you'd insist on my keeping my window open.'

'You shall have every window in the place sealed if you like.'

'I shall be all right tomorrow. I could have got up today, only I felt lazy.'

'Then you can very easily make the move. And then if you don't feel well at any time you can just go to bed, and I shall be there to look after you.'

'If it'll please you I'll come,' said Cronshaw, with his torpid not unpleasant smile.

'That'll be ripping.'

They settled that Philip should fetch Cronshaw next day, and Philip snatched an hour from his busy morning to arrange the change. He found Cronshaw dressed, sitting in his hat and great-coat on the bed, with a small, shabby portmanteau, containing his clothes and books, already packed: it was on the floor by his feet, and he looked as if he were sitting in the waiting-room of a station. Philip laughed at the sight of him. They went over to Kennington in a four-wheeler, of which the windows were carefully closed, and Philip installed his guest in his own room. He had gone out early in the morning and bought for himself a second-hand bedstead, a cheap chest of drawers, and a looking-glass. Cronshaw settled down at once to correct his proofs. He was much better.

Philip found him, except for the irritability which was a symptom of his disease, an easy guest. He had a lecture at nine in the morning, so did not see Cronshaw till the night. Once or twice Philip persuaded him to share the scrappy meal he prepared for himself in the evening, but Cronshaw was too restless to stay in, and preferred generally to get himself something to eat in one or other of the cheapest restaurants in Soho. Philip asked him to see Dr Tyrell, but he stoutly refused; he knew a doctor would tell him to stop drinking, and this he was resolved not to do. He always felt horribly ill in the morning, but his absinthe at midday put him on his feet again, and by the time he came home, at midnight, he was able to talk with the brilliancy which had astonished Philip when first he made his acquaintance. His proofs were corrected; and the volume was to come out among the publications of the early spring, when the public might be supposed to have recovered from the avalanche of Christmas books.

LXXXIV

AT the new year Philip became dresser in the surgical out-patients' department. The work was of the same character as that which he had just been engaged on, but with the greater directness which surgery has than medicine; and a larger proportion of the patients suffered from those two diseases which a supine public allows, in its prudishness, to be spread broadcast. The assistant-surgeon for whom Philip dressed was called Jacobs. He was a short, fat man, with an exuberant joviality, a bald head, and a loud voice; he had a cockney accent, and was generally described by the students as an 'awful bounder'; but his cleverness, both as a surgeon and as a teacher, caused some of them to overlook this. He had also a considerable facetiousness, which he exercised impartially on the patients and on the students. He took a great pleasure in making his dressers look foolish. Since they were ignorant, nervous, and could not answer as if he were their equal, this was not very difficult. He enjoyed his afternoons, with the home truths he permitted himself, much more than the students who had to put up with them with a smile. One day a case came up of a boy with a club-foot. His parents wanted to know whether anything could be done. Mr Jacobs turned to Philip.

'You'd better take this case, Carey. It's a subject you ought to know something about.'

Philip flushed, all the more because the surgeon spoke obviously with a humorous intention, and his brow-beaten dressers laughed obsequiously. It was in point of fact a subject which Philip, since coming to the hospital, had studied with anxious attention. He had read everything in the library which treated of talipes in its various forms. He made the boy take off his boot and stocking. He was fourteen, with a snub nose, blue eyes, and a freckled face. His father explained that they wanted something done if possible, it was such a hindrance to the kid in earning his living. Philip looked at him curiously. He was a jolly boy, not at all shy, but talkative and with a cheekiness which his father reproved. He was much interested in his foot.

'It's only for the looks of the thing, you know,' he said to Philip. 'I don't find it no trouble.'

'Be quiet, Ernie,' said his father. 'There's too much gas about you.'

Philip examined the foot and passed his hand slowly over the shapelessness of it. He could not understand why the boy felt none of the humiliation which always oppressed himself. He wondered why he could not take his deformity with that philosophic indifference. Presently Mr Jacobs came up to him. The boy was sitting on the edge of a couch, the surgeon and Philip stood on each side of him; and in a semi-circle, crowding round, were students. With accustomed brilliancy Jacobs gave a graphic little discourse upon the club-foot: he spoke of its varieties and of the forms which followed upon different anatomical conditions.

'I suppose you've got talipes equinus?' he said, turning suddenly to Philip.

'Yes.'

Philip felt the eyes of his fellow-students rest on him, and he cursed himself because he could not help blushing. He felt the sweat start up in the palms of his hands. The surgeon spoke with the fluency due to long practice and with the admirable perspicacity which distinguished him. He was tremendously interested in his profession. But Philip did not listen. He was only wishing that the fellow would get done quickly. Suddenly he realized that Jacobs was addressing him.

'You don't mind taking off your sock for a moment, Carey?'

Philip felt a shudder pass through him. He had an impulse to tell the surgeon to go to hell, but he had not the courage to make a scene. He feared his brutal ridicule. He forced himself to appear indifferent.

'Not a bit,' he said.

He sat down and unlaced his boot. His fingers were trembling, and he thought he should never untie the knot. He remembered how they had forced him at school to show his foot, and the misery which had eaten into his soul.

411

'He keeps his feet nice and clean, doesn't he?' said Jacobs, in his rasping, cockney voice.

The attendant students giggled. Philips noticed that the boy whom they were examining looked down at his foot with eager curiosity. Jacobs took the foot in his hands and said:

'Yes, that's what I thought. I see you've had an operation. When you were a child, I suppose?'

He went on with his fluent explanations. The students leaned over and looked at the foot. Two or three examined it minutely when Jacobs let it go.

'When you've quite done,' said Philip, with a smile, ironically.

He could have killed them all. He thought how jolly it would be to jab a chisel (he didn't know why that particular instrument came into his mind) into their necks. What beasts men were! He wished he could believe in hell so as to comfort himself with the thought of the horrible tortures which would be theirs. Mr Jacobs turned his attention to treatment. He talked partly to the boy's father and partly to the students. Philip put on his sock and laced his boot. At last the surgeon finished. But he seemed to have an afterthought and turned to Philip.

'You know, I think it might be worth your while to have an operation. Of course I couldn't give you a normal foot, but I think I can do something. You might think about it, and when you want a holiday you can just come into the hospital for a bit.'

Philip had often asked himself whether anything could be done, but his distaste for any reference to the subject had prevented him from consulting any of the surgeons at the hospital. His reading told him that, whatever might have been done when he was a small boy – and then treatment of talipes was not as skilful as in the present day – there was small chance now of any great benefit. Still it would be worth while if an operation made it possible for him to wear a more ordinary boot and to limp less. He remembered how passionately he had prayed for the miracle which his uncle had assured him was possible to omnipotence. He smiled ruefully.

'I was rather a simple soul in those days,' he thought.

Towards the end of February it was clear that Cronshaw was growing much worse. He was no longer able to get up. He lay in bed, insisting that the window should be closed always, and refused to see a doctor; he would take little nourishment, but demanded whisky and cigarettes: Philip knew that he should have neither, but Cronshaw's argument was unanswerable.

'I daresay they are killing me. I don't care. You've warned me, you've done all that was necessary: I ignore your warning. Give me something to drink and be damned to you.'

Leonard Upjohn blew in two or three times a week, and there was something of the dead leaf in his appearance which made that word exactly descriptive of the manner of his appearance. He was a weedy-looking fellow of five-and-thirty, with long pale hair and a white face; he had the look of a man who lived too little in the open air. He wore a hat like a dissenting minister's. Philip disliked him for his patronizing manner and was bored by his fluent conversation. Leonard Upjohn liked to hear himself talk. He was not sensitive to the interest of his listeners, which is the first requisite of the good talker; and he never realized that he was telling people what they knew already. With measured words he told Philip what to think of Rodin, Albert Samain, and César Franck. Philip's charwoman only came in for an hour in the morning, and since Philip was obliged to be at the hospital all day Cronshaw was left much alone. Upjohn told Philip that he thought someone should remain with him, but did not offer to make it possible.

'It's dreadful to think of that great poet alone. Why, he might die without a soul at hand.'

'I think he very probably will,' said Philip.

'How can you be so callous!'

'Why don't you come and do your work here every day, and then you'd be near if he wanted anything?' asked Philip drily.

'I? My dear fellow, I can only work in the surroundings I'm used to, and besides I go out so much.'

Upjohn was also a little put out because Philip had brought Cronshaw to his own rooms.

'I wish you had left him in Soho,' he said, with a wave of his long, thin hands. 'There was a touch of romance in that sordid attic. I could even bear it if it were Wapping or Shoreditch, but the respectability of Kennington! What a place for a poet to die!'

Cronshaw was often so ill-humoured that Philip could only keep his temper by remembering all the time that this irritability was a symptom of the disease. Upjohn came sometimes before Philip was in, and then Cronshaw would complain of him bitterly. Upjohn listened with complacency.

'The fact is that Carey has no sense of beauty,' he smiled. 'He has a middle-class mind.'

He was very sarcastic to Philip, and Philip exercised a good deal of self-control in his dealings with him. But one evening he could not contain himself. He had had a hard day at the hospital and was tired out. Leonard Upjohn came to him, while he was making himself a cup of tea in the kitchen, and said that Cronshaw was complaining of Philip's insistence that he should have a doctor.

'Don't you realize that you're enjoying a very rare, a very exquisite privilege? You ought to do everything in your power, surely, to show your sense of the greatness of your trust.'

'It's a rare and exquisite privilege which I can ill afford,' said Philip.

Whenever there was any question of money, Leonard Upjohn assumed a slightly disdainful expression. His sensitive temperament was offended by the reference.

'There's something fine in Cronshaw's attitude, and you disturb it by your importunity. You should make allowances for the delicate imaginings which you cannot feel.'

Philip's face darkened.

'Let us go in to Cronshaw,' he said frigidly.

The poet was lying on his back, reading a book, with a pipe in his mouth. The air was musty; and the room, notwithstanding Philip's tidying up, had the bedraggled look which seemed to accompany Cronshaw wherever he went. He took off his spectacles as they came in. Philip was in a towering rage.

'Upjohn tells me you've been complaining to him because I've urged you to have a doctor,' he said. 'I want you to have a doctor, because you may die any day, and if you hadn't been seen by anyone I shouldn't be able to get a certificate. There'd have to be an inquest and I should be blamed for not calling a doctor in.'

'I hadn't thought of that. I thought you wanted me to see a doctor for my sake and not for your own. I'll see a doctor whenever you like.'

Philip did not answer, but gave an almost imperceptible shrug of the shoulders. Cronshaw, watching him, gave a little chuckle.

'Don't look so angry, my dear. I know very well you want to do everything you can for me. Let's see your doctor, perhaps he can do something for me, and at any rate it'll comfort you.' He turned his eyes to Upjohn. 'You're a damned fool, Leonard. Why d'you want to worry the boy? He has quite enough to do to put up with me. You'll do nothing more for me than write a pretty article about me after my death. I know you.'

Next day Philip went to Dr Tyrell. He felt that he was the sort of man to be interested by the story, and as soon as Tyrell was free of his day's work he accompanied Philip to Kennington. He could only agree with what Philip had told him. The case was hopeless.

'I'll take him into the hospital if you like,' he said. 'He can have a small ward.'

'Nothing would induce him to come.'

'You know, he may die any minute, or else he may get another attack of pneumonia.'

Philip nodded. Dr Tyrell made one or two suggestions, and promised to come again whenever Philip wanted him to. He left his address. When Philip went back to Cronshaw he found him quietly reading. He did not trouble to enquire what the doctor had said.

'Are you satisfied now, dear boy?' he asked.

'I suppose nothing will induce you to do any of the things Tyrell advised?'

'Nothing,' smiled Cronshaw.

LXXXV

ABOUT a fortnight after this Philip, going home one evening after his day's work at the hospital, knocked at the door of Cronshaw's room. He got no answer and walked in. Cronshaw was lying huddled up on one side, and Philip went up to the bed. He did not know whether Cronshaw was asleep or merely lay there in one of his uncontrollable fits of irritability. He was surprised to see that his mouth was open. He touched his shoulder. Philip gave a cry of dismay. He slipped his hand under Cronshaw's shirt and felt his heart; he did not know what to do; helplessly, because he had heard of this being done, he held a looking-glass in front of his mouth. It startled him to be alone with Cronshaw. He had his hat and coat still on, and he ran down the stairs into the street; he hailed a cab and drove to Harley Street. Dr Tyrell was in.

'I say, would you mind coming at once? I think Cronshaw's dead.'

'If he is it's not much good my coming, is it?'

'I should be awfully grateful if you would. I've got a cab at the door. It'll only take half an hour.'

Tyrell put on his hat. In the cab he asked him one or two questions.

'He seemed no worse than usual when I left this morning,' said Philip. 'It gave me an awful shock when I went in just now. And the thought of his dying all alone ... D'you think he knew he was going to die?'

Philip remembered what Cronshaw had said. He wondered whether at that last moment he had been seized with the terror of death. Philip imagined himself in such a plight, knowing it was inevitable and with no one, not a soul, to give an encouraging word when the fear seized him.

'You're rather upset,' said Dr Tyrell.

He looked at him with his bright blue eyes. They were not unsympathetic. When he saw Cronshaw, he said:

'He must have been dead for some hours. I should think he died in his sleep. They do sometimes.'

The body looked shrunk and ignoble. It was not like anything human. Dr Tyrell looked at it dispassionately. With a mechanical gesture he took out his watch.

'Well, I must be getting along. I'll send the certificate round. I suppose you'll communicate with the relatives.'

'I don't think there are any,' said Philip.

'How about the funeral?'

'Oh, I'll see to that.'

Dr Tyrell gave Philip a glance. He wondered whether he ought to offer a couple of sovereigns towards it. He knew nothing of Philip's circumstances; perhaps he could well afford the expense; Philip might think it impertinent if he made any suggestion.

'Well, let me know if there's anything I can do,' he said.

Philip and he went out together, parting on the door-step, and Philip went to a telegraph office in order to send a message to Leonard Upjohn. Then he went to an undertaker whose shop he passed every day on his way to the hospital. His attention had been drawn to it often by the three words in silver lettering on a black cloth, which, with two model coffins, adorned the window: Economy, Celerity, Propriety. They had always diverted him. The undertaker was a little fat Jew with curly black hair, long and greasy, in black, with a large diamond ring on a podgy finger. He received Philip with a peculiar manner formed by the mingling of his natural blatancy with the subdued air proper to his calling. He quickly saw that Philip was very helpless and promised to send round a woman at once to perform the needful offices. His suggestions for the funeral were very magnificent; and Philip felt ashamed of himself when the undertaker seemed to think his objections mean. It was horrible to haggle on such a matter, and finally Philip consented to an expensiveness which he could ill afford.

'I quite understand, sir,' said the undertaker, 'you don't want any show and that – I'm not a believer in ostentation myself, mind you – but you want it done gentlemanly-like. You leave it to me, I'll do it as cheap as it can be done, 'aving regard to what's right and proper. I can't say more than that, can I?'

Philip went home to eat his supper, and while he ate the woman came along to lay out the corpse. Presently a telegram arrived from Leonard Upjohn:

Shocked and grieved beyond measure. Regret cannot come to-night. Dining out. With you early tomorrow. Deepest sympathy. Upjohn.

In a little while the woman knocked at the door of the sitting-room.

'I've done now, sir. Will you come and look at 'im and see it's all right?'

Philip followed her. Cronshaw was lying on his back, with his eyes closed and his hands folded piously across his chest.

'You ought by rights to 'ave a few flowers, sir.'

'I'll get some tomorrow.'

She gave the body a glance of satisfaction. She had performed her job, and now she rolled down her sleeves, took off her apron, and put on her bonnet. Philip asked how much he owed her.

'Well, sir, some give me two and sixpence and some give me five shillings.'

Philip was ashamed to give her less than the larger sum. She thanked him with just so much effusiveness as was seemly in presence of the grief he might be supposed to feel, and left him. Philip went back into his sitting-room, cleared away the remains of his supper, and sat down to read Walsham's *Surgery*. He found it difficult. He felt singularly nervous. When there was a sound on the stairs he jumped, and his heart beat violently. That thing in the adjoining room, which had been a man and now was nothing, frightened him. The silence seemed alive, as if some mysterious movement were taking place within it; the presence of death weighed upon these rooms, unearthly and terrifying: Philip felt a sudden horror for what had once been his friend. He tried to force himself to read, but presently pushed away his book in despair. What troubled him was the absolute futility of the life which had just ended. It did not matter if Cronshaw was alive or dead. It would have been just as well if he had never lived. Philip thought of Cronshaw young; and it needed an effort of imagination to picture him slender, with a springing step, and with hair on his head, buoyant and hopeful. Philip's rule of life, to follow one's instincts with due regard to the policeman round the corner, had not acted very well there: it was because Cronshaw had done this that he had made such a lamentable failure of existence. It seemed that the instincts could not be trusted. Philip was puzzled, and he asked himself what rule of life was there, if that one was useless, and why people acted in one way rather than in another. They acted according to their emotions, but their emotions might be good or bad; it seemed just a chance whether they led to triumph or disaster. Life seemed an inextricable confusion. Men hurried hither and thither, urged by forces they knew not; and the purpose of it all escaped them; they seemed to hurry just for hurrying's sake.

Next morning Leonard Upjohn appeared with a small wreath of laurel. He was pleased with his idea of crowning the dead poet with this; and attempted, notwithstanding Philip's disapproving silence, to fix it on the bald head; but the wreath fitted grotesquely. It looked like the brim of a hat worn by a low comedian in a music-hall.

'I'll put it over his heart instead,' said Upjohn.

'You've put it on his stomach,' remarked Philip.

Upjohn gave a thin smile.

'Only a poet knows where lies a poet's heart,' he answered.

They went back into the sitting-room, and Philip told him what arrangements he had made for the funeral.

'I hope you've spared no expense. I should like the hearse to be followed by a long string of empty coaches, and I should like the horses to wear tall nodding plumes, and there should be a vast number of mutes with long streamers on their hats. I like the thought of all those empty coaches.'

'As the cost of the funeral will apparently fall on me and I'm not over-flush just now, I've tried to make it as moderate as possible.'

'But, my dear fellow, in that case, why didn't you get him a pauper's funeral? There would have been something poetic in that. You have an unerring instinct for mediocrity.'

Philip flushed a little, but did not answer; and next day he and Upjohn followed the hearse in the one carriage which Philip had ordered. Lawson, unable to come, had sent a wreath;

and Philip, so that the coffin should not seem too neglected, had bought a couple. On the way back the coachman whipped up his horses. Philip was dog-tired and presently went to sleep. He was awakened by Upjohn's voice.

'It's rather lucky the poems haven't come out yet. I think we'd better hold them back a bit and I'll write a preface. I began thinking of it during the drive to the cemetery. I believe I can do something rather good. Anyhow I'll start with an article in *The Saturday*.'

Philip did not reply, and there was silence between them. At last Upjohn said:

'I daresay I'd be wiser not to whittle away my copy. I think I'll do an article for one of the reviews, and then I can just print it afterwards as a preface.'

Philip kept his eye on the monthlies, and a few weeks later it appeared. The article made something of a stir, and extracts from it were printed in many of the papers. It was a very good article, vaguely biographical, for no one knew much of Cronshaw's early life, but delicate, tender, and picturesque. Leonard Upjohn in his intricate style drew graceful little pictures of Cronshaw in the Latin Quarter, talking, writing poetry: Cronshaw became a picturesque figure, an English Verlaine; and Leonard Upjohn's coloured phrases took on a tremulous dignity, a more pathetic grandiloquence, as he described the sordid end, the shabby little room in Soho; and, with a reticence which was wholly charming and suggested a much greater generosity than modesty allowed him to state, the efforts he made to transport the poet to some cottage embowered with honeysuckle amid a flowering orchard. And the lack of sympathy, well-meaning but so tactless, which had taken the poet instead to the vulgar respectability of Kennington! Leonard Upjohn described Kennington with that restrained humour which a strict adherence to the vocabulary of Sir Thomas Browne necessitated. With delicate sarcasm he narrated the last weeks, the patience with which Cronshaw bore the well-meaning clumsiness of the young student who had appointed himself his nurse, and the pitifulness of that divine vagabond in those hopelessly middle-class surroundings. Beauty from ashes, he quoted from Isaiah. It was a triumph of irony for that outcast poet to die amid the trappings of vulgar respectability; it reminded Leonard Upjohn of Christ among the Pharisees, and the analogy gave him opportunity for an exquisite passage. And then he told how a friend – his good taste did not suffer him more than to hint subtly who the friend was with such gracious fancies – had laid a laurel wreath on the dead poet's heart; and the beautiful dead hands had seemed to rest with a voluptuous passion upon Apollo's leaves, fragrant with the fragrance of art, and more green than jade brought by swart mariners from the manifold, inexplicable China. And, an admirable contrast, the article ended with a description of the middle-class, ordinary, prosaic funeral of him who should have been buried like a prince or like a pauper. It was the crown-buffet, the final victory of Philistia over art, beauty, and immaterial things.

Leonard Upjohn had never written anything better. It was a miracle of charm, grace, and pity. He printed all Cronshaw's best poems in the course of the article, so that when the volume appeared much of its point was gone; but he advanced his own position a good deal. He was thenceforth a critic to be reckoned with. He had seemed before a little aloof; but there was a warm humanity about this article which was infinitely attractive.

LXXXVI

In the spring Philip, having finished his dressing in the out-patients' department, became an in-patients' clerk. This appointment lasted six months. The clerk spent every morning in the wards, first in the men's, then in the women's, with the house-physician; he wrote up cases, made tests, and passed the time of day with the nurses. On two afternoons a week the physician in charge went round with a little knot of students, examined the cases, and dispensed information. The work had not the excitement, the constant change, the intimate contact with reality, of the work in the out-patients' department; but Philip picked up a good deal of knowledge. He got on very well with the patients, and he was a little flattered at the pleasure they showed in his attendance on them. He was not conscious of any deep sympathy in their sufferings, but he liked them; and because he put on no airs he was more popular with them than other of the clerks. He was pleasant, encouraging, and friendly. Like everyone connected with hospitals he found that male patients were more easy to get on with than female. The women were often querulous and ill-tempered. They complained bitterly of the hard-worked nurses, who did not show them the attention they thought their right; and they were troublesome, ungrateful, and rude.

Presently Philip was fortunate enough to make a friend.

One morning the house-physician gave him a new case, a man; and, seating himself at the bedside, Philip proceeded to write down particulars on the 'letter'. He noticed on looking at this that the patient was described as a journalist: his name was Thorpe Athelny, an unusual one for a hospital patient, and his age was forty-eight. He was suffering from a sharp attack of jaundice, and had been taken into the ward on account of obscure symptoms which it seemed necessary to watch. He answered the various questions which it was Philip's duty to ask him in a pleasant, educated voice. Since he was lying in bed it was difficult to tell if he was short or tall, but his small head and small hands suggested that he was a man of less than average height. Philip had the habit of looking at people's hands, and Athelny's astonished him: they were very small, with long, tapering fingers and beautiful, rosy finger-nails; they were very smooth and except for the jaundice would have been of a surprising whiteness. The patient kept them outside the bed-clothes, one of them slightly spread out, the second and third fingers together, and, while he spoke to Philip, seemed to contemplate them with satisfaction. With a twinkle in his eyes Philip glanced at the man's face. Notwithstanding the yellowness it was distinguished; he had blue eyes, a nose of an imposing boldness, hooked, aggressive, but not clumsy, and a small beard, pointed and grey: he was rather bald, but his hair had evidently been quite fine, curling prettily, and he still wore it long.

'I see you're a journalist,' said Philip. 'What papers d'you write for?'

'I write for all the papers. You cannot open a paper without seeing some of my writing.'

There was one by the side of the bed and reaching for it he pointed out an advertisement. In large letters was the name of a firm well known to Philip: Lynn and Sedley, Regent Street, London; and below, in type smaller but still of some magnitude, was the dogmatic statement: Proscrastination is the Thief of Time. Then a question, startling because of its reasonableness: Why not order today? There was a repetition, in large letters, like the hammering of conscience on a murderer's heart: Why not? Then, boldly: Thousands of pairs of gloves from the leading markets of the world at astounding prices. Thousands of pairs of stockings from the most reliable manufacturers of the universe at sensational reductions. Finally the question recurred, but flung now like a challenging gauntlet in the lists: Why not order today?

'I'm the press representative of Lynn and Sedley.' He gave a little wave of his beautiful hand. 'To what base uses ...'

Philip went on asking the regulation questions, some a mere matter of routine, others artfully devised to lead the patient to discover things which he might be expected to desire to conceal.

'Have you ever lived abroad?' asked Philip.

'I was in Spain for eleven years.'

'What were you doing there?'

'I was secretary of the English water company at Toledo.'

Philip remembered that Clutton had spent some months in Toledo, and the journalist's answer made him look at him with more interest; but he felt it would be improper to show this: it was necessary to preserve the distance between the hospital patient and the staff. When he had finished his examination he went on to other beds.

Thorpe Athelny's illness was not grave, and, though remaining very yellow, he soon felt much better: he stayed in bed only because the physician thought he should be kept under observation till certain reactions became normal. One day, on entering the ward, Philip noticed that Athelny, pencil in hand, was reading a book. He put it down when Philip came to his bed.

'May I see what you're reading?' asked Philip, who could never pass a book without looking at it.

Philip took it up and saw that it was a volume of Spanish verse, the poems of San Juan de la Cruz, and as he opened it a sheet of paper fell out. Philip picked it up and noticed that verse was written upon it.

'You're not going to tell me you've been occupying your leisure in writing poetry? That's a most improper proceeding in a hospital patient.'

'I was trying to do some translations. D'you know Spanish?'

'No.'

'Well, you know all about San Juan de la Cruz, don't you?'

'I don't indeed.'

'He was one of the Spanish mystics. He's one of the best poets they've ever had. I thought it would be worth while translating him into English.'

'May I look at your translation?'

'It's very rough,' said Athelny, but he gave it to Philip with an alacrity which suggested that he was eager for him to read it.

It was written in pencil, in a fine but very peculiar handwriting, which was hard to read: it was just like black-letter.

'Doesn't it take you an awful time to write like that? It's wonderful.'

'I don't know why handwriting shouldn't be beautiful.'

Philip read the first verse:

> *In an obscure night*
> *With anxious love inflamed,*
> *O happy lot!*
> *Forth unobserved I went,*
> *My house being now at rest . . .*

Philip looked curiously at Thorpe Athelny. He did not know whether he felt a little shy with him or was attracted by him. He was conscious that his manner had been slightly patronizing, and he flushed as it struck him that Athelny might have thought him ridiculous.

'What an unusual name you've got,' he remarked, for something to say.

'It's a very old Yorkshire name. Once it took the head of my family a day's hard riding to make the circuit of his estates, but the mighty are fallen. Fast women and slow horses.'

He was short-sighted and when he spoke looked at you with a peculiar intensity. He took up his volume of poetry.

'You should read Spanish,' he said. 'It is a noble tongue. It has not the mellifluousness of Italian – Italian is the language of tenors and organ-grinders – but it has grandeur: it does not ripple like a brook in a garden, but it surges tumultuous like a mighty river in flood.'

His grandiloquence amused Philip, but he was sensitive to rhetoric; and he listened with pleasure while Athelny, with picturesque expressions and the fire of a real enthusiasm, described to him the rich delight of reading *Don Quixote* in the original and the music, romantic, limpid, passionate, of the enchanting Calderón.

'I must get on with my work,' said Philip presently.

'Oh, forgive me, I forgot. I will tell my wife to bring me a photograph of Toledo, and I will show it you. Come and talk to me when you have the chance. You don't know what a pleasure it gives me.'

During the next few days, in moments snatched whenever there was opportunity, Philip's acquaintance with the journalist increased. Thorpe Athelny was a good talker. He did not say brilliant things but he talked inspiringly, with an eager vividness which fired the imagination; Philip, living so much in a world of make-believe, found his fancy teeming with new pictures. Athelny had very good manners. He knew much more than Philip, both of the world and of books; he was a much older man; and the readiness of his conversation gave him a certain superiority; but he was in the hospital a recipient of charity, subject to strict rules; and he held himself between the two positions with ease and humour. Once Philip asked him why he had come to the hospital.

'Oh, my principle is to profit by all the benefits that society provides. I take advantage of the age I live in. When I'm ill I get myself patched up in a hospital, and I have no false shame, and I send my children to be educated at the board-school.'

'Do you really?' said Philip.

'And a capital education they get too, much better than I got at Winchester. How else do you think I could educate them at all? I've got nine. You must come and see them all when I get home again. Will you?'

'I'd like to very much,' said Philip.

LXXXVII

TEN days later Thorpe Athelny was well enough to leave the hospital. He gave Philip his address, and Philip promised to dine with him at one o'clock on the following Sunday. Athelny had told him that he lived in a house built by Inigo Jones; he had raved, as he raved over everything, over the balustrade of old oak; and when he came down to open the door for Philip he made him at once admire the elegant carving of the lintel. It was a shabby house, badly needing a coat of paint, but with the dignity of its period, in a little street between Chancery Lane and Holborn, which had once been fashionable but was now little better than a slum : there was a plan to pull it down in order to put up handsome offices; meanwhile the rents were small, and Athelny was able to get the two upper floors at a price which suited his income. Philip had not seen him up before and was surprised at his small size; he was not more than five feet and five inches high. He was dressed fantastically in blue linen trousers of the sort worn by working men in France, and a very old brown velvet coat; he wore a bright red sash round his waist, a low collar, and for tie a flowing bow of the kind used by the comic Frenchman in the pages of *Punch*. He greeted Philip with enthusiasm. He began talking at once of the house and passed his hand lovingly over the balusters.

'Look at it, feel it, it's like silk. What a miracle of grace! And in five years the house-breaker will sell it for firewood.'

He insisted on taking Philip into a room on the first floor, where a man in shirt-sleeves, a blousy woman, and three children were having their Sunday dinner.

'I've just brought this gentleman in to show him your ceiling. Did you ever see anything so wonderful? How are you, Mrs Hodgson? This is Mr Carey, who looked after me when I was in the hospital.'

'Come in, sir,' said the man. 'Any friend of Mr Athelny's is welcome. Mr Athelny shows the ceiling to all his friends. And it don't matter what we're doing, if we're in bed or if I'm 'aving a wash, in 'e comes.'

Philip could see that they looked upon Athelny as a little queer; but they liked him none the less; and they listened open-mouthed while he discoursed with his impetuous fluency on the beauty of the seventeenth-century ceiling.

'What a crime to pull this down, eh, Hodgson? You're an influential citizen, why don't you write to the papers and protest?'

The man in shirt-sleeves gave a laugh and said to Philip:

'Mr Athelny will 'ave his little joke. They do say these 'ouses are that insanitary, it's not safe to live in them.'

'Sanitation be damned, give me art,' cried Athelny. 'I've got nine children and they thrive on bad drains. No, no, I'm not going to take any risks. None of your new-fangled notions for me! When I move from here I'm going to make sure the drains are bad before I take anything.'

There was a knock at the door, and a little fair-haired girl opened it.

'Daddy, mummy says, do stop talking and come and eat your dinner.'

'This is my third daughter,' said Athelny, pointing to her with a dramatic forefinger. 'She is called María del Pilar, but she answers more willingly to the name of Jane. Jane, your nose wants blowing.'

'I haven't got a hanky, daddy.'

'Tut, tut, child,' he answered, as he produced a vast, brilliant bandanna, 'what do you suppose the Almighty gave you fingers for?'

They went upstairs, and Philip was taken into a room with walls panelled in dark oak. In the middle was a narrow table of teak on trestle legs, with two supporting bars of iron, of the kind called in Spain *mesa de bieraje*. They were to dine there, for two places were laid, and there were two large arm-chairs, with broad flat arms of oak and leathern backs, and leathern seats. They were severe, elegant, and uncomfortable. The only other piece of furniture was a *bargueno*, elaborately ornamented with gilt iron-work, on a stand of ecclesiastical design roughly but very finely carved. There stood on this two or three lustre plates, much broken but rich in colour; and on the walls were old masters of the Spanish school in beautiful though dilapidated frames : though gruesome in subject, ruined by age and bad treatment, and second-rate in their conception, they had a glow of passion. There was nothing in the room of any value, but the effect was lovely. It was magnificent and yet austere. Philip felt that it offered the very spirit of old Spain. Athelny was in the middle of showing him the inside of the *bargueno*, with its beautiful ornamentation and secret drawers, when a tall girl, with two plaits of bright brown hair hanging down her back, came in.

'Mother says dinner's ready and waiting and I'm to bring it in as soon as you sit down.'

'Come and shake hands with Mr Carey, Sally.' He turned to Philip. 'Isn't she enormous? She's my eldest. How old are you, Sally?'

'Fifteen, father, come next June.'

'I christened her María del Sol, because she was my first child and I dedicated her to the glorious sun of Castile; but her mother calls her Sally and her brother Pudding-face.'

The girl smiled shyly, she had even, white teeth, and blushed. She was well set-up, tall for her age, with pleasant grey eyes and a broad forehead. She had red cheeks.

'Go and tell your mother to come in and shake hands with Mr Carey before he sits down.'

'Mother says she'll come in after dinner. She hasn't washed herself yet.'

'Then we'll go in and see her ourselves. He mustn't eat the Yorkshire pudding till he's shaken the hand that made it.'

Philip followed his host into the kitchen. It was small and much overcrowded. There had been a lot of noise, but it stopped as soon as the stranger entered. There was a large table in the middle and round it, eager for dinner, were seated Athelny's children. A woman was standing at the oven, taking out baked potatoes one by one.

'Here's Mr Carey, Betty,' said Athelny.

426

'Fancy bringing him in here. What will he think?'

She wore a dirty apron, and the sleeves of her cotton dress were turned up above her elbows; she had curling pins in her hair Mrs Athelny was a large woman, a good three inches taller than her husband, fair, with blue eyes and a kindly expression; she had been a handsome creature, but advancing years and the bearing of many children had made her fat and blousy; her blue eyes had become pale, her skin was coarse and red, the colour had gone out of her hair. She straightened herself, wiped her hand on her apron, and held it out.

'You're welcome, sir,' she said, in a slow voice, with an accent that seemed oddly familiar to Philip. 'Athelny said you was very kind to him in the 'orspital.'

'Now you must be introduced to the live stock,' said Athelny. 'That is Thorpe,' he pointed to a chubby boy with curly hair; 'he is my eldest son, heir to the title, estates, and responsibilities of the family. There is Athelstan, Harold, Edward.' He pointed with his forefinger to three smaller boys, all rosy, healthy, and smiling, though when they felt Philip's smiling eyes upon them they looked shyly down at their plates. 'Now the girls in order: María del Sol . . .'

'Pudding-face,' said one of the small boys.

'Your sense of humour is rudimentary, my son. María de los Mercedes, María del Pilar, María de la Concepción, María del Rosario.'

'I call them Sally, Molly, Connie, Rosie, and Jane,' said Mrs Athelny. 'Now, Athelny, you go into your own room and I'll send you your dinner. I'll let the children come in afterwards for a bit when I've washed them.'

'My dear, if I'd had the naming of you I should have called you María of the Soapsuds. You're always torturing these wretched brats with soap.'

'You go first, Mr Carey, or I shall never get him to sit down and eat his dinner.'

Athelny and Philip installed themselves in the great monkish chairs, and Sally brought them in two plates of beef, Yorkshire pudding, baked potatoes, and cabbage. Athelny took sixpence out of his pocket and sent her for a jug of beer.

'I hope you didn't have the table laid here on my account,' said Philip. 'I should have been quite happy to eat with the children.'

'Oh no, I always have my meals by myself. I like these antique customs. I don't think that women ought to sit down at table with men. It ruins conversation and I'm sure it's very bad for them. It puts ideas in their heads, and women are never at ease with themselves when they have ideas.'

Both host and guest ate with a hearty appetite.

'Did you ever taste such Yorkshire pudding? No one can make it like my wife. That's the advantage of not marrying a lady. You noticed she wasn't a lady, didn't you?'

It was an awkward question, and Philip did not know how to answer it.

'I never thought about it,' he said lamely.

Athelny laughed. He had a peculiarly joyous laugh.

'No, she's not a lady, nor anything like it. Her father was a farmer, and she's never bothered about aitches in her life. We've had twelve children and nine of them are alive. I tell her it's about time she stopped, but she's an obstinate woman, she's got into the habit of it now, and I don't believe she'll be satisfied till she's had twenty.'

At that moment Sally came in with the beer, and, having poured out a glass for Philip, went to the other side of the table to pour some out for her father. He put his hand round her waist.

'Did you ever see such a handsome, strapping girl? Only fifteen and she might be twenty. Look at her cheeks. She's never had a day's illness in her life. It'll be a lucky man who marries her, won't it, Sally?'

Sally listened to all this with a slight, slow smile, not much embarrassed, for she was accustomed to her father's outbursts, but with an easy modesty which was very attractive.

'Don't let your dinner get cold, father,' she said, drawing herself away from his arm. 'You'll call when you're ready for your pudding, won't you?'

They were left alone, and Athelny lifted the pewter tankard to his lips. He drank long and deep.

'My word, is there anything better than English beer?' he said. 'Let us thank God for simple pleasures, roast beef and rice pudding, a good appetite and beer. I was married to a lady once. My God! Don't marry a lady, my boy.'

Philip laughed. He was exhilarated by the scene, the funny little man in his odd clothes, the panelled room and the Spanish furniture, the English fare: the whole thing had an exquisite incongruity.

'You laugh, my boy, you can't imagine marrying beneath you. You want a wife who's an intellectual equal. Your head is crammed full of ideas of comradeship. Stuff and nonsense, my boy! A man doesn't want to talk politics to his wife, and what do you think I care for Betty's views upon the Differential Calculus? A man wants a wife who can cook his dinner and look after his children. I've tried both and I know. Let's have the pudding in.'

He clapped his hands and presently Sally came. When she took away the plates, Philip wanted to get up and help her, but Athelny stopped him.

'Let her alone, my boy. She doesn't want you to fuss about, do you, Sally? And she won't think it rude of you to sit still while she waits upon you. She don't care a damn for chivalry, do you, Sally?'

'No, father,' answered Sally demurely.

'Do you know what I'm talking about, Sally?'

'No, father. But you know mother doesn't like you to swear.'

Athelny laughed boisterously. Sally brought them plates of rice pudding, rich, creamy, and luscious. Athelny attacked his with gusto.

'One of the rules of this house is that Sunday dinner should never alter. It is a ritual. Roast beef and rice pudding for fifty Sundays in the year. On Easter Sunday lamb and green peas, and at Michaelmas roast goose and apple sauce. Thus we preserve the traditions of our people. When Sally marries she will forget many of the wise things I have taught her, but she will never forget that if you want to be good and happy you must eat on Sundays roast beef and rice pudding.'

'You'll call when you're ready for cheese,' said Sally impassively.

'D'you know the legend of the halcyon?' said Athelny. Philip was growing used to his rapid leaping from one subject to another. 'When the kingfisher, flying over the sea, is exhausted, his mate places herself beneath him and bears him along upon her stronger wings. That is what a man wants in a wife, the halcyon. I lived with my first wife for three years. She was a lady, she had fifteen hundred a year, and we used to give nice little dinner-parties in our little red-brick house in Kensington. She was a charming woman; they all said so, the barristers and their wives who dined with us, and the literary stockbrokers, and the budding politicians; oh, she was a charming woman. She made me go to church in a silk hat and a frock-coat, she took me to classical concerts, and she was very fond of lectures on Sunday afternoon; and sat down to breakfast every morning at eight-thirty, and if I was late breakfast was cold; and she read the right books, admired the right pictures, and adored the right music. My God, how that woman bored me! She is charming still, and she lives in the little red-brick house in Kensington, with Morris papers and Whistler's etchings on the walls, and gives the same nice little dinner-parties, with veal creams and ices from Gunter's, as she did twenty years ago.'

Philip did not ask by what means the ill-matched couple had separated, but Athelny told him.

'Betty's not my wife, you know; my wife wouldn't divorce me. The children are bastards, every jack one of them, and are they any the worse for that? Betty was one of the maids in the little red-brick house in Kensington. Four or five years ago I was on my uppers, and I had seven children, and I went to my wife and asked her to help me. She said she'd make me an allowance if I'd give Betty up and go abroad. Can you see me giving Betty up? We starved for a while instead. My wife said I loved the gutter. I've degenerated; I've come down in the world; I earn three pounds a week as press agent to a linen-draper, and every day I thank God that I'm not in the little red-brick house in Kensington'

Sally brought in Cheddar cheese, and Athelny went on with his fluent conversation.

'It's the greatest mistake in the world to think that one needs money to bring up a family. You need money to make them gentlemen and ladies, but I don't want my children to be ladies and gentlemen. Sally's going to earn her living in another year. She's to be apprenticed to a dressmaker, aren't you, Sally? And the boys are going to serve their country. I want them all to go into the Navy; it's a jolly life and a healthy life, good food, good pay, and a pension to end their days on.'

Philip lit his pipe. Athelny smoked cigarettes of Havana tobacco, which he rolled himself. Sally cleared away. Philip was reserved, and it embarrassed him to be the recipient of so many confidences. Athelny, with his powerful voice in the diminutive body, with his bombast, with his foreign look, with his emphasis, was an astonishing creature. He reminded Philip a good deal of Cronshaw. He appeared to have the same independence of thought, the same bohemianism, but he had an infinitely more vivacious temperament; his mind was coarser, and he had not that interest in the abstract which made Cronshaw's conversation so captivating. Athelny was very proud of the county family to which he belonged; he showed Philip photographs of an Elizabethan mansion, and told him:

'The Athelnys have lived there for seven centuries, my boy. Ah, if you saw the chimney-pieces and the ceilings!'

There was a cupboard in the wainscoting and from this he took a family tree. He showed it to Philip with childlike satisfaction. It was indeed imposing.

'You see how the family names recur, Thorpe, Athelstan, Harold, Edward; I've used the family names for my sons. And the girls, you see, I've given Spanish names to.'

An uneasy feeling came to Philip that possibly the whole story was an elaborate imposture, not told with any base motive, but merely from a wish to impress, startle, and amaze. Athelny had told him that he was at Winchester; but Philip, sensitive to differences of manner, did not feel that his host had the characteristics of a man educated at a great public school. While he pointed out the great alliances which his ancestors had formed, Philip amused himself by wondering whether Athelny was not the son of some tradesman in Winchester, auctioneer or coal-merchant, and whether a similarity of surname was not his only connexion with the ancient family whose tree he was displaying.

LXXXVIII

THERE was a knock at the door and a troop of children came in. They were clean and tidy now; their faces shone with soap, and their hair was plastered down; they were going to Sunday school under Sally's charge. Athelny joked with them in his dramatic, exuberant fashion, and you could see that he was devoted to them all. His pride in their good health and their good looks was touching. Philip felt that they were a little shy in his presence, and when their father sent them off they fled from the room in evident relief. In a few minutes Mrs Athelny appeared. She had taken her hair out of the curling pins and now wore an elaborate fringe. She had on a plain black dress, a hat with cheap flowers, and was forcing her hands, red and coarse from much work, into black kid gloves.

'I'm going to church, Athelny,' she said. 'There's nothing you'll be wanting, is there?'

'Only your prayers, my Betty.'

'They won't do you much good, you're too far gone for that,' she smiled. Then, turning to Philip, she drawled: 'I can't get him to go to church. He's no better than an atheist.'

'Doesn't she look like Rubens's second wife?' cried Athelny. 'Wouldn't she look splendid in a seventeenth-century costume? That's the sort of wife to marry, my boy. Look at her.'

'I believe you'd talk the hind leg off a donkey, Athelny,' she answered calmly.

She succeeded in buttoning her gloves, but before she went she turned to Philip with a kindly, slightly embarrassed smile.

'You'll stay to tea, won't you? Athelny likes someone to talk to, and it's not often he gets anybody who's clever enough.'

'Of course he'll stay to tea,' said Athelny. Then when his wife had gone: 'I make a point of the children going to Sunday school, and I like Betty to go to church. I think women ought to be religious. I don't believe myself, but I like women and children to.'

Philip, strait-laced in matters of truth, was a little shocked by this airy attitude.

'But how can you look on while your children are being taught things which you don't think are true?'

'If they're beautiful I don't much mind if they're not true. It's asking a great deal that things should appeal to your reason as well as to your sense of the aesthetic. I wanted Betty to become a Roman Catholic; I should have liked to see her converted in a crown of paper flowers, but she's hopelessly Protestant. Besides, religion is a matter of temperament; you will believe anything if you have the religious turn of mind, and if you haven't it doesn't matter what beliefs were instilled into you, you will grow out of them. Perhaps religion is the best school of morality. It is like one of those drugs you gentlemen use in medicine which carries another in solution: it is of no efficacy in itself, but enables the other to be absorbed. You take your morality because it is combined with religion; you lose the religion and the morality stays behind. A man is more likely to be a good man if he has learned goodness through the love of God than through a perusal of Herbert Spencer.'

This was contrary to all Philip's ideas. He still looked upon Christianity as a degrading bondage that must be cast away at any cost: it was connected subconsciously in his mind with the dreary services in the cathedral at Tercanbury, and the long hours of boredom in the cold church at Blackstable; and the morality of which Athelny spoke was to him no more than a part of the religion which a halting intelligence preserved, when it had laid aside the beliefs which alone made it reasonable. But while he was meditating a reply Athelny, more interested in hearing himself speak than in discussion, broke into a tirade upon Roman Catholicism. For him it was an essential part of Spain; and Spain meant much to him, because he had escaped to it from the conventionality which during his married life he had found so irksome. With large gestures and in the emphatic tone which made what he said so striking, Athelny described to Philip the Spanish cathedrals with their vast dark spaces, the massive gold of the altar-pieces, and the sumptuous iron-work, gilt and faded, the air laden with incense, the silence: Philip almost saw the Canons in their short surplices of lawn, the acolytes in red, passing from the sacristy to the choir; he almost heard the monotonous chanting of vespers. The names which Athelny mentioned, Avila, Tarragona, Saragossa, Segovia, Cordoba, were like trumpets in his heart. He seemed to see the great grey piles of granite set in old Spanish towns amid a landscape tawny, wild, and windswept.

'I've always thought I should love to go to Seville,' he said casually, when Athelny, with one hand dramatically uplifted, paused for a moment.

'Seville!' cried Athelny. 'No, no, don't go there. Seville: it brings to the mind girls dancing with castanets, singing in gardens by the Guadalquivir, bull-fights, orange-blossom, mantillas, *mantones de Manila*. It is the Spain of comic opera and Montmartre. Its facile charm can offer permanent entertainment only to an intelligence which is superficial. Théophile Gautier got out of Seville all that it has to offer. We who come after him can only repeat his sensations. He put large fat hands on the obvious and there is nothing but the obvious there; and it is all finger-marked and frayed. Murillo is its painter.'

Athelny got up from his chair, walked over to the Spanish cabinet, let down the front with its great gilt hinges and gorgeous lock, and displayed a series of little drawers. He took out a bundle of photographs.

'Do you know El Greco?' he asked.

'Oh, I remember one of the men in Paris was awfully impressed by him.'

'El Greco was the painter of Toledo. Betty couldn't find the photograph I wanted to show you. It's a picture that El Greco painted of the city he loved, and it's truer than any photograph. Come and sit at the table.'

Philip dragged his chair forward, and Athelny set the photograph before him. He looked at it curiously, for a long time, in silence. He stretched out his hand for other photographs, and Athelny passed them to him. He had never before seen the work of that enigmatic master; and at the first glance he was bothered by the arbitrary drawing: the figures were extraordinarily elongated; the heads were very small; the attitudes were extravagant. This was not realism, and yet, and yet even in the photographs you had the impression of a troubling reality. Athelny was describing eagerly, with vivid phrases, but Philip only heard vaguely what he said. He was puzzled. He was curiously moved. These pictures seemed to offer some meaning to him, but he did not know what the meaning was. There were portraits of men with large, melancholy eyes which seemed to say you knew not what; there were long monks in the Franciscan habit or in the Dominican, with distraught faces, making gestures whose sense escaped you; there was an Assumption of the Virgin; there was a Crucifixion in which the painter by some magic of feeling had been able to suggest that the flesh of Christ's dead body was not human flesh only but divine; and there was an Ascension in which the Saviour seemed to surge up towards the empyrean and yet to stand upon the air as steadily as though it were solid ground: the uplifted arms of the Apostles, the sweep of their draperies, their ecstatic gestures, gave an impression of exultation and of holy joy. The background of nearly all was the sky by night, the dark night of the soul, with wild clouds swept by strange winds of hell and lit luridly by an uneasy moon.

'I've seen that sky in Toledo over and over again,' said Athelny. 'I have an idea that when first El Greco came to the city it was by such a night, and it made so vehement an impression upon him that he could never get away from it.'

Philip remembered how Clutton had been affected by this strange master, whose work he now saw for the first time. He thought that Clutton was the most interesting of all the people he had known in Paris. His sardonic manner, his hostile aloofness, had made it difficult to know him; but it seemed to Philip, looking back, that there had been in him a tragic force, which sought vainly to express itself in painting. He was a man of unusual character, mystical after the fashion of a time that had no leaning to mysticism, who was impatient with life because he found himself unable to say the things which the obscure impulses of his heart suggested. His intellect was not fashioned to the uses of the spirit. It was not surprising that he felt a deep sympathy with the Greek who had devised a new technique to express the yearnings of his soul. Philip looked again at the series of portraits of Spanish gentlemen, with ruffles and pointed beards, their faces pale against the sober black of their clothes and the darkness of the background. El Greco was the painter of the soul; and these gentlemen, wan and wasted, not by exhaustion but by restraint, with their tortured minds, seem to walk unaware of the beauty of the world; for their eyes

look only in their hearts, and they are dazzled by the glory
of the unseen. No painter has shown more pitilessly that the
world is but a place of passage. The souls of the men he
painted speak their strange longings through their eyes; their
senses are miraculously acute, not for sounds and odours and
colour, but for the very subtle sensations of the soul. The noble
walks with the monkish heart within him, and his eyes see
things which saints in their cells see too, and he is unastounded.
His lips are not lips that smile.

Philip, silent still, returned to the photograph of Toledo,
which seemed to him the most arresting picture of them all.
He could not take his eyes off it. He felt strangely that he was
on the threshold of some new discovery in life. He was tremulous with a sense of adventure. He thought for an instant of
the love that had consumed him: love seemed very trivial beside the excitement which now leaped in his heart. The picture
he looked at was a long one, with houses crowded upon a hill;
in one corner a boy was holding a large map of the town; in
another was a classical figure representing the River Tagus;
and in the sky was the Virgin surrounded by angels. It was a
landscape alien to all Philip's notions, for he had lived in circles
that worshipped exact realism; and yet here again, strangely
to himself, he felt a reality greater than any achieved by the
masters in whose steps humbly he had sought to walk. He
heard Athelny say that the representation was so precise that
when the citizens of Toledo came to look at the picture they
recognized their houses. The painter had painted exactly what
he saw, but he had seen with the eyes of the spirit. There was
something unearthly in that city of pale grey. It was a city of
the soul seen by a wan light that was neither that of night nor
day. It stood on a green hill, but of a green not of this world,
and it was surrounded by massive walls and bastions to be
stormed by no machines or engines of man's invention, but
by prayer and fasting, by contrite sighs and by mortifications
of the flesh. It was a stronghold of God. Those grey houses
were made of no stone known to masons, there was something
terrifying in their aspect, and you did not know what men
might live in them. You might walk through the streets and be
unamazed to find them all deserted, and yet not empty; for
you felt a presence invisible and yet manifest to every inner
sense. It was a mystical city in which the imagination faltered
like one who steps out of the light into darkness; the soul
walked naked to and fro, knowing the unknowable, and conscious strangely of experience, intimate but inexpressible, of

the absolute. And without surprise, in that blue sky, real with a reality that not the eye but the soul confesses, with its rack of light clouds driven by strange breezes, like the cries and the sighs of lost souls, you saw the Blessed Virgin with a gown of red and a cloak of blue, surrounded by winged angels. Philip felt that the inhabitants of that city would have seen the apparition without astonishment, reverent and thankful, and have gone their ways.

Athelny spoke of the mystical writers of Spain, of Teresa de Ávila, San Juan de la Cruz, Fray Diego de León; in all of them was that passion for the unseen which Philip felt in the pictures of El Greco: they seemed to have the power to touch the incorporeal and see the invisible. They were Spaniards of their age, in whom were tremulous all the mighty exploits of a great nation: their fancies were rich with the glories of America and the green islands of the Caribbean Sea; in their veins was the power that had come from age-long battling with the Moor; they were proud, for they were masters of the world; and they felt in themselves the wide distances, the tawny wastes, the snow-capped mountains of Castile, the sunshine and the blue sky, and the flowering plains of Andalusia. Life was passionate and manifold, and because it offered so much they felt a restless yearning for something more; because they were human they were unsatisfied; and they threw this eager vitality of theirs into a vehement striving after the ineffable. Athelny was not displeased to find someone to whom he could read the translations with which for some time he had amused his leisure; and in his fine, vibrating voice he recited the canticle of the Soul and Christ her lover, the lovely poem which begins with the words *en una noche oscura*, and the *noche serena* of Fray Luis de León. He had translated them quite simply, not without skill, and he had found words which at all events suggested the rough-hewn grandeur of the original. The pictures of El Greco explained them, and they explained the pictures.

Philip had cultivated a certain disdain for idealism. He had always had a passion for life, and the idealism he had come across seemed to him for the most part a cowardly shrinking from it. The idealist withdrew himself, because he could not suffer the jostling of the human crowd; he had not the strength to fight and so called the battle vulgar; he was vain, and since his fellows would not take him at his own estimate, consoled himself with despising his fellows. For Philip his type was Hayward, fair, languid, too fat now and rather bald, still cherishing the remains of his good looks and still delicately proposing to do exquisite things in the uncertain future; and at the back of this were whisky and vulgar *amours* of the street. It was in reaction from what Hayward represented that Philip clamoured for life as it stood; sordidness, vice, deformity, did not offend him; he declared that he wanted man in his nakedness; and he rubbed his hands when an instance came before him of meanness, cruelty, selfishness, or lust: that was the real thing. In Paris he had learned that there was neither ugliness nor beauty, but only truth: the search after beauty was sentimental. Had he not painted an advertisement of *chocolat Menier* in a landscape in order to escape from the tyranny of prettiness?

But here he seemed to divine something new. He had been coming to it, all hesitating, for some time, but only now was conscious of the fact; he felt himself on the brink of a discovery. He felt vaguely that here was something better than the realism which he had adored; but certainly it was not the bloodless idealism which stepped aside from life in weakness; it was too strong; it was virile; it accepted life in all its vivacity, ugliness and beauty, squalor and heroism; it was realism still; but it was realism carried to some higher pitch, in which facts were transformed by the more vivid light in which they were seen. He seemed to see things more profoundly through the grave eyes of those dead noblemen of Castile; and the gestures of the saints, which at first had seemed wild and distorted, appeared to have some mysterious significance. But he could not tell what that significance was. It was like a message which it was very important for him to receive, but it was given him in an unknown tongue, and he could not understand. He was always seeking for a meaning in life, and here it seemed to him that a meaning was offered; but it was obscure and vague. He was profoundly troubled. He saw what looked like the truth as by flashes of lightning on a dark, stormy night you might see a mountain range. He seemed to see that a man need not leave his life to chance, but that his will was powerful; he seemed to see that self-control might be as passionate and as active as the surrender to passion; he seemed to see that the inward life might be as manifold, as varied, as rich with experience, as the life of one who conquered realms and explored unknown lands.

THE conversation between Philip and Athelny was broken into by a clatter up the stairs. Athelny opened the door for the children coming back from Sunday school, and with laughter and shouting they came in. Gaily he asked them what they had learned. Sally appeared for a moment, with instructions from her mother that father was to amuse the children while she got tea ready; and Athelny began to tell them one of Hans Andersen's stories. They were not shy children, and they quickly came to the conclusion that Philip was not formidable. Jane came and stood by him and presently settled herself on his knees. It was the first time that Philip in his lonely life had been present in a family circle: his eyes smiled as they rested on the fair children engrossed in the fairy tale. The life of his new friend, eccentric as it appeared at first glance, seemed now to have the beauty of perfect naturalness. Sally came in once more.

'Now then, children, tea's ready,' she said.

Jane slipped off Philip's knees, and they all went back to the kitchen. Sally began to lay the cloth on the long Spanish table.

'Mother says, shall she come and have tea with you?' she asked. 'I can give the children their tea.'

'Tell your mother that we shall be proud and honoured if she will favour us with her company,' said Athelny.

It seemed to Philip that he could never say anything without an oratorical flourish.

'Then I'll lay for her,' said Sally.

She came back again in a moment with a tray on which were a cottage loaf, a slab of butter, and a jar of strawberry jam. While she placed the things on the table her father chaffed her. He said it was quite time she was walking out; he told Philip that she was very proud, and would have nothing to do with aspirants to that honour who lined up at the door, two by two, outside the Sunday school and craved the honour of escorting her home.

'You do talk, father,' said Sally, with her slow, good-natured smile.

'You wouldn't think to look at her that a tailor's assistant has enlisted in the army because she would not say how d'you do to him, and an electrical engineer, an electrical engineer, mind you, has taken to drink because she refused to share her hymn-book with him in church. I shudder to think what will happen when she puts her hair up.'

'Mother'll bring the tea along herself,' said Sally.

'Sally never pays any attention to me,' laughed Athelny, looking at her with fond, proud eyes. 'She goes about her business indifferent to wars, revolutions, and cataclysms. What a wife she'll make to an honest man!'

Mrs Athelny brought in the tea. She sat down and proceeded to cut bread and butter. It amused Philip to see that she treated her husband as though he were a child. She spread jam for him and cut up the bread and butter into convenient slices for him to eat. She had taken off her hat; and in her Sunday dress, which seemed a little tight for her, she looked like one of the farmer's wives whom Philip used to call on sometimes with his uncle when he was a small boy. Then he knew why the sound of her voice was familiar to him. She spoke just like the people round Blackstable.

'What part of the country d'you come from?' he asked her.

'I'm a Kentish woman. I come from Ferne.'

'I thought as much. My uncle's Vicar of Blackstable.'

'That's a funny thing now,' she said. 'I was wondering in church just now whether you was any connexion of Mr Carey. Many's the time I've seen 'im. A cousin of mine married Mr Barker of Roxley Farm, over by Blackstable Church, and I used to go and stay there often when I was a girl. Isn't that a funny thing now?'

She looked at him with a new interest, and a brightness came into her faded eyes. She asked him whether he knew Ferne. It was a pretty village about ten miles across country from Blackstable, and the Vicar had come over sometimes to Blackstable for the harvest thanksgiving. She mentioned names of various farmers in the neighbourhood. She was delighted to talk again of the country in which her youth was spent, and it was a pleasure to her to recall scenes and people that had remained in her memory with the tenacity peculiar to her class. It gave Philip a queer sensation too. A breath of the countryside seemed to be wafted into that panelled room in the middle of London. He seemed to see the flat Kentish fields with their stately elms; and his nostrils dilated with the scent of the air; it is laden with the salt of the North Sea, and that makes it keen and sharp.

Philip did not leave the Athelnys' till ten o'clock. The children came in to say good night at eight and quite naturally put up their faces for Philip to kiss. His heart went out to them. Sally only held out her hand.

'Sally never kisses gentlemen till she's seen them twice,' said her father.

'You must ask me again then,' said Philip.

'You mustn't take any notice of what father says,' remarked Sally, with a smile.

'She's a most self-possessed young woman,' added her parent.

They had supper of bread and cheese and beer while Mrs Athelny was putting the children to bed; and when Philip went into the kitchen to bid her good night (she had been sitting there, resting herself and reading *The Weekly Dispatch*) she invited him cordially to come again.

'There's always a good dinner on Sundays so long as Athelny's in work,' she said, 'and it's a charity to come and talk to him.'

On the following Saturday Philip received a postcard from Athelny saying that they were expecting him to dinner next day; but fearing their means were not such that Mr Athelny would desire him to accept, Philip wrote back that he would only come to tea. He bought a large plum cake so that his entertainment should cost nothing. He found the whole family glad to see him, and the cake completed his conquest of the children. He insisted that they should all have tea together in the kitchen, and the meal was noisy and hilarious.

Soon Philip got into the habit of going to Athelny's every Sunday. He became a great favourite with the children, because he was simple and unaffected and because it was so plain that he was fond of them. As soon as they heard his ring at the door one of them popped a head out of a window to make sure it was he, and then they all rushed downstairs tumultuously to let him in. They flung themselves into his arms. At tea they fought for the privilege of sitting next to him. Soon they began to call him Uncle Philip.

Athelny was very communicative, and little by little Philip learned the various stages of his life. He had followed many occupations, and it occurred to Philip that he managed to make a mess of everything he attempted. He had been on a tea plantation in Ceylon and a traveller in America for Italian wines; his secretaryship of the water company in Toledo had lasted longer than any of his employments; he had been a journalist and for some time had worked as police-court reporter for an evening paper; he had been sub-editor of a paper in the Midlands and editor of another on the Riviera. From all his occupations he had gathered amusing anecdotes, which he told with a keen pleasure in his own powers of entertainment. He had read a great deal, chiefly delighting in books which were unusual; and he poured forth his stores of abstruse knowledge with childlike enjoyment of the amazement of his hearers. Three or four years before, abject poverty had driven him to take the job of press-representative to a large firm of drapers; and though he felt the work unworthy his abilities, which he rated highly, the firmness of his wife and the needs of his family made him stick to it.

XC

WHEN he left the Athelnys' Philip walked down Chancery Lane and along the Strand to get a bus at the top of Parliament Street. One Sunday, when he had known them about six weeks, he did this as usual, but he found the Kennington bus full. It was June, but it had rained during the day and the night was raw and cold. He walked up to Piccadilly Circus in order to get a seat; the bus waited at the fountain, and when it arrived there seldom had more than two or three people in it. This service ran every quarter of an hour, and he had some time to wait. He looked idly at the crowd. The public-houses were closing, and there were many people about. His mind was busy with the ideas Athelny had the charming gift of suggesting.

Suddenly his heart stood still. He saw Mildred. He had not thought of her for weeks. She was crossing over from the corner of Shaftesbury Avenue and stopped at the shelter till a string of cabs passed by. She was watching her opportunity and had no eyes for anything else. She wore a large black straw hat with a mass of feathers on it and a black silk dress; at that time it was fashionable for women to wear trains; the road was clear, and Mildred crossed, her skirt trailing on the ground, and walked down Piccadilly. Philip, his heart beating excitedly, followed her. He did not wish to speak to her, but he wondered where she was going at that hour; he wanted to get a look at her face. She walked slowly along and turned down Air Street and so got through into Regent Street. She walked up again towards the Circus. Philip was puzzled. He could not make out what she was doing. Perhaps she was waiting for somebody, and he felt a great curiosity to know who it was. She overtook a short man in a bowler hat, who was strolling

441

very slowly in the same direction as herself; she gave him a sidelong glance as she passed. She walked a few steps more till she came to Swan and Edgar's, then stopped and waited, facing the road. When the man came up she smiled. The man stared at her for a moment, turned away his head, and sauntered on. Then Philip understood.

He was overwhelmed with horror. For a moment he felt such a weakness in his legs that he could hardly stand; then he walked after her quickly; he touched her on the arm.

'Mildred.'

She turned round with a violent start. He thought that she reddened, but in the obscurity he could not see very well. For a while they stood and looked at one another without speaking. At last she said:

'Fancy seeing you!'

He did not know what to answer; he was horribly shaken; and the phrases that chased one another through his brain seemed incredibly melodramatic.

'It's awful,' he gasped, almost to himself.

She did not say anything more, she turned away from him, and looked down at the pavement. He felt that his face was distorted with misery.

'Isn't there anywhere we can go and talk?'

'I don't want to talk,' she said sullenly. 'Leave me alone, can't you?'

The thought struck him that perhaps she was in urgent need of money and could not afford to go away at that hour.

'I've got a couple of sovereigns on me if you're hard up,' he blurted out.

'I don't know what you mean. I was just walking along here on my way back to my lodgings. I expected to meet one of the girls from where I work.'

'For God's sake don't lie now,' he said.

Then he saw that she was crying, and he repeated his question.

'Can't we go and talk somewhere? Can't I come back to your rooms?'

'No, you can't do that,' she sobbed. 'I'm not allowed to take gentlemen in there. If you like I'll meet you tomorrow.'

He felt certain that she would not keep an appointment. He was not going to let her go.

'No. You must take me somewhere now.'

'Well, there is a room I know, but they'll charge six shillings for it.'

'I don't mind that. Where is it?'

She gave him the address, and he called a cab. They drove to a shabby street beyond the British Museum in the neighbourhood of the Gray's Inn Road, and she stopped the cab at the corner.

'They don't like you to drive up to the door,' she said.

They were the first words either of them had spoken since getting into the cab. They walked a few yards and Mildred knocked three times, sharply, at a door. Philip noticed in the fanlight a cardboard on which was an announcement that apartments were to let. The door was opened quietly, and an elderly tall woman let them in. She gave Philip a stare and then spoke to Mildred in an undertone. Mildred led Philip along a passage to a room at the back. It was quite dark; she asked him for a match, and lit the gas; there was no globe, and the gas flared shrilly. Philip saw that he was in a dingy little bedroom with a suite of furniture painted to look like pine much too large for it; the lace curtains were very dirty; the grate was hidden by a large paper fan. Mildred sank on the chair which stood by the side of the chimney-piece. Philip sat on the edge of the bed. He felt ashamed. He saw now that Mildred's cheeks were thick with rouge, her eyebrows were blackened; but she looked thin and ill, and the red on her cheeks exaggerated the greenish pallor of her skin. She stared at the paper fan in a listless fashion. Philip could not think what to say, and he had a choking in his throat as if he were going to cry. He covered his eyes with his hands.

'My God, it is awful,' he groaned.

'I don't know what you've got to fuss about. I should have thought you'd have been rather pleased.'

Philip did not answer, and in a moment she broke into a sob.

'You don't think I do it because I like it, do you?'

'Oh, my dear,' he cried. 'I'm so sorry, I'm so awfully sorry.'

'That'll do me a fat lot of good.'

Again Philip found nothing to say. He was desperately afraid of saying anything which she might take for a reproach or a sneer.

'Where's the baby?' he asked at last.

'I've got her with me in London. I hadn't got the money to keep her on at Brighton, so I had to take her. I've got a room up Highbury way. I told them I was on the stage. It's a long way to have to come down to the West End every day, but it's a rare job to find anyone who'll let to ladies at all.'

'Wouldn't they take you back at the shop?'

'I couldn't get any work to do anywhere. I walked my legs off looking for work. I did get a job once, but I was off for a week because I was queer, and when I went back they said they didn't want me any more. You can't blame them either, can you? Them places, they can't afford to have girls that aren't strong.'

'You don't look very well now,' said Philip.

'I wasn't fit to come out tonight, but I couldn't help myself, I wanted the money. I wrote to Emil and told him I was broke, but he never even answered the letter.'

'You might have written to me.'

'I didn't like to, not after what happened, and I didn't want you to know I was in difficulties. I shouldn't have been surprised if you'd just told me I'd only got what I deserved.'

'You don't know me very well, do you, even now?'

For a moment he remembered all the anguish he had suffered on her account, and he was sick with the recollection of his pain. But it was no more than recollection. When he looked at her he knew that he no longer loved her. He was very sorry for her, but he was glad to be free. Watching her gravely, he asked himself why he had been so besotted with passion for her.

'You're a gentleman in every sense of the word,' she said. 'You're the only one I've ever met.' She paused for a minute and then flushed. 'I hate asking you, Philip, but can you spare me anything?'

'It's lucky I've got some money on me. I'm afraid I've only got two pounds.'

He gave her the sovereigns.

'I'll pay you back, Philip.'

'Oh, that's all right,' he smiled. 'You needn't worry.'

He had said nothing that he wanted to say. They had talked as if the whole thing were natural; and it looked as though she would go now, back to the horror of her life, and he would be able to do nothing to prevent it. She had got up to take the money, and they were both standing.

'Am I keeping you?' she asked. 'I suppose you want to be getting home.'

'No, I'm in no hurry,' he answered.

'I'm glad to have a chance of sitting down.'

Those words, with all they implied, tore his heart, and it was dreadfully painful to see the weary way in which she sank back into the chair. The silence lasted so long that Philip in his embarrassment lit a cigarette.

'It's very good of you not to have said anything disagreeable to me, Philip. I thought you might say I didn't know what all.'

He saw that she was crying again. He remembered how she had come to him when Emil Miller had deserted her and how she had wept. The recollection of her suffering and of his own humiliation seemed to render more overwhelming the compassion he felt now.

'If I could only get out of it!' she moaned. 'I hate it so. I'm unfit for the life, I'm not the sort of girl for that. I'd do anything to get away from it, I'd be a servant if I could. Oh, I wish I was dead.'

And in pity for herself she broke down now completely. She sobbed hysterically, and her thin body was shaken.

'Oh, you don't know what it is. Nobody knows till they've done it.'

Philip could not bear to see her cry. He was tortured by the horror of her position.

'Poor child,' he whispered. 'Poor child.'

He was deeply moved. Suddenly he had an inspiration. It filled him with a perfect ecstasy of happiness.

'Look here, if you want to get away from it, I've got an idea. I'm frightfully hard up just now, I've got to be as economical as I can; but I've got a sort of little flat in Kennington and I've got a spare room. If you like you and the baby can come and live there. I pay a woman three and sixpence a week to keep the place clean and to do a little cooking for me. You could do that and your food wouldn't come to much more than the money I should save on her. It doesn't cost any more to feed two than one, and I don't suppose the baby eats much.'

She stopped crying and looked at him.

'D'you mean to say that you could take me back after all that's happened?'

Philip flushed a little in embarrassment at what he had to say.

'I don't want you to mistake me. I'm just giving you a room which doesn't cost me anything and your food. I don't expect anything more from you than that you should do exactly the same as the woman I have in does. Except for that I don't want anything from you at all. I daresay you can cook well enough for that.'

She sprang to her feet and was about to come towards him.

'You are good to me, Philip.'

'No, please stop where you are,' he said hurriedly, putting out his hand as though to push her away.

He did not know why it was, but he could not bear the thought that she should touch him.

'I don't want to be anything more than a friend to you.'

'You are good to me,' she repeated. 'You are good to me.'

'Does that mean you'll come?'

'Oh, yes, I'd do anything to get away from this. You'll never regret what you've done, Philip, never. When can I come, Philip?'

'You'd better come tomorrow.'

Suddenly she burst into tears again.

'What on earth are you crying for now?' he smiled.

'I'm so grateful to you. I don't know how I can ever make it up to you.'

'Oh, that's all right. You'd better go home now.'

He wrote out the address and told her that if she came at half past five he would be ready for her. It was so late that he had to walk home, but it did not seem a long way, for he was intoxicated with delight; he seemed to walk on air.

XCI

NEXT day he got up early to make the room ready for Mildred. He told the woman who had looked after him that he would not want her any more. Mildred came about six, and Philip, who was watching from the window, went down to let her in and help her to bring up the luggage: it consisted now of no more than three large parcels wrapped in brown paper, for she had been obliged to sell everything that was not absolutely needful. She wore the same black silk dress she had worn the night before, and, though she had now no rouge on her cheeks, there was still about her eyes the black which remained after a perfunctory wash in the morning: it made her look very ill. She was a pathetic figure as she stepped out of the cab with the baby in her arms. She seemed a little shy, and they found nothing but commonplace things to say to one another.

'So you've got here all right.'

'I've never lived in this part of London before.'

Philip showed her the room. It was that in which Cronshaw had died. Philip, though he thought it absurd, had never liked the idea of going back to it; and since Cronshaw's death he had remained in the little room, sleeping on a fold-up bed, into which he had first moved in order to make his friend comfortable. The baby was sleeping placidly.

'You don't recognize her, I expect,' said Mildred.

'I've not seen her since we took her down to Brighton.'

'Where shall I put her? She's so heavy I can't carry her very long.'

'I'm afraid I haven't got a cradle,' said Philip, with a nervous laugh.

'Oh, she'll sleep with me. She always does.'

Mildred put the baby in an arm-chair and looked round the room. She recognized most of the things which she had known in his old diggings. Only one thing was new, a head and shoulders of Philip which Lawson had painted at the end of the preceding summer; it hung over the chimney-piece; Mildred looked at it critically.

'In some ways I like it and in some ways I don't. I think you're better-looking than that.'

'Things are looking up,' laughed Philip. 'You've never told me I was good-looking before.'

'I'm not one to worry myself about a man's looks. I don't like good-looking men. They're too conceited for me.'

Her eyes travelled round the room in an instinctive search for a looking-glass, but there was none; she put up her hand and patted her large fringe.

'What'll the other people in the house say to my being here?' she asked suddenly.

'Oh, there's only a man and his wife living here. He's out all day, and I never see her except on Saturday to pay my rent. They keep entirely to themselves. I've not spoken two words to either of them since I came.'

Mildred went into the bedroom to undo her things and put them away. Philip tried to read, but his spirits were too high: he leaned back in his chair, smoking a cigarette, and with smiling eyes looked at the sleeping child. He felt very happy. He was quite sure that he was not at all in love with Mildred. He was surprised that the old feeling had left him so completely; he discerned in himself a faint physical repulsion from her; and he thought that if he touched her it would give him goose-flesh. He could not understand himself. Presently, knocking at the door, she came in again.

'I say, you needn't knock,' he said. 'Have you made the tour of the mansion?'

'It's the smallest kitchen I've ever seen.'

'You'll find it large enough to cook our sumptuous repasts,' he retorted lightly.

'I see there's nothing in. I'd better go out and get something.'

'Yes, but I venture to remind you that we must be devilish economical.'

'What shall I get for supper?'

'You'd better get what you think you can cook,' laughed Philip.

He gave her some money and she went out. She came in half an hour later and put her purchases on the table. She was out of breath from climbing the stairs.

'I say, you are anaemic,' said Philip. 'I'll have to dose you with Blaud's Pills.'

'It took me some time to find the shops. I bought some liver. That's tasty, isn't it? And you can't eat much of it, so it's more economical than butcher's meat.'

There was a gas stove in the kitchen, and when she had put the liver on, Mildred came into the sitting-room to lay the cloth.

'Why are you only laying one place?' asked Philip. 'Aren't you going to eat anything?'

Mildred flushed.

'I thought you mightn't like me to have my meals with you.'

'Why on earth not?'

'Well, I'm only a servant, aren't I?'

'Don't be an ass. How can you be so silly?'

He smiled, but her humility gave him a curious twist in his heart. Poor thing! He remembered what she had been when first he knew her. He hesitated for an instant.

'Don't think I'm conferring any benefit on you,' he said. 'It's simply a business arrangement; I'm giving you board and lodging in return for your work. You don't owe me anything. And there's nothing humiliating to you in it.'

She did not answer, but tears rolled heavily down her cheeks. Philip knew from his experience at the hospital that women of her class looked upon service as degrading: he could not help feeling a little impatient with her; but he blamed himself, for it was clear that she was tired and ill. He got up and helped her to lay another place at the table. The baby was awake now, and Mildred had prepared some Mellin's Food for it. The liver and bacon were ready and they sat down. For economy's sake Philip had given up drinking anything but water, but he had in the house half a bottle of whisky, and he thought a little would do Mildred good. He did his best to make the supper pass cheerfully, but Mildred was subdued and exhausted. When they had finished she got up to put the baby to bed.

448

'I think you'll do well to turn in early yourself,' said Philip. 'You look absolutely done up.'

'I think I will after I've washed up.'

Philip lit his pipe and began to read. It was pleasant to hear somebody moving about in the next room. Sometimes his loneliness had oppressed him. Mildred came in to clear the table, and he heard the clatter of plates as she washed up. Philip smiled as he thought how characteristic it was of her that she should do all that in a black silk dress. But he had work to do, and he brought his book up to the table. He was reading Osler's *Medicine*, which had recently taken the place in the students' favour of Taylor's work, for many years the text-book most in use. Presently Mildred came in, rolling down her sleeves. Philip gave her a casual glance, but did not move; the occasion was curious, and he felt a little nervous. He feared that Mildred might imagine he was going to make a nuisance of himself, and he did not quite know how without brutality to reassure her.

'By the way, I've got a lecture at nine, so I should want breakfast at a quarter past eight. Can you manage that?'

'Oh, yes. Why, when I was in Parliament Street I used to catch the eight-twelve from Herne Hill every morning.'

'I hope you'll find your room comfortable. You'll be a different woman tomorrow after a long night in bed.'

'I suppose you work till late?'

'I generally work till about eleven or half past.'

'I'll say good night then.'

'Good night.'

The table was between them. He did not offer to shake hands with her. She shut the door quietly. He heard her moving about in the bedroom, and in a little while he heard the creaking of the bed as she got in.

XCII

The following day was Tuesday. Philip as usual hurried through his breakfast and dashed off to get to his lecture at nine. He had only time to exchange a few words with Mildred. When he came back in the evening he found her seated at the window, darning his socks.

'I say, you are industrious,' he smiled. 'What have you been doing with yourself all day?'

'Oh, I gave the place a good cleaning and then I took baby out for a little.'

She was wearing an old black dress, the same as she had worn as uniform when she served in the tea-shop; it was shabby, but she looked better in it than in the silk of the day before. The baby was sitting on the floor. She looked up at Philip with large, mysterious eyes and broke into a laugh when he sat down beside her and began playing with her bare toes. The afternoon sun came into the room and shed a mellow light.

'It's rather jolly to come back and find someone about the place. A woman and a baby make very good decoration in a room.'

He had gone to the hospital dispensary and got a bottle of Blaud's Pills. He gave them to Mildred and told her she must take them after each meal. It was a remedy she was used to, for she had taken it off and on ever since she was sixteen.

'I'm sure Lawson would love that green skin of yours,' said Philip. 'He'd say it was so paintable, but I'm terribly matter-of-fact nowadays, and I shan't be happy till you're as pink and white as a milkmaid.'

'I feel better already.'

After a frugal supper Philip filled his pouch with tobacco and put on his hat. It was on Tuesdays that he generally went to the tavern in Beak Street, and he was glad that this day came so soon after Mildred's arrival, for he wanted to make his relations with her perfectly clear.

'Are you going out?' she said.

'Yes, on Tuesdays I give myself a night off. I shall see you tomorrow. Good night.'

Philip always went to the tavern with a sense of pleasure. Macalister, the philosophic stockbroker, was generally there and glad to argue upon any subject under the sun; Hayward came regularly when he was in London; and though he and Macalister disliked one another they continued out of habit to meet on that one evening in the week. Macalister thought Hayward a poor creature, and sneered at his delicacies of sentiment: he asked satirically about Hayward's literary work and received with scornful smiles his vague suggestions of future masterpieces; their arguments were often heated; but the punch was good, and they were both fond of it; towards the end of the evening they generally composed their differences and thought each other capital fellows. This evening Philip found them both there, and Lawson also; Lawson came more seldom now that he was beginning to know people in London and went out to dinner a good deal. They were all on excellent terms with themselves, for Macalister had given them a good thing on the Stock Exchange, and Hayward and Lawson had made fifty pounds apiece. It was a great thing for Lawson, who was extravagant and earned little money: he had arrived at that stage of the portrait-painter's career when he was noticed a good deal by the critics and found a number of aristocratic ladies who were willing to allow him to paint them for nothing (it advertised them both, and gave the great ladies quite an air of patronesses of the arts); but he very seldom got hold of the solid philistine who was ready to pay good money for a portrait of his wife. Lawson was brimming over with satisfaction.

'It's the most ripping way of making money that I've ever struck,' he cried. 'I didn't have to put my hand in my pocket for sixpence.'

'You lost something by not being here last Tuesday, young man,' said Macalister to Philip.

'My God, why didn't you write to me?' said Philip. 'If you only knew how useful a hundred pounds would be to me.'

'Oh, there wasn't time for that. One has to be on the spot. I heard of a good thing last Tuesday, and I asked these fellows if they'd like to have a flutter. I bought them a thousand shares on Wednesday morning, and there was a rise in the afternoon, so I sold them at once. I made fifty pounds for each of them and a couple of hundred for myself.'

Philip was sick with envy. He had recently sold the last mortgage in which his small fortune had been invested and now had only six hundred pounds left. He was panic-stricken sometimes when he thought of the future. He had still to keep himself for two years before he could be qualified, and then he meant to try for hospital appointments, so that he could not expect to earn anything for three years at least. With the most rigid economy he would not have more than a hundred pounds left then. It was very little to have as a stand-by in case he was ill and could not earn money or found himself at any time without work. A lucky gamble would make all the difference to him.

'Oh, well, it doesn't matter,' said Macalister. 'Something is sure to turn up soon. There'll be a boom in South Africans again one of these days, and then I'll see what I can do for you.'

Macalister was in the Kaffir market and often told them stories of the sudden fortunes that had been made in the great boom of a year or two back.

'Well, don't forget next time.'

They sat on talking till nearly midnight, and Philip, who lived furthest off, was the first to go. If he did not catch the last tram he had to walk, and that made him very late. As it was he did not reach home till nearly half past twelve. When he got upstairs he was surprised to find Mildred still sitting in his arm-chair.

'Why on earth aren't you in bed?' he cried.

'I wasn't sleepy.'

'You ought to go to bed all the same. It would rest you.'

She did not move. He noticed that since supper she had changed into her black silk dress.

'I thought I'd rather wait up for you in case you wanted anything.'

She looked at him, and the shadow of a smile played upon her thin pale lips. Philip was not sure whether he understood or not. He was slightly embarrassed, but assumed a cheerful matter-of-fact air.

'It's very nice of you, but it's very naughty also. Run off to bed as fast as you can, or you won't be able to get up tomorrow morning.'

'I don't feel like going to bed.'

'Nonsense,' he said coldly.

She got up, a little sulkily, and went into her room. He smiled when he heard her lock the door loudly.

The next few days passed without incident. Mildred settled down in her new surroundings. When Philip hurried off after breakfast she had the whole morning to do the housework. They ate very simply, but she liked to take a long time to buy the few things they needed; she could not be bothered to cook anything for her dinner, but made herself some cocoa and ate bread and butter; then she took the baby out in the go-cart, and when she came in spent the rest of the afternoon in idleness. She was tired out, and it suited her to do so little. She made friends with Philip's forbidding landlady over the rent, which he left with Mildred to pay, and within a week was able to tell him more about his neighbours than he had learned in a year.

'She's a very nice woman,' said Mildred. 'Quite the lady. I told her we was married.'

'D'you think that was necessary?'

'Well, I had to tell her something. It looks so funny me being here and not married to you. I didn't know what she'd think of me.'

'I don't suppose she believed you for a moment.'

'That she did, I lay. I told her we'd been married two years – I had to say that, you know, because of baby – only your people wouldn't hear of it, because you was only a student' – she pronounced it stoodent – 'and so we had to keep it a secret, but they'd given way now and we were all going down to stay with them in the summer.'

'You're a past-mistress of the cock-and-bull story,' said Philip.

He was vaguely irritated that Mildred still had this passion for telling fibs. In the last two years she had learnt nothing. But he shrugged his shoulders.

'When all's said and done,' he reflected, 'she hasn't had much chance.'

It was a beautiful evening, warm and cloudless, and the people of South London seemed to have poured out into the streets. There was that restlessness in the air which seizes the cockney sometimes when a turn in the weather calls him into the open. After Mildred had cleared away the supper she went and stood at the window. The street noises came up to them, noises of people calling to one another, of the passing traffic, of a barrel-organ in the distance.

'I suppose you must work tonight, Philip?' she asked him, with a wistful expression.

'I ought, but I don't know that I must. Why, d'you want me to do anything else?'

'I'd like to go out for a bit. Couldn't we take a ride on the top of a tram?'

'If you like.'

'I'll just go and put on my hat,' she said joyfully.

The night made it almost impossible to stay indoors. The baby was asleep and could be safely left; Mildred said she had always left it alone at night when she went out; it never woke. She was in high spirits when she came back with her hat on. She had taken the opportunity to put on a little rouge. Philip thought it was excitement which had brought a faint colour to her pale cheeks; he was touched by her child-like delight, and reproached himself for the austerity with which he had treated her. She laughed when she got out into the air. The first tram they saw was going towards Westminster Bridge and they got on it. Philip smoked his pipe, and they looked at the crowded street. The shops were open, gaily lit, and people were doing their shopping for the next day. They passed a music-hall called the Canterbury and Mildred cried out:

'Oh, Philip, do let's go there. I haven't been to a music-hall for months.'

'We can't afford stalls, you know.'

'Oh, I don't mind, I shall be quite happy in the gallery.'

They got down and walked back a hundred yards till they came to the doors. They got capital seats for sixpence each, high up but not in the gallery, and the night was so fine that there was plenty of room. Mildred's eyes glistened. She enjoyed herself thoroughly. There was a simple-mindedness in her which touched Philip. She was a puzzle to him. Certain things in her still pleased him, and he thought that there was a lot in her which was very good: she had been badly brought up, and her life was hard; he had blamed her for much that she could not help; and it was his own fault if he had asked virtues from her which it was not in her power to give. Under different circumstances she might have been a charming girl. She was extraordinarily unfit for the battle of life. As he watched her now in profile, her mouth slightly open and that delicate flush on her cheeks, he thought she looked strangely virginal. He felt an overwhelming compassion for her, and with all his heart he forgave her for the misery she had caused him. The smoky atmosphere made Philip's eyes ache, but when he suggested going she turned to him with beseeching face and asked him to stay till the end. He smiled and consented. She took his hand and held it for the rest of the performance. When they streamed out with the audience into the crowded street she did not want to go home; they wandered up the Westminster Bridge Road, looking at the people.

'I've not had such a good time as this for months,' she said.

Philip's heart was full, and he was thankful to the fates because he had carried out his sudden impulse to take Mildred and her baby into his flat. It was very pleasant to see her happy gratitude. At last she tired and they jumped on a tram to go home; it was late now, and when they got down and turned into their own street there was no one about. Mildred slipped her arm through his.

'It's just like old times, Phil,' she said.

She had never called him Phil before, that was what Griffiths called him; and even now it gave him a curious pang. He remembered how much he had wanted to die then; his pain had been so great that he had thought quite seriously of committing suicide. It all seemed very long ago. He smiled at his past self. Now he felt nothing for Mildred but infinite pity. They reached the house, and when they got into the sitting-room Philip lit the gas.

'Is the baby all right?' he asked.

'I'll just go in and see.'

When she came back it was to say that it had not stirred since she left it. It was a wonderful child. Philip held out his hand.

'Well, good night.'

'D'you want to go to bed already?'

'It's nearly one. I'm not used to late hours these days,' said Philip.

She took his hand, and holding it looked into his eyes with a little smile.

'Phil, the other night in that room, when you asked me to come and stay here, I didn't mean what you thought I meant, when you said you didn't want me to be anything to you except just to cook and that sort of thing.'

'Didn't you?' answered Philip, withdrawing his hand. 'I did.'

'Don't be such an old silly,' she laughed.

He shook his head.

'I meant it quite seriously. I shouldn't have asked you to stay here on any other condition.'

'Why not?'

'I feel I couldn't. I can't explain it, but it would spoil it all.'

She shrugged her shoulders.

'Oh, very well, it's just as you choose. I'm not one to go down on my hands and knees for that, and chance it.'

She went out, slamming the door behind her.

XCIII

NEXT morning Mildred was sulky and taciturn. She remained in her room till it was time to get the dinner ready. She was a bad cook and could do little more than chops and steaks; and she did not know how to use up odds and ends, so that Philip was obliged to spend more money than he had expected. When she served up she sat down opposite Philip, but would eat nothing; he remarked on it; she said she had a bad headache and was not hungry. He was glad that he had somewhere to spend the rest of the day; the Athelnys were cheerful and friendly: it was a delightful and an unexpected thing to realize that everyone in that household looked forward with pleasure to his visit. Mildred had gone to bed when he came back, but next day she was still silent. At supper she sat with a haughty expression on her face and a little frown between her eyes. It made Philip impatient, but he told himself that he must be considerate to her; he was bound to make allowance.

'You're very silent,' he said, with a pleasant smile.

'I'm paid to cook and clean, I didn't know I was expected to talk as well.'

He thought it an ungracious answer, but if they were going to live together he must do all he could to make things go easily.

'I'm afraid you're cross with me about the other night,' he said.

It was an awkward thing to speak about, but apparently it was necessary to discuss it.

'I don't know what you mean,' she answered.

'Please don't be angry with me. I should never have asked you to come and live here if I'd not meant our relations to be merely friendly. I suggested it because I thought you wanted a home and you would have a chance of looking about for something to do.'

'Oh, don't think I care.'

'I don't for a moment,' he hastened to say. 'You mustn't think I'm ungrateful. I realize that you only proposed it for my sake. It's just a feeling I have, and I can't help it, it would make the whole thing ugly and horrid.'

'You are funny,' she said, looking at him curiously. 'I can't make you out.'

She was not angry with him now, but puzzled; she had no idea what he meant: she accepted the situation, she had indeed a vague feeling that he was behaving in a very noble fashion and that she ought to admire it; but also she felt inclined to laugh at him and perhaps even to despise him a little.

'He's a rum customer,' she thought.

Life went smoothly enough with them. Philip spent all day at the hospital and worked at home in the evening except when he went to the Athelnys' or to the tavern in Beak Street. Once the physician for whom he clerked asked him to a solemn dinner, and two or three times he went to parties given by fellow-students. Mildred accepted the monotony of her life. If she minded that Philip left her sometimes by herself in the evening she never mentioned it. Occasionally he took her to a music-hall. He carried out his intention that the only tie between them should be the domestic service she did in return for board and lodging. She had made up her mind that it was no use trying to get work that summer, and with Philip's approval determined to stay where she was till the autumn. She thought it would be easy to get something to do then.

'As far as I'm concerned you can stay on here when you've got a job if it's convenient. The room's there, and the woman who did for me before can come in to look after the baby.'

He grew very much attached to Mildred's child. He had a naturally affectionate disposition, which had had little opportunity to display itself. Mildred was not unkind to the little girl. She looked after her very well and once when she had a bad cold proved herself a devoted nurse; but the child bored her, and she spoke to her sharply when she bothered; she was fond of her, but had not the maternal passion which might have induced her to forget herself. Mildred had no demonstrativeness, and she found the manifestations of affection ridiculous. When Philip sat with the baby on his knees, playing with it and kissing it, she laughed at him.

'You couldn't make more fuss of her if you was her father,' she said. 'You're perfectly silly with the child.'

Philip flushed, for he hated to be laughed at. It was absurd to be so devoted to another man's baby, and he was a little ashamed of the overflowing of his heart. But the child, feeling Philip's attachment, would put her face against his or nestle in his arms.

'It's all very fine for you,' said Mildred. 'You don't have any of the disagreeable part of it. How would you like being kept awake for an hour in the middle of the night because her ladyship wouldn't go to sleep?'

Philip remembered all sorts of things of his childhood which he thought he had long forgotten. He took hold of the baby's toes.

'This little pig went to market, this little pig stayed at home.'

When he came home in the evening and entered the sitting-room his first glance was for the baby sprawling on the floor, and it gave him a little thrill of delight to hear the child's crow of pleasure at seeing him. Mildred taught her to call him daddy, and when the child did this for the first time of her own accord, laughed immoderately.

'I wonder if you're that stuck on baby because she's mine,' asked Mildred, 'or if you'd be the same with anybody's baby.'

'I've never known anybody else's baby, so I can't say,' said Philip.

Towards the end of his second term as in-patients' clerk a piece of good fortune befell Philip. It was the middle of July.

457

He went one Tuesday evening to the tavern in Beak Street and found nobody there but Macalister. They sat together, chatting about their absent friends, and after a while Macalister said to him:

'Oh, by the way, I heard of a rather good thing today, New Kleinfonteins; it's a gold mine in Rhodesia. If you'd like to have a flutter you might make a bit.'

Philip had been waiting anxiously for such an opportunity, but now that it came he hesitated. He was desperately afraid of losing money. He had little of the gambler's spirit.

'I'd love to, but I don't know if I dare risk it. How much could I lose if things went wrong?'

'I shouldn't have spoken of it, only you seemed so keen about it,' Macalister answered coldly.

Philip felt that Macalister looked upon him as rather a donkey.

'I'm awfully keen on making a bit,' he laughed.

'You can't make money unless you're prepared to risk money.'

Macalister began to talk of other things and Philip, while he was answering him, kept thinking that if the venture turned out well the stockbroker would be very facetious at his expense next time they met. Macalister had a sarcastic tongue.

'I think I will have a flutter if you don't mind,' said Philip anxiously.

'All right. I'll buy you two hundred and fifty shares and if I see a half-crown rise I'll sell them at once.'

Philip quickly reckoned out how much that would amount to, and his mouth watered; thirty pounds would be a godsend just then, and he thought the fates owed him something. He told Mildred what he had done when he saw her at breakfast next morning. She thought him very silly.

'I never knew anyone who made money on the Stock Exchange,' she said. 'That's what Emil always said; you can't expect to make money on the Stock Exchange, he said.'

Philip bought an evening paper on his way home and turned at once to the money columns. He knew nothing about these things and had difficulty in finding the stock which Macalister had spoken of. He saw they had advanced a quarter. His heart leaped, and then he felt sick with apprehension in case Macalister had forgotten or for some reason had not bought. Macalister had promised to telegraph. Philip could not wait to take a tram home. He jumped into a cab. It was an unwonted extravagance.

'Is there a telegram for me?' he said, as he burst in.

'No,' said Mildred.

His face fell, and in bitter disappointment he sank heavily into a chair.

'Then he didn't buy them for me after all. Curse him,' he added violently. 'What cruel luck! And I've been thinking all day of what I'd do with the money.'

'Why, what were you going to do?' she asked.

'What's the good of thinking about that now? Oh, I wanted the money so badly.'

She gave a laugh and handed him a telegram.

'I was only having a joke with you. I opened it.'

He tore it out of her hands. Macalister had bought him two hundred and fifty shares and sold them at the half-crown profit he had suggested. The commission note was to follow next day. For one moment Philip was furious with Mildred for her cruel jest, but then he could only think of his joy.

'It makes such a difference to me,' he cried. 'I'll stand you a new dress if you like.'

'I want it badly enough,' she answered.

'I'll tell you what I'm going to do. I'm going to be operated upon at the end of July.'

'Why, have you got something the matter with you?' she interrupted.

It struck her that an illness she did not know of might explain what had so much puzzled her. He flushed, for he hated to refer to his deformity.

'No, but they think they can do something to my foot. I couldn't spare the time before, but now it doesn't matter so much. I shall start my dressing in October instead of next month. I shall only be in hospital a few weeks and then we can go away to the seaside for the rest of the summer. It'll do us all good, you and the baby and me.'

'Oh, let's go to Brighton, Philip, I like Brighton, you get such a nice class of people there.'

Philip had vaguely thought of some little fishing village in Cornwall, but as she spoke it occurred to him that Mildred would be bored to death there.

'I don't mind where we go as long as I get the sea.'

He did not know why, but he had suddenly an irresistible longing for the sea. He wanted to bathe, and he thought with delight of splashing about in the salt water. He was a good swimmer, and nothing exhilarated him like a rough sea.

'I say, it will be jolly,' he cried.

'It'll be like a honeymoon, won't it?' she said. 'How much can I have for my new dress, Phil?'

XCIV

PHILIP asked Mr Jacobs, the assistant-surgeon for whom he had dressed, to do the operation. Jacobs accepted with pleasure, since he was interested just then in neglected talipes and was getting together materials for a paper. He warned Philip that he could not make his foot like the other, but he thought he could do a good deal; and though he would always limp he would be able to wear a boot less unsightly than that which he had been accustomed to. Philip remembered how he had prayed to a God who was able to remove mountains for him who had faith, and he smiled bitterly.

'I don't expect a miracle,' he answered.

'I think you're wise to let me try what I can do. You'll find a club-foot rather a handicap in practice. The layman is full of fads, and he doesn't like his doctor to have anything the matter with him.'

Philip went into a 'small ward', which was a room on the landing, outside each ward, reserved for special cases. He remained there a month, for the surgeon would not let him go till he could walk; and, bearing the operation very well, he had a pleasant enough time. Lawson and Athelny came to see him, and one day Mrs Athelny brought two of her children; students whom he knew looked in now and again to have a chat; Mildred came twice a week. Everyone was very kind to him, and Philip, always surprised when anyone took trouble with him, was touched and grateful. He enjoyed the relief from care; he need not worry there about the future, neither whether his money would last out nor whether he would pass his final examinations; and he could read to his heart's content. He had not been able to read much of late, since Mildred disturbed him: she would make an aimless remark when he was trying to concentrate his attention, and would not be satisfied unless he answered; whenever he was comfortably settled down with a book she would want something done and would come to him with a cork she could not draw or a hammer to drive in a nail.

They settled to go to Brighton in August. Philip wanted to take lodgings, but Mildred said that she would have to do housekeeping, and it would only be a holiday for her if they went to a boarding-house.

'I have to see about the food every day at home; I get that sick of it I want a thorough change.'

Philip agreed, and it happened that Mildred knew of a boarding-house at Kemp Town where they would not be charged more than twenty-five shillings a week each. She arranged with Philip to write about rooms, but when he got back to Kennington he found that she had done nothing. He was irritated.

'I shouldn't have thought you had so much to do as all that,' he said.

'Well, I can't think of everything. It's not my fault if I forget, is it?'

Philip was so anxious to get to the sea that he would not wait to communicate with the mistress of the boarding-house.

'We'll leave the luggage at the station and go to the house and see if they've got rooms, and if they have we can just send an outside porter for our traps.'

'You can please yourself,' said Mildred stiffly.

She did not like being reproached, and, retiring huffily into a haughty silence, she sat by listlessly while Philip made the preparations for their departure. The little flat was hot and stuffy under the August sun, and from the road beat up a malodorous sultriness. As he lay in his bed in the small ward with its red, distempered walls he had longed for fresh air and the splashing of the sea against his breast. He felt he would go mad if he had to spend another night in London. Mildred recovered her good temper when she saw the streets of Brighton crowded with people making holiday, and they were both in high spirits as they drove out to Kemp Town. Philip stroked the baby's cheek.

'We shall get a very different colour into them when we've been down here a few days,' he said, smiling.

They arrived at the boarding-house and dismissed the cab. An untidy maid opened the door and, when Philip asked if they had rooms, said she would inquire. She fetched her mistress. A middle-aged woman, stout and business-like, came downstairs, gave them the scrutinizing glance of her profession, and asked what accommodation they required.

'Two single rooms, and if you've got such a thing, we'd rather like a cot in one of them.'

'I'm afraid I haven't got that. I've got one nice large double room, and I could let you have a cot.'

'I don't think that would do,' said Philip.

'I could give you another room next week. Brighton's very full just now, and people have to take what they can get.'

461

'If it were only for a few days, Philip, I think we might be able to manage,' said Mildred.

'I think two rooms would be more convenient. Can you recommend any other place where they take boarders?'

'I can, but I don't suppose they'd have room any more than I have.'

'Perhaps you wouldn't mind giving me the address.'

The house the stout woman suggested was in the next street, and they walked towards it. Philip could walk quite well, though he had to lean on a stick, and he was rather weak. Mildred carried the baby. They went for a little in silence, and then he saw she was crying. It annoyed him, and he took no notice, but she forced his attention.

'Lend me a hanky, will you? I can't get at mine with baby,' she said in a voice strangled with sobs, turning her head away from him.

He gave her his handkerchief, but said nothing. She dried her eyes, and as he did not speak, went on:

'I might be poisonous.'

'Please don't make a scene in the street,' he said.

'It'll look so funny insisting on separate rooms like that. What'll they think of us?'

'If they knew the circumstances I imagine they'd think us surprisingly moral,' said Philip.

She gave him a sidelong glance.

'You're not going to give it away that we're not married?' she asked quickly.

'No.'

'Why won't you live with me as if we were married then?'

'My dear, I can't explain. I don't want to humiliate you, but I simply can't. I daresay it's very silly and unreasonable, but it's stronger than I am. I loved you so much that now ...' he broke off. 'After all, there's no accounting for that sort of thing.'

'A fat lot you must have loved me!' she exclaimed.

The boarding-house to which they had been directed was kept by a bustling maiden lady, with shrewd eyes and voluble speech. They could have one double room for twenty-five shillings a week each, and five shillings extra for the baby, or they could have two single rooms for a pound a week more.

'I have to charge that much more,' the woman explained apologetically, 'because if I'm pushed to it I can put two beds even in the single rooms.'

'I daresay that won't ruin us. What do you think, Mildred?'

'Oh, I don't mind. Anything's good enough for me,' she answered.

Philip passed off her sulky reply with a laugh, and, the landlady having arranged to send for their luggage, they sat down to rest themselves. Philip's foot was hurting him a little, and he was glad to put it up on a chair.

'I suppose you don't mind my sitting in the same room with you,' said Mildred aggressively.

'Don't let's quarrel, Mildred,' he said gently.

'I didn't know you was so well off you could afford to throw away a pound a week.'

'Don't be angry with me. I assure you it's the only way we can live together at all.'

'I suppose you despise me, that's it.'

'Of course I don't. Why should I?'

'It's so unnatural.'

'Is it? You're not in love with me, are you?'

'Me? Who d'you take me for?'

'It's not as if you were a very passionate woman, you're not that.'

'It's so humiliating,' she said sulkily.

'Oh, I wouldn't fuss about that if I were you.'

There were about a dozen people in the boarding-house. They ate in a narrow, dark room at a long table, at the head of which the landlady sat and carved. The food was bad. The landlady called it French cooking, by which she meant that the poor quality of the materials was disguised by ill-made sauces: plaice masqueraded as sole and New Zealand mutton as lamb. The kitchen was small and inconvenient, so that everything was served up lukewarm. The people were dull and pretentious; old ladies with elderly maiden daughters; funny old bachelors with mincing ways; pale-faced, middle-aged clerks with wives, who talked of their married daughters and their sons who were in a very good position in the Colonies. At table they discussed Miss Corelli's latest novel; some of them liked Lord Leighton better than Mr Alma-Tadema, and some of them liked Mr Alma-Tadema better than Lord Leighton. Mildred soon told the ladies of her romantic marriage with Philip; and he found himself an object of interest because his family, county people in a very good position, had cut him off with a shilling because he married while he was only a stoodent; and Mildred's father, who had a large place down Devonshire way, wouldn't do anything for them because she had married Philip. That was why they had come to a boarding-house and had not a nurse for the baby; but they had to have two rooms because they were both used to a good deal of accommodation and they didn't care to be cramped. The other visitors also had explanations of their presence: one of the single gentlemen generally went to the Metropole for his holiday, but he liked cheerful company and you couldn't get that at one of those expensive hotels; and the old lady with the middle-aged daughter was having her beautiful house in London done up and she said to her daughter: 'Gwennie, my dear, we must have a cheap holiday this year,' and so they had come there, though of course it wasn't at all the kind of thing they were used to. Mildred found them all very superior, and she hated a lot of common, rough people. She liked gentlemen to be gentlemen in every sense of the word.

'When people are gentlemen and ladies,' she said, 'I like them to be gentlemen and ladies.'

The remark seemed cryptic to Philip, but when he heard her say it two or three times to different persons, and found that it aroused hearty agreement, he came to the conclusion that it was only obscure to his own intelligence. It was the first time that Philip and Mildred had been thrown entirely together. In London he did not see her all day, and when he came home the household affairs, the baby, the neighbours, gave them something to talk about till he settled down to work. Now he spent the whole day with her. After breakfast they went down to the beach; the morning went easily enough with a bathe and a stroll along the front; the evening, which they spent on the pier, having put the baby to bed, was tolerable, for there was music to listen to and a constant stream of people to look at (Philip amused himself by imagining who they were and weaving little stories about them; he had got into the habit of answering Mildred's remarks with his mouth only so that his thoughts remained undisturbed); but the afternoons were long and dreary. They sat on the beach. Mildred said they must get all the benefit they could out of Doctor Brighton, and he could not read because Mildred made observations frequently about things in general. If he paid no attention she complained.

'Oh, leave that silly old book alone. It can't be good for you always reading. You'll addle your brain, that's what you'll do, Philip.'

'Oh, rot!' he answered.

'Besides, it's so unsociable.'

He discovered that it was difficult to talk to her. She had not even the power of attending to what she was herself saying, so that a dog running in front of her or the passing of a man in a loud blazer would call forth a remark and then she would forget what she had been speaking of. She had a bad memory for names. and it irritated her not to be able to think of them, so that she would pause in the middle of some story to rack her brains. Sometimes she had to give it up, but it often occurred to her afterwards, and when Philip was talking of something she would interrupt him.

'Collins, that was it. I knew it would come back to me some time. Collins, that's the name I couldn't remember.'

It exasperated him because it showed that she was not listening to anything he said, and yet, if he was silent, she reproached him for sulkiness. Her mind was of an order that could not deal for five minutes with the abstract, and when Philip gave way to his taste for generalizing she very quickly showed that she was bored. Mildred dreamt a great deal, and she had an accurate memory for her dreams, which she would relate every day with prolixity.

One morning he received a long letter from Thorpe Athelny. He was taking his holiday in the theatrical way, in which there was much sound sense, which characterized him. He had done the same thing for ten years. He took his whole family to a hop-field in Kent, not far from Mrs Athelny's home, and they spent three weeks hopping. It kept them in the open air, earned them money, much to Mrs Athelny's satisfaction, and renewed their contact with mother earth. It was upon this that Athelny laid stress. The sojourn in the fields gave them a new strength; it was like a magic ceremony, by which they renewed their youth and the power of their limbs and the sweetness of the spirit: Philip had heard him say many fantastic, rhetorical, and picturesque things on the subject. Now Athelny invited him to come over for a day, he had certain meditations on Shakespeare and the musical glasses which he desired to impart, and the children were clamouring for a sight of Uncle Philip. Philip read the letter again in the afternoon when he was sitting with Mildred on the beach. He thought of Mrs Athelny, cheerful mother of many children, with her kindly hospitality and her good humour; of Sally, grave for her years, with funny little maternal ways and an air of authority, with her long plait of fair hair and her broad forehead; and then in a bunch of all the others, merry, boisterous, healthy, and handsome. His heart went out to them. There was one quality which they had that he did not remember to have noticed in people before, and that was goodness. It had not occurred to him till now, but it was evidently the beauty of their goodness which attracted him. In theory he did not believe in it: if morality were no more than a matter of convenience good and evil had no meaning. He did not like to be illogical, but here was simple goodness, natural and without effort, and he thought it beautiful. Meditating, he slowly tore the letter into little pieces; he did not see how he could go without Mildred, and he did not want to go with her.

It was very hot, the sky was cloudless, and they had been driven to a shady corner. The baby was gravely playing with stones on the beach, and now and then she crawled up to Philip and gave him one to hold, then took it away again and placed it carefully down. She was playing a mysterious and complicated game known only to herself. Mildred was asleep. She lay with her head thrown back and her mouth slightly open; her legs were stretched out, and her boots protruded from her petticoats in a grotesque fashion. His eyes had been resting on her vaguely, but now he looked at her with peculiar attention. He remembered how passionately he had loved her, and he wondered why now he was entirely indifferent to her. The change in him filled him with dull pain. It seemed to him that all he had suffered had been sheer waste. The touch of her hand had filled him with ecstasy; he had desired to enter into her soul so that he could share every thought with her and every feeling; he had suffered acutely because, when silence had fallen between them, a remark of hers showed how far their thoughts had travelled apart, and he had rebelled against the unsurmountable wall which seemed to divide every personality from every other. He found it strangely tragic that he had loved her so madly and now loved her not at all. Sometimes he hated her. She was incapable of learning, and the experience of life had taught her nothing. She was as unmannerly as she had always been. It revolted Philip to hear the insolence with which she treated the hard-worked servant at the boarding-house.

Presently he considered his own plans. At the end of his fourth year he would be able to take his examination in mid-wifery, and a year more would see him qualified. Then he might manage a journey to Spain. He wanted to see the pictures which he knew only from photographs; he felt deeply that El Greco held a secret of peculiar moment to him; and he fancied that in Toledo he would surely find it out. He did not wish to do things grandly, and on a hundred pounds he might live for six months in Spain: if Macalister put him on to another good thing he could make that easily. His heart warmed at the thought of those old beautiful cities, and the tawny plains of Castile. He was convinced that more might be got out of life than offered itself at present, and he thought that in Spain he could live with greater intensity: it might be possible to practise in one of those old cities, there were a good many foreigners, passing or resident, and he should be able to pick up a living. But that would be much later; first he must get one or two hospital appointments; they gave experience and made it easy to get jobs afterwards. He wished to get a berth as ship's doctor on one of the large tramps that took things leisurely enough for a man to see something of the places at which they stopped. He wanted to go to the East; and his fancy was rich with pictures of Bangkok and Shanghai, and the ports of Japan: he pictured to himself palm-trees and skies blue and hot, dark-skinned people, pagodas; the scents of the Orient intoxicated his nostrils. His heart beat with passionate desire for the beauty and the strangeness of the world.

Mildred awoke.

'I do believe I've been asleep,' she said. 'Now then, you naughty girl, what have you been doing to yourself? Her dress was clean yesterday and just look at it now, Philip.'

XCV

WHEN they returned to London Philip began his dressing in the surgical wards. He was not so much interested in surgery as in medicine, which, a more empirical science, offered greater scope to the imagination. The work was a little harder than the corresponding work on the medical side. There was a lecture from nine till ten, when he went into the wards; there wounds had to be dressed, stitches taken out, bandages renewed: Philip prided himself a little on his skill in bandaging, and it amused him to wring a word of approval from a nurse. On certain afternoons in the week there were operations; and he stood in the well of the theatre, in a white jacket, ready to hand the operating surgeon any instrument he wanted or to sponge the blood away so that he could see what he was about. When some rare operation was to be performed the theatre would fill up, but generally there were not more than half a dozen students present, and then the proceedings had a cosiness which Philip enjoyed. At that time the world at large seemed to have a passion for appendicitis, and a good many cases came to the operating theatre for this complaint: the surgeon for whom Philip dressed was in friendly rivalry with a colleague as to which could remove an appendix in the shortest time and with the smallest incision.

In due course Philip was put on accident duty. The dressers took this in turn; it lasted three days, during which they lived in hospital and ate their meals in the common room; they had a room on the ground floor near the casualty ward, with a bed that shut up during the day into a cupboard. The dresser on duty had to be at hand day and night to see to any casualty that came in. You were on the move all the time, and not more than an hour or two passed during the night without the clanging of the bell just above your head, which made you leap out of bed instinctively. Saturday night was of course the busiest time and the closing of the public-houses the busiest hour. Men would be brought in by the police dead drunk and it would be necessary to administer a stomach-pump; women, rather the worse for liquor themselves, would come in with a wound on the head or a bleeding nose which their husbands had given them: some would vow to have the law on him, and others, ashamed, would declare that it had been an accident. What the dresser could manage himself he did, but if there was anything important he sent for the house-surgeon: he did this with care, since the house-surgeon was not vastly pleased to be dragged down five flights of stairs for nothing. The cases ranged from a cut finger to a cut throat. Boys came in with hands mangled by some machine, men were brought who had been knocked down by a cab, and children who had broken a limb while playing: now and then attempted suicides were carried in by the police: Philip saw a ghastly, wild-eyed man with a great gash from ear to ear, and he was in the ward for weeks afterwards in charge of a constable, silent, angry, because he was alive, and sullen; he made no secret of the fact that he would try again to kill himself as soon as he was released. The wards were crowded, and the house-surgeon was faced with a dilemma when patients were brought in by the police: if they were sent on to the station and died there disagreeable things were said in the papers; and it was very difficult sometimes to tell if a man was dying or drunk. Philip did not go to bed till he was tired out, so that he should not have the bother of getting up again in an hour; and he sat in the casualty ward talking in the intervals of work with the night-nurse. She was a grey-haired woman of masculine appearance, who had been night-nurse in the casualty department for twenty years. She liked the work because she was her own mistress and had no sister to bother her. Her movements were slow, but she was immensely capable and she never failed in an emergency. The dressers, often inexperienced or nervous, found her a tower of strength. She had seen thousands of them, and they made no impression upon her: she always called them Mr Brown; and when they expostulated and told her their real names, she merely nodded and went on calling them Mr Brown. It interested Philip to sit with her in the bare room, with its two horse-hair couches and the flaring gas, and listen to her. She had long ceased to look upon the people who came in as human beings; they were drunks, or broken arms, or cut throats. She took the vice and misery and cruelty of the world as a matter of course; she found nothing to praise or blame in human actions: she accepted. She had a certain grim humour.

'I remember one suicide,' she said to Philip, 'who threw himself into the Thames. They fished him out and brought him here, and ten days later he developed typhoid fever from swallowing Thames water.'

'Did he die?'

'Yes, he died all right. I could never make up my mind if it was suicide or not ... They're a funny lot, suicides. I remember one man who couldn't get any work to do and his wife died, so he pawned his clothes and bought a revolver; but he made a mess of it, he only shot out an eye and he got all right. And then, if you please, with an eye gone and a piece of his face blown away, he came to the conclusion that the world wasn't such a bad place after all, and he lived happily ever afterwards. Thing I've always noticed, people don't commit suicide for love, as you'd expect, that's just a fancy of novelists; they commit suicide because they haven't got any money. I wonder why that is.'

'I suppose money's more important than love,' suggested Philip.

Money was in any case occupying Philip's thoughts a good deal just then. He discovered the little truth there was in the airy saying, which himself had repeated, that two could live as cheaply as one, and his expenses were beginning to worry him. Mildred was not a good manager, and it cost them as much to live as if they had eaten in restaurants; the child needed clothes, and Mildred boots, an umbrella, and other small things which it was impossible for her to do without. When they returned from Brighton she had announced her intention of getting a job, but she took no definite steps, and presently a bad cold laid her up for a fortnight. When she was well she answered one or two advertisements, but nothing came of it: either she arrived too late and the vacant place was filled, or the work was more than she felt strong enough to do. Once she got an offer, but the wages were only fourteen shillings a week, and she thought she was worth more than that.

'It's no good letting oneself be put upon,' she remarked. 'People don't respect you if you let yourself go too cheap.'

'I don't think fourteen shillings is so bad,' answered Philip drily.

He could not help thinking how useful it would be towards the expenses of the household, and Mildred was already beginning to hint that she did not get a place because she had not got a decent dress to interview employers in. He gave her the dress, and she made one or two more attempts, but Philip came to the conclusion that they were not serious. She did not want to work. The only way he knew to make money was on the Stock Exchange, and he was very anxious to repeat the lucky experiment of the summer; but war had broken out with the Transvaal and nothing was doing in South Africans. Macalister told him that Redvers Buller would march into Pretoria in a month and then everything would boom. The only thing was to wait patiently. What they wanted was a British reverse to knock things down a bit, and then it might be worth while buying. Philip began reading assiduously the 'city chat' of his favourite newspaper. He was worried and irritable. Once or twice he spoke sharply to Mildred, and since she was neither tactful nor patient she answered with temper, and they quarrelled. Philip always expressed his regret for what he had said, but Mildred had not a forgiving nature, and she would sulk for a couple of days. She got on his nerves in all sorts of ways; by the manner in which she ate, and by the untidiness which made her leave articles of clothing about their sitting-room: Philip was excited by the war and devoured the papers, morning and evening; but she took no interest in anything that happened. She had made the acquaintance of two or three people who lived in the street, and one of them had asked if she would like the curate to call on her. She wore a wedding-ring and called herself Mrs Carey. On Philip's walls were two or three of the drawings which he had made in Paris, nudes, two of women and one of Miguel Ajuria, standing very square on his feet, with clenched fists. Philip kept them because they were the best things he had done, and they reminded him of happy days. Mildred had long looked at them with disfavour.

'I wish you'd take those drawings down, Philip,' she said to him at last. 'Mrs Foreman, of number thirteen, came in yesterday afternoon, and I didn't know which way to look. I saw her staring at them.'

'What's the matter with them?'

'They're indecent. Disgusting, that's what I call it, to have drawings of naked people about. And it isn't nice for baby either. She's beginning to notice things now.'

'How can you be so vulgar?'

'Vulgar? Modest, I call it. I've never said anything, but d'you think I like having to look at those naked people all day long.'

'Have you no sense of humour at all, Mildred?' he asked frigidly.

'I don't know what sense of humour's got to do with it. I've got a good mind to take them down myself. If you want to know what I think about them, I think they're disgusting.'

'I don't want to know what you think about them, and I forbid you to touch them.'

When Mildred was cross with him she punished him through the baby. The little girl was as fond of Philip as he was of her, and it was her great pleasure every morning to crawl into his room (she was getting on for two now and could walk pretty well), and be taken up into his bed. When Mildred stopped this the poor child would cry bitterly. To Philip's remonstrances she replied:

'I don't want her to get into habits.'

And if then he said anything more she said:

'It's nothing to do with you what I do with my child. To hear you talk one would think you was her father. I'm her mother, and I ought to know what's good for her, oughtn't I?'

Philip was exasperated by Mildred's stupidity; but he was so indifferent to her now that it was only at times she made him angry. He grew used to having her about. Christmas came, and with it a couple of days' holiday for Philip. He brought some holly in and decorated the flat, and on Christmas Day he gave small presents to Mildred and the baby. There were only two of them, so they could not have a turkey, but Mildred roasted a chicken and boiled a Christmas pudding which she had bought at a local grocer's. They stood themselves a bottle of wine. When they had dined Philip sat in his arm-chair by the fire, smoking his pipe; and the unaccustomed wine had made him forget for a while the anxiety about money which was so constantly with him. He felt happy and comfortable.

471

Presently Mildred came in to tell him that the baby wanted him to kiss her good night, and with a smile he went into Mildred's bedroom. Then, telling the child to go to sleep, he turned down the gas and, leaving the door open in case she cried, went back into the sitting-room.

'Where are you going to sit?' he asked Mildred.

'You sit in your chair. I'm going to sit on the floor.'

When he sat down she settled herself in front of the fire and leaned against his knees. He could not help remembering that this was how they had sat together in her rooms in the Vauxhall Bridge Road, but the positions had been reversed; it was he who had sat on the floor and leaned his head against her knee. How passionately he had loved her then! Now he felt for her a tenderness he had not known for a long time. He seemed still to feel twined round his neck the baby's soft little arms.

'Are you comfy?' he asked.

She looked up at him, gave a slight smile, and nodded. They gazed into the fire dreamily, without speaking to one another. At last she turned round and stared at him curiously.

'D'you know that you haven't kissed me once since I came here?' she said suddenly.

'D'you want me to?' he smiled.

'I suppose you don't care for me in that way any more?'

'I'm very fond of you.'

'You're much fonder of baby.'

He did not answer, and she laid her cheek against his hand.

'You're not angry with me any more?' she asked presently, with her eyes cast down.

'Why on earth should I be?'

'I've never cared for you as I do now. It's only since I passed through the fire that I've learnt to love you.'

It chilled Philip to hear her make use of the sort of phrase she read in the penny novelettes which she devoured. Then he wondered whether what she said had any meaning for her: perhaps she knew no other way to express her genuine feelings than the stilted language of *The Family Herald*.

'It seems so funny our living together like this.'

He did not reply for quite a long time, and silence fell upon them again; but at last he spoke and seemed conscious of no interval.

'You mustn't be angry with me. One can't help these things. I remember that I thought you wicked and cruel because you did this, that, and the other; but it was very silly of me. You didn't love me, and it was absurd to blame you for that. I thought I could make you love me, but I know now that was impossible. I don't know what it is that makes someone love you, but whatever it is, it's the only thing that matters, and if it isn't there you won't create it by kindness, or generosity, or anything of that sort.'

'I should have thought if you'd loved me really you'd have loved me still.'

'I should have thought so too. I remember how I used to think that it would last for ever; I felt I would rather die than be without you, and I used to long for the time when you would be faded and wrinkled so that nobody cared for you any more and I should have you all to myself.'

She did not answer, and presently she got up and said she was going to bed. She gave a timid little smile.

'It's Christmas Day, Philip, won't you kiss me good night?'

He gave a laugh, blushed slightly, and kissed her. She went to her bedroom and he began to read.

XCVI

THE climax came two or three weeks later. Mildred was driven by Philip's behaviour to a pitch of strange exasperation. There were many different emotions in her soul, and she passed from mood to mood with facility. She spent a great deal of time alone and brooded over her position. She did not put all her feelings into words, she did not even know what they were, but certain things stood out in her mind, and she thought of them over and over again. She had never understood Philip, nor had very much liked him; but she was pleased to have him about her because she thought he was a gentleman. She was impressed because his father had been a doctor and his uncle was a clergyman. She despised him a little because she had made such a fool of him, and at the same time was never quite comfortable in his presence; she could not let herself go, and she felt that he was criticizing her manners.

When she first came to live in the little rooms in Kennington she was tired out and ashamed. She was glad to be left alone. It was a comfort to think that there was no rent to pay; she need not go out in all weathers, and she could lie quietly in bed if she did not feel well. She had hated the life she led. It was horrible to have to be affable and subservient; and even now when it crossed her mind she cried with pity for herself as she thought of the roughness of men and their brutal language. But it crossed her mind very seldom. She was grateful to Philip for coming to her rescue, and when she remembered how honestly he had loved her and how badly she had treated him, she felt a pang of remorse. It was easy to make it up to him. It meant very little to her. She was surprised when he refused her suggestion, but she shrugged her shoulders: let him put on airs if he liked, she did not care, he would be anxious enough in a little while, and then it would be her turn to refuse; if he thought it was any deprivation to her he was very much mistaken. She had no doubt of her power over him. He was peculiar, but she knew him through and through. He had so often quarrelled with her and sworn he would never see her again, and then in a little while he had come on his knees begging to be forgiven. It gave her a thrill to think how he had cringed before her. He would have been glad to lie down on the ground for her to walk on him. She had seen him cry. She knew exactly how to treat him, pay no attention to him, just pretend you didn't notice his tempers, leave him severely alone, and in a little while he was sure to grovel. She laughed a little to herself, good humouredly, when she thought how he had come and eaten dirt before her. She had had her fling now. She knew what men were and did not want to have anything more to do with them. She was quite ready to settle down with Philip. When all was said, he was a gentleman in every sense of the word, and that was something not to be sneezed at, wasn't it? Anyhow, she was in no hurry, and she was not going to take the first step. She was glad to see how fond he was growing of the baby, though it tickled her a good deal; it was comic that he should set so much store on another man's child. He *was* peculiar and no mistake.

But one or two things surprised her. She had been used to his subservience: he was only too glad to do anything for her in the old days, she was accustomed to see him cast down by a cross word and in ecstasy at a kind one; he was different now, and she said to herself that he had not improved in the last year. It never struck her for a moment that there could be any change in his feelings, and she thought it was only acting when he paid no heed to her bad temper. He wanted to read sometimes and told her to stop talking: she did not know whether to flare up or to sulk, and was so puzzled that she did neither. Then came the conversation in which he told her that he intended their relations to be platonic, and, remembering an incident of their common past, it occurred to her that he

474

dreaded the possibility of her being pregnant. She took pains to reassure him. It made no difference. She was the sort of woman who was unable to realize that a man might not have her own obsession with sex; her relations with men had been purely on those lines; and she could not understand that they ever had other interests. The thought struck her that Philip was in love with somebody else, and she watched him, suspecting nurses at the hospital or people he met out; but artful questions led her to the conclusion that there was no one dangerous in the Athelny household; and it forced itself upon her also that Philip, like most medical students, was unconscious of the sex of the nurses with whom his work threw him in contact. They were associated in his mind with a faint odour of iodoform. Philip received no letters, and there was no girl's photograph among his belongings. If he was in love with someone, he was very clever at hiding it; and he answered all Mildred's questions with frankness and apparently without suspicion that there was any motive in them.

'I don't believe he's in love with anybody else,' she said to herself at last.

It was a relief, for in that case he was certainly still in love with her; but it made his behaviour very puzzling. If he was going to treat her like that, why did he ask her to come and live at the flat? It was unnatural. Mildred was not a woman who conceived the possibility of compassion, generosity, or kindness. Her only conclusion was that Philip was queer. She took it into her head that the reasons for his conduct were chivalrous; and, her imagination filled with the extravagances of cheap fiction, she pictured to herself all sorts of romantic explanations for his delicacy. Her fancy ran riot with bitter misunderstandings, purifications by fire, snow-white souls, and death in the cruel cold of a Christmas night. She made up her mind that when they went to Brighton she would put an end to all this nonsense; they would be alone there, everyone would think them husband and wife, and there would be the pier and the band. When she found that nothing would induce Philip to share the same room with her, when he spoke to her about it with a tone in his voice she had never heard before, she suddenly realized that he did not want her. She was astounded. She remembered all he had said in the past and how desperately he had loved her. She felt humiliated and angry, but she had a sort of native insolence which carried her through. He needn't think she was in love with him, because she wasn't. She hated him sometimes, and she longed to humble him; but she found herself singularly powerless; she did not know which way to handle him. She began to be a little nervous with him. Once or twice she cried. Once or twice she set herself to be particularly nice to him; but when she took his arm while they walked along the front at night he made some excuse in a while to release himself, as though it were unpleasant for him to be touched by her. She could not make it out. The only hold she had over him was through the baby, of whom he seemed to grow fonder and fonder: she could make him white with anger by giving the child a slap or a push; and the only time the old, tender smile came back into his eyes was when she stood with the baby in her arms. She noticed it when she was being photographed like that by a man on the beach, and afterwards she often stood in the same way for Philip to look at her.

When they got back to London Mildred began looking for the work she had asserted was so easy to find; she wanted now to be independent of Philip; and she thought of the satisfaction with which she would announce to him that she was going into rooms and would take the child with her. But her heart failed her when she came into closer contact with the possibility. She had grown unused to the long hours, she did not want to be at the beck and call of a manageress, and her dignity revolted at the thought of wearing once more a uniform. She had made out to such of the neighbours as she knew that they were comfortably off: it would be a come-down if they heard that she had to go out and work. Her natural indolence asserted itself. She did not want to leave Philip, and so long as he was willing to provide for her, she did not see why she should. There was no money to throw away, but she got her board and lodging, and he might get better off. His uncle was an old man and might die any day, he would come into a little then, and even as things were, it was better than slaving from morning till night for a few shillings a week. Her efforts relaxed; she kept on reading the advertisement columns of the daily paper merely to show that she wanted to do something if anything that was worth her while presented itself. But panic seized her, and she was afraid that Philip would grow tired of supporting her. She had no hold over him at all now, and she fancied that he only allowed her to stay there because he was fond of the baby. She brooded over it all, and she thought to herself angrily that she would make him pay for all this some day. She could not reconcile herself to the fact that he no longer cared for her. She would make him. She suffered from pique, and sometimes in a curious fashion she desired Philip. He was so cold now that it exasperated her. She thought of him in that way incessantly. She thought that he was treating her very badly, and she did not know what she had done to deserve it. She kept on saying to herself that it was unnatural they should live like that. Then she thought that if things were different and she were going to have a baby, he would be sure to marry her. He was funny, but he was a gentleman in every sense of the word, no one could deny that. At last it became an obsession with her, and she made up her mind to force a change in their relations. He never even kissed her now, and she wanted him to: she remembered how ardently he had been used to press her lips. It gave her a curious feeling to think of it. She often looked at his mouth.

One evening, at the beginning of February, Philip told her that he was dining with Lawson, who was giving a party in his studio to celebrate his birthday; and he would not be in till late; Lawson had bought a couple of bottles of the punch they favoured from the tavern in Beak Street, and they proposed to have a merry evening. Mildred asked if there were going to be women there, but Philip told her there were not; only men had been invited; and they were just going to sit and talk and smoke: Mildred did not think it sounded very amusing; if she were a painter she would have half a dozen models about. She went to bed, but could not sleep, and presently an idea struck her; she got up and fixed the catch on the wicket at the landing, so that Philip could not get in. He came back about one, and she heard him curse when he found that the wicket was closed. She got out of bed and opened.

'Why on earth did you shut yourself in? I'm sorry I've dragged you out of bed.'

'I left it open on purpose, I can't think how it came to be shut.'

'Hurry up and get back to bed, or you'll catch cold.'

He walked into the sitting-room and turned up the gas. She followed him in. She went up to the fire.'

'I want to warm my feet a bit. They're like ice.'

He sat down and began to take off his boots. His eyes were shining and his cheeks were flushed. She thought he had been drinking.

'Have you been enjoying yourself?' she asked, with a smile.

'Yes, I've had a ripping time.'

Philip was quite sober, but he had been talking and laughing, and he was excited still. An evening of that sort reminded him of the old days in Paris. He was in high spirits. He took his pipe out of his pocket and filled it.

'Aren't you going to bed?' she asked.

'Not yet, I'm not a bit sleepy. Lawson was in great form. He talked sixteen to the dozen from the moment I got there till the moment I left.'

'What did you talk about?'

'Heaven knows! Of every subject under the sun. You should have seen us all shouting at the tops of our voices and nobody listening.'

Philip laughed with pleasure at the recollection, and Mildred laughed too. She was pretty sure he had drunk more than was good for him. That was exactly what she had expected. She knew men.

'Can I sit down?' she said.

Before he could answer she settled herself on his knees.

'If you're not going to bed you'd better go and put on a dressing-gown.'

'Oh, I'm all right as I am.' Then putting her arms round his neck, she placed her face against his and said: 'Why are you so horrid to me, Phil?'

He tried to get up, but she would not let him.

'I do love you, Philip,' she said.

'Don't talk damned rot.'

'It isn't, it's true. I can't live without you. I want you.'

He released himself from her arms.

'Please get up. You're making a fool of yourself and you're making me feel a perfect idiot.'

'I love you, Philip. I want to make up for all the harm I did you. I can't go on like this, it's not in human nature.'

He slipped out of the chair and left her in it.

'I'm very sorry, but it's too late.'

She gave a heart-rending sob.

'But why? How can you be so cruel?'

'I suppose it's because I loved you too much. I wore the passion out. The thought of anything of that sort horrifies me. I can't look at you now without thinking of Emil and Griffiths. One can't help those things. I suppose it's just nerves.'

She seized his hand and covered it with kisses.

'Don't,' he cried.

She sank back into the chair.

'I can't go on like this. If you won't love me, I'd rather go away.'

478

'Don't be foolish, you haven't anywhere to go. You can stay here as long as you like, but it must be on the definite understanding that we're friends and nothing more.'

Then she dropped suddenly the vehemence of passion and gave a soft, insinuating laugh. She sidled up to Philip and put her arms round him. She made her voice low and wheedling.

'Don't be such an old silly. I believe you're nervous. You don't know how nice I can be.'

She put her face against his and rubbed his cheek with hers. To Philip her smile was an abominable leer, and the suggestive glitter of her eyes filled him with horror. He drew back instinctively.

'I won't,' he said.

But she would not let him go. She sought his mouth with her lips. He took her hands and tore them roughly apart and pushed her away.

'You disgust me,' he said.

'Me?'

She steadied herself with one hand on the chimney-piece. She looked at him for an instant, and two red spots suddenly appeared on her cheeks. She gave a shrill, angry laugh.

'I disgust *you*.'

She paused and drew in her breath sharply. Then she burst into a furious torrent of abuse. She shouted at the top of her voice. She called him every foul name she could think of. She used language so obscene that Philip was astounded; she was always so anxious to be refined, so shocked by coarseness, that it had never occurred to him that she knew the words she used now. She came up to him and thrust her face in his. It was distorted with passion, and in her tumultuous speech the spittle dribbled over her lips.

'I never cared for you, not once, I was making a fool of you always, you bored me, you bored me stiff, and I hated you, I would never have let you touch me only for the money, and it used to make me sick when I had to let you kiss me. We laughed at you, Griffiths and me, we laughed because you was such a mug. A mug! A mug!'

Then she burst again into abominable invective. She accused him of every mean fault; she said he was stingy, she said he was dull, she said he was vain, selfish; she cast virulent ridicule on everything upon which he was most sensitive. And at last she turned to go. She kept on, with hysterical violence, shouting at him an opprobrious, filthy epithet. She seized the handle of the door and flung it open. Then she turned round and hurled

479

at him the injury which she knew was the only one that really touched him. She threw into the word all the malice and all the venom of which she was capable. She flung it at him as though it were a blow.

'Cripple!'

XCVII

PHILIP awoke with a start next morning, conscious that it was late, and looking at his watch found it was nine o'clock. He jumped out of bed and went into the kitchen to get himself some hot water to shave with. There was no sign of Mildred, and the things which she had used for her supper the night before still lay in the sink unwashed. He knocked at her door.

'Wake up, Mildred. It's awfully late.'

She did not answer, even after a second louder knocking, and he concluded that she was sulking. He was in too great a hurry to bother about that. He put some water on to boil and jumped into his bath, which was always poured out the night before in order to take the chill off. He presumed that Mildred would cook his breakfast while he was dressing and leave it in the sitting-room. She had done that two or three times when she was out of temper. But he heard no sound of her moving, and realized that if he wanted anything to eat he would have to get it himself. He was irritated that she should play him such a trick on a morning when he had overslept himself. There was still no sign of her when he was ready, but he heard her moving about her room. She was evidently getting up. He made himself some tea and cut himself a couple of pieces of bread and butter, which he ate while he was putting on his boots, then bolted downstairs and along the street into the main road to catch his tram. While his eyes sought out the newspaper shops to see the war news on the placards, he thought of the scene of the night before: now that it was over and he had slept on it, he could not help thinking it grotesque; he supposed he had been ridiculous, but he was not master of his feelings; at the time they had been overwhelming. He was angry with Mildred because she had forced him into that absurd position, and then with renewed astonishment he thought of her outburst and the filthy language she had used. He could not help flushing when he remembered her final jibe; but he shrugged his shoulders contemptuously. He had long known that when his fellows were angry with him they never failed to taunt him with his deformity. He had seen men at the hospital imitate his walk, not before him as they used at school, but when they thought he was not looking. He knew now that they did it from no wilful unkindness, but because man is naturally an imitative animal, and because it was an easy way to make people laugh: he knew it, but he could never resign himself to it.

He was glad to throw himself into his work. The ward seemed pleasant and friendly when he entered it. The sister greeted him with a quick, business-like smile.

'You're very late, Mr Carey.'

'I was out on the loose last night.'

'You look it.'

'Thank you.'

Laughing, he went to the first of his cases, a boy with tuberculous ulcers, and removed his bandages. The boy was pleased to see him, and Philip chaffed him as he put a clean dressing on the wound. Philip was a favourite with the patients; he treated them good-humouredly; and he had gentle, sensitive hands which did not hurt them: some of the dressers were a little rough and happy-go-lucky in their methods. He lunched with his friends in the club-room, a frugal meal consisting of a scone and butter, with a cup of cocoa, and they talked of the war. Several men were going out, but the authorities were particular and refused everyone who had not had a hospital appointment. Someone suggested that, if the war went on, in a while they would be glad to take anyone who was qualified; but the general opinion was that it would be over in a month. Now that Roberts was there things would get all right in no time. This was Macalister's opinion too, and he had told Philip that they must watch their chance and buy just before peace was declared. There would be a boom then, and they might all make a bit of money. Philip had left with Macalister instructions to buy him stock whenever the opportunity presented itself. His appetite had been whetted by the thirty pounds he had made in the summer, and he wanted now to make a couple of hundred.

He finished his day's work and got on a tram to go back to Kennington. He wondered how Mildred would behave that evening. It was a nuisance to think that she would probably be surly and refuse to answer his questions. It was a warm evening for the time of year, and even in those grey streets of South London there was the languor of February; nature is restless then after the long winter months, growing things awake from their sleep, and there is a rustle in the earth, a forerunner of spring, as it resumes its eternal activities. Philip would have liked to drive on further, it was distasteful to him to go back to his rooms, and he wanted the air; but the desire to see the child clutched suddenly at his heart strings, and he smiled to himself as he thought of her toddling towards him with a crow of delight. He was surprised, when he reached the house and looked up mechanically at the windows, to see that there was no light. He went upstairs and knocked, but got no answer. When Mildred went out she left the key under the mat and he found it there now. He let himself in and going into the sitting-room struck a match. Something had happened, he did not at once know what; he turned the gas on full and lit it; the room was suddenly filled with the glare and he looked round. He gasped. The whole place was wrecked. Everything in it had been wilfully destroyed. Anger seized him, and he rushed into Mildred's room. It was dark and empty. When he had got a light he saw that she had taken away all her things and the baby's (he had noticed on entering that the go-cart was not in its usual place on the landing, but thought Mildred had taken the baby out); and all the things on the washing-stand had been broken, a knife had been drawn cross-ways through the seats of the two chairs, the pillow had been slit open, there were large gashes in the sheets and the counterpane, the looking-glass appeared to have been broken with a hammer. Philip was bewildered. He went into his own room, and here too everything was in confusion. The basin and the ewer had been smashed, the looking-glass was in fragments, and the sheets were in ribands. Mildred had made a slit large enough to put her hand into the pillow and had scattered the feathers about the room. She had jabbed a knife into the blankets. On the dressing-table were photographs of Philip's mother, the frames had been smashed and the glass shivered. Philip went into the tiny kitchen. Everything that was breakable was broken, glasses, pudding-basins, plates, dishes.

It took Philip's breath away. Mildred had left no letter, nothing but this ruin to mark her anger, and he could imagine the set face with which she had gone about her work. He went back into the sitting-room and looked about him. He was so astonished that he no longer felt angry. He looked curiously at the kitchen-knife and the coal-hammer, which were lying on the table where she had left them. Then his eye caught a large carving-knife in the fireplace which had been broken. It must have taken her a long time to do so much damage. Lawson's portrait of him had been cut cross-ways and gaped hideously. His own drawings had been ripped in pieces; and the photographs, Manet's *Olympia* and the *Odalisque* of Ingres, the portrait of Philip IV, had been smashed with great blows of the coal-hammer. There were gashes in the table-cloth and in the curtains and in the two arm-chairs. They were quite ruined. On one wall over the table which Philip used as his desk was the little bit of Persian rug which Cronshaw had given him. Mildred had always hated it.

'If it's a rug it ought to go on the floor,' she said, 'and it's a dirty stinking bit of stuff, that's all it is.'

It made her furious because Philip told her it contained the answer to a great riddle. She thought he was making fun of her. She had drawn the knife right through it three times, it must have required some strength, and it hung now in tatters. Philip had two or three blue and white plates, of no value, but he had bought them one by one for very small sums and liked them for their associations. They littered the floor in fragments. There were long gashes on the backs of his books, and she had taken the trouble to tear pages out of the unbound French ones. The little ornaments on the chimney-piece lay on the hearth in bits. Everything that it had been possible to destroy with a knife or a hammer was destroyed.

The whole of Philip's belongings would not have sold for thirty pounds, but most of them were old friends, and he was a domestic creature, attached to all those odds and ends because they were his; he had been proud of his little home, and on so little money had made it pretty and characteristic. He sank down now in despair. He asked himself how she could have been so cruel. A sudden fear got him on his feet again and into the passage, where stood a cupboard in which he kept his clothes. He opened it and gave a sigh of relief. She had apparently forgotten it and none of his things was touched.

He went back into the sitting-room and, surveying the scene, wondered what to do; he had not the heart to begin trying to set things straight; besides there was no food in the house, and he was hungry. He went out and got himself something to eat. When he came in he was cooler. A little pang seized him as he thought of the child, and he wondered whether she would miss him; at first perhaps, but in a week she would have forgotten him; and he was thankful to be rid of Mildred. He did not think of her with wrath, but with an overwhelming sense of boredom.

'I hope to God I never see her again,' he said aloud.

The only thing now was to leave the rooms, and he made up his mind to give notice the next morning. He could not afford to make good the damage done, and he had so little money left that he must find cheaper lodgings still. He would be glad to get out of them. The expense had worried him, and now the recollection of Mildred would be in them always. Philip was impatient and could never rest till he had put in action the plan which he had in mind; so on the following afternoon he got in a dealer in second-hand furniture who offered him three pounds for all his goods damaged and undamaged; and two days later he moved into the house opposite the hospital in which he had had rooms when first he became a medical student. The landlady was a very decent woman. He took a bedroom at the top, which she let him have for six shillings a week; it was small and shabby and looked on the yard of the house that backed on to it, but he had nothing now except his clothes and a box of books, and he was glad to lodge so cheaply.

XCVIII

AND now it happened that the fortunes of Philip Carey, of no consequence to any but himself, were affected by the events through which his country was passing. History was being made, and the process was so significant that it seemed absurd it should touch the life of an obscure medical student. Battle after battle, Magersfontein, Colenso, Spion Kop, lost on the playing fields of Eton, had humiliated the nation and dealt the death-blow to the prestige of the aristocracy and gentry who till then had found no one seriously to oppose their assertion that they possessed a natural instinct of government. The old order was being swept away: history was being made indeed. Then the colossus put forth his strength, and, blundering again, at last blundered into the semblance of victory. Cronje surrendered at Paardeberg, Ladysmith was relieved, and at the beginning of March Lord Roberts marched into Bloemfontein.

It was two or three days after the news of this reached London that Macalister came into the tavern in Beak Street and announced joyfully that things were looking brighter on the Stock Exchange. Peace was in sight, Roberts would march into Pretoria within a few weeks, and shares were going up already. There was bound to be a boom.

'Now's the time to come in,' he told Philip. 'It's no good waiting till the public gets on to it. It's now or never.'

He had inside information. The manager of a mine in South Africa had cabled to the senior partner of his firm that the plant was uninjured. They would start working again as soon as possible. It wasn't a speculation, it was an investment. To show how good a thing the senior partner thought it Macalister told Philip that he had bought five hundred shares for both his sisters; he never put them into anything that wasn't as safe as the Bank of England.

'I'm going to put my shirt on it myself,' he said.

The shares were two and an eighth to a quarter. He advised Philip not to be greedy, but to be satisfied with a ten-shilling rise. He was buying three hundred for himself and suggested that Philip should do the same. He would hold them and sell when he thought fit. Philip had great faith in him, partly because he was a Scotsman and therefore by nature cautious, and partly because he had been right before. He jumped at the suggestion.

'I daresay we shall be able to sell before the account,' said Macalister, 'but if not, I'll arrange to carry them over for you.'

It seemed a capital system to Philip. You held on till you got your profit, and you never even had to put your hand in your pocket. He began to watch the Stock Exchange columns of the paper with new interest. Next day everything was up a little, and Macalister wrote to say that he had had to pay two and a quarter for the shares. He said that the market was firm. But in a day or two there was a set-back. The news that came from South Africa was less reassuring, and Philip with anxiety saw that his shares had fallen to two; but Macalister was optimistic, the Boers couldn't hold out much longer, and he was willing to bet a top-hat that Roberts would march into Johannesburg before the middle of April. At the account Philip had to pay out nearly forty pounds. It worried him considerably, but he felt that the only course was to hold on: in his circumstances the loss was too great for him to pocket. For two or three weeks nothing happened; the Boers would not understand that they were beaten and nothing remained for them but to surrender: in fact they had one or two small successes, and Philip's shares fell half a crown more. It became evident that the war was not finished. There was a lot of selling. When Macalister saw Philip he was pessimistic.

'I'm not sure if the best thing wouldn't be to cut the loss. I've been paying out about as much as I want to in differences.'

485

Philip was sick with anxiety. He could not sleep at night; he bolted his breakfast, reduced now to tea and bread and butter, in order to get over to the club reading-room and see the paper; sometimes the news was bad, and sometimes there was no news at all, but when the shares moved it was to go down. He did not know what to do. If he sold now he would lose altogether hard on three hundred and fifty pounds; and that would leave him only eighty pounds to go on with. He wished with all his heart that he had never been such a fool as to dabble on the Stock Exchange, but the only thing was to hold on; something decisive might happen any day and the shares would go up; he did not hope now for a profit, but he wanted to make good his loss. It was his only chance of finishing his course at the hospital. The summer session was beginning in May, and at the end of it he meant to take the examination in midwifery. Then he would only have a year more; he reckoned it out carefully and came to the conclusion that he could manage it, fees and all, on a hundred and fifty pounds; but that was the least it could possibly be done on.

Early in April he went to the tavern in Beak Street anxious to see Macalister. It eased him a little to discuss the situation with him; and to realize that numerous people beside himself were suffering from loss of money made his own trouble a little less intolerable. But when Philip arrived no one was there but Hayward, and no sooner had Philip seated himself than he said:

'I'm sailing for the Cape on Sunday.'

'Are you!' exclaimed Philip.

Hayward was the last person he would have expected to do anything of the kind. At the hospital men were going out now in numbers; the Government was glad to get anyone who was qualified; and others, going out as troopers, wrote home that they had been put on hospital work as soon as it was learned that they were medical students. A wave of patriotic feeling had swept over the country, and volunteers were coming from all ranks of society.

'What are you going as?' asked Philip.

'Oh, in the Dorset Yeomanry. I'm going as a trooper.'

Philip had known Hayward for eight years. The youthful intimacy which had come from Philip's enthusiastic admiration for the man who could tell him of art and literature had long since vanished; but habit had taken its place; and when Hayward was in London they saw one another once or twice a week. He still talked about books with a delicate appreciation.

Philip was not yet tolerant, and sometimes Hayward's conversation irritated him. He no longer believed implicitly that nothing in the world was of consequence but art. He resented Hayward's contempt for action and success. Philip, stirring his punch, thought of his early friendship and his ardent expectation that Hayward would do great things; it was long since he had lost all such illusions, and he knew now that Hayward would never do anything but talk. He found his three hundred a year more difficult to live on now that he was thirty-five than he had when he was a young man; and his clothes, though still made by a good tailor, were worn a good deal longer than at one time he would have thought possible. He was too stout, and no artful arrangement of his fair hair could conceal the fact that he was bald. His blue eyes were dull and pale. It was not hard to guess that he drank too much.

'What on earth made you think of going out to the Cape?' asked Philip.

'Oh, I don't know, I thought I ought to.'

Philip was silent. He felt rather silly. He understood that Hayward was being driven by an uneasiness in his soul which he could not account for. Some power within him made it seem necessary to go and fight for his country. It was strange, since he considered patriotism no more than a prejudice, and, flattering himself on his cosmopolitanism, he had looked upon England as a place of exile. His countrymen in the mass wounded his susceptibilities. Philip wondered what it was that made people do things which were so contrary to all their theories of life. It would have been reasonable for Hayward to stand aside and watch with a smile while the barbarians slaughtered one another. It looked as though men were puppets in the hands of an unknown force, which drove them to do this and that; and sometimes they used their reason to justify their actions; and when this was impossible they did the actions in despite of reason.

'People are very extraordinary,' said Philip. 'I should never have expected you to go out as a trooper.'

Hayward smiled, slightly embarrassed, and said nothing.

'I was examined yesterday,' he remarked at last. 'It was worth while undergoing the *gêne* of it to know that one was perfectly fit.'

Philip noticed that he still used a French word in an affected way when an English one would have served. But just then Macalister came in.

'I wanted to see you, Carey,' he said. 'My people don't feel inclined to hold those shares any more, the market's in such an awful state, and they want you to take them up.'

Philip's heart sank. He knew that was impossible. It meant that he must accept the loss. His pride made him answer calmly:

'I don't know that I think that's worth while. You'd better sell them.'

'It's all very fine to say that, I'm not sure if I can. The market's stagnant, there are no buyers.'

'But they're marked down at one and an eighth.'

'Oh, yes, but that doesn't mean anything. You can't get that for them.'

Philip did not say anything for a moment. He was trying to collect himself.

'D'you mean to say they're worth nothing at all?'

'Oh, I don't say that. Of course they're worth something, but you see, nobody's buying them now.'

'Then you must just sell them for what you can get.'

Macalister looked at Philip narrowly. He wondered whether he was very hard hit.

'I'm awfully sorry, old man, but we're all in the same boat. No one thought the war was going to hang on this way. I put you into them, but I was in myself, too.'

'It doesn't matter at all,' said Philip. 'One has to take one's chance.'

He moved back to the table from which he had got up to talk to Macalister. He was dumbfounded; his head suddenly began to ache furiously; but he did not want them to think him unmanly. He sat on for an hour. He laughed feverishly at everything they said. At last he got up to go.

'You take it pretty coolly,' said Macalister, shaking hands with him. 'I don't suppose anyone likes losing between three and four hundred pounds.'

When Philip got back to his shabby little room he flung himself on his bed, and gave himself over to his despair. He kept on regretting his folly bitterly; and though he told himself that it was absurd to regret, for what had happened was inevitable just because it had happened, he could not help himself. He was utterly miserable. He could not sleep. He remembered all the ways he had wasted money during the last few years. His head ached dreadfully.

The following evening there came by the last post the statement of his account. He examined his passbook. He found that when he had paid everything he would have seven pounds left.

Seven pounds! He was thankful he had been able to pay. It would have been horrible to be obliged to confess to Macalister that he had not the money. He was dressing in the eye-department during the summer session, and he had bought an ophthalmoscope off a student who had one to sell. He had not paid for this, but he lacked the courage to tell the student that he wanted to go back on his bargain. Also he had to buy certain books. He had about five pounds to go on with. It lasted him six weeks; then he wrote to his uncle a letter which he thought very business-like; he said that owing to the war he had had grave losses and could not go on with his studies unless his uncle came to his help. He suggested that the Vicar should lend him a hundred and fifty pounds paid over the next eighteen months in monthly instalments; he would pay interest on this and promised to refund the capital by degrees when he began to earn money. He would be qualified in a year and a half at the latest, and he could be pretty sure then of getting an assistantship at three pounds a week. His uncle wrote back that he could do nothing. It was not fair to ask him to sell out when everything was at its worst, and the little he had he felt that his duty to himself made it necessary for him to keep in case of illness. He ended the letter with a little homily. He had warned Philip time after time, and Philip had never paid any attention to him; he could not honestly say he was surprised; he had long expected that this would be the end of Philip's extravagance and want of balance. Philip grew hot and cold when he read this. It had never occurred to him that his uncle would refuse, and he burst into furious anger; but this was succeeded by utter blankness: if his uncle would not help him he could not go on at the hospital. Panic seized him and, putting aside his pride, he wrote again to the Vicar of Blackstable, placing the case before him more urgently; but perhaps he did not explain himself properly and his uncle did not realize in what desperate straits he was, for he answered that he could not change his mind; Philip was twenty-five and really ought to be earning his living. When he died Philip would come into a little, but till then he refused to give him a penny. Philip felt in the letter the satisfaction of a man who for many years had disapproved of his courses and now saw himself justified.

PHILIP began to pawn his clothes. He reduced his expenses
by eating only one meal a day beside his breakfast; and he
ate it, bread and butter and cocoa, at four so that it should
last him till next morning. He was so hungry by nine o'clock
that he had to go to bed. He thought of borrowing money
from Lawson, but the fear of refusal held him back; at last he
asked him for five pounds. Lawson lent it with pleasure, but,
as he did so, said:

'You'll let me have it back in a week or so, won't you? I've
got to pay my framer, and I'm awfully broke just now.'

Philip knew he would not be able to return it, and the
thought of what Lawson would think made him so ashamed
that in a couple of days he took the money back untouched.
Lawson was just going out to luncheon and asked Philip to
come too. Philip could hardly eat, he was so glad to get some
solid food. On Sunday he was sure of a good dinner from
Athelny. He hesitated to tell the Athelnys what had happened
to him: they had always looked upon him as comparatively
well-to-do, and he had a dread that they would think less well
of him if they knew he was penniless.

Though he had always been poor, the possibility of not
having enough to eat had never occurred to him; it was not
the sort of thing that happened to the people among whom he
lived; and he was as ashamed as if he had some disgraceful
disease. The situation in which he found himself was quite
outside the range of his experience. He was so taken aback that
he did not know what else to do than to go on at the hospital;
he had a vague hope that something would turn up; he could
not quite believe that what was happening to him was true; and
he remembered how during his first term at school he had
often thought his life was a dream from which he would awake
to find himself once more at home. But very soon he foresaw
that in a week or so he would have no money at all. He must
set about trying to earn something at once. If he had been
qualified, even with a club-foot, he could have gone out to the
Cape, since the demand for medical men was now great. Except
for his deformity he might have enlisted in one of the Yeomanry regiments which were constantly being sent out. He
went to the secretary of the Medical School and asked if he
could give him the coaching of some backward student; but the

secretary held out no hope of getting him anything of the sort. Philip read the advertisement columns of the medical papers, and he applied for the post of unqualified assistant to a man who had a dispensary in the Fulham Road. When he went to see him, he saw the doctor glance at his club-foot; and on hearing that Philip was only in his fourth year at the hospital he said at once that his experience was insufficient: Philip understood that this was only an excuse; the man would not have an assistant who might not be as active as he wanted. Philip turned his attention to other means of earning money. He knew French and German and thought there might be some chance of finding a job as correspondence clerk; it made his heart sink, but he set his teeth; there was nothing else to do. Though too shy to answer the advertisements which demanded a personal application, he replied to those which asked for letters; but he had no experience to state and no recommendations: he was conscious that neither his German nor his French was commercial; he was ignorant of the terms used in business; he knew neither shorthand nor typewriting. He could not help recognizing that his case was hopeless. He thought of writing to the solicitor who had been his father's executor, but he could not bring himself to, for it was contrary to his express advice that he had sold the mortgages in which his money had been invested. He knew from his uncle that Mr Nixon thoroughly disapproved of him. He had gathered from Philip's year in the accountant's office that he was idle and incompetent.

'I'd sooner starve,' Philip muttered to himself.

Once or twice the possibility of suicide presented itself to him: it would be easy to get something from the hospital dispensary, and it was a comfort to think that if the worst came to the worst he had at hand the means of making a painless end of himself; but it was not a course that he considered seriously. When Mildred had left him to go with Griffiths his anguish had been so great that he wanted to die in order to get rid of the pain. He did not feel like that now. He remembered that the Casualty Sister had told him how people oftener did away with themselves for want of money than for want of love; and he chuckled when he thought that he was an exception. He wished only that he could talk his worries over with somebody, but he could not bring himself to confess them. He was ashamed. He went on looking for work. He left his rent unpaid for three weeks, explaining to his landlady that he would get money at the end of the month; she did not say anything, but pursed her lips and looked grim. When the end of the month came and she asked if it would be convenient for him to pay something on account, it made him feel very sick to say that he could not; he told her he would write to his uncle and was sure to be able to settle his bill on the following Saturday.

'Well, I 'ope you will, Mr Carey, because I 'ave my rent to pay, and I can't afford to let accounts run on.' She did not speak with anger, but a determination that was rather frightening. She paused for a moment and then said: 'If you don't pay next Saturday, I shall 'ave to complain to the secretary of the 'ospital.'

'Oh yes, that'll be all right.'

She looked at him for a little and glanced round the bare room. When she spoke it was without any emphasis, as though is were quite a natural thing to say.

'I've got a nice 'ot joint downstairs, and if you like to come down to the kitchen you're welcome to a bit of dinner.'

Philip felt himself redden to the soles of his feet, and a sob caught at his throat.

'Thank you very much, Mrs Higgins, but I'm not at all hungry.'

'Very good, sir.'

When she left the room Philip threw himself on his bed. He had to clench his fists in order to prevent himself from crying.

C

SATURDAY. It was the day on which he had promised to pay his landlady. He had been expecting something to turn up all through the week He had found no work. He had never been driven to extremities before, and he was so dazed that he did not know what to do. He had at the back of his mind a feeling that the whole thing was a preposterous joke. He had no more than a few coppers left, he had sold all the clothes he could do without; he had some books and one or two odds and ends upon which he might have got a shilling or two, but the landlady was keeping an eye on his comings and goings: he was afraid she would stop him if he took anything more from his room. The only thing was to tell her that he could not pay his bill. He had not the courage. It was the middle of June. The night was fine and warm. He made up his mind to stay out. He walked slowly along the Chelsea Embankment, because the river was restful and quiet, till he was tired, and then sat on a bench and dozed. He did not know how long he slept; he awoke with a start, dreaming that he was being shaken by a policeman and told to move on; but when he opened his eyes he found himself alone. He walked on, he did not know why, and at last came to Chiswick, where he slept again. Presently the hardness of the bench roused him. The night seemed very long. He shivered. He was seized with a sense of his misery; and he did not know what on earth to do: he was ashamed of having slept on the Embankment; it seemed peculiarly humiliating, and he felt his cheeks flush in the darkness. He remembered stories he had heard of those who did and how among them were officers, clergymen, and men who had been to universities: he wondered if he would become one of them, standing in a line to get soup from a charitable institution. It would be much better to commit suicide. He could not go on like that: Lawson would help him when he knew what straits he was in; it was absurd to let his pride prevent him from asking for assistance. He wondered why he had come such a cropper. He had always tried to do what he thought best, and everything had gone wrong. He had helped people when he could, he did not think he had been more selfish than anyone else, it seemed horribly unjust that he should be reduced to such a pass.

But it was no good thinking about it. He walked on. It was now light: the river was beautiful in the silence, and there was something mysterious in the early day; it was going to be very fine, and the sky, pale in the dawn, was cloudless. He felt very tired, and hunger was gnawing at his entrails, but he could not sit still; he was constantly afraid of being spoken to by a policeman. He dreaded the mortification of that. He felt dirty and wished he could have a wash. At last he found himself at Hampton Court. He felt that if he did not have something to eat he would cry. He chose a cheap eating-house and went in; there was a smell of hot things, and it made him feel slightly sick: he meant to eat something nourishing enough to keep him up for the rest of the day, but his stomach revolted at the sight of food. He had a cup of tea and some bread and butter. He remembered then that it was Sunday and he could go to the Athelnys; he thought of the roast beef and the Yorkshire pudding they would eat; but he was fearfully tired and could not face the happy, noisy family. He was feeling morose and wretched. He wanted to be left alone. He made up his mind that he would go into the gardens of the palace and lie down. His bones ached. Perhaps he could find a pump so that he could wash his hands and face and drink something; he was very thirsty; and now that he was no longer hungry he thought with pleasure of the flowers and the lawns and the great leafy trees. He felt that there he could think out better what he must do. He lay on the grass, in the shade, and lit his pipe. For economy's sake he had for a long time confined himself to two pipes a day; he was thankful now that his pouch was full. He did not know what people did when they had no money. Presently he fell asleep. When he awoke it was nearly midday, and he thought that soon he must be setting out for London so as to be there in the early morning and answer any advertisements which seemed to promise. He thought of his uncle, who had told him that he would leave him at his death the little he had; Philip did not in the least know how much this was: it could not be more than a few hundred pounds. He wondered whether he could raise money on the reversion. Not without the old man's consent, and that he would never give. 'The only thing I can do is to hang on somehow till he dies.' Philip reckoned his age. The Vicar of Blackstable was well over seventy. He had chronic bronchitis, but many old men had that and lived on indefinitely. Meanwhile something must turn up; Philip could not get away from the feeling that his position was altogether abnormal; people in his particular station did not starve. It was because he could not bring himself to believe in the reality of his experience that he did not give way to utter despair. He made up his mind to borrow half a sovereign from Lawson. He stayed in the garden all day and smoked when he felt very hungry; he did not mean to eat anything until he was setting out again for London: it was a long way and he must keep up his strength for that. He started when the day began to grow cooler, and slept on benches when he was tired. No one disturbed him. He had a wash and brush up, and a shave at Victoria, some tea and bread and butter, and while he was eating this read the advertisement columns of the morning paper. As he looked down them his eye fell upon an announcement asking for a salesman in the 'furnishing drapery' department of some well-known stores. He had a curious little sinking of the heart, for with his middle-class prejudices it seemed dreadful to go into a shop; but he shrugged his shoulders – after all what did it matter? – and he made up his mind to have a shot at it. He had a queer feeling that by accepting every humiliation, by going out to meet it even, he was forcing the hand of fate. When he presented himself, feeling horribly shy, in the department at nine o'clock he found that many others were there before him. They were of all ages, from boys of sixteen to men of forty; some were talking to one another in undertones, but most were silent; and when he took up his place those around him gave him a look of hostility. He heard one man say:

'The only thing I look forward to is getting my refusal soon enough to give me time to look elsewhere.'

The man standing next him glanced at Philip and asked:

'Had any experience?'

'No,' said Philip.

He paused a moment and then made a remark: 'Even the smaller houses won't see you without appointment after lunch.'

Philip looked at the assistants. Some were draping chintzes and cretonnes, and others, his neighbour told him, were preparing country orders that had come in by post. At about a quarter past nine the buyer arrived. He heard one of the men who were waiting say to another that it was Mr Gibbons. He was middle-aged, short and corpulent, with a black beard and dark, greasy hair. He had brisk movements and a clever face. He wore a silk hat and a frock coat, the lapel of which was adorned with a white geranium surrounded by leaves. He went into his office, leaving the door open; it was very small and contained only an American roll-desk in the corner, a bookcase, and a cupboard. The men standing outside watched him mechanically take the geranium out of his coat and put it in an ink-pot filled with water. It was against the rules to wear flowers in business.

(During the day the department men who wanted to keep in with the governor admired the flower.

'I've never seen better,' they said; 'you didn't grow it yourself?'

'Yes I did,' he smiled, and a gleam of pride filled his intelligent eyes.)

He took off his hat and changed his coat, glanced at the letters and then at the men who were waiting to see him. He made a slight sign with one finger, and the first in the queue stepped into the office. They filed past him one by one and answered his questions. He put them very briefly, keeping his eyes fixed on the applicant's face.

'Age? Experience? Why did you leave your job?'

He listened to the replies without expression. When it came to Philip's turn he fancied that Mr Gibbons stared at him curiously. Philip's clothes were neat and tolerably cut. He looked a little different from the others.

'Experience?'

'I'm afraid I haven't any,' said Philip.

'No good.'

Philip walked out of the office. The ordeal had been so much less painful that he expected that he felt no particular disappointment. He could hardly hope to succeed in getting a place the first time he tried. He had kept the newspaper and now he looked at the advertisements again: a shop in Holborn needed a salesman too, and he went there; but when he arrived he found that someone had already been engaged. If he wanted to get anything to eat that day he must go to Lawson's studio before he went out to luncheon, so he made his way along the Brompton Road to Yeoman's Row.

'I say, I'm rather broke till the end of the month,' he said, as soon as he found an opportunity. 'I wish you'd lend me half a sovereign, will you?'

It was incredible the difficulty he found in asking for money; and he remembered the casual way, as though almost they were conferring a favour, men at the hospital had extracted small sums out of him which they had no intention of repaying.

'Like a shot,' said Lawson.

But when he put his hand in his pocket he found that he had only eight shillings. Philip's heart sank.

'Oh well, lend me five bob, will you?' he said lightly.

'Here you are.'

Philip went to the public baths in Westminster and spent sixpence on a bath. Then he got himself something to eat. He did not know what to do with himself in the afternoon. He could not go back to the hospital in case anyone should ask him questions, and besides, he had nothing to do there now; they would wonder in the two or three departments he had work in why he did not come, but they must think what they chose, it did not matter: he would not be the first student who had dropped out without warning. He went to the free library, and looked at the papers till they wearied him, then he took out Stevenson's *New Arabian Nights*; but he found he could not read: the words meant nothing to him, and he continued to brood over his helplessness. He kept on thinking the same things all the time, and the fixity of his thoughts made his head ache. At last, craving for fresh air, he went into the Green Park and lay down on the grass. He thought miserably of his deformity, which made it impossible for him to go to the war. He went to sleep and dreamed that he was suddenly sound of foot and out at the Cape in a regiment of Yeomanry; the pictures he had looked at in the illustrated papers gave materials for his fancy; and he saw himself on the veldt, in khaki, sitting with other men round a fire at night. When he awoke he found that it was still quite light, and presently he heard Big Ben strike seven. He had twelve hours to get through with nothing to do. He dreaded the interminable night. The sky was overcast and he feared it would rain; he would have to go to a lodging-house where he could get a bed; he had seen them advertised on lamps outside houses in Lambeth: Good Beds, sixpence; he had never been inside one, and dreaded the foul smell and the vermin. He made up his mind to stay in the open air if he possibly could. He remained in the Park till it was closed and then began to walk about. He was very tired. The thought came to him that an accident would be a piece of luck, so that he could be taken to a hospital and lie there, in a clean bed, for weeks. At midnight he was so hungry that he could not go without food any more, so he went to a coffee stall at Hyde Park Corner and ate a couple of potatoes and had a cup of coffee. Then he walked again. He felt too restless to sleep, and he had a horrible dread of being moved on by the police. He noted that he was beginning to look upon the constable from quite a new angle. This was the third night he had spent out. Now and then he sat on the benches in Piccadilly and towards morning he strolled down to the Embankment. He listened to the striking of Big Ben, marking every quarter of an hour, and reckoned out how long it left till the City woke again. In the morning he spent a few coppers on making himself neat and clean, bought a paper to read the advertisements, and set out once more on the search for work.

He went on in this way for several days. He had very little food and began to feel weak and ill, so that he had hardly enough energy to go on looking for the work which seemed so desperately hard to find. He was growing used now to the long waiting at the back of a shop on the chance that he would be taken on, and the curt dismissal. He walked to all parts of London in answer to the advertisements, and he came to know by sight men who applied as fruitlessly as himself. One or two tried to make friends with him, but he was too tired and too wretched to accept their advances. He did not go any more to Lawson, because he owed him five shillings. He began to be too dazed to think clearly and ceased very much to care what would happen to him. He cried a good deal. At first he was very angry with himself for this and ashamed, but he found it relieved him and somehow made him feel less hungry. In the very early morning he suffered a good deal from cold. One night he went into his room to change his linen; he slipped in about three, when he was quite sure everyone would be asleep, and out again at five; he lay on the bed and its softness was enchanting; all his bones ached, and as he lay he revelled in the pleasure of it; it was so delicious that he did not want to go to sleep. He was growing used to want of food and did not feel very hungry, but only weak. Constantly now at the back of his mind was the thought of doing away with himself, but he used all the strength he had not to dwell on it, because he was afraid the temptation would get hold of him so that he would not be able to help himself. He kept on saying to himself that it would be absurd to commit suicide, since something must happen soon; he could not get over the impression that his situation was too preposterous to be taken quite seriously; it was like an illness which must be endured but from which he was bound to recover. Every night he swore that nothing would induce him to put up with such another and determined next morning to write to his uncle, or to Mr Nixon, the solicitor, or to Lawson; but when the time came he could not bring himself to make the humiliating confession of his utter failure. He did not know how Lawson would take it. In their friendship Lawson had been scatter-brained and he had prided himself on his common sense. He would have to tell the whole story of his folly. He had an uneasy feeling that Lawson, after helping him, would turn the cold shoulder on him. His uncle and the solicitor would of course do something for him, but he dreaded their reproaches. He did not want anyone to reproach him: he clenched his teeth and repeated that what had happened was inevitable just because it had happened. Regret was absurd.

The days were unending, and the five shillings Lawson had lent him would not last much longer. Philip longed for Sunday to come so that he could go to Athelny's. He did not know what prevented him from going there sooner, except perhaps that he wanted so badly to get through on his own; for Athelny, who had been in straits as desperate, was the only person who could do anything for him. Perhaps after dinner he could bring himself to tell Athelny that he was in difficulties. Philip repeated to himself over and over again what he should say. He was dreadfully afraid that Athelny would put him off with airy phrases: that would be so horrible that he wanted to delay as long as possible the putting of him to the test. Philip had lost all confidence in his fellows.

Saturday night was cold and raw. Philip suffered horribly.

From midday on Saturday till he dragged himself wearily to Athelny's house he ate nothing. He spent his last twopence on Sunday morning on a wash and a brush up in the lavatory at Charing Cross.

CI

WHEN Philip rang a head was put out of the window, and in a minute he heard a noisy clatter on the stairs as the children ran down to let him in. It was a pale, anxious, thin face that he bent down for them to kiss. He was so moved by their exuberant affection that, to give himself time to recover, he made excuses to linger on the stairs. He was in a hysterical state and almost anything was enough to make him cry. They asked him why he had not come on the previous Sunday, and he told them he had been ill; they wanted to know what was the matter with him; and Philip, to amuse them, suggested a mysterious ailment, the name of which, double-barrelled and barbarous with its mixture of Greek and Latin (medical nomenclature bristled with such), made them shriek with delight. They dragged Philip into the parlour and made him repeat it for their father's edification. Athelny got up and shook hands with him. He stared at Philip, but with his round, bulging eyes he always seemed to stare. Philip did not know why on this occasion it made him self-conscious.

'We missed you last Sunday,' he said.

Philip could never tell lies without embarrassment, and he was scarlet when he finished his explanation for not coming. Then Mrs Athelny entered and shook hands with him.

'I hope you're better, Mr Carey,' she said.

He did not know why she imagined that anything had been the matter with him, for the kitchen door was closed when he came up with the children, and they had not left him.

'Dinner won't be ready for another ten minutes,' she said, in her slow drawl. 'Won't you have an egg beaten up in a glass of milk while you're waiting?'

There was a look of concern on her face which made Philip uncomfortable. He forced a laugh and answered that he was not at all hungry. Sally came in to lay the table, and Philip began to chaff her. It was the family joke that she would be as fat as an aunt of Mrs Athelny, called Aunt Elizabeth, whom the children had never seen but regarded as the type of obscene corpulence.

'I say, what *has* happened since I saw you last, Sally?' Philip began.

'Nothing that I know of.'

'I believe you've been putting on weight.'

'I'm sure you haven't,' she retorted. 'You're a perfect skeleton.'

Philip reddened.

'That's a *tu quoque*, Sally,' cried her father. 'You will be fined one golden hair of your head. Jane, fetch the shears.'

'Well, he is thin, father,' remonstrated Sally. 'He's just skin and bone.'

'That's not the question, child. He is at perfect liberty to be thin, but your obesity is contrary to decorum.'

As he spoke he put his arm proudly round her waist and looked at her with admiring eyes.

'Let me get on with the table, father. If I am comfortable there are some who don't seem to mind it.'

'The hussy!' cried Athelny, with a dramatic wave of the hand. 'She taunts me with the notorious fact that Joseph, a son of Levi who sells jewels in Holborn, has made her an offer in marriage.'

'Have you accepted him, Sally?' asked Philip.

'Don't you know father better than that by this time? There's not a word of truth in it.'

'Well, if he hasn't made you an offer of marriage,' cried Athelny, 'by Saint George and Merry England, I will seize him by the nose and demand of him immediately what are his intentions.'

'Sit down, father, dinner's ready. Now then, you children, get along with you and wash your hands all of you, and don't shirk it, because I mean to look at them before you have a scrap of dinner, so there.'

Philip thought he was ravenous till he began to eat, but then discovered that his stomach turned against food, and he could eat hardly at all. His brain was weary; and he did not notice that Athelny, contrary to his habit, spoke very little. Philip was relieved to be sitting in a comfortable house, but every now and then he could not prevent himself from glancing out of the window. The day was tempestuous. The fine weather had broken; and it was cold, and there was a bitter wind; now and again gusts of rain drove against the window. Philip wondered what he should do that night. The Athelnys went to bed early, and he could not stay where he was after ten o'clock His heart sank at the thought of going out into the bleak

500

darkness. It seemed more terrible now that he was with his friends than when he was outside and alone. He kept on saying to himself that there were plenty more who would be spending the night out of doors. He strove to distract his mind by talking, but in the middle of his words a spatter of rain against the window would make him start.

'It's like March weather,' said Athelny. 'Not the sort of day one would like to be crossing the Channel.'

Presently they finished, and Sally came in and cleared away.

'Would you like a twopenny stinker?' said Athelny, handing him a cigar.

Philip took it and inhaled the smoke with delight. It soothed him extraordinarily. When Sally had finished Athelny told her to shut the door after her.

'Now we shan't be disturbed,' he said, turning to Philip. 'I've arranged with Betty not to let the children come in till I call them.'

Philip gave him a startled look, but before he could take in the meaning of his words, Athelny, fixing his glasses on his nose with the gesture habitual to him, went on.

'I wrote to you last Sunday to ask if anything was the matter with you, and as you didn't answer I went to your rooms on Wednesday.'

Philip turned his head away and did not answer. His heart began to beat violently. Athelny did not speak, and presently the silence seemed intolerable to Philip. He could not think of a single word to say.

'Your landlady told me you hadn't been in since Saturday night, and she said you owed her for the last month. Where have you been sleeping all this week?'

It made Philip sick to answer. He stared out of the window.

'Nowhere.'

'I tried to find you.'

'Why?' asked Philip.

'Betty and I have been just as broke in our day, only we had babies to look after. Why didn't you come here?'

'I couldn't.'

Philip was afraid he was going to cry. He felt very weak. He shut his eyes and frowned, trying to control himself. He felt a sudden flash of anger with Athelny because he would not leave him alone; but he was broken; and presently, his eyes still closed, slowly in order to keep his voice steady, he told him the story of his adventures during the last few weeks. As he spoke it seemed to him that he had behaved inanely, and it made it still harder to tell. He felt that Athelny would think him an utter fool.

'Now you're coming to live with us till you find something to do,' said Athelny, when he had finished.

Philip flushed, he knew not why.

'Oh, it's awfully kind of you, but I don't think I'll do that.'

'Why not?'

Philip did not answer. He had refused instinctively from fear that he would be a bother, and he had a natural bashfulness of accepting favours. He knew besides that the Athelnys lived from hand to mouth, and with their large family had neither space nor money to entertain a stranger.

'Of course you must come here,' said Athelny. 'Thorpe will tuck in with one of his brothers and you can sleep in his bed. You don't suppose your food's going to make any difference to us.'

Philip was afraid to speak, and Athelny, going to the door, called to his wife.

'Betty,' he said, when she came in. 'Mr Carey's coming to live with us.'

'Oh, that is nice,' she said. 'I'll go and get the bed ready.'

She spoke in such a hearty, friendly tone, taking everything for granted, that Philip was deeply touched. He never expected people to be kind to him, and when they were it surprised and moved him. Now he could not prevent two large tears from rolling down his cheeks. The Athelnys discussed the arrangements and pretended not to notice to what a state his weakness had brought him. When Mrs Athelny left them Philip leaned back in his chair, and looking out of the window laughed a little.

'It's not a very nice night to be out, is it?'

CII

ATHELNY told Philip that he could easily get him something to do in the large firm of linen-drapers in which he himself worked. Several of the assistants had gone to the war, and Lynn and Sedley with patriotic zeal had promised to keep their places open for them. They put the work of the heroes on those who remained, and since they did not increase the wages of these were able at once to exhibit public spirit and effect an economy; but the war continued and trade was less depressed; the holidays were coming, when numbers of the staff went away for a fortnight at a time: they were bound to engage more assistants. Philip's experience had made him doubtful whether even then they would engage him; but Athelny, representing himself as a person of consequence in the firm, insisted that the manager could refuse him nothing. Philip, with his training in Paris, would be very useful; it was only a matter of waiting a little and he was bound to get a well-paid job to design costumes and draw posters. Philip made a poster for the summer sale and Athelny took it away. Two days later he brought it back, saying that the manager admired it very much and regretted with all his heart that there was no vacancy just then in that department. Philip asked whether there was nothing else he could do.

'I'm afraid not.'

'Are you quite sure?'

'Well, the fact is they're advertising for a shop-walker tomorrow,' said Athelny, looking at him doubtfully through his glasses.

'D'you think I stand any chance of getting it?'

Athelny was a little confused; he had led Philip to expect something much more splendid; on the other hand he was too poor to go on providing him indefinitely with board and lodging.

'You might take it while you wait for something better. You always stand a better chance if you're engaged by the firm already.'

'I'm not proud, you know,' smiled Philip.

'If you decide on that you must be there at a quarter to nine tomorrow morning.'

Notwithstanding the war there was evidently much difficulty in finding work, for when Philip went to the shop many men were waiting already. He recognized some whom he had seen in his own searching, and there was one whom he had noticed lying about the Park in the afternoon. To Philip now that suggested that he was as homeless as himself and passed the night out of doors. The men were of all sorts, old and young, tall and short; but every one had tried to make himself smart for the interview with the manager: they had carefully brushed hair and scrupulously clean hands. They waited in a passage which Philip learnt afterwards led up to the dining-hall and the work rooms; it was broken every few yards by five or six steps. Though there was electric light in the shop here was only gas, with wire cages over it for protection, and it flared noisily. Philip arrived punctually, but it was nearly ten o'clock when he was admitted into the office. It was three-cornered, like a

cut of cheese lying on its side: on the walls were pictures of
women in corsets, and two poster-proofs, one of a man in
pyjamas, green and white in large stripes, and the other of a
ship in full sail ploughing an azure sea: on the sail was printed
in large letters 'great white sale'. The widest side of the office
was the back of one of the shop-windows, which was being
dressed at the time, and an assistant went to and fro during
the interview. The manager was reading a letter. He was a
florid man, with sandy hair and a large sandy moustache; from
the middle of his watch-chain hung a bunch of football medals.
He sat in his shirt-sleeves at a large desk with a telephone by
his side; before him were the day's advertisements, Athelny's
work, and cuttings from newspapers pasted on a card. He gave
Philip a glance but did not speak to him; he dictated a letter to
the typist, a girl who sat at a small table in one corner; then he
asked Philip his name, age, and what experience he had had.
He spoke with a cockney twang in a high, metallic voice which
he seemed not able always to control; Philip noticed that his
upper teeth were large and protruding; they gave you the impression that they were loose and would come out if you gave
them a sharp tug.

'I think Mr Athelny has spoken to you about me,' said
Philip.

'Oh, you are the young feller who did that poster?'

'Yes, sir.'

'No good to us, you know, not a bit of good.'

He looked Philip up and down. He seemed to notice that
Philip was in some way different from the men who had preceded him.

'You'd 'ave to get a frock coat, you know. I suppose you
'aven't got one. You seem a respectable young feller. I suppose
you found art didn't pay.'

Philip could not tell whether he meant to engage him or
not. He threw remarks at him in a hostile way.

'Where's your home?'

'My father and mother died when I was a child.'

'I like to give young fellers a chance. Many's the one I've
given their chance to and they're managers of departments
now. And they're grateful to me, I'll say that for them. They
know what I done for them. Start at the bottom of the ladder,
that's the only way to learn the business, and then if you stick
to it there's no knowing what it can lead to. If you suit, one of
these days you may find yourself in a position like what mine
is. Bear that in mind, young feller.'

'I'm very anxious to do my best, sir,' said Philip.

He knew that he must put in the 'sir' whenever he could, but it sounded odd to him, and he was afraid of overdoing it. The manager liked talking. It gave him a happy consciousness of his own importance, and he did not give Philip his decision till he had used a great many words.

'Well, I daresay you'll do,' he said at last, in a pompous way. 'Anyhow, I don't mind giving you a trial.'

'Thank you very much, sir.'

'You can start at once. I'll give you six shillings a week and your keep. Everything found, you know; the six shillings is only pocket money, to do what you like with, paid monthly. Start on Monday. I suppose you've got no cause of complaint with that?'

'No, sir.'

'Harrington Street – d'you know where that is? – Shaftesbury Avenue. That's where you sleep. Number ten, it is. You can sleep there on Sunday night, if you like; that's just as you please, or you can send your box there on Monday.' The manager nodded: 'Good morning.'

CIII

MRS ATHELNY lent Philip money to pay his landlady enough of her bill to let him take his things away. For five shillings and the pawn-ticket on a suit he was able to get from a pawnbroker a frock-coat which fitted him fairly well. He redeemed the rest of his clothes. He sent his box to Harrington Street by Carter Paterson and on Monday morning went with Athelny to the shop. Athelny introduced him to the buyer of the costumes and left him. The buyer was a pleasant, fussy little man of thirty, named Sampson; he shook hands with Philip, and, in order to show his own accomplishment of which he was very proud, asked him if he spoke French. He was surprised when Philip told him he did.

'Any other language?'

'I speak German.'

'Oh! I go over to Paris myself occasionally. *Parlez-vous français?* Ever been to Maxim's?'

Philip was stationed at the top of the stairs in the 'costumes'. His work consisted in directing people to the various departments. There seemed a great many of them as Mr Sampson tripped them off his tongue. Suddenly he noticed that Philip limped.

'What's the matter with your leg?' he asked.

'I've got a club-foot,' said Philip. 'But it doesn't prevent my walking or anything like that.'

The buyer looked at it for a moment doubtfully, and Philip surmised that he was wondering why the manager had engaged him. Philip knew that he had not noticed there was anything the matter with him.

'I don't expect you to get them all correct the first day. If you're in any doubt all you've got to do is to ask one of the young ladies.'

Mr Sampson turned away; and Philip, trying to remember where this or the other department was, watched anxiously for the customer in search of information. At one o'clock he went up to dinner. The dining-room, on the top floor of the vast building, was large, long, and well lit; but all the windows were shut to keep out the dust, and there was a horrid smell of cooking. There were long tables covered with cloths, with big glass bottles of water at intervals, and down the centre salt-cellars and bottles of vinegar. The assistants crowded in noisily, and sat down on forms still warm from those who had dined at twelve-thirty.

'No pickles,' remarked the man next to Philip.

He was a tall thin young man, with a hooked nose and a pasty face; he had a long head, unevenly shaped as though the skull had been pushed in here and there oddly, and on his forehead and neck were large acne spots red and inflamed. His name was Harris. Philip discovered that on some days there were large soup-plates down the table full of mixed pickles. They were very popular. There were no knives and forks, but in a minute a large fat boy in a white coat came in with a couple of handfuls of them and threw them loudly on the middle of the table. Each man took what he wanted; they were warm and greasy from recent washing in dirty water. Plates of meat swimming in gravy were handed round by boys in white jackets, and as they flung each plate down with the quick gesture of a prestidigitator the gravy slopped over on to the table-cloth. Then they brought large dishes of cabbages and potatoes; the sight of them turned Philip's stomach; he noticed that everyone poured quantities of vinegar over them. The noise was awful. They talked and laughed and shouted, and there was the clatter of knives and forks, and strange sounds of eating. Philip was glad to get back into the department. He was beginning to remember where each one was, and had less often to ask one of the assistants, when somebody wanted to know the way.

'First to the right. Second on the left, madam.'

One or two of the girls spoke to him, just a word when things were slack, and he felt they were taking his measure. At five he was sent up again to the dining-room for tea. He was glad to sit down. There were large slices of bread heavily spread with butter; and many had pots of jam, which were kept in the 'store' and had their names written on.

Philip was exhausted when work stopped at half past six. Harris, the man he had sat next to at dinner, offered to take him over to Harrington Street to show him where he was to sleep. He told Philip there was a spare bed in his room, and, as the other rooms were full, he expected Philip would be put there. The house in Harrington Street had been a bootmaker's; and the shop was used as a bedroom; but it was very dark, since the window had been boarded three parts up, and as this did not open the only ventilation came from a small skylight at the far end. There was a musty smell, and Philip was thankful that he would not have to sleep there. Harris took him up to the sitting-room, which was on the first floor; it had an old piano in it with a keyboard that looked like a row of decayed teeth; and on the table in a cigar-box without a lid was a set of dominoes; old numbers of *The Strand Magazine* and of *The Graphic* were lying about. The other rooms were used as bedrooms. That in which Philip was to sleep was at the top of the house. There were six beds in it, and a trunk or a box stood by the side of each. The only furniture was a chest of drawers: it had four large drawers and two small ones, and Philip as the newcomer had one of these; there were keys to them, but as they were all alike they were not of much use, and Harris advised him to keep his valuables in his trunk. There was a looking-glass on the chimney-piece. Harris showed Philip the lavatory, which was a fairly large room with eight basins in a row, and here all the inmates did their washing. It led into another room in which were two baths, discoloured, the woodwork stained with soap; and in them were dark rings at various intervals which indicated the water marks of different baths.

When Harris and Philip went back to their bedroom they found a tall man changing his clothes and a boy of sixteen whistling as loud as he could while he brushed his hair. In a minute or two without saying a word to anybody the tall man went out. Harris winked at the boy, and the boy, whistling

507

still, winked back. Harris told Philip that the man was called Prior; he had been in the army and now served in the silks; he kept pretty much to himself, and he went off every night, just like that, without so much as a good evening, to see his girl. Harris went out too, and only the boy remained to watch Philip curiously while he unpacked his things. His name was Bell and he was serving his time for nothing in the haberdashery. He was much interested in Philip's evening clothes. He told him about the other men in the room and asked him every sort of question about himself. He was a cheerful youth, and in the intervals of conversation sang in a half-broken voice snatches of music-hall songs. When Philip had finished he went out to walk about the streets and look at the crowd; occasionally he stopped outside the doors of restaurants and watched the people going in; he felt hungry, so he bought a bath bun and ate it while he strolled along. He had been given a latchkey by the prefect, the man who turned out the gas at a quarter past eleven, but afraid of being locked out he returned in good time; he had learned already the system of fines: you had to pay a shilling if you came in after eleven, and half a crown after a quarter past, and you were reported besides: if it happened three times you were dismissed.

All but the soldier were in when Philip arrived and two were already in bed. Philip was greeted with cries.

'Oh, Clarence! Naughty boy!'

He discovered that Bell had dressed up the bolster in his evening clothes. The boy was delighted with his joke.

'You must wear them at the social evening, Clarence.'

'He'll catch the belle of Lynn's, if he's not careful.'

Philip had already heard of the social evenings, for the money stopped from the wages to pay for them was one of the grievances of the staff. It was only two shillings a month, and it covered medical attendance and the use of a library of worn novels; but as four shillings a month besides was stopped for washing, Philip discovered that a quarter of his six shillings a week would never be paid to him.

Most of the men were eating thick slices of fat bacon between a roll of bread cut in two. These sandwiches, the assistants' usual supper, were supplied by a small shop a few doors off at twopence each. The soldier rolled in; silently, rapidly, took off his clothes and threw himself into bed. At ten minutes past eleven the gas gave a big jump and five minutes later went out. The soldier went to sleep, but the others crowded round the big window in their pyjamas and nightshirts and, throwing remains of their sandwiches at the women who passed in the street below, shouted to them facetious remarks. The house opposite, six storeys high, was a workshop for Jewish tailors who left off work at eleven; the rooms were brightly lit and there were no blinds to the windows. The sweater's daughter – the family consisted of father, mother, two small boys, and a girl of twenty – went round the house to put out the lights when work was over, and sometimes she allowed herself to be made love to by one of the tailors. The shop assistants in Philip's room got a lot of amusement out of watching the manoeuvres of one man or another to stay behind, and they made small bets on which would succeed. At midnight the people were turned out of the 'Harrington Arms' at the end of the street, and soon after they all went to bed: Bell, who slept nearest the door, made his way across the room by jumping from bed to bed, and even when he got to his own would not stop talking. At last everything was silent but for the steady snoring of the soldier, and Philip went to sleep.

He was awaked at seven by the loud ringing of a bell, and by a quarter to eight they were all dressed and hurrying downstairs in their stockinged feet to pick out their boots. They laced them as they ran along to the shop in Oxford Street for breakfast. If they were a minute later than eight they got none, nor, once in, were they allowed out to get themselves anything to eat. Sometimes, if they knew they could not get into the building in time, they stopped at the little shop near their quarters and bought a couple of buns; but this cost money, and most went without food till dinner. Philip ate some bread and butter, drank a cup of tea, and at half past eight began his day's work again.

'First to the right. Second on the left, madam.'

Soon he began to answer the questions quite mechanically. The work was monotonous and very tiring. After a few days his feet hurt him so that he could hardly stand: the thick soft carpets made them burn, and at night his socks were painful to remove. It was a common complaint, and his fellow 'floormen' told him that socks and boots just rotted away from the continual sweating. All the men in his room suffered in the same fashion, and they relieved the pain by sleeping with their feet outside the bedclothes. At first Philip could not walk at all and was obliged to spend a good many of his evenings in the sitting-room at Harrington Street with his feet in a pail of cold water. His companion on these occasions was Bell, the lad in the haberdashery, who stayed in often to arrange the stamps he collected. As he fastened them with little pieces of stamp paper he whistled monotonously.

CIV

THE social evenings took place on alternate Mondays. There was one at the beginning of Philip's second week at Lynn's. He arranged to go with one of the women in his department.

'Meet 'em 'alf-way,' she said, 'same as I do.'

This was Mrs Hodges, a little woman of five-and-forty, with badly dyed hair; she had a yellow face with a network of small red veins all over it, and yellow whites to her pale blue eyes. She took a fancy to Philip and called him by his Christian name before he had been in the shop a week.

'We've both known what it is to come down,' she said.

She told Philip that her real name was not Hodges, but she always referred to 'me 'usband Misterodges'; he was a barrister and he treated her simply shocking, so she left him as she preferred to be independent like; but she had known what it was to drive in her own carriage, dear – she called everyone dear – and they always had late dinner at home. She used to pick her teeth with the pin of an enormous silver brooch. It was in the form of a whip and a hunting-crop crossed, with two spurs in the middle. Philip was ill at ease in his new surroundings, and the girls in the shop called him 'sidey'. One addressed him as Phil, and he did not answer because he had not the least idea that she was speaking to him; so she tossed her head, saying he was a 'stuck-up thing', and next time with ironical emphasis called him Mister Carey. She was a Miss Jewell, and she was going to marry a doctor. The other girls had never seen him, but they said he must be a gentleman as he gave her such lovely presents.

'Never you mind what they say, dear,' said Mrs Hodges. 'I've 'ad to go through it same as you 'ave. They don't know any better, poor things. You take my word for it, they'll like you all right if you 'old your own same as I 'ave.'

The social evening was held in the restaurant in the basement. The tables were put on one side so that there might be room for dancing, and smaller ones were set out for progressive whist.

'The 'eads 'ave to get there early,' said Mrs Hodges.

She introduced him to Miss Bennett, who was the belle of Lynn's. She was the buyer in the 'Petticoats', and when Philip entered was engaged in conversation with the buyer in the 'Gentlemen's Hosiery'; Miss Bennett was a woman of massive proportions, with a very large red face heavily powdered and a bust of imposing dimensions; her flaxen hair was arranged with elaboration. She was overdressed, but not badly dressed, in black with a high collar, and she wore black *glacé* gloves, in which she played cards; she had several heavy gold chains round her neck, bangles on her wrists, and circular photograph pendants, one being of Queen Alexandra; she carried a black satin bag and chewed Sen-sens.

'Pleased to meet you, Mr Carey,' she said. 'This is your first visit to our social evenings, ain't it? I expect you feel a bit shy, but there's no cause to, I promise you that.'

She did her best to make people feel at home. She slapped them on the shoulders and laughed a great deal.

'Ain't I a pickle?' she cried, turning to Philip. 'What must you think of me? But I can't 'elp meself.'

Those who were going to take part in the social evening came in, the younger members of the staff mostly, boys who had not girls of their own, and girls who had not yet found anyone to walk with. Several of the young gentlemen wore lounge suits with white evening ties and red silk handkerchiefs; they were going to perform, and they had a busy, abstracted air; some were self-confident, but others were nervous, and they watched their public with an anxious eye. Presently a girl with a great deal of hair sat at the piano and ran her hands noisily across the keyboard. When the audience had settled itself she looked round and gave the name of her piece.

'*A Drive in Russia.*'

There was a round of clapping, during which she deftly fixed bells to her wrists. She smiled a little and immediately burst into energetic melody. There was a great deal more clapping when she finished, and when this was over, as an encore, she gave a piece which imitated the sea; there were little trills to represent the lapping waves and thundering chords, with the loud pedal down, to suggest a storm. After this a gentleman sang a song called *Bid me Good-bye*, and as an encore obliged with *Sing me to Sleep*. The audience measured their enthusiasm with a nice discrimination. Everyone was applauded till he gave an encore, and so that there might be no jealousy no one was applauded more than anyone else. Miss Bennett sailed up to Philip.

'I'm sure you play or sing, Mr Carey,' she said archly. 'I can see it in your face.'

'I'm afraid I don't.'

'Don't you even recite?'

'I have no parlour tricks.'

The buyer in the 'Gentlemen's Hosiery' was a well-known reciter, and he was called upon loudly to perform by all the assistants in his department. Needing no pressing, he gave a long poem of tragic character, in which he rolled his eyes, put his hand on his chest, and acted as though he were in great agony. The point, that he had eaten cucumber for supper, was divulged in the last line and was greeted with laughter, a little forced because everyone knew the poem well, but loud and long. Miss Bennett did not sing, play, or recite.

'Oh no, she 'as a little game of her own,' said Mrs Hodges.

'Now, don't you begin chaffing me. The fact is I know quite a lot about palmistry and second sight.'

'Oh, do tell my 'and, Miss Bennett,' cried the girls in her department, eager to please her.

'I don't like telling 'ands, I don't really. I've told people such terrible things and they've all come true, it makes one superstitious like.'

'Oh, Miss Bennett, just for once.'

A little crowd collected round her, and, amid screams of embarrassment, giggles, blushings, and cries of dismay or admiration, she talked mysteriously of fair and dark men, of money in a letter, and of journeys, till the sweat stood in heavy beads on her painted face.

'Look at me,' she said. 'I'm all of a perspiration.'

Supper was at nine. There were cakes, buns, sandwiches, tea, and coffee, all free; but if you wanted mineral water you had to pay for it. Gallantry often led young men to offer the ladies ginger beer, but common decency made them refuse. Miss Bennett was very fond of ginger beer, and she drank two and sometimes three bottles during the evening; but she insisted on paying for them herself. The men liked her for that.

'She's a rum old bird,' they said, 'but mind you, she's not a bad sort, she's not like what some are.'

After supper progressive whist was played. This was very noisy, and there was a great deal of laughing and shouting as people moved from table to table. Miss Bennett grew hotter and hotter.

'Look at me,' she said. 'I'm all of a perspiration.'

In due course one of the more dashing of the young men remarked that if they wanted to dance they'd better begin. The girl who had played the accompaniments sat at the piano and placed a decided foot on the loud pedal. She played a dreamy waltz, marking the time with the bass, while with the right hand she 'tiddled' in alternate octaves. By way of a change she crossed her hands and played the air in the bass.

'She does play well, doesn't she?' Mrs Hodges remarked to Philip. 'And what's more she's never 'ad a lesson in 'er life; it's all ear.'

Miss Bennett liked dancing and poetry better than anything in the world. She danced well, but very, very slowly, and an expression came into her eyes as though her thoughts were far, far away. She talked breathlessly of the floor and the heat and the supper. She said that the Portman Rooms had the best floor in London and she always liked the dances there; they were very select, and she couldn't bear dancing with all sorts of men you didn't know anything about; why, you might be exposing yourself to you didn't know what all. Nearly all the people danced very well, and they enjoyed themselves. Sweat poured down their faces, and the very high collars of the young men grew limp.

Philip looked on, and a greater depression seized him than he remembered to have felt for a long time. He felt intolerably alone. He did not go, because he was afraid to seem supercilious, and he talked with the girls and laughed, but in his heart was unhappiness. Miss Bennett asked him if he had a girl.

'No,' he smiled.

'Oh, well, there's plenty to choose from here. And they're very nice respectable girls, some of them. I expect you'll have a girl before you've been here long.'

She looked at him very archly.

'Meet 'em 'alf-way,' said Mrs Hodges. 'That's what I tell him.'

It was nearly eleven o'clock, and the party broke up. Philip could not get to sleep. Like the others he kept his aching feet outside the bedclothes. He tried with all his might not to think of the life he was leading. The soldier was snoring quietly.

CV

THE wages were paid once a month by the secretary. On payday each batch of assistants, coming down from tea, went into the passage and joined the long line of people waiting orderly like the audience in a queue outside a gallery door. One by one they entered the office. The secretary sat at a desk with wooden bowls of money in front of him, and he asked the employee's name; he referred to a book, quickly, after a suspicious glance at the assistant, said aloud the sum due, and taking money out of the bowl counted it into his hand.

'Thank you,' he said. 'Next.'

'Thank you,' was the reply.

The assistant passed on to the second secretary and before leaving the room paid him four shillings for washing money, two shillings for the club, and any fines that he might have incurred. With what he had left he went back into his department and there waited till it was time to go. Most of the men in Philip's house were in debt with the woman who sold the sandwiches they generally ate for supper. She was a funny old thing, very fat, with a broad, red face, and black hair plastered neatly on each side of the forehead in the fashion shown in early pictures of Queen Victoria. She always wore a little black bonnet and a white apron; her sleeves were tucked up to the elbow; she cut the sandwiches with large, dirty, greasy hands; and there was grease on her bodice, grease on her apron, grease on her skirt. She was called Mrs Fletcher, but everyone addressed her as 'Ma'; she was really fond of the shop assistants, whom she called her boys; she never minded giving credit towards the end of the month, and it was known that now and then she had lent someone or other a few shillings when he was in straits. She was a good woman. When they were leaving or when they came back from the holidays, the boys kissed her fat red cheek; and more than one, dismissed and unable to find another job, had got for nothing food to keep body and soul together. The boys were sensible of her large heart and repaid her with genuine affection. There was a story they liked to tell of a man who had done well for himself at Bradford, and had five shops of his own, and had come back after fifteen years and visited Ma Fletcher and given her a gold watch.

Philip found himself with eighteen shillings left out of his month's pay. It was the first money he had ever earned in his life. It gave him none of the pride which might have been expected, but merely a feeling of dismay. The smallness of the sum emphasized the hopelessness of his position. He took fifteen shillings to Mrs Athelny to pay back part of what he owed her, but she would not take more than half a sovereign.

'D'you know, at that rate it'll take me eight months to settle up with you.'

'As long as Athelny's in work I can afford to wait, and who knows, p'raps they'll give you a rise.'

Athelny kept on saying that he would speak to the manager about Philip, it was absurd that no use should be made of his talents; but he did nothing, and Philip soon came to the conclusion that the press agent was not a person of so much importance in the manager's eyes as in his own. Occasionally he saw Athelny in the shop. His flamboyance was extinguished; and in neat, commonplace, shabby clothes he hurried, a subdued, unassuming little man, through the departments as though anxious to escape notice.

'When I think of how I'm wasted there,' he said at home, 'I'm almost tempted to give in my notice. There's no scope for a man like me. I'm stunted, I'm starved.'

Mrs Athelny, quietly sewing, took no notice of his complaints. Her mouth tightened a little.

'It's very hard to get jobs in these times. It's regular and it's safe; I expect you'll stay there as long as you give satisfaction.'

It was evident that Athelny would. It was interesting to see the ascendancy which the uneducated woman, bound to him by no legal tie, had acquired over the brilliant, unstable man. Mrs Athelny treated Philip with motherly kindness now that he was in a different position, and he was touched by her anxiety that he should make a good meal. It was the solace of his life (and when he grew used to it, the monotony of it was what chiefly appalled him) that he could go every Sunday to that friendly house. It was a joy to sit in the stately Spanish chairs and discuss all manner of things with Athelny. Though his condition seemed so desperate he never left him to go back to Harrington Street without a feeling of exultation. At first Philip, in order not to forget what he had learned, tried to go on reading his medical books, but he found it useless; he could not fix his attention on them after the exhausting work of the day; and it seemed hopeless to continue working when he did not know in how long he would be able to go back to the hospital. He dreamed constantly that he was in the wards. The awakening was painful. The sensation of other people sleeping in the room was inexpressibly irksome to him; he had been used to solitude, and to be with others always, never to be by himself for an instant, was at these moments horrible to him. It was then that he found it most difficult to combat his despair. He saw himself going on with that life, 'First to the right, second on the left, madam', indefinitely; and having to be thankful if he was not sent away: the men who had gone

515

to the war would be coming home soon, the firm had guaranteed to take them back, and this must mean that others would be sacked; he would have to stir himself even to keep the wretched post he had.

There was only one thing to free him and that was the death of his uncle. He would get a few hundred pounds then, and on this he could finish his course at the hospital. Philip began to wish with all his might for the old man's death. He reckoned out how long he could possibly live; he was well over seventy. Philip did not know his exact age, but he must be at least seventy-five; he suffered from chronic bronchitis and every winter had a bad cough. Though he knew them by heart Philip read over and over again the details in his text-book of medicine of chronic bronchitis in the old. A severe winter might be too much for the old man. With all his heart Philip longed for cold and rain. He thought of it constantly, so that it became a monomania. Uncle William was affected by the great heat too, and in August they had three weeks of sweltering weather. Philip imagined to himself that one day perhaps a telegram would come saying that the Vicar had died suddenly, and he pictured to himself his unutterable relief. As he stood at the top of the stairs and directed people to the departments they wanted, he occupied his mind with thinking incessantly what he would do with the money. He did not know how much it would be, perhaps no more than five hundred pounds, but even that would be enough. He would leave the shop at once, he would not bother to give notice, he would pack his box and go without saying a word to anybody; and then he would return to the hospital. That was the first thing. Would he have forgotten much? In six months he could get it all back, and then he would take his three examinations as soon as he could, midwifery first, then medicine and surgery. The awful fear seized him that his uncle, notwithstanding his promises, might leave everything he had to the parish or the church. The thought made Philip sick. He could not be so cruel. But if that happened Philip was quite determined what to do, he would not go on in that way indefinitely; his life was only tolerable because he could look forward to something better. If he had no hope he would have no fear. The only brave thing to do then would be to commit suicide, and, thinking this over too, Philip decided minutely what painless drug he would take and how he would get hold of it. It encouraged him to think that if things became unendurable, he had at all events a way out.

'Second to the right, madam, and down the stairs. First on

the left and straight through. Mr Philips, forward please.'

Once a month, for a week, Philip was 'on duty'. He had to go to the department at seven in the morning and keep an eye on the sweepers. When they finished he had to take the sheets off the cases and the models. Then, in the evening when the assistants left, he had to put back the sheets on the models and the cases and 'gang' the sweepers again. It was a dusty, dirty job. He was not allowed to read or write or smoke, but just had to walk about, and the time hung heavily on his hands. When he went off at half past nine he had supper given him, and this was the only consolation; for tea at five o'clock had left him with a healthy appetite, and the bread and cheese, the abundant cocoa, which the firm provided, were welcome.

One day when Philip had been at Lynn's for three months, Mr Sampson, the buyer, came into the department, fuming with anger. The manager, happening to notice the costume window as he came in, had sent for the buyer and made satirical remarks upon the colour scheme. Forced to submit in silence to his superior's sarcasm, Mr Sampson took it out of the assistants; and he rated the wretched fellow whose duty it was to dress the window.

'If you want a thing well done you must do it yourself,' Mr Sampson stormed. 'I've always said it and I always shall. One can't leave anything to you chaps. Intelligent you call yourselves, do you? Intelligent!'

He threw the word at the assistants as though it were the bitterest term of reproach.

'Don't you know that if you put an electric blue in the window it'll kill all the other blues?'

He looked round the department ferociously, and his eye fell upon Philip.

'You'll dress the window next Friday, Carey. Let's see what you can make of it.'

He went into his office, muttering angrily. Philip's heart sank. When Friday morning came he went into the window with a sickening sense of shame. His cheeks were burning. It was horrible to display himself to the passers-by, and though he told himself it was foolish to give way to such a feeling he turned his back to the street. There was not much chance that any of the students at the hospital would pass along Oxford Street at that hour, and he knew hardly anyone else in London; but as Philip worked, with a huge lump in his throat, he fancied that on turning round he would catch the eye of some man he knew. He made all the haste he could. By the simple observation that all reds went together, and by spacing the costumes more than was usual, Philip got a very good effect; and when the buyer went into the street to look at the result he was obviously pleased.

'I knew I shouldn't go far wrong in putting you on the window. The fact is, you and me are gentlemen; mind you, I wouldn't say this in the department, but you and me are gentlemen, and that always tells. It's no good your telling me it doesn't tell, because I know it does tell.'

Philip was put on the job regularly, but he could not accustom himself to the publicity; and he dreaded Friday morning, on which the window was dressed, with a terror that made him awake at five o'clock and lie sleepless with sickness in his heart. The girls in the department noticed his shamefaced way, and they very soon discovered his trick of standing with his back to the street. They laughed at him and called him 'sidey'.

'I suppose you're afraid your aunt'll come along and cut you out of her will.'

On the whole he got on well enough with the girls. They thought him a little queer, but his club-foot seemed to excuse his not being like the rest, and they found in due course that he was good-natured. He never minded helping anyone, and he was polite and even-tempered.

'You can see he's a gentleman,' they said.

'Very reserved, isn't he?' said one young woman to whose passionate enthusiasm for the theatre he had listened unmoved.

Most of them had 'fellers', and those who hadn't said they had rather than have it supposed that no one had an inclination for them. One or two showed signs of being willing to start a flirtation with Philip, and he watched their manoeuvres with grave amusement. He had had enough of love-making for some time; and he was nearly aways tired and often hungry.

CVI

Philip avoided the places he had known in happier times. The little gatherings at the tavern in Beak Street were broken up: Macalister, having let down his friends, no longer went there, and Hayward was at the Cape. Only Lawson remained; and Philip, feeling that now the painter and he had nothing in common, did not wish to see him; but one Saturday afternoon, after dinner, having changed his clothes he walked down Regent Street to go to the free library in St Martin's Lane, meaning to spend the afternoon there, and suddenly found himself face to face with him. His first instinct was to pass on without a word, but Lawson did not give him the opportunity.

'Where on earth have you been all this time?' he cried.

'I?' said Philip.

'I wrote you and asked you to come to the studio for a beano and you never even answered.'

'I didn't get your letter.'

'No, I know. I went to the hospital to ask for you, and I saw my letter in the rack. Have you chucked the Medical?'

Philip hesitated for a moment. He was ashamed to tell the truth, but the shame he felt angered him, and he forced himself to speak. He could not help reddening.

'Yes, I lost the little money I had. I couldn't afford to go on with it.'

'I say, I'm awfully sorry. What are you doing?'

'I'm a shop-walker.'

The words choked Philip, but he was determined not to shirk the truth. He kept his eyes on Lawson and saw his embarrassment. Philip smiled savagely.

'If you went into Lynn and Sedley's, and made your way into the "Made Robes" department, you would see me in a frock-coat, walking about with a *dégagé* air and directing ladies who want to buy petticoats or stockings. "First to the right, madam, and second on the left." '

Lawson, seeing that Philip was making a jest of it, laughed awkwardly. He did not know what to say. The picture that Philip called up horrified him, but he was afraid to show his sympathy.

'That's a bit of a change for you,' he said.

His words seemed absurd to him, and immediately he wished he had not said them. Philip flushed darkly.

'A bit,' he said. 'By the way, I owe you five bob.'

He put his hand in his pocket and pulled out some silver.

'Oh, it doesn't matter. I'd forgotten all about it.'

'Go on, take it.'

Lawson received the money silently. They stood in the middle of the pavement, and people jostled them as they passed. There was a sardonic twinkle in Philip's eyes which made the painter intensely uncomfortable, and he could not tell that Philip's heart was heavy with despair. Lawson wanted dreadfully to do something, but he did not know what to do.

'I say, won't you come to the studio and have a talk?'

'No,' said Philip.

'Why not?'

'There's nothing to talk about.'

He saw the pain come into Lawson's eyes, he could not help it, he was sorry, but he had to think of himself; he could not bear the thought of discussing his situation, he could endure it only by determining resolutely not to think about it. He was afraid of his weakness if once he began to open his heart. Moreover, he took irresistible dislikes to the places where he had been miserable; he remembered the humiliation he had endured when he had waited in that studio, ravenous with hunger, for Lawson to offer him a meal, and the last occasion when he had taken the five shillings off him. He hated the sight of Lawson because he recalled those days of utter abasement.

'Then look here, come and dine with me one night. Choose your own evening.'

Philip was touched with the painter's kindness. All sorts of people were strangely kind to him, he thought.

'It's awfully good of you, old man, but I'd rather not.' He held out his hand. 'Good-bye.'

Lawson, troubled by a behaviour which seemed inexplicable, took his hand, and Philip quickly limped away. His heart was heavy; and, as was usual with him, he began to reproach himself for what he had done : he did not know what madness of pride made him refuse the offered friendship. But he heard someone running behind him and presently Lawson's voice calling him; he stopped and suddenly the feeling of hostility got the better of him; he presented to Lawson a cold, set face.

'What is it?'

'I suppose you heard about Hayward, didn't you?'

'I know he went to the Cape.'

'He died, you know, soon after landing.'

For a moment Philip did not answer. He could hardly believe his ears.

'How?' he asked.

'Oh, enteric. Hard luck, wasn't it? I thought you mightn't know. Gave me a bit of a turn when I heard it.'

Lawson nodded quickly and walked away. Philip felt a shiver pass through his heart. He had never before lost a friend of his own age, for the death of Cronshaw, a man so much older than himself, had seemed to come in the normal course of things. The news gave him a peculiar shock. It reminded him of his own mortality, for like everyone else Philip, knowing perfectly that all men must die, had no intimate feeling that the same must apply to himself; and Hayward's death, though he had long ceased to have any warm feeling for him, affected him deeply. He remembered on a sudden all the good talks they had had, and it pained him to think that they would never talk with one another again; he remembered their first meeting, and the pleasant months they had spent together in Heidelberg. Philip's heart sank as he thought of the lost years. He walked on mechanically, not noticing where he went, and realized suddenly, with a movement of irritation, that instead of turning down the Haymarket he had sauntered along Shaftesbury Avenue. It bored him to retrace his steps; and besides, with that news, he did not want to read, he wanted to sit alone and think. He made up his mind to go to the British Museum. Solitude was now his only luxury. Since he had been at Lynn's he had often gone there and sat in front of the groups from the Parthenon; and, not deliberately thinking, had allowed their divine masses to rest his troubled soul. But this afternoon they had nothing to say to him, and after a few minutes, impatiently, he wandered out of the room. There were too many people, provincials with foolish faces, foreigners poring over guide-books; their hideousness besmirched the everlasting masterpieces, their restlessness troubled the god's immortal repose. He went into another room and here there was hardly anyone. Philip sat down wearily. His nerves were on edge. He could not get the people out of his mind. Sometimes at Lynn's they affected him in the same way, and he looked at them file past him with horror; they were so ugly and there was such meanness in their faces, it was terrifying; their features were distorted with paltry desires, and you felt they were strange to any ideas of beauty. They had furtive eyes and weak chins. There was no wickedness in them, but only pettiness and vulgarity. Their humour was a low facetiousness. Sometimes he found himself looking at them to see what animal they resembled (he tried not to, for it quickly became an obsession), and he saw in them all the sheep or the horse or the fox or the goat. Human beings filled him with disgust.

But presently the influence of the place descended upon him. He felt quieter. He began to look absently at the tombstones with which the room was lined. They were the work of Athenian stone-masons of the fourth and fifth centuries before Christ, and they were very simple, work of no great talent but with the exquisite spirit of Athens upon them; time had mellowed the marble to the colour of honey, so that unconsciously one thought of the bees of Hymettus, and softened

521

their outlines. Some represented a nude figure, seated on a bench, some the departure of the dead from those who loved him, and some the dead clasping hands with one who remained behind. On all was the tragic word farewell; that and nothing more. Their simplicity was infinitely touching. Friend parted from friend, the son from his mother, and the restraint made the survivor's grief more poignant. It was so long, long ago, and century upon century had passed over that unhappiness; for two thousand years those who wept had been dust as those they wept for. Yet the woe was alive still, and it filled Philip's heart so that he felt compassion spring up in it, and he said:

'Poor things, poor things.'

And it came to him that the gaping sightseers and the fat strangers with their guide-books, and all those mean, common people who thronged the shop, with their trivial desires and vulgar cares, were mortal and must die. They too loved and must part from those they loved, the son from his mother, the wife from her husband; and perhaps it was more tragic because their lives were ugly and sordid, and they knew nothing that gave beauty to the world. There was one stone which was very beautiful, a bas-relief of two young men holding each other's hand; and the reticence of line, the simplicity, made one like to think that the sculptor here had been touched with a genuine emotion. It was an exquisite memorial to that than which the world offers but one thing more precious, to a friendship; and as Philip looked at it, he felt the tears come to his eyes. He thought of Hayward and his eager admiration for him when first they met, and how disillusion had come and then indifference, till nothing held them together but habit and old memories. It was one of the queer things of life that you saw a person every day for months and were so intimate with him that you could not imagine existence without him; then separation came and everything went on in the same way, and the companion who had seemed essential proved unnecessary. Your life proceeded and you did not even miss him. Philip thought of those early days in Heidelberg when Hayward, capable of great things, had been full of enthusiasm for the future, and how, little by little, achieving nothing, he had resigned himself to failure. Now he was dead. His death had been as futile as his life. He died ingloriously, of a stupid disease, failing once more, even at the end, to accomplish anything. It was just the same now as if he had never lived.

Philip asked himself desperately what was the use of living at all. It all seemed inane. It was the same with Cronshaw: it was quite unimportant that he had lived; he was dead and forgotten, his book of poems sold in remainder by second-hand booksellers; his life seemed to have served nothing except to give a pushing journalist occasion to write an article in a review. And Philip cried out in his soul:

'What is the use of it?'

The effort was so incommensurate with the result. The bright hopes of youth had to be paid for at such a bitter price of disillusionment. Pain and disease and unhappiness weighed down the scale so heavily. What did it all mean? He thought of his own life, the high hopes with which he had entered upon it, the limitations which his body forced upon him, his friendlessness, and the lack of affection which had surrounded his youth. He did not know that he had ever done anything but what seemed best to do, and what a cropper he had come! Other men, with no more advantages than he, succeeded, and others again, with many more, failed. It seemed pure chance. The rain fell alike upon the just and upon the unjust, and for nothing was there a why and a wherefore.

Thinking of Cronshaw, Philip remembered the Persian rug which he had given him, telling him that it offered an answer to his question upon the meaning of life; and suddenly the answer occurred to him: he chuckled: now that he had it, it was like one of the puzzles which you worry over till you are shown the solution and then cannot imagine how it could ever have escaped you. The answer was obvious. Life had no meaning. On the earth, satellite of a star speeding through space, living things had arisen under the influence of conditions which were part of the planet's history; and as there had been a beginning of life upon it, so, under the influence of other conditions, there would be an end: man, no more significant than other forms of life, had come not as the climax of creation but as a physical reaction to the environment. Philip remembered the story of the Eastern King who, desiring to know the history of man, was brought by a sage five hundred volumes; busy with affairs of state, he bade him go and condense it; in twenty years the sage returned and his history now was in no more than fifty volumes, but the King, too old then to read so many ponderous tomes, bade him go and shorten it once more; twenty years passed again and the sage, old and grey, brought a single book in which was the knowledge the King had sought; but the King lay on his death-bed, and he had no time to read even that; and then the sage gave him the history of man in a single line; it was this: he was born, he suffered, and he died. There was no meaning in life, and man by living served no end. It was immaterial whether he was born or not born, whether he lived or ceased to live. Life was insignificant and death without consequence. Philip exulted, as he had exulted in his boyhood when the weight of a belief in God was lifted from his shoulders: it seemed to him that the last burden of responsibility was taken from him; and for the first time he was utterly free. His insignificance was turned to power, and he felt himself suddenly equal with the cruel fate which had seemed to persecute him; for, if life was meaningless, the world was robbed of its cruelty. What he did or left undone did not matter. Failure was unimportant and success amounted to nothing. He was the most inconsiderable creature in that swarming mass of mankind which for a brief space occupied the surface of the earth; and he was almighty because he had wrenched from chaos the secret of its nothingness. Thoughts came tumbling over one another in Philip's eager fancy, and he took long breaths of joyous satisfaction. He felt inclined to leap and sing. He had not been so happy for months.

'Oh life,' he cried in his heart, 'oh life, where is thy sting?'

For the same uprush of fancy which had shown him with all the force of mathematical demonstration that life had no meaning, brought with it another idea; and that was why Cronshaw, he imagined, had given him the Persian rug. As the weaver elaborated his pattern for no end but the pleasure of his aesthetic sense, so might a man live his life, or if one was forced to believe that his actions were outside his choosing, so might a man look at his life, that it made a pattern. There was as little need to do this as there was use. It was merely something he did for his own pleasure. Out of the manifold events of his life, his deeds, his feelings, his thoughts, he might make a design, regular, elaborate, complicated, or beautiful; and though it might be no more than an illusion that he had the power of selection, though it might be no more than a fantastic legerdemain in which appearances were interwoven with moonbeams, that did not matter: it seemed, and so to him it was. In the vast warp of life (a river arising from no spring and flowing endlessly to no sea), with the background to his fancies that there was no meaning and that nothing was important, a man might get a personal satisfaction in selecting the various strands that worked out the pattern. There was one pattern, the most obvious, perfect, and beautiful, in which a man was born, grew to manhood, married, produced children, toiled for his bread, and died; but there were others, intricate and won-

derful, in which happiness did not enter and in which success
was not attempted; and in them might be discovered a more
troubling grace. Some lives, and Hayward's was among them,
the blind indifference of chance cut off while the design was
still imperfect; and then the solace was comfortable that it did
not matter; other lives, such as Cronshaw's, offered a pattern
which was difficult to follow: the point of view had to be
shifted and old standards had to be altered before one could
understand that such a life was its own justification. Philip
thought that in throwing over the desire for happiness he was
casting aside the last of his illusions. His life had seemed
horrible when it was measured by its happiness, but now he
seemed to gather strength as he realized that it might be
measured by something else. Happiness mattered as little as
pain. They came in, both of them, as all the other details of
his life came in, to the elaboration of the design. He seemed
for an instant to stand above the accidents of his existence, and
he felt that they could not affect him again as they had done
before. Whatever happened to him now would be more motive
to add to the complexity of the pattern, and when the end
approached he would rejoice in its completion. It would be a
work of art, and it would be none the less beautiful because he
alone knew of its existence, and with his death it would at
once cease to be.

Philip was happy.

CVII

MR SAMPSON, the buyer, took a fancy to Philip. Mr Sampson
was very dashing, and the girls in his department said they
would not be surprised if he married one of the rich customers.
He lived out of town and often impressed the assistants by
putting on his evening clothes in the office. Sometimes he would
be seen by those on sweeping duty coming in next morning
still dressed, and they would wink gravely to one another while
he went into his office and changed into a frock-coat. On these
occasions, having slipped out for a hurried breakfast, he also
would wink at Philip as he walked up the stairs on his way
back and rub his hands.

'What a night! What a night!' he said. 'My word!'

He told Philip that he was the only gentleman there, and he
and Philip were the only fellows who knew what life was.
Having said this, he changed his manner suddenly, called
Philip Mr Carey instead of old boy, assumed the importance

due to his position as buyer, and put Philip back into his place of shop-walker.

Lynn and Sedley received fashion papers from Paris once a week and adapted the costumes illustrated in them to the needs of their customers. Their clientele was peculiar. The most substantial part consisted of women from the smaller manufacturing towns, who were too elegant to have their frocks made locally and not sufficiently acquainted with London to discover good dressmakers within their means. Besides these, incongruously, was a large number of music-hall artistes. This was a connexion that Mr Sampson had worked up for himself and took great pride in. They had begun by getting their stage-costumes at Lynn's, and he had induced many of them to get their other clothes there as well.

'As good as Paquin and half the price,' he said.

He had a persuasive, hail-fellow-well-met air with him which appealed to customers of this sort, and they said to one another:

'What's the good of throwing money away when you can get a coat and skirt at Lynn's that nobody knows don't come from Paris?'

Mr Sampson was very proud of his friendship with the popular favourites whose frocks he made, and when he went out to dinner at two o'clock on Sunday with Miss Victoria Virgo – 'she was wearing that powder blue we made her and I lay she didn't let on it came from us, I 'ad to tell her meself that if I 'adn't designed it with my own hands I'd have said it must come from Paquin' – at her beautiful house in Tulse Hill, he regaled the department next day with abundant details. Philip had never paid much attention to women's clothes, but in course of time he began, a little amused at himself, to take a technical interest in them. He had an eye for colour which was more highly trained than that of anyone in the department, and he had kept from his student days in Paris some knowledge of line. Mr Sampson, an ignorant man conscious of his incompetence, but with a shrewdness that enabled him to combine other people's suggestions, constantly asked the opinion of the assistants in his department in making up new designs; and he had the quickness to see that Philip's criticisms were valuable. But he was very jealous, and would never allow that he took anyone's advice. When he had altered some drawing in accordance with Philip's suggestion, he always finished up by saying:

'Well, it comes round to my own idea in the end.'

One day, when Philip had been at the shop for five months,

Miss Alice Antonia, the well-known serio-comic, came in and asked to see Mr Sampson. She was a large woman, with flaxen hair, and a boldly painted face, a metallic voice, and the breezy manner of a *comédienne* accustomed to be on friendly terms with the gallery boys of provincial music-halls. She had a new song and wished Mr Sampson to design a costume for her.

'I want something striking,' she said. 'I don't want any old thing, you know. I want something different from what anybody else has.'

Mr Sampson, bland and familiar, said he was quite certain they could get her the very thing she required. He showed her sketches.

'I know there's nothing here that would do, but I just want to show you the kind of thing I would suggest.'

'Oh no, that's not the sort of thing at all,' she said, as she glanced at them impatiently. 'What I want is something that'll just hit 'em in the jaw and make their front teeth rattle.'

'Yes, I quite understand, Miss Antonia,' said the buyer, with a bland smile, but his eyes grew blank and stupid.

'I expect I shall 'ave to pop over to Paris for it in the end.'

'Oh, I think we can give you satisfaction, Miss Antonia. What you can get in Paris you can get here.'

When she had swept out of the department Mr Sampson, a little worried, discussed the matter with Mrs Hodges.

'She's a caution and no mistake,' said Mrs Hodges.

'Alice, where art thou?' remarked the buyer, irritably, and thought he had scored a point against her.

His ideas of music-hall costumes had never gone beyond short skirts, a swirl of lace, and glittering sequins; but Miss Antonia had expressed herself on that subject in no uncertain terms.

'Oh, my aunt!' she said.

And the invocation was uttered in such a tone as to indicate a rooted antipathy to anything so commonplace, even if she had not added that sequins gave her the sick. Mr Sampson 'got out' one or two ideas, but Mrs Hodges told him frankly she did not think they would do. It was she who gave Philip the suggestion:

'Can you draw, Phil? Why don't you try your 'and and see what you can do?'

Philip bought a cheap box of water colours, and in the evening while Bell, the noisy lad of sixteen, whistling three notes, busied himself with his stamps, he made one or two sketches. He remembered some of the costumes he had seen in Paris, and he adapted one of them, getting his effect from a combination of violent, unusual colours. The result amused him and next morning he showed it to Mrs Hodges. She was somewhat astonished, but took it at once to the buyer.

'It's unusual,' he said, 'there's no denying that.'

It puzzled him, and at the same time his trained eye saw that it would make up admirably. To save his face he began making suggestions for altering it, but Mrs Hodges, with more sense, advised him to show it to Miss Antonia as it was.

'It's neck or nothing with her, and she may take a fancy to it.'

'It's a good deal more nothing than neck,' said Mr Sampson, looking at the *décolletage*. 'He can draw, can't he? Fancy 'im keeping it dark all this time.'

When Miss Antonia was announced, the buyer placed the design on the table in such a position that it must catch her eye the moment she was shown into his office. She pounced on it at once.

'What's that?' she said. 'Why can't I 'ave that?'

'That's just an idea we got out for you,' said Mr Sampson casually. 'D'you like it?'

'Do I like it!' she said. 'Give me 'alf a pint with a little drop of gin in it.'

'Ah, you see, you don't have to go to Paris. You've only got to say what you want and there you are.'

The work was put in hand at once, and Philip felt quite a thrill of satisfaction when he saw the costume completed. The buyer and Mrs Hodges took all the credit of it; but he did not care, and when he went with them to the Tivoli to see Miss Antonia wear it for the first time he was filled with elation. In answer to her questions he at last told Mrs Hodges how he had learnt to draw – fearing that the people he lived with would think he wanted to put on airs, he had always taken the greatest care to say nothing about his past occupations – and she repeated the information to Mr Sampson. The buyer said nothing to him on the subject, but began to treat him a little more deferentially and presently gave him designs to do for two of the country customers. They met with satisfaction. Then he began to speak to his clients of a 'clever young feller, Paris art-student, you know', who worked for him; and soon Philip, ensconced behind a screen, in his shirt-sleeves, was drawing from morning till night. Sometimes he was so busy that he had to dine at three with the 'stragglers'. He liked it, because there were few of them and they were all too tired to talk; the food also was better, for it consisted of what was left over from the buyers' table. Philip's rise from shop-walker to designer of costumes had a great effect on the department. He realized that he was an object of envy. Harris, the assistant with the queer-shaped head, who was the first person he had known at the shop and had attached himself to Philip, could not conceal his bitterness.

'Some people 'ave all the luck,' he said. 'You'll be a buyer yourself one of these days, and we shall all be calling you "sir".'

He told Philip that he should demand higher wages, for not-withstanding the difficult work he was now engaged in, he received no more than the six shillings a week with which he started. But it was a ticklish matter to ask for a rise. The manager had a sardonic way of dealing with such applicants.

'Think you're worth more, do you? How much d'you think you're worth, eh?'

The assistant, with his heart in his mouth, would suggest that he thought he ought to have another two shillings a week.

'Oh, very well, if you think you're worth it. You can 'ave it.' Then he paused and sometimes, with a steely eye, added: 'And you can 'ave your notice too.'

It was no use then to withdraw your request, you had to go. The manager's idea was that assistants who were dissatisfied did not work properly, and if they were not worth a rise it was better to sack them at once. The result was that they never asked for one unless they were prepared to leave. Philip hesitated. He was a little suspicious of the men in his room who told him that the buyer could not do without him. They were decent fellows, but their sense of humour was primitive, and it would have seemed funny to them if they had persuaded Philip to ask for more wages and he were sacked. He could not forget the mortification he had suffered in looking for work, he did not wish to expose himself to that again, and he knew there was small chance of his getting elsewhere a post as designer: there were hundreds of people about who could draw as well as he. But he wanted money very badly; his clothes were worn out, and the heavy carpets rotted his socks and boots; he had almost persuaded himself to take the venture-some step when one morning, passing up from breakfast in the basement through the passage that led to the manager's office, he saw a queue of men waiting in answer to an advertisement. There were about a hundred of them, and whichever was engaged would be offered his keep and the same six shillings a week that Philip had. He saw some of them cast envious glances at him because he had employment. It made him shudder. He dared not risk it.

CVIII

THE winter passed. Now and then Philip went to the hospital, slinking in when it was late and there was little chance of meeting anyone he knew, to see whether there were letters for him. At Easter he received one from his uncle. He was surprised to hear from him, for the Vicar of Blackstable had never written him more than half a dozen letters in his whole life, and they were on business matters.

Dear Philip –

If you are thinking of taking a holiday soon and care to come down here I shall be pleased to see you. I was very ill with my bronchitis in the winter and Doctor Wigram never expected me to pull through. I have a wonderful constitution and I made, thank God, a marvellous recovery.

Yours affectionately,
William Carey

The letter made Philip angry. How did his uncle think he was living? He did not even trouble to inquire. He might have starved for all the old man cared. But as he walked home something struck him; he stopped under a lamp-post and read the letter again; the hand-writing had no longer the business-like firmness which had characterized it; it was larger and wavering: perhaps the illness had shaken him more than he was willing to confess, and he sought in that formal note to express a yearning to see the only relation he had in the world. Philip wrote back that he could come down to Blackstable for a fortnight in July. The invitation was convenient, for he had not known what to do with his brief holiday. The Athelnys went hopping in September, but he could not then be spared, since during that month the autumn models were prepared. The rule of Lynn's was that everyone must take a fortnight whether he wanted it or not; and during that time, if he had nowhere to go, the assistant might sleep in his room, but he was not allowed food. A number had no friends within reasonable distance of London, and to these the holiday was an awkward interval when they had to provide food out of their small wages and, with the whole day on their hands, had nothing to spend. Philip had not been out of London since his visit to

Brighton with Mildred, now two years before, and he longed for fresh air and the silence of the sea. He thought of it with such a passionate desire, all through May and June, that, when at length the time came for him to go, he was listless.

On his last evening, when he talked with the buyer of one or two jobs he had to leave over, Mr Sampson suddenly said to him:

'What wages have you been getting?'

'Six shillings.'

'I don't think it's enough. I'll see that you're put up to twelve when you come back.'

'Thank you very much,' smiled Philip. 'I'm beginning to want some new clothes badly.'

'If you stick to your work and don't go larking about with the girls like what some of them do, I'll look after you, Carey. Mind you, you've got a lot to learn, but you're promising, I'll say that for you, you're promising, and I'll see that you get a pound a week as soon as you deserve it.'

Philip wondered how long he would have to wait for that. Two years?

He was startled at the change in his uncle. When last he had seen him he was a stout man who held himself upright, clean-shaven, with a round, sensual face; but he had fallen in strangely, his skin was yellow; there were great bags under the eyes, and he was bent and old. He had grown a beard during his last illness, and he walked very slowly.

'I'm not at my best today,' he said, when Philip, having just arrived, was sitting with him in the dining-room. 'The heat upsets me.'

Philip, asking after the affairs of the parish, looked at him and wondered how much longer he could last. A hot summer would finish him; Philip noticed how thin his hands were; they trembled. It meant so much to Philip. If he died that summer he could go back to the hospital at the beginning of the winter session; his heart leaped at the thought of returning no more to Lynn's. At dinner the Vicar sat humped up on his chair, and the housekeeper who had been with him since his wife's death said:

'Shall Mr Philip carve, sir?'

The old man, who had been about to do so from disinclination to confess his weakness, seemed glad at the first suggestion to relinquish the attempt.

'You've got a very good appetite,' said Philip.

'Oh yes, I always eat well. But I'm thinner than when you

were here last. I'm glad to be thinner, I didn't like being so fat. Dr Wigram thinks I'm all the better for being thinner than I was.'

When dinner was over the housekeeper brought him some medicine.

'Show the prescription to Master Philip,' he said. 'He's a doctor too. I'd like him to see that he thinks it's all right. I told Dr Wigram that now you're studying to be a doctor he ought to make a reduction in his charges. It's dreadful the bills I've had to pay. He came every day for two months, and he charges five shillings a visit. It's a lot of money, isn't it? He comes twice a week still. I'm going to tell him he needn't come any more. I'll send for him if I want him.'

He looked at Philip eagerly while he read the prescriptions. They were narcotics. There were two of them, and one was a medicine which the Vicar explained he was to use only if his neuritis grew unendurable.

'I'm very careful,' he said. 'I don't want to get into the opium habit.'

He did not mention his nephew's affairs. Philip fancied that it was by way of precaution, in case he asked for money, that his uncle kept dwelling on the financial calls upon him. He had spent so much on the doctor and so much more on the chemist; while he was ill they had had to have a fire every day in his bedroom, and now on Sunday he needed a carriage to go to church in the evening as well as in the morning. Philip felt angrily inclined to say he need not be afraid, he was not going to borrow from him, but he held his tongue. It seemed to him that everything had left the old man now but two things, pleasure in his food and a grasping desire for money. It was a hideous old age.

In the afternoon Dr Wigram came, and after the visit Philip walked with him to the garden gate.

'How d'you think he is?' said Philip.

Dr Wigram was more anxious not to do wrong than to do right, and he never hazarded a definite opinion if he could help it. He had practised at Blackstable for five-and-thirty years. He had the reputation of being very safe, and many of his patients thought it much better that a doctor should be safe than clever. There was a new man at Blackstable – he had been settled there for ten years, but they still looked upon him as an interloper – and he was said to be very clever; but he had not much practice among the better people, because no one really knew anything about him.

'Oh, he's as well as can be expected,' said Dr Wigram in answer to Philip's inquiry.

'Has he got anything seriously the matter with him?'

'Well, Philip, your uncle is no longer a young man,' said the doctor with a cautious little smile, which suggested that after all the Vicar of Blackstable was not an old man either.

'He seems to think his heart's in a bad way.'

'I'm not satisfied with his heart,' hazarded the doctor, 'I think he should be careful, very careful.'

On the tip of Philip's tongue was the question: how much longer can he live? He was afraid it would shock. In these matters a periphrase was demanded by the decorum of life, but, as he asked another question instead, it flashed through him that the doctor must be accustomed to the impatience of a sick man's relatives. He must see through their sympathetic expressions. Philip, with a faint smile at his own hypocrisy, cast down his eyes.

'I suppose he's in no immediate danger?'

This was the kind of question the doctor hated. If you said a patient couldn't live another month the family prepared itself for a bereavement, and if then the patient lived on they visited the medical attendant with the resentment they felt at having tormented themselves before it was necessary. On the other hand, if you said the patient might live a year and he died in a week the family said you did not know your business. They thought of all the affection they would have lavished on the defunct if they had known the end was so near. Dr Wigram made the gesture of washing his hands.

'I don't think there's any grave risk so long as he – remains as he is,' he ventured at last. 'But on the other hand, we mustn't forget that he's no longer a young man, and – well, the machine is wearing out. If he gets over the hot weather I don't see why he shouldn't get on very comfortably till the winter, and then if the winter does not bother him too much, well, I don't see why anything should happen.'

Philip went back to the dining-room where his uncle was sitting. With his skull-cap and a crochet shawl over his shoulders he looked grotesque. His eyes had been fixed on the door, and they rested on Philip's face as he entered. Philip saw that his uncle had been waiting anxiously for his return.

'Well, what did he say about me?'

Philip understood suddenly that the old man was frightened of dying. It made Philip a little ashamed, so that he looked away involuntarily. He was always embarrassed by the weakness of human nature.

'He says he thinks you're much better,' said Philip.

A gleam of delight came into his uncle's eyes.

'I've got a wonderful constitution,' he said. 'What else did he say?' he added suspiciously.

Philip smiled.

'He said that if you take care of yourself there's no reason why you shouldn't live to be a hundred.'

'I don't know that I can expect to do that, but I don't see why I shouldn't see eighty. My mother lived till she was eighty-four.'

There was a little table by the side of Mr Carey's chair, and on it were a Bible and the large volume of the Common Prayer from which for so many years he had been accustomed to read to his household. He stretched out now his shaking hand and took his Bible.

'Those old patriarchs lived to a jolly good old age, didn't they?' he said, with a queer little laugh in which Philip read a sort of timid appeal.

The old man clung to life. Yet he believed implicitly all that his religion taught him. He had no doubt in the immortality of the soul, and he felt that he had conducted himself well enough, according to his capacities, to make it very likely that he would go to heaven. In his long career to how many dying persons must he have administered the consolations of religion! Perhaps he was like the doctor who could get no benefit from his own prescriptions. Philip was puzzled and shocked by that eager cleaving to the earth. He wondered what nameless horror was at the back of the old man's mind. He would have liked to probe into his soul so that he might see in its nakedness the dreadful dismay of the unknown which he suspected.

The fortnight passed quickly and Philip returned to London. He passed a sweltering August behind his screen in the costumes department, drawing in his shirt-sleeves. The assistants in relays went for their holidays. In the evening Philip generally went into Hyde Park and listened to the band. Growing more accustomed to his work it tired him less, and his mind recovering from its long stagnation, sought for fresh activity. His whole desire now was set on his uncle's death. He kept on dreaming the same dream: a telegram was handed to him one morning, early, which announced the Vicar's sudden demise, and freedom was in his grasp. When he awoke and found it was nothing but a dream he was filled with sombre rage. He occupied himself, now that the event seemed likely to happen at any time, with elaborate plans for the future. In these he passed rapidly over the year which he must spend before it was possible for him to be qualified and dwelt on the journey to Spain on which his heart was set. He read books about that country, which he borrowed from the free library, and already he knew from photographs exactly what each city looked like. He saw himself lingering in Cordova on the bridge that spanned the Guadalquivir; he wandered through tortuous streets in Toledo and sat in churches where he wrung from El Greco the secret which he felt the mysterious painter held for him. Athelny entered into his humour, and on Sunday afternoons they made out elaborate itineraries so that Philip should miss nothing that was noteworthy. To cheat his impatience Philip began to teach himself Spanish, and in the deserted sitting-room in Harrington Street he spent an hour every evening doing Spanish exercises and puzzling out with an English translation by his side the magnificent phrases of *Don Quixote*. Athelny gave him a lesson once a week, and Philip learned a few sentences to help him on his journey. Mrs Athelny laughed at them.

'You two and your Spanish!' she said. 'Why don't you do something useful?'

But Sally, who was growing up and was to put up her hair at Christmas, stood by sometimes and listened in her grave way while her father and Philip exchanged remarks in a language she did not understand. She thought her father the most wonderful man who had ever existed, and she expressed her opinion of Philip only through her father's commendations.

'Father thinks a rare lot of your Uncle Philip,' she remarked to her brothers and sisters.

Thorpe, the eldest boy, was old enough to go on the *Arethusa*, and Athelny regaled his family with magnificent descriptions of the appearance the lad would make when he came back in uniform for his holidays. As soon as Sally was seventeen she was to be apprenticed to a dressmaker. Athelny in his rhetorical way talked of the birds, strong enough to fly now, who were leaving the parental nest, and with tears in his eyes told them that the nest would be there still if ever they wished to return to it. A shake-down and a dinner would always be theirs, and the heart of a father would never be closed to the troubles of his children.

'You do talk, Athelny,' said his wife. 'I don't know what trouble they're likely to get into so long as they're steady. So long as you're honest and not afraid of work you'll never be out of a job, that's what I think, and I can tell you I shan't be sorry when I see the last of them earning their own living.'

Child-bearing, hard work, and constant anxiety were beginning to tell on Mrs Athelny; and sometimes her back ached in the evening so that she had to sit down and rest herself. Her ideal of happiness was to have a girl to do the rough work so that she need not herself get up before seven. Athelny waved his beautiful white hand.

'Ah, my Betty, we've deserved well of the state, you and I. We've reared nine healthy children, and the boys shall serve their king; the girls shall cook and sew and in their turn breed healthy children.' He turned to Sally, and to comfort her for the anti-climax of the contrast added grandiloquently: 'They also serve who only stand and wait.'

Athelny had lately added socialism to the other contradictory theories he vehemently believed in, and he stated now:

'In a socialist state we should be richly pensioned, you and I, Betty.'

'Oh, don't talk to me about your socialists, I've got no patience with them,' she cried. 'It only means that another lot of lazy loafers will make a good thing out of the working classes. My motto is, leave me alone; I don't want anyone interfering with me; I'll make the best of a bad job, and the devil take the hindmost.'

'D'you call life a bad job?' said Athelny. 'Never! We've had our ups and downs, we've had our struggles, we've always been poor, but it's been worth it, ay, worth it a hundred times I say when I look round at my children.'

'You do talk, Athelny,' she said, looking at him, not with anger but with scornful calm. 'You've had the pleasant part of the children, I've had the bearing of them, and the bearing with them. I don't say that I'm not fond of them, now they're there, but if I had my time over again I'd remain single. Why, if I'd remained single I might have a little shop by now, and four or five hundred pounds in the bank, and a girl to do the rough work. Oh, I wouldn't go over my life again, not for something.'

Philip thought of the countless millions to whom life is no more than unending labour, neither beautiful nor ugly, but just to be accepted in the same spirit as one accepts the changes of the seasons. Fury seized him because it all seemed useless. He could not reconcile himself to the belief that life had no meaning and yet everything he saw, all his thoughts, added to

536

the force of his conviction. But though fury seized him it was a joyful fury. Life was not so horrible if it was meaningless, and he faced it with a strange sense of power.

CIX

THE autumn passed into winter. Philip had left his address with Mrs Foster, his uncle's housekeeper, so that she might communicate with him, but still went once a week to the hospital on the chance of there being a letter. One evening he saw his name on an envelope in a handwriting he had hoped never to see again. It gave him a queer feeling. For a little while he could not bring himself to take it. It brought back a host of hateful memories. But at length, impatient with himself, he ripped open the envelope.

7 William Street
Fitzroy Square

Dear Phil –

Can I see you for a minute or two as soon as possible. I am in awful trouble and don't know what to do. It's not money.

Yours truly,

Mildred

He tore the letter into little bits and going out into the street scattered them in the darkness.

'I'll see her damned,' he muttered.

A feeling of disgust surged up in him at the thought of seeing her again. He did not care if she was in distress, it served her right whatever it was; he thought of her with hatred, and the love he had had for her aroused his loathing. His recollections filled him with nausea, and as he walked across the Thames he drew himself aside in an instinctive withdrawal from his thought of her. He went to bed, but he could not sleep; he wondered what was the matter with her, and he could not get out of his head the fear that she was ill and hungry; she would not have written to him unless she were desperate. He was angry with himself for his weakness, but he knew that he would have no peace unless he saw her. Next morning he wrote a letter-card and posted it on his way to the shop. He made it as stiff as he could and said merely that he was sorry she was in difficulties and would come to the address she had given at seven o'clock that evening.

It was that of a shabby lodging-house in a sordid street; and when, sick at the thought of seeing her, he asked whether she was in, a wild hope seized him that she had left. It looked the sort of place people moved in and out of frequently. He had not thought of looking at the postmark on her letter and did not know how many days it had lain in the rack. The woman who answered the bell did not reply to his inquiry, but silently preceded him along the passage and knocked on a door at the back.

'Mrs Miller, a gentleman to see you,' she called.

The door was slightly opened, and Mildred looked out suspiciously.

'Oh, it's you,' she said. 'Come in.'

He walked in and she closed the door. It was a very small bedroom, untidy as was every place she lived in; there was a pair of shoes on the floor, lying apart from one another and uncleaned; a hat was on the chest of drawers, with false curls beside it; and there was a blouse on the table. Philip looked for somewhere to put his hat. The hooks behind the door were laden with skirts, and he noticed that they were muddy at the hem.

'Sit down, won't you?' she said. Then she gave a little awkward laugh. 'I suppose you were surprised to hear from me again?'

'You're awfully hoarse,' he answered. 'Have you got a sore throat?'

'Yes, I have had for some time.'

He did not say anything. He waited for her to explain why she wanted to see him. The look of the room told him clearly enough that she had gone back to the life from which he had taken her. He wondered what had happened to the baby; there was a photograph of it on the chimney-piece, but no sign in the room that a child was ever there. Mildred was holding her handkerchief. She made it into a little ball, and passed it from hand to hand. He saw that she was very nervous. She was staring at the fire, and he could look at her without meeting her eyes. She was much thinner than when she had left him; and the skin, yellow and dryish, was drawn more tightly over her cheek-bones. She had dyed her hair and it was now flaxen: it altered her a good deal, and made her look more vulgar.

'I was relieved to get your letter, I can tell you,' she said at last. 'I thought p'raps you weren't at the 'ospital any more.'

Philip did not speak.

'I suppose you're qualified by now, aren't you?'

'No.'

'How's that?'

'I'm no longer at the hospital. I had to give it up eighteen months ago.'

'You are changeable. You don't seem as if you could stick to anything.'

, Philip was silent for another moment, and when he went on it was with coldness.

'I lost the little money I had in an unlucky speculation and I couldn't afford to go on with the Medical. I had to earn my living as best I could.'

'What are you doing then?'

'I'm in a shop.'

'Oh!'

She gave him a quick glance and turned her eyes away at once. He thought that she reddened. She dabbed her palms nervously with the handkerchief.

'You've not forgotten all your doctoring, have you?' She jerked the words out quite oddly.

'Not entirely.'

'Because that's why I wanted to see you.' Her voice sank to a hoarse whisper. 'I don't know what's the matter with me.'

'Why don't you go to a hospital?'

'I don't like to do that, and have all the stoodents staring at me, and I'm afraid they'd want to keep me.'

'What are you complaining of?' asked Philip coldly, with the stereotyped phrase used in the out-patients' room.

'Well, I've come out in a rash, and I can't get rid of it.'

Philip felt a twinge of horror in his heart. Sweat broke out on his forehead.

'Let me look at your throat.'

He took her over to the window and made such examination as he could. Suddenly he caught sight of her eyes. There was deadly fear in them. It was horrible to see. She was terrified. She wanted him to reassure her; she looked at him pleadingly, not daring to ask for words of comfort but with all her nerves astrung to receive them: he had none to offer her.

'I'm afraid you're very ill indeed,' he said.

'What d'you think it is?'

When he told her she grew deathly pale, and her lips even turned yellow: she began to cry, hopelessly, quietly at first and then with choking sobs.

'I'm awfully sorry,' he said at last. 'But I had to tell you.'

'I may just as well kill myself and have done with it.'

He took no notice of the threat.

'Have you got any money?' he asked.

539

'Six or seven pounds.'

'You must give up this life, you know. Don't you think you could find some work to do? I'm afraid I can't help you much, I only get twelve bob a week.'

'What is there I can do now?' she cried impatiently.

'Damn it all, you *must* try to get something.'

He spoke to her very gravely, telling her of her own danger and the danger to which she exposed others, and she listened sullenly. He tried to console her. At last he brought her to a sulky acquiescence in which she promised to do all he advised. He wrote a prescription, which he said he would leave at the nearest chemist's, and he impressed upon her the necessity of taking her medicine with the utmost regularity. Getting up to go, he held out his hand.

'Don't be downhearted, you'll soon get over your throat.'

But as he went her face became suddenly distorted, and she caught hold of his coat.

'Oh, don't leave me,' she cried hoarsely. 'I'm so afraid, don't leave me alone yet. Phil, please. There's no one else I can go to, you're the only friend I've ever had.'

He felt the terror of her soul, and it was strangely like that terror he had seen in his uncle's eyes when he feared that he might die. Philip looked down. Twice that woman had come into his life and made him wretched; she had no claim upon him; and yet, he knew not why, deep in his heart was a strange aching; it was that which, when he received her letter, had left him no peace till he obeyed her summons.

'I suppose I shall never really quite get over it,' he said to himself.

What perplexed him was that he felt a curious physical distaste, which made it uncomfortable for him to be near her.

'What do you want me to do?' he asked.

'Let's go out and dine together. I'll pay.'

He hesitated. He felt that she was creeping back again into his life when he thought she was gone out of it for ever. She watched him with sickening anxiety.

'Oh, I know I've treated you shocking, but don't leave me alone now. You've had your revenge. If you leave me by myself now I don't know what I shall do.'

'All right, I don't mind,' he said, 'but we shall have to do it on the cheap, I haven't got money to throw away these days.'

She sat down and put her shoes on, then changed her skirt and put on a hat; and they walked out together till they found a restaurant in the Tottenham Court Road. Philip had got out of the habit of eating at those hours, and Mildred's throat was so sore that she could not swallow. They had a little cold ham and Philip drank a glass of beer. They sat opposite one another, as they had so often sat before; he wondered if she remembered; they had nothing to say to one another and would have sat in silence if Philip had not forced himself to talk. In the bright light of the restaurant, with its vulgar looking-glasses that reflected in an endless series, she looked old and haggard. Philip was anxious to know about the child, but he had not the courage to ask. At last she said:

'You know baby died last summer.'

'Oh!' he said.

'You might say you're sorry.'

'I'm not,' he answered, 'I'm very glad.'

She glanced at him and, understanding what he meant, looked away.

'You were rare stuck on it at one time, weren't you? I always thought it funny like how you could see so much in another man's child.'

When they had finished eating they called at the chemist's for the medicine Philip had ordered, and going back to the shabby room he made her take a dose. Then they sat together till it was time for Philip to go back to Harrington Street. He was hideously bored.

Philip went to see her every day. She took the medicine he had prescribed and followed his directions, and soon the results were so apparent that she gained the greatest confidence in Philip's skill. As she grew better she grew less despondent. She talked more freely.

'As soon as I can get a job I shall be all right,' she said. 'I've had my lesson now and I mean to profit by it. No more racketing about for yours truly.'

Each time he saw her, Philip asked whether she had found work. She told him not to worry, she would find something to do as soon as she wanted it; she had several strings to her bow; it was all the better not to do anything for a week or two. He could not deny this, but at the end of that time he became more insistent. She laughed at him, she was much more cheerful now, and said he was a fussy old thing. She told him long stories of the manageresses she interviewed, for her idea was to get work at some eating-house; what they said and what she answered. Nothing definite was fixed, but she was sure to settle something at the beginning of the following week: there was no use hurrying, and it would be a mistake to take something unsuitable.

'It's absurd to talk like that,' he said impatiently. 'You must take anything you can get. I can't help you, and your money won't last for ever.'

'Oh, well, I've not come to the end of it yet and chance it.'

He looked at her sharply. It was three weeks since his first visit, and she had then less than seven pounds. Suspicion seized him. He remembered some of the things she had said. He put two and two together. He wondered whether she had made any attempt to find work. Perhaps she had been lying to him all the time. It was very strange that her money should have lastèd so long.

'What is your rent here?'

'Oh, the landlady's very nice, different from what some of them are; she's quite willing to wait till it's convenient for me to pay.'

He was silent. What he suspected was so horrible that he hesitated. It was no use to ask her, she would deny everything; if he wanted to know he must find out for himself. He was in the habit of leaving her every evening at eight, and when the clock struck he got up; but instead of going back to Harrington Street he stationed himself at the corner of Fitzroy Square so that he could see anyone who came along William Street. It seemed to him that he waited an interminable time, and he was on the point of going away, thinking his surmise had been mistaken, when the door of No. 7 opened and Mildred came out. He fell back into the darkness and watched her walk towards him. She had on the hat with a quantity of feathers on it which he had seen in her room, and she wore a dress he recognized, too showy for the street and unsuitable to the time of year. He followed her slowly till she came into Tottenham Court Road, where she slackened her pace; at the corner of Oxford Street she stopped, looked round, and crossed over to a music-hall. He went up to her and touched her on the arm. He saw that she had rouged her cheeks and painted her lips.

'Where are you going, Mildred?'

She started at the sound of his voice and reddened as she always did when she was caught in a lie; then the flash of anger which he knew so well came into her eyes as she instinctively sought to defend herself by abuse. But she did not say the words which were on the tip of her tongue.

'Oh, I was only going to see the show. It gives me the hump sitting every night by myself.'

He did not pretend to believe her.

'You mustn't. Good heavens, I've told you fifty times how dangerous it is. You must stop this sort of thing at once.'

'Oh, hold your jaw,' she cried roughly. 'How d'you suppose I'm going to live?'

He took hold of her arm and without thinking what he was doing tried to drag her away.

'For God's sake come along. Let me take you home. You don't know what you're doing. It's criminal.'

'What do I care? Let them take their chance. Men haven't been so good to me that I need bother my head about them.'

She pushed him away and walking up to the box-office put down her money. Philip had threepence in his pocket. He could not follow. He turned away and walked slowly down Oxford Street.

'I can't do anything more,' he said to himself.

That was the end. He did not see her again.

CX

CHRISTMAS that year falling on Thursday, the shop was to close for four days: Philip wrote to his uncle asking whether it would be convenient for him to spend the holidays at the vicarage. He received an answer from Mrs Foster, saying that Mr Carey was not well enough to write himself, but wished to see his nephew and would be glad if he came down. She met Philip at the door, and when she shook hands with him, said:

'You'll find him changed since you was here last, sir; but you'll pretend you don't notice anything, won't you, sir? He's that nervous about himself.'

Philip nodded, and she led him into the dining-room.

'Here's Mr Philip, sir.'

The Vicar of Blackstable was a dying man. There was no mistaking that when you looked at the hollow cheeks and the shrunken body. He sat huddled in the arm-chair, with his head strangely thrown back, and a shawl over his shoulders. He could not walk now without the help of sticks, and his hands trembled so that he could only feed himself with difficulty.

'He can't last long now,' thought Philip, as he looked at him.

'How d'you think I'm looking?' asked the Vicar. 'D'you think I've changed since you were here last?'

'I think you look stronger than you did last summer.'

543

'It was the heat. That always upsets me.'

Mr Carey's history of the last few months consisted in the number of weeks he had spent in his bedroom and the number of weeks he had spent downstairs. He had a hand-bell by his side and while he talked he rang it for Mrs Foster, who sat in the next room ready to attend to his wants, to ask on what day of the month he had first left his room.

'On the seventh of November, sir.'

Mr Carey looked at Philip to see how he took the information.

'But I eat well still, don't I, Mrs Foster?'

'Yes, sir, you've got a wonderful appetite.'

'I don't seem to put on flesh though.'

Nothing interested him now but his health. He was set upon one thing indomitably and that was living, just living, notwithstanding the monotony of his life and the constant pain which allowed him to sleep only when he was under the influence of morphia.

'It's terrible the amount of money I have to spend on doctor's bills.' He tinkled his bell again. 'Mrs Foster, show Master Philip the chemist's bill.'

Patiently she took it off the chimney-piece and handed it to Philip.

'That's only one month. I was wondering if as you're doctoring yourself you couldn't get me the drugs cheaper. I thought of getting them down from the stores, but then there's the postage.'

Though apparently taking so little interest in him that he did not trouble to inquire what Philip was doing, he seemed glad to have him there. He asked how long he could stay, and when Philip told him he must leave on Tuesday morning, expressed a wish that the visit might have been longer. He told him minutely all his symptoms and repeated what the doctor had said of him. He broke off to ring his bell, and when Mrs Foster came in, said:

'Oh, I wasn't sure if you were there. I only rang to see if you were.'

When she had gone he explained to Philip that it made him uneasy if he was not certain that Mrs Foster was within earshot; she knew exactly what to do with him if anything happened. Philip, seeing that she was tired and that her eyes were heavy from want of sleep, suggested that he was working her too hard.

'Oh, nonsense,' said the Vicar, 'she's as strong as a horse.'

544

And when next she came in to give him his medicine he said to her:

'Master Philip says you've got too much to do, Mrs Foster. You like looking after me, don't you?'

'Oh, I don't mind, sir. I want to do everything I can.'

Presently the medicine took effect and Mr Carey fell asleep. Philip went into the kitchen and asked Mrs Foster whether she could stand the work. He saw that for some months she had had little peace.

'Well, sir, what can I do?' she answered. 'The poor old gentleman's so dependent on me, and, although he is troublesome sometimes, you can't help liking him, can you? I've been here so many years now, I don't know what I shall do when he comes to go.'

Philip saw that she was really fond of the old man. She washed and dressed him, gave him his food, and was up half a dozen times in the night; for she slept in the next room to his and whenever he awoke he tinkled his little bell till she came in. He might die at any moment, but he might live for months. It was wonderful that she should look after a stranger with such patient tenderness, and it was tragic and pitiful that she should be alone in the world to care for him.

It seemed to Philip that the religion which his uncle had preached all his life was now of no more than formal importance to him: every Sunday the curate came and administered to him Holy Communion, and he often read his Bible; but it was clear that he looked upon death with horror. He believed that it was the gateway to life everlasting, but he did not want to enter upon that life. In constant pain, chained to his chair, and having given up the hope of ever getting out into the open again, like a child in the hands of a woman to whom he paid wages, he clung to the world he knew.

In Philip's head was a question he could not ask, because he was aware that his uncle would never give any but a conventional answer: he wondered whether at the very end, now that the machine was painfully wearing itself out, the clergyman still believed in immortality; perhaps at the bottom of his soul, not allowed to shape itself into words in case it became urgent, was the conviction that there was no God and after this life nothing.

On the evening of Boxing Day Philip sat in the dining-room with his uncle. He had to start very early next morning in order to get to the shop by nine, and he was to say good-night to Mr Carey then. The Vicar of Blackstable was dozing and

Philip, lying on the sofa by the window, let his book fall on his knees and looked idly round the room. He asked himself how much the furniture would fetch. He had walked round the house and looked at the things he had known from his childhood; there were a few pieces of china which might go for a decent price and Philip wondered if it would be worth while to take them up to London; but the furniture was of the Victorian order, of mahogany, solid and ugly; it would go for nothing at an auction. There were three or four thousand books, but everyone knew how badly they sold, and it was not probable that they would fetch more than a hundred pounds. Philip did not know how much his uncle would leave, and he reckoned out for the hundredth time what was the least sum upon which he could finish the curriculum at the hospital, take his degree, and live during the time he wished to spend on hospital appointments. He looked at the old man, sleeping restlessly: there was no humanity left in that shrivelled face; it was the face of some queer animal. Philip thought how easy it would be to finish that useless life. He had thought it each evening when Mrs Foster prepared for his uncle the medicine which was to give him an easy night. There were two bottles: one contained a drug which he took regularly, and the other an opiate if the pain grew unendurable. This was poured out for him and left by his bedside. He generally took it at three or four in the morning. It would be a simple thing to double the dose; he would die in the night, and no one would suspect anything; for that was how Doctor Wigram expected him to die. The end would be painless. Philip clenched his hands as he thought of the money he wanted so badly. A few more months of that wretched life could matter nothing to the old man, but the few more months meant everything to him: he was getting to the end of his endurance, and when he thought of going back to work in the morning he shuddered with horror. His heart beat quickly at the thought which obsessed him, and though he made an effort to put it out of his mind he could not. It would be so easy, so desperately easy. He had no feeling for the old man, he had never liked him; he had been selfish all his life, selfish to his wife who adored him, indifferent to the boy who had been put in his charge; he was not a cruel man, but a stupid, hard man, eaten up with a small sensuality. It would be easy, desperately easy. Philip did not dare. He was afraid of remorse; it would be no good having the money if he regretted all his life what he had done. Though he had told himself so often that regret was futile, there were

546

certain things that came back to him occasionally and worried him. He wished they were not on his conscience.

His uncle opened his eyes; Philip was glad, for he looked a little more human then. He was frankly horrified at the idea that had come to him, it was murder that he was meditating; and he wondered if other people had such thoughts or whether he was abnormal and depraved. He supposed he could not have done it when it came to the point, but there the thought was, constantly recurring: if he held his hand it was from fear. His uncle spoke.

'You're not looking forward to my death, Philip?'

Philip felt his heart beat against his chest.

'Good heavens, no.'

'That's a good boy. I shouldn't like you to do that. You'll get a little bit of money when I pass away, but you mustn't look forward to it. It wouldn't profit you if you did.'

He spoke in a low voice, and there was a curious anxiety in his tone. It sent a pang in Philip's heart. He wondered what strange insight might have led the old man to surmise what strange desires were in Philip's mind.

'I hope you'll live for another twenty years,' he said.

'Oh, well, I can't expect to do that, but if I take care of myself I don't see why I shouldn't last another three or four.'

He was silent for a while, and Philip found nothing to say. Then, as if he had been thinking it all over, the old man spoke again.

'Everyone has the right to live as long as he can.'

Philip wanted to distract his mind.

'By the way, I suppose you never hear from Miss Wilkinson now?'

'Yes, I had a letter some time this year. She's married, you know.'

'Really?'

'Yes, she married a widower. I believe they're quite comfortable.'

CXI

NEXT day Philip began work again, but the end which he expected within a few weeks did not come. The weeks passed into months. The winter wore away, and in the parks the trees burst into bud and into leaf. A terrible lassitude settled upon Philip. Time was passing, though it went with such heavy feet, and he thought that his youth was going and soon he would have lost it and nothing would have been accomplished. His work seemed more aimless now that there was the certainty of his leaving it. He became skilful in the designing of costumes, and though he had no inventive faculty acquired quickness in the adaptation of French fashions to the English market. Sometimes he was not displeased with his drawings, but they always bungled them in the execution. He was amused to notice that he suffered from a lively irritation when his ideas were not adequately carried out. He had to walk warily. Whenever he suggested something original Mr Sampson turned it down: their customers did not want anything *outré*, it was a very respectable class of business, and when you had a connexion of that sort it wasn't worth while taking liberties with it. Once or twice he spoke sharply to Philip; he thought the young man was getting a bit above himself because Philip's ideas did not always coincide with his own.

'You jolly well take care, my fine young fellow, or one of these days you'll find yourself in the street.'

Philip longed to give him a punch on the nose, but he restrained himself. After all it could not possibly last much longer, and then he would be done with all these people for ever. Sometimes in comic desperation he cried out that his uncle must be made of iron. What a constitution! The ills he suffered from would have killed any decent person twelve months before. When at last the news came that the Vicar was dying Philip, who had been thinking of other things, was taken by surprise. It was in July, and in another fortnight he was to have gone for his holiday. He received a letter from Mrs Foster to say the doctor did not give Mr Carey many days to live, and if Philip wished to see him again he must come at once. Philip went to the buyer and told him he wanted to leave. Mr Sampson was a decent fellow, and when he knew the circumstances made no difficulties. Philip said good-bye to the people in his department; the reason of his leaving had spread among them in an exaggerated form, and they thought he had come into a fortune. Mrs Hodges had tears in her eyes when she shook hands with him.

'I suppose we shan't often see you again,' she said.

'I'm glad to get away from Lynn's,' he answered.

It was strange, but he was actually sorry to leave these people whom he thought he had loathed, and when he drove away from the house in Harrington Street it was with no exultation. He had so anticipated the emotions he would experience on this occasion that now he felt nothing: he was as unconcerned as though he were going for a few days' holiday.

'I've got a rotten nature,' he said to himself. 'I look forward to things awfully, and then when they come I'm always disappointed.'

He reached Blackstable early in the afternoon. Mrs Foster met him at the door, and her face told him that his uncle was not yet dead.

'He's a little better today,' she said. 'He's got a wonderful constitution.'

She led him into the bedroom where Mr Carey lay on his back. He gave Philip a slight smile, in which was a trace of satisfied cunning at having circumvented his enemy once more.

'I thought it was all up with me yesterday,' he said, in an exhausted voice. 'They'd all given me up, hadn't you, Mrs Foster?'

'You've got a wonderful constitution, there's no denying that.'

'There's life in the old dog yet.'

Mrs Foster said that the Vicar must not talk, it would tire him; she treated him like a child, with kindly despotism; and there was something childish in the old man's satisfaction at having cheated all their expectations. It struck him at once that Philip had been sent for, and he was amused that he had been brought on a fool's errand. If he could only avoid another of his heart attacks he would get well enough in a week or two; and he had had the attacks several times before; he always felt as if he were going to die, but he never did. They all talked of his constitution, but they none of them knew how strong it was.

'Are you going to stay a day or two?' he asked Philip, pretending to believe he had come down for a holiday.

'I was thinking of it,' Philip answered cheerfully.

'A breath of sea-air will do you good.'

Presently Dr Wigram came, and after he had seen the Vicar talked with Philip. He adopted an appropriate manner.

'I'm afraid it is the end this time, Philip,' he said. 'It'll be a great loss to all of us. I've known him for five-and-thirty years.'

'He seems well enough now,' said Philip.

'I'm keeping him alive on drugs, but it can't last. It was dreadful these last two days, I thought he was dead half a dozen times.'

The doctor was silent for a minute or two, but at the gate he said suddenly to Philip:

'Has Mrs Foster said anything to you?'

'What d'you mean?'

'They're very superstitious, these people: she's got hold of an idea that he's got something on his mind, and he can't die till he gets rid of it; and he can't bring himself to confess it.'

Philip did not answer, and the doctor went on.

'Of course it's nonsense. He's led a very good life, he's done his duty, he's been a good parish priest, and I'm sure we shall all miss him; he can't have anything to reproach himself with. I very much doubt whether the next vicar will suit us half so well.'

For several days Mr Carey continued without change. His appetite which had been excellent left him, and he could eat little. Dr Wigram did not hesitate now to still the pain of the neuritis which tormented him; and that, with the constant shaking of his palsied limbs, was gradually exhausting him. His mind remained clear. Philip and Mrs Foster nursed him between them. She was so tired by the many months during which she had been attentive to all his wants that Philip insisted on sitting up with the patient so that she might have her night's rest. He passed the long hours in an arm-chair so that he should not sleep soundly, and read by the light of shaded candles *The Thousand and One Nights*. He had not read them since he was a little boy, and they brought back his childhood to him. Sometimes he sat and listened to the silence of the night. When the effects of the opiate wore off Mr Carey grew restless and kept him constantly busy.

At last, early one morning, when the birds were chattering noisily in the trees, he heard his name called. He went up to the bed. Mr Carey was lying on his back, with his eyes looking at the ceiling; he did not turn them on Philip. Philip saw that sweat was on his forehead, and he took a towel and wiped it.

'Is that you, Philip?' the old man asked.

Philip was startled because the voice was suddenly changed. It was hoarse and low. So would a man speak if he was cold with fear.

'Yes, d'you want anything?'

There was a pause, and still the unseeing eyes stared at the ceiling. Then a twitch passed over the face.

'I think I'm going to die,' he said.

'Oh, what nonsense!' cried Philip. 'You're not going to die for years.'

Two tears were wrung from the old man's eyes. They moved Philip horribly. His uncle had never betrayed any particular emotion in the affairs of life; and it was dreadful to see them now, for they signified a terror that was unspeakable.

'Send for Mr Simmonds,' he said. 'I want to take the Communion.'

Mr Simmonds was the curate.

'Now?' asked Philip.

'Soon, or else it'll be too late.'

Philip went to awake Mrs Foster, but it was later than he thought and she was up already. He told her to send the gardener with a message, and he went back to his uncle's room.

'Have you sent for Mr Simmonds?'

'Yes.'

There was a silence. Philip sat by the bedside, and occasionally wiped the sweating forehead.

'Let me hold your hand, Philip,' the old man said at last.

Philip gave him his hand and he clung to it as to life, for comfort in his extremity. Perhaps he had never really loved anyone in all his days, but now he turned instinctively to a human being. His hand was wet and cold. It grasped Philip's with feeble, despairing energy. The old man was fighting with the fear of death. And Philip thought that all must go through that. Oh, how monstrous it was, and they could believe in a God that allowed His creatures to suffer such a cruel torture! He had never cared for his uncle, and for two years he had longed every day for his death; but now he could not overcome the compassion that filled his heart. What a price it was to pay for being other than the beasts!

They remained in silence broken only once by a low inquiry from Mr Carey:

'Hasn't he come yet?'

At last the housekeeper came in softly to say that Mr Simmonds was there. He carried a bag in which were his surplice and his hood. Mrs Foster brought the Communion plate. Mr Simmonds shook hands silently with Philip, and then with professional gravity went to the sick man's side. Philip and the maid went out of the room.

Philip walked round the garden all fresh and dewy in the morning. The birds were singing gaily. The sky was blue, but the air, salt-laden, was sweet and cool. The roses were in full bloom. The green of the trees, the green of the lawns, was eager and brilliant. Philip walked, and as he walked he thought of the mystery which was proceeding in that bedroom. It gave him a peculiar emotion. Presently Mrs Foster came out to him and said that his uncle wished to see him. The curate was putting his things back into the black bag. The sick man turned his head a little and greeted him with a smile. Philip was astonished, for there was a change in him, an extraordinary change; his eyes had no longer the terror-stricken look, and the pinching of his face had gone: he looked happy and serene.

'I'm quite prepared now,' he said, and his voice had a different tone in it. 'When the Lord sees fit to call me I am ready to give my soul into His hands.'

Philip did not speak. He could see that his uncle was sincere. It was almost a miracle. He had taken the body and blood of his Saviour, and they had given him strength so that he no longer feared the inevitable passage into the night. He knew he was going to die: he was resigned. He only said one thing more:

'I shall rejoin my dear wife.'

It startled Philip. He remembered with what a callous selfishness his uncle had treated her, how obtuse he had been to her humble, devoted love. The curate, deeply moved, went away, and Mrs Foster, weeping, accompanied him to the door. Mr Carey, exhausted by his effort, fell into a light doze, and Philip sat down by the bed and waited for the end. The morning wore on, and the old man's breathing grew stertorous. The doctor came and said he was dying. He was unconscious and he pecked feebly at the sheets; he was restless and he cried out. Dr Wigram gave him a hypodermic injection.

'It can't do any good now, he may die at any moment.'

The doctor looked at his watch and then at the patient. Philip saw that it was one o'clock. Dr Wigram was thinking of his dinner.

'It's no use your waiting,' he said.

'There's nothing I can do,' said the doctor.

When he was gone Mrs Foster asked Philip if he would go to the carpenter, who was also the undertaker, and tell him to send up a woman to lay out the body.

'You want a little fresh air,' she said, 'it'll do you good.'

The undertaker lived half a mile away. When Philip gave him his message, he said:

'When did the poor old gentleman die?'

Philip hesitated. It occurred to him that it would seem brutal to fetch a woman to wash the body while his uncle still lived, he wondered why Mrs Foster had asked him to come. They would think he was in a great hurry to kill the old man off. He thought the undertaker looked at him oddly. He repeated the question. It irritated Philip. It was no business of his.

'When did the Vicar pass away?'

Philip's first impulse was to say that it had just happened, but then it would seem inexplicable if the sick man lingered for several hours. He reddened and answered awkwardly:

'Oh, he isn't exactly dead yet.'

The undertaker looked at him in perplexity, and he hurried to explain.

'Mrs Foster is all alone and she wants a woman there. You understand, don't you? He may be dead by now.'

The undertaker nodded.

'Oh, yes, I see. I'll send someone up at once.'

When Philip got back to the vicarage he went up to the bedroom. Mrs Foster rose from her chair by the bedside.

'He's just as he was when you left,' she said.

She went down to get herself something to eat, and Philip watched curiously the process of death. There was nothing human now in the unconscious being that struggled feebly. Sometimes a muttered ejaculation issued from the loose mouth. The sun beat down hotly from a cloudless sky, but the trees in the garden were pleasant and cool. It was a lovely day. A bluebottle buzzed against the window-pane. Suddenly there was a loud rattle, it made Philip start, it was horribly frightening, a movement passed through the limbs and the old man was dead. The machine had run down. The bluebottle buzzed, buzzed noisily against the window-pane.

CXII

JOSIAH GRAVES in his masterful way made arrangements, becoming but economical, for the funeral; and when it was over came back to the vicarage with Philip. The will was in his charge, and with a due sense of the fitness of things he read it to Philip over an early cup of tea. It was written on half a sheet of paper and left everything Mr Carey had to his nephew. There was the furniture, about eighty pounds at the bank, twenty shares in the A.B.C. company, a few in Allsop's brewery, some in the Oxford music-hall, and a few more in a London restaurant. They had been bought under Mr Graves's direction, and he told Philip with satisfaction:

'You see, people must eat, they will drink, and they want amusement. You're always safe if you put your money in what the public thinks necessities.'

His words showed a nice discrimination between the grossness of the vulgar, which he deplored but accepted, and the finer taste of the elect. Altogether in investments there was about five hundred pounds; and to that must be added the balance at the bank and what the furniture would fetch. It was riches to Philip. He was not happy but infinitely relieved.

Mr Graves left him, after they had discussed the auction which must be held as soon as possible, and Philip sat himself down to go through the papers of the deceased. The Rev. William Carey had prided himself on never destroying anything and there were piles of correspondence dating back for fifty years and bundle upon bundle of neatly docketed bills. He had kept not only letters addressed to him, but letters which he himself had written. There was a yellow packet of letters which he had written to his father in the forties, when as an Oxford undergraduate he had gone to Germany for the long vacation. Philip read them idly. It was a different William Carey from the William Carey he had known, and yet there were traces in the boy which might to an acute observer have suggested the man. The letters were formal and a little stilted. He showed himself strenuous to see all that was noteworthy, and he described with a fine enthusiasm the castles of the Rhine. The falls of Schaffhausen made him 'offer reverent thanks to the all-powerful Creator of the universe, whose works were wondrous and beautiful,' and he could not help thinking that they who lived in sight of 'this handiwork of their blessed Maker must be moved by the contemplation to lead pure and holy lives.' Among some bills Philip found a miniature which had been painted of William Carey soon after he was ordained. It represented a thin young curate, with long hair that fell over his head in natural curls, with dark eyes, large and dreamy, and a pale ascetic face. Philip remembered the chuckle with which his uncle used to tell of the dozens of slippers which were worked for him by adoring ladies.

The rest of the afternoon and all the evening Philip toiled through the innumerable correspondence. He glanced at the address and at the signature, then tore the letter in two and threw it into the washing-basket by his side. Suddenly he came upon one signed Helen. He did not know the writing. It was thin, angular, and old-fashioned. It began: my dear William, and ended: your affectionate sister. Then it struck him that it was from his own mother! He had never seen a letter of hers before, and her handwriting was strange to him. It was about himself.

My dear William,

Stephen wrote to you to thank you for your congratulations on the birth of our son and your kind wishes to myself. Thank God we are both well and I am deeply thankful for the great mercy which has been shown me. Now that I can hold a pen I want to tell you and dear Louisa myself how truly grateful I am to you both for all your kindness to me now and always since my marriage. I am going to ask you to do me a great favour. Both Stephen and I wish you to be the boy's godfather, and we hope that you will consent. I know I am not asking a small thing, for I am sure you will take the responsibilities of the position very seriously, but I am especially anxious that you should undertake this office because you are a clergyman as well as the boy's uncle. I am very anxious for the boy's welfare and I pray God night and day that he may grow into a good, honest, and Christian man. With you to guide him I hope that he will become a soldier in Christ's Faith and be all the days of his life God-fearing, humble, and pious.

Your affectionate sister,

Helen

Philip pushed the letter away and, leaning forward, rested his face on his hands. It deeply touched and at the same time surprised him. He was astonished at its religious tone, which seemed to him neither mawkish nor sentimental. He knew nothing of his mother, dead now for nearly twenty years, but that she was beautiful and it was strange to learn that she was simple and pious. He had never thought of that side of her. He read again what she said about him, what she expected and thought about him; he had turned out very differently; he looked at himself for a moment; perhaps it was better that she was dead. Then a sudden impulse caused him to tear up the letter; its tenderness and simplicity made it seem peculiarly private; he had a queer feeling that there was something indecent in his reading what exposed his mother's gentle soul. He went on with the Vicar's dreary correspondence.

A few days later he went up to London, and for the first time for two years entered by day the hall of St Luke's Hospital. He went to see the secretary of the Medical School; he was surprised to see him and asked Philip curiously what he had been doing. Philip's experiences had given him a certain confidence in himself and a different outlook upon many things: such a question would have embarrassed him before; but now he answered coolly, with a deliberate vagueness which prevented further inquiry, that private affairs had obliged him to make a break in the curriculum; he was now anxious to qualify as soon as possible. The first examination he could take was in Midwifery and the Diseases of Women, and he put his name down to be a clerk in the ward devoted to feminine ailments; since it was holiday time there happened to be no difficulty in getting a post as obstetric clerk; he arranged to undertake that duty during the last week of August and the first two of September. After this interview Philip walked through the Medical School, more or less deserted, for the examinations at the end of the summer session were all over; and he wandered along the terrace by the riverside. His heart was full. He thought that now he could begin a new life, and he would put behind him all the errors, follies, and miseries of the past. The flowing river suggested that everything passed, was passing always, and nothing mattered; the future was before him rich with possibilities.

He went back to Blackstable and busied himself with the settling up of his uncle's estate. The auction was fixed for the middle of August, when the presence of visitors for the summer holidays would make it possible to get better prices. Catalogues were made out and sent to the various dealers in second-hand books at Tercanbury, Maidstone, and Ashford.

One afternoon Philip took it into his head to go over to Tercanbury and see his old school. He had not been there since the day when, with relief in his heart, he had left it with the feeling that thenceforward he was his own master. It was strange to wander through the narrow streets of Tercanbury which he had known so well for so many years. He looked at the old shops, still there, still selling the same things; the book-sellers with school-books, pious works, and the latest novels in one window, and photographs of the Cathedral and of the city in the other; the games shop, with its cricket bats, fishing tackle, tennis rackets, and footballs; the tailor from whom he had got clothes all through his boyhood; and the fishmonger where his uncle whenever he came to Tercanbury bought fish. He wandered along the sordid street in which, behind a high wall, lay the red-brick house which was the preparatory school. Further on was the gateway that led into King's School, and he stood in the quadrangle round which were the various buildings. It was just four and the boys were hurrying out of school. He saw the masters in their gowns and mortar-boards, and they were strange to him. It was more than ten years since he had left and many changes had taken place. He saw the headmaster; he walked slowly down from the schoolhouse to his own, talking to a big boy who Philip supposed was in the sixth; he was little changed, tall, cadaverous, romantic as Philip remembered him, with the same wild eyes; but the black beard was streaked with grey now and the dark, sallow face was more deeply lined. Philip had an impulse to go up and speak to him, but he was afraid he would have forgotten him, and he hated the thought of explaining who he was.

Boys lingered talking to one another, and presently some who had hurried to change came out to play fives; others straggled out in twos and threes and went out of the gateway: Philip knew they were going up to the cricket ground; others again went into the precincts to bat at the nets. Philip stood among them a stranger; one or two gave him an indifferent glance; but visitors, attracted by the Norman staircase, were not rare and excited little attention. Philip looked at them curiously. He thought with melancholy of the distance that separated him from them, and he thought bitterly how much he had wanted to do and how little done. It seemed to him that all those years, vanished beyond recall, had been utterly wasted. The boys, fresh and buoyant, were doing the same things that he had done; it seemed that not a day had passed since he left the school, and yet in that place where at least by name he had known everybody, now he knew not a soul. In a few years these too, others taking their place, would stand alien as he stood; but the reflection brought him no solace; it merely impressed upon him the futility of human existence. Each generation repeated the trivial round. He wondered what had become of the boys who were his companions: they were nearly thirty now; some would be dead, but others were married and had children; they were soldiers and parsons, doctors, lawyers; they were staid men who were beginning to put youth behind them. Had any of them made such a hash of life as he? He thought of the boy he had been devoted to; it was funny, he could not recall his name; he remembered exactly what he looked like, he had been his greatest friend; but his name would not come back to him. He looked back with amusement on the jealous emotions he had suffered on his account. It was irritating not to recollect his name. He longed to be a boy again, like those he saw sauntering through the quadrangle, so that, avoiding his mistakes, he might start afresh and make something more out of life. He felt an intolerable loneliness. He almost regretted the penury which he had suffered during the last two years, since the desperate struggle merely to keep body and soul together had deadened the pain of living. *In the sweat of thy brow shalt thou earn thy daily bread:* it was not a curse upon mankind, but the balm which reconciled it to existence.

But Philip was impatient with himself; he called to mind his idea of the pattern of life: the unhappiness he had suffered was no more than part of a decoration which was elaborate and beautiful; he told himself strenuously that he must accept with gaiety everything, dreariness and excitement, pleasure and pain, because it added to the richness of the design. He sought for beauty consciously, and he remembered how even as a boy he had taken pleasure in the Gothic cathedral as one saw it from the precincts; he went there and looked at the massive pile, grey under the cloudy sky, with the central tower that rose like the praise of men to their God; but the boys were batting at the nets, and they were lissom and strong and active; he could not help hearing their shouts and laughter. The cry of youth was insistent, and he saw the beautiful thing before him only with his eyes.

CXIII

AT the beginning of the last week in August Philip entered upon his duties in the 'district'. They were arduous, for he had to attend on an average three confinements a day. The patient had obtained a 'card' from the hospital some time before; and when her time came it was taken to the porter by a messenger, generally a little girl, who was then sent across the road to the house in which Philip lodged. At night the porter, who had a latchkey, himself came over and awoke Philip. It was mysterious then to get up in the darkness and walk through the deserted streets of the South Side. At those hours it was generally the husband who brought the card. If there had been a number of babies before, he took it for the most part with surly indifference, but if newly married he was nervous and then sometimes strove to allay his anxiety by getting drunk. Often there was a mile or more to walk, during which Philip and the messenger discussed the conditions of labour and the cost of living; Philip learned about the various trades which were practised on that side of the river. He inspired confidence in the people among whom he was thrown, and during the long hours that he waited in a stuffy room, the woman in labour lying on a large bed that took up half of it, her mother and the midwife talked to him as naturally as they talked to one another. The circumstances in which he had lived during the last two years had taught him several things about the life of the very poor, which it amused them to find he knew; and they were impressed because he was not deceived by their little subterfuges. He was kind, and he had gentle hands, and he did not lose his temper. They were pleased because he was not above drinking a cup of tea with them, and when the dawn came and they were still waiting they offered him a slice of bread and dripping; he was not squeamish and could eat most things now with a good appetite. Some of the houses he went to, in filthy courts off a dingy street, huddled against one another without light or air, were merely squalid; but others, unexpectedly, though dilapidated, with worm-eaten floors and leaking roofs, had the grand air: you found in them oak balusters exquisitely carved, and the walls had still their panelling. These were thickly inhabited. One family lived in each room, and in the daytime there was the incessant noise of children playing in the court. The old walls were the breeding-place of vermin; the air was so foul that often, feeling sick, Philip had to light his pipe. The people who dwelt here lived from hand to mouth. Babies were unwelcome, the man received them with surly anger, the mother with despair; it was one more mouth to feed, and there was little enough wherewith to feed those already there. Philip often discerned the wish that the child might be born dead or might die quickly. He delivered one woman of twins (a source of humour to the facetious) and when she was told she burst into a long, shrill wail of misery. Her mother said outright:

'I don't know how they're going to feed 'em.'

'Maybe the Lord'll see fit to take 'em to 'imself,' said the midwife.

Philip caught sight of the husband's face as he looked at the tiny pair lying side by side, and there was a ferocious sullenness in it which startled him. He felt in the family assembled there a hideous resentment against those poor atoms who had come into the world unwished for; and he had a suspicion that if he did not speak firmly an 'accident' would occur. Accidents occurred often; mothers 'overlaid' their babies, and perhaps errors of diet were not always the result of carelessness.

'I shall come every day,' he said. 'I warn you that if anything happens to them there'll have to be an inquest.'

The father made no reply, but he gave Philip a scowl. There was murder in his soul.

'Bless their little 'earts,' said the grandmother, 'what should 'appen to them?'

The great difficulty was to keep the mothers in bed for ten days, which was the minimum upon which the hospital practice insisted. It was awkward to look after the family, no one would see to the children without payment, and the husband grumbled because his tea was not right when he came home tired from his work and hungry. Philip had heard that the poor helped one another, but woman after woman complained to him that she could not get anyone in to clean up and see to the children's dinner without paying for the service, and she could not afford to pay. By listening to the women as they talked and by chance remarks from which he could deduce much that was left unsaid, Philip learned how little there was in common between the poor and the classes above them. They did not envy their betters, for the life was too different, and they had an ideal of ease which made the existence of the middle classes seem formal and stiff; moreover, they had a certain contempt for them because they were soft and did not work with their hands. The proud merely wished to be left alone, but the majority looked upon the well-to-do as people to be exploited; they knew what to say in order to get such advantages as the charitable put at their disposal, and they accepted benefits as a right which came to them from the folly of their superiors and their own astuteness. They bore the curate with contemptuous indifference, but the district visitor excited their bitter hatred. She came in and opened your windows without so much as a 'by your leave' or 'with your leave', 'and me with my bronchitis, enough to give me my death of cold;' she poked her nose into corners, and if she didn't say the place was dirty you saw what she thought right enough, 'an' it's all very well for them as 'as servants, but I'd like to see what she'd make of 'er room if she 'ad four children, and 'ad to do the cookin', and mend their clothes, and wash them.'

Philip discovered that the greatest tragedy of life to these people was not separation or death, that was natural and the grief of it could be assuaged with tears, but loss of work. He saw a man come home one afternoon, three days after his wife's confinement, and tell her he had been dismissed; he was a builder and at that time work was slack; he stated the fact, and sat down to his tea.

'Oh, Jim,' she said.

The man ate stolidly some mess which had been stewing in a sauce-pan against his coming; he stared at his plate; his wife looked at him two or three times, with little startled glances, and then quite silently began to cry. The builder was an uncouth little fellow with a rough, weather-beaten face and a long white scar on his forehead; he had large, stubbly hands. Presently he pushed aside his plate as if he must give up the effort to force himself to eat, and turned a fixed gaze out of the window. The room was at the top of the house, at the back, and one saw nothing but sullen clouds. The silence seemed heavy with despair. Philip felt that there was nothing to be said, he could only go; and as he walked away, wearily, for he had been up most of the night, his heart was filled with rage against the cruelty of the world. He knew the hopelessness of the search for work and the desolation which is harder to bear than hunger. He was thankful not to have to believe in God, for then such a condition of things would be intolerable; one could reconcile oneself to existence only because it was meaningless.

It seemed to Philip that the people who spent their time in helping the poorer classes erred, because they sought to remedy things which would harass them if they themselves had to endure them without thinking that they did not in the least disturb those who were used to them. The poor did not want large airy rooms; they suffered from cold, for their food was not nourishing and their circulation bad; space gave them a feeling of chilliness, and they wanted to burn as little coal as need be; there was no hardship for several to sleep in one room, they preferred it; they were never alone for a moment, from the time they were born to the time they died, and loneliness oppressed them; they enjoyed the promiscuity in which they dwelt, and the constant noise of their surroundings pressed upon their ears unnoticed. They did not feel the need of taking a bath constantly, and Philip often heard them speak with indignation of the necessity to do so with which they were faced on entering the hospital: it was both an affront and a discomfort. They wanted chiefly to be left alone; then if the man was in regular work life went easily and was not without its pleasures: there was plenty of time for gossip, after the day's work a glass of beer was very good to drink, the streets were a constant source of entertainment, if you wanted to read there was *Reynolds's* or the *News of the World*; 'but there, you couldn't make out 'ow the time did fly, the truth was and that's a fact, you was a rare one for reading when you was a girl, but what with one thing and another you didn't get no time now not even to read the paper.'

The usual practice was to pay three visits after a confinement, and one Sunday Philip went to see a patient at the dinner hour. She was up for the first time.

'I couldn't stay in bed no longer, I really couldn't. I'm not one for idling, and it gives me the fidgets to be there and do nothing all day long, so I said to 'Erb, I'm just going to get up and cook your dinner for you.'

'Erb was sitting at table with his knife and fork already in

561

his hands. He was a young man, with an open face and blue eyes. He was earning good money, and as things went the couple were in easy circumstances. They had only been married a few months, and were both delighted with the rosy boy who lay in the cradle at the foot of the bed. There was a savoury smell of beefsteak in the room and Philip's eyes turned to the range.

'I was just going to dish up this minute,' said the woman.

'Fire away,' said Philip. 'I'll just have a look at the son and heir and then I'll take myself off.'

Husband and wife laughed at Philip's expression, and 'Erb getting up went over with Philip to the cradle. He looked at his baby proudly.

'There doesn't seem much wrong with him, does there?' said Philip.

He took up his hat, and by this time 'Erb's wife had dished up the beefsteak and put on the table a plate of green peas.

'You're going to have a nice dinner,' smiled Philip.

'He's only in of a Sunday and I like to 'ave something special for him, so as he shall miss his 'ome when he's out at work.'

'I suppose you'd be above sittin' down and 'avin' a bit of dinner with us?' said 'Erb.

'Oh, 'Erb,' said his wife, in a shocked tone.

'Not if you ask me,' answered Philip, with his attractive smile.

'Well, that's what I call friendly; I knew 'e wouldn't take offence, Polly. Just get another plate, my girl.'

Polly was flustered, and she thought 'Erb a regular caution, you never knew what ideas 'e'd get in 'is 'ead next; but she got a plate and wiped it quickly with her apron, then took a new knife and fork from the chest of drawers, where her best cutlery rested among her best clothes. There was a jug of stout on the table, and 'Erb poured Philip out a glass. He wanted to give him the lion's share of the beefsteak, but Philip insisted that they should share alike. It was a sunny room with two windows that reached to the floor; it had been the parlour of a house which at one time was if not fashionable at least respectable : it might have been inhabited fifty years before by a well-to-do tradesman or an officer on half pay. 'Erb had been a football player before he married, and there were photographs on the wall of various teams in self-conscious attitudes, with neatly plastered hair, the captain seated proudly in the middle holding a cup. There were other signs of prosperity : photographs of the relations of 'Erb and his wife in Sunday clothes;

on the chimney-piece an elaborate arrangement of shells stuck on a miniature rock; and on each side mugs, 'A present from Southend' in Gothic letters, with pictures of a pier and a parade on them. 'Erb was something of a character; he was a non-union man and expressed himself with indignation at the efforts of the union to force him to join. The union wasn't no good to him, he never found no difficulty in getting work, and there was good wages for anyone as 'ad a head on his shoulders and wasn't above puttin' 'is 'and to anything as come 'is way. Polly was timorous. If she was 'im she'd join the union, the last time there was a strike she was expectin' 'im to be brought back in an ambulance every time he went out. She turned to Philip.

'He's that obstinate, there's no doing anything with 'im.'

'Well, what I say is it's a free country, and I won't be dictated to.'

'It's no good saying it's a free country,' said Polly, 'that won't prevent 'em bashin' your 'ead in if they get the chanst.'

When they had finished Philip passed his pouch over to 'Erb and they lit their pipes; then he got up, for a 'call' might be waiting for him at his rooms, and shook hands. He saw that it had given them pleasure that he shared their meal, and they saw that he had thoroughly enjoyed it.

'Well, good-bye, sir,' said 'Erb, 'and I 'ope we shall 'ave as nice a doctor next time the missus disgraces 'erself.'

'Go on with you, 'Erb,' she retorted. ' 'Ow d'you know there's going to be a next time?'

CXIV

THE three weeks which the appointment lasted drew to an end. Philip had attended sixty-two cases, and he was tired out. When he came home about ten o'clock on his last night he hoped with all his heart that he would not be called out again. He had not had a whole night's rest for ten days. The case which he had just come from was horrible. He had been fetched by a huge, burly man, the worse for liquor, and taken to a room in an evil-smelling court, which was filthier than any he had seen: it was a tiny attic; most of the space was taken up by a wooden bed, with a canopy of dirty red hangings, and the ceiling was so low that Philip could touch it with the tips of his fingers; with the solitary candle that afforded what light there was he went over it, frizzling up the bugs that crawled upon it. The woman was a blowzy creature of middle age, who had had a long succession of still-born children. It was a story that Philip was not unaccustomed to: the husband had been a soldier in India; the legislation forced upon that country by the prudery of the English public had given a free run to the most distressing of all diseases; the innocent suffered. Yawning, Philip undressed and took a bath, then shook his clothes over the water and watched the animals that fell out wriggling. He was just going to get into bed when there was a knock at the door, and the hospital porter brought him a card.

'Curse you,' said Philip. 'You're the last person I wanted to see tonight. Who's brought it?'

'I think it's the 'usband, sir. Shall I tell him to wait?'

Philip looked at the address, saw that the street was familiar to him, and told the porter that he would find his own way. He dressed himself and in five minutes, with his black bag in his hand, stepped into the street. A man, whom he could not see in the darkness, came up to him and said he was the husband.

'I thought I'd better wait, sir,' he said. 'It's a pretty rough neighbour'ood, and them not knowing who you was.'

Philip laughed.

'Bless your heart, they all know the doctor. I've been in some damned sight rougher places than Waver Street.'

It was quite true. The black bag was a passport through wretched alleys and down foul-smelling courts into which a policeman was not ready to venture by himself. Once or twice a little group of men had looked at Philip curiously as he passed; he heard a mutter of observations and then one say:

'It's the 'ospital doctor.'

As he went by one or two of them said: 'Good night, sir.'

'We shall 'ave to step out if you don't mind, sir,' said the man who accompanied him now. 'They told me there was no time to lose.'

'Why did you leave it so late?' asked Philip, as he quickened his pace.

He glanced at the fellow as they passed a lamp-post.

'You look awfully young,' he said.

'I'm turned eighteen, sir.'

He was fair, and he had not a hair on his face, he looked no more than a boy; he was short, but thick-set.

'You're young to be married,' said Philip.

'We 'ad to.'

'How much d'you earn?'

'Sixteen, sir.'

Sixteen shillings a week was not much to keep a wife and child on. The room the couple lived in showed that their poverty was extreme. It was a fair size, but it looked quite large, since there was hardly any furniture in it; there was no carpet on the floor; there were no pictures on the walls; and most rooms had something, photographs or supplements in cheap frames from the Christmas numbers of the illustrated papers. The patient lay on a little iron bed of the cheapest sort. It startled Philip to see how young she was.

'By Jove, she can't be more than sixteen,' he said to the woman who had come in to 'see her through'.

She had given her age as eighteen on the card, but when they were very young they often put on a year or two. Also she was pretty, which was rare in those classes in which the constitution has been undermined by bad food, bad air, and unhealthy occupations; she had delicate features and large blue eyes, and a mass of dark hair done in the elaborate fashion of the coster girl. She and her husband were very nervous.

'You'd better wait outside, so as to be at hand if I want you,' Philip said to him.

Now that he saw him better Philip was surprised again at his boyish air: you felt that he should be larking in the street with the other lads instead of waiting anxiously for the birth of a child. The hours passed, and it was not till nearly two that the baby was born. Everything seemed to be going satisfactorily; the husband was called in, and it touched Philip to see the awkward, shy way in which he kissed his wife; Philip packed up his things. Before going he felt once more his patient's pulse.

'Hulloa!' he said.

He looked at her quickly: something had happened. In cases of emergency the S.O.C. – senior obstetric clerk – had to be sent for; he was a qualified man, and the 'district' was in his charge. Philip scribbled a note, and giving it to the husband told him to run with it to the hospital; he bade him hurry, for his wife was in a dangerous state. The man set off. Philip waited anxiously; he knew the woman was bleeding to death; he was afraid she would die before his chief arrived; he took what steps he could. He hoped fervently that the S.O.C. would not have been called elsewhere. The minutes were interminable. He came at last, and, while he examined the patient, in a low voice asked Philip questions. Philip saw by his face that he thought the case very grave. His name was Chandler. He was a tall man of few words, with a long nose and a thin face much lined for his age. He shook his head.

'It was hopeless from the beginning. Where's the husband?'

'I told him to wait on the stairs,' said Philip.

'You'd better bring him in.'

Philip opened the door and called him. He was sitting in the dark on the first step of the flight that led to the next floor. He came up to the bed.

'What's the matter?' he said.

'Why, there's internal bleeding. It's impossible to stop it.' The S.O.C. hesitated a moment, and because it was a painful thing to say he forced his voice to become brusque. 'She's dying.'

The man did not say a word; he stopped quite still, looking at his wife, who lay, pale and unconscious, on the bed. It was the midwife who spoke.

'The gentlemen 'ave done all they could, 'Arry,' she said. 'I saw what was comin' from the first.'

'Shut up,' said Chandler.

There were no curtains on the windows, and gradually the night seemed to lighten; it was not yet the dawn, but the dawn was at hand. Chandler was keeping the woman alive by all the means in his power, but life was slipping away from her, and suddenly she died. The boy who was her husband stood at the end of the cheap iron bed with his hands resting on the rail; he did not speak; but he looked very pale and once or twice Chandler gave him an uneasy glance, thinking he was going to faint: his lips were grey. The midwife sobbed noisily, but he took no notice of her. His eyes were fixed upon his wife, and in them was an utter bewilderment. He reminded you of a dog whipped for something he did not know was wrong. When Chandler and Philip had gathered together their things Chandler turned to the husband.

'You'd better lie down for a bit. I expect you're about done up.'

'There's nowhere for me to lie down, sir,' he answered, and there was in his voice a humbleness which was very distressing.

'Don't you know anyone in the house who'll give you a shake-down?'

'No, sir.'

'They only moved in last week,' said the midwife. 'They don't know nobody yet.'

Chandler hesitated a moment awkwardly, then he went up to the man and said:

'I'm very sorry this has happened.'

He held out his hand and the man, with an instinctive glance at his own to see if it was clean, shook it.

'Thank you, sir.'

Philip shook hands with him too. Chandler told the midwife to come and fetch the certificate in the morning. They left the house and walked along together in silence.

'It upsets one a bit at first, doesn't it?' said Chandler at last.

'A bit,' answered Philip.

'If you like I'll tell the porter not to bring you any more calls tonight.'

'I'm off duty at eight in the morning in any case.'

'How many cases have you had?'

'Sixty-three.'

'Good. You'll get your certificate then.'

They arrived at the hospital, and the S.O.C. went in to see if anyone wanted him. Philip walked on. It had been very hot all the day before, and even now in the early morning there was a balminess in the air. The street was very still. Philip did not feel inclined to go to bed. It was the end of his work and he need not hurry. He strolled along, glad of the fresh air and the silence; he thought that he would go on to the bridge and look at daybreak on the river. A policeman at the corner bade him good morning. He knew who Philip was from his bag.

'Out late tonight, sir,' he said.

Philip nodded and passed. He leaned against the parapet and looked towards the morning. At that hour the great city was like a city of the dead. The sky was cloudless, but the stars were dim at the approach of day; there was a light mist on the river, and the great buildings on the north side were like palaces in an enchanted island. A group of barges were moored in midstream. It was all of an unearthly violet, troubling somehow and awe-inspiring; but quickly everything grew pale, and cold, and grey. Then the sun rose, a ray of yellow gold stole across the sky, and the sky was iridescent. Philip could not get out of his eyes the dead girl lying on the bed, wan and white, and the boy who stood at the end of it like a stricken beast. The bareness of the squalid room made the pain of it more poignant. It was cruel that a stupid chance should have cut off her life when she was just entering upon it; but in the very moment of saying this to himself, Philip thought of the life which had been in store for her, the bearing of children, the dreary fight with poverty, the youth broken by toil and deprivation into a slatternly middle age – he saw the pretty face

567

grow thin and white, the hair grow scanty, the pretty hands, worn down brutally by work, become like the claws of an old animal – then, when the man was past his prime, the difficulty of getting jobs, the small wages he had to take; and the inevitable, abject penury of the end: she might be energetic, thrifty, industrious, it would not have saved her; in the end was the workhouse or subsistence on the charity of her children. Who could pity her because she had died when life offered so little?

But pity was inane. Philip felt it was not that which these people needed. They did not pity themselves. They accepted their fate. It was the natural order of things. Otherwise, good heavens! otherwise they would swarm over the river in their multitude to the side where those great buildings were, secure and stately; and they would pillage, burn, and sack. But the day, tender and pale, had broken now, and the mist was tenuous; it bathed everything in a soft radiance; and the Thames was grey, rosy, and green; grey like mother-of-pearl and green like the heart of a yellow rose. The wharves and storehouses of the Surrey side were massed in disorderly loveliness. The scene was so exquisite that Philip's heart beat passionately. He was overwhelmed by the beauty of the world. Beside that nothing seemed to matter.

CXV

PHILIP spent the few weeks that remained before the beginning of the winter session in the out-patients' department, and in October settled down to regular work. He had been away from the hospital for so long that he found himself very largely among new people; the men of different years had little to do with one another, and his contemporaries were now mostly qualified: some had left to take up assistantships or posts in country hospitals and infirmaries, and some held appointments at St Luke's. The two years during which his mind had lain fallow had refreshed him, he fancied, and he was able now to work with energy.

The Athelnys were delighted with his change of fortune. He had kept aside a few things from the sale of his uncle's effects and gave them all presents. He gave Sally a gold chain that had belonged to his aunt. She was now grown up. She was apprenticed to a dressmaker and set out every morning at eight to work all day in a shop in Regent Street. Sally had frank blue eyes, a broad brow, and plentiful shining hair; she was buxom, with broad hips and full breasts; and her father, who was fond of discussing her appearance, warned her constantly that she must not grow fat. She attracted because she was healthy, animal, and feminine. She had many admirers, but they left her unmoved; she gave one the impression that she looked upon love-making as nonsense; and it was easy to imagine that young men found her unapproachable. Sally was old for her years: she had been used to help her mother in the household work and in the care of the children, so that she had acquired a managing air, which made her mother say that Sally was a bit too fond of having things her own way. She did not speak very much, but as she grew older she seemed to be acquiring a quiet sense of humour, and sometimes uttered a remark which suggested that beneath her impassive exterior she was quietly bubbling with amusement at her fellow-creatures. Philip found that with her he never got on the terms of affectionate intimacy upon which he was with the rest of Athelny's huge family. Now and then her indifference slightly irritated him. There was something enigmatic in her.

When Philip gave her the necklace Athelny in his boisterous way insisted that she must kiss him; but Sally reddened and drew back.

'No, I'm not going to,' she said.

'Ungrateful hussy!' cried Athelny. 'Why not?'

'I don't like being kissed by men,' she said.

Philip saw her embarrassment, and, amused, turned Athelny's attention to something else. That was never a very difficult thing to do. But evidently her mother spoke of the matter later, for next time Philip came she took the opportunity when they were alone for a couple of minutes to refer to it.

'You didn't think it disagreeable of me last week when I wouldn't kiss you?'

'Not a bit,' he laughed.

'It's not because I wasn't grateful.' She blushed a little as she uttered the formal phrase which she had prepared. 'I shall always value the necklace, and it was very kind of you to give it me.'

Philip found it always a little difficult to talk to her. She did all that she had to do very competently, but seemed to feel no need of conversation; yet there was nothing unsociable in her. One Sunday afternoon when Athelny and his wife had gone out together and Philip, treated as one of the family, sat reading in the parlour, Sally came in and sat by the window to sew. The girls' clothes were made at home and Sally could not afford to spend Sundays in idleness. Philip thought she wished to talk and put down his book.

'Go on reading,' she said. 'I only thought as you were alone I'd come and sit with you.'

'You're the most silent person I've ever struck,' said Philip.

'We don't want another one who's talkative in this house,' she said.

There was no irony in her tone: she was merely stating a fact. But it suggested to Philip that she measured her father, alas, no longer the hero he was to her childhood, and in her mind joined together his entertaining conversation and the thriftlessness which often brought difficulties into their life; she compared his rhetoric with her mother's practical common sense; and though the liveliness of her father amused her she was perhaps sometimes a little impatient with it. Philip looked at her as she bent over her work; she was healthy, strong, and normal; it must be odd to see her among the other girls in the shop with their flat chests and anaemic faces. Mildred suffered from anaemia.

After a time it appeared that Sally had a suitor. She went out occasionally with friends she had made in the workroom, and had met a young man, an electrical engineer in a very good way of business, who was a most eligible person. One day she told her mother that he had asked her to marry him.

'What did you say?' said her mother.

'Oh, I told him I wasn't over-anxious to marry anyone just yet awhile.' She paused a little as was her habit between observations. 'He took on so that I said he might come to tea on Sunday.'

It was an occasion that thoroughly appealed to Athelny. He rehearsed all the afternoon how he should play the heavy father for the young man's edification till he reduced his children to helpless giggling. Just before he was due Athelny routed out an Egyptian tarboosh and insisted on putting it on.

'Go on with you, Athelny,' said his wife, who was in her best, which was of black velvet, and, since she was growing stouter every year, very tight for her. 'You'll spoil the girl's chances.'

She tried to pull it off, but the little man skipped nimbly out of her way.

'Unhand me, woman. Nothing will induce me to take it off.

This young man must be shown at once that it is no ordinary family he is preparing to enter.'

'Let him keep it on, mother,' said Sally, in her even, indifferent fashion. 'If Mr Donaldson doesn't take it the way it's meant he can take himself off, and good riddance.'

Philip thought it was a severe ordeal that the young man was being exposed to, since Athelny, in his brown velvet jacket, flowing black tie, and red tarboosh, was a startling spectacle for an innocent electrical engineer. When he came he was greeted by his host with the proud courtesy of a Spanish grandee and by Mrs Athelny in an altogether homely and natural fashion. They sat down at the old ironing-table in the high-backed monkish chairs, and Mrs Athelny poured tea out of a lustre teapot which gave a note of England and the countryside to the festivity. She had made little cakes with her own hand, and on the table was home-made jam. It was a farmhouse tea, and to Philip very quaint and charming in that Jacobean house. Athelny for some fantastic reason took it into his head to discourse upon Byzantine history; he had been reading the later volumes of the *Decline and Fall*; and, his forefinger dramatically extended, he poured into the astonished ears of the suitor scandalous stories about Theodora and Irene. He addressed himself directly to his guest with a torrent of rhodomontade; and the young man, reduced to helpless silence and shy, nodded his head at intervals to show that he took an intelligent interest. Mrs Athelny paid no attention to Thorpe's conversation, but interrupted now and then to offer the young man more tea or to press upon him cake and jam. Philip watched Sally; she sat with downcast eyes, calm, silent, and observant; and her long eyelashes cast a pretty shadow on her cheek. You could not tell whether she was amused at the scene or if she cared for the young man. She was inscrutable. But one thing was certain: the electrical engineer was good-looking, fair and clean-shaven, with pleasant, regular features, and an honest face; he was tall and well made. Philip could not help thinking he would make an excellent mate for her, and he felt a pang of envy for the happiness which he fancied was in store for them.

Presently the suitor said he thought it was about time he was getting along. Sally rose to her feet without a word and accompanied him to the door. When she came back her father burst out:

'Well, Sally, we think your young man very nice. We are prepared to welcome him into our family. Let the banns be called and I will compose a nuptial song.'

Sally set about clearing away the tea things. She did not answer. Suddenly she shot a swift glance at Philip.

'What did you think of him, Mr Philip?'

She had always refused to call him Uncle Phil as the other children did, and would not call him Philip.

'I think you'd make an awfully handsome pair.'

She looked at him quickly once more, and then with a slight blush went on with her business.

'I thought him a very nice civil-spoken young fellow,' said Mrs Athelny, 'and I think he's just the sort to make any girl happy.'

Sally did not reply for a minute or two, and Philip looked at her curiously: it might be thought that she was meditating upon what her mother had said, and on the other hand she might be thinking of the man in the moon.

'Why don't you answer when you're spoken to, Sally?' remarked her mother, a little irritably.

'I thought he was a silly.'

'Aren't you going to have him then?'

'No, I'm not.'

'I don't know how much more you want,' said Mrs Athelny, and it was quite clear now that she was put out. 'He's a very decent young fellow and he can afford to give you a thorough good home. We've got quite enough to feed here without you. If you get a chance like that it's wicked not to take it. And I daresay you'd be able to have a girl to do the rough work.'

Philip had never before heard Mrs Athelny refer so directly to the difficulties of her life. He saw how important it was that each child should be provided for.

'It's no good your carrying on, mother,' said Sally in her quiet way. 'I'm not going to marry him.'

'I think you're a very hard-hearted, cruel, selfish girl.'

'If you want me to earn my own living, mother, I can always go into service.'

'Don't be so silly, you know your father would never let you do that.'

Philip caught Sally's eye, and he thought there was in it a glimmer of amusement. He wondered what there had been in the conversation to touch her sense of humour. She was an odd girl.

CXVI

DURING his last year at St Luke's Philip had to work hard. He was contented with life. He found it very comfortable to be heart-free and to have enough money for his needs. He had heard people speak contemptuously of money: he wondered if they had ever tried to do without it. He knew that the lack made a man petty, mean, grasping; it distorted his character and caused him to view the world from a vulgar angle; when you had to consider every penny, money became of grotesque importance: you needed a competency to rate it at its proper value. He lived a solitary life, seeing no one except the Athelnys, but he was not lonely; he busied himself with plans for the future, and sometimes he thought of the past. His recollection dwelt now and then on old friends, but he made no effort to see them. He would have liked to know what was become of Norah Nesbit; she was Norah something else now, but he could not remember the name of the man she was going to marry; he was glad to have known her: she was a good and a brave soul. One evening about half past eleven he saw Lawson walking along Piccadilly; he was in evening clothes and might be supposed to be coming back from a theatre. Philip gave way to a sudden impulse and quickly turned down a side street. He had not seen him for two years and felt that he could not now take up again the interrupted friendship. He and Lawson had nothing more to say to one another. Philip was no longer interested in art; it seemed to him that he was able to enjoy beauty with greater force than when he was a boy; but art appeared to him unimportant. He was occupied with the forming of a pattern out of the manifold chaos of life, and the materials with which he worked seemed to make preoccupation with pigments and words very trivial. Lawson had served his turn. Philip's friendship with him had been a motive in the design he was elaborating: it was merely sentimental to ignore the fact that the painter was of no further interest to him.

Sometimes Philip thought of Mildred. He avoided deliberately the streets in which there was a chance of seeing her; but occasionally some feeling, perhaps curiosity, perhaps something deeper which he would not acknowledge, made him wander about Piccadilly and Regent Street during the hours when she might be expected to be there. He did not know then whether he wished to see her or dreaded it. Once he saw a back which reminded him of hers, and for a moment he thought it was she; it gave him a curious sensation: it was a strange sharp pain in his heart, there was fear in it and a sickening dismay; and when he hurried on and found that he was mistaken he did not know whether it was relief that he experienced or disappointment.

At the beginning of August Philip passed his Surgery, his last examination, and received his diploma. It was seven years since he had entered St Luke's Hospital. He was nearly thirty. He walked down the stairs of the Royal College of Surgeons with the roll in his hand which qualified him to practise, and his heart beat with satisfaction.

'Now I'm really going to begin life,' he thought.

Next day he went to the secretary's office to put his name down for one of the hospital appointments. The secretary was a pleasant little man with a black beard, whom Philip had always found very affable. He congratulated him on his success, and then said:

'I suppose you wouldn't like to do a *locum* for a month on the South coast? Three guineas a week with board and lodging.'

'I wouldn't mind,' said Philip.

'It's at Farnley, in Dorsetshire. Doctor South. You'd have to go down at once; his assistant has developed mumps. I believe it's a very pleasant place.'

There was something in the secretary's manner that puzzled Philip. It was a little doubtful.

'What's the crab in it?' he asked.

The secretary hesitated a moment and laughed in a conciliating fashion.

'Well, the fact is, I understand he's rather a crusty, funny old fellow. The agencies won't send him anyone any more. He speaks his mind very openly, and men don't like it.'

'But d'you think he'll be satisfied with a man who's only just qualified? After all I have no experience.'

'He ought to be glad to get you,' said the secretary diplomatically.

Philip thought for a moment. He had nothing to do for the next few weeks, and he was glad of the chance to earn a bit of money. He could put it aside for the holiday in Spain which he had promised himself when he had finished his appointment at St Luke's or, if they would not give him anything there, at some other hospital.

'All right. I'll go.'

'The only thing is, you must go this afternoon. Will that suit you? If so, I'll send a wire at once.'

Philip would have liked a few days to himself; but he had seen the Athelnys the night before (he had gone at once to take them his good news) and there was really no reason why he should not start immediately. He had little luggage to pack. Soon after seven that evening he got out of the station at Farnley and took a cab to Doctor South's. It was a broad low stucco house, with a Virginia creeper growing over it. He was shown into the consulting-room. An old man was writing at a desk. He looked up as the maid ushered Philip in. He did not get up, and he did not speak; he merely stared at Philip. Philip was taken aback.

'I think you're expecting me,' he said. 'The secretary of St Luke's wired to you this morning.'

'I kept dinner back for half an hour. D'you want to wash?'

'I do,' said Philip.

Doctor South amused him by his odd manner. He got up now, and Philip saw that he was a man of middle height, thin, with white hair cut very short and a long mouth closed so tightly that he seemed to have no lips at all; he was clean-shaven but for small white whiskers, and they increased the squareness of face which his firm jaw gave him. He wore a brown tweed suit and a white stock. His clothes hung loosely about him as though they had been made for a much larger man. He looked like a respectable farmer of the middle of the nineteenth century. He opened the door.

'There is the dining-room,' he said, pointing to the door opposite. 'Your bedroom is the first door you come to when you get on the landing. Come downstairs when you're ready.'

During dinner Philip knew that Doctor South was examining him, but he spoke little, and Philip felt that he did not want to hear his assistant talk.

'When were you qualified?' he asked suddenly.

'Yesterday.'

'Were you at a university?'

'No.'

'Last year when my assistant took a holiday they sent me a 'Varsity man. I told 'em not to do it again. Too damned gentlemanly for me.'

There was another pause. The dinner was very simple and

575

very good. Philip preserved a sedate exterior, but in his heart he was bubbling over with excitement. He was immensely elated at being engaged as a *locum*; it made him feel extremely grown-up; he had an insane desire to laugh at nothing in particular; and the more he thought of his professional dignity the more he was inclined to chuckle.

But Doctor South broke suddenly into his thoughts.

'How old are you?'

'Getting on for thirty.'

'How is it you're only just qualified?'

'I didn't go in for the Medical till I was nearly twenty-three, and I had to give it up for two years in the middle.'

'Why?'

'Poverty.'

Doctor South gave him an odd look and relapsed into silence. At the end of dinner he got up from the table.

'D'you know what sort of a practice this is?'

'No,' answered Philip.

'Mostly fishermen and their families. I have the Union and the Seamen's Hospital. I used to be alone here, but since they tried to make this into a fashionable seaside resort a man has set up on the cliff, and the well-to-do people go to him. I only have those who can't afford to pay for a doctor at all.'

Philip saw that the rivalry was a sore point with the old man.

'You know that I have no experience,' said Philip.

'You none of you know anything.'

He walked out of the room without another word and left Philip by himself. When the maid came in to clear away she told Philip that Doctor South saw patients from six till seven. Work for that night was over. Philip fetched a book from his room, lit his pipe, and settled himself down to read. It was a great comfort, since he had read nothing but medical books for the last few months. At ten o'clock Doctor South came in and looked at him. Philip hated not to have his feet up, and he had dragged up a chair for them.

'You seem able to make yourself pretty comfortable,' said Doctor South, with a grimness which would have disturbed Philip if he had not been in such high spirits.

Philip's eyes twinkled as he answered:

'Have you any objection?'

Doctor South gave him a look, but did not reply directly.

'What's that you're reading?'

'*Peregrine Pickle*. Smollett.'

'I happen to know that Smollett wrote *Peregrine Pickle*.'

'I beg your pardon. Medical men aren't much interested in literature, are they?'

Philip had put the book down on the table, and Doctor South took it up. It was a volume of an edition which had belonged to the Vicar of Blackstable. It was a thin book bound in faded morocco, with a copper-plate engraving as a frontispiece; the pages were musty with age and stained with mould. Philip, without meaning to, started forward a little as Doctor South took the volume in his hands, and a slight smile came into his eyes. Very little escaped the old doctor.

'Do I amuse you?' he asked icily.

'I see you're fond of books. You can always tell by the way people handle them.'

Doctor South put down the novel immediately.

'Breakfast at eight-thirty,' he said, and left the room.

'What a funny old fellow!' thought Philip.

He soon discovered why Doctor South's assistants found it difficult to get on with him. In the first place, he set his face firmly against all the discoveries of the last thirty years: he had no patience with the drugs which became modish, were thought to work marvellous cures, and in a few years were discarded; he had stock mixtures which he had brought from St Luke's, where he had been a student, and had used all his life; he found them just as efficacious as anything that had come into fashion since. Philip was startled at Doctor South's suspicion of asepsis; he had accepted it in deference to universal opinion; but he used the precautions which Philip had known were insisted upon so scrupulously at the hospital, with the disdainful tolerance of a man playing at soldiers with children.

'I've seen antiseptics come along and sweep everything before them, and then I've seen asepsis take their place. Bunkum!'

The young men who were sent down to him knew only hospital practice; and they came with the unconcealed scorn for the General Practitioner which they had absorbed in the air at the hospital; but they had seen only the complicated cases which appeared in the wards; they knew how to treat an obscure disease of the suprarenal bodies, but were helpless when consulted for a cold in the head. Their knowledge was theoretical and their self-assurance unbounded. Doctor South watched them with tightened lips; he took a savage pleasure in showing them how great was their ignorance and how unjustified their conceit. It was a poor practice, of fishing folk, and the doctor made up his own prescriptions. Doctor South asked his assistant how he expected to make both ends meet if he gave a fisherman with a stomach-ache a mixture consisting of half a dozen expensive drugs. He complained too that the young medical men were uneducated: their reading consisted of *The Sporting Times* and *The British Medical Journal*; they could neither write a legible hand nor spell correctly. For two or three days Doctor South watched Philip closely, ready to fall on him with acid sarcasm if he gave him the opportunity; and Philip, aware of this, went about his work with a quiet sense of amusement. He was pleased with the change of occupation. He liked the feeling of independence and of responsibility. All sorts of people came to the consulting-room. He was gratified because he seemed able to inspire his patients with confidence; and it was entertaining to watch the process of cure which at a hospital necessarily could be watched only at distant intervals. His rounds took him into low-roofed cottages in which were fishing tackle and sails and here and there mementoes of deep-sea travelling, a lacquer box from Japan, spears and oars from Melanesia, or daggers from the bazaars of Stamboul; there was an air of romance in the stuffy little rooms, and the salt of the sea gave them a bitter freshness. Philip liked to talk to the sailor men, and when they found that he was not supercilious they told him long yarns of the distant journeys of their youth.

Once or twice he made a mistake in diagnosis (he had never seen a case of measles before, and when he was confronted with the rash took it for an obscure disease of the skin), and once or twice his ideas of treatment differed from Doctor South's. The first time this happened Doctor South attacked him with savage irony; but Philip took it with good humour; he had some gift for repartee, and he made one or two answers which caused Doctor South to stop and look at him curiously. Philip's face was grave, but his eyes were twinkling. The old gentleman could not avoid the impression that Philip was chaffing him. He was used to being disliked and feared by his assistants, and this was a new experience. He had half a mind to fly into a passion and pack Philip off by the next train, he had done that before with his assistants; but he had an uneasy feeling that Philip then would simply laugh at him outright; and suddenly he felt amused. His mouth formed itself into a smile against his will, and he turned away. In a little while he grew conscious that Philip was amusing himself systematically at his expense. He was taken aback at first and then diverted.

'Damn his impudence,' he chuckled to himself. 'Damn his impudence.'

PHILIP had written to Athelny to tell him that he was doing a *locum* in Dorsetshire and in due course received an answer from him. It was written in the formal manner he affected, studded with pompous epithets as a Persian diadem was studded with precious stones; and in the beautiful hand, like black-letter and as difficult to read, upon which he prided himself. He suggested that Philip should join him and his family in the Kentish hop-field to which he went every year; and to persuade him said various beautiful and complicated things about Philip's soul and the winding tendrils of the hops. Philip replied at once that he would come on the first day he was free. Though not born there, he had a peculiar affection for the Isle of Thanet, and he was fired with enthusiasm at the thought of spending a fortnight so close to the earth and amid conditions which needed only a blue sky to be as idyllic as the olive groves of Arcady.

The four weeks of his engagement at Farnley passed quickly. On the cliff a new town was springing up, with red-brick villas round the golf links, and a large hotel had recently been opened to cater for the summer visitors; but Philip went there seldom. Down below, by the harbour, the little stone houses of a past century were clustered in a delightful confusion, and the narrow streets, climbing down steeply, had an air of antiquity which appealed to the imagination. By the water's edge were neat cottages with trim, tiny gardens in front of them; they were inhabited by retired captains in the merchant service, and by mothers or widows of men who had gained their living by the sea; and they had an appearance which was quaint and peaceful. Into the little harbour came tramps from Spain and the Levant, ships of small tonnage; and now and then a wind-jammer was borne in by the winds of romance. It reminded Philip of the dirty little harbour with its colliers at Blackstable, and he thought that there he had first acquired the desire, which was now an obsession, for Eastern lands and sunlit islands in a tropic sea. But here you felt yourself closer to the wide, deep ocean than on the shore of that North Sea which seemed always circumscribed; here you could draw a long breath as you looked out upon the even vastness; and the west wind, the dear soft salt wind of England, uplifted the heart and at the same time melted it to tenderness.

One evening, when Philip had reached his last week with Doctor South, a child came to the surgery door while the old doctor and Philip were making up prescriptions. It was a little ragged girl with a dirty face and bare feet. Philip opened the door.

'Please, sir, will you come to Mrs Fletcher's in Ivy Lane at once?'

'What's the matter with Mrs Fletcher?' called out Doctor South in his rasping voice.

The child took no notice of him, but addressed herself again to Philip.

'Please, sir, her little boy's had an accident and will you come at once?'

'Tell Mrs Fletcher I'm coming,' called out Doctor South.

The little girl hesitated for a moment, and putting a dirty finger in a dirty mouth stood still and looked at Philip.

'What's the matter, kid?' said Philip, smiling.

'Please, sir, Mrs Fletcher says, will the new doctor come?'

There was a sound in the dispensary and Doctor South came out into the passage.

'Isn't Mrs Fletcher satisfied with me?' he barked. 'I've attended Mrs Fletcher since she was born. Why aren't I good enough to attend her filthy brat?'

The little girl looked for a moment as though she were going to cry, then she thought better of it; she put out her tongue deliberately at Doctor South, and, before he could recover from his astonishment, bolted off as fast as she could run. Philip saw that the old gentleman was annoyed.

'You look rather fagged, and it's a goodish way to Ivy Lane,' he said, by way of giving him an excuse not to go himself.

Doctor South gave a low snarl.

'It's a damned sight nearer for a man who's got the use of both legs than for a man who's only got one and a half.'

Philip reddened and stood silent for a while.

'Do you wish me to go or will you go yourself?' he said at last frigidly.

'What's the good of my going? They want you.'

Philip took up his hat and went to see the patient. It was hard upon eight o'clock when he came back. Doctor South was standing in the dining-room with his back to the fireplace.

'You've been a long time,' he said.

'I'm sorry. Why didn't you start dinner?'

'Because I chose to wait. Have you been all this while at Mrs Fletcher's?'

'No, I'm afraid I haven't. I stopped to look at the sunset on my way back, and I didn't think of the time.'

Doctor South did not reply, and the servant brought in some grilled sprats. Philip ate them with an excellent appetite. Suddenly Doctor South shot a question at him.

'Why did you look at the sunset?'

Philip answered with his mouth full:

'Because I was happy.'

Doctor South gave him an odd look, and the shadow of a smile flickered across his old, tired face. They ate the rest of the dinner in silence; but when the maid had given them the port and left the room, the old man leaned back and fixed his sharp eyes on Philip.

'It stung you up a bit when I spoke of your game leg, young fellow?' he said.

'People always do, directly or indirectly, when they get angry with me.'

'I suppose they know it's your weak point.'

Philip faced him and looked at him steadily.

'Are you very glad to have discovered it?'

The doctor did not answer, but he gave a chuckle of bitter mirth. They sat for a while staring at one another. Then Doctor South surprised Philip extremely.

'Why don't you stay here and I'll get rid of that damned fool with his mumps?'

'It's very kind of you, but I hope to get an appointment at the hospital in the autumn. It'll help me so much in getting other work later.'

'I'm offering you a partnership,' said Doctor South grumpily.

'Why?' asked Philip, with surprise.

'They seem to like you down here.'

'I didn't think that was a fact which altogether met with your approval,' Philip said drily.

'D'you suppose that after forty years' practice I care a twopenny damn whether people prefer my assistant to me? No, my friend. There's no sentiment between my patients and me. I don't expect gratitude from them. I expect them to pay my fees. Well, what d'you say to it?'

Philip made no reply, not because he was thinking over the proposal, but because he was astonished. It was evidently very unusual for someone to offer a partnership to a newly qualified man; and he realized with wonder that, although nothing would induce him to say so, Doctor South had taken a fancy to him.

He thought how amused the secretary at St Luke's would be when he told him.

'The practice brings in about seven hundred a year. We can reckon out how much your share would be worth, and you can pay me off by degrees. And when I die you can succeed me. I think that's better than knocking about hospitals for two or three years, and then taking assistantships until you can afford to set up for yourself.'

Philip knew it was a chance that most people in his profession would jump at; the profession was overcrowded, and half the men he knew would be thankful to accept the certainty of even so modest a competence as that.

'I'm awfully sorry, but I can't,' he said. 'It means giving up everything I've aimed at for years. In one way and another I've had a roughish time, but I always had that one hope before me, to get qualified so that I might travel; and now, when I wake in the morning, my bones simply ache to get off, I don't mind where particularly, but just away, to places I've never been to.'

Now the goal seemed very near. He would have finished his appointment at St Luke's by the middle of the following year, and then he would go to Spain; he could afford to spend several months there, rambling up and down the land which stood to him for romance; after that he would get a ship and go to the East. Life was before him and time of no account. He could wander, for years if he chose, in unfrequented places, amid strange peoples, where life was led in strange ways. He did not know what he sought or what his journeys would bring him; but he had a feeling that he would learn something new about life and gain some clue to the mystery that he had solved only to find more mysterious. And even if he found nothing he would allay the unrest which gnawed at his heart. But Doctor South was showing him a great kindness, and it seemed ungrateful to refuse his offer for no adequate reason; so in his shy way, trying to appear as matter-of-fact as possible, he made some attempt to explain why it was so important to him to carry out the plans he had cherished so passionately.

Doctor South listened quietly, and a gentle look came into his shrewd old eyes. It seemed to Philip an added kindness that he did not press him to accept his offer. Benevolence is often very peremptory. He appeared to look upon Philip's reasons as sound. Dropping the subject, he began to talk of his own youth; he had been in the Royal Navy, and it was his long connexion with the sea that, when he retired, had made him settle at Farnley. He told Philip of old days in the Pacific and of wild adventures in China. He had taken part in an expedition against the head-hunters of Borneo and had known Samoa when it was still an independent state. He had touched at coral islands. Philip listened to him entranced. Little by little he told Philip about himself. Doctor South was a widower, his wife had died thirty years before, and his daughter had married a farmer in Rhodesia; he had quarrelled with him, and she had not come to England for ten years. It was just as if he had never had wife or child. He was very lonely. His gruffness was little more than a protection which he wore to hide a complete disillusionment; and to Philip it seemed tragic to see him just waiting for death, not impatiently, but rather with loathing for it, hating old age and unable to resign himself to its limitations, and yet with the feeling that death was the only solution of the bitterness of his life. Philip crossed his path, and the natural affection which long separation from his daughter had killed – she had taken her husband's part in the quarrel and her children he had never seen – settled itself upon Philip. At first it made him angry, he told himself it was a sign of dotage; but there was something in Philip that attracted him, and he found himself smiling at him he knew not why. Philip did not bore him. Once or twice he put his hand on his shoulder: it was as near a caress as he had got since his daughter left England so many years before. When the time came for Philip to go Doctor South accompanied him to the station: he found himself unaccountably depressed.

'I've had a ripping time here,' said Philip. 'You've been awfully kind to me.'

'I suppose you're very glad to go?'

'I've enjoyed myself here.'

'But you want to get out into the world? Ah, you have youth.' He hesitated a moment. 'I want you to remember that if you change your mind my offer still stands.'

'That's awfully kind of you.'

Philip shook hands with him out of the carriage window, and the train steamed out of the station. Philip thought of the fortnight he was going to spend in the hop-field: he was happy at the idea of seeing his friends again, and he rejoiced because the day was fine. But Doctor South walked slowly back to his empty house. He felt very old and very lonely.

CXVIII

It was late in the evening when Philip arrived at Ferne. It was Mrs Athelny's native village, and she had been accustomed from her childhood to pick in the hop-field to which with her husband and her children she still went every year. Like many Kentish folk her family had gone out regularly, glad to earn a little money, but especially regarding the annual outing, looked forward to for months, as the best of holidays. The work was not hard, it was done in common, in the open air, and for the children it was a long, delightful picnic; here the young men met the maidens; in the long evenings when work was over they wandered about the lanes, making love; and the hopping season was generally followed by weddings. They went out in carts with bedding, pots and pans, chairs and tables; and Ferne while the hopping lasted was deserted. They were very exclusive and would have resented the intrusion of foreigners, as they called the people who came from London; they looked down upon them and feared them too; they were a rough lot, and the respectable country folk did not want to mix with them. In the old days the hoppers slept in barns, but ten years ago a row of huts had been erected at the side of a meadow; and the Athelnys, like many others, had the same hut every year.

Athelny met Philip at the station in a cart he had borrowed from the public-house at which he had got a room for Philip. It was a quarter of a mile from the hop-field. They left his bag there and walked over to the meadow in which were the huts. They were nothing more than a long, low shed, divided into little rooms about twelve feet square. In front of each was a fire of sticks, round which a family was grouped, eagerly watching the cooking of supper. The sea-air and the sun had browned already the faces of Athelny's children. Mrs Athelny seemed a different woman in her sunbonnet: you felt that the long years in the city had made no real difference to her; she was the country woman born and bred, and you could see how much at home she found herself in the country. She was frying bacon and at the same time keeping an eye on the younger children, but she had a hearty handshake and a jolly smile for Philip. Athelny was enthusiastic over the delights of a rural existence.

'We're starved for sun and light in the cities we live in. It isn't life, it's a long imprisonment. Let us sell all we have, Betty, and take a farm in the country.'

'I can see you in the country,' she answered with good-humoured scorn. 'Why, the first rainy day we had in the winter you'd be crying for London.' She turned to Philip. 'Athelny's always like this when we come down here. Country, I like that! Why, he don't know a swede from a mangel-wurzel.'

'Daddy was lazy today,' remarked Jane, with the frankness which characterized her, 'he didn't fill one bin.'

'I'm getting into practice, child, and tomorrow I shall fill more bins than all of you put together.'

'Come and eat your supper, children,' said Mrs Athelny. 'Where's Sally?'

'Here I am, mother.'

She stepped out of their little hut, and the flames of the wood fire leaped up and cast sharp colour upon her face. Of late Philip had only seen her in the trim frocks she had taken to since she was at the dressmaker's, and there was something very charming in the print dress she wore now, loose and easy to work in; the sleeves were tucked up and showed her strong, round arms. She too had a sunbonnet.

'You look like a milkmaid in a fairy story,' said Philip, as he shook hands with her.

'She's the belle of the hop-fields,' said Athelny. 'My word, if the Squire's son sees you he'll make you an offer of marriage before you can say Jack Robinson.'

'The Squire hasn't got a son, father,' said Sally.

She looked about for a place to sit down in, and Philip made room for her beside him. She looked wonderful in the night lit by wood fires. She was like some rural goddess, and you thought of those fresh, strong girls whom old Herrick had praised in exquisite numbers. The supper was simple – bread and butter, crisp bacon, tea for the children, and beer for Mr and Mrs Athelny and Philip. Athelny, eating hungrily, praised loudly all he ate. He flung words of scorn at Lucullus and piled invectives upon Brillat-Savarin.

'There's one thing one can say for you, Athelny,' said his wife, 'you do enjoy your food and no mistake!'

'Cooked by your hand, my Betty,' he said, stretching out an eloquent forefinger.

Philip felt himself very comfortable. He looked happily at the line of fires, with people grouped about them, and the colour of the flames against the night; at the end of the meadow was a line of great elms, and above the starry sky.

The children talked and laughed, and Athelny, a child among them, made them roar by his tricks and fancies.

'They think a rare lot of Athelny down here,' said his wife. 'Why, Mrs Bridges said to me, I don't know what we should do without Mr Athelny now, she said. He's always up to something, he's more like a schoolboy than the father of a family.'

Sally sat in silence, but she attended to Philip's wants in a thoughtful fashion that charmed him. It was pleasant to have her beside him, and now and then he glanced at her sunburned, healthy face. Once he caught her eyes, and she smiled quietly. When supper was over Jane and a small brother were sent down to a brook that ran at the bottom of the meadow to fetch a pail of water for washing up.

'You children, show your Uncle Philip where we sleep, and then you must be thinking of going to bed.'

Small hands seized Philip, and he was dragged towards the hut. He went in and struck a match. There was no furniture in it; and beside a tin box, in which clothes were kept, there was nothing but the beds; there were three of them, one against each wall. Athelny followed Philip in and showed them proudly.

'That's the stuff to sleep on,' he cried. 'None of your spring-mattresses and swansdown. I never sleep so soundly anywhere as here. *You* will sleep between sheets. My dear fellow, I pity you from the bottom of my soul.'

The beds consisted of a thick layer of hopbine, on the top of which was a coating of straw, and this was covered with a blanket. After a day in the open air, with the aromatic scent of the hops all round them, the happy pickers slept like tops. By nine o'clock all was quiet in the meadow and everyone in bed but one or two men who still lingered in the public-house and would not come back till it was closed at ten. Athelny walked there with Philip. But before he went Mrs Athelny said to him:

'We breakfast about a quarter to six, but I daresay you won't want to get up as early as that. You see, we have to set to work at six.'

'Of course he must get up early,' cried Athelny, 'and he must work like the rest of us. He's got to earn his board. No work, no dinner, my lad.'

'The children go down to bathe before breakfast, and they can give you a call on their way back. They pass "The Jolly Sailor".'

'If they'll wake me I'll come and bathe with them,' said Philip.

Jane and Harold and Edward shouted with delight at the prospect, and next morning Philip was awakened out of a sound sleep by their bursting into his room. The boys jumped on his bed, and he had to chase them out with his slippers. He put on a coat and a pair of trousers and went down. The day had only just broken, and there was a nip in the air; but the sky was cloudless, and the sun was shining yellow. Sally, holding Connie's hand, was standing in the middle of the road, with a towel and a bathing-dress over her arm. He saw now that her sunbonnet was of the colour of lavender, and against it her face, red and brown, was like an apple. She greeted him with her slow, sweet smile, and he noticed suddenly that her teeth were small and regular and very white. He wondered why they had never caught his attention before.

'I was for letting you sleep on,' she said, 'but they would go up and wake you. I said you didn't really want to come.'

'Oh, yes, I did.'

They walked down the road and then cut across the marshes. That way it was under a mile to the sea. The water looked cold and grey, and Philip shivered at the sight of it; but the others tore off their clothes and ran in shouting. Sally did everything a little slowly, and she did not come into the water till all the rest were splashing round Philip. Swimming was his only accomplishment; he felt at home in the water; and soon he had them all imitating him as he played at being a porpoise, and a drowning man, and a fat lady afraid of wetting her hair. The bathe was uproarious, and it was necessary for Sally to be very severe to induce them all to come out.

'You're as bad as any of them,' she said to Philip, in her grave, maternal way, which was at once comic and touching. 'They're not anything like so naughty when you're not here.'

They walked back, Sally with her bright hair streaming over one shoulder and her sunbonnet in her hand, but when they got to the huts Mrs Athelny had already started for the hop-garden. Athelny, in a pair of the oldest trousers anyone had ever worn, his jacket buttoned up to show he had no shirt on, and in a wide-brimmed soft hat, was frying kippers over a fire of sticks. He was delighted with himself: he looked every inch a brigand. As soon as he saw the party he began to shout the witches' chorus from *Macbeth* over the odorous kippers.

'You mustn't dawdle over your breakfast or mother will be angry,' he said, when they came up.

And in a few minutes, Harold and Jane with pieces of bread and butter in their hands, they sauntered through the meadow into the hop-field. They were the last to leave. A hop-garden was one of the sights connected with Philip's boyhood and the oast-houses to him the most typical feature of the Kentish scene. It was with no sense of strangeness, but as though he were at home, that Philip followed Sally through the long lines of the hops. The sun was bright now and cast a sharp shadow. Philip feasted his eyes on the richness of the green leaves. The hops were yellowing, and to him they had the beauty and the passion which poets in Sicily have found in the purple grape. As they walked along Philip felt himself overwhelmed by the rich luxuriance. A sweet scent arose from the fat Kentish soil, and the fitful September breeze was heavy with the goodly perfume of the hops. Athelstan felt the exhilaration instinctively, for he lifted up his voice and sang; it was the cracked voice of the boy of fifteen, and Sally turned round.

'You be quiet, Athelstan, or we shall have a thunder-storm.'

In a moment they heard the hum of voices, and in a moment more came upon the pickers. They were all hard at work, talking and laughing as they picked. They sat on chairs, on stools, on boxes, with their baskets by their sides, and some stood by the bin throwing the hops they picked straight into it. There were a lot of children about and a good many babies, some in makeshift cradles, some tucked up in a rug on the soft brown dry earth. The children picked a little and played a great deal. The women worked busily, they had been pickers from childhood, and they could pick twice as fast as foreigners from London. They boasted about the number of bushels they had picked in a day, but they complained you could not make money now as in former times: then they paid you a shilling for five bushels, but now the rate was eight and even nine bushels to the shilling. In the old days a good picker could earn enough in the season to keep her for the rest of the year, but now there was nothing in it; you got a holiday for nothing, and that was about all. Mrs Hill had bought herself a pianner out of what she made picking, so she said, but she was very near, one wouldn't like to be near like that, and most people thought it was only what she said; if the truth was known perhaps it would be found that she had put a bit of money from the savings bank towards it.

The hoppers were divided into bin companies of ten pickers, not counting children, and Athelny loudly boasted of the day when he would have a company consisting entirely of his own family. Each company had a bin-man, whose duty it was to supply it with strings of hops at their bins (the bin was a large sack on a wooden frame, about seven feet high, and long rows of them were placed between the rows of hops); and it was to this position that Athelny aspired when his family was old enough to form a company. Meanwhile he worked rather by encouraging others than by exertions of his own. He sauntered up to Mrs Athelny, who had been busy for half an hour and had already emptied a basket into the bin, and with his cigarette between his lips began to pick. He asserted that he was going to pick more than anyone that day but mother; of course no one could pick so much as mother; that reminded him of the trials which Aphrodite put upon the curious Psyche, and he began to tell his children the story of her love for the unseen bridegroom. He told it very well. It seemed to Philip, listening with a smile on his lips, that the old tale fitted in with the scene. The sky was very blue now, and he thought it could not be more lovely even in Greece. The children with their fair hair and rosy cheeks, strong, healthy, and vivacious; the delicate form of the hops; the challenging emerald of the leaves, like a blare of trumpets; the magic of the green alley, narrowing to a point as you looked down the row, with the pickers in their sunbonnets: perhaps there was more of the Greek spirit there than you could find in the books of professors or in museums. He was thankful for the beauty of England. He thought of the winding white roads and the hedgerows, the green meadows with their elm-trees, the delicate line of the hills and the copses that crowned them, the flatness of the marshes, and the melancholy of the North Sea. He was very glad that he felt its loveliness. But presently Athelny grew restless and announced that he would go and ask how Robert Kemp's mother was. He knew everyone in the garden and called them all by their Christian names; he knew their family histories and all that had happened to them from birth. With harmless vanity he played the fine gentleman among them, and there was a touch of condescension in his familiarity. Philip would not go with him.

'I'm going to earn my dinner,' he said.

'Quite right, my boy,' answered Athelny, with a wave of the hand, as he strolled away. 'No work, no dinner.'

CXIX

PHILIP had not a basket of his own, but sat with Sally. Jane thought it monstrous that he should help her elder sister rather than herself, and he had to promise to pick for her when Sally's basket was full. Sally was almost as quick as her mother.

'Won't it hurt your hands for sewing?' asked Philip.

'Oh, no, it wants soft hands. That's why women pick better than men. If your hands are hard and your fingers are stiff with a lot of rough work you can't pick near so well.'

He liked to see her deft movements, and she watched him too now and then with that maternal spirit of hers which was so amusing and yet so charming. He was clumsy at first, and she laughed at him. When she bent over and showed him how best to deal with a whole line their hands met. He was surprised to see her blush. He could not persuade himself that she was a woman; because he had known her as a flapper, he could not help looking upon her as a child still; yet the number of her admirers showed that she was a child no longer; and though they had only been down a few days one of Sally's cousins was already so attentive that she had to endure a lot of chaffing. His name was Peter Gann, and he was the son of Mrs Athelny's sister, who had married a farmer near Ferne. Everyone knew why he found it necessary to walk through the hop-field every day.

A call-off by the sounding of a horn was made for breakfast at eight, and though Mrs Athelny told them they had not deserved it, they ate it very heartily. They set to work again and worked till twelve, when the horn sounded once more for dinner. At intervals the measurer went his round from bin to bin, accompanied by the booker, who entered first in his own book and then in the hopper's the number of bushels picked. As each bin was filled it was measured out in bushel baskets into a huge bag called a poke; and this the measurer and the pole-puller carried off between them and put on the wagon. Athelny came back now and then with stories of how much Mrs Heath or Mrs Jones had picked, and he conjured his family to beat her: he was always wanting to make records, and sometimes in his enthusiasm picked steadily for an hour. His chief amusement in it, however, was that it showed the beauty of his graceful hands, of which he was excessively proud. He spent much time manicuring them. He told Philip, as he stretched out his tapering fingers, that the Spanish grandees had always slept in oiled gloves to preserve their whiteness. The hand that wrung the throat of Europe, he remarked dramatically, was as shapely and exquisite as a woman's; and he looked at his own, as he delicately picked the hops, and sighed with self-satisfaction. When he grew tired of this he rolled himself a cigarette and discoursed to Philip of art and literature. In the afternoon it grew very hot. Work did not proceed so actively and conversation halted. The incessant chatter of the morning dwindled now to desultory remarks. Tiny beads of sweat stood on Sally's upper lip, and as she worked her lips were slightly parted. She was like a rosebud bursting into flower.

Calling-off time depended on the state of the oast-house. Sometimes it was filled early, and as many hops had been picked by three or four as could be dried during the night. Then work was stopped. But generally the last measuring of the day began at five. As each company had its bin measured it gathered up its things and, chatting again now that work was over, sauntered out of the garden. The women went back to the huts to clean up and prepare the supper, while a good many of the men strolled down the road to the public-house. A glass of beer was very pleasant after the day's work.

The Athelnys' bin was the last to be dealt with. When the measurer came Mrs Athelny, with a sigh of relief, stood up and stretched her arms: she had been sitting in the same position for many hours and was stiff.

'Now, let's go to "The Jolly Sailor",' said Athelny. 'The rites of the day must be duly performed, and there is none more sacred than that.'

'Take a jug with you, Athelny,' said his wife, 'and bring back a pint and a half for supper.'

She gave him the money, copper by copper. The bar-parlour was already well filled. It had a sanded floor, benches round it, and yellow pictures of Victorian prize-fighters on the walls. The licensee knew all his customers by name, and he leaned over his bar smiling benignly at two young men who were throwing rings on a stick that stood up from the floor: their failure was greeted with a good deal of hearty chaff from the rest of the company. Room was made for the new arrivals. Philip found himself sitting between an old labourer in corduroys, with string tied under his knees, and a shiny-faced lad of seventeen with a love-lock neatly plastered on his red forehead. Athelny insisted on trying his hand at the throwing of

591

rings. He backed himself for half a pint and won it. As he drank the loser's health he said:

'I would sooner have won this than won the Derby, my boy.'

He was an outlandish figure, with his wide-brimmed hat and pointed beard, among those country folk, and it was easy to see that they thought him very queer, but his spirits were so high, his enthusiasm so contagious, that it was impossible not to like him. Conversation went easily. A certain number of pleasantries were exchanged in the broad, slow accent of the Isle of Thanet, and there was uproarious laughter at the sallies of the local wag. A pleasant gathering! It would have been a hard-hearted person who did not feel a glow of satisfaction in his fellows. Philip's eyes wandered out of the window, where it was bright and sunny still; there were little white curtains in it tied up with red ribbon like those of a cottage window, and on the sill were pots of geraniums. In due course one by one the idlers got up and sauntered back to the meadow where supper was cooking.

'I expect you'll be ready for your bed,' said Mrs Athelny to Philip. 'You're not used to getting up at five and staying in the open air all day.'

'You're coming to bathe with us, Uncle Phil, aren't you?' the boys cried.

'Rather.'

He was tired and happy. After supper, balancing himself against the wall of the hut on a chair without a back, he smoked his pipe and looked at the night. Sally was busy. She passed in and out of the hut, and he lazily watched her methodical actions. Her walk attracted his notice; it was not particularly graceful, but it was easy and assured; she swung her legs from the hips, and her feet seemed to tread the earth with decision. Athelny had gone off to gossip with one of the neighbours, and presently Philip heard his wife address the world in general.

'There now, I'm out of tea and I wanted Athelny to go down to Mrs Black's and get some.' A pause, and then her voice was raised: 'Sally, just run down to Mrs Black's and get me half a pound of tea, will you? I've run quite out of it.'

'All right, mother.'

Mrs Black had a cottage about half a mile along the road, and she combined the office of postmistress with that of universal provider. Sally came out of the hut, turning down her sleeves.

'Shall I come with you, Sally?' asked Philip.

'Don't you trouble. I'm not afraid to go alone.'

'I didn't think you were; but it's getting near my bedtime, and I was just thinking I'd like to stretch my legs.'

Sally did not answer, and they set out together. The road was white and silent. There was not a sound in the summer night. They did not speak much.

'It's quite hot even now, isn't it?' said Philip.

'I think it's wonderful for the time of year.'

But their silence did not seem awkward. They found it was pleasant to walk side by side and felt no need of words. Suddenly at a stile in the hedgerow they heard a low murmur of voices, and in the darkness they saw the outline of two people. They were sitting very close to one another and did not move as Philip and Sally passed.

'I wonder who that was,' said Sally.

'They looked happy enough, didn't they?'

'I expect they took us for lovers too.'

They saw the light of the cottage in front of them, and in a minute went into the little shop. The glare dazzled them for a moment.

'You are late,' said Mrs Black. 'I was just going to shut up.' She looked at the clock. 'Getting on for nine.'

Sally asked for her half pound of tea (Mrs Athelny could never bring herself to buy more than half a pound at a time), and they set off up the road again. Now and then some beast of the night made a short, sharp sound, but it seemed only to make the silence more marked.

'I believe if you stood still you could hear the sea,' said Sally.

They strained their ears, and their fancy presented them with a faint sound of little waves lapping up against the shingle. When they passed the stile again the lovers were still there, but now they were not speaking; they were in one another's arms, and the man's lips were pressed against the girl's.

'They seem busy,' said Sally.

They turned a corner, and a breath of warm wind beat for a moment against their faces. The earth gave forth its freshness. There was something strange in the tremulous night, and something, you knew not what, seemed to be waiting; the silence was on a sudden pregnant with meaning. Philip had a queer feeling in his heart, it seemed very full, it seemed to melt (the hackneyed phrases expressed precisely the curious sensation), he felt happy and anxious and expectant. To his memory came back those lines in which Jessica and Lorenzo murmur melodious words to one another, capping each other's utterance; but passion shines bright and clear through the conceits that amuse them. He did not know what there was in the air that made his senses so strangely alert; it seemed to him that he was pure soul to enjoy the scents and the sounds and the savours of the earth. He had never felt such an exquisite capacity for beauty. He was afraid that Sally by speaking would break the spell, but she said never a word, and he wanted to hear the sound of her voice. Its low richness was the voice of the country night itself.

They arrived at the field through which she had to walk to get back to the huts. Philip went in to hold the gate open for her.

'Well, here I think I'll say good night.'

'Thank you for coming all that way with me.'

She gave him her hand, and as he took it, he said: 'If you were very nice you'd kiss me good night like the rest of the family.'

'I don't mind,' she said.

Philip had spoken in jest. He merely wanted to kiss her because he was happy and he liked her and the night was so lovely.

'Good night then,' he said, with a little laugh, drawing her towards him.

She gave him her lips; they were warm and full and soft; he lingered a little, they were like a flower; then, he knew not how, without meaning it, he flung his arms round her. She yielded quite silently. Her body was firm and strong. He felt her heart beat against his. Then he lost his head. His senses overwhelmed him like a flood of rushing waters. He drew her into the darker shadow of the hedge.

CXX

PHILIP slept like a log and awoke with a start to find Harold tickling his face with a feather. There was a shout of delight when he opened his eyes. He was drunken with sleep.

'Come on, lazy bones,' said Jane. 'Sally says she won't wait for you unless you hurry up.'

Then he remembered what had happened. His heart sank, and, half out of bed already, he stopped; he did not know how he was going to face her; he was overwhelmed with a sudden rush of self-reproach, and bitterly, bitterly, he regretted what he

594

had done. What would she say to him that morning? He dreaded meeting her, and he asked himself how he could have been such a fool. But the children gave him no time; Edward took his bathing-drawers and his towel, Athelstan tore the bed-clothes away; and in three minutes they all clattered down into the road. Sally gave him a smile. It was as sweet and innocent as it had ever been.

'You do take a time to dress yourself,' she said. 'I thought you was never coming.'

There was not a particle of difference in her manner. He had expected some change, subtle or abrupt; he fancied that there would be shame in the way she treated him, or anger, or perhaps some increase of familiarity; but there was nothing. She was exactly the same as before. They walked towards the sea all together, talking and laughing; and Sally was quiet, but she was always that, reserved, but he had never seen her other-wise, and gentle. She neither sought conversation with him nor avoided it. Philip was astounded. He had expected the incident of the night before to have caused some revolution in her, but it was just as though nothing had happened; it might have been a dream; and as he walked along, a little girl holding on to one hand and a little boy to the other, while he chatted as uncon-cernedly as he could, he sought for an explanation. He won-dered whether Sally meant the affair to be forgotten. Perhaps her senses had run away with her just as his had, and, treating what had occurred as an accident due to unusual circum-stances, it might be that she had decided to put the matter out of her mind. It was ascribing to her a power of thought and a mature wisdom which fitted neither with her age nor with her character. But he realized that he knew nothing of her. There had been in her always something enigmatic.

They played leap-frog in the water, and the bathe was as uproarious as on the previous day. Sally mothered them all, keeping a watchful eye on them, and calling to them when they went out too far. She swam staidly backwards and forwards while the others got up to their larks, and now and then turned on her back to float. Presently she went out and began drying herself; she called to the others more or less peremptorily, and at last only Philip was left in the water. He took the oppor-tunity to have a good hard swim. He was more used to the cold water this second morning, and he revelled in its salt fresh-ness; it rejoiced him to use his limbs freely, and he covered the water with long, firm strokes. But Sally, with a towel round her, went down to the water's edge.

'You're to come out this minute, Philip,' she called, as though he were a small boy under her charge.

And when, smiling with amusement at her authoritative way, he came towards her, she upbraided him.

'It is naughty of you to stay in so long. Your lips are quite blue, and just look at your teeth, they're chattering.'

'All right. I'll come out.'

She had never talked to him in that manner before. It was as though what had happened gave her a sort of right over him, and she looked upon him as a child to be cared for. In a few minutes they were dressed, and they started to walk back. Sally noticed his hands.

'Just look, they're quite blue.'

'Oh, that's all right. It's only the circulation. I shall get the blood back in a minute.'

'Give them to me.'

She took his hands in hers and rubbed them, first one and then the other, till the colour returned. Philip, touched and puzzled, watched her. He could not say anything to her on account of the children, and he did not meet her eyes; but he was sure they did not avoid his purposely, it just happened that they did not meet. And during the day there was nothing in her behaviour to suggest a consciousness in her that anything had passed between them. Perhaps she was a little more talkative than usual. When they were all sitting again in the hop-field she told her mother how naughty Philip had been in not coming out of the water till he was blue with cold. It was incredible, and yet it seemed that the only effect of the incident of the night before was to arouse in her a feeling of protection towards him: she had the same instinctive desire to mother him as she had with regard to her brothers and sisters.

It was not till the evening that he found himself alone with her. She was cooking the supper, and Philip was sitting on the grass by the side of the fire. Mrs Athelny had gone down to the village to do some shopping, and the children were scattered in various pursuits of their own. Philip hesitated to speak. He was very nervous. Sally attended to her business with serene competence, and she accepted placidly the silence which to him was so embarrassing. He did not know how to begin. Sally seldom spoke unless she was spoken to or had something particular to say. At last he could not bear it any longer.

'You're not angry with me, Sally?' he blurted out suddenly.

She raised her eyes quietly and looked at him without emotion.

596

'Me? No. Why should I be?'

He was taken aback and did not reply. She took the lid off the pot, stirred the contents, and put it on again. A savoury smell spread over the air. She looked at him once more, with a quiet smile which barely separated her lips; it was more a smile of the eyes.

'I always liked you,' she said.

His heart gave a great thump against his ribs, and he felt the blood rushing to his cheeks. He forced a faint laugh.

'I didn't know that.'

'That's because you're a silly.'

'I don't know why you liked me.'

'I don't either.' She put a little more wood on the fire. 'I knew I liked you that day you came when you'd been sleeping out and hadn't had anything to eat, d'you remember? And me and mother, we got Thorpy's bed ready for you.'

He flushed again, for he did not know that she was aware of that incident. He remembered it himself with horror and shame.

'That's why I wouldn't have anything to do with the others. You remember that young fellow mother wanted me to have? I let him come to tea because he bothered me so, but I knew I'd say no.'

Philip was so surprised that he found nothing to say. There was a queer feeling in his heart; he did not know what it was, unless it was happiness. Sally stirred the pot once more.

'I wish those children would make haste and come. I don't know where they've got to. Supper's ready now.'

'Shall I go and see if I can find them?' said Philip.

It was a relief to talk about practical things.

'Well, it wouldn't be a bad idea, I must say.... There's mother coming.'

Then, as he got up, she looked at him without embarrassment.

'Shall I come for a walk with you tonight when I've put the children to bed?'

'Yes.'

'Well, you wait for me down by the stile, and I'll come when I'm ready.'

He waited under the stars, sitting on the stile, and the hedges with their ripening blackberries were high on each side of him. From the earth rose rich scents of the night, and the air was soft and still. His heart was beating madly. He could not understand anything of what happened to him. He associated passion with cries and tears and vehemence, and there was nothing of this in Sally; but he did not know what else but passion could have caused her to give herself. But passion for him? He would not have been surprised if she had fallen to her cousin, Peter Gann, tall, spare, and straight, with his sunburned face and long, easy stride. Philip wondered what she saw in him. He did not know if she loved him as he reckoned love. And yet? He was convinced of her purity. He had a vague inkling that many things had combined, things that she felt though was unconscious of, the intoxication of the air and the hops and the night, the healthy instincts of the natural woman, a tenderness that overflowed, and an affection that had in it something maternal and something sisterly! and she gave all she had to give because her heart was full of charity.

He heard a step on the road, and a figure came out of the darkness.

'Sally,' he murmured.

She stopped and came to the stile, and with her came sweet, clean odours of the countryside. She seemed to carry with her scents of the new-mown hay, and the savour of ripe hops, and the freshness of young grass. Her lips were soft and full against his, and her lovely, strong body was firm within his arms.

'Milk and honey,' he said. 'You're like milk and honey.'

He made her close her eyes and kissed her eyelids, first one and then the other. Her arm, strong and muscular, was bare to the elbow; he passed his hand over it and wondered at its beauty; it gleamed in the darkness; she had the skin that Rubens painted, astonishingly fair and transparent, and on one side were little golden hairs. It was the arm of a Saxon goddess; but no immortal had that exquisite, homely naturalness; and Philip thought of a cottage garden with the dear flowers which bloom in all men's hearts, of the hollyhock and the red and white rose which is called York and Lancaster, and of love-in-a-mist and Sweet William, and honeysuckle, larkspur, and London Pride.

'How can you care for me?' he said. 'I'm insignificant and crippled and ordinary and ugly.'

She took his face in both her hands and kissed his lips.

'You're an old silly, that's what you are,' she said.

598

CXXI

WHEN the hops were picked, Philip, with the news in his pocket that he had got the appointment as assistant house-physician at St Luke's, accompanied the Athelnys back to London. He took modest rooms in Westminster and at the beginning of October entered upon his duties. The work was interesting and varied; every day he learned something new; he felt himself of some consequence; and he saw a good deal of Sally. He found life uncommonly pleasant. He was free about six, except on the days on which he had out-patients, and then he went to the shop at which Sally worked to meet her when she came out. There were several young men, who hung about opposite the 'trade entrance' or a little further along, at the first corner; and the girls, coming out two and two or in little groups, nudged one another and giggled as they recognized them. Sally in her plain black dress looked very different from the country lass who had picked hops side by side with him. She walked away from the shop quickly, but she slackened her pace when they met, and greeted him with a quiet smile. They walked together through the busy street. He talked to her of his work at the hospital, and she told him what she had been doing in the shop that day. He came to know the names of the girls she worked with. He found that Sally had a restrained, but keen, sense of the ridiculous, and she made remarks about the girls or the men who were set over them which amused him by their unexpected drollery. She had a way of saying a thing which was very characteristic, quite gravely, as though there were nothing funny in it at all, and yet it was so sharp-sighted that Philip broke into delighted laughter. Then she would give him a little glance in which the smiling eyes showed she was not unaware of her own humour. They met with a handshake and parted as formally. Once Philip asked her to come and have tea with him in his rooms, but she refused.

'No, I won't do that. It would look funny.'

Never a word of love passed between them. She seemed not to desire anything more than the companionship of those walks. Yet Philip was positive that she was glad to be with him. She puzzled him as much as she had done at the beginning. He did not begin to understand her conduct; but the more he knew her the fonder he grew of her; she was competent and self-controlled, and there was a charming honesty in her: you felt that you could rely upon her in every circumstance.

'You are an awfully good sort,' he said to her once apropos of nothing at all.

'I expect I'm just the same as everyone else,' she answered.

He knew that he did not love her. It was a great affection that he felt for her, and he liked her company; it was curiously soothing; and he had a feeling for her which seemed to him ridiculous to entertain towards a shop-girl of nineteen: he respected her. And he admired her magnificent healthiness. She was a splendid animal, without defect; and physical perfection filled him always with admiring awe. She made him feel unworthy.

Then one day, about three weeks after they had come back to London as they walked together, he noticed that she was unusually silent. The serenity of her expression was altered by a slight line between the eyebrows: it was the beginning of a frown.

'What's the matter, Sally?' he asked.

She did not look at him, but straight in front of her, and her colour darkened.

'I don't know.'

He understood at once what she meant. His heart gave a sudden, quick beat, and he felt the colour leave his cheeks.

'What d'you mean? Are you afraid that . . . ?'

He stopped. He could not go on. The possibility that anything of the sort could happen had never crossed his mind. Then he saw that her lips were trembling, and she was trying not to cry.

'I'm not certain yet. Perhaps it'll be all right.'

They walked on in silence till they came to the corner of Chancery Lane, where he always left her. She held out her hand and smiled.

'Don't worry about it yet. Let's hope for the best.'

He walked away with a tumult of thoughts in his head. What a fool he had been! That was the first thing that struck him, an abject, miserable fool, and he repeated it to himself a dozen times in a rush of angry feeling. He despised himself. How could he have got into such a mess? But at the same time, for his thoughts chased one another through his brain and yet seemed to stand together, in a hopeless confusion, like the pieces of a jigsaw puzzle seen in a nightmare, he asked himself what he was going to do. Everything was so clear before him, all he had aimed at so long within reach at last, and now his inconceivable stupidity had erected this new obstacle. Philip had never been able to surmount what he acknowledged was a defect in his resolute desire for a well-ordered life, and that was his passion for living in the future; and no sooner was he settled in his work at the hospital than he had busied himself with arrangements for his travels. In the past he had often tried not to think too circumstantially of his plans for the future, it was only discouraging; but now that his goal was so near he saw no harm in giving way to a longing that was so difficult to resist. First of all he meant to go to Spain. That was the land of his heart; and by now he was imbued with its spirit, its romance and colour and history and grandeur; he felt that it had a message for him in particular which no other country could give. He knew the fine old cities already as though he had trodden their tortuous streets from childhood, Cordova, Seville, Toledo, León, Tarragona, Burgos. The great painters of Spain were the painters of his soul, and his pulse beat quickly as he pictured his ecstasy on standing face to face with those works which were more significant than any others to his own tortured, restless heart. He had read the great poets, more characteristic of their race than the poets of other lands; for they seemed to have drawn their inspiration not at all from the general currents of the world's literature but directly from the torrid, scented plains and the bleak mountains of their country. A few short months now, and he would hear with his own ears all around him the language which seemed most apt for grandeur of soul and passion. His fine taste had given him an inkling that Andalusia was too soft and sensuous, a little vulgar even, to satisfy his ardour; and his imagination dwelt more willingly among the wind-swept distances of Castile and the rugged magnificence of Aragon and León. He did not know quite what those unknown contacts would give him, but he felt that he would gather from them a strength and a purpose which would make him more capable of affronting and comprehending the manifold wonders of places more distant and more strange.

For this was only a beginning. He had got into communica-with the various companies which took surgeons out on their ships, and knew exactly what were their routes, and from men who had been on them what were the advantages and disadvantages of each line. He put aside the Orient and the P. & O. It was difficult to get a berth with them; and besides their passenger traffic allowed the medical officer little freedom; but there were other services which sent large tramps on leisurely expeditions to the East, stopping at all sorts of ports for various periods, from a day or two to a fortnight, so that you had plenty of time, and it was often possible to make a trip inland. The pay was poor and the food no more than adequate, so that there was not much demand for the posts, and a man with a London degree was pretty sure to get one if he applied. Since there were no passengers other than a casual man or so, shipping on business from some out-of-the-way port to another, the life on board was friendly and pleasant. Philip knew by heart the list of places at which they touched; and each one called up in him visions of tropical sunshine, and magic colour, and of a teeming, mysterious, intense life. Life! That was what he wanted. At last he would come to close quarters with life. And perhaps, from Tokio or Shanghai, it would be possible to tranship into some other line and drop down to the islands of the South Pacific. A doctor was useful anywhere. There might be an opportunity to go up country in Burma, and what rich jungles in Sumatra or Borneo might he not visit? He was young still and time was no object to him. He had no ties in England, no friends; he could go up and down the world for years, learning the beauty and the wonder and the variedness of life.

Now this thing had come. He put aside the possibility that Sally was mistaken; he felt strangely certain that she was right; after all, it was so likely; anyone could see that Nature had built her to be the mother of children. He knew what he ought to do. He ought not to let the incident divert him a hair's breadth from his path. He thought of Griffiths; he could easily imagine with what indifference that young man would have received such a piece of news; he would have thought it an awful nuisance and would at once have taken to his heels, like a wise fellow; he would have left the girl to deal with her troubles as best she could. Philip told himself that if this had happened it was because it was inevitable. He was no more to blame than Sally; she was a girl who knew the world and the facts of life, and she had taken the risk with her eyes open. It would be madness to allow such an accident to disturb the whole pattern of his life. He was one of the few people who was acutely conscious of the transitoriness of life, and how necessary it was to make the most of it. He would do what he could for Sally; he could afford to give her a sufficient sum of money. A strong man would never allow himself to be turned from his purpose.

Philip said all this to himself, but he knew he could not do it. He simply could not. He knew himself.

602

'I'm so damned weak,' he muttered despairingly.

She had trusted him and been kind to him. He simply could not do a thing which, notwithstanding all his reason, he felt was horrible. He knew he would have no peace on his travels if he had the thought constantly with him that she was wretched. Besides, there were her father and mother: they had always treated him well; it was not possible to repay them with ingratitude. The only thing was to marry Sally as quickly as possible. He would write to Doctor South, tell him he was going to be married at once, and say that if his offer still held he was willing to accept it. That sort of practice, among poor people, was the only one possible for him; there his deformity did not matter, and they would not sneer at the simple manners of his wife. It was curious to think of her as his wife, it gave him a queer, soft feeling; and a wave of emotion spread over him as he thought of the child which was his. He had little doubt that Doctor South would be glad to have him, and he pictured to himself the life he would lead with Sally in the fishing village. They would have a little house within sight of the sea, and he would watch the mighty ships passing to the lands he would never know. Perhaps that was the wisest thing. Cronshaw had told him that the facts of life mattered nothing to him who by the power of fancy held in fee the twin realms of space and time. It was true. *Forever wilt thou love and she be fair!*

His wedding present to his wife would be all his high hopes. Self-sacrifice! Philip was uplifted by its beauty, and all through the evening he thought of it. He was so excited that he could not read. He seemed to be driven out of his rooms into the streets, and he walked up and down Birdcage Walk, his heart throbbing with joy. He could hardly bear his impatience. He wanted to see Sally's happiness when he made her his offer, and if it had not been so late he would have gone to her there and then. He pictured to himself the long evenings he would spend with Sally in the cosy sitting-room, the blinds undrawn so that they could watch the sea; he with his books, while she bent over her work, and the shaded lamp made her sweet face more fair. They would talk over the growing child, and when she turned her eyes to his there was in them the light of love. And the fishermen and their wives who were his patients would come to feel a great affection for them, and they in their turn would enter into the pleasures and pains of those simple lives. But his thoughts returned to the son who would be his and hers. Already he felt in himself a passionate devotion to it. He thought of passing his hands over his little perfect limbs, he knew he would be beautiful; and he would make over to him all his dreams of a rich and varied life. And thinking over the long pilgrimage of his past he accepted it joyfully. He accepted the deformity which had made life so hard for him; he knew that it had warped his character, but now he saw also that by reason of it he had acquired that power of introspection which had given him so much delight. Without it he would never have had his keen appreciation of beauty, his passion for art and literature, and his interest in the varied spectacle of life. The ridicule and the contempt which had so often been heaped upon him had turned his mind inward and called forth those flowers which he felt would never lose their fragrance. Then he saw that the normal was the rarest thing in the world. Everyone had some defect, of body or of mind: he thought of all the people he had known (the whole world was like a sick-house, and there was no rhyme or reason in it), he saw a long procession, deformed in body and warped in mind, some with illness of the flesh, weak hearts or weak lungs, and some with illness of the spirit, languor of will, or a craving for liquor. At this moment he could feel a holy compassion for them all. They were the helpless instruments of blind chance. He could pardon Griffiths for his treachery and Mildred for the pain she had caused him. They could not help themselves. The only reasonable thing was to accept the good of men and be patient with their faults. The words of the dying God crossed his memory:

Forgive them, for they know not what they do.

CXXII

He had arranged to meet Sally on Saturday in the National Gallery. She was to come there as soon as she was released from the shop and had agreed to lunch with him. Two days had passed since he had seen her, and his exultation had not left him for a moment. It was because he rejoiced in the feeling that he had not attempted to see her. He had repeated to himself exactly what he would say to her and how he would say it. Now his impatience was unbearable. He had written to Doctor South and had in his pocket a telegram from him received that morning: *'Sacking the mumpish fool. When will you come?'* Philip walked along Parliament Street. It was a fine day, and there was a bright, frosty sun which made the light dance in the street. It was crowded. There was a tenuous mist in the distance, and it softened exquisitely the noble lines of the buildings. He crossed Trafalgar Square. Suddenly his heart gave a sort of twist in his body; he saw a woman in front of him who he thought was Mildred. She had the same figure, and she walked with that slight dragging of the feet which was so characteristic of her. Without thinking, but with a beating heart, he hurried till he came alongside, and then, when the woman turned, he saw it was someone unknown to him. It was the face of a much older person, with a lined, yellow skin. He slackened his pace. He was infinitely relieved, but it was not only relief that he felt; it was disappointment too; he was seized with horror of himself. Would he never be free from that passion? At the bottom of his heart, notwithstanding everything, he felt that a strange, desperate thirst for that vile woman would always linger. That love had caused him so much suffering that he knew he would never, never quite be free of it. Only death could finally assuage his desire.

But he wrenched the pang from his heart. He thought of Sally, with her kind blue eyes; and his lips unconsciously formed themselves into a smile. He walked up the steps of the National Gallery and sat down in the first room, so that he should see her the moment she came in. It always comforted him to get among pictures. He looked at none in particular, but allowed the magnificence of their colour, the beauty of their lines, to work upon his soul. His imagination was busy with Sally. It would be pleasant to take her away from that London in which she seemed an unusual figure, like a cornflower in a shop among orchids and azaleas; he had learned in the Kentish hop-field that she did not belong to the town; and he was sure that she would blossom under the soft skies of Dorset to a rarer beauty. She came in, and he got up to meet her. She was in black, with white cuffs at her wrists and a lawn collar round her neck. They shook hands.

'Have you been waiting long?'

'No. Ten minutes. Are you hungry?'

'Not very.'

'Let's sit here for a bit, shall we?'

'If you like.'

They sat quietly, side by side, without speaking. Philip enjoyed having her near him. He was warmed by her radiant health. A glow of life seemed like an aureole to shine about her.

'Well, how have you been?' he said at last, with a little smile.

'Oh, it's all right. It was a false alarm.'

'Was it?'

'Aren't you glad?'

An extraordinary sensation filled him. He had felt certain that Sally's suspicion was well founded; it had never occurred to him for an instant that there was a possibility of error. All his plans were suddenly overthrown, and the existence, so elaborately pictured, was no more than a dream which would never be realized. He was free once more. Free! He need give up none of his projects, and life still was in his hands for him to do what he liked with. He felt no exhilaration, but only dismay. His heart sank. The future stretched out before him in desolate emptiness. It was as though he had sailed for many years over a great waste of waters, with peril and privation, and at last had come upon a fair haven, but as he was about to enter, some contrary wind had arisen and drove him out again into the open sea; and because he had let his mind dwell on these soft meads and pleasant woods of the land, the vast deserts of the ocean filled him with anguish. He could not confront again the loneliness and the tempest. Sally looked at him with her clear eyes.

'Aren't you glad?' she asked again. 'I thought you'd be as pleased as Punch.'

He met her gaze haggardly.

'I'm not sure,' he muttered.

'You are funny. Most men would.'

He realized that he had deceived himself; it was no self-sacrifice that had driven him to think of marrying, but the desire for a wife and a home and love; and now that it all seemed to slip through his fingers he was seized with despair. He wanted all that more than anything in the world. What did he care for Spain and its cities, Cordova, Toledo, León; what to him were the pagodas of Burma and the lagoons of South Sea Islands? America was here and now. It seemed to him that all his life he had followed the ideals that other people, by their words or their writings, had instilled into him, and never the desires of his own heart. Always his course had been swayed by what he thought he should do and never by what he wanted with his whole soul to do. He put all that aside now with a gesture of impatience. He had lived always in the future, and the present always, always had slipped through his fingers. His ideals? He thought of his desire to make a design, intricate and beautiful, out of the myriad, meaningless facts of life: had he not seen also that the simplest pattern, that in

606

which a man was born, worked, married, had children, and died, was likewise the most perfect? It might be that to surrender to happiness was to accept defeat, but it was a defeat better than many victories.

He glanced quickly at Sally, he wondered what she was thinking, and then looked away again.

'I was going to ask you to marry me,' he said.

'I thought p'raps you might, but I shouldn't have liked to stand in your way.'

'You wouldn't have done that.'

'How about your travels, Spain and all that?'

'How d'you know I want to travel?'

'I ought to know something about it. I've heard you and Dad talk about it till you were blue in the face.'

'I don't care a damn about all that.' He paused for an instant and then spoke in a low, hoarse whisper. 'I don't want to leave you! I can't leave you.'

She did not answer. He could not tell what she thought.

'I wonder if you'll marry me, Sally.'

She did not move and there was no flicker of emotion on her face, but she did not look at him when she answered:

'If you like.'

'Don't you want to?'

'Oh, of course I'd like to have a house of my own, and it's about time I was settling down.'

He smiled a little. He knew her pretty well by now, and her manner did not surprise him.

'But don't you want to marry *me*?'

'There's no one else I would marry.'

'Then that settles it.'

'Mother and Dad will be surprised, won't they?'

'I'm so happy.'

'I want my lunch,' she said.

'Dear!'

He smiled and took her hand and pressed it. They got up and walked out of the gallery. They stood for a moment at the balustrade and looked at Trafalgar Square. Cabs and omnibuses hurried to and fro, and crowds passed, hastening in every direction, and the sun was shining.

EXPLANATORY NOTES

23 "dissenting ministers": "Dissenters" or "Nonconformists" refer to members of Protestant sects that have separated themselves from the established Church of England.

24 "Bismarck": Otto von Bismarck (1815–1898), founder and first Chancellor of the German Empire.

63 "General Gordon": Charles George Gordon (1833–1885), British general who, after distinguishing himself in the "Arrow" War in China, became a martyr-hero when killed by Sudanese rebels in the siege of Khartoum.

81 "Perugino": Pietro di Cristoforo Vanucci (1450–1523), early Renaissance Italian painter.

92 *"Anlage"*: public park.

95 *"Burschenshaft"*: student organization at German universities, active in the 1848 revolution and strongly nationalistic.
"Kneipe": bar, saloon.

99 *"Walpurgisnacht"*: The eve of May 1, when witches were said to meet to celebrate the eighth-century Saint Walpurgis and hold revels with the devil.
"Gravelotte": At the Battle of Gravelotte, August 16–18, 1870, the French army failed to break through the Prussian lines and was subsequently trapped at Sedan.

102 "Garibaldi": Giuseppe Garibaldi (1807–1882), an Italian military revolutionary leader, who played a central role in the revolution of 1848 and the unification of Italy in 1860.

103 *"Stadtgarten"*: municipal or city garden.
"Maibowle": white wine punch.

105 *"Marius"*: Walter Pater (1839–1894) published *Marius the Epicurean* in 1885.

112 "Mr. Gladstone": William Ewart Gladstone (1809–1898), British statesman who was four times prime minister.

114 "Renan's *Vie de Jésus*": Ernest Renan's (1823–1892) *Vie de Jésus* (1863) argues that Christianity was the creation of the human imagination rather than divine intervention.

118 "pomatum": scented hair and skin ointment.

121 *"hetaira"*: courtesan, mistress.

129 "Kuno Fischer": Ernst Kuno Berthold Fischer (1824–1907), German philosopher and educator who founded Neo-Kantian thought and was a leading exponent of the philosophy of aesthetics.

133 "Alphonse Daudet": Alphonse Daudet (1840–1897), French short-story writer and novelist.

139 *"La Vie de Bohème"*: Louis-Henri Murger's (1822–1861) *Scènes de la vie bohème* (1847–1849), which depicted bohemian life, was made into operas by Leoncavallo and Puccini.

173 *"massière"*: a student in charge of a French art school.

175 "Latin Quarter": the section of Paris surrounding the university, known for centuries for its intellectual, cultural, and bohemian life.

184 *"Absinthe"*: a highly aromatic liqueur, banned in France and many other countries in 1915 because of its dangerously high alcoholic content (68 percent by volume).

186 "Zola": Emile Zola (1840–1902), a controversial French novelist critic and leader of the Naturalist movement in literature, published a defense of Manet in 1867.

189 *"The Yellow Book"*: An illustrated quarterly (1894–97), which came to represent the Decadent and *fin de siècle* movements in the 1890s.

190 *"bock"*: Strong dark German beer.

193 *"tas de farceurs"*: Literally, a pile of jokers or humbugs.

194 *"bonne à toute faire"*: Maid-of-all-work.

210 "Mrs. Grundy": Fictional English character who has come to represent the repressive force of conventional, respectable public opinion.

224 "Mrs. Warren": The central figure, a prostitute, of George Bernard Shaw's (1856–1950) play *Mrs. Warren's Profession* (1902).

228 "sedulous ape": One who acquires an artistic style by assiduous imitation.

243 "A.R.A.": Associate of the Royal Academy.
"cénacle": Literary or artistic coterie.

259 "Cook's tickets": Thomas Cook is a leading British travel agency.

281 "dog-cart": Two-wheeled, horse-drawn wagon, with seats back to back.

351 "The Flying Dutchman": Legendary ghost ship doomed to sail the seas forever.

354 *"viva voce"*: Orally.

432 "Herbert Spencer": Herbert Spencer (1820–1903), English philosopher whose theories of evolution preceded those of Charles Darwin.

433 *"mantones de Manila"*: Manila shawls.

470 "war had broken out with the Transvaal": The South African (Boer) war (1899–1902).

487 *"gêne"*: Torture.

500 "a *tu quoque*": A retort meaning "so are you."

509 "The sweater's daughter": Daughter of an exacting and exploitative employer.

510 "sidey": Assuming superiority.

574 *"locum"*: Colloquial for *locum tenens*, one who substitutes for a doctor.

585 "mangel-wurzel": Large type of beet, used to feed cattle.

590 "flapper": Girl in her late teens.

CLICK ON A CLASSIC
www.penguinclassics.com

The world's greatest literature at your fingertips

Constantly updated information on more than a thousand titles,
from Icelandic sagas to ancient Indian epics, Russian drama to
Italian romance, American greats to African masterpieces

•

The latest news on recent additions to the list, updated
editions, and specially commissioned translations

•

Original essays by leading writers

•

A wealth of background material, including biographies
of every classic author from Aristotle to Zamyatin, plot
synopses, readers' and teachers' guides, useful web links

•

Online desk and examination copy assistance for academics

•

Trivia quizzes, competitions, giveaways, news on
forthcoming screen adaptations

> "Maugham has given infinite pleasure and
> left us a splendor of writing" —Dirk Bogarde

Collected Short Stories
Volume 1
These thirty stories, including the piece "Rain," are set in the Pacific
Islands, England, France, and Spain.   *ISBN 0-14-018589-5*

Collected Short Stories
Volume 2
The stories collected here, including "The Alien Corn," "Flotsam and
Jetsam," and "The Vessel of Wrath," reconfirm Maugham's stature as
one of the masters of the short story.   *ISBN 0-14-018590-9*

Collected Short Stories
Volume 3
Maugham learned his craft from Maupassant, and these stories, featuring his alter-ego Ashenden, display the unique and remarkable talent that made him an unsurpassed storyteller.   *ISBN 0-14-018591-7*

Collected Short Stories
Volume 4
These thirty stories—most set in the colonies at a time when the
Empire was still assured, in a world in which men and women were
caught between their own essentially European values and the richness and ambiguity of their unfamiliar surroundings—show a master
of the genre at the peak of his power.   *ISBN 0-14-018592-5*

The Magician
The Magician is one of Maugham's most complex and perceptive novels. Running through it is the theme of evil, deftly woven into a story
as memorable for its action as for its astonishingly vivid characters.
                                        ISBN 0-14-018595-X

The Moon and Sixpence
Charles Strickland, a dull bourgeois city gent, is driven to abandon his home, wife, and children to devote himself slavishly to painting. In a tiny studio in Paris, he fills canvas after canvas, refusing to sell his works. He drifts to Marseilles and, finally, to Tahiti, where, even after being blinded by leprosy, he produces some of his most passionate and mysterious works of art.   *ISBN 0-14-018597-6*

Mrs. Craddock
In this penetrating study of an unequal marriage, Maugham explores the nature of love and happiness and finds that the two rarely coincide.   *ISBN 0-14-018594-1*

The Narrow Corner
First published in 1932, this volume recalls many of Maugham's best short stories, featuring a story of love, money, and mutiny.
       ISBN 0-14-018598-4

The Painted Veil
Set in Hong Kong during the heart of a cholera epidemic, this novel portrays a young woman as she learns the true meaning of love—but her discovery comes too late.   *ISBN 0-14-018599-2*

The Summing Up
Written to give some account of how Maugham learned his craft and why he became such an acute observer of human beings, *The Summing Up* is like an intimate conversation with one of the great cultured minds of the century.   *ISBN 0-14-018600-X*